Exemplary Novels

Exemplary Novels

MIGUEL DE CERVANTES

TRANSLATED FROM THE SPANISH
BY EDITH GROSSMAN

EDITED BY ROBERTO GONZÁLEZ ECHEVARRÍA

YALE UNIVERSITY PRESS ■ NEW HAVEN & LONDON

A MARGELLOS
WORLD REPUBLIC OF LETTERS BOOK

The Margellos World Republic of Letters is dedicated to making literary works from around the globe available in English through translation. It brings to the English-speaking world the work of leading poets, novelists, essayists, philosophers, and playwrights from Europe, Latin America, Africa, Asia, and the Middle East to stimulate international discourse and creative exchange.

Yale University Press books may be purchased in quantity for educational, business, or promotional use. For information, please e-mail sales.press@yale.edu (U.S. office) or sales@yaleup.co.uk (U.K. office).

Set in Electra and Nobel type by Westchester Publishing Services

Printed in the United States of America.

ISBN 978-0-300-12586-3 (hardcover : alk. paper)

Library of Congress Control Number: 2016937056

A catalogue record for this book is available from the British Library.

This paper meets the requirements of ANSI/NISO Z39.48-1992 (Permanence of Paper).

10 9 8 7 6 5 4 3 2 1

CONTENTS

INTRODUCTION

Roberto González Echevarría

Twelve brilliant short novels, packed with compelling plots and fascinating characters, redolent with literary games of the greatest variety and sophistication, were the author of *Don Quixote*'s response to his suddenly acquired fame. It was a new kind of book, never seen before in the Spanish language, rivaling the influential collections of Italian novellas then circulating in the Iberian Peninsula, and on a par with the best writing by the literary giants among whom its author lived in early seventeenth-century Madrid. When Miguel de Cervantes published *Exemplary Novels* in 1613, he was sixty-six years old, an advanced age for the time. He would die three years later, on April 22, 1616, coincidentally on nearly the same date as Shakespeare, but a few days apart because Spain followed the Gregorian calendar and England the Julian. The fact that this book, his third masterpiece if we count the two parts of the *Don Quixote* (published in 1605 and 1615, respectively) as separate novels, appeared so late in his life says much about Cervantes and the collection of novels that it contains.

In spite of the success that he had with the first part of *Don Quixote* in 1605, Cervantes did not profit enough from it to overcome the life of penury and disappointment that he had endured until then. Publishers did become willing to bring out his work, and he managed to bring out in short order a collection of his theater, *Eight Comedies and Eight New Interludes Never Before Published*, in 1615, and in the same year Part Two of *Don Quixote*. But much of the profit remained with the editors, who also printed posthumously, in 1617, *The Trials of Persiles and Sigismunda*, the Byzantine romance that Cervantes labored over and enthused about during the last years of his life. Collecting the twelve novels separately in one volume was probably due in some measure to the criticism that he endured for having inserted similar stories in the first *Don Quixote*, something he refrained from doing in Part Two.

But *Exemplary Novels* is a work of genius in its own right and would have secured its author a prominent place in the history of Western literature even if he had not written any of his other books. It was an instant success in Spain, where the novels even found their way into the musical theater (*zarzuelas*), and had an immediate and lasting impact on English literature. Cervantes was a hit in England and elsewhere. Thomas Shelton brought out his translation of *Don Quixote* in 1612, and César Ouidan, the first complete French translation of the novel in 1614. Shakespeare wrote a play based on the character Cardenio, from *Don Quixote*, which has never been found. People dressed as Don Quixote and Sancho Panza for fairs and carnivals in Germany and Peru. *Exemplary Novels* did not fall far behind. Jacobean playwrights Thomas Middleton, William Rowley, and John Fletcher adapted some of the novellas for the stage. Neglected until the last decade of his life, Cervantes then became a prolific literary celebrity.

Exemplary Novels spans nearly the whole creative life of Cervantes. Studies have shown that some of the stories go back at least twenty years from the date of publication, if not more, while others were written in that productive period between the two parts of *Don Quixote*, 1605 to 1615. The book is like a summing up of Cervantes's fiction, displaying its broad range of topics, characters, styles, and plots. The order in which the novels appear in the book is not the one in which they were written, to be sure. For that reason, it is tempting to wonder if Cervantes encrypted a message in the sequence that he gave to the book, and the place that each story occupies with reference to the others. The order may also have been determined by the publisher, though even then Cervantes must have had a hand in it. One story, "The Pretended Aunt," published separately and anonymously but that critics now are almost sure is Cervantes's, was left out of the volume, which adds a significant detail about the process of selection followed. It is very salacious and somewhat clumsy (an early work?). The resemblances of some of the exemplary novels to the ones that he included in Part One of *Don Quixote* also adds an intriguing dimension to the arrangement of this collection. It appears to be certain, to me in any case, that the book constitutes a review and totaling up of his oeuvre by an author who knows that he is near the end of his life and wants to leave a significant legacy for posterity, showing the full spectrum of his creative mind.

The stories are an assemblage of literary artifacts of the utmost complexity and sophistication, as *Don Quixote* had been, presented in such a light, entertaining way that the reader, entranced by the twists and turns of the plots and the antics of the protagonists, hardly notices their artistry. Some of the novels, like "The English Spanishwoman," are lengthy for the genre, that of the Italian *novella*, which is how Cervantes uses the term. *Novela* was not yet available in Spanish in its present sense, it only meant a long short story in the style of Boccaccio, as Covarrubias, who cites the Italian, explains in his 1611 *Tesoro de la lengua castellana o española.* The geographic settings range from England to the Mediterranean. Italy is featured often, with a focus on Spain, especially Castile and Andalusia, regions of the peninsula that Cervantes knew firsthand, as he did Italy. The historical period is roughly Cervantes's present. The language, as in all of his work, is elegant without being pedantic, with a rich lexical range reflecting the social and native provenance of the characters. The narrators engage the reader in a friendly, complicit manner that invites following along with the narrative. Cervantes's style and language are highly accessible to today's Spanish speakers. Some of the novels in the collection are well-known and widely recognized throughout Spain and Latin America, where they are included in school curricula.

Love is the overarching theme of *Exemplary Novels*. The plots focus on the adventures of young men and women on their way to adulthood and matrimony. As in most literature of the Spanish Golden Age, everything that happens before marriage is the stuff of comedy while all that happens after, of tragedy. In *Exemplary Novels* Cervantes offers highly original variants of this broad scheme, sometimes based on traditional tales, such as that of the old man married to a young woman, or new stories, like that of a young man married to a seasoned prostitute who fools him, steals his jewels, and infects him with syphilis. The variety of the stories, as much in plot and character as in their following the available narrative molds of the period, is one of the appeals of the book, which may get its title from being a collection of samples (*ejemplos*) of novelistic possibilities: picaresque, byzantine, Italianate (comic-erotic), and even one, the last one, a dialogue featuring two dogs as protagonists. One way to see Cervantes's project in this book is as a miniaturization of extant prose-fictional genres that probes into their artfulness and draws out their literary essence by compression. They are exemplary in that way, it seems to me, though there has been much discussion about the adjective "exemplary," in which some want to see a moralistic intention. But Cervantes never wrote that kind of story. He declares in the prologue: "My intention has been to bring out into the public square of our nation a magician's table where each person can be entertained, with no harm to anyone; I mean, with no harm to soul or body, because honest, pleasant pastimes are profitable rather than harmful."

Cervantes knew the works of Giovanni Boccaccio and Matteo Bandello, the premier novella writers, particularly the first. He was familiar with Italian literature which, even this late in the Renaissance, continued to be the defining one in Europe and provided models for poetry—mostly the epic—and prose. When Cervantes boasts in the prologue to *Exemplary Novels* that he is "the first to have written novellas in Castilian," he means that he is the first Spanish writer to publish stories whose form, content, and style followed those of the Italian masters, particularly Boccaccio, who was well-known in Spain in the original as well as in translations. (The verb that Cervantes uses, *novelar*, is a neologism.) But he needed no translations from the Italian, having spent several years in an Italy that was still in no small measure part of the Spanish Empire, obviously learning the language. These stories, or *novelle*, were what, by today's standards, are called long short stories or short novels. "Daisy Miller," by Henry James, and "The Old Man and the Sea," by Ernest Hemingway, come to mind as modern examples in English. One could imagine some of Cervantes's novels in today's *New Yorker*. Boccaccian stories were sophisticated, lascivious, often humorous, and involved mostly one or two protagonists with a supporting cast of accomplices or victims. They dealt with sexual promiscuity involving sinful activities such as adultery and concubinage, dwelling in a delightful way upon the guiles of young men and women seeking erotic satisfaction against societal and religious restrictions. Priests were often participants in the shenanigans. Bandello was even more daring and lewd, and his stories became a source for writers from other lands, like Shakespeare, who took from him the plot of *Romeo and Juliet*. Cervantes was never as bawdy as Boccaccio or Bandello, but he was daring by Spanish standards.

Cervantes added a strong dose of realism to the Italian features of some of his stories that he derived from the Spanish picaresque, which involved settings in low-class environments, such as sordid inns and town squares, and characters like criminals and prostitutes. But in other stories the setting is idealistic, reminiscent of pastoral and Byzantine romances, the latter redolent with sea voyages and their inevitable shipwrecks, unexpected encounters and re-encounters, discoveries of their identities, and other conventional narrative devices. In several stories he manages to merge these two trends, as he did in *Don Quixote*, producing a brilliant synthesis of styles that is one of the most recognizable features of his work. Some have tried to divide the stories into idealistic and realistic, but Cervantes threw them all together in the volume, and not a few stories have features of both.

In Italian, the short novels go back to *Il Novellino*, the Florentine collection of tales written in the late thirteenth century and published in 1525, and ultimately, like all brief stories, to *The Thousand and One Nights* and the dawn of narrative fiction. In Spanish, their antecedents are those stories included in *Libro de los ejemplos del conde Lucanor y de Patronio* ("Book of the Examples of Count Lucanor and of Patronio") by Don Juan Manuel, first written in 1335.

The length and structure of these texts are probably determined by their oral beginnings, which means that they should be read aloud in one sitting and that listeners ought to be able to remember and connect details of the narrative as they followed the speaker. A silent reading can also be finished in one session, with the same effect. This relative brevity leads to the text's taut artistry, which is still a feature of the modern short story. Cervantes dramatizes this foundational scene in *Don Quixote*, when the priest reads to the group assembled at the inn the story of "The Man Who Was Recklessly Curious." His *Exemplary Novels* and the novels he inserted in *Don Quixote* owe much to this previous history and to the assiduous practice of storytelling by the Italians and their followers. I suspect that he also learned a good deal from listening to tales told by people of all ranks and backgrounds as he roamed through the Castilian and Andalusian towns doing his work as a tax collector. Some of the novels retain the freshness of something heard from real people.

What Cervantes did not need from the Italians or from literary tradition in general were plots and characters. He was full of ideas for stories and seems to have favored the short novel as the preferred length for plots, to judge by the many that he included or worked into his longer works, such as Part One of *Don Quixote* and *The Trials of Persiles and Sigismunda*. In all likelihood *Don Quixote* started as a brief novel which was going to end after the scrutiny of the hidalgo's library or thereabouts. Cervantes planned a separate collection of novels, to be called *Semanas del jardín*, or *Weeks in the Garden*, which by its title seems to have had an overarching narrative conceit like that of Boccaccio's *Decameron*; a group of storytellers retire to a garden fleeing some catastrophe to tell their tales. But it was never published and instead probably morphed into *Exemplary Novels*, which did not need such a contrivance to buttress it but simply appeared as the work of Miguel de Cervantes because of his newly acquired fame and authority.

Critics of the intercalated stories in Part One of *Don Quixote* have not realized that the experiment that Cervantes was carrying out was merging two broad narrative schemes into his book. On the one hand the sequential, epic-style plot of the chivalric romance, which he was parodying and therefore copying, as it were. On the other, the collection of short novels in the style of Boccaccio. He carried it off brilliantly, particularly in the amalgam of narrative threads that intertwine at the inn, involving the story of Fernando and Dorotea, Dorotea's paranoid version of the story of the giant Pandafilando de la Fosca Vista, the imbroglio of Cardenio and Luscinda, and the main plot of the novel in which Don Quixote and Sancho are protagonists. All of the conflicts in those narratives are resolved in yet another story, Don Quixote's dream, in which he slays the giant, but has really slashed the wine skins that the inn-keeper hangs in the room where the knight sleeps. The nightmare of a mad-man brings harmony to all. This is a spark of literary genius that went unnoticed by Cervantes's detractors, but it shows the preeminent role that short novels played in his creative mind.

Cervantes's imagination also seemed to be filled with characters; there is the vast array of those in both parts of *Don Quixote,* who range from the pair of unforgettable protagonists to Juan Palomeque, the innkeeper in Part One, to Maritornes, the ugly but kind prostitute accosted by Don Quixote in the dark of night, and to the Duke and Duchess in Part Two. With a mere brush-stroke, Cervantes created the galley slave (I, 22), a serial seducer who has im-pregnated two of his cousins, and the Gentleman in Green, a contented petty nobleman who invites the knight to his home. Then there are those charac-ters imagined by other characters, like Dulcinea in her various guises, the en-chanters, and the spectral residents of Montesinos Cave. The same variety and originality prevails in *Exemplary Novels,* where we find a madman who believes that he is made of glass, the wily and wise Monipodio who runs a brotherhood of thugs from his house in Seville, eloquent witches, dogs who live picaresque lives and talk about them, and a delightful Gypsy orphan who turns out to be the stolen daughter of aristocrats. In his fiction, Cervantes is like a minor god, creating individuals who are colorful, unique, entertaining, and often highly articulate.

Miguel de Cervantes Saavedra had been born in September 1547, probably on the 29th, the feast of St. Michael, to judge by the Christian name with which he was baptized, in Alcalá de Henares, a town near Madrid, hence in Castile and the center of the Spanish Peninsula. In 1498 an impressive university had been founded there, but Miguel and his family had nothing to do with it, as far as is known. Cervantes's father was a surgeon, which at the time did not require a university degree and was an occupation closer to that of a barber than to what a surgeon is today. He was often in debt, moving his family from city to city to escape from debt collectors. It exposed the young Miguel to Madrid, Valladolid, and Seville, cities in which he would live during signifi-cant periods of his adult life.

We know very little about Miguel's childhood and education. Because of his praiseful references to them, it seems possible that he attended Jesuit schools. He is believed to have matriculated at some point in a school run by Juan López de Hoyos, who published some of his early verse, reputed to be a follower of Desiderius Erasmus, which has led much scholarship to associate

Cervantes with the captivating philosophy of that prominent humanist. This is all based on speculation, questionable readings of his works, and even more questionable critical practices. Cervantes never attended university. We must assume that the considerable humanistic education that he evinces in his writings was self-acquired and resign ourselves to the fact that it is useless to judge him by the standards we use for ordinary individuals like ourselves. He was obviously brilliant, a genius, motivated, disciplined, and ambitious, all while desperately trying to make a living and secure a decent place in society. Cervantes was also fortunate to have found himself immersed in a high-powered, active, literary, intellectual, and artistic world, packed with first-rate, prolific minds. This was his university. For all the clichés about Spain being intellectually cut off from European trends, the likes of Fray Luis de León, Lope de Vega, Luis de Góngora, Tirso de Molina, Mateo Alemán, Francisco de Quevedo, and Calderón de la Barca constituted an array of literary geniuses without peer in the Continent. Among the painters there were, of course, Diego Velázquez, El Greco, Francisco de Zurbarán, and Juan de Herrera who topped the list of architects (he designed El Escorial). Precariously propped up economically by wealth arriving from its American colonies and ruinous loans from foreign bankers, Spain and the newly designated capital Madrid were undergoing a construction boom in which the arts thrived. In addition, Spain's interests and control over substantial parts of Italy opened wide a door to artistic and philosophical movements that were at the cutting edge in the West. Cervantes profited artistically and intellectually, though not financially, from this enriching environment because he had the intelligence, dedication, and drive to do so.

There are quite a few young characters in *Exemplary Novels* who display these qualities as they mature and look for a place in the world. These novels, as the rest of Cervantes's works, are full of students at various levels of their education. Most are witty, ingenuous, and bent on learning as much as possible from books as well as from life. The most memorable is Tomás Rodaja, the young man who, poisoned by a spurned woman, winds up insane, believing himself to be made of glass. He had earlier managed to acquire a superb education by becoming the servant of well-to-do students at the University of Salamanca, where he became a notable legal scholar. Perhaps in all these students Cervantes portrays the young man that he would have liked to have been. But fate took him in the direction of the military, and the debate between arms and letters will resonate throughout his fiction, no doubt reflecting his own destiny.

Chance would intervene, as it often does in Cervantes's fiction. In 1569 he fled to Italy, accused of wounding a man in a duel, a practice that was forbidden and severely punished by the right hand being cut off. Cervantes would not return to Spain until 1580. In Rome he joined the household of Cardinal Acquaviva as chamberlain. What qualifications he had for the job is anyone's guess. It was likely a question of influences. But Cervantes was expanding his Italian education. In 1570, however, he enlisted in a Spanish regiment stationed in Naples, part of the vast naval force gathered by the Holy League under John of Austria for the purpose of stopping the Ottoman Turks. On October 7, 1571, Cervantes fought bravely in the Battle of Lepanto, in which the Turks were soundly defeated. In the fierce close combat from ship to ship he was shot in the left arm, forever losing the use of that hand. He would always mention with pride his participation in this battle, which eventually led to his acquiring the rhyming moniker by which he is known in the Spanish-speaking world: "el Manco de Lepanto," or "The One-Handed Man of Lepanto." It was the high point of his military career, which continued in spite of his being partially maimed. In 1575 he attempted to return home with his brother Rodrigo, who was also a soldier, but was captured at sea by Barbary pirates and sold into slavery in Algiers. Because he carried with him letters of recommendation from important people, his captors thought Cervantes to be an important person and set his ransom very high. He spent five years in captivity, during which he made four unsuccessful escape attempts. In 1580 Cervantes was finally ransomed for 500 ducats paid by his struggling family and Trinitarian monks. Captivity left a deep impression on the writer he would become, appearing in his theater and famously in *Don Quixote*, in which he tells his story in the captive's tale (I, 39–41). María Antonia Garcés has written the most thorough account of this period in Cervantes's life and its impact on his writing.

Cervantes's experiences as a soldier and captive in the Mediterranean enriched his life with characters and stories, some of which would emerge not just in his longer fictions but also in *Exemplary Novels* and his theater. The decade away from home, however, had put his literary career and ordinary life on hold. In 1580 Cervantes was thirty-three, unmarried, putatively childless (he may have left an illegitimate son in Italy), and had yet to publish a book or stage a play. It was this late start that likely provoked his late blooming in the last ten years of his work. Ana de Villafranca, a married woman who was his mistress in Madrid, gave him a daughter, Isabel, around 1584. In that same year, Cervantes, who was by now thirty-eight, married Catalina de Salazar, an eighteen-year-old from Esquivias, a wine-producing region near Madrid. Her family owned some land. The next year, in 1585, he published his first book, *La Galatea*, a pastoral romance, and sold two plays which have not survived.

The romance showed promise, particularly because we now know what came after, but it would not have made Cervantes famous. To judge by the theater that did reach us, the plays were not successful because he made the wrong choice at a crucial juncture in the history of the Spanish stage. He sided with those who would follow Aristotle's *Poetics*, as they were being touted by theorists like Alfonso López Pinciano—keeping to the three units of action, time, and space. Lope de Vega (1562–1635), who would emerge as the unsurpassed playwright of the period, was founder of the national theater and had develped his own formula, which disregarded the unities. Lope became a thorn in Cervantes's side throughout his career. He lorded over the literary landscape and did not hold the author of *Don Quixote* in high regard. And as the theater was the only literary activity from which Cervantes could hope to derive a profit, he was, as he would be for much of his life, out of money and without work.

Cervantes found a job as king's purchasing agent in Andalusia, part of the effort to provision the great Spanish Armada that Philip II was assembling to finally put away the English. He spent seven years all told in this activity, as tax collector in the same area after the defeat of the Armada in 1588. This occupation would allow him to come to know intimately the Andalusian countryside, with its dusty roads, ramshackle inns, and its quarrelsome small towns, where the residents resented his presence and occupation. Cervantes also spent a great deal of time in Seville, gateway to the New World, a bustling port thriving with all the legal and illegal activities typical of such a place. Cervantes was jailed twice for apparent irregularities in his accounts. In 1597–98 he spent several months in Seville's jail, where he purportedly conceived the idea for *Don Quixote*.

Miguel and Catalina did not live together for long periods during these years, and the marriage remained barren. He came to grief because of the illicit activities of his sister Magdalena and his daughter Isabel, who had a variety of affairs with wealthy men, in part no doubt due to their precarious financial situation. In 1604 the family moved to Valladolid, which had become the capital of Spain for a brief period, obviously looking for ways to make a living. The women worked as seamstresses. It was then that Cervantes finished *Don Quixote*, which was published in early 1605 to great acclaim. It was a distillation of his vast readings including, of course, the romances of chivalry, and his intense engagement with the realities that he had experienced as a soldier, captive, itinerant tax collector, and aspiring author. Spain had begun its decline, and the catastrophe of the Armada in 1588 was a clear sign of it. The economy was beset by inflation, which was partly due to the riches arriving from the Indies, as well as demographic changes that soon would include the expulsion of the *moriscos*, or the Muslims who remained in the Peninsula after the fall of Granada in 1492. (The best account of all this in English continues to be J. H. Elliott's magnificent *Imperial Spain*.) *Don Quixote* was not, in spite of it all, a disillusioned book, in great measure because of its humor and the humane way in which Cervantes portrays people from all ranks and occupations. No character in Cervantes is uniformly evil. He is not a pessimistic writer, like his contemporary Shakespeare. As Melveena McKendrick puts it in her excellent book *Cervantes*, addressing the misguided opinion that in *Exemplary Novels* there is a progression from idealism to pessimism, "Cervantes's literary disillusion is never cruel and is usually good humored; and in his work as a whole he balances his exposure to the folly of man with an affirmation of right values and right behavior—just as in *Don Quixote* his parody of the literature of knight errantry is underpinned by his assertions of what literature ought to be: responsible, congruous, and truthful" (172). The several happy endings in *Exemplary Novels* attest to this.

McKendrick also points out that toward the end of his life Cervantes seems to have found solace in religion. In 1609 he joined the brotherhood called the Confraternity of Slaves of the Most Blessed Sacrament. He had never been the religious rebel that some have tried to make him out to be. As McKendrick also writes, "throughout his life and work Cervantes gives us no reason to believe that he was not as true a son of the Church as he was a fervent patriot" (123). It is tempting to make Cervantes into a modern thinker because of his emphasis on ambiguity, perspectivism, the fragility and elusiveness of the self and of the truth, and the shiftiness of the literary text. He takes these issues as far as they can go even today, and they may appear to have been heretical in the Spain of his time. But Cervantes never had any trouble with the Inquisition and none of his works suffered from censorship. I believe that in these matters he practiced a double truth, as Américo Castro suggests in *El pensamiento de Cervantes*, where he disavows the idea that the author of the *Quixote* was an *ingenio lego*, an unlettered wit. The two truths were those emerging from the new ideas that developed in the Renaissance and beyond, leading to modernity, and Catholic doctrine, particularly the Spanish kind, which seemed to favor a return to the Middle Ages and scholasticism. Cervantes found a way to harmonize both without straining either. Nothing shook him from his faith, as he expounds in the prologue to the *Persiles*, practically written on his deathbed. Cervantes had extreme unction, the last sacrament of the Church, administered, and he was buried in Madrid's Convent of the Barefoot Trinitarian Nuns, where his bones have apparently just been found to the foolish glee of the Spanish state.

A characteristic that makes Cervantes sound like one of us is his delightful self-deprecation, which seems sincere, not a mere rhetorical convention to garner the reader's approval. In the prologue to the 1605 *Don Quixote*, he takes self-effacement to a high philosophical level, questioning what it means to begin a book, pretending to disavow his authorship of it, inventing a friend who advises him to dispense with the conventions of a prologue and with literary tradition as a whole, and making the difficulties of writing the prologue its very subject. The prologue to *Exemplary Novels*, in which he alludes to the previous one, is much more personal and his self-mockery more humorous and physical. To tell the reader how he looks, Cervantes writes what a friend of his would write if asked to describe a portrait of him:

> The man you see here, with the aquiline face, chestnut hair, smooth
> clear brow, joyful eyes, curved yet well-proportioned nose, silver beard
> that was golden not twenty years ago, large mustache, small mouth,
> teeth neither short nor long because he has only six, and those are worn
> down and badly placed since they are not distributed in a symmetrical
> manner; his body lies between the two extremes, neither large nor
> small, his coloring is vivid, more fair than dark, and he is somewhat
> stoop-shouldered and not very light on his feet; this, I say, is the appear-
> ance of the author of *La Galatea* and *Don Quixote de la Mancha*, and
> of the man who made the *Viaje del Parnaso*, imitating the one by Cesare
> Caporali of Perugia, as well as other works that have gone astray and
> perhaps are missing the name of their owner, who is commonly called
> Miguel de Cervantes Saavedra. He was a soldier for many years, and a
> captive for five and a half, when he learned to be patient in adversity. In
> the naval battle of Lepanto he lost his left hand to a harquebus, a wound
> that, although it looks ugly, he considers beautiful because it was
> acquired on the highest, most memorable occasion witnessed by past
> centuries or that future centuries can hope to see, as he served under
> the victorious banners of the son of the thunderbolt of war, Charles the
> Fifth, of happy memory.

It is typical of Cervantes that he does not write directly about himself but, as in the 1605 *Don Quixote* prologue, invents a friend who does it for him, pretending to take his distance. But what is so charming is the description of his well-worn body and how it has suffered the ravages of time and of war—missing teeth, gray beard, hunched back, and crippled hand—compared to his long gone, youthful attractive attributes such as an aquiline profile, happy eyes, well-proportioned nose, brown hair, and blond beard. The description is similar to those he would write of some of his characters, deftly combining physical and moral features, all in a state of flux that renders the combination mildly comical. In some instances a physical trait defines a character like Preciosa's cleft chin in "The Novel of the Little Gypsy Girl," or Ginés de Pasamonte's crossed eyes in *Don Quixote*. It is the Cervantes portrayed in the prologue, with all his faults and physical defects, who is the author of the "inventions" (as he calls them) that the reader will find in *Exemplary Novels*; not an intellectual or physical giant, but an ordinary fellow who is near the end of his life. Age and experience have given him an unembellished, ironic perspective of himself and the world, but not a pessimistic one, to which the humor attests.

In the front matter to the book, specifically in the poems that serve the function of today's literary endorsements, and which Cervantes composed himself of course, he refers to the novels in the book as "twelve labyrinths" (8) and "fables" with a "secret" (9). He was well aware and justifiably proud of the depth and deftness of the fictions that he had created, of their sophistication and originality. And he was right to be so. From the first to the last, all the tales carry the Cervantean imprint of unobtrusive self-reflexiveness and an invitation to do the keenest interpretive reading, like both parts of *Don Quixote*, particularly the second with its several internal authors and readers of the first. The *Exemplary Novels* engage literary and philosophical issues of the highest complexity and reach, augmented by their relative brevity which demands critical concentration. Even the opening novel, which has the air of being just an entertaining romance about a charming character, the young Gypsy girl Preciosa, who turns out to be the daughter of aristocrats, and who is virtuous and adept at singing and dancing, is a complex and challenging work. That it was chosen to open the volume seems to suggest that it announces the collection's main premises and themes, and it does.

The story hinges on anagnorisis, the discovery by the young woman of who she truly is, which restrospectively explains her principled ways and physical beauty (Cervantes, like his contemporaries, believed in the power of heredity). This is a traditional motif and has as background the story of Cinderella. Self-discovery is a serious matter, as Oedipus, and Segismundo in Calderón de la Barca's mastepiece *Life Is a Dream*, famously show. Just as important are Preciosa's and Andrés's creation of identities; he, a young nobleman, willfully turns into a Gypsy to gain Preciosa's love and acceptance by her people. The idea of undergoing a rigorous test to make oneself worthy of a woman is also a traditional motif. Preciosa plays to the hilt the role of the captivating young Gypsy woman, endowed with the talents of such an individual. She can sing, dance, and be alluring to all, particularly to men, which makes her seductive and profitable, a crucial trait for Gypsies, whose main occupation is robbery, but also charming others out of their wealth. Later, Preciosa will have to learn to be the young aristocrat that she was from birth, but this comes easy to her.

The restitution of her true kinship at the end follows precise legal strictures, as if to underline the gravity of the matter which, after all, began with a crime: her abduction by the Gypsies. The juridical allusion also highlights the picaresque setting of the story, with and against which Cervantes is working. The Gypsy camp appears as a scaled-down prototype of picaresque fiction, being that its denizens are criminal by nature and adhere to the rules of a self-invented but strict organization, like those of a novel. The main conceit of picaresque novels is that they portray the disorder of criminal low life, in contrast to mainstream society's order, but Cervantes's representation of it shows that the lower classes have, too, their own very rigorous internal organization. (It is in this feature that the brilliant Spanish criminologist Rafael Salillas found in Cervantes's works the origins of modern social science.) The Gypsy band is the inverted image of society, and the counterpart of the Neoplatonic perfection displayed by Preciosa and her mores, whose backdrop is the pastoral. This conflicting combination of the real and the ideal is Cervantes's signature.

In "The Novel of the Little Gypsy Girl" Cervantes has rewritten the picaresque, mixing its strongest traits with features of Neoplatonic, idealist literature like the pastoral. But he has shown, in the character of Andrés, that the picaresque, which draws stories and characters from the legal archive purported to reflect reality and not literature, has turned into a literary paradigm, even providing a new role to play, like that of knight or shepherd. Andrés willfully becomes a kind of *pícaro* when he joins the Gypsies. When Cervantes returns to the picaresque in "The Novel of Rinconete and Cortadillo" and "The Novel of the Illustrious Scullery Maid," he again underscores that the protagonists of these novels choose to become rogues in a similar way to Alonso Quijano, the hidalgo who becomes Don Quixote, chose to become a knight. Picaresque life appeals to these young men, as it did to the first innkeeper in *Don Quixote* (a retired *pícaro*), because it is a life of freedom, without society's rules and restrictions. This is a constant in Cervantes: characters exercise their free will to turn themselves into whatever they want to be, which is often to play the role of literary characters.

In "Rinconete and Cortadillo," Cervantes sets the action in Seville, the capital of picaresque life, a bustling port through which Spain communicated with its vast empire, and a place were he spent a good deal of time sampling its most sordid sectors, including the city's jail. There is an immediacy in the portrayal of Seville that betrays these autobiographical elements. But, as in "La Gitanilla," Cervantes avails himself of literary, including most importantly theatrical, conventions. The eponymous young men join a gang of thugs run authoritatively by Monipodio, who rules crime in Seville like a business venture centered around his house, within which Cervantes sets memorable scenes that give the novel the air of a play, perhaps an interlude ("entremés") like those he excelled in writing. The action includes a sophisticated and hilarious altercation between Cariharta (Full Face), a prostitute, and her pimp Repolido (Hairless). He, whose baldness suggests a venereal disease, has beaten her badly, she claims, but it turns out that they engaged in consensual sado-masochistic sexual play. "The Novel of Rinconete and Cortadillo" does not have a very satisfactory ending; it reads like the prelude to a longer story. The young men leave the confraternity to get on with their lives, closing the picaresque period which took the form of a fun-filled education.

But the wake of "The Novel of the Little Gypsy Girl" is felt most strongly in two stories that rely on anagnorises and a young man's effort to gain the love of a young woman by passing an arduous test. They both center on a female protagonist made up of contradictory qualities that give titles to the novels: "The Novel of the Illustrious Scullery Maid" and "The Novel of the English Spanishwoman." How can anybody be an "illustrious" scullery maid, or even more implausibly, an "English Spanish" lady? Costanza, the product of the rape of an aristocratic widow, lives unaware of who she really is while working as a maid at the notorious "Sevillian's Inn" in Toledo. Isabella was abducted as an infant during the English raid on Cadiz and brought up in London by an English family. Both young women are gorgeous, of course, as well as virtuous. Isabella, brought up by covert Catholics, remains true to her Spanish roots, though she otherwise becomes a young English lady, soon courted by two young men of quality. Costanza is so famous for her beauty that two young men who have left home with a servant to study in Salamanca divert to Toledo to see her. They had, in any case, decided to abandon their studies to become *pícaros* in Seville. One of them, Tomás, falls madly in love with Costanza and devotes all his energies to making her his wife. He manages to do this after much effort and the unexpected appearance of Costanza's mother, which leads to the discovery of her true origins, and makes the marriage possible. The portrayal of life at the inn and its environs, featuring working-class people of the lowest classes, particularly carriers, is as detailed as that in "The Novel of Rinconete and Cortadillo." It includes much card playing. In one such game, Tomás loses his precious donkey, which he wanted to use to earn a living by carrying water, and recovers it through an elaborate trick that encrypts the very nature of the complicated text of the novel and the role chance plays in life, as Katherine L. Brown has shown in a brilliant essay. Meanwhile, Isabella's suitor, Ricaredo, to meet conditions to attain her established by none other than the English Virgin Queen Elizabeth herself, is forced to captain a fleet of ships that attack Spanish vessels. He is in the predicament of fighting against his own, meaning Catholics. After protracted adventures reminiscent of Byzantine romances that include a very conventional stopover in Rome, and the return of Isabella to her parents in Cadiz, they marry and live happily ever after, as did Preciosa with her Andrés.

The way Cervantes closed the volume of *Exemplary Novels* could not have been the result of chance or the editor's intervention. It is a very significant conclusion to the book because it involves two interconnected novels, and the final one is left unfinished, with a second part still to be told. It is as open-ended as can be. We have here Cervantes returning to his games of authorship by playing with the origins of his text, its reliability, and the roles of author and reader. To top it all off, the last novella is about two dogs who tell their stories to each other. The potentially fantastic element and the framing-tale structure hearken back to the origins of fiction, so it is clear to me that Cervantes is winding up his book with a meditation on storytelling and on writing. Although the enveloping novel appears to be a conventional one with, again, a realistic setting reminiscent of the picaresque, it is anything but that.

The protagonist is lieutenant Campuzano, who is staggering out of the Hospital of La Resurrección in Valladolid, where he has been treated for a bout of syphilis. He stumbles upon his old friend Licentiate Peralta, a lawyer, who invites him to his place for a meal to help him recover. There, Campuzano tells his friend how one night, while half asleep in the hospital, he overheard a conversation between two dogs, Cipión and Berganza, which he had committed to memory and then written down in a manuscript that he pulls out of his bosom and hands over to the licentiate. He also tells him how he came to be in the hospital, which is "The Novel of the Deceitful Marriage," the eleventh story in the book. That frame tale, for all its apparently standard adventures, is a novel told backwards. Whereas nearly all the other novels in the volume lead to a marriage (except the one about the old man married to the young woman, "The Novel of the Jealous Extremaduran"), here the action nearly begins with a wedding. The soldier, to have a good time, picks up an attractive woman—she is not beautiful—whom he plans to marry, and after a while, skip town and return to the army. She seems quite willing and offers the use of a substantial house where she seemingly lives. The woman, Estefanía, who is a prostitute, plans to bilk the soldier out of his money and jewels. Under these false pretenses they marry and move into the house, where they enjoy a brief period of matrimonial bliss. But the true owners of the house show up unexpectedly, Estefanía disappears with the jewels which Campuzano regrets—but not so much because he knows that they are fakes anyway. It is Estefanía, however, who has the last laugh because Campuzano winds up in the hospital with syphilis. So marriage, which in the *Exemplary Novels* stands for order, is used here for deceit and leaves the protagonists in a social, moral, and physical wilderness. Though quite funny, this is a very depressing ending. But all is saved by literature because, in the hospital, the ensign is inspired to write "The Dogs' Colloquy," a truly remarkable novel that is arguably the masterpiece of *Exemplary Novels*. It is, as it were, the child of the fraudulent marriage.

The debate as to whether the dogs could actually speak, or whether the ensign suffered a hallucination or (most probably) that he just wrote the story himself and created a fiction about its origins, is never resolved. The soldier has asked his lawyer friend, presumably trained in reading for the truth, to tell him if he should write the second part, for only Berganza's story is told, and the dogs had agreed that Cipión would go ahead with his tale the following night. Peralta tells him that he should proceed; that whatever the nature of the tale, it is good enough to deserve being completed.

Berganza's story is like a picaresque autobiography, and it includes a story about the dogs' origins and their ability to speak. They are presumably children of a famous witch who appears in the novel, but no conclusive evidence of this is given. The action takes place in Seville, of course, and the picaresque convention of a rogue serving several masters is easily worked into the tale because the dogs, naturally, have various owners who use them for different tasks, some illegal, to be sure. Their early lives center on Seville's slaughterhouse, filled with violence and blood, not all from animals, and peopled by criminals of all sorts. Cervantes's perversion of the picaresque is original, brilliant even, as people are observed from the perspective of dogs that can assume and express a detached critical attitude. Some of the episodes are hilarious. Cipión, meanwhile, is an informed, skeptical, and pedantic interlocutor who keeps Berganza to his story line by criticizing digressions, distractions, and unnecessary moralizing. He is a very funny editor in action who, with the lawyer Peralta, represents us, the readers, in the story.

If any writer encouraged his readers to read behind the story being told, it is Cervantes. In the case of Berganza's account of his life, it is possible to discern the ensign Campuzano's own veiled autobiography. His mother may have been a whore, we are led to suspect, like the witch who presumably gave birth to both dogs, and his childhood may very well have been like those of the animals in

Seville's sordid slaughterhouse. The untold life of Cipión, because of the dog's martial name (two famous Roman soldiers were named Scipio), could be Campuzano's embellished soldierly adventures, a Quixote-like life of heroic deeds, though, because of his punctilious concern with narrative form, it would also contain a bookish side. Cipión could then represent the marriage of arms and letters that Cervantes himself embodied, and provide through his story a synthesis of their timeless quarrel, potentially, as well as a mirthful self-portrait. But the reader is left waiting for it, eagerly anticipating that next night when Cervantes's fictional world would again awaken to bring us, the readers, renewed joy.

I cannot finish this introduction without acknowledging the crucial assistance that I have enjoyed from Matthew Tanico. This young *cervantista* helped me not just with technical issues and bibliographical queries, but was my interlocutor throughout. His observations and criticisms were invaluable and are reflected in the final product, whose failings are all my own, of course. I thank him sincerely and wish him well in what will no doubt be a distinguished career as a scholar and professor.

BIBLIOGRAPHY

Brown, Katherine L. "Invento del 'quinto cuarto': La conciencia dividida, la fragmentación textual y la paradoja de la lectura en 'La ilustre fregona.'" *Cervantes* (Fall 2016) 36.2.

Burningham, Bruce R. *Tilting Cervantes: Baroque Reflections on Postmodern Culture*. Nashville: Vanderbilt University Press, 2008.

Canavaggio, Jean. *Cervantes*. Trans. J. R. Jones. New York: W. W. Norton, 1990.

Cascardi, Anthony J. *The Cambridge Companion to Cervantes*. Cambridge: Cambridge University Press, 2002.

Castro, Américo. *El pensamiento de Cervantes*, nueva edición y con notas del autor y de Julio Rodríguez Puértolas. Barcelona-Madrid: Editorial Noguer, 1972. [1925]

de Armas, Frederick A. *Cervantes, Raphael and the Classics*. Cambridge: Cambridge University Press, 1998.

——. *Quixotic Frescoes: Cervantes and Italian Renaissance Art*. Toronto: University of Toronto Press, 2006.

Durán, Manuel. *Cervantes*. New York: Twayne, 1974.

Elliott, J. H. *Imperial Spain 1469–1716*. New York: St. Martin's Press, 1963.

El Saffar, Ruth S. *Novel to Romance: A Study of Cervantes' Novelas ejemplares*. Baltimore: Johns Hopkins University Press, 1974.

Flores, Ángel, and M. J. Bernardete, eds. *Cervantes across the Centuries*. New York: Dryden Press, 1947.

Forcione, Alban. *Cervantes and the Humanist Vision: A Study of Four "Exemplary Novels."* Princeton, NJ: Princeton University Press, 1982.

———. *Cervantes and the Mystery of Lawlessness: A Study of "El casamiento enga-ñoso" and "El coloquio de los perros."* Princeton, NJ: Princeton University Press, 1984.

Fuchs, Barbara. *Passing for Spain: Cervantes and the Fictions of Identity.* Urbana: University of Illinois Press, 2003.

Garcés, María Antonia. *Cervantes in Algiers: A Captive's Tale.* Nashville: Vanderbilt University Press, 2002.

González Echevarría, Roberto. *Celestina's Brood: Continuities of the Baroque in Spanish and Latin American Literature.* Durham, NC: Duke University Press, 1993.

———, ed. *Cervantes' Don Quixote: A Casebook.* New York: Oxford University Press, 2005.

———. *Love and the Law in Cervantes.* New Haven, CT, and London: Yale University Press, 2005.

———. *Miguel de Cervantes.* CD-ROM. Primary Source Media, 1998.

———. *Miguel de Cervantes's Don Quixote.* New Haven, CT: Yale University Press, 2015.

Hart, Thomas R. *Cervantes' Exemplary Fictions: A Study of the* Novelas ejemplares. Lexington: University of Kentucky Press, 1994.

McKendrick, Melveena. *Cervantes.* Boston: Little, Brown, 1980.

Nelson, Lowry, Jr., ed. *Cervantes: A Collection of Critical Essays.* Englewood Cliffs, NJ: Prentice Hall, 1969.

Riley, E. C. *Cervantes' Theory of the Novel.* Oxford: Oxford University Press, 1962.

Exemplary Novels

I should like, if it were possible, to spare myself the writing of this prologue, because matters did not go well enough for me following the one I
wrote for my *Don Quixote* that I should wish to repeat the experience with
this one. The fault lies with a friend, one of the many I have acquired in the
course of my life, more as a result of my good nature than my shrewdness; this
friend, as is the usual custom, could have engraved my likeness on the first
page of this book, and for that purpose I could have given him my portrait by
the famous Don Juan de Jáuregui. And that would have satisfied my ambition
as well as the desire of some who might have wished to know what kind of
looks and appearance belonged to one who dares to send out into the world so
many inventions and set them before people's eyes, writing beneath the likeness: "The man you see here, with the aquiline face, chestnut hair, smooth,
clear brow, joyful eyes, curved yet well-proportioned nose, silver beard that was
golden not twenty years ago, large mustache, small mouth, teeth neither short
nor long because he has only six, and those are worn down and badly placed
since they are not distributed in a symmetrical manner; his body lies between
the two extremes, neither large nor small, his coloring is vivid, more fair than
dark, and he is somewhat stoop-shouldered and not very light on his feet; this,
I say, is the appearance of the author of *La Galatea* and of *Don Quixote de la
Mancha*, and of the man who made the *Viaje del Parnaso*, imitating the one
by Cesare Caporali of Perugia, as well as other works that have gone astray and
perhaps are missing the name of their owner, who is commonly called Miguel
de Cervantes Saavedra. He was a soldier for many years, and a captive for five
and a half, when he learned to be patient in adversity. In the naval battle of
Lepanto he lost his left hand to a harquebus, a wound that, although it looks
ugly, he considers beautiful because it was acquired on the highest, most
memorable occasion witnessed by past centuries or that future centuries can
hope to see, as he served under the victorious banners of the son of the thun-
derbolt of war, Charles the Fifth, of happy memory." And when the memory
of my friend, about whom I am complaining, cannot summon anything else
to say about me except what has been said here, I myself could find two dozen
testimonies and tell them to him in secret, so that my name would be made

known and my talent recognized. For thinking that such panegyrics tell the exact truth is foolishness, because neither the praise nor the censure has a precise, specific limit.

Well, since this opportunity has passed, and I have been left unsatisfied and without a portrait, I will be obliged to speak for myself, using my own voice, which lacks eloquence but is fine for telling truths that even when told with gestures tend to be understood. And so I tell you again, kind reader, that in no way will you be able to make hash of these novels I offer you, for they have no feet, head, innards, or anything that resembles them. I mean that the amorous remarks you will find in some of them are so chaste and so moderated by reason and Christian discourse that they will not move either the careless or the attentive reader to any ignoble thought.

I have called them exemplary, and if you consider this carefully, there is none from which one cannot derive some edifying example; and if only not to prolong this matter too much, perhaps I could show you the delightful and virtuous profit that can be derived from all of them taken together as well as from each one by itself. My intention has been to bring out into the public square of our nation a gaming table where each person can be entertained, with no harm to anyone; I mean, with no harm to soul or body, because honest, pleasant pastimes are profitable rather than harmful.

Certainly people are not always in churches; they are not always found in small chapels; they are not always attending to their affairs, no matter how important those may be. There are times of recreation, when the afflicted spirit can rest. That is why walks are planted with trees, fountains are sought out, hills are leveled and gardens cultivated with care. One thing I shall dare say to you: if it happened somehow that the reading of these *Novels* could encourage the person reading them to any evil desire or thought, I would rather cut off the hand that wrote them than make them public. I am too old now to gamble with the next life, for at fifty-five I win nine more and my hand allows me to advance.[1]

My mind applied itself to this, my inclination leads me here, and what I believe is that I am the first to have written novellas in Castilian, for the many that have been published in this language have all been translated from for-

---

1. Born in September of 1547, the sixty-four years that Cervantes accounts for would bring us as late as the summer of 1612, approximately one year before the publication of the collection. The phrase "my hand allows me to advance" ("*gano . . . por la mano*") refers to the author's approaching birthday, which would add one more year to the count.

eign languages, while these are my own, neither imitated nor stolen; my wit engendered them, and my pen gave birth to them, and they are maturing in the arms of print. After them, if life allows, I shall offer you the *Trials of Persiles*, a book that dares compete with Heliodorus, unless, because of its boldness, it fares badly; and first you will see, and soon, the continuation of the deeds of Don Quixote and the delights of Sancho Panza, and then the *Weeks in the Garden*.

I promise a great deal, with the small strength I have, but who can rein in desires? I wish only that you consider this, that since I have had the courage to dedicate these *Novels* to the great Count of Lemos, they hide a mystery that elevates them.

That is all, except for this: may God keep you and give me the patience to endure the bad things that will be said of me by more than a few faultfinders and mollycoddles. Farewell.

TO DON PEDRO FERNÁNDEZ DE CASTRO

Count of Lemos, Andrade, and Villalba; Marquis of Sarria;
Gentleman-in-waiting to His Majesty; Viceroy, Governor, and
Captain General of the Kingdom of Naples; Knight-Commander
of La Zarza of the Order of Alcántara

Those who dedicate their works to princes almost always fall into two errors. The first is that, carried away either by truth or flattery, they expand the
letter called Dedicatory, which should be brief, succinct, very much to the
point, and circumspect, by recalling the deeds not only of the princes' fathers
and grandfathers but all their family members, friends, and benefactors as
well. The second is saying that they place their works under the princes' protection and care so that malicious, gossiping tongues will not dare to slash and
wound them. And therefore I, avoiding these two difficulties, do hereby pass
over the great deeds and titles of Your Excellency's ancient and royal house
with its infinite virtues, both natural and acquired, relinquishing them until a
new Phidias or Lysippus finds the marbles and bronzes to engrave and sculpt
them so they may endure for all time. Nor do I plead with Your Excellency to
place this book under your protection, because I know that if it is not good,
even if set under the wings of Astolfo's hippogriff or in the shadow of Hercules's club, those like Zoilus, the Cynics, Aretino, and Bernia will not fail to put
a keen edge on their condemnation, with no regard for anyone. I ask only that
Your Excellency observe that I am sending you, as if it were of no importance,
twelve stories, which, if they had not been composed in the workshop of my
mind, might presume to stand beside the most accomplished tales. There they
go, just as they are, and here I remain, very content, because I believe I am in
this way demonstrating the desire I have to serve Your Excellency as my true
lord and benefactor. May God keep Your Excellency.

From Madrid, the fourteenth of July of 1613.

Your Excellency's servant,
Miguel de Cervantes Saavedra

From the Marqués de Alcañices
to Miguel de Cervantes

Sonnet

If in the moral example and gentle
admonition of your deft and solemn lyre,
Cervantes, the reader observes the concept
in learned style, a paradise portrayed;

    let him look more carefully, for with art
your genius wished to derive from the lie
the truth, whose flame aspires only to make
the voluntary a necessity.

Memories offered up, it dedicates time
to the matter, so that in so brief a sum
all the extremes, made succinct, can find room;

    and a noble quality of your glories
is that one of them is due to your pen,
and the other to the grandeur of Lemos.

From Fernando Bermúdez y Caravajal,
Chamberlain to the Duke of Sesa,
to Miguel de Cervantes

    Bright, clear memory has made
the famous labyrinth of
that ingenious Daedalus
a work that is rare and strange;
but if your name were to reach
Crete and its monster so cruel,
they would award bronze and brush
to it when in different terms
they saw in twelve labyrinths
more skill and art than in his one.
    And if fair nature, in her
grand variety reveals
greater beauty and greater
artifice and artistry,

let Cervantes celebrate,
subtle, rare, and with more haste
this flowering April whose
variety astonishes
fast-moving fame that sees in him
a thousand varieties.

From Don Fernando de Lodeña
to Miguel de Cervantes

Sonnet

Abandon, oh Nereids, the chambers
built of crystal in your shadowy home,
their ceilings poorly made of lightest foam,
although with precious coral nicely trimmed;
    leave behind your most amenable spot,
oh Dryads, in the uncharted forest,
and you, oh most celebrated Muses!
abandon the overflowing fountains;
    all together bring a single branch of the
tree into which Daphne, metamorphosed,
showed the golden-haired god so much hardness,
    for though not intended for Apollo,
today she would be a green laurel wreath
circling the head of Miguel de Cervantes.

From Juan de Solís Mejía,
a Gentleman and Courtier,
to the Readers

Sonnet

You, oh reader, who have perused these fables,
if you contemplate the secret in them,
you will see they are the mounting for truth,
which puts on this disguise for your delight!
    Illustrious Cervantes, you knew well
our human inclination when you mixed

the sweet with the virtuous, and tempered it
to make silver armor for body and soul.
    Rich and sumptuous you stride, Philosophy,
now moral doctrine, for in this raiment
there will be none to despise you or to mock;
    if now you lack a company around you,
never expect the mortal human line
to honor your virtue and your majesty.

THE NOVEL OF THE LITTLE GYPSY GIRL

It seems that Gypsies were born into the world only to be thieves; they are born of thieving parents, grow up with thieves, study to be thieves, and finally, in the end, become very common thieves under any and all circumstances, and desiring to steal and stealing are, in them, like inseparable accidental qualities that cannot be shed except in death. An old Gypsy woman of this nation, who could hold a professor's chair in the science of Cacus,[1] brought up a girl as if she were her granddaughter, gave her the name of Preciosa, and taught her all her Gypsy tricks, forms of deception, and ways of stealing. This girl Preciosa turned out to be the most extraordinary dancer in all of Gypsydom, and the most beautiful and discerning girl that one could find, not only among the Gypsies but also all those girls renowned for their beauty and good judgment. Neither the sun, nor the wind, nor all the inclement weather of heaven to which the Gypsies, more than other people, are subject could blemish her face or roughen her hands; what is more, the coarse surroundings in which she grew up revealed only that she had been born with greater gifts and qualities than other Gypsies, because she was extremely courteous and judicious. And with it all, she was somewhat bold, but not in a manner that would reveal any kind of immodesty. On the contrary, along with her cleverness, she was so virtuous that in her presence no Gypsy woman, old or young, dared to sing lascivious songs or say indecent words. In short, her grandmother knew the treasure she had in her granddaughter, and so the old eagle decided to take her eaglet out to fly and teach her how to survive by her own efforts.

As it turned out, Preciosa possessed a wealth of carols, songs, sarabandes, and other verses, especially ballads, which she sang with particular charm. For her cunning grandmother realized that such songs and skills in her granddaughter, given her youth and great beauty, would be desirable attractions and incentives to increase her fortune; and therefore she obtained the songs

1. According to Roman mythology, Cacus was the fire-breathing son of Vulcan. He is known for having stolen cattle from the giant Geryon, which led to his death at the hand of Hercules. Thus, the "science of Cacus" is thievery.

and searched for them wherever she could, and there was no lack of poets who gave them to her, for there are also poets who get along with Gypsies and sell them their works, as there are poets for the blind who counterfeit their miracles and give the poets a share of their earnings. Everything exists in the world, and the fact of hunger perhaps forces intellects to venture into areas not found on the map.

Preciosa grew up in various parts of Castilla, and when she was fifteen the girl's supposed grandmother returned her to the capital and her old encampment on the fields of Santa Bárbara, where the Gypsies usually locate their camps, planning to sell her merchandise in the capital, where everything is bought and sold. And Preciosa's first appearance in Madrid was on the day of Santa Ana, patron saint and defender of the city, in a dance with eight Gypsy women, four old and four young, and one man, a great dancer, who led them. And although they were all clean and well dressed, the charm of Preciosa was so great that little by little the eyes of everyone who looked at her succumbed to love. From the notes of the tabour and castanets and the most intense moment of the dance came a sound that heightened the beauty and grace of the Gypsy girl, and the boys ran to see her and the men to watch her. But when they heard her sing, for there was singing along with the dance, that was the high point, that was when the fame of the Gypsy girl took its first breath, and by the mutual agreement of the festival officials she was distinguished immediately as the treasure and jewel of the best dance; and when it was time to perform in the Church of Santa María, before the image of Santa Ana, after all the others had danced, Preciosa took a small tambourine, and to its sound, making long, light turns, she sang this ballad:

> O, most precious tree
> late in bearing fruit,
> years that could have dressed
> her in mourning black,
> and made the pure
> desires of her consort
> not very certain,
> countered to their hope;
> and from that delay
> was born the chagrin
> that ejected from
> the temple a most

just and righteous man;
barren sainted earth,
that at last produced
the rich plenitude
that sustains the world;
the mint where the mold
was forged that gave to
God the form He had
as a man; mother
of a daughter in
whom God chose to show
His grandeur divine
in a human coin.
For your own sake and
for hers, Ana, you are
the refuge where our
afflictions and woes
seek a remedy.
In a certain way
you, I have no doubt,
over your grandson
have just and clement
sway. Belonging to
that supernal line
you would give consent
to myriad kin.
What a daughter she was!
What a grandson! And
what a son-in-law!
With no delay, and
with just cause, you might
triumphant have sung.
But you, humbly, went
with your daughter to
learn humility,
and now at her side,
closest to God, you
delight in bliss I
can only surmise.

Preciosa's singing filled everyone who heard her with admiration. Some said: "God bless you, girl!" Others said: "What a shame this child is a Gypsy. The truth is, the truth is she deserves to be the daughter of a great lord." Others were coarser and said: "Let the youngster grow up and she'll have her little tricks! She's weaving a nice tight net inside to ensnare hearts!" Another, more amiable, coarser, and more foolish, seeing her move so nimbly in the dance, said: "Go on, child, go on! Enough about love, and stamp that dust fine!" And she replied, still dancing: "I will, the finest dust!"

Vespers and the Feast of Santa Ana were over, and Preciosa was somewhat tired, but so celebrated for her beauty, cleverness, and discernment, and for her dancing, that clusters of people were talking about her throughout the capital. Two weeks later she returned to Madrid with three other girls who had tambourines and a new dance, all of them well prepared with ballads and joyful tunes, but all of them modest; for Preciosa did not allow the girls in her company to sing indecent songs, and she never sang them either; and many people noticed this and thought very highly of her. Always with her was the old Gypsy woman, who watched over her like Argos, afraid that someone would steal away the girl she called her granddaughter; and the girl considered the old woman her grandmother. They began to dance in the shade on Calle de Toledo, and those who followed them grew into a large crowd; and as they danced, the old woman asked the onlookers for money, and *ochavos* and *cuartos* rained down like stones against a wooden target; for beauty also has the power to awaken sleeping charity.

When the dance was concluded, Preciosa said:

"If you give me a few *cuartos*, I'll sing a very pretty ballad for you about when Her Majesty Queen Margarita went to Mass for a Newborn in Valladolid, at the Church of San Llorente. I say that it's famous, composed by a professional poet with a rank like that of a battalion captain."

As soon as she said this, almost all those in the encircling crowd called out: "Sing it, Preciosa, and here are my *cuartos*!"

And the coins fell around her like hail, and the old woman had no rest picking them up. And so, having reaped her harvest, Preciosa took her tambourine, and in the manner of a *corrido*, sang this ballad:

> The greatest queen in Europe
> went to a Mass for the Newborn,
> and in her valor and her name
> she was a rich and noble jewel.
> As she captivates every eye,

she captivates too all the souls
of those who see and admire
her piety and her splendor.
And to reveal to all the world
that she is a part of heaven,
Austria's sun is on one side,
on the other, the tender Dawn.[2]
At her back a bright star attends;
it appeared unforeseen the night
of the day heaven and earth both
weep. If in heaven there are stars
that form bright shining chariots,
in others living stars adorn
their heaven. Ancient Saturn here
tends and ministers to his beard,
belated, but he moves apace,
for pleasure is the cure for gout.
The eloquent god comes in tongues
that flatter, amatorious;
Cupid is in diverse drawings
'broidered in rubies and pearls.
There goes the wrathful god of war
Mars, in the vigilant person
of more than one gallant young man
shaken by his own shadow.
Next to the house of the sun goes
Jupiter, for naught is toilsome
to favor based on prudent acts.
The Moon is found on the cheeks of
various human goddesses;
chaste Venus, in the comeliness
of those who compose this heaven.
Minute Ganymedes like cherubs
cross over, go, come back, return
along the ornamented waist

2. "Austria's sun" is King Philip III, the husband of Queen Margarita, and "the tender Dawn" is their daughter Anne of Austria. Many of the mythological references that follow correspond to various members of Philip's court.

of this most miraculous sphere.
For everything to amaze
and everything to astonish,
all generosity transforms
into utmost extravagance.
Milan with its opulent stuffs
goes there, a prodigious sight with
the Indies and their diamonds,
Arabia with its perfumes.
With those who are malicious goes
the slandering tongue of envy,
and kind goodness in the bosoms
filled with the loyalty of Spain.
Limitless gaiety and joy,
fleeing sorrow and affliction,
run through the streets and the plazas
unruly, wild, and almost mad.
Silence opens wide its mouth for
a thousand soundless blessings,
and the boys echo and repeat
whatever the men may intone.
One says: "O fertile grapevine, grow,
climb, embrace, and touch your joyous
elm, may it give you shade for a
thousand centuries, for your own
glory, for the greater honor
of Spain, for the defense of the
Church, for the terror of Islam."
Another tongue cries out and says:
"Long life to you, oh milk-white dove!
For you will give to us as heirs
two-headed eagles and their crowns,
to drive out of the air the rage
of ravening birds of prey,
and cover over with their wings
all their fearsome, threatening traits."
Another, more prudent and grave,
more wise and fine, more elegant,
joy pouring from his eyes and mouth,

says: "This pearl that you gave to us,
unique nacre of Austria,
how many schemes has she broken!
How many intrigues cut off!
How many hopes she inspires!
How many desires she thwarts!
How many fears she increases!
How many plights she overcomes!"
And then they came to the temple
of the holy Phoenix who in Rome
was burned and yet went on to live
in fame and radiant glory.
To the image of life, to the
lady of heaven, to the
one, who because she was humble
now steps on the stars up above.
To the mother who was Virgin,
to the daughter and the consort
of God, Margarita sinks to
her knees and says this in prayer:
"What you have given to me I
shall give to you, a hand always
bountiful; where your favor is
absent, there misery abounds.
My first fruits I offer up to
you, oh most beautiful Virgin,
just as they are, look at them,
accept them, help and better them.
To you I commend their father,
a human Atlas, whose back curves
under the weight of so many
kingdoms and places so remote.
I know that the heart of the king
abides in the hands of God,
and I know that you, merciful,
intercede with God all you wish."
When she came to the end of this
prayer, another like it is
intoned in hymns and by voices

that show glory is on earth.
When the offices are ended
with regal ceremonies this
heaven, this marvelous sphere,
returned to its starting point.

No sooner had Preciosa ended her ballad than from the illustrious audience listening to her, as serious-minded as a senate, a single voice arose and said:

"Sing again, dear Preciosa, you'll have no lack of *cuartos!*"

More than two hundred people were watching the dance and listening to the song of the Gypsy girls, and as that transpired one of the deputy mayors happened to pass by, and seeing so many people gathered together he asked what was going on, and they replied that they were listening to the singing of the beautiful Gypsy girl. The Deputy Mayor approached, for he was curious, and listened for a while, and to preserve his dignity, he did not listen to the ballad until the end; and since the Gypsy girl had seemed fine on all counts, he sent one of his pages to tell the old Gypsy woman to come to his house at nightfall with the Gypsy girls, for he wanted his wife, Doña Clara, to hear them. The page complied, and the old woman said she would come.

When they finished dancing and singing, they moved to another place, and as they did so, a very well-dressed page came up to Preciosa, handed her a folded paper, and said:

"Preciosa, sing the ballad written here because it is very good, and I shall give you others from time to time, and with them you will become famous as the best ballad singer in the world."

"I'll learn that very willingly," replied Preciosa, "and look, Señor, be sure to give me the ballads you've mentioned as long as they're decent, and if you want me to pay for them, let us agree to a dozen, a dozen sung and a dozen paid for; because thinking that I'll pay you in advance is thinking the impossible."

"Even if you give me money only for the paper, Señora Preciosa," said the page, "I'll be happy; and, if it turns out that the ballad is not good and decent, you will not have to pay for it."

"All I have to do now is choose them."

And with this they continued along the street, and from behind a grille some gentlemen called to the Gypsy girls. Preciosa went up to the grille, which was not high, and saw a good number of gentlemen passing the time in a newly decorated, very handsome room, strolling about or playing various games.

"Do you, Theñoreth, with to give me a tip?" said Preciosa who, as a Gypsy, spoke with a lisp, which is a trick of theirs, and not natural.

At the sound of Preciosa's voice, and a glimpse of her face, those who were gambling left their game and the walkers their stroll, and all of them came over to the grille to see her, for they had already heard about her, and they said:

"Come in, come in girls, in here we'll give you a tip."

"You'll pay dearly if you try to pinch us," replied Preciosa.

"No, our word as gentlemen," replied one, "you can come in, certain that no one will touch the welt of your shoe; no, by the insignia I wear on my chest."

And he put his hand over the insignia of the Order of Calatrava.

"If you want to go in, Preciosa," said one of the three Gypsy girls who were with her, "then go in and good luck to you, but I don't intend to go where there are so many men."

"Look, Cristina," replied Preciosa, "what you have to look out for is being alone with one man, not with so many together; on the contrary, when there are many of them it takes away our fear and suspicion of being offended. Know this, Cristina, and be certain of one thing: the woman who's determined to be upright succeeds even in the midst of an army of soldiers. It's true that it's good to stay away from dangerous situations, but those are secret, not public ones."

"Let's go in, Preciosa," said Cristina, "for you know more than a wise man."

The old woman encouraged them, and they went in; and as soon as Preciosa had entered, the gentleman with the insignia saw the paper she carried in her bodice, and going up to her he took it, and Preciosa said:

"Don't take that, Señor, it's a ballad that was just given to me, and I haven't read it yet!"

"And do you know how to read, my girl?" one of them said.

"And write," said the old woman; "I've brought up my granddaughter like the child of an educated man."

The gentleman opened the paper and saw a gold *escudo* inside, and he said:

"The truth is, Preciosa, this letter carries its postage on the inside; take this *escudo* that was inside the ballad."

"It's enough," said Preciosa, "that the poet has treated me like a poor girl. Because it's certainly true that a poet giving me an *escudo* is more of a miracle than my taking it; if his ballads come with this addition, let him copy all of the *General Ballad Collection* and send them to me one by one, and I'll take their pulse, and if they're harsh, I'll be gentle when I receive them."

Those who heard the Gypsy girl were astonished, not only by her good judgment but by the grace with which she spoke.

"Read it, Señor, and read it aloud; we'll see if this poet is as clever as he is generous."

And this is what the gentleman read:

> Sweet Gypsy girl, for your beauty
> people can pay you compliments,
> and for your stony attributes,
> Preciosa, they call you precious.
> One fact assures me this is true
> as you can see in yourself:
> lack of compassion and beauty
> is never divided, never.
> If as your worth is augmented
> your arrogance keeps increasing,
> to the age in which you were born
> I shall give nothing for the gain;
> for a basilisk grows in you
> and its merest glance is lethal;
> and dominion that although mild
> can seem like tyranny to us.
> Among poor folk and Gypsy camps
> how did such beauty come to be?
> How did the humble Manzanares
> give rise to this fine work of art?
> Because of this it will gain fame
> like that of the golden Tagus,
> and for the precious Preciosa
> more fame than the swelling Ganges.
> You say good luck and good fortune,
> but constantly bestow the bad,
> for your beauty and intention
> do not travel the same path.
> Because in the weighty danger
> of looking or gazing at you,
> your intention will excuse you
> and your beauty will lead to death.
> They say all the women of your
> nation are witches but your spells
> are the most powerful and real;
> after carrying away the
> spoils of every man who sees you,
> you place your spells on your own eyes.

With your powers you move forward,
for with your dancing you astound
us, kill us if you look at us,
enchant us if you trill a tune.
You cast spells in a thousand ways
whether you speak or are silent,
whether you sing or merely gaze,
or come near or move away,
you stir up the fire of love.
Over the most unfettered heart
you have dominion and command,
to which my own heart bears witness,
satisfied with your mastery.
Preciosa, precious gem of love,
this is written most humbly by
the man who dies and lives for you:
a humble lover, although poor.

"The last verse ends with 'poor,'" Preciosa said then, "a bad sign. Lovers should never say that they are poor, because, first of all, in my opinion poverty is the bitter enemy of love."

"Who taught you that, girl?" said one of the gentlemen.

"Who has to teach it to me?" replied Preciosa. "Don't I have a soul in my body? Aren't I fifteen years old? I'm not maimed, or crippled, or a fool. The wits of Gypsies follow a polestar different from that of other people: they are always older than their years; no Gypsy man is a dullard, no Gypsy woman is stupid. Since earning their living consists of being clever, astute, and good liars, they sharpen their wits constantly and don't let moss grow anywhere. Do you see these girls, my companions, who keep quiet and look like idiots? Well, put your fingers in their mouths and feel their wisdom teeth, and you'll see what you shall see. There's no girl of twelve who doesn't know what you know at twenty-five, because she has had the devil and experience for her teachers and mentors, and they teach in an hour what you may learn in a year."

What the Gypsy girl said astonished her listeners, and those who were gambling gave her a tip, and so did those who weren't. The old woman's purse picked up more than thirty *reales*, and richer and happier than an Easter Sunday, she gathered together her lambs and moved them ahead of her and to the house of the Deputy Mayor, agreeing that on another day she would return with her flock to the delight of those generous gentlemen.

Señora Doña Clara, the wife of the Deputy Mayor, already had been informed that the Gypsy girls would be coming to her house, and she was waiting for them with great eagerness, along with her ladies and duennas, as well as those of a neighbor of hers, all of them together to see Preciosa. And as soon as the Gypsy girls came in, Preciosa shone among them like the light of a torch among other, lesser lights. And so everyone hurried toward her: some ladies embraced her, others looked at her, some blessed her, others praised her. Doña Clara said:

"This really is hair of gold! These really are emerald eyes!"

Her neighbor analyzed Preciosa minutely and made a jumble of all her traits and features. And when she began to praise a small dimple that Preciosa had on her chin, she said:

"Oh, what a dimple! Every eye that looks at her will stumble into that dimple."

A squire with a long beard and longer years accompanied Señora Doña Clara, and when he heard this, he said:

"My lady, does your grace call that a dimple? Well, either I don't know much about dimples, or that's not a dimple but the grave of living desires. By God, the Gypsy girl is so pretty that if she were made of silver or sugar icing she couldn't be better! Can you read my fortune, my girl?"

"In three or four different ways," replied Preciosa.

"That too?" said Doña Clara. "By the life of my husband, the Deputy Mayor, you have to tell me mine, girl of gold, and girl of silver, and girl of pearls, and girl of carbuncles, and girl of heaven, which is the most that I can say."

"Touch her, touch the girl's palm, and as long as you make the sign of the cross there with a coin," said the old woman, "you'll see all the things she'll tell you; she knows more than any doctor of medicine."

The wife of the Deputy Mayor opened her change purse and discovered that she had no money. She asked her maids for a *cuarto*, but none of them had any money, and neither did her neighbor. Seeing this, Preciosa said:

"All crosses, because they are crosses, are good; but the ones made of silver or gold are better; and your graces should know that crossing a palm with a copper coin tarnishes the fortune, at least the ones I tell; and so I prefer to have my palm crossed first with a gold *escudo*, or a piece of eight, or a piece of four, at least; for I'm like the sacristans, who rejoice when there's a good offering."

"By your life, girl, you have wit," said the neighbor.

And turning to the squire she said:

"Señor Contreras, do you happen to have a piece of four? Give it to me, and when my husband the doctor comes back, I'll return it to you."

"Yes, I do," Contreras replied, "but I owe twenty-two *maravedís* for my supper last night. If you give that to me, I'll fly to get the piece of four."

"We don't have a *cuarto* among us," said Doña Clara, "and you're asking for twenty-two *maravedís*? Go on, Contreras, you always were impertinent."

One of the ladies-in-waiting, seeing how barren the house was, said to Preciosa:

"Girl, will it help to cross your palm with a silver thimble?"

"You can make the best crosses in the world with silver thimbles," replied Preciosa, "as long as there are a lot of them."

"I have one," responded the lady-in-waiting, "and if this will do, here it is, on the condition that you'll tell my fortune as well."

"So many fortunes for a thimble?" said the old Gypsy. "Granddaughter, finish up here, it's getting dark."

Preciosa took the thimble and the hand of the Deputy Mayor's wife, and said:

> Pretty lady, pretty lady,
> lady with silvery hands,
> your husband loves you more than
> the king of Las Alpujarras.[3]
> You are a dove without gall,
> but at times you are as untamed
> as a lioness of Oran,
> or a tigress of Ocaña.
> But in the wink of an eye
> all your ill temper is gone, and
> you are as sweet as spun sugar,
> as tame as a mild little lamb.
> You argue a great deal, and you
> do not eat very much, and you
> are always just a tad jealous;
> the Deputy is frolicsome,
> and wants to bring his staff close.
> When you were a maiden a man
> with a good face loved you dearly;
> bad luck to all the third parties

3. Hernando de Valor y Córdoba, also known as Abén Humeya, was the elected leader of a Morisco rebellion, the War of the Alpujarras (1568–71).

who destroy the tastes of others.
If by chance you had been a nun,
today you would rule your convent,
because more than four hundred lines
of an abbess adorn your palm.
I do not wish to tell you this,
but it is of no importance,
you will be widowed, then again,
and you will marry two more times.
Don't cry, Señora, my lady,
we Gypsy girls don't always say
the gospel truth; enough, don't cry.
If you should die first, that's enough
to cure a looming widowhood.
You will inherit, and soon,
a very large fortune; you will
have a son, a canon; the church
is not revealed. Impossible
in Toledo. You will have a
daughter, blonde and fair, and if she
enters an order, she will be
an abbess too. If your husband
does not die within four weeks,
you will see him become mayor
of Burgos, or Salamanca.
You have a mole like a moon, how
pretty it is! Ah, Jesus, what
a bright moon! What a sun that shines
its light on dark valleys there
in the Antipodes! More than
two blind men would give more than four
blancas to see it. Now is the
time for a titter! May the joke
be blessed! Be careful of falling,
in particular on your back;
that tends to be a great danger
to important, high-born ladies.
I have more things to say to you;
if you wait for me on Friday

you will hear them, they are pleasant,
and a few tell of misfortunes.

Preciosa concluded her fortune-telling, and at the same time aroused the desire of all the other ladies to know their fortunes, and all of them begged her; but she put them off until Friday, and they promised her they would have silver coins for crossing her palm.

Then the Deputy Mayor came in; he had been told marvels about the Gypsy girl; he had the girls dance a little and confirmed as true and accurate the praise that Preciosa had received, and placing his hand in his change purse, he indicated his desire to give her something, and having examined and shaken and scraped it many times, he finally pulled out his empty hand and said:

"By God, I don't have a penny! Doña Clara, give Preciosa a *real* and I'll repay you later."

"That's certainly a good idea, Señor! Yes, as if anybody here had a *real*! None of us ladies had even a *cuarto* for crossing her palm, and you want us to come up with a *real*?"

"Well, give her a little scarf of yours, or some other trifle; Preciosa will see us again another day, and we'll give her a better reward."

To which Doña Clara responded:

"So that she'll come back, I don't want to give Preciosa anything now."

"If you don't give me something," said Preciosa, "I'll never come here again. Of course I'll come back to please such important gentlefolk; but I'll know ahead of time that they won't give me anything, and I'll save myself the trouble of expecting it. Your grace should harvest a few bribes and then, Señor Deputy, after the harvest you'll have money, and don't take up new ways or you'll starve to death. Look, Señora, I've heard it said (and though I'm a girl, I know it's nothing good) that you have to get money from your office to pay for leaving that office and taking up a new one."

"That's what cold-hearted men say and do," replied the Deputy Mayor, "but the judge who reviews the case will not have to pay any judgment at all, and if you have performed your office well, he will be the advocate for their giving you another."

"Your grace speaks in a very saintly way, Señor Deputy," Preciosa responded. "You keep it up and we'll cut off pieces of your rags as relics."

"You know a great deal, Preciosa," said the Deputy Mayor. "Be still, and I'll arrange for their majesties to see you, because you're like one of the king's jesters."

"They'll want me to be a buffoon," replied Preciosa, "and I won't know how, and I'll lose everything. If they wanted me for my insight, they might still have me; but in some palaces buffoons prosper more than discerning people. I'm very happy being a Gypsy and being poor, and let my fate be whatever heaven wills."

"Oh, girl," said the old Gypsy woman, "don't say anymore, you've talked a great deal and know more than I've taught you. Don't be so subtle that you outsmart yourself; talk about what's right for your years, and don't be so proud that you fly too high, because every flight ends in a fall."

"These Gypsy women have the devil inside them!" said the Deputy Mayor.

The Gypsies said goodbye, and as they were leaving, the lady-in-waiting with the thimble said:

"Preciosa, tell me my fortune or give me back my thimble, because I don't have another one for my needlework."

"Señora," responded Preciosa, "pretend that I did and find another thimble, or don't do any embroidery until Friday, when I'll come back and tell you more fortunes and misfortunes than a book of chivalry."

They left and joined the many peasant girls who generally leave Madrid at dusk to return to their villages, and many others who come into the city, so that the Gypsy women were always accompanied, and returned home safe, because the old Gypsy lived in constant fear that her Preciosa would be stolen away from her.

It so happened one morning, as they were returning to Madrid with the rest of the Gypsy girls to collect their tributes in a small valley about five hundred steps before you reach the city, they saw an elegant young man richly dressed for traveling. The sword and dagger he carried were, as they say, like embers of gold, and his hat had a richly ornamented band adorned with feathers of various colors. The Gypsy women noticed him and began to stare, surprised that so handsome a young man would be in that place, at that time, alone and on foot.

He approached them, and speaking to the older Gypsy, he said:

"By your life, my friend, will you and Preciosa be so kind as to let me say a few words in private to you both, which will be to your benefit?"

"As long as it doesn't take us out of our way or take too long, that will be fine."

And calling to Preciosa, they moved about twenty steps away from the others, and as they were standing there, the young man said:

"I come humbly devoted to the good judgment and beauty of Preciosa, for after a great effort to avoid reaching this point, in the end I find myself more devoted and less able to avoid it. I, my ladies, for I shall always call you that if heaven favors my desire, I am a gentleman, as this insignia can demonstrate," and moving aside his short cape, he revealed on his chest one of the highest in

Spain. "I am the son of someone whose name, for good reasons, I shall not declare here; I am under his guardianship and protection; I am his only son, one who expects a reasonable inheritance. My father is here at court seeking an office; he has already been proposed and is almost certain of receiving it. And being of the quality and nobility that I have indicated, and which must be clear to you, with all of that, I should like to be a great lord in order to raise up with my rank the low-born status of Preciosa, making her my equal and my lady. I have no desire to mock her, and within the confines of the love I have for her, no kind of mockery has a place; I want only to serve her in the manner most pleasing to her; her wish is mine. For her my soul is of wax, where she can imprint whatever she desires; and to preserve and keep it, it will be not as if imprinted on wax but sculpted in marble, whose hardness withstands the passage of time. If the two of you believe this truth, my hope will not admit any discouragement; but if you do not believe me, your doubt will always keep me fearful. This is my name," and he told them his name. "My father's I have already told you. The house in which he lives is on this street, and this is its description; he has neighbors and you can get information from them, and even from those people who are not neighbors, for the quality of my father or his name and mine are not so obscure that they are not known in the courtyards of the palace, and even throughout the city. I have one hundred gold *escudos* here to give you as a dowry and guarantee of what I plan to give to you; for the man who gives his soul does not hold back his wealth."

While the gentleman was saying this, Preciosa looked at him attentively, and no doubt his words and appearance did not seem unattractive to her; and turning to the old woman, she said:

"Forgive me, Grandmother, for taking the liberty of responding to this gentleman who is so much in love."

"Respond however you wish, Granddaughter," replied the old woman, "for I know you have enough discretion for everything."

And Preciosa said:

"I, Señor, though a poor Gypsy girl and humbly born, have a certain creative spirit here inside, which leads me to great things. Promises do not move me, gifts do not make me fall to pieces, offerings do not sway me, and loving words do not astound me; and although I am fifteen years old or, according to my grandmother's count, I shall turn fifteen this day of San Miguel, I am already old in my thoughts and achieve more in that regard than my age promises, more because of my innate disposition than my experience. But because of one or the other, I know that amorous passions in those who have recently fallen in love are like unthinking impulses that put the will out of kilter, so that trampling over all obstacles, it throws itself madly after its desire, and thinking it will encounter the apple of its eye, it falls into a hell of sorrows instead. If it reaches what it desires, desire wanes with possession of the desired object, and perhaps opening then the eyes of its understanding, it sees clearly that it despises what it once adored. This fear engenders in me so much wariness that I do not believe any words and doubt a good number of works. I possess only one jewel, which I value more than life, and that is my wholeness and virginity, and I do not intend to sell it for promises or gifts, because in the end, that would mean selling it, and if it can be bought, it will not be valued very highly; and it will not be taken from me by schemes or lies; instead, I intend to take it with me to the grave, and perhaps to heaven, rather than endangering it and allowing chimeras and dreamed fantasies to assault or lay hands upon it. The flower of virginity is one that, as much as possible, should not be offended even in the imagination. When the rose is cut from the rosebush, how quickly and easily does it wither! One man touches it, another smells it, yet another pulls off its petals, and finally, it crumbles in rough hands. If you, Señor, have come only for this prize, you will not carry it away except attached to the bonds and ties of matrimony; for if virginity is to bend down, it will be for this holy yoke; for then it would not mean losing it but using it in festivities that promise joyous gains. If you should like to be my spouse, I shall be yours; but first there must be many conditions and assurances. First, I have to know whether you are who you say; then, this truth confirmed, you must leave your parents' house and move to our encampments, and putting on the clothes of a Gypsy, spend two years in our schools, and during that time I shall find out about your character, and you will find out about mine; after this, if you are satisfied with me and I with you, I shall give myself as your wife; but until then I must be your sister in our dealings with each other, as well as your humble servant. And you must consider that in the time of this novitiate, you may recover your sight, which is now lost, or at least clouded, and you will see that you ought to flee from what you pursue now with so much eagerness. And recovering your lost liberty, with honest repentance any fault will be pardoned. If, under these conditions, you wish to join our militia as a soldier, the decision is in your hands, for if any of these conditions is missing, you will not touch a finger of mine."

The young man was dumbfounded at Preciosa's words and seemed enthralled, looking at the ground, giving signs that he was considering how he should respond. And seeing this, Preciosa spoke to him again, saying:

"This case is not of so little importance that it can or should be resolved in the brief moments offered us here by time. Return, Señor, to the city, and consider slowly what suits you best, and in this same spot you can speak to me on any feast day you wish, as we go to or leave Madrid."

To which the gentleman responded:

"When heaven disposed that I should love you, my Preciosa, I resolved to do for you whatever your will should happen to ask of me, although it never occurred to me that you would ask what you have asked. But, since it is your pleasure that mine should adjust and accommodate itself to yours, count me as a Gypsy from now on, and have me experience whatever you wish; for you will always find me the same as I appear to you now. Tell me when you want me to change my attire, for I should like it to happen immediately; I shall deceive my parents and tell them that I am leaving for Flanders as a soldier and take enough money for a few days, and I can delay my departure for up to eight days. I shall be able to deceive the men who go with me so that I can achieve my purpose. What I ask of you (if I can dare now to ask and beg anything of you) is that if it is not today, that you do not return to Madrid to learn about my quality and that of my parents, because I would not wish for any of the countless opportunities that may arise there to waylay the good fortune that will cost me so much."

"Not that, young gallant," replied Preciosa; "you should know that with me liberty must always be untrammeled, not stifled or troubled by the weight of jealousy; and understand that I shall not take it as excessive if you notice from a good distance that virtue accompanies my boldness; and the first thing I want to ask of you and for which I would be grateful is that you must have confidence in me. For lovers who come demanding jealousy are either simple or presumptuous."

"You have Satan in your heart, girl," said the old Gypsy woman. "You say things a student at Salamanca wouldn't say! You know about love, you know about jealousy, you know about confidence; how is it that you've made me crazed and I listen to you as if you were a person possessed who speaks Latin without knowing it?"

"Be still, Grandmother," responded Preciosa, "and know that all the things you hear from me are trifling and not serious compared to the many truer things that remain in my heart."

Everything Preciosa said, and all the perception she displayed, added wood to the fire burning in the heart of the enamored gentleman. Finally, they agreed that in a week's time they would see each other in that same spot, where he would come to give an account of the state of his affairs, and the women would have had time to find out the truth of what he had told them. The young man took out a brocade purse that he said contained one hundred gold *escudos* and offered it to the old woman, but Preciosa did not want her to take it under any circumstances, to which the Gypsy woman said:

"Be still, girl; the best sign this gentleman has given of his surrender is turning over his weapons as a sign of his submission; and no matter the occasion, giving has always indicated a generous heart. And remember the proverb that says: 'God helps those who help themselves.' And besides, I don't want to be responsible for Gypsy women losing the reputation they've had for centuries for being greedy and shrewd. You want me to turn down a hundred *escudos* of golden gold that can be sewn into the gathers of a petticoat worth less than two *reales* and kept there like a landholding someone has in the pastures of Extremadura? And if through some misfortune one of our children, grandchildren, or kin fell into the hands of the law, would there be any help as good as the sound of these *escudos* reaching the ears of the judge and the court clerk and then their purses? Three times, for three different offenses, I've found myself on the point of being publicly flogged and humiliated and was saved from one by a silver jug, and the other by a string of pearls, and the third by forty pieces of eight that I had changed for pieces of four, giving twenty *reales* more for the exchange. Look, girl, we're in a very dangerous trade full of obstacles and unavoidable circumstances, and there are no defenses that help and assist us faster than the invincible weapons of the great king money: cases don't go past his *plus ultra*.[4] For a *doblón* with two faces, the sad face of the prosecutor and all the ministers of death look contentedly on us; they are the harpies of us poor Gypsy women and would rather fleece us and skin us alive than a highwayman would; never, no matter how ragged and wretched we are, do they think we're poor; they say we're like the doublets of the Frenchies from Belmonte: torn and greasy and filled with *doblones*."

"On your life, Grandmother, say no more; you're on your way to claiming so many laws in favor of keeping the money that we'll run out of the laws of the emperors; keep them, and may they do you good, and pray that God buries them in a grave where they may never see the light of day again, or have any need to. It will be necessary to give our friends here something; they've been waiting for us a long time, and by now they must be annoyed."

---

4. *Plus Ultra* ("Further Beyond") was the Latin motto of the Spanish monarchs beginning with Charles I. The motto was printed on Spanish coins as a banner adorning the Pillars of Hercules, the geographical point located at the Strait of Gibraltar that was thought to be impassable until the discovery of the Americas. Cervantes is alluding to bribery and corruption in the justice system.

"They're as likely to see a single coin of all these," replied the old woman, "as they are to see the Turk right now! This good gentleman will see if he has some silver coins left, some *cuartos,* and he can distribute them, because these women will be satisfied with very little."

"I do have some," said the young man.

And he took from his purse three pieces of eight, which he divided among the three Gypsy girls, and they were happier and more satisfied than a playwright when, in competition with another, his name is written on the walls with the words "Victor, Victor."[5]

In short, they agreed, as we have said, to meet there in a week's time, and that when he was a Gypsy his name would be Andrés Caballero, because there were Gypsy men among them with that last name.

Andrés, which is what we shall call him from now on, did not dare embrace Preciosa; instead, he sent his soul to her with his eyes, and without it, in a manner of speaking, he left them and entered Madrid, and the Gypsies, feeling very happy, did the same. Preciosa, tending to favor, more out of benevolence than love, the gallant disposition of Andrés, wanted to find out if he was who he'd said he was. She entered Madrid, and after walking past a few streets, she encountered the page, poet of the ballads and the *escudo,* and when he saw her he approached and said:

"You've come at just the right time, Preciosa; did you happen to read the verses I gave you the other day?"

To which Preciosa replied:

"Before I say a word to you, you have to tell me the truth about something, on the life of what you love best."

"That's an oath," the page responded, "that even if saying it were to cost me my life, I would never deny under any circumstances."

"Well, the truth I want you to tell me," said Preciosa, "is if by some good fortune you happen to be a poet."

"If I were," the page replied, "of necessity it would be good fortune. But you should know, Preciosa, that the name of poet is deserved by very few; and so, I'm not a poet but a lover of poetry. And for what I need I'm not going to ask or search for anyone else's verses; the ones I gave you are mine, and these I'm giving you now are too; but that does not mean I'm a poet, God forbid."

"Is it so bad being a poet?" replied Preciosa.

---

5. This tradition began in universities where the names of students who passed examinations for high-level degrees would be written in red on the walls.

"It isn't bad," said the page, "but I don't think that being a poet who's alone is very good. Poetry should be used, like a precious jewel whose owner doesn't bring it out every day or show it off to everyone all the time, but only when it's right and proper to do so. Poetry is a beautiful maiden, chaste, moral, discerning, intelligent, modest, who remains within the limits of the highest discretion. She is a friend of solitude; fountains entertain her, meadows console her, trees calm her, flowers bring her joy; in short, she delights and teaches everyone with whom she communicates."

"With all that," Preciosa responded, "I've heard she is very poor, almost a beggar."

"Just the opposite is true, in fact," said the page, "because there is no poet who isn't rich, for all of them live content in their state, a wisdom that few achieve. But, Preciosa, what has moved you to ask the question?"

"I was moved," responded Preciosa, "because as I consider all or most poets to be poor, I was amazed by the gold *escudo* wrapped in the verses you gave me; but now, knowing you're not a poet but rather a lover of poetry, you might be rich, though I doubt it, because the part of you that writes verses must consume any wealth you might have; for there is no poet, they say, who knows how to retain the wealth he has, or acquire the wealth he doesn't have."

"Well, I'm not one of them," replied the page. "I write verses, and I'm neither rich nor poor; without regretting or ignoring it, as the Genoese do with their guests,[6] I can easily give an *escudo* or two to whomever I choose. Here, Precious Pearl, take this second paper and the second *escudo* inside it, without thinking about whether I'm a poet or not; I want only for you to think and believe that the man who gives you this would like to have the riches of Midas to give to you."

And he handed her a paper, and Preciosa felt it and found an *escudo* inside, and said:

"This paper will live for many years because it brings two souls with it: the soul of the *escudo* and that of the verses, which always are full of *souls* and *hearts*. But Señor Page should know I don't want so many souls with me, and if he doesn't remove one, there's no chance I'll receive the other; I love him as a poet, not as a generous man, and in this way we shall have a lasting friendship; for an *escudo* may be missed, no matter how heavy, more easily than the charm of a ballad."

"Well, if what you want, Preciosa," replied the page, "is for me to be poor of necessity, do not reject the soul I send to you in this paper and return the

6. It was a common stereotype in Spain that the Genovese were stingy despite their economic prosperity.

escudo; for since you have touched it with your hand, I shall consider it a relic for as long as I live."

Preciosa removed the *escudo* from the paper and kept the paper, and did not wish to read it on the street. The page said goodbye and left very happily, believing that Preciosa had already surrendered since she had spoken to him so amiably.

And as she was determined to find the house of Andrés's father, and did not wish to stop and dance anywhere, she was soon on the street where the residence was located, a street she knew very well; and having walked half its length, she looked up at a gilded iron balcony that she had been told was a feature of the house, and saw a gentleman of fifty or so who had venerable gravity and presence, and wore the insignia of a red cross on his chest; as soon as he saw the Gypsy girl, he said:

"Come up, girls, you'll be given alms here."

After he spoke three other gentlemen came out to the balcony, and among them was the enamored Andrés who, when he saw Preciosa, paled and almost passed out, so great was his shock at seeing her. All the Gypsies went up except the old Gypsy, who remained below to learn from the servants the truth about Andrés.

When the Gypsy girls entered the salon, the old gentleman was saying to the others:

"She undoubtedly is the beautiful Gypsy girl people say is now in Madrid."

"She is," replied Andrés, "and no doubt is the most beautiful creature ever seen."

"That's what they say," said Preciosa, who heard their conversation as she came in, "but the truth is they are sadly mistaken. Pretty, I do think I'm that, but as beautiful as they say, I wouldn't think so."

"By the life of my son, Don Juanico," said the old man, "you're even more beautiful than they say, lovely Gypsy!"

"And who is your son, Don Juanico?" asked Preciosa.

"That elegant young man beside you," responded the gentleman.

"The truth is I thought," said Preciosa, "that your grace was swearing by a child of two. Look at what a Don Juanico he is, what a jewel! I believe he might already be married, and as he has a few lines on his forehead, not three years will pass before he is, and very happily if from now on he doesn't lose his way or change his mind."

"That's enough!" said one of the gentlemen. "What does the Gypsy girl know about lines?"

This was when the three Gypsy girls with Preciosa all gathered in a corner of the room, and imposing silence on one another, huddled together in order not to be heard.

Cristina said:

"Girls, this is the gentleman who gave us three pieces of eight this morning."

"That's true," they replied, "but let's not mention it or say anything to him, if he doesn't speak to us. Who knows? Perhaps he wants to conceal it."

As the three girls were talking, Preciosa responded to the question about lines:

"What I see with my eyes, I guess at with my finger; without lines, what I know about Don Juanico is that he's easily infatuated, impetuous and reckless, and likely to promise things that seem impossible; and please God that he's not deceitful, which would be the worst of all. He's supposed to travel now, very far from here, but the bay thinks one thing and the man saddling him another; man proposes, and God disposes; perhaps he thinks he'll be with the Oñez faction and meets up with the Gamboa party instead."[7]

To which Don Juan responded:

"In truth, Gypsy, you're right about many aspects of my nature; but as for my being deceitful, you're very far from correct, because I boast of always telling the truth. As for the long trip, you're right, for God willing, within four or five days I shall leave for Flanders, though you threaten I'll lose my way, and I shouldn't want any mishap to occur that might hinder me."

"Be still, young gentleman," responded Preciosa, "and put your trust in God that everything will be fine. You should know that I don't know anything about what I say, and it's no wonder that since I talk a great deal about a great many things, I'm right about some things at times, and I would like to be right about persuading you not to leave but to calm your heart and remain with your parents and give them a good old age, because I'm not comfortable with this going back and forth to Flanders, particularly in lads as young as you; wait until you're a little older, so that you can bear the difficulties of war, especially because you have a good deal of war in your house; a good number of amorous battles assail your heart. Be calm, be calm, impetuous boy, and consider what you're doing before you marry, and give us some alms for the love of God and for the sake of who you are, for the truth is I believe you are well born. And if this is combined with your being truthful, I'll celebrate everything that happens with the victory of having been correct in everything I've told you."

"I'll tell you again, my girl," responded Don Juan who was to be Andrés Caballero, "that you are correct in everything except the fear you have that

---

7. The Oñez and Gamboa were rival clans from the Basque region.

I'm not very truthful; about this you are deceived, there can be no doubt. The promise I give in the countryside I'll keep in the city and any place else, without being asked, for no one can consider himself a gentleman who engages in the vice of lying. My father will give you alms for God's sake and for mine; for the truth is that this morning I gave all I had to some ladies, who because they were as pleasing as they were beautiful, especially one of them, I don't regret their gain."

Cristina, hearing this, with the same caution as before, said to the other Gypsies:

"Oh, girls, let them kill me if he's not saying this because of the three pieces of eight he gave us this morning!"

"That isn't so," responded one of the two other girls, "because he said they were ladies, and we aren't. And if he's as truthful as he says, he wouldn't lie about this."

"It isn't so serious a lie," responded Cristina, "when it's told without harming anyone, and to the advantage and credit of the person who says it. But even so, I see that they're not giving us anything or having us dance."

The old Gypsy woman came up and said:

"Granddaughter, finish up, it's late and there's a great deal to do and more to say."

"What's the news, Grandmother?" asked Preciosa. "Is it a boy or a girl?"

"A boy, and a very handsome one," responded the old woman. "Come, Preciosa, and you'll hear true marvels."

"Pray God she doesn't die of the lying-in!" said Preciosa.

"Everything will be fine," replied the old woman, "especially because so far everything has been straightforward, and the infant is pure gold."

"Has someone given birth?" asked the father of Andrés Caballero.

"Yes, Señor," responded the Gypsy, "but the birth has been so secret that only Preciosa and I, and one other person, know about it; and so we can't tell you who the lady is."

"Nor do we wish to know that here," said one of the men present, "but woe to her who entrusts her secret to your tongues and her honor to your assistance."

"Not all of us are bad," responded Preciosa. "Perhaps there is one among us who values her discretion and truthfulness as much as the most admirable man in this room. Let's go, Grandmother, they don't think very highly of us here. And the truth is that we're not thieves and don't beg anything from anyone!"

"Don't be angry, Preciosa," said the father, "for, at least as far as you're concerned, I imagine no one can presume anything bad, for your virtuous face is the guarantor and surety of your good works. By Preciosita's life, dance a while with your companions, and I have here a gold *doblón* with two heads, and neither one is like yours, even though they belong to two monarchs."

As soon as the old woman heard this, she said:

"Come along, girls, tuck up your skirts and do what these gentlemen ask!"

Preciosa picked up the castanets, and the girls made their turns and danced their figures with so much charm and ease that their feet were followed by the eyes of everyone watching, in particular those of Andrés, fixed on Preciosa's feet as if the center of his glory were to be found there. But as luck would have it, that glory turned into an inferno for him; for in the movements of the dance Preciosa let fall the paper the page had given her, and as soon as it fell, the man who did not have a good opinion of the Gypsies picked it up, opened it immediately, and said:

"Well, well, we have ourselves a sonnet. Stop the dance and listen to it, because according to the first line, it really isn't foolish at all."

To Preciosa's sorrow, she did not know what was in it, and she begged them not to read it and return it to her, and all the urgency she brought to her plea was like spurs to Andrés's desire to hear it. Finally, the gentleman read it aloud, and this is what it said:

> When Preciosa plays the tambourine
> and its sweet sound pierces the empty air,
> those are pearls pouring from her hands; and
> those are flowers flowing from her mouth;
>   my soul is left perplexed, my mind made mad
> by those gentle gestures, unearthly actions
> which are so pure, so modest, so honest
> that her fame reaches up to highest heaven.
>   Hanging from the least of her strands of hair
> she bears a thousand souls, and at her feet
> Love has humbled both the arrows he shoots.
>   Her beautiful suns blind and illuminate,
> Love maintains his empire with those arrows,
> and suspects even more grandeur in her.

"By God," said the man who read the sonnet, "the poet who wrote this has great charm!"

"He isn't a poet, Señor, he's a very gallant and honest page," said Preciosa.

(Consider what you've said, Preciosa, and what you are going to say, for these are not praises of the page but lances that run through the heart of

Andrés, who hears them. Do you want to see it, my girl? Well, look around and you will see him collapsed on the chair, in a deathly sweat. Do not think, young maiden, that Andrés's love for you is so casual that the slightest careless-ness on your part does not strike and wound him. Go up to him at a fortunate moment and say a few words in his ear that will go straight to his heart and bring him back from his swoon. No, just bring sonnets every day written in your praise, and you will see what a state they put him in.)

All this occurred as it has been described: Andrés, upon hearing the son-net, was assailed by a thousand jealous imaginings. He did not faint but paled so much that his father, on seeing him, said:

"What is it, Don Juan? You look as if you're about to faint, you've turned so white."

"Wait a moment," said Preciosa, "let me say some words in his ear, and you'll see that he won't lose consciousness."

And going up to him, she said, almost without moving her lips:

"A fine spirit for a Gypsy! Andrés, how will you withstand the water torture when you can't bear the one of paper?"

And making the sign of the cross half a dozen times over his heart, she moved away from him, and then Andrés breathed a little and made it clear that Preciosa's words had done him good.

Finally, the *doblón* with two heads was given to Preciosa, and she told her companions she would change it and generously share it with them. Andrés's father told her to write down for him the words she had said to Don Juan, for he wanted to keep them always. She said she would be happy to say them, and those present should understand that, although they might seem a joke, they had a special virtue to protect against heartache and vertigo, and the words were:

> Oh dear sweet head, oh dear sweet head,
> endure, and don't be downhearted,
> and prepare at least two supports
> for blessed patience, a virtue.
> Ask and pray for
> an engaging
> self-reliance;
> don't be inclined
> to vicious thoughts;
> you will see things
> that may touch on miraculous,

> may God and His
> giant, St. Christopher, help you.

"Say half of these words, and make the sign of the cross six times over the heart of the person with vertigo," said Preciosa, "and he will be as sound as an apple."

When the old Gypsy woman heard the incantation and the lie, she was dumbfounded, and Andrés even more so, for he saw that it was all an invention of her sharp wit. They kept the sonnet, because Preciosa did not wish to ask for it to avoid giving Andrés another shock; for she already knew, without being taught, what it meant to give shocks and blows and fits of jealousy to devoted lovers.

The Gypsies said goodbye, and as they were leaving, Preciosa said to Don Juan:

"Look, Señor, every day this week is favorable for departures, and none is ill-omened. Plan to leave as soon as you can, for a full, free, and very pleasurable life awaits you if you wish to accommodate to it."

"In my opinion the soldier's life is not so free that it doesn't have more controls than freedom; but even so, when in Rome I'll do as the Romans do."

"You'll do more than you think," responded Preciosa, "and may God take you and bring you back with success, as your good bearing deserves."

With these final words, Andrés was happy, and the Gypsy women were very happy too, when they left.

The *doblón* was changed and divided equally among them, although the old chaperone always took one-and-a-half parts of what they collected, not only because of her age but because she was the compass that guided them through the abundant labyrinths of their dances, their charms, and even their deceptions.

The day finally arrived when Andrés Caballero appeared one morning in the place he had first come into, riding a rented mule and with no servants at all. There he found Preciosa and her grandmother, and being known to them, they received him with great pleasure. He told them to lead him to the encampment before it got any later and show him how to get there, in case someone came looking for him. The women, as if they had been warned, had come alone, and they turned and soon reached their shacks.

Andrés went into one, which was the largest in the encampment, and then ten or twelve Gypsies came to see him, all of them young men, high-spirited and handsome, whom the old woman had told about the new companion who would be arriving, with no need to tell them his secret; for, as we have already said, they obeyed her with uncommon sagacity and promptness. Then they looked at the mule, and one of them said:

"We'll be able to sell this on Thursday in Toledo."

"No," said Andrés, "because there's no rental mule that isn't known to all the mule drivers who move around Spain."

"By God, Señor Andrés!" said one of the Gypsies, "even if the mule had more signs than those that will appear before the Day of Judgment, we'll transform her here so she won't be recognized even by the mother that bore her or the owner that raised her."

"Even so," responded Andrés, "this time you have to accept and follow what I say. This mule must be killed and buried where not even her bones will be found."

"What a sin!" said another Gypsy. "Take an innocent's life? Don't say such a thing, my good Andrés, but do one thing: look at her very carefully now, so that all her markings will be etched in your memory, and let me take her, and if you recognize her in two hours, let them baste me like a runaway black."

"In no way shall I consent," said Andrés, "to the mule not dying, no matter how you assure me of her transformation. I'm afraid of being found out if she's not in the ground. And if you do it for the profit you can earn from selling her, I haven't come to this brotherhood so naked that I can't pay more than a few mules are worth to get in."

"Well, if that's what Señor Andrés Caballero wants," said another Gypsy, "let the blameless mule die, and God knows how much it pains me, as much for her youth, for her teeth haven't evened out yet, not a usual thing among rental mules, as for the fact that she must be a good one since she doesn't have scabs on her flanks or sores from spurs."

Her death was put off until evening, and in what remained of the day they performed the ceremonies for Andrés becoming a Gypsy, which were these: they immediately stripped one of the best shacks in the encampment and decorated it with branches and fragrant sedge, and sitting Andrés on half a cork oak, placed in his hands a hammer and tongs, and to the sound of two guitars played by two Gypsies, they had him leap twice; then they bared one arm, and with a strip of new silk and a garrote they gave it two gentle turns.

Preciosa witnessed everything, and many other Gypsy women, old and young, looked at him, some with amazement and others with love; Andrés's nature was so elegant that even the Gypsy men were taken with him.

When these ceremonies were completed, an old Gypsy man took Preciosa by the hand and, standing in front of Andrés, he said:

"This girl, who is the cream of all the beautiful Gypsy girls who we know live in Spain, we give to you as your wife or your lover; as far as that's concerned, you can do whatever you choose, because this free life of ours isn't subject to affectations or many ceremonies. Look at her carefully, and see if she pleases you or if you see in her something you don't like, and if you do, choose among the girls who are here the one you like best, and we will give you the one you prefer; but you must know that once you have chosen her, you cannot leave her for another or interfere or meddle with either married women or maidens. We hold the law of friendship inviolable; no man solicits the darling of another; we live free of the bitter pestilence of jealousy. With us, although there is a good deal of incest, there is no adultery; and when there is adultery in our own wife, or some cheating in our lover, we don't go to the law to ask for punishment; we are the judges and executioners of our wives or lovers; we kill them and bury them in the mountains and wastelands as easily as if they were dangerous animals; no relative avenges them, no parents ask for their death. Because of this fear and dread, the women do their best to be chaste, and we, as I've said, live securely. We have few things not held in common, except for wives or lovers, for we want each to belong to the man she was given to by fate. For us, age or death can be a reason for divorce. The man who wishes to can leave his old wife, if he's young, and choose another who corresponds to the taste of his years. With these and other laws and statutes we maintain ourselves and live happily; we are lords of the countryside, the sown fields, the forests, the woods, the fountains, and the rivers. The woods offer us free firewood; the trees their fruits; the vines their grapes; the gardens their produce; the fountains their water; the rivers their fish; the preserves their game; the rocks their shade; the ravines cool air; and the caves our houses. For us the inclemencies of heaven are gentle breezes; snowfalls are refreshment; the rain our baths; the thunder our music; and lightning our axes. For us the hard ground is a soft featherbed; the tanned leather of our bodies serves as impenetrable armor that protects us; shackles do not impede our agility, ravines do not stop it, walls do not limit it; our spirit is not stretched on the rack, impaired by the strappado, drowned in the water torture, or broken by wild horses. We do not differentiate between yes and no when it suits us; we pride ourselves more on being martyrs than confessors. Beasts of burden are raised in the fields for us, and purses are cut in the cities. There is no eagle or any other bird of prey that attacks its quarry more rapidly than we swoop down on profitable opportunities when they present themselves; and, finally, we have many abilities that promise us a happy ending; because in prison we sing, on the rack we're silent, we work by day, and we steal by night or, to put it another way, we advise no one to live negligently, careless about his wealth. Fear of losing our honor does not weary us, nor does the ambition to increase it keep us awake, nor do we ever take sides, nor do we wake at dawn to present petitions for employment, or to accompany magnates, or to solicit favors. We deem these shacks and movable encampments to be gilded ceilings and sumptuous palaces; our Flemish landscapes are those given to us by nature in the high crags and snowy peaks, broad meadows and thick forests, which meet our eyes at every step. We are rustic astronomers, because, since we almost always sleep outdoors, we always know the time by day and by night; we see how dawn corners and sweeps the stars from the sky, and how she comes out with her companion daybreak, gladdening the air, cooling the water, and dampening the earth, and then, behind them, the sun *gilding mountaintops*, as the poet said, *and crimping woodlands*; nor do we fear being frozen by the sun's absence when it wounds us askance with its rays, or burned when they touch us in particular. We turn the same face to the sun and to ice; to scarcity and to abundance. In short, we are people who live by our industry and our patter, and we do not follow the old saying about a man's future: 'Church, or sea, or royal house.' We have what we want, because we're content with what we have. I have told you all this, generous youth, so that you will not be ignorant of the life to which you have come and the kind of behavior you must put into practice, all of which I have sketched out for you; you'll discover an infinite number of other things in time, no less worthy of consideration than those you have already heard."

Saying this, the eloquent old Gypsy stopped speaking, and the new one said he was very happy to have learned such praiseworthy statutes, and that he intended to join an order so committed to reason and civilized basic principles, and that he regretted only not having come sooner into knowledge of so joyful a life, and from that moment on he renounced the profession of gentleman and the vainglory of his illustrious lineage and placed it all under the yoke, or rather, under the laws they lived by, for with such high recompense they satisfied his desire to serve them by giving him the divine Preciosa, for whom he would abandon crowns and empires and desire them only in her service.

To which Preciosa responded:

"Since these honorable legislators have determined by means of their laws that I am yours, and as yours they have given me to you, I have determined by means of the law of my will, which is the strongest of all, that I do not wish to be yours except on the conditions we both agreed to before you came here. You are to live for two years in our company before you enjoy mine, so that you do not repent of your haste and I am not deceived by mine. Conditions break laws; you know the ones I have laid down for you; if you wish to adhere to them, it may be that I shall be yours and you will be mine, and if not, the mule is not dead yet, your clothes are not torn, and you're not missing a penny of your money; you have been absent for less than a day, and you can use what's left of it to consider the best thing for you to do. These gentlemen can certainly give you my body, but not my soul, which is free and was born free and will remain free for as long as I should wish. If you stay, I shall think very highly of you; if you go back, I shall think no less of you; because, in my opinion, amorous impulses run free, until they come up against reason or disillusion; and I wouldn't want you to be with me like the hunter who, upon reaching the hare he is pursuing, catches it and then leaves it to pursue another that is running away from him. Eyes have been deceived that, at first glance, also mistake glitter for gold; but soon they know very well the difference between what is fine and what is false. This beauty of mine, which you say I possess and you value more than the sun and praise more than gold, how do I know that at close quarters it won't seem like darkness to you and, when you touch it, you will realize it is counterfeit? I give you two years to consider and ponder what will be good for you to choose or right for you to reject; for the article that, once purchased, you can never get rid of except in death, must be looked at and looked at again to see its faults and virtues; for I am not governed by the barbaric, insolent license these kinfolk of mine have taken in leaving their wives, or punishing them, whenever it suits them; and since I do not intend to do anything that calls for punishment, I do not wish the companionship of anyone who can cast me aside whenever he pleases."

"Oh, Preciosa, you are right," Andrés said, "and therefore, if you wish me to dispel your fears and dissipate your suspicions by swearing that I shall not deviate one iota from whatever you command, choose the oath you wish me to take, or any other security I can give you, for you shall find me prepared to do anything."

"The oaths and promises the captive makes to obtain his liberty rarely are kept when he is free," said Preciosa, "and the same is true, I think, of the lover's; for, in order to attain his desire, he will promise the wings of Mercury and the thunderbolts of Jupiter, which is what a certain poet promised me, and he swore by the River Styx. I do not want oaths, Señor Andrés, and I do not want promises; I want only to submit everything to the experience of this novitiate, and my obligation will be to protect myself when you may think yours is to offend me."

"So be it," responded Andrés. "I ask only one thing of these gentlemen and companions of mine, which is that they not force me to steal anything, at least for a month, because I don't think I'll be a very good thief if I don't have a good number of lessons first."

"Be still, my boy," said the old Gypsy, "for here we'll teach you to be an expert at the trade; and when you know it, you'll like it so much you'll eat it up with both hands. It's fun to leave empty-handed in the morning and return to the encampment at night loaded down with goods."

"I've seen some of those with empty hands return full of floggings," said Andrés.

"Nothing ventured, nothing gained," replied the old man. "Everything in this life is subject to a variety of dangers, and the thief's actions are subject to galleys, floggings, and the gallows; but because one ship runs into a storm or sinks, others will not stop sailing. It would be a fine thing if there would be no more soldiers because war devours men and horses! Besides, for us, the one flogged under the law wears an insignia on his back that seems better to him than the good ones worn on the chest. The point is for the flower of our youth not to end up kicking in midair for their first crime; because we don't think swatting flies on someone's back or beating water in the galleys are worth a bean.[8] Andrés my boy, rest now in the nest beneath our wings, and in due course we shall take you out to fly, and in a place where you won't come back without prey, and I mean what I said: you'll lick your fingers after each theft."

"Well, to compensate you," said Andrés, "for what I could have stolen in this time you've granted me, I want to divide two hundred gold *escudos* among all those in the encampment."

As soon as he said this, many Gypsy men ran toward him, picked him up, placed him on their shoulders, and chanted, "Victor, victor!" and "The great Andrés!" as well as "And long live Preciosa, his beloved wife!" The Gypsy women did the same with Preciosa, not without the envy of Cristina and some other girls who were present; for envy resides in the camps of barbarians and the hovels of shepherds as well as in the palaces of princes, and seeing my neighbor prosper when he doesn't seem more meritorious than I am can be very wearing.

After this, they ate lavishly; the promised money was divided with equity and justice; they renewed their praises of Andrés and extolled Preciosa's beauty to the skies.

Night fell, they killed the mule with a blow to the back of the head and buried her so that Andrés could be sure he would not be discovered on her

8. Swatting flies off one's back is a colloquial expression for being whipped.

account; and with her they also buried all her trappings, the saddle and bit and cinches, as the Indians do, who bury the dead with their most prized possessions.

Andrés marveled at everything he had seen and heard, and at the Gypsies' cleverness, and intended to follow and succeed in his undertaking without becoming involved in any way with their customs or, at least, to excuse himself from taking part by every means he could, intending to use his money to free himself of the obligation to obey them in any unjust thing they might tell him to do.

The next day Andrés asked them to change their camp and move away from Madrid because he feared being recognized there; they said they had already decided to go to the forests of Toledo and from there to steal and beg in the surrounding territory.

And so they broke camp and gave Andrés a young mule to ride, but he refused, going on foot instead, acting as attendant to Preciosa, who rode another mule; she was delighted to see how she had triumphed over her gallant squire, and he was similarly delighted to find himself next to the one he had made mistress of his will.

Oh powerful force of the one called sweet god of bitterness—a title given to him by our idleness and negligence—how truly you subjugate us, and how disrespectfully you treat us! Andrés is a gentleman, a young man of very good understanding brought up almost his entire life at court and indulged by his wealthy parents, and since yesterday he has changed so much that he deceived his servants and friends, disappointed his parents' hopes in him, left the road to Flanders, where he was to exercise his own valor and increase the honor of his lineage, and came to prostrate himself at the feet of a girl and be her lackey, and even though very beautiful, she was, after all, a Gypsy; a privilege of beauty that brings, grudgingly and unwillingly, the most liberated will to her feet.

Four days later they reached a village two leagues from Toledo, where they set up camp, first giving a few silver objects to the mayor of the town as a pledge they would steal nothing there or in the immediate vicinity. Having done this, all the old Gypsy women, and some young ones, and the Gypsy men, spread out through all the villages or, at least, those situated four or five leagues from the one where they had made their encampment. Andrés went with them for his first instruction in thievery, but although they taught him many lessons on that excursion, none were to his liking; rather, as was appropriate to his noble blood, each theft committed by his teachers tore at his soul, and on occasion he paid with his own money for the thefts his companions had committed, moved by the tears of the owners; the Gypsies despaired of this, saying it was contrary to their statutes and ordinances, which forbade the presence of charity in their hearts, for if they had it, they would have to stop being thieves, something that would not benefit them at all. And seeing this, Andrés said he wanted to steal by himself and not in anyone's presence, because he had the agility to flee danger and did not lack the courage to face it; and so he wanted the reward or punishment for what he might steal to be his alone.

The Gypsies succeeded in dissuading him from this resolve, telling him that occasions might arise when others would be necessary, both for attack and defense, and that one person on his own could not obtain great spoils. But no matter what they said, Andrés wanted to be a lone and solitary thief, intending to move away from the band and buy with his money something he could then say he had stolen, and in this way have as little as possible weighing on his conscience.

Using this stratagem, in less than a month he brought more profit to the company than four of its proudest thieves, which brought no small joy to Preciosa, seeing that her tender lover was so excellent and skillful a thief; and yet she feared some misfortune and did not wish to see him in disgrace for all the treasure of Venice, feeling obliged to show goodwill for the many services and gifts her Andrés had given her.

They spent a little more than a month in the environs of Toledo, where their August harvest was good even though the month was September, and from there they went on to Extremadura, for it was a rich, warm land. Andrés had modest, discerning, and loving conversations with Preciosa, and she gradually was falling in love with the judiciousness and fine manner of her lover, and similarly, if it was possible for his love to grow, it was growing; such was the virtue, good judgment, and beauty of his Preciosa. Wherever they went, he won the prizes and the wagers, running faster and jumping higher than anyone else; he played ninepins and hit a ball with great skill; he threw a short spear with great power and singular dexterity; in brief, in a short time his fame spread throughout Extremadura, and there was no village where they did not speak of the gallant disposition of the Gypsy Andrés Caballero and of his congeniality and ability, and along with his fame the renown of the Gypsy girl's beauty also grew; and there was no town, village or hamlet where they were not called upon to brighten the fiestas for their patron saints or for other, private celebrations. In this manner the encampment grew rich, prosperous, and content, and the lovers were happy just looking at each other.

As it happened, the encampment was in a grove of oak trees, some distance from the royal highway, and one night, in the small hours, they heard their dogs barking very urgently and more than they usually did; some of the

Gypsies went out, Andrés with them, to find out why they were barking, and they saw a man dressed in white trying to fend them off, for two of the dogs had him by the leg; the Gypsies arrived and freed him, and one of the Gypsies said:

"What the devil brought you here at this hour and so far from the road? Have you come to steal something? Because, my man, you really have reached a good port."

"I haven't come to steal," replied the man who had been bitten, "and I don't know whether I'm off the road, though I see very clearly that I'm lost. But tell me, Señores, is there an inn or a village nearby that can take me in and treat the wounds your dogs have made?"

"There is no village or inn where we could send you," responded Andrés, "but you will lack no comfort at our camp, where we can treat your wounds and give you lodging for the night; come with us, for we may be Gypsies but won't seem so in our charity to you."

"May God show the same charity to you," replied the man, "and take me where you choose, for the pain in this leg is bothering me a good deal."

Andrés approached him along with another charitable Gypsy—for even among demons some are worse than others, and among many bad men there is usually one who is good—and the two of them lifted him up to carry him.

The moon was bright and they could see he was a young man with an agreeable face and figure; he was dressed all in white linen, and across his shoulders and encircling his chest he had a kind of linen bag or purse. They reached Andrés's shack or tent and quickly lit a lamp, and then Preciosa's grandmother came to treat the wounded man, for they had already told her about him. She took some hairs from the dogs, fried them in oil, washed the two bites he had on his left leg with wine, placed the hairs and oil on the bites and then a little chewed green rosemary; over that she very carefully tied clean cloths, and making the sign of the cross over the wounds, she said to him:

"Sleep, friend, with God's help it won't be anything."

Preciosa was present while his wound was being treated, and she was looking at him very closely, and he was looking at her just as closely; Andrés noticed the attention with which the young man looked at her but assumed it was because Preciosa's great beauty attracted all eyes. In short, after the youth had been treated, they left him alone on a bed of straw; they did not wish to ask him where he was going or any other question at that time.

As soon as they had left him, Preciosa called Andrés aside and said:

"Do you remember, Andrés, that I dropped a paper in your house when I was dancing with my companions, which, I believe, you found unpleasant?"

"Yes, I do remember," responded Andrés, "and it was a sonnet praising you, and not a bad one."

"Well you should know, Andrés," replied Preciosa, "that the person who wrote that sonnet is this young man who has been bitten and left in the hut; I can't be mistaken, because he spoke to me two or three times in Madrid and even gave me a very good ballad. He was there, I believe, as a page, not an ordinary page but one favored by some prince; and I tell you the truth, Andrés, that the lad is clever and well spoken and exceedingly modest, and I can't imagine why he has come here in this way and in those clothes."

"What can't you imagine, Preciosa?" responded Andrés. "The same power that made me a Gypsy has simply made him look like a miller and come here to find you. Ah, Preciosa, Preciosa, how we keep learning that you wish to boast of having humbled more than one man! And if this is true, finish me off first, and then kill this other one, and don't try to sacrifice us together on the altar of your deceit or your beauty."

"Lord save me, Andrés," responded Preciosa, "how delicately you move and from what a slender hair you've hung your hopes and my good name, for the hard sword of jealousy has entered your soul so easily! Tell me, Andrés, if there were artifice or any deceit in this, wouldn't I know how to be quiet about him and conceal who this young man is? Am I by chance so foolish that I would give you reason to doubt my virtue and good word? Be still, Andrés, on your life, and tomorrow try to remove from your heart this anguish over who comes and goes; it might be that your suspicion was deceived, as I am not, and he is who I've said he is. And for your greater satisfaction, for I have reached the limits of satisfying you, no matter how and with what intention this young man has come here, bid him farewell and have him leave, for all our people obey you, and no one will want to give him shelter against your will; and if this isn't true, I give you my word that I will not leave my shack, or let myself be seen by his eyes, or any others that you do not want to see me. Look, Andrés, it does not make me sad to see you jealous, but it will make me very sad if I see you lacking in good judgment."

"As long as you don't see me crazed, Preciosa," responded Andrés, "any other evidence will be worth little or nothing to indicate how far the bitter, hard presumption of jealousy can go, and how wearying it can be. But even so, I shall do as you command, and find out, if possible, what this page poet wants, where he is going, or what he is searching for; it might be that by means of a thread he carelessly displays, I may find the entire ball of twine with which I fear he has come to entangle me."

"I imagine," said Preciosa, "that jealousy never leaves the mind free to judge things as they are; jealousy always looks through spectacles that enlarge, making small things big; dwarves turn into giants, and suspicions into truths. By your life and by mine, Andrés, proceed in this and in everything that has to do with our arrangement, with good sense and understanding; if you do, I know you will have to grant that I have carried the day in modesty and prudence, and am faithful in the extreme."

Saying this, she took her leave of Andrés, and he continued waiting for daylight to take the confession of the wounded man, his soul filled with confusion and a thousand contrary imaginings. He could not help believing that the page had come there attracted by Preciosa's beauty because the thief believes everyone is like him. On the other hand, the satisfaction Preciosa had given him seemed so strong that it obliged him to be steadfast and leave his entire fate in the hands of her virtue.

Daylight came, he went to see the bitten man, asked his name and where he was going, and why he was walking so late and so far from the road, though he first asked how he was and whether he felt any pain from the bites. To which the young man replied that he was better and felt no pain at all and so could be on his way. As for his name and where he was going, he said only that his name was Alonso Hurtado, that he was going to Our Lady of la Peña de Francia to take care of a piece of business, and to get there sooner he had traveled by night; on the previous night he had lost his way and happened into the encampment by accident, where the guard dogs had done what he had already seen.

Andrés did not think this statement was legitimate but very much a bastard, and suspicions began to plague his soul again, and so he said:

"Brother, if I were a judge and you had come under my jurisdiction because of some crime that demanded that I ask you the questions I've asked you, the answer you've given would oblige me to tighten the cords of the rack. I don't want to know who you are, what your name is, or where you are going, but I'll give you some advice: if you have to lie during your journey, make your lie seem more like the truth. You say you're going to Peña de Francia, and that's to our right, a good thirty leagues behind the place where we are now; you travel by night to arrive more quickly, and you go off the road, through woods and oak groves that barely have trails, let alone roads. Friend, get up and learn to lie, and go with God. But in exchange for the good advice I've given you, won't you tell me one truth? You'll say yes since you know how to lie so badly. Tell me, are you by chance a person I've often seen in the capital, part page and part gentleman, who was known as a great poet, one who wrote a ballad and a sonnet for a Gypsy girl who was recently in Madrid and thought to be singularly beautiful? Tell me, and I promise by my faith as a Gypsy gentleman to keep the secret that it suits you to keep. And denying the truth that you are who I say you are is no escape, because the face I see here is the one I saw in Madrid. There's no doubt that the great fame of your understanding made me look at you very often as a singular and celebrated man; and so your appearance remained in my memory and because of that I recognized you, even though your clothes are different from what you wore when I saw you then. Don't worry, cheer up, and don't think you've come to a den of thieves; this is a refuge that will protect and defend you against the whole world. Look, there's something I imagine, and if the truth is as I imagine it, you have found your good luck in finding me. What I imagine is that, in love with Preciosa, that beautiful Gypsy girl for whom you wrote your verses, you came looking for her, for which I do not think less of you, but much, much more; for, although a Gypsy, experience has shown me how far the powerful force of love extends and the transformations it imposes on those it takes under its jurisdiction and command. If this is so, as I believe it undoubtedly is, the Gypsy girl is here."

"Yes, she is here, for I saw her last night," said the bitten man; a statement that left Andrés like a dead man, for it seemed to him that he had finally confirmed his suspicions. "I saw her last night," the young man said again, "but I didn't dare tell her who I was, because it wasn't to my advantage."

"That means," said Andrés, "you are the poet I mentioned."

"Yes I am," the young man replied, "I cannot deny it, nor do I wish to. Perhaps it may be that where I thought to lose myself I have found myself, if it is true that there is fidelity in the forests and a good welcome in the woods."

"There is, undoubtedly," responded Andrés, "and among us Gypsies, the greatest secrecy in the world. With this confidence, Señor, you can open your heart to me; for you will find in mine what you see, with no duplicity at all. The Gypsy girl is related to me and is subject to whatever I wish to do with her; if you want her as your wife, I and all her kin will be pleased; and if as a lover, we will raise no objection, as long as you have money, for greed never leaves our encampments."

"I have brought money," the young man responded. "There are four hundred gold *escudos* in these cloth bags tied around my body."

This was another mortal shock for Andrés, since carrying so much money could only be for conquering or buying the woman he loved; and with an already troubled tongue he said:

"That's a nice sum; you have to reveal yourself and get to work, for the girl is no fool and she'll see how advantageous it would be for her to be yours."

"Oh, my friend," the young man said. "I want you to know that the force that has made me change my clothing is not the power of love, as you say, or desire for Preciosa, for Madrid has beautiful girls who can and know how to steal hearts and subdue souls as well as and better than the most beautiful Gypsies; though I confess, the beauty of your relation is greater than that of all the girls I have seen. It is not love that has me in these clothes, on foot, and bitten by dogs, but my misfortune."

As the young man spoke these words, Andrés recovered the breath he had lost, for it seemed to him that the matter was moving to a conclusion different from the one he had imagined; and wanting to leave that confusion behind, Andrés reassured him again that he could make a clean breast of it, and so the young man continued, saying:

"I was in Madrid in the house of a nobleman, whom I served not as my master but as my kin. He had a son, his only heir, who, not only because we were related but because our ages and natures were the same, treated me with great familiarity and friendship. As it happened, this gentleman fell in love with a high-ranking girl whom he would gladly have chosen as his wife if, as a good son, his will were not subject to that of his parents, who aspired to arrange an even higher-ranking marriage for him; but he served her in secret, hidden from all the eyes, not to mention the tongues, that could have made his desires public; only I witnessed his intention. And on a night that misfortune must have chosen for the event I'll tell you about now, as the two of us were passing by the street door of this lady, we saw two men who appeared to be of good aspect leaning against it. My kinsman wanted to find out who they were, and as soon as he started toward them they very quickly put their hands on their swords and two small shields and came toward us; we did the same and attacked with similar weapons. The dispute did not last very long because the lives of our two opponents did not last very long: two thrusts guided by the jealousy of my kinsman, and my defense of him, were their downfall; a strange, rarely seen occurrence. In a triumph we did not desire we returned home, and secretly taking all the money we could, sought sanctuary in the monastery of San Jerónimo, waiting for daybreak, the discovery of what had happened, and the presumptions that would be made about the killers. We learned there were no clues at all about us, and the prudent clerics advised us to return home and not give or awaken with our absence any suspicion about us; and when we had decided to follow their advice, they told us that the magistrates had arrested the girl's parents and the girl herself in their house, and that among the servants whose testimony they heard, one of her maids told how my kinsman courted her mistress night and day; and with this clue they had come to look for us, and finding not us but many signs of our having fled, it was confirmed throughout the city that we had killed those two gentlemen, which is what they were, and very high-ranking too. Finally, following the opinion of the count my kinsman, and of the clerics, after hiding in the monastery for two weeks my comrade, in a friar's habit, went toward Aragón with another friar, intending to go to Italy, and from there to Flanders, until they saw how the case progressed. I wanted to divide and separate our fortunes so that our fates would not follow the same path; I took a road different from theirs, and in the habit of a friar's servant, I traveled with a cleric who left me in Talavera. From there I came here alone, off the road, until last night, when I reached this oak grove, where what you have seen happened to me. And if I asked for the road to Peña de Francia, it was to give an answer to what I was asked; for the truth is I don't know where Peña de Francia is, though I know it's above Salamanca."

"That's true," responded Andrés, "and it's on the right, almost twenty leagues from here; and you'll see what a straight road it is if you go there."

"The one I intended to take, however," replied the young man, "goes to Sevilla; I have a Genoan gentleman there, a great friend of the count and my kinsman, who usually sends a great quantity of silver to Genoa, and my plan is for him to find a place for me with the men who usually carry it; and with this scheme I'll surely be able to get to Cartagena and from there to Italy, because two galleys will arrive shortly to carry this silver. This, my good friend, is my story; you see that I can say it is born more of pure misfortune than painful love. But if these Gypsy gentlemen would like to take me with them to Sevilla, if they're going there, I'll pay them very well; my understanding is that in their company I'll travel more securely and won't be afraid."

"Yes, they'll take you," responded Andrés. "And if you don't go with our encampment, because I don't know whether we're going to Andalucía, you can go with another that I think we'll meet up with in a couple of days, and if you give them some of the money you're carrying, you'll make other, even greater difficulties easier."

Andrés left him and went to recount to the other Gypsies what the young man had told him and what he planned, with the offer he had made of good payment and recompense. Everyone thought he should stay with their encampment. Only Preciosa thought otherwise, and the grandmother said she couldn't go to Sevilla or its environs because some years earlier she had played a trick on a ne'er-do-well named Triguillos, who was well known in the city, having him stand in a large earthen jar of water up to his neck, naked and with a crown of cypress on his head, waiting for midnight to get out of the jar and dig up a great treasure she had made him think was somewhere in his house. She said as soon as the good ne'er-do-well heard the call to matins, in order not to miss his chance he tried to climb out of the jar so quickly that he and it

both fell to the ground, and the blow and the pieces of broken jar left him battered and bruised, all the water poured out, and he was left floundering in it
and shouting that he was drowning. His wife and neighbors came with lights
and found him gesturing like a swimmer, huffing and puffing and dragging
his belly along the ground, and moving his arms and legs very quickly, and
crying out, "Help, everyone, I'm drowning!" He was so overwhelmed by fear
that he really thought he was drowning. They put their arms around him, got
him out of that danger, he recovered his senses, told them about the Gypsy
woman's trick, and despite that, he dug a hole more than a meter and a half
deep in the spot she had indicated, even though everyone told him she had
deceived him; and if his neighbor hadn't stopped him, if he had allowed him
to dig as much as he wanted to, he would have brought both buildings down,
for he was digging at the foundations of his house. Everyone in the city heard
the story, and even the children pointed their fingers at him and talked about
his credulity and the old Gypsy's deception.

She told this story and gave it as her excuse for not going to Sevilla. The
Gypsies, who had already heard from Andrés Caballero that the young man
had a good amount of money, easily welcomed him into their company, offered to guard and conceal him for as long as he wished, and decided to take
the road to the left into La Mancha and the kingdom of Murcia.

They called to the young man and told him what they intended to do for
him; he thanked them and gave them one hundred gold *escudos* to divide
among themselves. This gift made them softer than fine leather; only Preciosa was not very happy about the sojourn of Don Sancho, which is what the
young man said his name was; but the Gypsies changed it to Clemente, which
is what they called him from then on. Andrés was also somewhat unhappy, not
satisfied with Clemente remaining, for it seemed to him that with little reason
he had abandoned his original plans; but Clemente, as if he had read Andrés's
mind, told him among other things that he was glad to be going to the kingdom of Murcia, since it was close to Cartagena, where, if the galleys arrived,
as he thought they would, he would easily be able to travel to Italy. Finally, in
order to keep an eye on him and watch what he did and scrutinize his thoughts,
Andrés wanted Clemente to be his friend and companion, and Clemente considered this friendship a great favor. They were always together, spent freely, poured
down *escudos*, ran, jumped, danced, and threw the bar better than all the other
Gypsies; the Gypsy women were more than a little in love with them, and the
Gypsy men respected them in every way.

And so they left Extremadura and entered La Mancha, and gradually they
reached the kingdom of Murcia. In all the villages and towns they passed

through, there were competitions in ball playing, fencing, running, jumping, throwing the bar, and other exercises of strength, skill, and agility, and Andrés and Clemente won all of them, which was also true of Andrés alone. And in all this time, which was more than a month and a half, Clemente never had occasion, nor did he seek one out, to speak to Preciosa, until one day, when she and Andrés were together, he came into the conversation because they called him over, and Preciosa said to him:

"Since the first time you came to our encampment I knew you, Clemente, and I remembered the verses you gave me in Madrid; but I didn't want to say anything because I didn't know what your intention was when you came to our settlement. And when I learned your misfortune I regretted it very much, and my heart grew calm, for it was alarmed, thinking that if there were Don Juans in the world who turned into Andréses, there might also be Don Sanchos who changed into other names. I am speaking to you in this way because Andrés has told me that you have realized who he is and his intention in becoming a Gypsy"—and that was true, for Andrés had made him aware of his history in order to communicate his thoughts—"and don't think that his knowing you was of little advantage to you, for out of regard for me, and because of what I said about you, it became easier to welcome you and take you into our company where, may it please God, you will have the good fortune you desire. I would like you to repay these good wishes by not speaking ill of the lowliness of his intention to Andrés, or describing for him how harmful it is for him to persist in this condition; for even though I imagine that his will lies under the locks of mine, even so it would grieve me to see him show signs, no matter how small, of any regret."

To which Clemente replied:

"Do not think, my most unusual Preciosa, that Don Juan revealed to me who he was lightly; first I met him, and first his eyes revealed to me his intention; first I told him who I was, and first I guessed the imprisonment of his will, which you have pointed out; and he, giving me the credit it was reasonable for him to give me, entrusted his secret to mine, and he is a good witness if I praised his determination and dedication to love; for I am not, oh Preciosa, of such limited intelligence that I cannot conceive of how far the powers of beauty extend, and yours, passing the limits of the greatest extremes of loveliness, is enough excuse for greater errors, if the ones committed for such inescapable reasons ought to be called errors. I thank you, Señora, for what you said to my credit, and I intend to repay you by desiring that these amorous complications turn out happily, and that you enjoy your Andrés, and Andrés his Preciosa, in conformity with and at the pleasure of his parents, because from so beautiful a union let us see in the world the handsomest shoots that well-intentioned nature can form. This I desire, Preciosa, and this shall I always say to your Andrés, not anything that can divert him from his well-directed thoughts."

Clemente said these words with so much affection that Andrés doubted whether he had said them as a lover or as a prudent man; for the infernal disease of jealousy is so delicate and constructed in such a way that it is preoccupied with the atoms of the sun, and the lover is vexed by and made desperate by those that touch the beloved creature. But even so, his jealousy was not corroborated, trusting more in the goodness of Preciosa than in his own good fortune, for those in love always consider themselves unlucky until they achieve their desire. In short, Andrés and Clemente were comrades and great friends, all of it assured by the good intentions of Clemente and the discretion and prudence of Preciosa, who never gave Andrés occasion to be jealous of her.

Clemente had his traces of the poet, as he had demonstrated in the verses he had given to Preciosa, and Andrés had his pretensions as well, and both were fond of music. And so it happened, when the camp was set up in a valley four leagues from Murcia, that one night, to pass the time, the two of them sat down, each with a guitar, Andrés at the foot of a cork tree and Clemente under an oak, and invited by the silence of the night, with Andrés beginning and Clemente responding, they sang these verses:

Andrés

Look, Clemente, at the starry curtain
that this gelid night wishes
to use to vie with the day,
adorning heaven with beauteous lights;
and in this calm concordance,
if your divine wit can achieve so much,
that visage surely appears
where the extreme of beauty does attend.

Clemente

Where the extreme of beauty does attend,
and wherever Preciosa
hastens with every extreme of goodness
and beautiful purity
all in a single creature,
no human wit can begin to praise her

that does not touch on divine,
on high, on rare, on grave, on perfect grace.

Andrés

On high, on rare, on grave, on perfect grace,
a never-before-used style
elevated to heaven,
sweet to the world, and lacking the same path,
your name, lovely Gypsy girl!
causing surprise, amazement, and wonder,
I would like fame to carry
as high as the eighth sphere of the fixed stars.

Clemente

As high as the eighth sphere of the fixed stars
would be both proper and right,
giving joy to the heavens
when the sound of her name was heard on high,
and creating here on earth,
wherever her dulcet name might resound
music in our human ears,
peace in our souls, glory in our senses.

Andrés

Peace in our souls, glory in our senses,
is felt when the Siren sings,
beguiling guilelessly and
lulling the most cautious, the most forewarned,
and such is my Preciosa,
that beauty is the least of her virtues,
delicate treasure of mine,
the crown of grace, the honor of spirit.

Clemente

The crown of grace, the honor of spirit
is what you are, sweet Gypsy,
the coolness of the morning,
a gentle breeze in the burning summer,
a bolt that blindfolded Love

uses to turn the coldest heart to flame;
a power that does just this,
that kindly kills and softly satisfies.

The free man and the captive gave signs of not concluding very quickly if the voice of Preciosa had not sounded behind them, for she had listened to their songs. They stopped when they heard her, and without moving, paying marvelous attention, they listened to her. She (and I do not know whether they were improvised or whether the verses she sang had ever been written), with extraordinary charm, sang the following lines as if they had been composed in response to theirs:

In this amorous enterprise
where I while away love, amused,
I deem my good fortune greater
if I'm modest, not beautiful.
        The one that is the humblest plant
if she keeps her climb unswerving,
through grace or because of nature
ascends straight up to the heavens.
        In this coin, my lowly copper,
with its enamel of modesty,
no good desire is lacking,
no wealth that is not in excess.
        Not having your love or esteem
causes me no sorrow at all,
for I intend to fabricate
my own luck, my own good fortune.
        Let me do what's in my power,
I'm on the road to being good,
and let heaven do and decide
what it wishes to afterward.
        I want to see if beauty has
so great a prerogative that
it raises me so high, so far
that I strive for a greater height.
        If souls are created equal,
that of a peasant may be worth
and even have the value of
exalted, imperial souls.

What I regret about mine will
raise me to a higher degree,
because royal majesty and love
do not occupy the same seat.

Here Preciosa brought her song to an end, and Andrés and Clemente stood to receive her. The three of them conversed with discernment, and Preciosa discovered in their words their good judgment, modesty, and intelligence, so that in Clemente she found an excuse for Andrés's intention, which until then she had not found, having judged his daring decision to be more an effect of his youth than his good sense.

That morning they broke camp and went to stay in a village in the jurisdiction of Murcia, three leagues from the city, where Andrés suffered a misfortune that almost cost him his life. What happened was that after presenting to the village some vases and silver objects as a deposit, which was their custom, Preciosa and her grandmother, and Cristina with two other girls, and both Clemente and Andrés lodged in an inn owned by a wealthy widow who had a daughter of seventeen or eighteen, rather more brazen than beautiful and, apparently, named Juana Carducha. She, having seen the Gypsy women and men dancing, was seized by the devil and fell in love with Andrés so madly that she decided to tell him and take him for her husband, if he wished, even though all his kin might object; and so she looked for the opportunity to speak to him and found it in a corral where Andrés had gone to look at two donkeys. She went up to him and quickly, in order not to be seen, she said:

"Andrés"—for she already knew his name—"I'm a maiden and I'm rich, for my mother has no other child except me, and this inn is hers; besides this she has a good number of new vines planted and two other houses; answer me quickly, and if you're clever, stay here and you'll see the life we can have."

Andrés was astonished at the Carducha girl's resolve, and with the speed she had requested, he replied:

"Señora maiden, I've already arranged to marry, and Gypsies marry only Gypsies; may God keep you for the favor you wished to grant me and which I do not deserve."

The Carducha girl almost died at Andrés's harsh response, to which she would have replied if she hadn't seen some other Gypsy girls entering the corral. She left, insulted and hurt, and she would gladly have taken her revenge if she could have. Andrés, an intelligent man, decided to put some distance between himself and the girl and get away from the opportunity the devil had offered him; for he read clearly in the Carducha girl's eyes that even without the bonds of matrimony she would willingly give herself to him, and he did not want to find himself alone and without help in that situation; and so he asked all the Gypsies to leave the village that night. They, who always obeyed him, immediately did as he asked, collected their deposit that afternoon, and left.

The Carducha girl, who saw that with Andrés leaving half her soul was leaving too, did not have time to solicit the satisfaction of her desires and gave orders that Andrés be kept there by force, since she could not have him stay willingly; and so, with the industry, sagacity, and secrecy that her evil intention taught her, she placed among Andrés's prized possessions, which she knew were his, some rich corals, two silver medallions, and other small gems of hers. And as soon as they left the inn, she began to shout, saying that those Gypsies who were leaving had stolen her jewelry, and in response the law and all the people in the village came to her assistance.

The Gypsies halted and all of them swore they had stolen nothing and would open all the bags and baggage they were carrying. The old Gypsy woman became extremely distressed when she heard this, fearing that in the search Preciosa's jewelry and Andrés's clothes would be discovered, which she had hidden with great care and caution, but the good Carducha quickly saved the situation because at the second bundle they looked into she said they should ask which one belonged to that Gypsy who was such a great dancer, for she had seen him go into her room twice and he might be the one who had taken her things. Andrés understood she was talking about him, and he laughed and said:

"Señora Maiden, this is my baggage and this is my donkey, and if you find what you are missing in either one, I shall pay you an extra fine, aside from subjecting myself to the punishment the law gives to thieves."

Then the officers of the law came to unpack the donkey, and after rummaging around a few times they found what was missing; Andrés was so amazed at this and so preoccupied that he looked like a statue, mute and made of stone.

At this point the Carducha girl said, "Wasn't I right to suspect him? Look what a good face hides so great a thief!"

The mayor, who was present, began to hurl a thousand insults at Andrés and all the Gypsies, calling them public thieves and highwaymen. Andrés said nothing to all of this; indecisive and thoughtful, he had not yet realized the Carducha girl's betrayal. At this point an elegant soldier, nephew to the mayor, stepped forward and said:

"Don't you see the state of this wretched Gypsy rotten with thievery? I'll wager he's putting on an act and denying the theft even though he's been caught red-handed; my blessings on the man who would send all of you to the galleys. Just think how much better this villain would be there, serving His Majesty, than dancing from place to place and stealing everything in sight! By my faith as a soldier, I'd like to give him a slap that would knock him down, here at my feet."

And saying this, without further ado, he raised his hand and slapped Andrés so hard that he brought him out of his self-absorption and made him remember that he was not Andrés Caballero but Don Juan, and a gentleman; and rushing at the soldier with great speed and even greater rage, he pulled his own sword from its sheath and buried it in the soldier's body, leaving him dead on the ground.

And then came the shouts of the villagers, the anger of the uncle mayor, the fainting of Preciosa, the agitation of Andrés at seeing her in a faint, and then everyone calling for weapons to go after the murderer. The confusion increased, the shouting increased; and because Andrés attended to Preciosa's faint, he failed to attend to his own defense; and as luck would have it, Clemente was not present at these disastrous events, for he had already left the village with the mules. In the end, so many people fell on Andrés that they took him and shackled him with two very heavy chains. The mayor was ready to hang him then and there, if it had been up to him, but he was obliged to transfer Andrés to Murcia, since they were in that jurisdiction. They did not take him away until the next day, and in the time he was there Andrés endured many tortures and vituperations inflicted on him by the indignant mayor and his ministers and all the inhabitants of the village. The mayor arrested all the Gypsy men and women he could, but most had fled, among them Clemente, who feared being caught and discovered.

Finally, at the preliminary hearing and with a multitude of Gypsies present, among them Preciosa and poor Andrés wrapped in chains, with his hands manacled to his waist and unable to move his head, the mayor and his ministers, with many other armed people, entered Murcia. All of Murcia came out to see the prisoners, for they had already heard about the death of the soldier. But that day the beauty of Preciosa was so great that no one looked at her without blessing her, and word of her beauty reached the ears of the Señora Corregidora, the magistrate's wife, who, curious to see her, had the Corregidor, her husband, give the order that the Gypsy girl was not to be sent to prison, but all the others were; and they put Andrés in a narrow dungeon where the darkness and the lack of Preciosa's light made him think he would never leave there except to go to his grave. They brought Preciosa and her grandmother to the Corregidora, and as soon as she saw the girl she said:

"They have reason to praise her beauty."

And drawing her close, she embraced her tenderly and could not get her fill of looking at her, and she asked the grandmother how old the girl was.

"Fifteen years," responded the Gypsy, "and two months, more or less."

"That's the age my poor Costanza would be now. Oh, my friends, this child has revived my misfortune," said the Corregidora.

When she heard this Preciosa took hold of the Corregidora's hands, and kissing them over and over again, she bathed them in tears, and said to her:

"My lady, the Gypsy held prisoner is not guilty, because he was provoked; he was called a thief, and he is not; he was slapped in the face where the goodness of his spirit is revealed. For the sake of God and of who you are, Señora, help him avoid judgment and tell the Señor Corregidor not to rush to impose the punishment that the law threatens; and in the event my beauty has given you some pleasure, linger over it by having the prisoner linger too, because the end of his life is the end of mine. He is to be my husband, and just and moral impediments have prevented us from being betrothed until now. If money is necessary for the accused to be pardoned, our entire encampment will be sold at public auction, and we shall give even more than is asked for. My lady, if you know what love is, and if you ever felt it, and now you have your husband, take pity on me, for I love mine tenderly and chastely."

As she was saying this, she never let go of the Corregidora's hands or allowed her eyes to stop looking at her very attentively, shedding bitter and pious tears in great abundance. By the same token, the Corregidora clasped the girl's hands, looking at her as intently, with no less urgency and no fewer tears. Then the Corregidor came in, and finding his wife and Preciosa weeping so fervently and so closely joined, he was perplexed, both by their tears and their beauty. He asked the reason for their emotion, and Preciosa's answer was to release the hands of the Corregidora and clasp the feet of the Corregidor, saying:

"Señor, have mercy, have mercy! If my husband dies, I die. The fault is not his; but if it is, inflict the punishment on me; and if this cannot be done, at least postpone the hearing while all possible means for a solution are sought and striven for; it may be that the man who did not commit the sin of wickedness will be saved by the grace of heaven."

The Corregidor was again perplexed when he heard the discerning words of the Gypsy girl, and he would have joined her in shedding tears if it were not that he did not wish to show any signs of weakness. While this was going on, the old Gypsy woman was considering many great and varied matters, and at the end of all this perplexity and imagining, she said:

"Wait for me, your graces, my lord and lady, just a little, and I shall make these tears turn into laughter, even if it costs me my life."

And so, with a rapid step, she left the room, leaving all those present confused by what she had said.

As they waited for her to return, Preciosa never ceased weeping or pleading that her husband's case be delayed, intending to advise his father that he should come and be part of it. The Gypsy woman returned with a small chest under her arm, and she told the Corregidor that he, his wife, and she should go into another room, for she had great things to tell them in secret. The Corregidor, thinking she wanted to tell him about some robberies by the Gypsies so that he would favor the prisoner during the trial, withdrew with her and his wife into his private chamber, where the Gypsy, kneeling before the two of them, said:

"If the good news I wish to give you, my lord and lady, does not deserve the reward of having a great sin of mine pardoned, here I am to receive whatever punishment you may wish to give me; but before I confess it, I want you to tell me first, my lord and my lady, whether you recognize these jewels."

And showing them a small chest that contained Preciosa's jewels, she placed it in the hands of the Corregidor, and when he opened it he saw those child's trinkets but did not grasp what they could mean. The Corregidora looked at them too, but she did not grasp their meaning either; she simply said:

"These are the ornaments of some small infant."

"That is true," said the Gypsy, "and the infant they belong to is written here on this folded paper."

The Corregidor opened it quickly and read what it said:

> The girl was named Doña Costanza de Azevedo y de Meneses; her mother, Doña Guiomar de Meneses, and her father, Don Fernando de Azevedo, a knight of the Order of Calatrava; I abducted her on the Day of the Ascension of Our Lord, at eight in the morning, in the year 1595. The girl was wearing the jewels that are kept in this chest.

As soon as the Corregidora heard the words written on the paper, and when she recognized the jewels, she placed them on her lips, giving them infinite kisses, and fell into a swoon. The Corregidor hurried to help her before asking the Gypsy about his daughter, and when his wife recovered consciousness, she said:

"Good woman, angel rather than Gypsy, where is the owner, I mean the child to whom these trinkets belonged?"

"Where, Señora?" responded the Gypsy. "You have her here in your house: that Gypsy girl who brought tears to your eyes is the owner, and she undoubtedly is your daughter; I stole her from your house in Madrid on the day and at the hour that the paper says."

Hearing this, the agitated lady threw caution to the wind and eagerly raced to the room where she had left Preciosa, and found her still weeping, surrounded by the Corregidora's ladies and servants. She hurried to her, and without saying anything, quickly unfastened her bodice and looked to see whether beneath her left breast she had a small mark, a kind of white mole that she had been born with, and she found it, large now, for it had grown over time. Then, with the same haste, she took off her shoes and revealed a rounded foot of snow and ivory, and saw what she was looking for, which was that the last two toes on the right foot were connected by a tiny bit of flesh, which they had never wanted to cut when she was a girl in order not to hurt her. Her breast, her toes, the jewels, the day of the abduction, the Gypsy woman's confession, and the shock and joy her parents had felt when they saw her rightfully confirmed in the soul of the Corregidora that Preciosa was her daughter; and so, taking her in her arms, she returned with her to where the Corregidor and the old Gypsy woman were waiting.

Preciosa was bewildered, for she did not know the reason for these proceedings, in particular finding herself carried in the arms of the Corregidora, who gave her countless kisses. Finally, Doña Guiomar and her precious burden came into the presence of her husband, and transferring Preciosa from her arms to his, she said:

"Receive, Señor, your daughter Costanza, for it is doubtless she; do not doubt it in any way, for I have seen the sign of her joined toes and the mark under her breast; and besides, my soul has been telling me this is so from the moment I laid eyes upon her."

"I don't doubt it," responded the Corregidor, holding Preciosa in his arms, "for the same effects have passed through my soul as through yours; and besides, so many coincidences taken together, how could that happen if not by a miracle?"

All the people in the house were enthralled, asking one another what it could be about, and none of them hit the mark; for who could have imagined that the Gypsy girl was the daughter of their lord and lady?

The Corregidor said to his wife and daughter, and to the old Gypsy woman, that the matter should remain secret until he revealed it; and he also said to the old woman that he forgave the wrong she had done him in stealing away his soul, for the recompense of having returned it to him deserved a greater reward, and he was aggrieved only by her having, knowing the quality of Preciosa's birth, betrothed her to a Gypsy, especially one who was a thief and a murderer.

"Oh," said Preciosa, "my lord, he is neither a Gypsy nor a thief, but he is a killer, though of one who took his honor, and he could do no less than kill him to show who he was."

"What do you mean he's not a Gypsy, my daughter?" said Doña Guiomar.

Then the old Gypsy woman briefly recounted the story of Andrés Caballero, who was the son of Don Francisco de Cárcamo, a knight of the Order of Santiago, and whose name was Don Juan de Cárcamo, also of the same order, and she still had his clothes from the moment he changed them for those of a Gypsy. She also recounted the agreement made between Preciosa and Don Juan to wait two years before deciding whether or not to marry. She spoke of the purity of both and the agreeable character of Don Juan. They were as astonished at this as at the discovery of their daughter, and the Corregidor told the old Gypsy to get Don Juan's clothes. She did so, and returned with another Gypsy, a man who carried them.

While she left and returned, her parents asked Preciosa a hundred thousand questions, to which she responded with so much astuteness and charm that even if they had not recognized her as their daughter, she would have inspired their love. They asked if she felt any affection for Don Juan. She responded that she felt no more than that to which she was obliged by gratitude to one who had lowered himself to be a Gypsy for her sake, but that it would not extend to more than her honored parents might desire.

"Be still, my daughter Preciosa," said her father, "for I want you to keep this name of Preciosa in memory of your loss and your discovery; for I, as your father, take on the responsibility of placing you in a position where it does not contradict who you are."

Preciosa sighed when she heard this, and her mother, who was perceptive, understood that she was sighing for love of Don Juan, and she said to her husband:

"Señor, since Don Juan de Cárcamo is so illustrious, and loves our daughter so much, it would not be a bad idea for us to give her to him in marriage."

And he replied:

"Only today we have found her, and already you want us to lose her? Let us enjoy her for a while; for when she is married she will not be ours but her husband's."

"You are right, Señor," she replied, "but give the order to release Don Juan, who must be in some dungeon."

"Yes, he must be," said Preciosa, "for they would have given no better to a thief and a murderer, especially one who was a Gypsy."

"I want to see him as if I were going to take his confession," responded the Corregidor, "and once more I charge you, Señora, let no one know this story until I choose to reveal it."

And embracing Preciosa, he went to the prison and entered the dungeon where Don Juan was being kept, and he did not allow anyone to enter with him. He found him with both feet in a pillory and his hands cuffed, and they had not yet removed the wooden board that immobilized his head. The chamber was dark, but he had them open a skylight through which some light could enter, but not very much; and so, when he saw him, he said:

"How is the scoundrel? This is how I would like to have all the Gypsies in Spain leashed together, and put an end to them in one day, as Nero wished to do with Rome, giving only one blow! You should know, suspicious thief, that I am the Corregidor of this city, and I have come to find out, man to man, if it is true that your wife is a Gypsy girl who is traveling with you."

When Andrés heard this, he imagined the Corregidor must have fallen in love with Preciosa; for jealousy is an almost immaterial body and enters other bodies without breaking, separating, or dividing them; but, even so, he responded:

"If she has said that I am her husband, it is perfectly true; and if she has said that I am not, she has also told the truth, because it is not possible for Preciosa to tell a lie."

"Is she so truthful?" replied the Corregidor. "That's no small thing, for a Gypsy. Well now, young man, she has said that she's your wife but has never given you her hand. She has learned that on account of your crime you are to die, and she has asked that before your death I marry the two of you, because she wants the honor of being the widow of a thief as great as you."

"Well, your grace, Señor Corregidor, do as she asks; for if I am married to her, I shall go happily to the next life as long as I leave this one known for being hers."

"You must love her a great deal!" said the Corregidor.

"So much," responded the prisoner, "that saying it means nothing. In short, Señor Corregidor, there is nothing more to say: I killed the man who tried to take away my honor; I adore that Gypsy girl; I shall die happy if I die in her favor, and I know we shall not lack the grace of God, for both of us will have kept, virtuously and faithfully, the promises we made to each other."

"Well, tonight I shall send for you," said the Corregidor, "and in my house I shall marry you to Preciosa, and tomorrow at noon you will be on the gallows; in this way I shall fulfill what the law demands and both your desires."

Andrés thanked him, and the Corregidor returned to his house and told his wife what had happened with Don Juan, and about something else that he planned to do.

While he had been away, Preciosa told her mother about the course of her life, and how she had always believed she was a Gypsy, the granddaughter of the old woman; but that she had always valued herself much more than one would expect of a Gypsy. Her mother asked her to be truthful and tell her whether she loved Don Juan de Cárcamo. She, with embarrassment and lowered eyes, said that because she thought she was a Gypsy and would improve her lot if she married a member of a military order, and one as prominent as Don Juan de Cárcamo, and having seen for herself his good character and virtuous behavior, she had looked at him with fond eyes; but, in a word, she had already said that she had no will other than what her parents might desire.

Night fell, and when it was almost ten o'clock, they took Andrés out of prison, without the handcuffs and the board but with a large chain wrapped around his entire body, beginning with his feet. In this way he arrived at the house of the Corregidor, not seen by anyone except those who brought him, and silently and cautiously they took him into a room and left him there alone. A short while later a priest came in and told him to make his confession, because he was to die the next day. To which Andrés replied:

"I shall confess very gladly, but why aren't I being married first? And if I am being married, it surely is a very poor nuptial bed that awaits me."

Doña Guiomar, who knew everything, told her husband that he was giving too many shocks to Don Juan and he should moderate them, because he might cause the young man to lose his life. The Corregidor thought this was good advice, and so he went in and called to the priest who was confessing him and said that first they would marry the Gypsy boy to Preciosa, the Gypsy girl, and afterward the boy would make his confession and commend himself wholeheartedly to God since His mercies often rain down when hope is at its driest.

In effect, Andrés went into a drawing room where only Doña Guiomar, the Corregidor, Preciosa, and two servants were present. But when Preciosa saw Don Juan restrained and shackled with such a large chain, his face pale and his eyes showing signs of having wept, her heart sank and she leaned on the arm of her mother, who was beside her and who embraced her and said:

"Calm yourself, my girl, for everything you see will lead to your joy and benefit."

Preciosa, who had no knowledge of what was going to happen, could not be consoled, and the old Gypsy woman was perturbed, and the others present were in suspense regarding how things would turn out.

The Corregidor said:

"Señor auxiliary priest, these two Gypsies are the ones your grace is to marry."

"I cannot do that if certain necessary particulars are not taken care of first. Where were the banns published? Where is the license from my superior permitting this marriage to take place?"

"That was my oversight," responded the Corregidor, "but I shall arrange for the vicar to give it to you."

"Well, until I see it," responded the auxiliary priest, "these ladies and gentlemen will excuse me."

And without another word, and so that a scandal would not ensue, he walked out of the house and left them all in a state of astonishment.

"The priest has done very well," said the Corregidor, "and this might be Divine Providence, to delay Andrés's punishment, because, in fact, he will marry Preciosa, and before that the banns must be published, which is a leisurely process that usually provides a sweet ending for many bitter difficulties; and with all this, I should like to hear from Andrés whether, if fate guides his affairs so that, without these shocks and surprises, he finds himself Preciosa's husband, he will consider himself fortunate either as Andrés Caballero or as Don Juan de Cárcamo."

As soon as Andrés heard his real name, he said:

"Since Preciosa has not wanted to be restrained by the limits of silence and has revealed who I am, although that good fortune might find me sovereign of the world, I would consider it so great that it would end all my desires, and I would not dare to desire any other good except heaven."

"Well, because of this good spirit that you have demonstrated, Señor Don Juan de Cárcamo, in due course I shall make Preciosa your legitimate wife, and now I give to you, with that hope, the richest jewel of my house, and my life, and my soul; and esteem her as you say you will, because in her I present you with Doña Costanza de Meneses, my only daughter, who, if she equals you in love, in no way is unworthy of you in lineage."

Andrés marveled when he saw the love they were showing him, and very briefly Doña Guiomar recounted how they had lost their daughter and found her again, with the incontrovertible details the old Gypsy woman had given about her abduction, and at this Don Juan was amazed and astounded, but his happiness went beyond all bounds; he embraced his in-laws and called them his parents, his lord and lady; he kissed Preciosa's hands, and she, in tears, asked for his. The secret was out, the news left the house as the servants who had been present also left; when the mayor, the dead man's uncle, heard the news, he saw that the paths to his revenge had been closed off, for the rigor of the law would not be imposed on the son-in-law of the Corregidor.

Don Juan put on the traveling clothes that the Gypsy woman had brought in; prison cells and iron chains were transformed into freedom and chains of gold; the sadness of the Gypsy prisoners turned to joy, for the next day they were freed on bail. The dead man's uncle received the promise of two thousand *ducados* if he would drop his complaint and pardon Don Juan; he, not forgetting his comrade Clemente, had him searched for; but no one found him or knew anything about him until four days later, when he received reliable word that Clemente had boarded one of the two galleys from Genoa that had been in the port of Cartagena, and had already sailed.

The Corregidor told Don Juan that he had it on good authority that his father, Don Francisco de Cárcamo, had been named Corregidor of his city and that it would be advisable to wait for him so that the nuptials would take place with his approval and consent. Don Juan said he would do exactly as he wished, but before anything else, he had to marry Preciosa.

The archbishop gave permission for them to marry with the publication of only one bann. The city celebrated, since the Corregidor was well loved, with illuminations, bullfights, and mock battles on the day of the betrothal; the old Gypsy woman stayed in the house, for she did not want to be away from her granddaughter Preciosa.

The news of the case and the marriage of the Gypsy girl reached the capital; Don Francisco de Cárcamo learned that his son was the Gypsy lad and Preciosa the Gypsy girl he had seen, and her beauty excused the frivolity of his son, whom he had considered lost when he learned that he had not gone to Flanders; and even more so because of how good it was for him to marry the daughter of a gentleman as great and wealthy as Don Fernando de Azevedo. He hurried his departure, wanting to see his children soon, and within twenty days he was in Murcia, and with his arrival the celebrations were repeated, the nuptials took place, their lives were recounted; and the poets in the city, for there are some, and very good ones, took it upon themselves to celebrate this strange story, along with the unequaled beauty of the Gypsy girl. And the famous licentiate Pozo wrote about it in such a way that the fame of Preciosa will endure forever and a day.

I forgot to say how the enamored innkeeper revealed to the police that the theft by Andrés the Gypsy was not true, and she confessed her love and her fault, but there was no penalty imposed because in the joy of the discovery of the bride and groom, vengeance was buried and mercy resurrected.

"Oh, pitiable ruins of unfortunate Nicosia, the blood of your valorous and ill-fated defenders only recently washed away! You lack feeling, but if you had it now, in this our solitude, we might lament our misfortunes together, and perhaps finding a companion in our lamentations might alleviate our torment. This hope may have remained in you, sadly demolished towers, that once more, though not for so righteous a defense as the one in which you were toppled, you may see yourselves rebuilt. But I, poor wretch, what good can I hope for in the miserable straits in which I find myself, even if I return to my earlier state? Such is my misfortune that in freedom I had no happiness, and in captivity I neither have it nor hope for it."

These words were spoken by a Christian captive, looking down from a height at the fallen walls of the lost Nicosia, speaking to them in this way and comparing his miseries to theirs, as if they could understand him: a condition peculiar to the afflicted who, carried away by their imaginations, do and say things alien to all reason and fair speech.

As he was speaking, out of a pavilion or tent, one of four standing in the field, came a Turk, a very well-favored and elegant young man who approached the Christian and said:

"I would wager, Ricardo my friend, that your constant thoughts bring you to these places."

"Yes, they do," responded Ricardo, for this was the name of the captive, "but what good does it do if, no matter where I go, I find neither peace nor rest? Instead, these ruins that you can see from here have intensified them."

"You must be speaking of the ruins of Nicosia," said the Turk.

"Well, which ones would I be speaking of?" Ricardo repeated, "There are no others to be seen around here."

"You really will have something to weep over," replied the Turk, "if you follow that train of thought, because two years ago our eyes saw this renowned, rich island of Cyprus in all its calm and tranquility, its residents enjoying all that human felicity can grant to men, and those who see or contemplate it now are its exiles or miserable captives, and how can one help but feel sad about its calamity and misfortune? But let us put these things aside, for they have no remedy, and turn to your sorrows, for I wish to see if yours do, and so I beg you for the sake of what you owe to the goodwill I have shown you, and for the sake of what you are obliged to do by the fact that both of us are from the same nation and were brought up together as boys, to tell me what makes you so extremely sad; for although captivity alone is enough to sadden the most joyful heart in the world, I still imagine that the current of your misfortunes flows from an earlier time. Because generous spirits like yours do not normally surrender so fully to common sorrows that they show signs of extraordinary feelings; and what makes me believe this is knowing that you are not so poor that you do not have the sum they have demanded for your ransom; nor are you in the towers on the Black Sea as an important captive who achieves his desired freedom either late or never.[1] And so, bad luck not having taken from you the hope of finding yourself free, and yet seeing you humbled into giving wretched signs of your misfortune, it is not difficult for me to imagine that your sorrow proceeds from some reason other than the freedom you lost, and that reason I beg you to tell me, offering you all I can and all I am worth; perhaps, to help you, chance brought about the circumstance in which I find myself wearing an outfit that I despise. As you know, Ricardo, my master is the magistrate of this city, which is the same as being its bishop. You know too how much he is worth and how far I can go with him. Further, you are not ignorant of the burning desire I have not to die in this state that I seem to profess, for when I can stand it no longer, I have to confess and shout aloud the faith of Jesus Christ, from which I was separated by my youth and lack of understanding, since I know that such a confession would cost me my life; and in exchange for not losing the life of my soul, I shall think it a good exchange to lose the life of my body. This being said, I want you to infer and consider that my friendship can be useful to you, and so that I may know what remedies or relief your affliction may have, you have to tell me about it, just as the patient's history is necessary to the physician, and I assure you that I shall confine it to the most hidden part of silence."

Ricardo said nothing in the face of all these words, yet finding himself obliged by them and by necessity, this was his reply:

"Oh, Mahamut my friend!"—for that was the Turk's name—"if you are as correct in its remedy as you are in what you imagine my misfortune is, I would consider my freedom well lost and not trade my misfortune for the greatest happiness one could imagine; but I know it is such that everyone can very well

1. Yedikule Fortress or the Fortress of the Seven Towers housed, among other things, an Ottoman prison on the Black Sea.

know the cause from which it proceeds, but not a single person will dare find the remedy or even any relief. And so that you may be persuaded of this truth, I shall tell you about it in the fewest words possible; but before I enter the confused labyrinth of my woes, I want you to tell me why Hazán Pasha, my master, set up tents and pavilions in this field before he entered Nicosia, where he has been named viceroy, or pasha, which is what the Turks call viceroys."

"I shall answer you briefly," responded Mahamut. "You should know it is the custom among the Turks that those who are named viceroys in some province do not enter the city where their predecessor is living until he leaves and allows the one coming in to review freely the public accounts; and while the new pasha is doing this, the old one waits in the field for the results of this scrutiny, carried out without his being able to intervene and make use of bribes or friendship, if he has not done so already. When the review is complete, it is presented in a sealed, stamped parchment to the one leaving office, who then takes it to the Gate of the Great Lord, that is to say, to the court of the Great Council of the Turks; and there, before the vizier pasha and the other four lesser pashas, as if we were to say, before the President of the Royal Council and judges, they either reward or punish him, according to the results of the review; if he is culpable, with money he can be excused and exempted from punishment; if he is not culpable and they do not reward him, which is what ordinarily happens, with gifts and presents he achieves the position he most desires, because positions and offices are granted not on the basis of merit but of money; everything is sold and everything is bought. The providers of positions rob those they benefit and skin them alive; from this purchased office comes the means to buy another that promises even more profit. Everything happens as I say, all of this empire is violent, a sign that promises it will not endure; but I believe, and it must be true, that our sins carry it on their shoulders, I mean, the sins of those who brazenly and blatantly offend God, as do I. May He remember me for the sake of who He is! For the reason I have told you, your master Hazán Pasha has been in this field for four days, and if he has not left Nicosia as he was supposed to, it was because he was very ill; but he is better now and will undoubtedly leave today or tomorrow and stay in some tents you have not seen behind this slope, and then your master will enter the city. And this is what you must know about what you asked."

"Listen, then," said Ricardo, "but I don't know whether I can do what I said earlier about telling you of my misfortune in a few words, for it is so extensive and excessive it cannot be measured with one's reason; but I shall do what I can, and what time allows. And so, I ask you first if in our town of Trápana you know a maiden to whom fame has given the title of the most beautiful woman in all of Sicily; a maiden, I say, about whom all curious tongues said, and the most extraordinary minds affirmed, that hers was the most perfect beauty of the past age, the present one, and the age to come; a maiden about whom the poets sang that her hair was gold, her eyes two radiant suns, and her cheeks scarlet roses, her teeth pearls, her lips rubies, her throat alabaster, and that in her the parts with the whole and the whole with its parts created a marvelous, consonant harmony, nature strewing over everything a delicacy of colors so natural and perfect that envy could never find any flaw in her. What, Mahamut, is it possible you have not told me yet who she is or what her name is? I certainly believe you either don't hear me or that you were unconscious when you were in Trápana."

"The truth is, Ricardo," responded Mahamut, "that if the woman you have depicted with such extremes of beauty is not Leonisa, the daughter of Rodolfo Florencio, then I don't know who it can be; for she alone had the fame you describe."

"It is she, oh Mahamut!" responded Ricardo. "It is she, my friend, the principal cause of all my good and all my misfortune; it is she, and not the freedom I have lost, for whom my eyes have shed numberless tears, shed them now, and will shed them in the future, the one for whom my sighs heat the air, near and far, the one for whom my words weary the heaven that listens to them and the ears that hear them; it is she for whose sake you have judged me mad or, at least, as having little courage and less spirit; this Leonisa—to me a lioness and to another a gentle lamb—is the one who has me in this miserable state. Because you should know that since a tender age, or, at least, since I had the use of my reason, I have not only loved but adored and served her with as much solicitude as if I did not have on earth or in heaven another deity to serve or adore. Her kin and parents knew of my desires and never gave a sign of being aggrieved by them, considering that their purpose was upright and virtuous; and I know they often said so to Leonisa, to inspire her to accept me as her husband. But she had her eyes set on Cornelio, the son of Ascanio Rótulo, whom you know very well: an elegant youth, smartly dressed, with soft hands and curled hair, a mellifluous voice and amorous words, in short, all made of perfume and sugar paste and adorned with rich fabrics and decorated with gold brocades; she did not wish to set her eyes on my face, which is not as delicate as Cornelio's, nor did she choose to even thank me for my many continual services, repaying my desire with scorn and contempt; my love for her reached such an extreme that I would have taken it as a stroke of good fortune if I had died simply because of her disdain and ingratitude, as long as her favors to Cornelio, no matter how virtuous, were not made public. Think, then, if to the anguish of disdain and aversion was added the greater and crueler agony of jealousy, how my soul was assailed by two mortal plagues! Leonisa's parents concealed the favors she granted Cornelio, believing, as it was reasonable for them to believe, that the young man, attracted by her incomparably beautiful loveliness, would choose her as his wife, and they would acquire a son-in-law much richer than I; and it might well have been true, if it had happened that way; but, and I say this without arrogance, they would not have acquired one of better character than mine, or more elevated thoughts, or more recognized valor. And so it happened, while I was courting her, that I learned that one day in the past month of May, and today it is one year, three days, and five hours since that day, Leonisa and her parents and Cornelio and his parents went on a pleasure trip, with all their kin and servants, to the garden of Ascanio, close to the shore on the road to the salt marshes."

"I know it very well," said Mahamut. "Go ahead, Ricardo, I spent some days there, when God wished it, quite a few times."

"I learned this," replied Ricardo, "and at that very moment my soul was overrun so vehemently and intensely by fury, rage, and an inferno of jealousy that I lost all control, as you will see from what I did then, which was to go to the garden where I had been told they were, and found most of the people enjoying themselves, and Cornelio and Leonisa sitting under a walnut tree a little off to the side. I don't know what they felt when they saw me; for myself, I can say I was so thunderstruck at seeing them that I lost my sight and was like a statue, unable to speak or move. But it did not take very long for vexation to incite anger, and anger the blood of my heart, and blood to incite rage, and rage to incite my hands and tongue; my hands were tied by the respect I thought was owed to the beautiful face I had before me, but my tongue broke the silence with these words:

'You must be pleased, oh mortal enemy of my repose, to have so calmly before your eyes the cause that will make mine live in perpetual and sorrowful weeping. Come, come a little closer, oh cruel one, and wind your ivy around this useless trunk that searches for you; comb or curl the hair of that new Ganymede of yours, who courts you so tepidly; it is time to stop giving yourself to the immature years of this boy in whom you take so much pleasure, because for me, losing the hope of winning you means ending the life I detest. Do you by chance think, proud and thoughtless maiden, that in your case alone the usual laws and statutes can be broken and ignored? I mean, do you think this boy, haughty because of his wealth, arrogant because of his good looks, inexperienced because of his youth, presumptuous because of his lineage, will desire, or be able to, or know how to be firm in his love, or esteem the inestimable, or know what mature and experienced men know? If you do think so, be disabused of the thought, because the only good thing the world has is always to act in the same way so that no one is deceived except by his own ignorance. In few years there is much inconstancy; in the rich, pride; vanity, in the arrogant; in the beautiful, disdain; and in those who have all of these, folly, which is mother to every unfortunate event. And you, boy, who so unassailably intend to carry off the prize that more rightly belongs to my honest desires than to your idle ones, why don't you get up from that bed of flowers where you are lying and come rip out my soul, which so despises yours? And not because what you are doing offends me, but because you do not know how to value the treasure that fortune has granted you; it is plain to see you think little of it, for you do not wish to take action to defend it so as not to run the risk of ruining the careful ornamentation of your pretty clothes. If Achilles had been as quiet as you, Ulysses would have been certain he would not succeed in his undertaking. Go, go, and take your pleasure with your mother's ladies, and be careful there of your hair and your hands, more clever at spinning soft silk than at grasping the hard sword.'

"None of these words made Cornelio get up from the place where I had found him sitting; instead he was passive, looking at me as if enchanted, not moving; at the sound of the raised voice in which I told him what you have heard, the people who were walking in the garden approached and began to listen to the other insults I directed at Cornelio; and he, encouraged by the people who had come near, because all or most of them were his kin, his servants, or his friends, showed signs of standing; but before he rose to his feet, I placed my hand on my sword and rushed at him, and not only at him but at everyone there. But Leonisa fell into a deep swoon as soon as she saw the flash of my sword, which made me even more incensed and more violent. I cannot tell you whether the many who attacked me wanted only to defend themselves, as one defends against an enraged madman, or whether it was my good luck or diligence, or that heaven wanted to save me for greater misfortunes, because in fact I wounded seven or eight of those closest to me. Cornelio's effort protected him, for he put so much into his feet as he fled that he escaped my hands.

"Finding myself in such present danger, surrounded by enemies who wanted revenge as if they had been attacked, fortune came to my assistance with a remedy, and it would have been better if I had lost my life there rather than having it saved in such an unprecedented manner, and then losing it thousands of times each day. What happened was that, without warning, a large number of Turks stormed into the garden from two corsairs' galleys from

Bizerta; they had disembarked on a nearby beach without being detected by the sentinels at the naval towers or discovered by the coastal scouts or cavalry. When my opponents saw them, they left me alone and quickly hid in a safe place. Of all those in the garden, the Turks could capture only three and Leonisa, who was still in a faint. They captured me with four huge wounds, avenged by my own hand on four Turks, and I left another four lying on the ground, lifeless.

"The Turks carried out this assault with their usual diligence, and not very happy with the outcome, they returned to their ships and then headed out to sea, and using sails and oars soon reached the island of Favignana. They took an inventory to see who was missing, and seeing that the dead were four soldiers of the kind they call *leventes*, or naval soldiers, among the best and most respected they had with them, they wanted to wreak vengeance on me, and so the captain of the flagship ordered the lateen yard lowered so they could hang me.

"Leonisa, who had regained consciousness, watched all this, and finding herself a prisoner of the corsairs, shed an abundance of beautiful tears, and wringing her delicate hands, not saying a word, she listened closely, trying to see if she could understand what the Turks were saying. But one of the Christian galley slaves told her in Italian how the captain had ordered the hanging of the Christian, pointing to me, because he had killed in his defense four of the best soldiers on the galleys. This was heard and understood by Leonisa who, showing me compassion for the first time, said to the captive that he should tell the Turks not to hang me because they would lose a large ransom, and that she was asking them to return to Trápana, where I would soon be ransomed. This, as I say, was the first and perhaps the last charity Leonisa showed me, all to my greater misfortune. And so the Turks heard what the captive said, believed him, and the desire for profit tempered their anger. The next morning, flying a flag of peace, they returned to Trápana. I spent that night in pain that you can imagine, not so much because of my wounds as from imagining the danger to my cruel beloved enemy among those barbarians.

"Having reached the city, as I say, one of the galleys sailed into the port and the other remained outside; soon the entire port and shoreline were crowded with Christians, and from a distance pretty Cornelio watched events on the galley. One of my stewards arrived to negotiate my ransom, and to him I said that in no way was it a matter of my freedom but Leonisa's, and he should give my entire fortune for her; further, I ordered him to go back on land and tell Leonisa's parents to allow him to negotiate their daughter's freedom and not to do anything on her account. When this was done, the principal captain, a

Greek renegade named Yzuf, asked six thousand *escudos* for Leonisa and four thousand for me, adding that he wouldn't give up one without the other; he asked for this huge sum, as I learned afterward, because he had fallen in love with Leonisa and did not want a ransom for her; instead, he wanted to give me to the captain of the other galley, with whom he was supposed to divide the money evenly, for four thousand *escudos*, and a thousand in silver and copper, which added up to five thousand, and keep Leonisa for another five thousand. And this was the reason why they valued the two of us at ten thousand *escudos*.

"Leonisa's parents offered nothing, mindful of the promise my steward had made to them on my behalf; and Cornelio did not say a word for her sake; and so, after many demands and responses, my steward concluded by paying five thousand *escudos* for Leonisa and three thousand for me. Yzuf accepted this division, forced by the arguments of his companion and by what all his soldiers were telling him. But my steward did not have the entire sum, and he asked for three days to obtain it, intending to sell my possessions for less than they were worth until he had amassed the ransom. Yzuf rejoiced at this, thinking this would give him time to find the opportunity to prevent the agreement from going forward. And returning to the island of Favignana, he said that at the conclusion of three days he would return for the money. But ungrateful fortune, never tired of mistreating me, ordained that a Turkish sentinel, keeping watch at the highest part of the island, saw six lateen sails not far out to sea and believed, and it was true, that they must be either the squadron of Malta or ships from Sicily. He ran down to give the news, and in the blink of an eye the Turks who were on land, whether cooking their food or washing their clothes, set sail, and weighing anchor with uncommon speed, turned their oars to the water and their sails to the wind, and with their prows heading toward Barbary, in less than two hours they lost sight of the galleys; and so, hidden by the island and approaching night, they conquered the fear that had overwhelmed them.

"I leave it up to you, oh Mahamut, my friend, to consider my state of mind on that journey so contrary to the one I had hoped for; and more so the next day, when the two small galleys reached Pantelleria, and the Turks leaped onto land on the south side of the island for firewood and meat, as they call taking on provisions, and even more so when I saw that the captains leaped onto land and began to divide up the captives they had taken. Each of these actions was for me a slow death. Coming to me and Leonisa, Yzuf gave Fetala, which was the name of the captain of the other ship, six Christians, four for the oars and two beautiful Corsican boys, and me with them, so that he could keep Leonisa, and Fetala was content with this, and though I was present throughout I could not understand what they were saying, but I knew what they were doing, and I would not have understood then the division they were making if Fetala had not come up to me and said in Italian:

"'Christian, you mine now, for two thousand gold *escudos* they give me you, and if you want freedom, you give four thousand; if not, death here for you.'

"I asked him if the Christian woman was his as well; he said no, but that Yzuf was keeping her, intending to make her a Moor and marry her. And this was true, because one of the galley slaves, who understood Turkish very well, told me it was, and he had heard Yzuf and Fetala negotiating. I told my master to do whatever necessary to keep the Christian woman, and I would give him ten thousand solid gold *escudos* for her ransom. He replied it was not possible, but he would let Yzuf know the large sum he was offering for the Christian woman; perhaps, carried away by a desire for profit, he would change his mind and ransom her.

"He did so, and ordered everyone on his galley to set sail immediately, because he wanted to leave Barbary and go to Tripoli, which was his home. Yzuf for his part decided to go to Bizerta; and so they left with the same speed as when they discover either galleys to fear or commercial vessels to rob; they were moved to make haste because they thought the weather was changing, with signs of a storm. Leonisa was on land, but not where I could see her, though when it was time to set sail we came down to the shore at the same moment. Her new master and newest suitor held her by the hand, and when she stepped on the ladder going up to the galley, she turned her eyes to look at me, and my eyes, which never moved from her, looked at her with so much tender sentiment and sorrow that, without knowing how, a cloud passed in front of them so that I could not see; and without sight or sense I fell to the ground. They told me afterward that the same thing happened to Leonisa, because they saw her fall from the ladder into the sea, and Yzuf dove in after her and carried her out in his arms.

"They told me this afterward on my master's galley, where they had placed me without my being aware of it; but when I recovered from my swoon and found myself alone on the galley while the other one, on another course, moved away from us, taking with it half my soul, I mean to say, all of it, my heart went into mourning again, and again I cursed my fate and called for death; and I grieved so much that my master, annoyed at hearing me, threatened me with a heavy stick and said he would hurt me if I did not keep still. I repressed my tears and held back my sighs, believing I did so with such force that they would explode and open a doorway for my soul, which so wanted to abandon this miserable body; but fate, not content with placing me in such dire straits, ordered the end of everything, taking from me completely all hope of finding a remedy. In an instant the anticipated storm broke, and the wind that blew from the south and assailed our prow began to intensify so vigorously that it was necessary to turn the prow and allow the ship to go wherever the wind wished to take it.

"The captain intended to sail around the island and take shelter on the northern end, but his plan suffered a reversal because the wind attacked with so much fury that, in spite of all the distance we had sailed in two days, in a little more than fourteen hours we found ourselves six or seven miles from the same island we had left, and it seemed inevitable that we would crash into it, and not onto a beach but against some towering rocks that loomed before us, threatening our lives. Beside us we saw our companion ship, with Leonisa on it, and all its Turks and captive rowers struggling with the oars to hold off shattering against the rocks. Those on our small galley did the same, with greater success and effort, it seemed, than the men on the other ship who, wearied by the exertion and conquered by the ferocity of the wind, let go of the oars and before our very eyes surrendered and allowed themselves to smash into the rocks with so much devastating force that the galley broke into pieces. Night began to fall, and the cries of those who were lost were so great, as was the shock of those on our vessel in fear of losing their lives, that none of our captain's orders was understood or carried out; all that anyone cared about was not letting the oars slip from their hands, and they came upon the solution of turning the prow into the wind and dropping both anchors to delay for a while the death they considered certain. And although the fear of dying was general in everyone, my plight was just the opposite, for with the illusory hope of seeing in the next world the girl who had so recently departed this one, each moment that the galley did not sink or crash into the rocks was for me a century of the most grievous death. The huge waves that passed over the vessel and my head made me watch to see if the body of the unfortunate Leonisa was carried in one of them.

"I don't want to stop now, oh Mahamut, to recount in detail the shocks, the fears, the anguish, the thoughts I had and suffered during that long, bitter night, in order not to contradict what I intended at first, which was to tell you briefly of my misfortune. It is enough to say they were so numerous and of such a nature that if death had come then, it would have had to do very little to take my life.

"Day came with indications of a storm greater than the previous one, and we discovered that the vessel had made a huge turn away from the rocks and arrived at a promontory on the island; and finding that we were so close to having sailed around it, after six hours Turks and Christians, with new hope and strength, rounded the cape and found the sea calmer and more benign, allowing us to use the oars more easily; sheltered by the island, the Turks had the opportunity to go on land to see if anything was left of the galley that had crashed onto the rocks the night before. But heaven still did not wish to grant me the relief I hoped for of holding Leonisa's body in my arms, which, even if dead and broken, I would have been happy to see if only to break the impossibility fate had imposed on me of ever uniting with her, as my virtuous desires deserved; and so I asked a renegade who wanted to disembark to look and see if the ocean had tossed her ashore. But, as I have said, all this heaven denied me, for at that same instant the wind became angry again so that the island no longer provided shelter. Seeing this, Fetala did not wish to brave the storm that had pursued him, and so he ordered the foresail unfurled and the rowers to stop using the oars; he turned the prow toward the ocean and the stern to the wind; taking over the rudder himself, he let the ship run on the open sea, certain no obstacle would block its way. The oars were raised on the midship gangway and all the people sat on the benches and rails, and no one was visible anywhere on the galley except the galley–slave driver, who for greater security had himself tied tightly to the post in the stern. The vessel raced with so much speed that in three days and three nights, passing within sight of Trápana, Milazzo, and Palermo, it entered the waters of the Lighthouse of Messina, to the astonishment of those inside and those watching from land.

"In short, in order not to be as long in recounting the storm as the storm was in its persistence, I'll say that tired, hungry, and exhausted by a detour that meant sailing around almost the entire island of Sicily, we reached Tripoli in Barbary, where my master, before counting the booty with his corsairs and giving them their share, along with a fifth to the king, which is the custom, suffered a pain in his side so severe that within three days it sent him down to hell. Then the king of Tripoli took over his fortune, as did the superintendent of the dead kept there by the Great Turk who, as you know, is heir to those who do not leave him anything at their death; those two took control of the estate of Fetala, my master, and I fell to the superintendent, who at the time was the viceroy of Tripoli, and two weeks later the title of viceroy of Cyprus came to him, and I have come here with him not intending to ransom myself, though he has often told me I should, for I am an important gentleman, according to Fetala's soldiers, but I have never responded; instead, I have said that those who told him great things about my possibilities deceived him. And Mahamut, if you want me to tell you all my thinking, you should know I do not wish to return to a place where there is any possibility that something may console me, and by joining to a life in captivity, I want the thoughts and memories of the death of Leonisa, which never leave me, to become the reason I never enjoy anything. And if it is true that constant sorrows must of necessity come to an end or end the person who suffers them, mine will have to kill me because I plan to give them free rein so that in a few days they will catch up with the wretched life I so unwillingly sustain.

"This is, Mahamut my brother, my sad story; this is the cause of my sighs and my tears; look now and consider whether it is enough to take them from the depths of my soul and engender them in the despondency of my wounded heart. Leonisa died, and with her my hope, and even though, when she was alive, that hope survived on a slender thread, still, still. . . ."

And with this last "still" his tongue cleaved to the roof of his mouth so that he could not speak another word or stop the tears that, as they say, streamed down his cheeks so abundantly that they dampened the earth. In this Mahamut joined him; but when the paroxysm, caused by renewed memory in the bitter story, had passed, Mahamut attempted to console Ricardo with the most eloquent words he knew; but Ricardo stopped him, saying:

"What you must do, my friend, is tell me what I should do to fall into disgrace with my master and all those with whom I may communicate, so that, being despised by him and them, they all will mistreat and persecute me, and by adding sorrow to sorrow and grief to grief, I shall quickly achieve what I desire, which is the end of my life."

"Now I know," said Mahamut, "that what people say is true, that what can be felt can be said, though sometimes sentiment silences the tongue; whatever the case, Ricardo, whether your sorrow reaches your words or they keep ahead of it, you will always find in me a true friend, either for help or for advice; even if my youth and my stupidity in putting on these clothes cry out that you cannot trust or hope for anything from those two things I offer you, I shall do what I can to keep that suspicion from being true and show you that one cannot assume this opinion is valid, and even though you do not wish to be advised or favored, I shall not for that reason stop doing what is best for you, as one does with a sick man to whom one gives what is good for him and not what he asks for. There is no one in the entire city who can do as much or is worth as much as the magistrate, my master; not even yours, who will be viceroy here, can do as much; and this being true, I say I am the one who can do most in the city, for I can achieve whatever I wish with my master. I say this because I may be able to find a way to persuade him to take you as his servant, and when you are with me, time will tell us what we must do for you to be consoled, if you wish to or can be consoled, and for me to leave this life for a better one or, at least, learn the direction to take to have a life that is more secure."

"I thank you, Mahamut," replied Ricardo, "for the friendship you offer, though I am certain that no matter how much you do, you will not be able to do anything that can benefit me. But let us leave this for now and go to the tents, because I see that many people are leaving the city, and no doubt it is the former viceroy who has come out to the countryside to allow my master to enter the city and take up residence."

"That is true," said Mahamut. "Come, then, Ricardo, and you will see the ceremonies to welcome him, for I know you will enjoy watching them."

"Let us go quickly," said Ricardo. "I may need you if the warden of my master's captives has noticed my absence, for he is a renegade Corsican and doesn't have a very merciful nature."

They stopped chatting and reached the tents at the same time that the old pasha arrived and the new one came out to greet him at the door of the tent.

Alí Pasha, which was the name of the one leaving office, was accompanied by all the Janizaries who had been quartered in Nicosia since the Turkish conquest, and who numbered some five hundred men. They came in two wings or lines, some with rifles and others with naked scimitars. They reached the door of Hazán, the new pasha, surrounded it, and Alí Pasha, bending down, bowed to Hazán, who, bending less, greeted him in turn. Then Alí entered Hazán's tent, and the Turks placed Hazán on a powerful horse with rich trappings and led him around the tents and through a good portion of the countryside, calling and shouting and saying in their language:

"Hurrah, long live Suleiman the Sultan and Hazán Pasha in his name!"

This was repeated a good many times, the voices and the war cries growing stronger, and then they returned him to the tent, where Alí Pasha had remained, and he, the magistrate, and Hazán closed the tent door and were alone for an hour.

Mahamut told Ricardo they were there to discuss what should be done in the city in the vicinity of the construction that Alí had begun.

A short while later the magistrate came to the door of the tent and called out in Turkish, Arabic, and Greek that all those who wished to enter to ask for justice or any other matter having to do with Alí Pasha, could enter freely, for there was Hazán Pasha, whom the Great Lord had sent to be viceroy of Cyprus, and who would preserve reason and justice. With this license, the Janizaries stopped blocking the door of the tent and allowed those who so wished to enter. Mahamut had Ricardo go in with him, and since he was Hazán's slave, they did not prevent his entering.

Greek Christians went in to ask for justice, as well as some Turks, and all for matters of so little importance that the magistrate dispatched most of them without juridical bureaucracy, with no discovery of evidence, orders from the judge, or legal questions or their responses, for all trials, except matrimonial ones, are taken care of quickly and without delay, more through the judgment of a good man than any law. And among those barbarians, if they are barbarians in this matter, the magistrate is the competent judge in all trials, for he hears and decides them on the spot, and gives his verdict in an instant, and there is no appealing his sentence in any other court.

At this point a *chauz*, which is like a bailiff, came in and said that a Jew at the door of the tent had come to sell a very beautiful Christian girl. The magistrate said to have him come in. The *chauz* went out and returned immediately, and with him was a venerable Jew who held by the hand a girl dressed in Berber clothing, so beautifully adorned and arranged that the richest Moorish women from Fez or Morocco could not have looked as beautiful, though they are better dressed than all the other women in Africa, even those from Algiers with all their many pearls. Her face was covered by scarlet taffeta; around her bare insteps appeared two *carcajes*—what they call bracelets in Arabic—which seemed to be pure gold, and on her arms, seen or surmised through a shirt of fine silk, she wore other gold *carcajes* studded with many pearls; in short, as far as her clothing was concerned, she was richly and elegantly adorned.

Marveling at this first glimpse of her, the magistrate and the other pashas, before saying or asking anything else, ordered the Jew to have the Christian girl remove her veil. He did so, and a face was revealed that both dazzled the eyes and brought joy to the hearts of all those present, like the sun, after long darkness, shining through heavy clouds and offering itself to the eyes of all who desire it; such was the beauty of the captive Christian, and such her charm and elegance. But the one on whom the marvelous light that had been revealed made the greatest impression was the doleful Ricardo, the man who knew her better than any other, for it was his cruel and dearly loved Leonisa whom so often and with so many tears he had considered and wept for as dead. At the unexpected sight of the Christian's singular beauty, Alí's heart was transfixed and conquered, and Hazán's was wounded to the same degree, and the heart of the magistrate did not escape the amorous wound, and more enthralled than any of the others, he could not move his eyes away from the beautiful eyes of Leonisa. And to insist on the powerful force of love, you should know that at that same moment, in the hearts of all three, what seemed to each a firm hope of winning and enjoying her was born; and so, without wanting to know how, or where, or when she had come into the Jew's power, they asked him how much he wanted for her.

The covetous Jew responded four thousand *doblas*, which amounted to two thousand *escudos*; but no sooner had he declared the price than Alí Pasha said he would pay that for her, and they should go quickly to his tent to count the money; but Hazán Pasha, who did not intend to lose her, even if it cost him his life, said:

"I too shall pay the four thousand *doblas* the Jew is asking, and I would not give them or contradict what Alí has said if I were not forced to by what he himself would say rightly obliges and forces me to do so, and it is that this exquisite slave is not for either of us but for the Great Lord only; and so I say that in his name I buy her; now let us see who is rash enough to take her from me."

"I am," replied Alí, "because I shall buy her for the same reason, and it is more appropriate for me to give the Great Lord this present because I can take her to Constantinople immediately, thereby earning the goodwill of the Great Lord; for, Hazán, being the man I am, as you see, with no position at all, I need to find ways to earn one, while you are sure of yours, for three years since today you begin to rule and govern this rich kingdom of Cyprus; for these reasons and because I was the first to offer the price of the captive, it stands to reason, oh Hazán, that you will let me have her."

"I should be thanked even more," responded Hazán, "for procuring and sending her to the Great Lord, which I do unmoved by my own interests, and as for the ease of taking her there, I shall provide a small galley staffed with only my servants and slaves."

Alí, incensed by these words, rose to his feet, put his hand on his scimitar, and said:

"My purpose being clear, oh Hazán, which is to take this Christian to the Great Lord and give her to him as a gift, and having been the first buyer, it is reasonable and just that you leave her to me; and if you intend something else, this scimitar I am holding will defend my right and punish your boldness."

The magistrate listened to all this and, no less inflamed than the other two, and fearful of losing the Christian girl, he imagined how he could stop the fire that had been lit and at the same time keep the captive and not give any hint of his hypocritical intention, and so, getting to his feet, he placed himself between the two, who were already standing, and said:

"Calm down, Hazán, and you, Alí, be still; for I am here and know how to and am able to settle your differences, so that the two of you achieve your desires and the Great Lord, as you intend, is served."

They immediately obeyed the words of the magistrate, and even if he had ordered them to do something more difficult, they still would have obeyed, so great is the respect those of that damaged sect have for his white hairs. The magistrate continued, saying:

"You say, Alí, that you want this Christian for the Great Lord, and Hazán says the same; you allege that because you were the first to offer the price, she must be yours; Hazán contradicts you, and although he does not know how to support his reasoning, I find that his is the same as yours, that is, his intention, which undoubtedly must have been born at the same time as yours, to buy the slave for the same reason; you had only the advantage of speaking first, and this must not be a motive for Hazán to be completely disappointed in his honest desire; and so I think it a good idea to reconcile the two of you in this way: let the slave belong to both of you, and since how she is used depends on the will of the Great Lord, for whom she was bought, he must dispose of her; and so you will pay, Hazán, two thousand *doblas*, and Alí another two thousand, and the captive will remain under my authority so that in both your names I shall send her to Constantinople, so that I am not left without any reward, even for having been present; and therefore I offer to send her at my cost, with the authority and decency owed to the person to whom she is sent, writing to the Great Lord and telling him everything that has occurred here and the desire the two of you have shown to serve him."

The two enamored Turks did not know how to contradict him, nor could they, nor did they wish to, and even though they saw that with his plan they would not achieve their desires, they had to submit to the magistrate's opinion, each forming and tending to a hope in his soul which, though doubtful, promised that they could reach the goal of their burning desires. Hazán, now viceroy of Cyprus, planned to give so many gifts to the magistrate that he would be won over and in his debt and then would give him the captive; Alí imagined doing something that guaranteed his obtaining what he desired; each thought his plan was certain, and they easily agreed to what the magistrate wished, and with the consent and will of both they gave her to him immediately, and then each paid the Jew two thousand *doblas*.

The Jew said he could not give her to them in the clothes she was wearing, because they were worth another two thousand *doblas*, and this was true, because in her hair—part of which hung loose down her back and part tied and bound with ribbons at her forehead—there were strings of pearls very charmingly wound through her tresses. The bracelets on her feet and hands were also covered with large pearls, her dress was a full-length Moorish robe of green satin, embroidered and covered in gold braid; in short, everyone thought the price the Jew asked for her attire was too low, and the magistrate, not wishing to seem less generous than the two pashas, said he would pay for the clothes so that the Christian would appear before the Great Lord dressed as she was. The two rivals thought this was a good idea, each believing that everything would go his way.

Now what Ricardo felt at seeing his soul put up for public auction must be mentioned, and the thoughts he had at that moment, and the fears that assailed him at seeing that having found his beloved darling only meant losing her even more. He could not tell if he was asleep or awake, he could not believe what his own eyes saw, because he thought it impossible to see so unexpectedly the girl he thought had closed her eyes forever. He went up to his friend Mahamut and said:

"Don't you recognize her, my friend?"

"No, I don't," said Mahamut.

"Well, you must know," replied Ricardo, "that she is Leonisa."

"What are you saying, Ricardo?" said Mahamut.

"What you have heard," said Ricardo.

"Well, be quiet and don't expose her," said Mahamut, "because fortune is arranging for you to have her in a good and prosperous state since she is going to my master."

"Do you think that it would be a good idea," said Ricardo, "to stand where she can see me?"

"No," said Mahamut, "don't alarm her or become alarmed yourself, and don't give any sign that you know her or have seen her; that might work to the detriment of my plan."

"I'll do as you say," responded Ricardo.

And so he did not allow his eyes to meet Leonisa's, and she kept hers, while this was going on, fixed on the ground, shedding a few tears. The magistrate approached her, took her by the hand, and handed her over to Mahamut, ordering him to take her to the city, deliver her to his lady Halima, and tell her to treat the girl as a slave of the Great Lord. Mahamut did so and left Ricardo alone, who followed his star with his eyes until she went behind the cloud of the walls of Nicosia. He went up to the Jew and asked him where he had bought her, or how that Christian captive had come into his hands. The Jew responded that on the island of Pantanalea he had bought her from some Turks who had been shipwrecked there; and wanting to continue on his way, he was stopped by a summons from the pashas, who wanted to ask him what Ricardo had desired to know; and with this he took his leave.

On the road from the tents to the city, Mahamut had the opportunity to ask Leonisa, in Italian, where she was from, and she answered from the city of Trápana. Mahamut also asked if she knew a rich and noble gentleman from that city named Ricardo. Hearing this, Leonisa gave a great sigh and said:

"Yes, I do, to my woe."

"Why to your woe?" asked Mahamut.

"Because he knew me to both his and my misfortune," responded Leonisa.

"And by chance," asked Mahamut, "did you also know in the same city another gentleman of gallant disposition, the son of very wealthy parents, and in his own person very valiant, very generous, and very discerning, whose name was Cornelio?"

"I know him as well," responded Leonisa, "and I can say more to my woe than to Ricardo's; but who are you, Señor, who know them and ask me about them?"

"I am," said Mahamut, "a native of Palermo who, through a series of accidents, am wearing this clothing and attire different from what I normally wore, and I know them because not many days ago both were in my hands; Moors from Tripoli in Barbary captured Cornelio and sold him to a Turk, a merchant from Rhodes, who brought him to this island with merchandise to sell, and he entrusted all his goods to Cornelio."

"He'll know how to care for them very well," said Leonisa, "because he knows how to take good care of what is his; but tell me, Señor, how or with whom did Ricardo come to this island?"

"He came," responded Mahamut, "with a corsair who had captured him while he was in a seaside garden in Trápana, and with him he said they had captured a girl whose name he never wanted to tell me. He was here a few days with his master, who went to visit the tomb of Muhammad, in the city of Medina, and when it was time to leave Ricardo became very sick and indisposed, and his master left him with me because he was from my country and said I was to nurse him and take care of him until he returned, and if by chance he did not come back, I was to send him to Constantinople, and he would let me know when he had arrived there; but heaven had other plans, for though he took no turn for the worse, in only a few days the days of the unlucky Ricardo's life came to an end, and he was always calling the name of Leonisa, whom he said he loved more than his own life and soul; this Leonisa, he told me, had drowned in a small galley that had foundered on the island of Pantanalea, and he always cried over and lamented her death, until it brought him to the point that he lost his life, for I did not think he had a sickness in his body but gave signs of a sorrow in his soul."

"Tell me, Señor," replied Leonisa, "this boy you're talking about, in the conversations he had with you, which, since you were from the same country, must have been many, did he ever name this Leonisa and say how she and Ricardo were captured?"

"Yes, he did," said Mahamut, "and he asked me if a Christian girl by that name and with such and such characteristics had been brought to this island, for he would be happy to find her and ransom her, if it happened that her master had been disappointed because she was not as rich as he had thought, although it might be that because he had enjoyed her, he would value her less; and if it were no more than three or four hundred *escudos*, he would pay that very gladly for her, because at one time he had felt some love for her."

"It must have been very little," said Leonisa, "since he did not go over four hundred *escudos*; Ricardo is more generous, and more valiant, and more courteous. May God forgive the person responsible for his death; it is I, I am the unfortunate woman he wept over and took for dead, and God knows I would be happy to repay him if he were alive and could see I felt the same sentiment because of his adversity that he felt because of mine. I, Señor, as I have already told you, am the only-slightly-loved of Cornelio and the well-wept-for of Ricardo, and for very many and varied reasons, I have come to this wretched state in which I find myself; and though it is so dangerous, through the grace of God I have maintained the entirety of my honor, and so I live content in my misery. Now I don't know where I am, or who my master is, or where my adverse fate will take me, and therefore I beg you, Señor, perhaps for the sake of the Christian blood you have, to advise me in my travails; for since they are so many, they have made me somewhat wary; so many of the most difficult kind happen so suddenly that I do not know how I am to adapt to them."

To which Mahamut responded that he would do what he could to serve her, advising and helping her with his ingenuity and his strength; he told her about the disagreement of the two pashas on her account, and how she was in the hands of the magistrate, his master, who would take her to Constantinople and present her as a gift to the Great Turk Selim; but before that happened he had hope that the true God, in whom he believed though he was a poor Christian, would dispose matters differently, and he advised her to get on very well with Halima, the wife of the magistrate, his master, in whose hands she would be until she was sent to Constantinople, and he told her about Halima's character and said these and other things to her benefit, until he left her at the house and in the hands of Halima, to whom he gave his master's message.

The Moorish woman welcomed her, seeing that she was so well dressed and so beautiful. Mahumut returned to the tents to tell Ricardo what had happened with Leonisa; and when he found him he recounted everything, point by point, and when he came to what Leonisa had felt when she was told that he was dead, tears almost came to his eyes. He said he had invented the story of Cornelio's captivity to see what she felt; he told him about the indifference and suspicion with which she had spoken about Cornelio, all of which was a poultice for the afflicted heart of Ricardo, who said to Mahamut:

"I recall, Mahamut my friend, a story my father told me; you know already how much curiosity he had and have heard how much honor was paid him by the Emperor Carlos V, whom he always served in honorable wartime positions. And so, he told me that when the emperor was just outside Tunis and took it with the fortress of La Goleta, he was in his tent on campaign one day when they brought him as a gift a Moorish girl who was singularly beautiful, and when she was given to him some rays of sun came in through parts of the tent and shone on her hair, its gold competing with that of the sun, something new in Moorish women, who always valued having black hair. He recounted that on this occasion, among many other people in the tent, were two Spanish knights: one Andalusian and the other Catalan, both very clever and both of them poets. And the Andalusian, having seen her, began with admiration to recite some verses they call *coplas*, with some difficult consonants and consonant rhyme, and stopping at the five verses of the *copla*, he did not finish either the stanza or the verse because he could not think so spontaneously of the consonants he needed to finish it; but the other gentleman, who was beside him and heard the verses, seeing him indecisive, as if half the *copla* had been stolen out of his mouth, continued it and finished with the same consonant rhymes. And this came to mind when I saw the beautiful Leonisa come into the pasha's tent, darkening not only the rays of the sun, if they touched her, but the entire sky with its stars."

"Be quiet, now," said Mahamut, "that's enough, Ricardo my friend, with each thing you say I'm afraid you will go so far in your praise of the beautiful Leonisa that you will no longer resemble a Christian and begin to resemble a pagan. If you like, tell me those verses or *coplas* or whatever you call them, and afterward we'll talk about other things that are more pleasant and perhaps even more profitable."

"All right," said Ricardo, "and I'll tell you again that one person said the first five verses, and another the second five, all of it extemporized, and these are the verses:

> Just as when the sun peers out
> behind a low-rising hill,

and without warning takes us
and with its gaze overcomes
our gaze, and then slackens it;

like a precious, costly gem
that allows no splintering,
such is your visage, Aja,
steadfast lance of Muhammad,
that splits my inmost heart in two.

"They sound good to me," said Mahamut, "and it sounds and seems even better to me that you're able to recite verses, Ricardo, because reciting or writing them requires a dispassionate mind."

"Dirges are normally wept, just as hymns are sung, and all of it is reciting verses. But leaving that aside, tell me what you plan to do about our concerns, for since I didn't understand what the pashas were saying in the tent, while you were taking Leonisa away one of my master's renegades, a Venetian who was present and understands Turkish very well, told me about it. And what must be done before anything else is find a way to stop Leonisa from falling into the hands of the Great Lord."

"The first thing that must be done," responded Mahamut, "is for you to become my master's slave; once that's accomplished, we can consult and decide what our best course of action may be."

At this point the guardian for Hazán's Christian captives came in and took Ricardo away with him. The magistrate returned to the city with Hazán, who in only a few days had taken on the duties of Alí and considered it certain that he would go to Constantinople. And then Hazán left, urging the magistrate to lose no time in sending the captive girl to the Great Lord and writing to him in support of Hazán's aspirations. The magistrate promised with his traitor's heart, which was burning for her. Alí left, filled with false hopes, and Hazán remained, not free of them, and Mahamut took steps so that Ricardo would come into his master's hands. The days passed, and the desire to see Leonisa gripped Ricardo so tightly that he did not have a moment's peace. Ricardo changed his name to Mario so his name would not reach Leonisa's ears before he saw her, and seeing her was very difficult because the Moors are exceedingly jealous, and the men completely cover the faces of their women, though they do not mind Christian men seeing them, perhaps because they do not consider them real men since they are captives.

One day it happened that Señora Halima saw her slave Mario, and she looked at him so hard and long that he was etched in her heart and fixed in her memory; and perhaps not very happy with the weak embraces of her ancient husband, she easily gave in to a sinful desire, and just as easily confessed it to Leonisa, for whom she had already developed deep affection because of her pleasant disposition and discerning behavior, and whom she treated with great respect because she belonged to the Great Lord. She told her that the magistrate had brought to the house a Christian captive so gallant in his charm and good looks that she had never laid eyes on a handsomer man in her life, and they said he was a *chelebí*, which means a gentleman, and from the same country as Mahamut, her renegade, and she did not know how to tell him of her love without the Christian thinking less of her for having declared her feelings. Leonisa asked the captive's name, and Halima said his name was Mario, to which Leonisa replied:

"If he were a gentleman and from the place they say, I would know him; but there is no gentleman in Trápana named Mario; Señora, let me see him and speak to him, and I shall tell you who he is and what you can expect from him."

"All right," said Halima, "then on Friday, when the magistrate is at prayer in the mosque, I shall have the captive brought here, where you can speak to him alone, and if you think it appropriate to hint at my desire, then do so the best way you can."

Halima said this to Leonisa, and less than two hours later the magistrate summoned Mahamut and Mario, and just as effectively as Halima had revealed her heart to Leonisa, the enamored old man revealed his to his two slaves, asking their advice about what to do so that he could enjoy the Christian girl and fulfill his obligations to the Great Lord, to whom she belonged, saying he would die a thousand deaths before presenting her to the Great Turk still a virgin. The religious Moor recounted his passion so vividly that it entered the hearts of his two slaves, who thought just the opposite of what he thought. They agreed that Mario, as a man from her country, though he had said he did not know her, would take the lead in appealing to her and declaring the magistrate's desire, and if she could not be persuaded in this way, then he would use force, for she was in his power. And if it came to that, he would say she was dead and not send her to Constantinople.

The magistrate was delighted with the thinking of his slaves, and imagining his joy he immediately offered Mahamut his freedom and half his fortune when he died. By the same token, he promised Mario, if he achieved what the magistrate desired, freedom and enough money to return home rich, honored, and content. If he was generous in his promises, his captives were prodigal in offering to obtain for him the moon in the sky, not to mention Leonisa, as long as he gave them the opportunity to speak to her.

"I shall give that to Mario as often as he wishes," responded the magistrate, "because I shall have Halima go to the house of her parents, who are Greek Christians, for a few days, and while she is away, I shall tell the gatekeeper to let Mario enter the house as often as he wishes, and I shall tell Leonisa that she can speak with her countryman whenever she so desires."

In this way the wind of fortune began to turn for Ricardo and blow in his favor, not knowing what his own masters were doing.

The three of them having made this arrangement, the one who first put it into practice was Halima, who, just like a woman, had a pliant nature easily persuaded to do everything she enjoyed. That same day the magistrate told Halima that whenever she wished she could go to her parents' house to rest with them for as many days as she liked. But since she was delighted with the hope that Leonisa had given her, she not only would not go to her parents' house, but did not even wish to go to the feigned paradise of Muhammad; and so she replied that for the moment she had no desire to leave, and when she did, she would tell him, but she would have to take the Christian captive with her.

"No, not that," replied the magistrate, "it isn't a good idea for the prize of the Great Lord to be seen by anyone, even more so if she converses with Christians, for you know that when she is in the power of the Great Lord, she will be locked in the seraglio and made a Turk whether she wishes it or not."

"Since she will be with me," replied Halima, "it does not matter whether she is in my parents' house or communicates with them, for I communicate with them even more than she will and that does not stop me from being a good Turk; besides, I do not plan to stay in their house more than four or five days, because my love for you will not allow me to be absent from you and not see you for so long."

The magistrate did not wish to reply so as not to give her a reason for harboring any suspicion of his intention.

Friday came, and he went to the mosque but could not leave for almost four hours; and as soon as Halima saw him cross the threshold she sent for Mario, but a Corsican Christian who guarded the door to the courtyard would not let him enter until Halima called to him to let Mario in; and so he came in, confused and trembling, as if he were about to do battle with an army of enemies.

Leonisa was dressed just as she had been when she entered the pasha's tent, sitting at the foot of a large marble staircase that led to the upper passageways. Her head was resting on the palm of her right hand, and her arm was on her knees, her eyes on the area opposite to the door through which Mario had come in, and so although he walked toward the place where she was sitting, she did not see him. As soon as Ricardo came in, he looked around the house and found nothing in it but still, peaceful silence, until his eyes came to rest on the place where Leonisa was sitting. In an instant, so many thoughts overwhelmed the enamored Ricardo, enraptured and overjoyed to think he was twenty steps, or perhaps a little more, from his happiness and contentment; he considered himself a captive, his glory in someone else's hands. With these thoughts whirling around in his mind, he moved, slowly and fearfully, alarmed, happy and sad, fearful and courageous, approaching the center of his joy, when Leonisa turned her head unexpectedly and her eyes met those of Mario, who was looking at her fixedly. But when their eyes met, they revealed in different ways what their souls had been feeling. Ricardo stopped and could not take another step; Leonisa thought Ricardo was dead because of what Mahamut had told her, and seeing him alive so unexpectedly filled her with fear and horror, and not taking her eyes off him or turning her back to him, she moved up four or five steps, and taking a small cross from her bodice, kissed it many times and made the sign of the cross an infinite number of times, as if she were seeing a phantom or something else from the next world. Ricardo recovered from his daze, inferred from what Leonisa was doing the true cause of her fear, and said to her:

"It grieves me, oh beautiful Leonisa, that the news of my death given to you by Mahamut was not true, because that might excuse the fears I now have that the harshness you always used with me is still as strong in you. Be calm, Señora, and come down, and if you have the courage to do what you have never done, which is to come to me, then do so and you will see that I am not a phantom body; I am Ricardo, Leonisa; Ricardo, the man who is as fortunate as you wish him to be."

At this point Leonisa placed her finger over her mouth, and Ricardo understood it was a sign that he should be silent or lower his voice; and finding a little more courage, he came close enough to her to hear these words:

"Speak quietly and slowly, Mario, for I think that's your name now, and don't talk about anything except what I talk about; and be aware that our having been heard might be a reason for our never seeing each other again. I believe that Halima, our mistress, is listening, and she told me she adores you; she has made me the intermediary for her desire. If you wish to reciprocate, you must concentrate more on the body than on the soul; and if you do not wish to, you must pretend, if only because I beg you to, and because of what a woman's stated desires deserve."

To which Ricardo responded:

"I never thought and never could have imagined, oh beautiful Leonisa, that anything you asked of me could also be impossible for me to do, but what you are asking has made me realize the truth. Is desire by any chance so light a thing that it can be moved and carried wherever one might wish to carry it, or is it good for a true and honorable man to pretend in matters that are so weighty? If you believe that any of these things should or can be done, then do as you wish, for you are mistress of my will; but I know you are deceiving me in this as well, for you have never known desire, and therefore you do not know what you should do with it. But in exchange for your not saying that, in the first thing you told me to do, I failed to obey you, I shall lose the right I owe to being the man I am, and I shall satisfy your desire and Halima's, pretending, as you say, if in this way I can acquire the greater good of seeing you; and so invent the answers as you wish, for from now on my feigned desire affirms and confirms them. And in payment for what I am doing for you, which is the most, in my opinion, I can do, even if I give you again the soul I have so often given to you, I beg you to tell me briefly how you escaped from the hands of the corsairs and came into those of the Jew who sold you."

"The story of my misfortunes demands more time; despite that, I wish to satisfy you in some way. And so, a day after we were separated, Yzuf's ship returned with favorable winds to the island of Pantanalea, where we also saw your galley, but ours, unable to avoid it, foundered on the rocks. And my master, seeing his perdition so near, quickly emptied two barrels that were filled with water, closed them very carefully, and tied them together with rope; he put me between them, then undressed and, holding another barrel in his arms, tied his body to it with a cord, and tied the same cord around my barrels, and with great courage threw himself into the sea, taking me after him. I did not have the courage to throw myself in, and another Turk gave me a shove and tossed me in behind Yzuf, and I fell, senseless, and did not recover until I found myself on land in the arms of two Turks who, holding me face down, had me spew out the great quantity of water I had swallowed. I opened my eyes, astounded and horrified, and saw Yzuf next to me, his head shattered; as I learned later, when he reached land he crashed head first into the rocks, and there his life ended. The Turks also told me that by pulling on the cord, they brought me to land, almost drowned; only eight people escaped the doomed galley.

"We were on the island for a week, the Turks showing me as much respect as if I had been their sister, and perhaps even more. We hid in a cave, for they were fearful a squadron of Christians on the island would come down and capture them; they survived on the wet hardtack that the ocean washed ashore; it had been on the ship and they went out at night to search for it. As luck would have it, and to my greater sorrow, the squadron was without its captain, who had been killed a few days earlier, and in the squadron there were only twenty soldiers; they learned this from a boy the Turks had captured who left the squadron and came down to gather shellfish on the beach. After a week a Moorish ship, the kind they call a *caramoussal*, reached the coast; the Turks saw it and came out of hiding, signaling the vessel when it was close to shore so those on board would know they were Turks. They recounted their misfortunes, and the Moors welcomed them onto their ship; a Jew was traveling with them, a very rich merchant, and all or most of the merchandise on the ship was his; it consisted of wool cloth and cloth of wool and cotton, and other things carried from Barbary to the Levant. The Turks went to Tripoli on the ship, and on the way they sold me to the Jew, who paid two thousand *doblas* for me, an excessive price if the love the Jew revealed to me had not made him generous.

"Leaving the Turks in Tripoli, the ship resumed its course, and the Jew began to importune me shamelessly. I offered the resistance his base desires deserved. Seeing that achieving them was hopeless, he decided to get rid of me as soon as he could; and knowing that the two pashas, Alí and Hazán, were on this island, where he could sell his goods as easily as on Chios, where he had originally intended to go, he came here planning to sell me to one of them, which is why he dressed me as you see me now, to make them enthusiastic about buying me. I have learned that this magistrate bought me to make a present of me to the Great Turk, about which I am more than a little fearful. Here I learned of your feigned death, and I can tell you, if you choose to believe it, that it pained my soul, and that I envied you more than I mourned you, and not because I did not love you—for although I am unresponsive, I am neither ungrateful nor unappreciative—but because you were finished with the tragedy of your life."

"What you say might be true, Señora," responded Ricardo, "if death had not interfered with the good of seeing you again; for now I esteem this instant of glory when I look at you more than any other fate, except the eternal one, which my desire could secure for me in life or in death. The desire of my master the magistrate, into whose hands I have come by means of no fewer mishaps than you have suffered, is the same for you as Halima's desire for me; he has made me the interpreter of his thoughts. I accepted, not to give him pleasure but for the sake of the pleasure I would enjoy in speaking to you, so you can see, Leonisa, the end to which our misfortunes have brought us, you to be intermediary for the impossible, which is what you are asking of me, as you know, and I to do the same for the last thing I ever thought of; in order not to achieve it, I would give the life I now value for the extreme happiness of seeing you."

"I don't know what to say to you, Ricardo," replied Leonisa, "or what path to take to get out of the labyrinth where, as you say, our bad luck has placed us. I know only that in this circumstance it is necessary to use what cannot be expected of our natures, which is pretense and deceit; and so I say that I shall give to Halima a few words from you that will entertain her rather than drive her to despair. For my part, you can tell the magistrate that to protect my honor and his deception, you will see what else should be done. And since I place my honor in your hands, you can certainly believe in its integrity and truth, which might be placed in doubt considering the many roads I have traveled and the many reverses I have suffered. It will be easy for us to talk to each other, and it will give me great pleasure to do so, on the condition that you never speak to me of anything that has to do with your declared desires, for the moment you do so is the moment I shall stop seeing you, because I do not want you to think I am worth so little that captivity can do what liberty could not; with the grace of God, I must be like gold: the more it is refined, the purer and cleaner it becomes. Be satisfied with my having said that seeing you will not annoy me, as it used to, because I tell you, Ricardo, I always thought you were disagreeable and arrogant, prouder of yourself than you should have been. I confess as well that I was deceived, and it might be that now, having this knowledge, I shall realize the truth that will place reality before my eyes, and realizing the truth, I shall be not only virtuous but more compassionate as well. Go with God, for I am afraid that Halima may have heard us, and she understands some of the Christian language, at least that mixture of languages that allows all of us to understand one another."

"Very nicely put, Señora," responded Ricardo, "and I am infinitely grateful for your helping me to realize the truth, and my esteem for you matches the favor you do me in allowing me to see you; and as you say, perhaps knowledge and experience will help you understand how simple my nature is, and how humble, especially when it comes to adoring you; and without your putting a boundary or limit on my behavior with you, may it be so virtuous that you could not find any better. As for putting off the magistrate, do not worry; do the same with Halima and know, Señora, that after seeing you a hope has been born in me and it assures me that very soon we shall achieve the liberty we desire. And with this, go with God, and I shall tell you at another time about the twists and turns by which fortune brought me to this state after I left you, I mean to say, after I was forced to leave."

They said goodbye, and Leonisa was happy and satisfied with Ricardo's candid behavior, and he was extremely happy to have heard a kind word from Leonisa's mouth.

Halima was in her room, praying to Muhammad that Leonisa would bring good news in the message that had been entrusted to her. The magistrate was in the mosque with his people, rewarding his wife's desires with his own, thinking them easy to deal with, and anticipating the answer he expected from his slave, whom he had charged with speaking to Leonisa, which Mahamut would facilitate even if Halima were at home. Leonisa increased Halima's foolish desire and love, giving her very good reasons to hope that Mario would do everything she asked; but first he said he had to let two Mondays go by before what he desired much more than she did could be granted, and he asked for this amount of time because he was imploring and beseeching God for his freedom. Halima was satisfied with the response and explanation from her beloved Mario, to whom she would give his freedom before his time of obligation was over, if he would accede to her desire; and so she asked Leonisa to ask him to shorten his time of obligation and lessen the delay, and she would offer him whatever the magistrate was asking for his ransom.

Before Ricardo replied to his master, he consulted with Mahamut regarding how he should answer; and the two of them agreed to drive him to despair and advise him to take her to Constantinople as soon as he could, and on the way, either with her consent or by force, he would achieve his desire. As for the problem he might have in fulfilling his obligations to the Great Lord, it would be a good thing to buy another slave girl, and on the journey pretend that Leonisa had fallen ill and then toss the Christian girl he had bought into the sea one night, saying it was Leonisa, captive of the Great Lord, who had died; and this could be done and would be done in such a way that the truth would never be discovered, and he would be blameless in the eyes of the Great Lord, and his desire would be satisfied, and a way would be found and devised afterward to prolong his pleasure. The wretched old magistrate, who would have believed another thousand pieces of nonsense if they served to fulfill his hopes, believed everything they said, especially because it seemed that everything they told him pointed in the right direction and promised success; and that would have been true if the intention of his two advisers had not been to take over the vessel and kill him as payment for his mad ideas. Another difficulty occurred to the magistrate, in his opinion greater than any of the others, and it was the thought that his wife Halima would not allow him to go to Constantinople if he did not take her along; but he soon resolved it, saying that instead of buying a Christian girl to die instead of Leonisa, they could use Halima, whom he wished to be free of more than he wished to be free of death.

Mahamut and Ricardo supported him in this as easily as he had thought of it; and all three in agreement, that same day the magistrate told Halima about the trip he planned to take to Constantinople to bring the Christian girl to the Great Lord, whose generosity he expected to make him the chief magistrate of Cairo or Constantinople. Halima told him she thought his decision was a good one, believing he would leave Ricardo at home; but when the magistrate declared that he planned to take him along as well as Mahamut, she changed her mind and tried to dissuade him from what she had at first approved. In short, she concluded that if he did not take her with him, she had no intention of allowing him to go. The magistrate was content to do as she wished, because he thought he would soon shake off what was for him a very heavy weight around his neck.

During this time Pasha Hazán had not neglected to ask the magistrate to give him the slave girl, offering him mountains of gold; and having given him Ricardo for nothing, whose ransom was estimated at two thousand *escudos*, he facilitated the gift as industriously as he had imagined killing the captive whenever the Great Turk sent for her. All these gifts and promises inclined the magistrate to accelerate his departure; and so, importuned by his desire and the urging of Hazán, and even Halima, who also harbored vain hopes created out of thin air, in twenty days he outfitted a brig with fifteen rowers' benches and hired good oarsmen, Moors and a few Greek Christians. He loaded all his wealth aboard the ship, and Halima did not leave any significant object in her house, and she asked her husband to allow her to take along her parents so they could see Constantinople. Halima's intention was the same as Mahamut's: to plan with him and Ricardo to take control of the brig on the way, but she did not wish to state her idea until she had embarked, for she wished to go to a Christian land, become what she had been earlier, and marry Ricardo; for it seemed obvious that if she had so much wealth with her and became a Christian, he could not fail to take her as his wife.

At this time Ricardo spoke again with Leonisa and told her what they intended, and she told him her mistress's intention, for Halima had told her about it. They both promised to keep the secret, and putting themselves in the hands of God, waited for the day of departure. And when that day arrived, Hazán came out and accompanied them to the shore with all his soldiers and did not leave them until their sails were unfurled, and did not even take his eyes off the brig until it was lost from sight. And it seems that the breeze of sighs emitted by the enamored Moor impelled with greater force the sails that took away and made off with his soul. But, like one who had loved for a long time, he could find no repose, and thinking of what he had to do in order not to die at the hands of his desires, he put into effect what he had thought about with long reflection and resolute determination. And so, in a ship with seventeen benches, which he had prepared in another port, he placed fifty soldiers, all of them his friends and acquaintances who were under obligation to him because of his many gifts and promises, and ordered them to cut off and capture the magistrate's vessel and all its riches, and put to the knife everyone on board except the captive, Leonisa; for he wanted only her, a prize superior to the many goods the brig was carrying. He also ordered them to sink the ship so nothing would remain to indicate that it had been captured. Greed for the booty put wings on their feet and strength in their hearts, though they saw clearly how little resistance they would find in the crew of the brig, who were unarmed and did not suspect this kind of occurrence.

The brig had been sailing for two days, which seemed like two centuries to the magistrate, for on the first day he had wanted to put his plan into effect, but his slaves advised him that he should first arrange for Leonisa to fall ill; to make her death believable, she had to be sick for several days. He had wanted to say simply that she had died suddenly and have it over and done with quickly, and get rid of his wife, and put out the fire in his entrails that was slowly consuming him; but, in fact, he had to yield to the opinion of his two slaves.

By now Halima had declared her intention to Mahamut and Ricardo, and they had agreed to put it into effect when they passed the Crosses of Alexandria, or entered the castles of Anatolia;[2] but the magistrate was pressing them so urgently that they offered to do it at the first opportunity. And after six days of sailing, when it seemed to the magistrate that he had pretended long enough that Leonisa was ill, he importuned his slaves to finish off Halima the next day and throw her shrouded body into the sea, saying she was the captive of the Great Lord.

Waking at dawn, then, on the day that, according to Mahamut and Ricardo's intention, was to be the fulfillment of their desires or the end of their days, they saw a vessel pursuing them with sail and oar. They feared it belonged to Christian corsairs, from whom neither group could expect anything good, because the Moors feared being captured, and the Christians, though they might have their freedom, would be left naked and robbed; but Mahamut and Ricardo were content with Leonisa's freedom and their own; with everything they imagined, they feared the insolence of corsairs, for anyone who gives himself over to such actions, regardless of his faith or language, always has a cruel spirit and an insolent nature. They went on the defensive without dropping the oars, doing everything they could; but in just a few hours they saw that the

2. The Crosses of Alexandria are in Alexandria Troas on the Aegean Sea, not in Egyptian Alexandria. Hence its proximity to Anatolia.

corsairs were gaining on them, and in less than two hours they were within range of their cannon. Seeing this, they changed what they were doing, dropped the oars, took up their weapons and waited, even though the magistrate told them not to be afraid, because the vessel was Turkish and would do them no harm. Then he ordered a white flag of peace placed on the lateen yard so that it would be seen by those who now, blinded by greed, were coming so furiously to attack the poorly defended brig. At this point Mahamut turned his head and saw a small galley, coming from the west, that seemed to have twenty benches; he told the magistrate, and some Christians on the oars said that this ship belonged to Christians; all of which doubled their turmoil and fear, and they were confused, not knowing what they would do, both fearing and hoping for whatever outcome God chose to grant them.

It seems to me that at this moment the magistrate would have given everything his desire had hoped to achieve to be back in Nicosia: so great was the confusion in which he found himself, though the first ship quickly relieved him of that, for disregarding the flags of peace, or what they owed to their religion, they attacked the magistrate's ship with so much fury that it did not take them long to sink it. Then the magistrate recognized those who were attacking and saw that they were soldiers from Nicosia; he guessed what it might be and considered himself lost and dead. And if the soldiers had not robbed before they killed, no one would have been left alive; but when they were most ardently and attentively involved in their robbery, a Turk called out, saying:

"To arms, soldiers, a Christian ship is attacking us!"

And this was true, because the vessel spotted by the magistrate's brig was flying Christian flags and banners, and it came at full speed to attack Hazán's ship; but before it reached them, someone called from the prow in Turkish, asking whose ship it was. They answered that it belonged to Hazán Pasha, viceroy of Cyprus.

"Well, why," replied the Turk, "being Muslims, do you attack and rob that ship, when we know it carries the magistrate of Nicosia?"

To which they responded that they knew only that they had been ordered to take the ship, and being soldiers and subordinates, they had obeyed.

Having found out what he wanted to know, the captain of the second ship, which came under Christian guise, allowed it to attack Hazán's ship and come to the aid of the magistrate's, and at the first shots they fired they killed more than ten Turks, and then they boarded with great spirit and speed; but no sooner had they boarded than the magistrate knew that the man who had attacked Hazán's ship was not a Christian but Alí Pasha, enamored of Leonisa, and he, with the same intention as Hazán, had been awaiting his arrival; to avoid being recognized, he had dressed his soldiers as Christians, so that by means of this strategy, his theft would be better hidden. The magistrate, who knew the intentions of lovers and traitors, began to shout their iniquities in a loud voice, saying:

"What is this, traitor Alí Pasha, that you, being a Muslim—which means a Turk—assault me as a Christian? And you, traitorous soldiers of Hazán, what demon has moved you to commit so great an insult? Why, in order to satisfy the lascivious appetite of the one who sends you here, do you wish to go against your natural lord?"

At these words, all firing stopped, and the men looked at one another and recognized one another, because all of them had been soldiers under one captain and fought under one flag; perplexed by the magistrate's words and the damage they had done, they sheathed their scimitars and their spirits fell; only Alí closed his eyes and ears to everything and, charging the magistrate, slashed his head so fiercely that if not for the protection of one hundred yards of cloth in his turban, it undoubtedly would have been cut in two; but then he was knocked down among the benches on the ship, and as he fell the magistrate said:

"Oh cruel renegade, enemy of my prophet! Is it possible there will be no one to punish your cruelty and great insolence? How, accursed man, have you dared raise hands and arms against your magistrate, and a minister of Muhammad?"

These words added great strength to his first ones, and were heard by Hazán's soldiers, who were moved by the fear that Alí's soldiers would take their plunder, which they already considered their own, and decided to risk everything. And beginning with one, and all the rest following, they attacked Alí's soldiers with so much speed, rancor, and energy that in a short time—although Alí's soldiers numbered many more than Hazán's—they were reduced to a small number; but those who remained, coming back to themselves, avenged their comrades, leaving only a few of Hazán's men alive, and those few severely wounded.

Ricardo and Mahamut from time to time peered out of the hatchway to the cabin in the stern to see how that great confusion and uproar would end; and seeing how almost all the Turks were dead, and those still alive badly wounded, and how easily they could finish off all of them, Ricardo called to Mahamut and Halima's two nephews, whom she had told to board with him to help besiege the ship, and with them and their father, taking scimitars from the dead, they leaped to the midship gangway and shouted, "Freedom, freedom!" and helped by good fortune and the Greek Christians, they easily, and without receiving a single wound, decapitated all the Turks; and passing over to Alí's galley, which was undefended, they took it with everything it contained. Of those who died in the second encounter, one of the first was Alí Pasha, whom a Turk, to avenge the magistrate, had stabbed to death.

Then, following Ricardo's advice, everyone began to transfer everything of value from their vessel and Hazán's to Alí's galley, which was a larger ship and suitable for any cargo or voyage, and with Christian rowers who, happy with the freedom they had obtained and with the many items that Ricardo distributed among them, offered to take him to Trápana and even to the ends of the earth, if he should wish it. And so Mahamut and Ricardo, delighted with their success, went to the Moorish woman Halima and told her that if she wanted to return to Cyprus, with their good fortune they would outfit a vessel of her own and give her half the riches they had on board; but she, who through so much calamity still had not lost the affection and love she had for Ricardo, said that she wanted to go with them to Christian lands, regarding which her parents were extremely happy.

The magistrate regained consciousness, and they treated his wounds the best they could; to him they said that he could choose one of two courses of action: allow himself to be taken to Christian lands, or return to Nicosia in his own ship. He responded that since fortune had brought him to such a condition, he thanked them for the freedom they had given him and said he wished to go to Constantinople and complain to the Great Lord of the injury done to him by Hazán and Alí; but when he learned that Halima was leaving him and wanted to become a Christian again, he was very close to losing his mind. In brief, they outfitted a ship for him and provided all the things needed for his voyage, and even gave him some of the gold coins that had been his, and taking his leave of everyone, having decided to return to Nicosia, he asked that before he set sail Leonisa embrace him, and that kindness and favor would be enough to make him forget all his misfortune. Everyone begged Leonisa to grant that favor to one who loved her so much, and said it would not go against the decorum of her virtue. Leonisa did as they asked, and the magistrate asked her to place her hands on his head, so that he could take away with him the hope that his wound would heal; Leonisa satisfied his every wish.

Having done this, and after drilling a hole in Hazán's ship and being favored by a fresh east wind that seemed to call to the sails in order to give itself to them, they set sail and in a short time lost sight of the magistrate's ship, and he, with tears in his eyes, watched as the wind carried away his fortune, his delight, his wife, and his soul.

Ricardo and Mahamut sailed with thoughts different from those of the magistrate; not wishing to go ashore anywhere, they quickly passed within sight of Alexandria, and without shortening the sails or needing to use the oars, they reached the craggy island of Corfu, where they took on fresh water and then, without stopping, passed the infamous Acroceraunos cliffs, and from a distance on the second day they could see Pachino, a promontory of fertile Sicily, and with the sight of this and the celebrated island of Malta, they flew, and the fortunate ship sailed with no less speed.

In short, navigating around the island, four days later they saw Lampedusa, and then the island where they had been lost, at the sight of which Leonisa began to tremble, remembering the danger she had been in. The next day they saw before them their longed for, beloved homeland; joy returned to their hearts; their spirits were aroused at their new happiness, which is one of the greatest one can have in this life: to reach one's homeland safe and sound after long captivity. Another happiness that can equal this is the happiness of victory achieved over one's enemies.

In the galley they found a box filled with pennants and small flags of different colored silks, which Ricardo used to decorate the ship. It was shortly after dawn when they found themselves less than a league from the city, and alternating their turns at the oars, and from time to time raising joyous shouts and calls, they approached the port, where in an instant an infinite number of people from the town appeared; having seen how that beautifully adorned vessel was approaching land so slowly, not a person in the city failed to come down to the shore.

In the meantime, Ricardo had begged and pleaded with Leonisa to dress and adorn herself in the same manner as when she entered the pashas' tent, because he wanted to play an amusing trick on his parents. She did so, and adding finery to finery, pearls to pearls, and beauty to beauty, which tends to increase with happiness, she dressed so that she once again caused admiration and surprise. Ricardo also dressed in the Turkish style, as did Mahamut and all the Christians on the oars, for there were enough of the dead Turks' clothes for everyone.

They arrived in port at about eight on a morning so peaceful and clear that it seemed to be watching that joyful entrance attentively. Before entering the port, Ricardo had the men fire the artillery on the galley: a cannon on the midship gangway and two small cannons or falconets; the city responded in kind.

The people were bewildered as they waited for the decorated ship to arrive. But when it was close enough for them to see that it was Turkish, because they saw the white turbans worn by men who seemed to be Moors, they became fearful, and suspecting some deception, all those in the city who were in the militia took up their weapons and went to the port, and those on horseback lined up along the shore; all of which cheered those who were approaching gradually as they entered the port, dropped anchor close to land, lowered the gangplank, dropped their oars all at once, and one by one, as if in a procession, walked ashore, and with tears of joy in their eyes, kissed the land over and over again, a clear sign that they were Christians and had stolen the ship. Finally, Halima's father and mother came out, and her two nephews, all of them, as has been said, dressed in the Turkish style; at the very end came the beautiful Leonisa, her face covered with scarlet taffeta; she came down between Ricardo and Mahamut, a sight followed by the eyes of the entire multitude that watched them. When they were ashore, they did what all the others had done, prostrating themselves and kissing the ground.

At this point the captain-governor of the city arrived, and he knew very well who the principals were, but no sooner had he arrived than he recognized Ricardo and ran with arms spread wide and signs of great happiness to embrace him. Cornelio and his father came with the governor, and Leonisa's parents and all her kin, and Ricardo's, for all of them were the leading people in the city. Ricardo embraced the governor, and responded to everyone's greetings; he grasped Cornelio's hand, and he, knowing Ricardo and finding himself held by him, lost all the color in his face and almost began to tremble with fear, and Ricardo, holding Leonisa's hand as well, said:

"As a courtesy I beg you, gentlemen, before we enter the city and the temple to give the thanks due to Our Lord for the great mercies He has showed us in our misfortune, to hear certain words I wish to say to you."

To which the governor responded that he should say whatever he wished, that everyone would listen to him with pleasure and in silence. Then all the leading citizens surrounded him, and he, raising his voice slightly, said:

"Surely you remember, gentlemen, the misfortune that befell me a few months ago in the garden at the salt marshes with the loss of Leonisa; and you also will not have forgotten how diligently I attempted to procure her freedom; forgetting about mine, I offered my entire fortune for her ransom, although this apparent generosity cannot and should not redound in my praise, since I was offering it for the ransom of my soul. What happened to the two of us afterward requires more time, another occasion, and a tongue less perturbed than mine; it is enough for now to tell you that after various strange events, and after a thousand lost hopes of finding a remedy for our misfortunes, merciful heaven, with no merit on our part, has returned us to our longed for homeland, filled with joy and overflowing with riches. And the unequaled happiness I feel is born not of those riches or the freedom I have achieved but of the happiness I imagine this sweet enemy of mine in peace and in war is feeling, as much for finding herself free as for seeing, as she sees now, the man whose portrait is in her soul; I still rejoice at the general joy of those who have been my companions in misery. And although misfortunes and sad events tend to alter dispositions and annihilate valiant spirits, this has not been the case with the executioner of my virtuous hopes; because with more courage and fortitude than I can say, she has endured the shipwreck of her afflictions and the encounters with my importunities as ardent as they are honest, which verifies that those who once were established in certain customs change heaven and not their customs. From everything I have said I want to infer that I offered her my fortune as a ransom, and my soul in my desires; I schemed for her freedom and risked my life for it more than for my own; and all of this in another more grateful individual might have amounted to burdens of some significance, but I do not want that except in this person whom I present to you now."

And saying this, he raised his hand and with honest delicacy removed the veil from Leonisa's face, which was like lifting the cloud that perhaps covers the beautiful brightness of the sun, and then continued speaking:

"You see here, oh Cornelio, that I hand to you the prize you should value above all things worthy of being valued; and see here, beautiful Leonisa, I give to you the one you have always had in your mind. This I do want you to consider as generosity, compared to which giving one's fortune, one's life, and one's honor is nothing. Receive her, oh fortunate young man, receive her, and if your knowledge can reach as far as knowing such great worth, consider yourself the most fortunate man on earth. Along with her I shall also give you my entire share of what heaven has given to all of us, which I believe amounts to more than thirty thousand *escudos*; you can enjoy it all however you choose, with freedom, serenity, and rest, and may it please heaven that it will be for long, happy years. I, alas, am left without Leonisa and prefer to be poor; for the man who lacks Leonisa, life is excessive."

And upon saying this he fell silent, as if his tongue were sticking to his palate; but then, before anyone else could speak, he said:

"Lord save me, how difficult tribulations upset one's understanding! I, gentlemen, with the desire I have to do what is right, have not thought carefully about what I said, because it is not possible for anyone to be generous with what belongs to someone else. What jurisdiction do I have over Leonisa that I give her to another? Or how can I offer what is so far from being mine? Leonisa is her own person, and so much so that if she had no parents, and may they live many happy years, she would have no opposition to her will; and if, as a judicious woman, she would consider her obligations to me, from this moment on I wipe them out, cancel them, and consider them nothing; and so I unsay what I have said and give nothing to Cornelio, because I cannot; I confirm only the gift of my estate to Leonisa, wanting no compensation other than that she consider my virtuous thoughts as true, and believe they never were directed toward or wanted anything other than what her incomparable virtue, her great courage, and her infinite beauty ask for."

Ricardo fell silent after saying this, to which Leonisa responded in this manner:

"Oh Ricardo, if you imagine that I granted some favor to Cornelio at the time you were in love with me and jealous, imagine it was as virtuous as if guided by the will and command of my parents who, attentive to moving him to be my husband, permitted them to be offered; if you are satisfied with this, you must also be very satisfied with what experience has shown you regarding my virtue and prudence. I say this so you will understand, Ricardo, that I was always my own person, not subject to anyone but my parents, whom I now humbly beseech, and it is right that I do so, to give me license and liberty to dispose of what your great courage and generosity have given to me."

Her parents said they did, because they trusted in her discernment and in her using it in a way that would always redound to her honor and benefit.

"Well, with that license," the discerning Leonisa continued, "I want not to be considered forward in exchange for not being ungrateful; and so, oh valiant Ricardo, my will, until now concealed, perplexing, and doubtful, declares in your favor; and by showing myself grateful, let men know that not all women are ungrateful. I am yours, Ricardo, and I shall be yours until death, if another better love does not move you to refuse the hand I ask of you as my husband."

Ricardo was beside himself when he heard these words, and he could not respond to Leonisa with more words, but only kneeled before her and kissed her hands, which he grasped at very often, bathing them in tender and loving tears. Cornelio shed them with grief, and Leonisa's parents with joy, and everyone present with astonishment and happiness.

The bishop or archbishop of the city was present, and with his blessing and permission he led them to the temple, and dispensing with certain rules, married them on the spot. Joy spread throughout the city, as demonstrated that night by infinite illuminations, and for many more days there were games and celebrations sponsored by Ricardo's kin and Leonisa's. Mahamut and Halima reconciled with the Church, and she, unable to fulfill her desire to be Ricardo's wife, was content to be Mahamut's. To Halima's parents and nephews Ricardo's generosity gave from his share of the spoils enough for them to live on. In short, everyone was content, free, and satisfied, and Ricardo's fame, going beyond the boundaries of Sicily, extended throughout Italy and many other places under the name of the Generous Lover, and it endures today in the many children he had with Leonisa, who was a singular example of discernment, virtue, prudence, and beauty.

THE NOVEL OF RINCONETE AND CORTADILLO

In Molinillo's Inn at the end of the famous fields of Alcudia as we travel from Castilla to Andalucía, two boys of about fourteen or fifteen happened to be there on a hot summer day, neither older than seventeen and both nice looking but very ragged, tattered, and ill-treated. They had no cloak, their breeches were canvas, and their stockings were their own flesh. It is very true that their shoes compensated for all this, because one wore espadrilles as torn as they were worn, and the other's shoes were in bits and pieces and missing their soles, so that they were more like wooden shackles than footwear. One wore a green hunter's cap, the other, a hat with no band, a low crown, and a wide brim. On his back, and tight across his chest, one carried a chamois-colored shirt wrapped up in a vagabond's bundle; the other was unencumbered by any knapsack, although on his chest there was a large shape that, as it turned out, was the kind of collar called Van Dyck, starched with grease and so threadbare it was all in shreds. Some oval-shaped playing cards were wrapped up and kept in it; their corners had been worn out with so much handling, and they had been cut into that shape so they would last longer. Both boys were sunburned and had long nails edged in black and hands that were not very clean. One had a short sword and the other a knife with a yellow handle, the kind generally called a slaughterer's knife.

The two came out to rest in the shade under a portico or lean-to in front of the inn, and sitting face to face, the one who seemed older said to the younger:

"What land does your grace come from, my good sir, and where are you going?"

"My land, kind sir," he responded, "I do not know, and I do not know where I am going, either."

"Well, in truth," said the older one, "your grace does not appear to be in the right place, since one cannot settle here, and you will be obliged to keep moving."

"That is so," replied the younger one, "but what I have said is true because my land is not mine, for there I have only a father who does not consider me his son, and a stepmother who treats me like a stepson; my travels have no fixed plan, and I would end them wherever I found someone to give me what I need to live out this miserable life."

"And does your grace know some trade?" asked the bigger boy.

And the smaller one responded:

"The only one I know is that I can run like a hare, and leap like a deer, and make very fine cuts with a scissors."

"All of that is very good, useful, and beneficial," said the bigger one, "because there must be a sacristan who will give your grace the offerings for All Saints' Day so that you'll cut some paper rosettes for the monument on Maundy Thursday."

"That isn't the kind of cutting I do," responded the smaller one, "but my father, by the grace of God, is a tailor and hosier, and he taught me to cut gaiters that, as your grace knows very well, are half stockings with spats, which are usually called leggings; and I cut them so well that I could pass the examination for maestro, except that bad luck has me in a corner."

"All of that and more happens for no reason," responded the older boy, "and I have always heard that good skills are most easily wasted; but your grace is still young enough to alter your life. But, if I am not mistaken and my eye does not deceive me, your grace has other secret talents that your grace does not wish to reveal."

"Yes, I do," replied the younger, "but they are not to be made public, as your grace has very correctly pointed out."

To which the older boy responded:

"Well, I can tell you that I am one of the most secretive boys you can find anywhere; and to oblige your grace to open your heart and let down your guard with me, I want to oblige your grace by revealing mine first, because I imagine that not without mystery has fate brought us together here, and I think we shall be, until the last day of our lives, true friends. I, my dear sir, am a native of Fuenfrida, a place known and famous for the distinguished travelers who continually pass through it; my name is Pedro del Rincón; my father is a person of quality because he is a minister of the Holy Crusade, I mean to say, a pardoner, or parner, as the common people say. Some days I accompanied him in his trade, and I learned it so well that even those who brag the most cannot issue an indulgence better than I. But one day, having grown fonder of the money paid for the indulgences than of the indulgences themselves, I embraced a small purse and found myself, and it, in Madrid, where, with all the comforts ordinarily offered there, in a few days I had removed the innards of the purse and left it more wrinkled than a newlywed's handkerchief. The man responsible for the money came after me; I was arrested; I had little protection, although those gentlemen, seeing how young I was, were satisfied with tying me to a post and having the flies swatted off my back for a while, and then banning me from the capital for four years. I was patient, shrugged my shoulders, suffered the fly-swatting, and went into exile so quickly I did not have time to look for a beast to ride. I took what I could of my prized possessions, the ones that seemed most necessary, among them these cards"—and at that point he revealed the ones about which it has been said that he carried them in his collar—"and with them I have earned my living playing twenty-one in the taverns and inns from here to Madrid; and even though your grace sees them so ragged and worn, they have a marvelous quality for the one who understands them, for they will not play unless there is a hidden ace. And if your grace knows the game, your grace will see what an advantage is had by the one who knows he has an ace at the first card, which he can use as a one or an eleven; and with this advantage, and a wager on twenty-one, the money stays at home. Aside from that, I learned from the cook to a certain ambassador certain tricks in the games of reversis and lansquenet, which is also called faro; for just as your grace can be examined in the court of your gaiters, I can be a maestro in the science of cards. With this I can be sure not to die of hunger, because even if I come to a farmhouse, there is always someone who wants to pass the time playing cards, and both of us will experience this later. Let us spread the net and see whether a bird among the mule drivers here falls into it; I mean, let's you and I play twenty-one, as if it were a real game, and if anyone wants to be the third, he will be the first to leave his money behind."

"May we have good luck," said the other boy, "and I take it as a very great kindness your grace has done me in recounting your life, which has obliged me not to hide mine, which, very briefly, is this. I was born in the pious village located between Salamanca and Medina del Campo. My father is a tailor, he taught me his trade, and with my intelligence I leaped from learning to cut with a scissors to cutting purses. The mean-spirited village life and unloving treatment from my stepmother bedeviled me. I left my village, came to Toledo to practice my trade, and there I have done marvels; because no memento dangles so high on a headdress and no purse is so hidden that my fingers do not visit it and my scissors cut it, even if it is watched over with the eyes of Argos. And in the few months I spent in that city, I was never caught or taken by surprise or chased by agents of the law or squealed on by any snitches. True, some eight days ago an informer told the magistrate about my skills, and he, taken with my talents, wanted to see me; but I, being humble and not wishing to have dealings with such important persons, did my best not to see him and left the city so quickly I did not have the opportunity to obtain a mount or money or hire a coach, or at least a wagon."

"Forget about that," said Rincón, "and since we know each other now, there's no need for pride or arrogance: let us confess openly that we don't have a *blanca* or even shoes."

"Fine," responded Diego Cortado, for that is what the younger boy said his name was, "and since our friendship, as your grace, Señor Rincón, has said, will last forever, let us begin it with sacred and praiseworthy ceremonies."

And Diego Cortado stood and embraced Rincón, who returned the embrace, tenderly and tightly, and then the two of them began to play twenty-one with the above-mentioned cards, free of dust and straw but not of grease and malice; and after a few hands, Cortado could hide the ace as well as Rincón, his teacher.

A mule driver came out to take the air under the portico and said he wanted to play as well. They welcomed him willingly and in less than half an hour had won twelve *reales* and twenty-two *maravedís*, which meant giving the mule driver twelve thrusts with a lance and twenty-two sorrows. And believing that because they were boys they would not be able to stop him, the mule driver tried to take the money from them; but they, one placing a hand on his half sword and the other on his slaughterer's knife, kept him so busy that if his companions had not come out, he would undoubtedly have had a very bad time.

At this moment a troop of men on horseback happened to pass on the road, going to spend the hottest hours of the afternoon at the inn of the Alcalde, half a league farther on; and seeing the dispute between the mule driver and the two boys, they calmed them down and said that if by any chance they were going to Sevilla, then they should go together.

"We are going there," said Rincón, "and we shall serve your graces in everything you ask of us."

And without stopping again, they jumped in front of the mules and made off with them, leaving the mule driver aggrieved and angry and the innkeeper's wife amazed at the good manners of the scoundrels, for she had been listening to their talk without their knowledge. And when she told the mule driver that she had heard them say that the cards they were carrying were marked, he was enraged and humiliated and wanted to go after them to the inn to take back his money, because he said it was a huge affront and a slur upon his honor for two boys to have deceived a tall, strapping fellow like him. His companions stopped him and advised him not to go, if only not to make public his ineptitude and simple-mindedness. In short, their words did not console him but neither did they oblige him to remain where he was.

In the meantime, Cortado and Rincón were so skillful in serving the travelers that for most of the way they rode behind them on the mules, and even though they had several opportunities to probe the bags of their demi-masters, they did not in order not to miss so favorable a circumstance for traveling to Sevilla, where they had the greatest desire to be.

Even so, in the late afternoon, as the group entered the city at the Customs Gate because of the registry and import duty they had to pay on the goods they were carrying, Cortado could not resist cutting the bag or pouch that a Frenchman in the group carried behind him; and with his slaughterer's knife he gave it so long and deep a wound that its entrails were exposed, and he very cunningly removed two good shirts, a sundial, and a small notebook, things that, when the boys saw them, did not afford them much pleasure; and they thought that if the Frenchman carried that bag behind him, it would not be filled only with objects of so little value, and they wanted to try again but did not, imagining that he must have missed those things already and placed what remained in a safe place.

They had taken their leave, before the theft, of those who had fed them so far, and the next day sold the shirts in the secondhand market outside the Sandy Ground Gate and earned twenty *reales*. And then they went to see the city and marveled at the grandeur and magnificence of its largest church and the great crowd of people on the river, for it was a period when the merchant fleet was in and there were six galleys on the river, the sight of which made them sigh and even fear the day when their offenses would cause them to serve as galley slaves for life. They saw the great number of boys working as porters; they learned about the job from one of the boys: whether it was very difficult, and how much he earned.

The Asturian boy whom they questioned responded that it was restful work, you did not have to pay a sales tax, and some days he earned five or six *reales*, with which he ate and drank and was as happy as a king, free of having to find a master to give a guarantee to and certain of eating whenever he liked, because the tiniest shop in the city sold prepared food at any hour of the day or night.

The account of the young Asturian did not seem bad to the two friends, and they were not unhappy with the work, because they thought it was perfectly suited to plying their own trades with secrecy and safety since it allowed them to enter every house, and then they decided to buy the implements they would need, since they could do the work with no prior testing. And they asked the Asturian what they should buy, and he answered that each of them needed a small cloth sack, clean or new, and three two-handled baskets made of esparto grass, two large and one small, in which they carried meat, fish, and fruit, and bread in the sack; and he led them to the place where they were sold, and, with the money from the sale of what they had stolen from the Frenchman, they bought everything, and in less than two hours were handing the baskets and hoisting the sacks so well they could have been graduates in their new trade. Their guide told them of the places where they had to go: in the mornings, to the Meat Market and the Plaza de San Salvador; on Fridays, to the Fish Market and the Costanilla Market; every afternoon, to the river; on Thursdays, to the Fair.

They committed the entire lesson to memory and the next day, very early in the morning, they stood on the Plaza de San Salvador. And no sooner had they arrived than they were surrounded by other boys in the trade who saw the brand new sacks and baskets and asked them a thousand questions, and they responded to all of them with discernment and good manners. Then a student and a soldier arrived, and attracted by the clean baskets of the two beginners, the one who looked like a student called to Cortado and the soldier called Rincón.

"In the name of God," they both said.

"The work is off to a good start," said Rincón, "since your grace is my first customer, Señor."

To which the soldier replied:

"Your initiation will not be bad because I am shopping and am in love, and today I have to give a banquet for some of my lady's friends."

"Well, put in as much as your grace desires, for I have the fortitude and strength to carry away this whole square, and if it should be necessary to help you cook it, I shall do that very willingly."

The soldier was pleased with the boy's affability and told him that if he wished to serve him, he would take him away from that lowly job; to which Rincón responded that since this was the first day he was working at it, he did not wish to leave it so quickly until he could at least see its good points and its bad; and whenever he became unhappy with it, he gave his word he would rather be the soldier's servant than a canon's.

The soldier laughed; he loaded him down and showed him his lady's house so that Rincón would know it in the future and the soldier would not have to accompany him the next time he sent him there. Rincón promised him faithfulness and good behavior. The soldier gave him three *cuartos*, and in a trice he returned to the square so as not to lose an opportunity, for the Asturian had also told them about that, and also that when they were carrying small fish, for instance bleak fish or sardines or plaice, they could easily take a few and be the first to try them and save on that day's expenses; but this had to be done with absolute shrewdness and care so as not to lose their reputation, which was the most important thing in their work.

Rincón returned quickly and found Cortado back in the same place. Cortado came up to Rincón and asked how things had gone for him. Rincón opened his hand and showed him the three *cuartos*. Cortado put his hand inside his shirt and took out a small purse that gave signs of having been tanned with amber; it was somewhat swollen, and he said:

"His reverence the student paid me with this and two *cuartos*; but you take it, Rincón, just in case."

And having slipped it to him, you can see now where the student returns in a sweat and worried to death, and seeing Cortado, asked whether he had happened to see a missing purse of such and such a size and color, containing fifteen *escudos* of pure gold and three coins worth two *reales* each and any number of *maravedís* in *cuartos* and *ochavos*, and to tell him whether he had taken it while they had been shopping together. To which, with admirable dissembling, without changing his expression or behavior at all, Cortado responded:

"What I can say about that purse is that it probably isn't lost, unless your grace put it in an unsafe place."

"That's the problem, sinner that I am," responded the student, "I must have put it in an unsafe place, because it's been stolen!"

"That's what I say," said Cortado, "but there's a remedy for everything except death, and what your grace can do, first and foremost, is have patience, never say die, one day follows the next, and what goes around comes around; it might happen that, in time, the one who took the purse will repent and return it to your grace as full as he found it."

"Then all would be forgiven," replied the student.

And Cortado responded, saying:

"Furthermore, there are papal letters of excommunication, and diligence is the mother of good fortune; yet, if truth be told, I wouldn't want to be the one carrying that purse, because if your grace happens to have holy orders, it would seem to me he had committed some great incest, or sacrilege."

"Indeed, he has committed sacrilege," said the afflicted student, "for though I am not a priest but the sacristan to some nuns, the money in the purse was the third of the income from the use of a chapel, which a priest I know had asked me to collect, and it is holy and blessed money."

"Then it's his problem," said Rincón, "I wouldn't give anything for his gains; the Day of Judgment will come, and then all truth will out, and we'll know what's what and who's who and who dared to take, steal, and diminish the third of the chapel income. And how much does it come to each year? Tell me, Señor Sacristan, on your life."

"Damn the whore who bore me! Now do I have to tell you the income?" responded the sacristan, with a little too much rage. "Tell me, brothers, if you know something; if not, God be with you, because I want to make this public."

"That seems like a good solution," said Cortado, "but be advised, your grace, not to forget a description of the purse and the exact amount of money in it, because if your grace is off by even one centavo, it will never turn up, and that is what I foresee."

"You don't have to fear that," replied the sacristan, "for it's clearer in my memory than the ringing of the bells; I won't be wrong in the smallest detail."

And then he removed from his pocket a lace-trimmed handkerchief to wipe away the perspiration that poured from his face as if it were a distillery, and as soon as Cortado saw it, he marked it as his own. The sacristan left and Cortado followed him and caught up with him on the cathedral steps, where he called to him and moved him off to the side, and there he began to tell him endless nonsense, of the kind called addled, about the theft and recovery of his purse, giving him good hope, and never finishing anything he began to say, so that the poor sacristan was in a daze listening to him. And since he really did not understand what Cortado was saying to him, he had him repeat each phrase two or three times.

Cortado stared into the sacristan's face and did not move his own eyes away from his. The sacristan looked at him the same way, hanging onto each word. This allowed Cortado to complete his work and very carefully remove the handkerchief from the sacristan's pocket, and then take his leave, saying that in the afternoon he would try to see him in the same spot, because he seemed to recall that a boy doing his kind of work and his same size, who was something of a thief, had taken his purse, and he pledged to find out for sure in just a few days, or perhaps more than that.

This comforted the sacristan somewhat, and he said goodbye to Cortado, who then came over to Rincón, who had seen everything from just a little distance away; and farther down the steps was another boy, a porter, who saw everything that had happened and how Cortado had given the handkerchief to Rincón, and coming up to them he said:

"Tell me, my good fellows, are you in the game or what?"

"We don't understand the question, my good fellow," responded Rincón.

"You don't get it, my good filchers?" responded the other boy.

"We're not from Gedit or from Filcha," said Cortado. "If there's something else you want, say so, and if not, go with God."

"You don't understand?" said the boy. "Well, I'll explain it all to you and feed it to you with a silver spoon. I mean, gentlemen, are your graces thieves?

But I don't know why I bother to ask, since I already know you are. But tell me, why haven't you cleared customs with Señor Monipodio?"

"Do thieves pay a quota around here, my good fellow?" said Rincón.

"If they don't pay," responded the boy, "at least they sign in with Señor Monipodio, who is their father, their teacher, and their protector; and so, I advise you to come with me and swear obedience to him, and if not, don't dare steal anything without his permission, or else you'll pay for it."

"I thought," said Cortado, "that stealing was an immune trade, free of taxes and duties, and if they were paid it was all together and only once, stretching your neck and swatting your back; but if this is the case, and every place has its own customs, we shall obey the ones here, which, being the greatest place in the world, must also be the most correct. And so, your grace may lead us to that gentleman you mentioned, because I have a feeling, according to what I've heard, that he is very noble and generous, and extremely skilled in his trade."

"Of course he's noble, skilled, and competent," responded the boy. "So much so that in the four years he's been our superior and father, only four have gone to the gallows, and something like thirty have been swatted, and sixty-two have picked up the oars."

"The truth is, Señor," said Rincón, "we don't understand those words any more than we know how to fly."

"Let's start walking, and on the way I'll tell you what they mean," responded the boy, "along with some others you ought to know as well as the bread in your mouth."

And so he walked along, saying and explaining other words of the kind they call *germanesco*, or thieves' argot, as they talked, and their conversation was not brief because the way was long. And Rincón said to their guide:

"Does your grace happen to be a thief?"

"Yes," he replied, "may it please God and all good people, but I'm not one of the very learned ones, for I'm still in my novitiate year."

To which Cortado responded:

"It's news to me that there are thieves in the world to please God and good people."

To which the boy replied:

"Señor, I don't stick my nose into tologies; what I do know is that each one in his trade can praise God, and even more so in the order that Monipodio has made for all his godchildren."

"No doubt," said Rincón, "it must be a good and holy one, since it makes thieves please God."

"It's so holy and good," replied the boy, "that I don't know if it could be improved in our craft. He has ordered us to give a part of what we steal, some alms, for the oil in the lamp of a very revered image in this city, and the truth is we've seen very great things because of this good work; because a few days ago they gave three rounds of dolor to a rustler who stole two whinnies and, having a weak character and quartan fever, he suffered them without singing a note. And those of us in the craft attribute this to his devotion, because his strength wasn't enough to endure the first flicks of the line. And because I know you'll ask me about some of the words I've said, I want to take the cure before I get sick and tell you before you ask. Let me tell you that a *rustler* is an animal thief, *dolor* is torture, *whinnies* are asses, excuse the expression; *flicks of the line* are the first lashes of the whip. We have more, for we say our allotted rosary every day of the week, and many of us don't steal on Fridays, and don't have any kind of intercourse with any woman named María on Saturdays."

"All this seems pure gold to me," said Cortado, "but tell me, your grace, is there any restitution or penance other than what you have said?"

"As far as restitution is concerned, there's nothing to say," the boy answered, "because it's impossible on account of the many parts the loot is divided into, each of the ministers and contracting parties receiving his share; and so the first thief cannot return anything, especially because there is no one who tells us to take that step, because we never make confession, and if letters of excommunication are issued, they never come to our attention, because we never go to church when they are read, unless it's a day of indulgence, when the gathering of so many people offers us a profit."

"And with no more than this, those gentlemen," said Cortadillo, "claim that their life is holy and good?"

"Well, what's bad about it?" replied the boy. "Isn't it worse to be a heretic or a renegade, or kill your father and mother, or be a solomite?"

"Your grace must mean a sodomite," responded Rincón.

"That's what I said," said the boy.

"It's all bad," replied Cortado, "but since it's our fate to join this brotherhood, please hurry, for I'm dying to meet Señor Monipodio who, they say, has so many virtues."

"Your desire will soon be satisfied," said the boy, "for you can see his house from here. Your graces stay at the door, and I'll go in to see if he's free, for this is the time he usually grants audiences."

"Good luck," said Rincón.

And moving ahead of them, the boy went into a house that had a very shabby appearance, and the other two stood waiting at the door. He soon came out again and called to them, and they went in, and their guide told them to wait in a small brick courtyard so clean and polished it seemed to overflow with the finest carmine. To one side was a three-legged bench and on the other a broken-mouthed vessel and on top of it a jug as broken as the vessel; in another section was a rush mat, and in the middle of that the kind of flowerpot called a *maceta* in Sevilla, filled with sweet basil.

The boys looked carefully at the fine furnishings in the house while Señor Monipodio was coming down; and seeing that he was delayed, Rincón dared to go into one of the two low rooms off the courtyard, and in it he saw two fencing swords and two small cork shields hanging from four nails, and a large chest without a lid or anything else to cover it, and another three rush mats on the floor. A poorly printed image of Our Lady was fastened to the front wall, and below that hung a small palm-leaf basket, and inserted in the wall was a white basin, which led Rincón to assume that the basket was used to hold a slotted container for alms and the basin for holding holy water, and he was correct.

As he was doing this, two young men of about twenty and dressed as students came in the house, and soon afterward two more carrying a basket, along with a blind man; and without any of them saying a word, they began to walk around the courtyard. Not long after them, in came two old men in mourning, wearing eyeglasses that made them look serious and worthy of respect, each holding in his hand a rosary with large, noisy beads. Behind them came an old woman in full skirts, and not saying anything, she went into the room; and having taken some holy water, with enormous devotion she kneeled before the image, and after a long time, first having kissed the floor three times and raised her arms and her eyes to heaven another three times, she stood and put her alms into the basket, and went to join the others in the courtyard. In brief, in a short period of time at least fourteen people wearing different kinds of clothes and following different trades were gathered in the courtyard. Among the last to arrive were two brave and gallant fellows with long mustaches, broad-brimmed hats, Van Dyck collars, colored stockings, large, showy garters, swords longer than the legal standard, pistols instead of daggers, and shields hanging from a leather strap; as soon as they came in, they looked sideways at Rincón and Cortado, indicating that they were strangers and didn't know them. And coming up to them, they asked if they belonged to the brotherhood. Rincón replied that they did, at the service of their graces.

This was the precise moment when Señor Monipodio came down, waited for and well thought of by that entire virtuous company. He seemed to be forty-five or forty-six years old, tall, dark-skinned, with bushy brows, a dark, heavy beard, and deep-set eyes. He wore a shirt, and the front opening revealed a forest: that was how thick the hair on his chest was. He had on a cape of thin mourning cloth almost down to his feet, on which he wore shoes without heels, like slippers, and his legs were covered by wide, pleated canvas breeches that came to his ankles; he had on a vagrant's hat, with a bell-shaped crown and drooping brim; a leather strap crossed his back and chest, and from it hung a short, wide sword, the well-known kind forged by the converted dog of Toledo;[1] his hands were short and hairy, his fingers fat, and his nails short and flat; his legs were not visible, but his feet were uncommonly wide with enormous bunions. In fact, he was the crudest and most misshapen barbarian in the world. The guide of the two boys came down with him, and grasping their hands, he presented them to Monipodio, saying:

"These are the two good lads I mentioned to your grace, my Señor Monipodio; examine them, your grace, and your grace will see that they are worthy of joining our congregation."

"That I shall do very willingly," responded Monipodio.

I forgot to mention that as soon as Monipodio came down, everyone waiting for him made a deep long bow, except for the two blustering ones who, very carelessly and in a half-baked way, as they say, removed their birettas, and then they returned to their walk around one part of the courtyard; around the other walked Monipodio, who asked the newcomers their trade, where they came from, and who their parents were.

To which Rincón replied:

"Our trade is already known, for we have come before your grace; I do not think it is very important to say where we come from, or who our parents were, for that is the kind of information required for entrance into some honorable order."

To which Monipodio responded:

"You, my son, are correct, and it is very proper to hide the things you say; because if your luck doesn't run as it should, it's not good for such things to be recorded above the sign of the scribe, or entered in a register: 'So-and-so, son of so-and-so, resident in such-and-such a place, hanged or whipped on such-and-such a day,' or something similar which, at the very least, does not sound good to good ears; and so, I say again that it is good advice to hide where one comes from, not say who one's parents are, and change one's name; although

1. Julián del Rey, known as "*el perrillo*," was a Morisco arms manufacturer from Toledo. The sobriquet, a derogatory term for a convert, also corresponded to the image of a dog used as the insignia on his swords.

among ourselves there should be nothing hidden, and now I want only to know your names."

Rincón said his name, and so did Cortado.

"Well, from now on," responded Monipodio, "I wish, and it is my will, that you, Rincón, will be called Rinconete, and you, Cortado, will be known as Cortadillo, which are names that suit your ages and our ordinances, under which falls the need to know the names of our members' parents, because it is our custom to have certain masses said each year for the souls of our dead and our benefactors, taking the cost of the stupend for the person who says them from a part of what we steal, and these masses, as many as we pay for, they say are to the benefit of those souls who are suffraging *per modum sufragii*, and support our benefactors: the prosecutor who defends us, the constable who advises us, the hangman who has pity on us, and, when one of us is running down the street and people run after us shouting 'Thief! Thief! Stop thief! Stop thief!' one man steps in and opposes the crowd in pursuit, saying: 'Leave the wretch alone, he has nothing but bad luck! Let him suffer the consequences, punish his sin!' The ladies are also our benefactors, those who support us by the sweat of their brow, in jail and in the galleys; and our fathers and mothers, who bring us into the world, and the scribe, for whom, if he's in a good mood, no crime has a punishment, and no punishment is very painful; and for all these people I've mentioned our brotherhood celebrates their anversry each year with all the pop and circus-dance that we can."

"Certainly," said Rinconete, his new name confirmed, "this is a work worthy of the most high and deep intelligence that we have heard your grace, Señor Monipodio, possesses. But our parents still enjoy this life; if we learn otherwise, we shall immediately inform this happy and protective fraternity, so that for the sake of their souls, it may do the usual suffrage or torment, or that anversry that you say, with the usual pomp and circumstance; unless it's done better with pop and circus-dance, as your grace also noted in your words."

"It will be done, or there will be nothing left of me," replied Monipodio.

And calling to the guide, he said:

"Come here, Ganchuelo; are the guards at their posts?"

"Yes," said the guide, for Ganchuelo was his name, "three sentries are on the lookout, and there's no fear that anybody will take us by surprise."

"Well, then, as I was saying," said Monipodio, "I should like to know, children, what you know so I can give you the trade and practice that match your inclinations and abilities."

"I," responded Rinconete, "know a little about stacking a deck; I can palm a card; I have a good eye for greasing the cards; I can play without tricks, or by hiding cards, or by other tricks; I don't run away from scratching or pricking the cards with a pin or a boar's tooth; I go into the lion's den as if it were my own house and let the sucker win in the beginning, and I'd rather help out in a caper than caper in the infantry in Naples, and give a change in the order of the cards to the best cardsharp rather than lend him the change of two *reales*."

"It's a beginning," said Monipodio, "but all that is no more valuable than dried sprigs of lavender, and used so often there's not a beginner who doesn't know them, and they're good only for somebody so green he lets himself be taken after midnight; but time will pass and we'll see; with half a dozen lessons building on this foundation, my devout wish is that you'll turn out to be a famous craftsman, and maybe even a master."

"It will all be to serve your grace and the gentlemen of the brotherhood."

"And you, Cortadillo, what do you know?" asked Monipodio.

"I," responded Cortadillo, "know the trick they call putting in two and taking out five, and I know how to drink from a purse with a good deal of skill and confidence."

"Do you know anything else?" said Monipodio.

"No, great sinner that I am," responded Cortadillo.

"Don't be distressed, son," replied Monipodio, "for you have come to a port and a school where you will not drown and will surely come out very well provided with everything you need to know. And as for courage, how is that in you, my boys?"

"How should it be," replied Rinconete, "except very good? We have the courage to undertake any enterprise that touches on our art and craft."

"That's good," replied Monipodio, "but I should also like you to have the courage to suffer, if necessary, half a dozen flicks without opening your lips or saying a word."

"We already know, Señor Monipodio," said Cortadillo, "what flicks mean, and we have courage for everything, because we are not so ignorant that we don't know that what the tongue says the neck pays for, and heaven is kind to the bold man, not to call him anything else, who leaves his life or his death on his tongue: as if it took more time to say *no* than *yes!*"

"Stop, there's no need for more!" said Monipodio. "I say that phrase alone convinces me, obliges me, persuades me, and forces me to tell you to consider yourselves members of the brotherhood right now and that you are excused from serving the year of your novitiate."

"I agree with that," said one of the blusterers.

And with one voice all those present confirmed it, for they had been listening to the entire conversation, and they asked Monipodio to grant the boys permission immediately to enjoy all the immunities of their brotherhood, because their agreeable presence and good talk deserved it all.

He responded that in order to make everyone happy, he granted his permission from that moment on, and told them to esteem those immunities, because they meant not paying an assessment on their first theft; not doing an apprentice's work for an entire year, namely, not taking bail money to prison for any older brother or to his brothel on behalf of his clients; being able to guzzle unwatered wine; having a feast whenever, however, and wherever they wished, without asking their superior's permission; as members receiving their share of their brothers' loot right away; and other things they considered a remarkable kindness, and with very courteous words, they expressed their gratitude.

As this was happening, a boy ran in, breathless, and said:

"The vagrants' bailiff is walking toward this house, but he doesn't have any cops with him."

"Nobody get excited," said Monipodio, "because he's a friend and never comes here to do us harm. Calm down, and I'll go out to talk to him."

Everyone settled down, for they had been somewhat alarmed, and Monipodio went to the door, where he found the bailiff, with whom he spoke for a while, and then Monipodio came back in and asked:

"Whose turn was it today at the Plaza de San Salvador?"

"Mine," said the boy who had been their guide.

"Well, how is it," said Monipodio, "that I haven't been shown an amber purse that was lifted there this morning and had fifteen gold *escudos* and two pieces worth two *reales* each, and I don't know how many *cuartos*?"

"It's true," said the guide, "today that purse went missing, but I didn't take it, and I can't imagine who did."

"Don't try any tricks with me!" replied Monipodio. "The purse has to appear, because the bailiff is asking for it, and he's a friend and does us a thousand favors a year!"

The boy swore again that he didn't know anything about it. Monipodio became so enraged that fire seemed to shoot out of his eyes, and he said:

"Nobody should play at breaking the tiniest rule of our order, because it will cost him his life. The purse had better appear, and if someone's hiding it so as not to pay his taxes, I'll give him the entire amount that's due him, and I'll put up my house for the rest, because no matter what, the bailiff has to leave here happy."

The boy swore again and cursed, saying he hadn't taken that purse or even seen it with his own eyes; all of which added fuel to the fire of Monipodio's rage and was the reason the entire assembly became agitated, seeing that their statutes and good laws were being broken.

Rinconete, in the face of so much dissension and disorder, thought it would be a good idea to calm his leader down and please him, since he was exploding with anger; and consulting with his friend Cortadillo, who was of the same mind, Rinconete took out the sacristan's purse and said:

"Let the quarreling end, gentlemen, for this is the purse, and it contains everything the bailiff said, for today my comrade Cortadillo stole it, along with a handkerchief that he also lifted from the owner."

Then Cortadillo took out the handkerchief and showed it; seeing this, Monipodio said:

"Cortadillo the Good, for with this title and fame he shall be known from now on, can keep the handkerchief, and the satisfaction of his providing this service will be paid into my account; and the bailiff will take the purse, for it belongs to a relative of his who is a sacristan, and it's a good idea to follow the old saying: 'It isn't much to give a leg to the person who gave you the whole chicken.' This good bailiff turns more of a blind eye in one day than we could in a hundred."

By common consent everyone approved of the newcomers' nobility and the judgment and opinion of their leader, who went out to give the purse to the bailiff; and Cortadillo was confirmed as having the surname *Good*, just as if he were Don Alonso Pérez de Guzmán the *Good*, who threw the knife over the walls of Tarifa so his only son could be beheaded.[2]

When Monipodio returned, two girls came in with him, their faces painted, their lips full of color, their breasts powdered white; they wore half capes of serge and were filled with immodesty and shamelessness, clear signs by which Rinconete and Cortadillo knew when they saw them that they were in the life and were in no way deceived. And as soon as the girls came in they opened their arms, and one went to Chiquiznaque and the other to Maniferro, for these were the names of the two toughs; and Maniferro got his name because he had a metal hand instead of the one cut off by the law. They embraced the two girls with great rejoicing and asked if they had brought anything to wet their whistles.

2. Alonso Pérez de Guzmán (1256–1309) defended the recently recaptured town of Tarifa against a siege of Moors and the Infante Don Juan. Legend has it that when his youngest son was taken captive, Pérez de Guzmán threw his own knife over the walls to his enemies, claiming that the sacrifice of his son for the town was an honorable death.

"How could I not, my trusty blade?" responded one, who was called La Gananciosa. "Your servant, Silbatillo, will be here soon with the laundry basket full of whatever God wills."

And that was true, because a boy came in at that moment carrying a laundry basket covered with a sheet.

Everyone was happy when Silbato came in, and Monipodio immediately ordered that one of the rush mats in the house be placed in the middle of the courtyard. And he also ordered everyone to sit around it so that, after they had something to eat, they could take care of some business. At this the old woman who had prayed to the image said:

"Monipodio, my son, I'm in no mood for parties because I've had vertigo for two days and it's making me crazy; besides, before midday I have to say my prayers and light my candles to Our Lady of the Waters and to the Holy Crucifix of Santo Agustín, and I wouldn't fail to do that even if it was snowing and the wind was blowing. The reason I came is because last night El Renegado and Centopiés brought a laundry basket to my house, a little bigger than this one, filled with linens, and by God and my soul, it still had the ashes for bleaching in it; the poor things probably didn't have time to remove it, and they were sweating so much it made me sorry just to see them come in all out of breath, and with water running down their faces, they looked like little angels. They told me they were following a cattleman who had weighed certain sheep at the Meat Market to see if they could get their hands on a huge purse filled with *reales* that he was carrying. They didn't take the linens out of the basket or count them, trusting to my good conscience; and so may God fulfill my honest desires and free all of us from the power of the law, for I haven't laid a finger on the basket, and it is as untouched and whole as the day it was born."

"My lady mother, I believe everything you say," responded Monipodio, "and leave the basket there, and I'll go at dusk and take stock of what it contains and give to each one his due, well and faithfully, as is my custom."

"Let it be as you have ordered, son," responded the old woman, "and since it's getting late, give me a little drink, if you have anything, to comfort this stomach of mine that is constantly upset."

"Drink it in good health, mother!" said Escalanta, for that was the name of Gananciosa's companion.

And opening the basket, she revealed a leather wineskin with about thirty-two liters of wine and a cork cup that could easily hold, with room left over, a little more than two liters; Escalanta filled it and placed it in the hands of the blessedly devout old woman who, taking it in both hands and blowing away the froth a little, said:

"You poured in a great deal, Escalanta my daughter, but God will give us strength for everything."

And placing her lips to the rim, in a single swallow, without taking a breath, she decanted the wine from the cup to her stomach, and when she was finished she said:

"It's from Guadalcanal, and the gentleman still has a touch of plaster in it. May God comfort you, daughter, as you have comforted me, though I'm afraid it will make me sick because I haven't had breakfast yet."

"It won't, mother," responded Monipodio, "because it's more than three years old."

"And so I place my trust in the Virgin," responded the old woman.

And she added:

"Girls, look and see if you have a *cuarto* to buy candles for my prayers, because I was in such a hurry and wanted so much to come here with news about the basket that I left my purse at home."

"I do, Señora Pipota" (for this was the name of the good old woman), replied Gananciosa. "Here, take two *cuartos*, and I beg you to buy one for me and light it for Señor San Miguel; and if you can buy two, light the other one for Señor San Blas, for they're my mediators. I'd like you to light another one for Señora Santa Lucía, because of my eyes I'm also devoted to her, but I don't have more change, but we'll have enough another day to light candles for all of them."

"You'll do the right thing, my daughter, and look, don't be tightfisted, it's very important for a person to carry the candles herself before she dies and not wait for heirs or executors to light them for her."

"Well said, Mother Pipota," said Escalanta.

And putting her hand in her purse, she gave her another *cuarto* and asked her to light another two candles for the saints she thought the most beneficial and grateful. And then Pipota left, saying:

"Enjoy yourselves, my children, now while you have time; for age will come and then you'll cry over the chances you wasted in your youth, as I do now; and mention me in your prayers, and I'll do the same for myself and for you, so that God saves and preserves us in our dangerous dealings, with no surprises from the law."

And with this, she left.

When the old woman had gone, they all sat around the mat and Gananciosa spread the sheet as a tablecloth; and the first thing she took from the basket was a large bunch of radishes and some two dozen oranges and lemons, and then a large casserole filled with slices of fried cod. Then half a Flemish cheese appeared, and a pot of first-rate olives, and a dish of prawns, and a large number of crabs, with their side dish of caper berries smothered in peppers, and three large, snow-white loaves from Gandul. There were about fourteen people at the lunch, and each pulled out a yellow-handled knife except Rinconete, who took out his half sword. It fell to the two old men with cloths and the guide to pour the wine. But just as they began their assault on the oranges, loud knocking at the door startled all of them. Monipodio told them to calm down, and going into the downstairs room, and taking down a small shield and placing his hand on his sword, he walked up to the door, and in a resounding, frightening voice he asked:

"Who's knocking?"

From outside the answer came:

"It's me, it's nobody, Señor Monipodio. It's Tagarete, this morning's sentry, and I came to tell you that Juliana la Cariharta is on her way here, all messy and weepy, so it looks like some disaster has happened to her."

Just then, the woman he had mentioned arrived, sobbing, and when Monipodio heard her, he opened the door and ordered Tagarete back to his post, and from then on to let him know what he saw with less commotion and noise. Tagarete said he would. Cariharta came in, a girl of the same type as the others, and in the same trade. Her hair was disheveled and her face was covered with black and blue marks, and as soon as she walked into the courtyard she fell to the ground in a faint. Gananciosa and Escalanta came to help her, and loosening her bodice, they found her battered and bruised. They sprinkled water on her face, and she regained consciousness, shouting:

"May the justice of God and the king fall on the head of that worthless thief, that killer for hire, that underhanded coward, that flea-bitten crook, I've saved him from the gallows more times than he has hairs in his beard! Woe is me! I've lost and wasted my youth and the flower of my years on a heartless villain, an incorrigible desperado!"

"Calm down, Cariharta," said Monipodio, "for I'm here and I'll see that justice is done. Tell us the offense, and you'll need more time to tell it than I will in avenging you; tell me if it has something to do with your admirer, and if it does and you want vengeance, you only have to say so."

"What admirer?" responded Juliana. "I'll be admired in hell before I let that lion among sheep and lamb among men admire me. Eat more bread of affliction with that man, or go to bed with him? I'd rather see jackals eat this flesh of mine, and now you'll see what he's done to it!"

And immediately raising her skirts to the knee, and even a little higher, she showed that they were covered in welts.

"This is how," she went on, "that ingrate Repolido has left me, owing me more than he owes the mother who bore him. And why do you think he did it? As if I gave him any reason! No, of course not, he did it just because when he was gambling and losing, he sent Cabrillas, his servant, to ask me for thirty *reales*, and I sent him only twenty-four. I pray to heaven that the hard work and exhaustion that went into my earning them helps to discount my sins. And to pay for this courtesy and good deed, thinking I had filched something from the account that in his imagination he had made of how much I might have, this morning he took me out to the field behind La Huerta del Rey, and there in the olive groves he stripped me, and with a leather belt, the buckle still attached—and may I live to see him in shackles and irons!—he hit me so many times that he left me for dead. And these welts you're looking at are good witnesses to the truth of this story."

And here voices were raised again, and she asked again for justice, and again Monipodio and all the rough men there promised it to her. Gananciosa offered her hand to console her, saying that she would gladly give one of her most valuable possessions, because the same thing had happened to her with her sweetheart.

"Because," she said, "I want you to know, my sister Cariharta, if you don't know already, that we always hurt the one we love; and when these scoundrels hit us and beat us and kick us around, they adore us afterward; if not, tell me the truth on your life: after Repolido beat and bruised you, didn't he give you a caress?"

"What do you mean, one?" responded the weeping woman. "He gave me a hundred thousand and said he'd give a finger for me to go with him to his lodgings, and I even think tears almost fell from his eyes after he beat me."

"There's no doubt about that," replied Gananciosa. "And he'd cry with grief at seeing what he did to you; because in these men, and in these cases, no sooner do they commit the offense then they're full of remorse. And you'll see, my sister, if he doesn't come to find you before we leave here, and beg your pardon for everything that happened, and be as meek as a lamb."

"The truth is," responded Monipodio, "that cowardly batterer will not pass through these doors if he doesn't first repent publicly for the crime he's committed. He dared to lay hands on Cariharta's face and body when she is a person who can compete in cleanliness and earnings with Gananciosa herself, here before us, who has them to the nth degree."

"Ay!" said Juliana at that moment. "Your grace, Señor Monipodio, should not speak ill of that accursed man, for even though he's so bad, I love him with all my heart; and the words in his favor that my friend Gananciosa has said have returned my soul to my body, and the truth is I'm ready to go out and find him."

"That you won't do, and that's my advice!" replied Gananciosa, "because he'll swell and puff up and slash at you as if you were a fencing dummy. Control yourself, sister, and before long you'll see him as repentant as I've said; and if he doesn't come, we'll write him some lines of poetry, and that will be painful for him."

"Oh yes," said Cariharta, "and I have a thousand things to write to him!"

"I'll be the secretary whenever you need me," said Monipodio, "and though I'm no kind of poet, still, if I set my mind to it, I'm the man to make two thousand verses in the wink of an eye; and if they don't turn out as they should, I have a barber friend who's a great poet who will say what we want to say any time, and right now, at this time, let's finish what we began at lunch, and then everything will work out fine."

Juliana was happy to obey her mentor; and so, everyone returned to their *gaudeamus*, and soon they saw the bottom of the basket and the dregs of the wineskin.[3] The older people drank without restraint, the young in abundance, and the ladies to excess. The older people asked permission to leave. Monipodio gave it immediately, charging them to come back and report in detail everything they saw that might be useful and profitable to the community. They responded that they would be careful to do so, and they left.

Rinconete, who was curious by nature, first begged pardon and permission and then asked Monipodio what two persons so gray-haired, so dignified and serious in appearance, did in the brotherhood. To which Monipodio responded that in their slang and manner of speaking, they were called hornets, and they spent the day walking through the city, deciding which houses they could sting at night, and following those who took money from the House of Trade or the Mint to see which house they took it to, and even the place where they hid it; and knowing this, they tested the thickness of the walls of the house and marked the best places to make openings to facilitate entry. In short, he said, they were among the most valuable people in his band and received a fifth of what was stolen as a result of their skill, just as His Majesty received his share of treasures; and with all that, they were very truthful and honorable men, who led virtuous lives and had good reputations—God-fearing men of conscience—and every day they heard Mass with admirable devotion.

"And some are so considerate, especially the two who are leaving now, that they are happy with much less than the portion we think is theirs. There are two

---

3. A *gaudeamus* (Latin for "Let us rejoice") refers to a celebration.

others who are thieves and they, since they are constantly moving, know the entrances and exits of all the houses in the city, and which can be profitable and which ones not."

"I think everything's gold," said Rinconete, "and I'd like to be useful to so famous a brotherhood."

"Heaven always favors virtuous desires," said Monipodio.

As they were chatting, there was a knock at the door; Monipodio went to see who it was, and when he asked, the response was:

"Open up, Señor Monipodio, it's Repolido."

Cariharta heard the voice, and raising hers to heaven, she said:

"Don't let that ogle in, your grace, Señor Monipodo, don't let that muenster in!"

Monipodio let Repolido in anyway, but when Cariharta saw him opening the door, she leaped to her feet, ran to the room with the shields, locked the door from the inside, and shouted:

"Get him away from me, that bogeyman, that beater of innocents, that oppressor of his girls, those tame doves!"

Maniferro and Chiquiznaque held Repolido, who kept trying to go into the room where Cariharta was, but since they wouldn't let him, he said from outside:

"That's enough, my angry girl, on your life calm down, and you'll find yourself married."

"Me, married, you villain?" responded Cariharta. "Just see what he's come up with now! You want me to marry you; I'd rather be married to death himself than to you!"

"Hey, you fool," replied Repolido, "that's enough now, it's getting late, and don't get a swelled head because I'm talking so nice and came here so humble, because, by God, if the anger goes up to my belfry, the second fall will be worse than the first! Be humble, let's all be humble, and let's not feed the devil."

"I'd even give him supper," said Cariharta, "if he'd take you away to where these eyes would never see you again."

"Didn't I tell all of you?" said Repolido. "By God, I'm figuring out, Señora Slut, that this time I won't hold anything back no matter what!"

Then Monipodio said:

"In my presence there will be no insults; Cariharta will come out, not because of threats but for love of me, and everything will be fine, for arguments between those who really love each other are the reason for even greater joy when they make peace. Ah Juliana! Ah my girl! Ah Cariharta! Come out here, for my sake, and I'll have Repolido get down on his knees and beg your forgiveness."

"If he does that," said Escalanta, "all of us girls will be in his favor and beg Juliana to come out here."

"If this path of submission begins to smell of belittling my person," said Repolido, "I won't surrender to an army of Swiss mercenaries, but if it's a path that Cariharta likes, I don't say I'll kneel down, but I'd walk on knife blades in her service to prove I'm telling the truth."

Chiquiznaque and Maniferro laughed at this, which made Repolido so angry, thinking they were making fun of him, that with indications of infinite rage, he said:

"Anybody who laughs or thinks about laughing at what Cariharta said against me, or I said against her, or what we have said or may say, I say he's lying and will lie every time he laughs or thinks about laughing, as I've said already."

Chiquiznaque and Maniferro looked at each other with such evil humor that Monipodio knew it would end very badly if he didn't take care of it, and so, immediately placing himself among them, he said:

"Don't go any further, Señores; let strong words stop now and crumble between your teeth; and since the ones that have been said aren't important, no one should think they're aimed at him."

"We're sure," responded Chiquiznaque, "that no words like that were said or will ever be said about us, and if anyone imagined that they were, then the tambourine's in his hands and let him play it if he knows how."

"We have a tambourine here too, Señor Chiquiznaque," replied Repolido, "and, if necessary, we'll also know how to play the bells, and I've already said whoever laughs is lying; and whoever thinks different, follow me, and with a different brand of sword this man will turn words into deeds."

And saying this, he walked to the door to go outside.

Cariharta was listening to him, and when she heard that he was leaving early, she came out and said:

"Hold him, don't let him go, he'll get up to his old tricks! Don't you see he's angry, and he's a Judas Macabeen as far as courage is concerned?[4] Come back here, brave man of the world and of my eyes!"

And holding him, she seized his cape, and Monipodio also held him, and the two of them stopped him.

Chiquiznaque and Maniferro did not know whether or not to be angry, and they were quiet, waiting to see what Repolido would do; and he, begged by both Cariharta and Monipodio, came back saying:

4. The first of several "mispronounced" names that reveal the ignorance of the characters. Judas Maccabeus was a Jewish priest who fought against the Seleucid armies to preserve the Jewish religion in Judea and restore the Temple of Jerusalem.

"Friends should never make friends angry, or make fun of their friends, especially when they see that their friends are angry."

"There is no friend here," responded Maniferro, "who wants to anger or make fun of another friend, and since we're all friends, let friends give one another their hands."

At this, Monipodio said: "All of you have spoken like good friends, and as friends take the hands of your friends."

They gave one another their hands right away, and Escalanta, removing one of her clogs, began to play on it as if it were a tambourine. Gananciosa picked up a new palmetto broom that she happened to find there, and by scratching it she made a sound that, although rough and harsh, harmonized with the sound of the clog. Monipodio broke a plate and made two crude castanets, which, placed between the fingers and clicked very rapidly, created a counterpoint to the clog and the broom.

Rinconete and Cortadillo marveled at the new use for the broom, because they had never seen it before. Maniferro realized this and said:

"Are you surprised at the broom? Well, good for them, because no one in the world has invented music that is faster, less trouble, or cheaper; in fact, the other day I heard a student say that not even Negrorpheus who got Yuridis out of hell,[5] or that Marión who climbed on the dolphin and rode out of the ocean like he was on the back of a rental mule,[6] or that other great musician who made a city that had a hundred gates and the same number of posterns,[7] ever invented a better kind of music, so easy to learn, so simple to play, so free of frets, pegs, strings, and there's no need for tuning; and I'd even swear they say it was invented by a young man in this city who boasts of being a Hector in music."

"I believe it," responded Rinconete, "but let's listen to what our musicians want to sing, because it looks like Gananciosa is spitting, a sure sign she's going to sing."

5. Negrorpheus and Yuridis are deformations of Orpheus and Eurydice. Orpheus tried to bring Eurydice back from the underworld, persuading Hades and Persephone with his lyre. He failed, however, when he looked back to see if she was behind him, breaking the conditions of her release.

6. Marión seems to be Arion, the mythological horse fathered by Poseidon and known for its speed. The description does not accord with any known account of Arion, which may be intentional.

7. The "other great musician" is Amphion. He built the walls of Cadmea by playing his lyre, which moved the stones into place. He is also known to have added three strings to his lyre, which explains the "better kind of music."

And that was true, because Monipodio had asked her to sing some popular seguidillas;[8] but the one who began first was Escalanta, and in a high-pitched, trilling voice, this is what she sang:

> That good-looking Sevillano,
> in breeches and collar so wide
> has set my heart on fire,
> and still he's not satisfied.

Gananciosa continued, singing:

> For a dark-skinned boy
> who has eyes of green,
> the fiery girl who's not lost
> hasn't ever been seen.

And then Monipodio, playing his castanets even faster, added:

> Two lovers argue then set things right;
> the sharper their anger, the greater their delight.

Cariharta did not wish to pass over her desire in silence, because taking the other clog, she began to dance, and accompanied the rest by singing:

> Stop, you're angry, don't hit me again;
> just think: it's your own flesh you tan.

"Sing without spite," Repolido said at this point, "and don't bring up old stories, there's no reason to; let the past be past, and take another tack, and that's enough now."

They did not seem about to finish the singing very quickly, but they heard rapid knocking at the door; Monipodio went out to see who it was, and the sentry told him that at the end of the street the magistrate had appeared and in front of him came Tordillo and Cernícalo, unbribed bailiffs. Those inside heard this and all of them became so agitated that Cariharta and Escalanta put their clogs on backwards, Gananciosa dropped the broom and Monipodio his castanets, and all the music fell into troubled silence; Chiquiznaque was mute, Repolido froze, Maniferro suspended all activity, and everyone, some in one direction and some in the other, disappeared, climbing to the flat roofs and eaves to escape, and using them to reach another street. No harquebus has ever been fired so inopportunely,

8. Seguidillas are Spanish folksongs.

no sudden clap of thunder ever frightened a flock of careless pigeons as much, as the news of the arrival of the magistrate upset and frightened that entire gathering of good people. The two novices, Rinconete and Cortadillo, did not know what to do, and they stood still waiting to see how that sudden storm would end, and all it amounted to was that the sentry returned to say that the magistrate had passed by, showing no sign or symptom of any suspicion at all.

And as he was telling this to Monipodio, a young gentleman came to the door, dressed, as they say, for the neighborhood, in a careless manner. Monipodio brought him inside, and sent for Chiquiznaque, Maniferro, and Repolido, saying that no one else should come down. Since they had stayed in the courtyard, Rinconete and Cortadillo could hear everything said by Monipodio and the recently arrived gentleman, who asked Monipodio why the task he had entrusted to him had been performed so badly. Monipodio replied that he did not know yet what had been done, but here was the official assigned to his affair, who would account for himself very well.

Chiquiznaque came down and Monipodio asked him whether he had completed the job he had been assigned regarding the fourteen-stitch knifing.

"Which one?" responded Chiquiznaque. "Was it the merchant at the crossroads?"

"That's it," said the gentleman.

"Well, what happened with that," responded Chiquiznaque, "is that I waited for him last night at the door to his house, and he came before nightfall; I got close to him, studied his face, and saw that it was so small that a fourteen-stitch slash would never fit on it, and finding it impossible to do what had been promised and what I had been destructed to do . . ."

"Your grace means *instructed*," said the gentleman, "not *destructed*."

"That's what I meant to say," responded Chiquiznaque. "So seeing that on that tiny, narrow face the proposed stitches wouldn't fit, and so that my trip wouldn't be in vain, I slashed a servant of his, and there's no question they'll be able to sew him up with more than the standard fourteen stitches."

"I would have preferred," said the gentleman, "you to give the master a seven-stitch slash rather than a fourteen-stitch one to the servant. In effect, you haven't fulfilled your obligation to me in a reasonable way, but it doesn't matter; I won't miss the thirty *ducados* I left here as an advance. I kiss the hands of your graces."

And saying this, he doffed his hat and turned around to leave; but Monipodio grasped the varicolored cape he was wearing and said:

"You better stop and keep your word, because we've kept ours very honorably and diligently; you owe twenty *ducados* and you won't leave here without giving us the money, or goods worth that much."

"Is this what your grace calls keeping your word," responded the gentleman, "cutting the servant when you were supposed to cut the master?"

"The gentleman certainly doesn't seem to understand," said Chiquiznaque. "He doesn't seem to remember the proverb that says 'Love me, love my dog.'"

"Well, how does that proverb apply here?" replied the gentleman.

"Well, isn't it the same as saying," Chiquiznaque continued, "'Hate me, hate my dog'? And so 'me' is the merchant, you hate him, the servant is his dog, and by hurting the dog you hurt 'me,' and the debt is clear and supposes that the work has been completed; and therefore the only thing for you to do is pay immediately with no petition for an end to the debt."

"I'll swear to that," added Monipodio, "and, Chiquiznaque my friend, you have taken from my own mouth everything you've said here; and so you, my gallant gentleman, don't quibble over trifles with your servants and friends, but take my advice and pay right now for the work that has been done, and if you're of a mind to slash the master the number of stitches his face can hold, know he's already being treated for that."

"If that's the case," responded the elegant young man, "I shall very willingly and happily make complete payment for both."

"Have no doubts about it," said Monipodio, "but being a Christian, Chiquiznaque will give him a perfect one that will look very good on him."

"Well, with that certainty and promise," the gentleman replied, "take this chain as a pledge for the twenty remaining *ducados* and for the forty I'm offering for the future slashing. It's worth a thousand *reales*, and it's possible it won't be enough, because I suspect another fourteen stitches will be needed before long."

At this point he removed a small-linked chain from around his neck and handed it to Monipodio, who could tell from its touch and weight that it was not made of tin. Monipodio accepted it very happily and courteously, because he was very well brought up; execution was in the hands of Chiquiznaque, who took that night only as an installment. The gentleman was very satisfied when he left, and then Monipodio called all those who were absent and had been frightened. Everyone came down, and placing himself in the middle of them, Monipodio took a small notebook from the hood of his cape, and gave it to Rinconete to read, because he did not know how. Rinconete opened it, and on the first page it said:

> Note on the knife slashes to be completed this week. The first is the merchant at the crossroads; worth fifty escudos, thirty have been received as a down payment. Executator, Chiquiznaque.

"I don't think there's another one, my boy," said Monipodio, "keep looking and find where it says: *Note on beatings.*"

Rinconete turned the page, and saw that on the next one was written: *Note on beatings.*

And under that it said:

> *Tavern keeper on Plaza de la Alfalfa, twelve blows with a cudgel at the highest rate of one* escudo *each. Eight have already been given. Time limit, six days. Executator, Maniferro.*

"You can erase that note, said Maniferro, "because tonight I'll close the account."

"Is there anything else, son?" said Monipodio.

"Yes, one more," responded Rinconete, "and this is what it says:

> *The hunchback tailor, nicknamed the Canary, six blows with a cudgel at the highest rate at the request of the lady who left her necklace. Executator, Desmochado."*

"I'm amazed," said Monipodio, "that this note still hasn't been taken care of. No doubt about it: Desmochado must be sick, because it's two days past the time limit and he hasn't done anything about this."

"I ran into him yesterday," said Maniferro, "and he said that since the hunchback was in bed because he was sick, he hadn't done his duty."

"I believe that," said Monipodio, "because I think Desmochado is such a good officer that if it wasn't for this very reasonable stumbling block, he'd have already completed even bigger jobs. Is there anything else, kid?"

"No, Señor," answered Rinconete.

"Well, go ahead," said Monipodio, "and look where it says: *Note on common offenses."*

Rinconete turned the pages until he found this written:

> *Note on common offenses, to wit, blows given with flasks filled with foul-smelling liquids, ointments made with strong-smelling juniper tar, tacking on doors signs for Jews and horns for cuckolds, rackets, frights, disturbances and fake knife fights, publication of libels, etc.*

"What does it say lower down?" said Monipodio.

"It says," said Rinconete: "*Juniper tar on the house* . . . "

"Don't read the house, I already know where it is," responded Monipodio, "and I'm the key person and executator of that little trifle, four *escudos* as a down payment and the sum is eight."

"That's true," said Rinconete, "it's all written down here; and further down it even says *Tacking on horns."*

"And don't read," said Monipodio, "the house or where it is, it's enough for the offense to be done without saying it in public, for that's a great burden on one's conscience. At least, I'd rather tack up a hundred horns and the same number of punishment lists for the Inquis'tion and be paid for my work than say it just one time, even if it was to the mother who bore me."

"The executator of this," said Rinconete, "is Narigueta."

"That's already done and paid for," said Monipodio. "Look and see if there's more, for if I remember correctly, there should be a twenty-*escudo* fright; half has been paid, and the executator is the entire community, and the time limit is this whole month, and it has to be carried out exactly, with a dot over every *i*, and it will be one of the best things to happen in this city for a long time. Give me the book, young man, because I know there's nothing else, and I also know that business is very slow; but another time will come after this one and there will be more to do than we could want, for God's eye is on the sparrow and we don't need to force anyone here; besides, every man is brave in his own defense and doesn't want to pay for work that he can do with his own hands."

"That's true," said Repolido. "But look, your grace, Señor Monipodio, give us your orders and directions, because it's late and getting hotter very fast."

"This is what has to be done," responded Monipodio. "All of you go to your posts and nobody move until Sunday, when we'll all meet right here and divide everything that's come in, without wronging anybody. Rinconete the Good and Cortadillo will have as their area, until Sunday, from the Torre del Oro, outside the city, to the postern gate of the Alcázar, where you can work your tricks blindfolded; for I've seen others with less skill end each day with more than twenty *reales* in small change, besides the silver, with just one shuffle and four cards missing. Ganchoso will show you the district; and even if you go as far as San Sebastián and Santelmo, it doesn't matter since it's just simple justice that nobody becomes another man's possession."

The two boys kissed his hand for the good turn he was doing them and offered to ply their trade well and faithfully, with all due diligence and discretion.

Then Monipodio took a folded paper from the hood of his cloak, which contained the list of members of the brotherhood, and told Rinconete to add his name and Cortadillo's to the list; but since they had no inkwell, he gave him the paper to take with him and write the names in the first pharmacy they came to, saying, 'Rinconete and Cortadillo, members; no novitiate; Rinconete, cardsharp; Cortadillo, cutpurse'; and the day, month, and year, omitting parentage and birthplace.

Just then one of the old hornets came in and said:

"I've come to tell your graces how right now, just this minute, I ran into Lobillo el de Málaga in Gradas, and he tells me his art's improved so much that with an unmarked card he'll take the money of Satan himself; and because he's so ragged, he isn't coming right away to register and offer his usual obedience, but that on Sunday he'll be here without fail."

"I always firmly believed," said Monipodio, "that this Lobillo had to be unique in his art, because he has the best and most suitable hands for it that one could desire; to be a good official in his trade, good instruments for exercising it are as necessary as the intelligence to learn it."

"And in a boarding house on Calle de Tintores," said the old man, "I also ran into the Jew in a priest's habit who took a room there because he heard that two very rich men were staying in the same house, and he wanted to see if he could start to gamble with them, even if it was for a small sum, because that could grow into a large one. He also says that on Sunday he won't miss the assembly and will give an account of his person."

"That Jew," said Monipodio, "is also a great saker falcon and has great knowledge. I haven't seen him for days, and that isn't right, and I swear if he doesn't change his ways, I'll take apart his tonsure, because that thief has no more orders than a Turk, and he knows no more Latin than my mother. Any other news?"

"No," said the old man, "at least as far as I know."

"Well, it will all work out," said Monipodio. "All of you take this pittance," and he divided some forty *reales* among them, "and everybody be here on Sunday, and everything that's been stolen will be here too."

Everyone thanked him. Repolido and Cariharta embraced again, as did Escalanta and Maniferro, and Gananciosa and Chiquiznaque, arranging to see one another that night, after finishing their work in the brothel, at Pipota's, where Monipodio also said he would go, to examine the bleaching basket and then he had to do his duty and erase the juniper tar certificate. He embraced Rinconete and Cortadillo, and giving them his blessing, sent them on their way, telling them not to ever have a fixed or permanent residence, because that was best for everyone's health. Ganchoso accompanied them to show them their posts, reminding them not to miss Sunday, because he believed and thought that Monipodio would read a lesson in a public comp'tition regarding things having to do with their art. With this he left, leaving the two companions amazed at what they had seen.

It was Rinconete who, though a boy, had a very sharp intelligence and a good disposition, and had accompanied his father in the sale of indulgences and knew something about fine language, and it made him laugh to think about the words he had heard spoken by Monipodio and the rest of his company and blessed community. And even more so when, in order to say *per modum sufragii* [by way of prayer], he had said *per modo de naufragio* [by way of shipwreck], and that they collected the *stupend* instead of the *stipend* when they meant what they had stolen; and when Cariharta said that Repolido was like an ogle and a muenster, with another thousand effronteries (he thought it especially funny when she said that all the trouble she had gone to in order to earn the twenty-four *reales* would be received in heaven as a reduction of her sins), these and others even worse; and, above all, he marveled at the certainty and confidence they had that they would go to heaven if they said their prayers when they were so full of thefts and homicides and offenses against God. And he laughed at the other good old woman, Pipota, who left the basket of stolen laundry in her house and went to light wax candles before the images of the saints and thought with that she would go to heaven and have nothing else to worry about. And he was no less surprised at the obedience and respect that everyone showed Monipodio, when he was a barbaric man, rough and heartless. He considered what he had read in his notebook, and the practices all of them were engaged in. Finally, he exaggerated how careless the law was in that famous city of Sevilla, because such pernicious people, so contrary to nature itself, lived there almost in the open, and he proposed to himself to advise his companion that they not stay too long in a life that was so lost and so bad, so unsettled, so free and so dissolute. But, even so, carried along by his youth and lack of experience, he spent a few more months in it, during which time things happened to him that demand to be written about, and so recounting his life and miracles is left for another occasion, along with those of his teacher Monipodio, and other events that took place in the infamous academy, for they will all be of great consequence and can serve as a caution and warning to those who read them.

Among the spoils the English carried away from the city of Cádiz, Clotaldo, an English gentleman and captain of a squadron of ships, took to London a girl approximately seven years old, much against the will and the wisdom of the Count of Leste, who very diligently searched for the girl in order to return her to her parents; they had complained to him of their daughter's absence, asking him that, since he was satisfied with property and left persons free, they should not be so unfortunate as to be left not only impoverished but without their daughter, who was the apple of their eye and the most beautiful child in the entire city.

The count had an edict issued to his entire fleet stating that, under pain of death, whoever had the girl should return her; but no punishments or fears were enough for Clotaldo to obey the order, and he kept her hidden on his ship, for he was taken, though in a Christian way, with the incomparable beauty of Isabel, which was the girl's name. In short, her parents, sad and disconsolate, were left without her, and Clotaldo, extraordinarily happy, reached London and gave the beautiful girl to his wife as the richest of his spoils.

As good luck would have it, all the members of Clotaldo's household were secret Catholics, although in public they seemed to follow the opinion of their queen. Clotaldo had a son named Ricaredo, who was twelve years old and taught by his parents to love and fear God, and to be very steadfast in the truths of the Catholic faith. Catalina, Clotaldo's wife, a noble, Christian, and prudent lady, felt so much love for Isabel that, as if she were her own daughter, she reared her, cared for her, and taught her; and the girl was so gifted that she easily learned everything she was taught. With time and all the kindness shown her, she began to forget all that her true parents had done for her, but not to the extent that she stopped recalling them often and sighing for them; and though she was learning the English language, she did not lose Spanish, because Clotaldo was careful to bring to the house in secret Spaniards who would speak with her. In this way, without forgetting her own language, as we have said, she spoke English as if she had been born in London.

After teaching her all the kinds of needlework that a wellborn girl can and should know, she was taught to read and write more than passably well; but her greatest achievement lay in playing all the instruments it is licit for a woman to know, and she did this with so much musical perfection, and accompanied her playing with a voice so perfected by heaven, that she enchanted when she sang.

All these charms, acquired and added to her own nature, gradually began to set fire to the heart of Ricaredo, whom she loved and served as the son of her master. At first love surprised him with a way to enjoy and take pleasure in seeing Isabel's unequaled beauty and to consider her infinite virtues and graces, loving her as if she were his sister, his desires not going beyond honorable and virtuous boundaries. But as Isabel grew, for by the time Ricaredo burned with love she was twelve years old, that early benevolence, that pleasure and joy in looking at her, turned into an ardent desire to enjoy and possess her; not because he aspired to this by means other than being her husband, for because of the incomparable virtue of Isabella—which is what they called her—nothing else could be hoped for, nor did he wish to hope for it, even if he could, because his own nobility and the esteem in which he held Isabella would not allow any evil thought to take root in his soul.

A thousand times he decided to reveal his desires to his parents, and another thousand times he did not confirm his decision because he knew they had determined he should marry a very rich and prominent Scottish girl, like them a secret Christian; and it was clear, as he said, that they would not wish to give to a slave—if this name could be given to Isabella—what they had already agreed to give to a lady. And so, perplexed and pensive, not knowing which road to take to reach his virtuous desire, he lived his life in such a way that he almost lost it. But thinking it would be great cowardice to let himself die without attempting some kind of remedy for his suffering, he took courage and made the effort to declare his intentions to Isabella.

Everyone in the house was saddened and agitated by Ricaredo's malady, for he was loved by everyone, and by his parents as much as anyone could love, not only because they had no other son but because his great virtue and valor and intelligence deserved it. In short, determined to break through all the difficulties he could imagine, one day when Isabella came in to tend to him he saw she was alone, and with a faint voice and stumbling tongue, he said:

"Beautiful Isabella, your worth, your great virtue and beauty have brought me to this state; if you do not wish me to leave my life in the hands of the greatest suffering imaginable, let your virtuous desire respond to mine, which is no other than to receive you as my wife behind the back of my parents, who, I'm afraid, since they don't know your worth as I do, will deny me the good that matters so much to me. If you give your word that you will be mine, I shall immediately give you mine, as a true and Catholic Christian, to be yours; for, since I shall not enjoy you, as I shall not, until it is with the blessing of the Church and my parents, imagining that you are surely mine will be enough to give me back my health and keep me happy and contented until the joyous moment I desire arrives."

As Ricaredo said this, Isabella listened to him, her eyes lowered, showing in this that her virtue equaled her beauty, and her great discernment her modesty. And so, seeing that Ricaredo fell silent, the virtuous, beautiful, and perceptive girl responded in this way:

"After the severity or clemency of heaven, for I do not know which of those extremes to call it, willed that I should be taken from my parents, Señor Ricaredo, and given to yours, and grateful for the infinite kindnesses they have shown me, I decided that my will should never differ from theirs; and so, without that, I should consider the inestimable favor you wish to do me not good fortune but bad. If in their wisdom they deem me fortunate enough to deserve you, from this moment on I offer you the will they give me; and for as long as this takes, or if it does not happen at all, let your desires be allayed knowing that mine will be eternal and pure in wishing for you the good that heaven can afford you."

And here Isabella called a halt to her virtuous and wise words, and here Ricaredo's health began to return and the hopes of his parents, which in his illness had died, began to revive.

The two took courteous leave of each other; he, with tears in his eyes; she, with surprise in her soul to see how submissive Ricaredo's soul was to her love. And he, risen from his bed, miraculously in their opinion, did not wish to keep his thoughts hidden from his parents any longer. And so, he revealed them to his mother one day, telling her at the end of his explanation, which was long, that if they did not marry him to Isabella, denying him and killing him were one and the same thing. With this kind of insistent language Ricaredo praised Isabella's virtues to the skies, until it seemed to his mother that Isabella might be making a mistake in not taking her son as a husband. She gave her son hope that his father would be disposed to favor what she already did; and this was so, for by telling her husband the same words their son had said to her, she easily moved him to want what their son so desired, inventing excuses to prevent the marriage that had almost been arranged with the young lady from Scotland.

At this time Isabella was fourteen and Ricaredo was twenty; and in this green and flowering age, their great discernment and distinct prudence made them old. It was four days until the day when Ricaredo's parents had wanted their son to bend his neck to the holy yoke of matrimony, thinking themselves wise and very fortunate to have turned their prisoner into their daughter, placing more value on the dowry of her virtues than on the great wealth the Scotswoman offered. Wedding preparations had been made, kinfolk and friends had been invited, and there was nothing left to do but inform the queen of their arrangement, because without her will and consent among people of noble blood, no marriage could take place; but they had no doubts about her permission and had postponed requesting it. And so, this being the situation just four days before the wedding, a minister of the queen disturbed all their good cheer one afternoon with a message for Clotaldo: Her Majesty commanded that the next day, in the morning, he bring into her presence his prisoner, the Spanish girl from Cádiz. Clotaldo responded that he very gladly would do what Her Majesty commanded. The minister departed, leaving everyone's bosom filled with perturbation, alarm, and fear.

"Oh," said Lady Catalina, "if the queen knows I've brought this girl up a Catholic, and then infers that all of us in this house are Christians! Well, if the queen asks her what she has learned in the eight years she's been a prisoner, what can the distressed girl say that won't condemn us, no matter how judicious she is?"

Hearing this, Isabella said:

"Do not let that fear cause you any grief at all, my lady, for I trust that heaven, in its divine mercy, will give me words at that moment that not only will not condemn us but will benefit all of you."

Ricaredo was trembling, almost as if he foresaw some evil occurrence. Clotaldo searched for ways to allay his great fear with courage and did not find them except in his great trust in God and in the prudence of Isabella, whom he charged with using all the ways she could to avoid condemning them as Catholics; for, although they were ready in spirit to accept martyrdom, their weak flesh rejected that bitter path. Over and over again, Isabella assured them they could be certain that what they feared and suspected would not happen on her account, because, although she did not know at that moment how she would respond to the questions she might be asked, she had a sure and certain hope, as she had said before, that her answers would be to their advantage.

That night they talked about many things, especially the fact that if the queen knew they were Catholic, she would not have sent so gentle a message, and from this they could infer that she wished only to see Isabella, whose unequaled beauty and abilities no doubt had reached her ears, as well as everyone else's in the city. But they realized their fault in not having presented her to the queen earlier, and thought it might be correct to say that, since she had come under their control, they had chosen and designated her to be the wife of their son Ricaredo. But in this they were also at fault for having arranged the wedding without the queen's permission, although this fault did not seem to merit severe punishment.

This helped to console them, and they agreed that Isabella should not be dressed humbly, as a prisoner, but as a bride, for she was already betrothed to a groom as distinguished as their son.

Having resolved this, the next day they dressed Isabella in the Spanish style, in a skirt and bodice of green satin slashed and lined in rich cloth of gold, the slashes caught up with links of pearls, and all of it embroidered with sumptuous pearls; a necklace and corselet of diamonds, and a fan in the fashion of Spanish ladies; and her hair, which was thick, blonde, and long, was intertwined and scattered with diamonds and pearls, and this served as her headdress. With this resplendent adornment and her charming disposition and miraculous beauty, she appeared that day in London in a beautiful carriage, taking with her the astonished souls and eyes of everyone who saw her. Clotaldo, his wife, and Ricaredo rode with her in the carriage, and many distinguished relatives of theirs accompanied them on horseback. Clotaldo wanted to honor his prisoner in all these ways in order to oblige the queen to treat her as his son's bride.

Having reached the palace and a large salon where the queen was sitting, Isabella entered the room, presenting herself in the most beautiful way imaginable. The salon was large and spacious, and her escort remained two steps behind her; and by herself she resembled the star or shooting star that moves through the region of fire on a serene and quiet night, or the ray of sunlight that can be seen between two mountains at daybreak. All of this she appeared to be, and even a comet that predicted the blaze in more than one soul present there whom Love inflamed with the rays of Isabella's beautiful suns, and she, filled with humility and courtesy, went to kneel before the queen, and in English she said:

"Your Majesty, give your hands to this your servant, and beginning today she will consider herself more of a lady, for she has been fortunate enough to see your greatness."

The queen looked at her for a long time, not saying a word, thinking, as she said afterward to her lady-in-waiting, that before her she had a starry sky, the stars being the many pearls and diamonds that Isabella wore; her lovely face and her eyes the sun and the moon, and all of her a startling marvel of beauty. The ladies who were with the queen would have liked to be all eyes so they would not miss any part of Isabella. One praised the sparkle in her eyes, another the color of her face, another the gracefulness of her body, and another the sweetness of her speech, and there was even one who, out of pure envy, said:

"The Spanish girl's all right, but I don't like her dress."

After the queen's astonishment had passed somewhat, she had Isabella stand and said to her:

"Speak to me in Spanish, young lady, for I understand it and would enjoy that."

And turning to Clotaldo, she said:

"Clotaldo, you have offended me by keeping this treasure hidden from me for so many years; it is understandable that you were moved by covetousness; you are obliged to restore it to me, because it is mine by right."

"My lady," responded Clotaldo, "there is much truth in what Your Majesty says; I confess my fault, if keeping this treasure until she had reached the perfection suitable for appearing before Your Majesty's eyes is a fault, and now that she has I intended to improve her even more by asking Your Majesty's permission for Isabella to be the wife of my son Ricaredo, and to offer to Your Majesty all that I can offer in the two of them."

"I even like her name," responded the queen, "and she has to be called Isabella *the Spanishwoman* so that there is no perfection left for me to desire in her; but be advised, Clotaldo, I know that without my permission you promised her to your son."

"That is true, my lady," responded Clotaldo, "it was with confidence that the many significant services I and my forebears have performed for this crown would secure from Your Majesty other kindnesses more difficult than those surrounding this permission; moreover, my son is not yet betrothed."

"And he will not be to Isabella," said the queen, "until he deserves it on his own merits. I mean, I do not wish your services or those of your ancestors to benefit him; he has to be prepared to serve me on his own and be worthy of this prize by himself, for I already esteem her as if she were my own daughter."

As soon as she heard this last word, Isabella kneeled again before the queen and said to her in Spanish:

"The misfortunes that such compensations bring, Most Serene Highness, should be thought of as joys rather than as afflictions. Your Majesty has called me daughter; with such security, what evils can I fear or what benefits can I not expect?"

Isabella said what she said with so much grace and charm that the queen became extremely fond of her and ordered that she enter her service. And she handed her over to a great lady, her oldest lady-in-waiting, to teach her their way of life.

Ricaredo, who saw his life taken away when they took Isabella away from him, was about to lose his reason; and so, trembling and alarmed, he went to kneel before the queen, to whom he said:

"For me to serve Your Majesty there is no need to induce me with rewards other than those my parents and forebears have achieved for having served their sovereigns, but since it pleases Your Majesty that I serve her with new desires and aspirations, I should like to know in what manner and in which activity can I show that I am satisfying the obligation Your Majesty has placed on me."

"Two ships," responded the queen, "are about to leave to privateer, and I have made Baron Lansac their commander. I make you captain of one of them, because the line you come from assures me that it will compensate for your youth. And be aware of the kindness I am doing you, for I am giving you the opportunity, corresponding to who you are, to show in the service of your queen the worth of your intelligence and your person, and to win the best reward that, in my opinion, you can ever hope to desire. I myself shall be Isabella's guardian, although she has shown that her virtue will be her truest guardian. Go with God, and as I imagine you are in love, I expect great things from your deeds. Happy the warrior monarch who has ten thousand lover soldiers in the army who hope that the reward for their victories will be to enjoy their ladies. Arise, Ricaredo, and see whether you have to or wish to say anything to Isabella, because your departure is tomorrow."

Ricaredo kissed the queen's hands, valuing greatly the kindness she had done him, and he went to kneel before Isabella, and wishing to speak he could not because a lump in his throat tied his tongue, and tears filled his eyes, and he attempted to hide them as much as possible; but, even so, he could not hide them from the eyes of the queen, who said:

"Do not be ashamed, Ricaredo, to cry, and do not think less of yourself for having given in this critical moment such tender demonstrations of your heart, for it is one thing to fight with enemies and quite another to say goodbye to one you love very much. Isabella, embrace Ricaredo and give him your blessing, for his sentiment surely deserves it."

Isabella, who was astonished and amazed to see Ricaredo's humility and pain, for she loved him as her husband, did not understand what the queen commanded but began to shed tears, not thinking about what she was doing, and so quietly and with no movement at all, it was as if an alabaster statue were weeping. These emotions on the part of the two lovers, so young and so much in love, made many of those present shed tears, and without Ricaredo saying another word, and without his having said anything to Isabella, Clotaldo, and those who accompanied him, he bowed to the queen and left the salon, filled with compassion, chagrin, and tears.

Isabella was left like an orphan who has just buried her parents and is fearful her new mistress might want to change the customs in which the first had reared her. In short, she remained at court, and two days later Ricaredo set sail, shaken by two thoughts, among many others, that made him frantic. One was considering that it was to his advantage to perform deeds that would make him deserving of Isabella, and the other, that he could not perform a single one if it challenged his Catholic intention, which prevented him from drawing his sword against Catholics; and if he did not, he would be noted as a Christian or a coward, and all of that would be to the detriment of his life and an obstacle to his aspiration. But at last he decided to give preference to his joy in being a lover to his joy in being a Catholic, and in his heart he asked heaven to furnish him with occasions in which, by being brave, he would fulfill his Christian duty, satisfy his queen, and prove worthy of Isabella.

The two ships sailed for six days before a favorable wind, following the route of the Azores, a place where there are always either Portuguese ships from the East Indies or some proceeding from the West Indies. And after six days, they were hit broadside by a strong wind that in the Atlantic has a name different from the one used in the Mediterranean, where it is called the *mediodía*, or southern wind; this wind was so long-lasting and robust that it did not allow them to reach the islands, and they were obliged to sail to Spain; and near that coast, at the mouth of the Strait of Gibraltar, they discovered three ships, one large and powerful, and two small ones. Ricaredo sailed his vessel up to the flagship to find out whether the admiral wanted to attack the three ships, but before he could reach it, he saw them raise above the largest topsail a black flag, and coming closer, he heard them playing bugles and blaring trumpets on board, clear signs that the admiral or some other important person on the ship was dead. After this shock, they were able to speak to one another, which they had not done after leaving port. They called from the flagship, saying that Captain Ricaredo should come aboard because the admiral had died of apoplexy the night before. Everyone became very sad except Ricaredo, who felt happy, not because of the harm to his admiral but at seeing he was free to command the two ships, for it was the queen's order that, in the absence of the admiral, Ricaredo should take his place; he quickly boarded the flagship, where he found that some wept for the dead admiral and others rejoiced over the living one. Then they all vowed obedience to their admiral and celebrated him with brief ceremonies, two of the three vessels they had seen not allowing for anything else, for moving away from the large one, they were approaching the two ships under Ricaredo's command.

Then, because of the half-moons on their flags, they saw that they were Turkish galleys, which pleased Ricaredo very much, for it seemed to him that the prize, if heaven should grant it to him, would be considerable without his having to offend any Catholic. The two Turkish galleys approached and recognized the ships as English, although they were flying not the emblems of England but of Spain to deceive anyone who attempted to identify them, and in order not to be mistaken for corsairs' ships. The Turks believed they were ships en route from the Indies and could easily be taken. They gradually came in closer, and Ricaredo intentionally allowed them to approach until they were within range of his artillery, which he ordered to fire in such good time that five cannon balls hit the middle of one of the galleys with so much fury that a hole was opened directly through the vessel. Then it tilted to one side and began to go down, and there was no way to stop it. The other galley, seeing the disastrous turn of events, tossed a cable to be placed under the side of the great ship; but Ricaredo, whose ships were fast and agile and came and went as if they had oars, ordered all the artillery reloaded and followed them, raining countless cannonballs down on them.

As soon as the men aboard the sinking ship were near the English vessel, they abandoned theirs and with speed and dispatch attempted to take it over. Ricaredo saw this, and that the undamaged galley was also attacking, and he bore down on it with his two ships, and not allowing it to maneuver or take advantage of its oars, pursued it relentlessly, for the Turks were also taking advantage of the possibility of boarding the English ship, not to defend themselves but to escape and save their lives.

The Christians carried on the galleys tore away their shackles, broke their chains, mixed in with the Turks, and also sought refuge on the ship, and as they were climbing up the side, the harquebuses on the ships shot at them as if they were targets, but only at the Turks, for Ricaredo ordered that no one should shoot at the Christians. In this way, almost all the Turks were killed, and those who boarded the ship were cut to pieces with their own weapons by the Christians who had mixed with them; for the strength of the brave, when they fall, passes to the weakness of those who rise up. And so, with the ardor the Christians felt at the thought that the English ships were Spanish, they performed miracles for their freedom. Finally, having killed almost all the Turks, some Spaniards drew up alongside the ship, and shouted to those they thought were Spaniards to come and enjoy the prize of their conquest.

Ricaredo asked them in Spanish what ship that was. They replied it was a vessel from the Portuguese East Indies carrying spices, and countless pearls and diamonds worth more than a million in gold, and storms had carried them there, ruined and without artillery because the crew, sick and almost dead from thirst and hunger, had thrown the guns overboard, and those two galleys, which belonged to the corsair Arnaúte Mamí, had surrendered the day before, having no possibility of defending themselves, and according to what they had heard, since so much wealth could not be passed to their two vessels, they were towing it in order to place it in the river at Larache, which was nearby.

Ricaredo replied that if they thought those two ships were Spanish, they were mistaken, for they belonged to none other than the queen of England, a piece of news that gave those who heard it a great deal to think about and to fear, thinking, as it was reasonable to think, that they had fallen from one hazard into another. But Ricaredo told them not to fear any harm and to be certain of their freedom as long as they made no effort to defend themselves.

"It isn't even possible for us to do that," was the response, "because, as we've said, this ship has no artillery and we have no weapons; and so we are obliged to rely on the gallantry and generosity of your admiral; for it is only just that the person who has freed us from the insufferable captivity of the Turks will continue that great kindness and benefit, for it could make him famous in all the places, and they must be infinite, where the news of this memorable victory and his generosity, more hoped for than feared by us, may travel."

The Spaniard's words seemed reasonable to Ricaredo, and he consulted with the men on his ship, asking how they could send all the Christians to Spain without exposing themselves to any sinister action in the event their numbers gave them the courage to rebel. Some were of the opinion that he should have them board the ship one by one, and as they came aboard, they should each be killed below decks, and in this way all would be dead and they could take the great ship to London with no fears or worries whatsoever.

To which Ricaredo responded:

"Since God has done us the great kindness of giving us so much treasure, I don't want to respond with a cruel and ungrateful spirit, and if I can solve something with skill, it is not good to solve it with the sword. And so it is my opinion that no Catholic Christian should die, not because I am so fond of them but because I am very fond of myself, and I should not like today's deed to bring us, either myself or you who have been my companions in the undertaking, the fame of being cruel along with the name of brave men, because cruelty never was in accord with valor. What we must do is have all the artillery on one of these ships passed to the large Portuguese vessel, not leaving on that ship weapons or anything other than food; and not abandoning our people's ship, we shall take it to England, and the Spaniards will go to Spain."

No one dared contradict what Ricaredo had proposed; some thought him valiant and magnanimous, with a good understanding, while others judged him in their hearts as more Catholic than he should have been. Having made this decision, Ricaredo took fifty harquebusiers with him onto the Portuguese vessel, all of them alert and with their hemp fuses lit. On the vessel he found almost three hundred men who had escaped from the galleys. Then he asked for the ship's record book, and the same man who had spoken to him first from the side of the ship replied that the corsair who commanded the vessels had taken it, and it had gone down with him. He immediately put the tackle in order, and bringing his second ship alongside the great vessel, with surprising speed and using the strength of very powerful capstans, they moved the artillery from the small ship to the larger vessel. Then, speaking briefly to the Christians, he ordered them to pass to the stripped vessel, where they would find enough provisions for more than a month and for more people; and as they were boarding, he gave each of them four Spanish gold *escudos*, which he had brought from his ship, to take partial care of their needs when they reached land, which was so close that the high mountains of Gibraltar and Djebel Musa were visible. They all thanked him profusely for the kindness he had shown them, and the last to board was the man who had spoken for the others, and he said to him:

"For the sake of your good fortune, valiant gentleman, take me with you to England and don't send me to Spain, because although it is my country and I left it only six days ago, I shall not find anything there that does not give rise to sadness and solitude for me. You should know, Señor, that in the fall of Cádiz, which occurred fifteen years ago, I lost a daughter whom the English must have taken to England, and with her I lost the rest for my old age and the light of my eyes, for after they did not see her, they never again saw anything that pleased them. The deep sadness caused by her loss, and the loss of my fortune, also taken from me, put me into such a state that I did not wish to, nor could I, practice the trade that had brought me the reputation of being the richest merchant in the entire city. And it was true, because aside from my credit, which amounted to many hundreds of thousands of *escudos*, my wealth behind the doors of my house was valued at more than fifty thousand *ducados*. I lost everything, and none of it would have been a loss if I had not lost my daughter too. After the general misfortune, and mine in particular, poverty came to pursue me, so much so that, unable to resist, my wife and I—she is that sad woman sitting over there—decided to go to the Indies, a common shelter for impoverished nobility. And having embarked on a dispatch boat six days ago, as we left Cádiz these two pirate ships came after ours, and captured us, repeating our misfortune and confirming our bad luck. And it would have been worse if the pirates had not taken that Portuguese vessel, which held them off until what you had seen occurred."

Ricaredo asked what his daughter's name was. He replied that it was Isabel. With this, Ricaredo confirmed what he had suspected, which was that the man telling him the story was the father of his beloved Isabella. And without giving him any news about her, he said he would very gladly take him and his wife to London, where they might hear something they wished to hear. He had them board his flagship, and placed enough sailors and guards on the Portuguese vessel.

That night they set sail and hurried to move away from the Spanish coast, and on the ship with the freed captives—among them some twenty Turks to whom Ricaredo had also given their freedom to show that he had been generous more because of his good moral sense and elevated spirit than any obligatory love he might feel for Catholics—he asked the Spaniards to let the Turks go at the first opportunity, and they too expressed their gratitude to him.

The wind, which had shown signs of being favorable and steady, began to die down a little, and this calm raised a storm of fear in the English, who blamed Ricaredo and his generosity, saying the freed men could tell them in Spain about what had happened, and if by chance there were battle galleons in port they might come looking for them and cause them trouble, and they would be lost. Ricaredo knew very well they were right, but winning them over with his words, he calmed them; the wind calmed them even more, because it began to freshen so that with all sails unfurled, with no need to shorten or trim them, in nine days' time they found themselves within sight of London, and when they returned to the city, victorious, they had been away for thirty days.

Ricaredo did not wish to sail into port with displays of joy because of the death of his admiral, and so he combined the joyful with the sad. At times rejoicing bugles, other times, harsh trumpets; sometimes cheerful drums played surprising rhythms, to which fifes responded with sad, lamenting sounds; from one topsail a flag covered with half-moons hung upside down; from another one could see a long standard of black taffeta, its ends kissing the water. Finally, with these extreme opposites, he entered the river of London on his ship, because the draft of the larger ship was too deep for it, and it remained anchored at sea, parallel to the coast.

These contrasting signs and signals baffled the huge crowd watching them from the bank. Because of certain insignia, they were well aware that the smaller ship was the flagship of the Baron de Lansac, but they could not grasp why the other one had replaced the powerful vessel left at sea because it could not enter the river; but all doubt was removed from their minds when the valiant Ricaredo, armed with every rich and resplendent piece of armor, leaped into the skiff and then went by foot to the palace, not waiting for any attendants other than the countless common folk who followed him, and there the queen, informed by scouts, waited to hear news of the ships.

Isabella, along with the other ladies-in-waiting, was with the queen, and she was dressed in the English style, which suited her as well as the Spanish. Before Ricaredo arrived, someone came to tell the queen how Ricaredo was walking to the palace. Isabella was overjoyed when she heard Ricaredo's name, and at that moment she feared the bad and hoped for the good outcomes that might result from his arrival.

Ricaredo was a tall, gallant, and well-proportioned man. And as he was armed with breastplate, back plate, gorget, brassarts, and cuisse, all of it shining Milanese armor, engraved and gilded, he seemed extremely handsome to everyone who looked at him; his head was not covered by any helmet but by a broad-brimmed reddish hat that had a great diversity of feathers slanting across the crown; his sword was broad; his sword belt, rich; his tights, in the Swiss style. With these adornments, and his spirited step, there were some who compared him to Mars, the god of battles, and others, taken with the beauty of his face, say that they compared him to Venus, who, to mock Mars, had disguised herself in that way. In short, he came before the queen. He kneeled and said to her:

"Your Majesty, by dint of your good fortune and the attainment of my desire, after Admiral Lansac died of apoplexy, and I was in his place, thanks to your generosity, luck furnished me with two Turkish galleys towing that large vessel you see over there. I attacked; your soldiers fought as always, and the corsairs' ships sank; on one of ours, in your royal name, I freed the Christians who had escaped the power of the Turks; I brought back with me only a Spanish man and woman who wished to come and see your grandeur. That vessel is one of those that come from the Portuguese Indies, driven by a storm into the hands of the Turks who, with not much effort, I should say, with none at all, captured it, and according to some of the Portuguese on board, the value of the pearls and diamonds and other goods it was carrying amounts to more that a million in gold. None of it has been touched, and the Turks never laid hands on it because heaven offered all of it, and I gave orders to keep it for

Your Majesty, to whom, with only one jewel that you give me, I shall be in debt for another ten ships; that jewel Your Majesty has already promised me, and she is my good Isabella. With her I shall be rich and rewarded, not only for this service, whatever it may be, that I have performed for Your Majesty, but for many others I intend to perform in partial payment of the almost infinite price of this jewel that Your Majesty has offered me."

"Arise, Ricaredo," responded the queen, "and believe me, if I had given you Isabella for a price, considering how much I esteem her, you would not have been able to pay it either with what that vessel is carrying or what remains in the Indies. I am giving her to you because I promised to and because she is worthy of you and you of her; your valor alone deserves her. If you have kept the jewels from the ship for me, I have kept your jewel for you. And even if you think I am not doing much by returning what is yours, I know that I am showing you a great kindness; articles that are purchased with desire and find their value in the soul of the buyer, are worth as much as a soul, and there is no price on earth that can calculate its value. Isabella is yours, see her there; whenever you wish you can take full possession of her, and I believe it will be to her liking, because she is discerning and will know how to weigh the friendship you bring her, for I do not wish to call it kindness but rather friendship, because I wish to elevate myself by saying that only I can do her kindnesses. Go and rest and come to see me tomorrow, for I wish to hear your deeds in greater detail. And bring me those two who, you say, of their own free will wished to come to see me, for I wish to thank them."

Ricaredo kissed her hands for the many kindnesses she had done him. The queen went into another room, and the ladies surrounded Ricaredo, and one of them, named Lady Tansi, who had become Isabella's great friend and was considered the most intelligent, confident, and charming of them all, said to Ricaredo:

"What is this, Sir Ricaredo, what armor is this? Did you think by chance that you were coming to do battle with your enemies? Well, the truth is that all of us ladies here are your friends, except for Lady Isabella who, as a Spaniard, is obliged to bear you ill will."

"Remind her, Lady Tansi, not to feel any toward me, for as long as I am in her memory," said Ricaredo, "I know that her will is to be good, for there is no place in her great worth and understanding and rare beauty for the ugliness of being ungrateful."

To which Isabella responded:

"Sir Ricaredo, since I am to be yours, it is up to you to take from me all the satisfaction you may wish as recompense for the praise you have given me and the kindnesses you intend to do for me."

These and other virtuous words passed between Ricaredo and Isabella and the ladies, among them a very young girl who did nothing but look at Ricaredo while he was there. She raised his cuisses to see what he was wearing underneath, she felt his sword, and with the simplicity of a child wanted his armor to serve as her mirror, coming very close to look at herself; and when he left, she turned to the ladies and said:

"Now, ladies, I imagine that war must be a very beautiful thing, because even women think that men in armor look good."

"They certainly do look good!" responded Lady Tansi. "If you don't think so, look at Ricaredo, for it seems that the sun has come down to earth and is walking along the street in that attire."

Everyone laughed at the girl's witticism and Tansi's nonsensical simile, and there were even grumblers who thought it an impertinence that Ricaredo had come to the palace in armor, but there were those who excused it, saying that as a soldier, he could do that to demonstrate his gallantry and courage.

Ricaredo was welcomed with displays of deep love and affection by his parents, friends, relatives, and acquaintances. That night there was general rejoicing in London because of his success.

Isabella's parents were in Clotaldo's house now, for Ricaredo had told him who they were, but asked that they not be given news about Isabella until he gave it to them himself. Lady Catalina, his mother, and all the servants in the house were told the same thing. That night, with a good number of ships, sloops, and boats, and the same number of eyes watching, they began to unload the large vessel, which in a week had not produced all its stores of pepper and other rich goods hidden away in the hold.

The next day Ricaredo went to the palace, taking with him Isabella's father and mother, dressed for the first time in the English style, and saying that the queen wished to see them. They all came to where the queen was surrounded by her ladies, waiting for Ricaredo, whom she wished to please and favor by having Isabella near her, wearing the same dress she had worn the first time, and looking no less beautiful now than she had then. Isabella's parents were astonished, marveling at the sight of so much grandeur and luxury together. They turned their eyes toward Isabella and did not know her, although their hearts in a presentiment of the good they had so close to them began to pound, not with a fright that would sadden them but with a kind of joy they could not understand. The queen did not permit Ricaredo to remain kneeling before her; instead, she had him stand and then sit on an armless chair placed there for that sole purpose, an unusual kindness given the queen's high status. And one person said to another:

"Ricaredo isn't sitting today on the chair they've given him but on the pepper he brought here."

Someone else replied:

"Now this proves what people say, that gifts can shatter rock, for the ones presented by Ricaredo have softened the hard heart of our queen."

Another agreed, and said:

"Now that he's so firmly in the saddle, nobody will dare try to unseat him."

Indeed, this new honor that the queen offered to Ricaredo was the occasion for the birth of envy in the hearts of those who saw it, because there is no kindness the prince can do for a favorite that does not become a lance through the heart of the envious man.

The queen wished to know from Ricaredo the details of the battle with the corsairs' vessels. He recounted them again, attributing the victory to God and the valiant arms of his soldiers, praising all of them together and specifying the deeds of some who had stood out more than the others, thereby obliging the queen to show kindness to all of them, in particular those who had distinguished themselves; and when he began to tell of the freedom he had given to the Turks and Christians in the name of Her Majesty, he said:

"That woman and man over there," and he indicated Isabella's parents, "are the ones I told Your Majesty about yesterday, who, wishing to see your grandeur, earnestly requested that I take them with me; they are from Cádiz, and according to what they have told me, and what I have seen and observed in them, I know they are distinguished, outstanding people."

The queen ordered them to approach. Isabella looked up to see people who were Spaniards, and in particular from Cádiz, and wanted to know if by chance they knew her parents. As Isabella looked up, her mother looked at her, and stopped to look at her more carefully, and in Isabella's memory confused recollections began to awaken which led her to understand that she had seen the woman before her long ago. Her father was in the same state of confusion, not daring to credit the truth his eyes were showing him. Ricaredo very attentively watched the emotions and feelings of the three doubtful, perplexed souls so perturbed by the question of whether or not they recognized one another. The queen perceived their indecision and even Isabella's uneasiness, because she saw her cold perspiration and how she kept raising her hands to arrange her hair.

By now Isabella wanted the woman she thought was her mother to speak: perhaps her ears would settle the doubt caused by her eyes. The queen told Isabella to speak to that woman and man in Spanish and ask them the reason for their not wanting to enjoy the freedom Ricaredo had given them, since freedom was the thing loved best not only by rational people but even by animals that are deprived of it.

Isabella asked her mother all of this, and not saying a word, moving wildly and almost stumbling, she came up to Isabella, and with no concern for courtly circumspection or solicitude, put her hand on Isabella's right ear and found a black mole there, which finally confirmed her suspicion. And seeing clearly that Isabella was her daughter, she embraced her and cried out, saying:

"Oh daughter of my heart. Oh dear jewel of my soul!"

And unable to take another step, she fainted in Isabella's arms.

Her father, no less tender than prudent, showed signs of his feelings not with more words but by shedding tears that quietly bathed his venerable face and beard. Isabella placed her head next to her mother's, and turning her eyes toward her father, looked at him in a way that let him understand the pleasure and uneasiness in her soul at seeing them there. The queen, astonished at this turn of events, said to Ricaredo:

"I think, Ricaredo, that your judgment arranged these encounters, and do not let it be said they were correct, for we know that sudden joy kills as often as sudden sorrow."

And saying this, she turned to Isabella and moved her away from her mother who, having had water sprinkled on her face, had regained consciousness and, recovered from her faint, kneeled before the queen and said:

"Your Majesty, forgive my boldness, for fainting is not a great thing considering the joy of finding this dearly loved treasure."

The queen answered that she was right, using Isabella as her interpreter in order to be understood; Isabella, in the manner that has been recounted, recognized her parents and her parents recognized her, and the queen commanded all of them to stay in the palace so they could talk calmly to their daughter and rejoice with her, which pleased Ricaredo a great deal, and he again asked the queen to fulfill her promise of giving Isabella to him if he by chance deserved her; and if he did not deserve her, he begged the queen to order him to accomplish things that would make him worthy of what he desired. The queen understood very well that Ricaredo was satisfied with himself and his great courage, that there was no need for new tests to make him worthy, and so she said that in four days she would give Isabella to him, honoring both of them as much as she could.

Then Ricaredo took his leave, very happy about the proximate hope of possessing Isabella with no fear of losing her, which is the ultimate desire of all lovers.

Time passed, but not with the speed he desired, for those who live with hopes of future promises always imagine not that time is flying but creeping on the feet of sloth itself. But at last the day arrived, not when Ricaredo thought to put an end to his desires but to find in Isabella new charms that would move him to love her more, if more were possible. In that brief time, however, when he thought the ship of his good fortune was sailing before a favorable wind toward the desired port, bad luck raised on his sea a storm so great he feared a thousand times that it would sink him.

What happened, in fact, was that the queen's principal lady-in-waiting, in whose charge Isabella had been placed, had a son, twenty-two years of age, named Count Arnesto. The grandeur of his condition, the nobility of his blood, the great favor his mother enjoyed with the queen: these things, I say, made him arrogant, haughty, and presumptuous beyond all reason. This Arnesto, then, fell so passionately in love with Isabella that the light from her eyes set his soul ablaze; and although in the time Ricaredo had been absent Arnesto had revealed his desire by certain signs, Isabella never accepted him. And even though aversion and scorn at the beginning of love usually cause the lovers to abandon the enterprise, in Arnesto the many open rejections from Isabella had the opposite effect, because her devotion made him burn and her modesty set him on fire. And when he saw that Ricaredo, in the queen's opinion, had deserved Isabella and that in a very short time she would be given to him as his wife, Arnesto wanted to commit suicide; but before he reached so base and cowardly a remedy, he spoke to his mother, telling her to ask the queen to make Isabella his wife; if not, she should think that death was knocking at the doors of his life. The lady-in-waiting was taken aback at her son's words, and since she knew the asperity of his insolent nature, and the tenacity with which desires became obsessive in his soul, she feared that his love would lead to some unhappy consequence. Therefore, as a mother, in whom it is natural to desire and procure her children's welfare, she promised her son that she would speak to the queen, not with the hope of obtaining from her the impossibility of breaking her word, but in order not to fail to attempt, even if it proved hopeless, the ultimate remedy.

And that morning, with Isabella, by order of the queen, being so richly dressed that the pen does not dare tell about it, and the queen herself having placed around her neck a string of the best pearls the ship had brought, valued at twenty thousand *ducados*, and slipped on her finger a diamond ring valued at six thousand *ducados*, and the ladies being elated because of the celebration they expected of the nuptial vows that were close at hand, the queen's principal lady-in-waiting came in, and on her knees begged her to postpone the marriage for two more days, and she would consider this one kindness from Her Majesty satisfaction and payment for all the kindnesses she deserved and expected because of her services.

The queen wanted to know, first of all, why she was asking so fervently for a delay that went so directly against the word she had given Ricaredo, but the lady-in-waiting would not tell her until she had granted what she asked; the queen so wanted to know the reason for her request that, after the lady-in-waiting had obtained what she desired, she told the queen about her son's love and her fear that if Isabella were not given to him in marriage, he would kill himself or commit some other scandalous act; and if she had requested those two days, it was to give Her Majesty time to think about the means that would be fitting and creditable for giving her son relief.

The queen responded that if her royal word were not involved, she would find a way out of so impenetrable a labyrinth, but that she would not break it or disappoint the hopes of Ricaredo for all the advantage in the world. The lady-in-waiting repeated this answer to her son who, not stopping for an instant, burning with love and jealousy, put on complete armor, and mounted on a strong, beautiful horse, appeared before Clotaldo's house, and shouted for Ricaredo to appear at the window; and at that moment he was dressed in the finery of a bridegroom and ready to go to the palace with the entourage the ceremony required; but having heard the shouts and been told who was shouting and how he was armed, with some alarm he went to a window and, when Arnesto saw him, he said:

"Ricaredo, listen to what I want to say to you. The queen, my lady, told you to go and serve her and do deeds that would make you worthy of the incomparable Isabella. You went, and returned with ships filled with gold, with which you thought you had bought and deserved Isabella; and although the queen, my lady, has promised her to you, it was because she believed there was no man in her court who serves her better than you, and no one who to a greater degree deserves Isabella, and in this she may very well have been deceived; and so, having come to believe what I consider a proven truth, I say that you have not done deeds that make you deserve Isabella, and you could not do anything that would raise you to such a prize; and since you do not deserve her, if you wish to contradict me, I challenge you to a battle to the death."

The count fell silent and this is how Ricaredo replied:

"In no way am I inspired to come out and meet your challenge, Sir Count, because I confess not only that I do not deserve Isabella, but that no man living in the world today deserves her; and so confessing what you have said, once again I say that your challenge does not inspire me; but I accept it because of your insolence in challenging me."

With this he left the window and quickly asked for his armor. His relatives and all those who had come to accompany him to the palace became agitated. Of the many people who had seen Count Arnesto in his armor and had heard him shout his challenge, there was no lack of those who went to tell the queen, who ordered the captain of her guard to go and arrest the count. The captain hurried so much that he arrived just as Ricaredo came out of his house in the armor he wore when he had disembarked, and mounted on a beautiful horse.

When the count saw the captain, he immediately knew why he had come and decided not to allow himself to be arrested, and shouting again at Ricaredo, he said:

"You see, Ricaredo, the obstacle that hinders us. If you wish to chastise me, you will look for me; and because I desire to chastise you, I shall look for you; and since two men looking easily find each other, let us leave until then the completion of our desires."

"Agreed," responded Ricaredo.

At this moment the captain arrived with all his guards, and he said to the count that he was arrested in the name of Her Majesty. The count replied he would allow himself to be arrested, but only if he were taken into the presence of the queen. This satisfied the captain, and surrounding him with guards, he took him to the palace and to the queen, who had already been informed by her lady-in-waiting of the great love her son had for Isabella, and, in tears, pleaded with the queen to pardon the count who, as a young man in love, was prey to even greater errors.

Arnesto came before the queen, and she, exchanging no words with him, ordered him to remove his sword and had him taken to a tower as a prisoner.

All these things tormented the hearts of Isabella and her parents, who saw the sea of their tranquility so quickly agitated. The lady-in-waiting advised the queen that to assuage the ill-feeling that might arise between her kin and Ricaredo's, the cause, which was Isabella, should be removed by sending her to Spain, and in this way the effects that should be feared would cease, adding to this that Isabella was Catholic, and so Christian that none of her exhortations, and there had been many, had succeeded in turning her away in the slightest from her Catholic intention. To which the queen responded that for this reason she esteemed her even more, for she knew so well how to keep the precepts her parents had taught her, and under no circumstances would she be sent to Spain because her beautiful presence and many graces and virtues pleased her greatly, and there was no question that, if not on this day then on another, she would be given to Ricaredo as his wife, as he had been promised.

The queen's resolution left the lady-in-waiting so disconsolate that she did not say a word. And thinking the same as before, that if Isabella were not removed there was no way at all that her son's rigid disposition would soften or change enough for him to make peace with Ricaredo, she decided to commit one of the greatest cruelties that ever crossed the mind of a distinguished woman, especially one as prominent as she was. And her decision was to poison Isabella, and since it is generally the nature of women to be prompt and determined, that same afternoon she gave Isabella poison in a preserve that she offered her, urging her to eat it because it was good for the heartache she was feeling.

Not long after she had eaten it, Isabella's tongue and throat began to swell, her lips turned black, her voice became hoarse, her eyes burned, and her chest felt constricted: all the well-known signs that one has been poisoned. The ladies hurried to the queen to tell her what had happened and affirm that the lady-in-waiting had committed that terrible crime. Not much convincing was needed for the queen to believe it, and so she went to see Isabella, who was on the point of dying.

The queen quickly sent for her physicians, and while waiting for them she had Isabella take a large quantity of powdered unicorn horn and many other antidotes that great princes generally have ready for such occasions. The physicians arrived, increased the remedies, and asked the queen to have the lady-in-waiting say what kind of poison she had given the girl so there would be no doubt that another person might have poisoned her. She confessed, and with this news the physicians applied so many effective remedies that with them and the help of God, Isabella regained her life or, at least, the hope of keeping it.

The queen ordered her lady-in-waiting arrested and locked in a narrow chamber of the palace, intending to punish her as her crime deserved, for she excused herself by saying that in killing Isabella she was making a sacrifice to heaven by removing a Catholic from the earth and, with her, the reason for her son's disputes.

This sad news, when Ricaredo heard it, brought him to the verge of madness, such were the things he did and the doleful words with which he complained. In the end, Isabella did not lose her life, but nature tempered her keeping it by leaving her with no eyebrows, lashes, or hair, her face swollen, her complexion ruined, her skin blistered, and her eyes tearing. In short, she was left so ugly that just as before she had seemed a miracle of beauty, she now seemed a monster of ugliness. Those who knew her thought that her surviving in this way was a greater misfortune than if the poison had killed her. Even so, Ricaredo asked and pleaded with the queen to allow him to take Isabella to his house, because the love he had for her passed beyond the body to the soul; and if she had lost her beauty, she could not have lost her infinite virtues.

"That is true," said the queen, "and take her, Ricaredo; know you are taking a priceless jewel encased in a rough wooden box; God knows how I wish I could give her to you as you gave her to me, but since that is not possible, forgive me; perhaps the punishment I shall impose on the woman responsible for this crime will satisfy in part your desire for vengeance."

Ricaredo said many things to the queen, excusing the lady-in-waiting and begging her to pardon her, for the apologies she gave were enough to pardon greater affronts. Finally, Isabella and her parents were placed in his care, and Ricaredo took them to his house, I mean, to his parents' house. The queen added other jewels to the rich pearls and diamonds, and other dresses, revealing the great love she had for Isabella, who remained in her ugliness for two months, giving no sign of being able to return to her earlier comeliness; but after this period of time the blisters began to disappear, revealing her lovely complexion.

During this time Ricaredo's parents, thinking it was not possible for Isabella to recover her beauty, decided to send for the young lady from Scotland whom they had originally arranged for Ricaredo to marry before Isabella, and they did this without his knowledge, certain that the present beauty of the new bride would make their son forget the past beauty of Isabella, whom they planned to send to Spain with her parents, giving them so much wealth and so many riches that they would be recompensed for their past losses. In less than a month and a half, without Ricaredo's knowing it, the new bride appeared unannounced, accompanied in a fitting manner, and so beautiful that, after the Isabella who used to be, there was no girl as beautiful in all of London.

Ricaredo was startled at the unexpected sight of the young lady, and he feared that the shock of her arrival might end Isabella's life; and so, to ease this fear, he went to Isabella's bedside, and found her with her parents, before whom he said:

"Isabella of my soul: my parents, with the great love they have for me but not yet really aware of how much I have for you, have brought to the house the Scottish young lady whom they had arranged for me to marry before I learned of your great merits. And I believe they have done this with the intention that her great beauty will erase yours from my soul, where it is imprinted. Isabella, from the moment I fell in love with you it was with a love different from the one whose goal and purpose is the satisfaction of the sensual appetite; for, although your corporeal beauty captivated my senses, your infinite virtues captured my soul, so that if I loved you when you were beautiful, I adore you when you are ugly; and to confirm this truth, give me your hand."

She gave him her right hand and, grasping it with his, he continued speaking:

"By the Catholic faith that my Christian parents taught me, and if that is lacking the required integrity, I swear by the faith of the Roman Pontiff, which in my heart is the one I profess, believe, and uphold, and by the true God who hears us, I promise, oh Isabella, the other half of my soul, to be your husband, which I am, naturally, if you wish to raise me to the height of belonging to you."

Isabella was taken aback at Ricaredo's words, and her parents amazed and astonished. She did not know what to say, and could do nothing but kiss Ricaredo's hand over and over again and say, in a tearful voice, that she accepted him as hers and gave herself to be his slave. Ricaredo kissed her ugly face, never having dared to move close to it when it was beautiful.

Isabella's parents solemnized with many tenderhearted tears the celebration of their betrothal. Ricaredo told them he would delay his marriage to the Scotswoman, who now was in the house, and afterward they would see; and when his father wanted to send all three of them to Spain, they should not refuse but go and wait for him in Cádiz or Sevilla for two years, and in that time he gave them his word he would be with them, if heaven granted him that much life, and if he went past that time limit, they could be certain that some great obstacle, or death, which was more probable, had been placed in his path.

Isabella responded that she would wait for him not only two years but all the years of her life until she learned that he no longer had his, because the moment she knew that would be the moment of her death. With these tender words they all shed tears again, and Ricaredo went out to tell his parents that under no circumstances would he marry or give his hand to his bride the Scotswoman without having first gone to Rome to keep his conscience out of harm's way. The words he said to them and to the kin who had come with Clisterna—for that was the Scotswoman's name—they believed without difficulty for they were all Catholics, and Clisterna was content to stay in the house of her father-in-law until Ricaredo's return, which she asked would be in one year's time.

This having been established and arranged, Clotaldo told Ricaredo that he had decided to send Isabella and her parents to Spain, if the queen gave her permission: perhaps the air of her homeland would hasten and facilitate the health she was beginning to regain. Ricaredo, in order not to give any indication of his plans, responded indifferently to his father and said he should do whatever he thought best; he asked only that Isabella not lose any part of the riches that the queen had given her. Clotaldo gave him his promise, and that same day he went to request the queen's permission, not only to marry his son to Clisterna but to send Isabella and her parents to Spain. The queen was pleased with everything, and thought Clotaldo's decision was the right one. And that very day, without the participation of attorneys, and without subjecting her lady-in-waiting to questioning, she condemned her to not serving again in the palace and to paying Isabella ten thousand gold *escudos*; and because of his challenge, she exiled Count Arnesto from England for six years.

In fewer than four days Arnesto was ready to go into exile and the money had been secured. The queen summoned a wealthy French merchant who lived in London and had representatives in France, Italy, and Spain, and gave him the ten thousand *escudos* and requested bills of exchange that would be given to Isabella's father in Sevilla or any other financial center in Spain. The merchant, having discounted the interest and his profit, told the queen he would transmit the bills, safe and guaranteed, to Sevilla to another French merchant, his representative, in this way: he would write to Paris so that the bills would be prepared there by another representative of his, in order to show a French date, not an English one, since communication between Spain and England was against the law, and an undated letter of notification from him, bearing his countersigns, would be enough for the merchant in Sevilla, who would have been notified by the one in Paris, to hand over the money. In short, the queen accepted the guarantees of the merchant, who had no doubts regarding the security of the transfer; not content with this, she sent for the owner of a Flemish ship scheduled to leave the next day for France, and told him to obtain in a French port evidence that the ship had sailed from France and not England so it could enter Spain; and she earnestly asked him to take Isabella and her parents on his ship, and with absolute security and good treatment bring them to a Spanish port, the first one he came to. The owner, who wanted to please the queen, said he would and that he would take them to Lisbon, Cádiz, or Sevilla. Having the merchant's documents, the queen sent a message to Clotaldo telling him not to take from Isabella any of the things, whether jewels or gowns, that she had given her.

The next day Isabella and her parents came to take their leave of the queen, who received them very lovingly. The queen gave them the merchant's letter and many other gifts, money as well as other presents for the trip. Isabella thanked her with words that once again obliged the queen to always show her kindness. She said goodbye to the ladies who, since she was ugly now, did not wish her to go, finding themselves free of the envy that her beauty had caused in them, and happy to enjoy her grace and intelligence. The queen embraced the three of them, and commending them to good fortune and to the owner of the ship, and asking Isabella to let her know when they had arrived safely in Spain, and to tell her about her health through the French merchant, she said goodbye to Isabella and her parents; that same afternoon they embarked, not without the tears of Clotaldo and his wife and everyone in their house, for she was dearly loved by all of them. Ricaredo was not present at this farewell, for in order to show no signs of tender sentiment, he had arranged to go hunting that day with some friends. The gifts that Lady Catalina gave to Isabella for the voyage were many; the embraces, infinite; the tears, abundant; the requests that she write, innumerable; and the thanks of Isabella and her parents matched it all; so that, although they were weeping, they were satisfied.

That night the vessel set sail, and having reached France before a favorable wind and obtained the necessary documents for going to Spain, thirty days later it entered near the reefs of Cádiz, where Isabella and her parents disembarked, and being known to everyone in the city, they were welcomed with displays of great joy. They received a thousand congratulations for having found Isabella and for the freedom they had achieved, both from the Moors who had captured them—having learned all about the captives that Ricaredo's generosity had freed—and from the English.

At this time Isabella was beginning to have great hopes of regaining her earlier beauty. They were in Cádiz a little more than a month, recovering from the fatigue of the journey, and then they went to Sevilla to see whether the payment of ten thousand *ducados* from the French merchant turned out to be true. Two days after they arrived in Sevilla they looked for him, found him, and gave him the letter from the French merchant in the city of London. He accepted it and said that until he received the bills of payment and letter of notification, he could not disburse the money, but that he expected an order of payment very soon.

Isabella's parents rented an elegant house across from the convent of Santa Paula where, as it happened, a niece of theirs with a singularly beautiful voice was a nun in that holy monastery; and so to be close to her, and because Isabella had told Ricaredo that if he went to look for her, he would find her in Sevilla and her cousin, a sister of Santa Paula, would tell him where her house was, and to find her all he had to do was ask for the nun with the best voice in the convent, because these were directions he could not forget.

It took another forty days for the documents to arrive from Paris, and two days later the French merchant gave the ten thousand *ducados* to Isabella, and she gave them to her parents, and with that money and a little more that they obtained by selling some of Isabella's many jewels, her father returned to his work as a merchant, much to the surprise of those who knew about his great losses. In short, in a few months his lost credit was being restored and Isabella's beauty returned to what it had been, so that when speaking of beautiful women, everyone gave the laurel to the English Spanishwoman, known as much by that name as for her beauty throughout the city. By means of the warrant of the French merchant in Sevilla, Isabella and her parents wrote to the queen of England telling of their arrival, and of the gratitude and deference owed for the many kindnesses received from her. They also wrote to Clotaldo and Lady Catalina, Isabella calling them parents, and her parents calling them their lords. They received no answer from the queen, but they did from Clotaldo and his wife, who congratulated them on their safe arrival and told them that their son Ricaredo, on the day after they set sail, had left for France, and from there had gone to other places where it was advisable for him to go for the benefit of his conscience, adding to these words others of great love and devotion. And Isabella and her parents responded to this letter with another no less courteous and loving than it was grateful.

Then Isabella imagined that Ricaredo must have left England to look for her in Spain, and encouraged by this hope, she was as happy as could be and attempted to live in such a manner that when Ricaredo arrived in Sevilla, he would hear first about the fame of her virtues before he found out where her house was. Rarely, if ever, did she leave her house except to go to the convent; she received no indulgences other than those granted in the convent. In her house and her small private chapel she meditated, on Fridays during Lent, on the holy Station of the Cross and the Holy Spirit's seven days to come. She never visited the river, or went to Triana, or saw the public festival in the Campo de Tablada and the Puerta de Jerez—if the weather was fine—on the day of San Sebastián, celebrated by so many people that it can hardly be converted to a number.[1] In short, she saw no public celebration or other festivities in Sevilla; she placed her trust in her seclusion, and in her prayers and virtuous desires as she waited for Ricaredo. Her extreme withdrawal set fire to the desires not

1. Triana was and still is a neighborhood in Sevilla, Campo de Tablada was the site of the hermitage of San Sebastián, and the Puerta de Jerez was one of the gated entrances to the walled city of Sevilla.

only of the neighborhood dandies but of all those who had ever seen her even once, giving rise to serenades at night and promenades by day on her street; from not allowing herself to be seen, and from many men desiring it, there was an increase in the number of gifts from go-betweens who promised to be the first and only ones to court Isabella, and there were some who wanted to take advantage of what are called charms, which are nothing but lies and foolishness, but faced with all this Isabella was like a rock in the middle of the sea, touched but not moved by the waves and the winds.

A year and a half had passed when the proximate hope of the two years promised by Ricaredo began to agitate Isabella's heart more fervently than before. And when it already seemed to her that her husband was arriving and that he was before her and she was asking him what obstacles had detained him so long, and when she could already hear her husband's apologies, and when she was forgiving him and embracing him and welcoming him to the center of her soul, a letter came from Lady Catalina, dated in London fifty days earlier. It was written in English, but reading it in Spanish, she saw that it said:

> *Daughter of my soul, you knew Guillarte, Ricaredo's page, very well. He went traveling with him, which I had told you about in another letter, when Ricaredo left for France and other places the day after you left. Well, this same Guillarte, after sixteen months of not hearing anything from my son, walked through our door yesterday with the news that Count Arnesto had treacherously killed Ricaredo in France. Imagine, my daughter, how his father and I, his wife, responded to this news, which, I tell you, did not permit us to doubt our misfortune. What Clotaldo and I beg of you again, daughter of my soul, is that you very sincerely commend Ricaredo's soul to God, for the man who loved you so well, as you know, deserves this favor. I hope you will also ask Our Lord to grant us patience and a good death, and we also ask Him and beg Him to grant you and your parents long years of life.*

The handwriting and the signature left no doubt in Isabella, and she believed her husband was dead. She knew the page Guillarte very well and knew he was a truthful man and would not have wanted or been obliged to lie about that death, nor would his mother, Lady Catalina, have lied about it or not cared about sending her such sad news. In the end, no reasoning and nothing she imagined could relieve her of the thought that this news of her misfortune was true.

When she had finished reading the letter, without shedding tears or giving signs of painful emotion, with a calm face and, apparently, with a tranquil bosom, she got up from the chair where she was sitting and went into a chapel, and kneeling before the image of a venerable crucifix, she made a vow to become a nun, which she could do because she considered herself a widow. Her parents dissimulated, and with discretion they concealed the grief that the sad news had caused in them in order to console Isabella in the bitterness she felt; she, almost as if satisfied with her sorrow, and tempering it with the holy, Christian decision she had made, consoled her parents. She revealed her intention to them, and they advised her not to do anything until the two years Ricaredo had set for his return had passed, which would confirm the truth of Ricaredo's death, and she could change her status with more certainty. This Isabella did, and she spent the six-and-a-half months remaining until the two years were over in the practices of a religious woman and in arrangements for entering the convent, having selected Santa Paula, where her cousin was a nun.

The period of two years passed and the day for her taking the veil arrived, and this news spread throughout the city, and those who had seen Isabella and those who knew her only because of her fame filled the convent and the short distance that lay between it and Isabella's house. And her father, having invited his friends, and they having invited others, had made for Isabella one of the most honorable entourages ever seen in Sevilla for similar ceremonies. The Magistrate was there, and the vicar of the Archbishop, along with all the noble ladies and gentlemen in the city; such was the desire in everyone to see the sun of Isabella's beauty, which had been eclipsed for so many months. And since it is the custom of young ladies going to take the veil to be as elegant and beautifully dressed as possible, like one who at that moment sheds her beauty and bids it farewell, Isabella wanted to look as beautiful as possible; and so she put on the same dress she had worn when she went to see the queen of England, and we have already said how rich and attractive it was. On display were the pearls and the famous diamond, along with the necklace and corselet, which were also very valuable. With this adornment and her comeliness, giving everyone the opportunity to praise God in her, Isabella walked out of her house, which was so close to the convent there was no need for coaches and carriages. The gathering of people was so large that they regretted not having come in coaches, for no one would let them through to the convent. Some blessed her parents; others blessed heaven for having granted her so much beauty; some stood on tiptoe to see her; others, having seen her once, ran ahead to see her twice. And the man who was most insistent, to the extent that many noticed it, was dressed in the habit of those who have been ransomed from captivity, with an insignia of the Trinity on the bosom, as a sign that they have been ransomed through the charity of their redeemers.[2] This captive, then, at the moment that Isabella had a foot inside the door of the convent, where, as is the custom, the prioress and the nuns carrying the cross had come out to receive her, called to her in a loud voice:

"Stop, Isabella, stop, for as long as I am alive you cannot be a religious!"

At this, Isabella and her parents turned to look and saw that, making his way through all the people, the captive was coming toward them, and a round blue hat that he was wearing having fallen off, he revealed a confused tangle of golden ringlets and a red and white face like the rose and the snow, signs that immediately made him known and judged a foreigner by everyone. And falling down and picking himself up, he came to where Isabella was standing, and grasping her hand, he said:

"Do you know me, Isabella? Look, I'm Ricaredo, your husband."

"Yes, I know you," said Isabella, "unless you're a ghost come to disturb my tranquility."

Her parents seized hold of him and looked at him carefully, and, in short, they knew the captive was Ricaredo; he, with tears in his eyes, kneeling before Isabella, begged her not to let the strangeness of the clothes he was wearing interfere with her good judgment, or allow ill fortune to hinder her compliance with the promise the two of them had made to each other. Isabella, in spite of the impression made in her memory by the letter Ricaredo's mother had written to her giving her the news of his death, wanted to give more credit to her eyes and the truth she had in front of her, and so, embracing the captive, she said:

"You, dear sir, are beyond any doubt the only man who could interfere with my Christian decision; you, sir, are undoubtedly half of my soul, for you are my true husband; I have you stamped in my memory and protected in my soul. My lady, your mother, wrote me of the news of your death, and since that did not take my life, it forced me to choose the religious life, which at this point I wanted to enter. But since God with so just an obstacle shows that He wishes something else, I cannot, nor is it fitting on my account to hamper that. Come, sir, to my parent's house, which is yours, and there I shall be yours according to the terms demanded by our Holy Catholic Faith."

The bystanders heard everything they said, including the Magistrate, vicar, and ecclesiastical judge of the Archbishop, and they were amazed and startled

2. The Trinitarian friars dedicated themselves to the rescue of Spanish captives by collecting alms for ransom. The order had rescued Cervantes from his captivity in Algiers in 1580.

by what they heard and then wanted to be told what story this was, and who the stranger was, and what marriage they were talking about. To all of which Isabella's father responded, saying that the story demanded another place and some time to be told. And so he asked everyone who wanted to know the tale to turn around and come to his house, since it was so close by, and there it would be recounted, and they would be satisfied with the truth, and astonished at the greatness and strangeness of what had occurred. At this point, one of those present raised his voice, saying:

"Gentlemen, this young man is a great English corsair; I know him, and he is the one who, a little more than two years ago, took from Algerian pirates the Portuguese ship coming back from the Indies. There is no doubt that it is he; I know him because he gave me my freedom and money to come to Spain, and not only me but three hundred other captives as well."

At these words the people became animated, and the desire they all had to know and see such intricate matters clearly was inflamed. Finally, the most illustrious people, along with the Magistrate and the two ecclesiastical gentlemen, turned and accompanied Isabella to her house, leaving the nuns sad, confused, and weeping for what they were losing in not having the beautiful Isabella in their company. She, being in her house, in a large salon, had those gentlemen sit down; and although Ricaredo wanted to take the lead in recounting their story, he still thought it better to trust in the language and discretion of Isabella rather than his own, for he did not speak Castilian very expertly.

Everyone present fell silent, and with their souls hanging on Isabella's words, she began her tale, which I summarize by saying that she told everything that had happened to her since the day Clotaldo captured her in Cádiz until her return there, recounting as well the battle Ricaredo had waged with the Turks, the generosity he had shown the Christians, the promise each had made to the other to be husband and wife, the two-year promise, and the news she had received of his death, so true in her opinion that it had brought her to the point of becoming a nun. She praised the generosity of the queen, the Christianity of Ricaredo and his parents, and ended by saying that Ricaredo should recount what had happened to him after he left London and up to the present moment, when he was dressed in the clothes of a captive and with indications that he had been ransomed by means of charity.

"That is true," said Ricaredo, "and in just a few words I shall summarize my adventures and hardships.

"After I left London to avoid the marriage I could not have with Clisterna, the Scottish Catholic young lady whom, as Isabella has said, my parents wanted me to marry, and taking with me Guillarte, the page who, as my mother writes, brought to London the news of my death, and crossing France, I reached Rome, where my soul rejoiced and my faith was strengthened. I kissed the feet of the Supreme Pontiff, confessed my sins with the chief confessor, who absolved me and gave me the necessary sureties that would attest to my confession and penitence, and the return I had made to our universal mother the Church. Having done this, I visited the places, as holy as they are countless, in that holy city, and of the two thousand gold *escudos* I had, I gave sixteen hundred to a money exchange who issued them to a Florentine named Roqui. With the four hundred I had left, intending to travel to Spain, I left for Genoa, where I had heard there were two galleys belonging to that signory that were leaving for Spain. With Guillarte, my servant, I came to a place called Aquapendente, which going from Rome to Florence is the Pope's last possession, and in a small inn or hostelry where I dismounted, I discovered Count Arnesto, my mortal enemy, who with four servants, disguised and hidden, was going to Rome, I understand, more because he was curious than because he was Catholic. I believed he surely had not recognized me. I withdrew to a room with my servant, and I was concerned and determined to move to another inn in the dead of night. I did not, because the great carelessness I noted in the count and his servants assured me they had not recognized me. I ate supper in my room, locked the door, prepared my sword, commending myself to God, and did not lie down. My servant fell asleep and I dozed on a chair. But shortly after midnight, I was awakened to send me to an eternal sleep: four pistols, as I learned later, were fired at me by the count and his servants; and leaving me for dead, and already having readied their horses, they left, telling the innkeeper to bury me because I was an important man. And with this they left.

"My servant, as the innkeeper said later, awoke at the noise, and in fear jumped out a window that led to a courtyard, saying, 'Woe is me, they killed my master!' And he left the inn. And it must have been with so much fear that he did not stop till he reached London, for he was the one who carried the news of my death.

"The people in the inn came up and found me pierced by four bullets and a good number of pellets, but all of them lodged in places where the wound was not mortal. As a Christian Catholic, I asked for confession and all the sacraments; they were given to me, I was treated, and was in no condition to travel for two months, at the end of which I went to Genoa, where the only passage I found was two tenders that I and two other high-ranking Spaniards chartered; one to sail ahead as a scout, and the other on which we would travel.

"With this assurance we embarked, sailing along the coast and not intending to enter the high seas; but coming to a place called Las Tres Marías on the coast of France, while our first boat was exploring, suddenly two small Turkish galleys came out of a cove and approached us, one on the side of the sea, the other on the side of land, and as we prepared to attack, they cut us off and captured us. When we boarded the galley, they stripped us naked. They took everything the tenders were carrying and let them crash onto land without sinking them, saying they would use them another time to carry more *galima*, which is what they call the loot they steal from Christians. You can believe me when I say that I felt my captivity in my soul, and especially the loss of the documents from Rome that I carried in a tin cylinder, along with the certificate for the sixteen hundred *ducados*; but as good luck would have it, the cylinder came into the hands of a Christian captive, a Spaniard, who kept it; if the Turks had taken it, they would have demanded for my ransom the amount on the certificate at the very least, for they would find out whose it was.

"They took us to Algiers, where I learned that the fathers of the Holy Trinity were ransoming prisoners. I spoke to them, told them who I was, and moved by charity, even though I was a foreigner, they ransomed me in this way: they would pay three hundred *ducados* for me, one hundred in cash and two hundred when the ship arrived carrying the charity for ransoming the redeeming priest who was being held in Algiers for four hundred *ducados*, for he had spent more than he had brought with him. Because, in addition to all this mercy and generosity, there is the charity of these priests who give their liberty in exchange for someone else's and become captives in order to ransom other captives. Along with the good of my liberty, I found the lost cylinder with the documents and the certificate. I showed it to the blessed priest who had ransomed me and offered him five hundred *ducados* more than my ransom to help him meet his debt. The ship with the charity took almost a year to return, and if I were to tell you now what happened to me during that year, it would be another history. I shall say only that I became acquainted with one of the twenty Turks whom I freed along with the rest of the Christians I've already mentioned, and he was so grateful and such a virtuous man that he did not wish to reveal who I was; because if the Turks had learned I was the man who had sunk their two ships and taken from them the great ship from the Indies, they would either have given me as a present to the Grand Turk or taken my life; and if I had been given to the Great Lord, I would have never been free again in my life. Finally, the redeeming priest came to Spain with me and fifty other ransomed Christians. In Valencia we had the general procession, and from there everyone went where he chose with the insignias of his freedom, which are these clothes. Today I arrived in this city, with so much desire to see Isabella, my wife, that without stopping for anything else I asked for this convent, where they could give me news of my wife. What has happened to me here you have all seen. What remains to be seen are these documents, so that you can accept my story as true, for it is as miraculous as it is factual."

And then, saying this, he took out of a tin cylinder the documents he had mentioned and placed them in the hands of the vicar general, who saw them along with the Magistrate, and he found nothing in them that would make him doubt the truth of what Ricaredo had recounted. And in further confirmation, heaven ordained that present at these events was the Florentine merchant who held the certificate for the sixteen hundred *ducados*, and he asked to see the certificate, and when they showed it to him he recognized it immediately, for he had received the order of payment many months earlier. All of this added surprise to surprise and astonishment to astonishment. Ricaredo said he again offered the five hundred *ducados* he had promised. The Magistrate embraced Ricaredo, and Isabella's parents, and Isabella, offering himself to them with courteous words. The two ecclesiastical gentlemen did the same and asked Isabella to write down that entire history so that the Archbishop could read it, and she promised she would.

The great silence that everyone present had kept listening to the strange case broke into praises to God for His great marvels, and from the oldest to the youngest they gave congratulations to Isabella, to Ricaredo and his parents, and left them; and then they asked the Magistrate to honor their wedding, which they planned to have in a week's time. The Magistrate was happy to accept, and one week later, accompanied by the most illustrious residents of the city, he was at the wedding.

By these twists and turns and these circumstances, Isabella's parents recovered their daughter and restored their fortune; and she, favored by heaven and helped by her many virtues, in spite of so many difficulties, found a husband as distinguished as Ricaredo, in whose company it is thought she still lives today in the houses they rented across from Santa Paula, which they later bought from the heirs of a gentleman from Burgos named Hernando de Cifuentes.

This tale could teach us how much virtue can accomplish and how much beauty can do, for they are fairly close and each by itself can inspire love even in enemies, and how heaven knows how to extract from our greatest adversities our greatest benefits.

THE NOVEL OF THE GLASS LAWYER

Two gentlemen students were walking along the banks of the Tormes when they came across a boy of about eleven sleeping under a tree and dressed like a farm laborer. They sent a servant to wake him. He awoke, and they asked him where he was from and why he was sleeping in that lonely spot. To which the boy responded that he had forgotten the name of his native land, and that he was going to the city of Salamanca to find a master to serve in exchange for instruction. They asked if he knew how to read; he said he did, and how to write, too.

"That means," said one of the gentlemen, "it is not lack of memory that has made you forget the name of your native land."

"Whatever the reason," responded the boy, "no one will know that or the homeland of my parents until I can honor them and it."

"Well, then, how do you intend to honor them?" asked the other gentleman.

"With my studies," answered the boy, "by being famous for them. Because I've heard that bishops are made of men."

This reply moved the two gentlemen to accept him as their pupil and they took him with them, giving him instruction in the usual way in that university for those who serve. The boy said his name was Tomás Rodaja, which led his masters to infer from his name and clothing that he must be the son of some poor farm laborer. In a few days they dressed him in black, and in a few weeks Tomás gave signs of having uncommon intelligence, serving his masters with so much fidelity, punctuality, and diligence that, without falling behind in any way in his studies, it seemed that his only concern was to serve them. And since good service from the servant moves the will of the master to treat him well, Tomás was no longer the servant of his masters but their companion. In short, in the eight years he was with them, he became so famous in the university for his good mind and notable skill that he was esteemed and loved by all kinds of people.

His principal field of study was the law, but where he really shone was in humanistic letters; his memory was so good it was startling, and his fine intelligence illuminated his memory in a way that made him as famous for one as for the other.

Then the time came when his masters completed their studies and returned to their home, which was one of the best cities in Andalucía. They took Tomás with them, and he was with them for some days. But he was vexed by desires to return to his studies and to Salamanca, a city that bewitches the will to return in everyone who has enjoyed the tranquility of its way of life, and he asked his masters for permission to go back. They, being courteous and generous, gave it, arranging matters so that, with the money they gave him, he could live there for three years.

He took his leave, showing his gratitude in his words, and left Málaga, which was his masters' home. And as he descended the slope of La Zambra, on the way to Antequera, he met a gentleman on horseback, dressed elegantly for traveling, with two servants also on horseback. He rode beside him and learned that they had the same destination. They struck up a friendship, spoke of various matters, and Tomás soon gave indications of his uncommon intelligence, and the gentleman demonstrated his nobility and courteous manner. He said he was a captain of his majesty's infantry, and his second lieutenant was recruiting a company of soldiers in Salamanca. He praised the soldier's life; he painted a lively picture of the beauty of the city of Naples, the pleasures of Palermo, the abundance of Milan, the festivities of Lombardy, the splendid meals in the inns; he depicted for him, sweetly and exactly, the *Hey you, landlord, Manigoldo, bring on the meatballs, the chickens, the macaronis.* He praised to the sky the free life of the soldier, and the freedom of Italy. But he said nothing about the sentries' cold, the danger of attacks, the terror of battles, or the hunger, the sieges, or the destruction caused by mines, along with other matters of the kind that some deem and consider additions to the weight of being a soldier, but which are its principal burden. In short, he told him so many things, and said them so well, that the good judgment of our Tomás Rodaja began to waver, and his will became enthusiastic about a life that keeps death so close.

The captain, whose name was Don Diego de Valdivia, delighted with Tomás's fine presence, intelligence, and assurance, asked him to go to Italy with him, if he so desired, just out of curiosity; he offered him his table, and if necessary, even his standard, because his second lieutenant would soon be leaving. Little was needed for Tomás to accept, rapidly thinking to himself that it would be good to travel to Italy and Flanders and various other lands and countries, for extensive travel makes men wise, and he could spend three or four years at most doing this, which, added to his few years, would not come to enough to keep him from returning to his studies. And as if everything had to happen as it suited him, he told the captain that he did want to go with him to Italy, but it had to be on condition that he not be conscripted under a standard or included on the list of soldiers in the company, so he would not be obliged to follow their flag, even though the captain said being on the list did not matter, for it meant only that he would enjoy the assistance and pay given to the company, and the captain would give him a furlough every time he asked for one.

"That would mean," said Tomás, "going against my conscience and that of the captain. And so, I prefer to go free rather than under obligation."

"So scrupulous a conscience," said Don Diego, "belongs more to a religious man than to a soldier. But be that as it may, now we are comrades."

That night they arrived in Antequera, and after a few days of long hours of travel, they reached the company, which was now complete and preparing to leave for Cartagena, billeting, along with four other companies, in the towns they passed through. There Tomás noticed the authority of the commissaries, the bad character of some of the captains, the demands of the billeting officers, the administrative work of the paymasters, the complaints of the townspeople, the trading of billeting vouchers, the insolence of the recruits, the quarrels between host and lodgers, the demand for more beasts of burden than necessary, and, in brief, the necessity, almost the obligation, to do everything he noticed and that seemed wrong to him.

Tomás had dressed like a parrot, renouncing the student's attire and putting on the clothes of a ruffian ready to swear that God is Christ, as they say. His many books he had reduced to a *Book of Prayers to Our Lady* and a *Garcilaso* without commentary, and these he carried in two pockets.[1]

They arrived in Cartagena sooner than they might have wished, because the billeted life is varied and filled with possibilities, and every day one encounters pleasant new things. There they embarked on four galleys from the fleet in Naples, and Tomás Rodaja also observed the strange life in those maritime dwellings, where most of the time bedbugs abuse, galley slaves steal, sailors irritate, mice destroy, and rough seas harass. The severe squalls and tempests filled him with fear, especially in the Gulf of León, where they

---

1. Garcilaso de la Vega (d. 1536) was the most influential poet of the Spanish Golden Age. He is known for having brought Italian verse forms and poetic themes to Spanish poetry. His poems were published for the first time posthumously in 1543 alongside the works of another poet, Juan Boscán. Two annotated editions of his work existed by 1613: that of Francisco Sánchez de las Brozas or "El Brocense," first published in 1574 and subsequently revised and republished in a number of editions; and that of Fernando de Herrera, published in 1580.

suffered two storms; one drove them to Corsica and the other returned them to Toulon in France. Finally, haggard, drenched, and with circles under their eyes, they reached the beautiful, captivating city of Genoa, and disembarking in its sheltered Mandrache, and visiting a church, the captain with all his companions went to an inn, where they forgot all the storms of the past in their present *gaudeamus*.

There they came to know the smoothness of Trebiano, the audacity of Montefiascone, the strength of Asperino, the nobility of the two Greeks, Candia and Soma, the majesty of the one from Cinco Viñas, the sweetness and mildness of Señora Guarnacha, and the rusticity of Centola, while the lowliness of Romanesco did not dare appear among all this nobility. And the innkeeper, having reviewed so many different kinds of wines, offered to introduce there, with no tricks or deceptions but really and truly, Madrigal, Coca, Alaejos, and the imperial rather than the royal city, the antechamber of the god of laughter; he offered Esquivias, Alanía, Cazalla, Guadalcanal, and Membrilla, not forgetting Ribadavia and Descargamaría. In short, the innkeeper named more wines and offered more than Bacchus himself could have kept in his wine cellar.[2]

The good Tomás admired the blonde hair of the Genoese women, the gallantry and elegant disposition of the men, and the admirable beauty of the city, which seems to have houses set on its crags like diamonds in gold.

The next day all the companies that were to go to the Piedmont disembarked, but Tomás did not wish to make this trip; rather, he wanted to go by land to Rome and Naples, which is what he did, agreeing to return by way of Venice and Loreto to Milan and the Piedmont, where Don Diego de Valdivia said he would find him unless he had already been taken to Flanders, as the saying goes. Two days later Tomás took his leave of the captain, and in five days he arrived in Florence, having first seen Luca, a small but very well-constructed city, where Spaniards are viewed more favorably and better received than in other parts of Italy.

He was extremely pleased with Florence, as much for its pleasant setting as for its cleanliness, sumptuous buildings, bright river, and peaceful streets. He spent four days there and then left for Rome, queen of cities and mistress of the world. He visited its temples, worshiped its relics, and was in awe of its grandeur. And just as one comes to know the lion's greatness and ferocity through its claws, he deduced Rome's through its broken marbles, partial and

2. The list of wines is an indication of the autobiographical basis of this part of the story. Cervantes obviously became very familiar with Italian wines while living there.

complete statues, damaged arches, and ruined baths; its magnificent porticoes and great amphitheaters; its famous, holy river that is always filled to its banks with water and beatifies them with infinite relics from the bodies of martyrs who found their graves there; its bridges that seem to look at one another; and its streets whose names alone give them authority over all the streets of other cities in the world: the Via Apia, the Flaminia, the Giulia, along with others of the same kind. And he admired no less the distribution of its hills: Monte Celio, Monte Quirinal, Monte Vaticano, as well as the other four whose names make manifest the greatness and majesty of Rome. He also observed the authority of the College of Cardinals, the majesty of the Supreme Pontiff, the assemblage and variety of peoples and nations. He looked at and noted and appreciated everything. And having made his pilgrimage to the seven churches and confessed to a penitentiary priest and kissed the foot of His Holiness, and with an abundance of Agnus Dei images and rosary beads, he decided to leave for Naples; and since it was the bad, dangerous season for everyone who enters or leaves Rome if they have traveled by land, he went by sea to Naples, where, to the admiration he felt after having seen Rome, he added that caused by seeing Naples, in his opinion and in the opinion of all who have seen it, the best city in Europe and even the entire world.

From there he went to Sicily and saw Palermo and then Messina. He liked the setting and beauty of Palermo, and Messina's port, and the abundance he saw on the island, which appropriately and truly is called the granary of Italy. He returned to Naples, and to Rome, and from there he went to Our Lady of Loreto, in whose holy temple he saw no interior or exterior walls because they all were covered with crutches, winding sheets, chains, shackles, manacles, hair, half figures of wax, and paintings and altar-pieces, which gave a clear indication of the countless mercies received by many from the hand of God through the intercession of His divine Mother, whose sacrosanct image He wished to enlarge and authorize with a host of miracles as recompense for the devotion of those who, with similar hangings, decorate the walls of their houses. He saw the very lodging and room where the highest and most important message was delivered, seen and not understood by all the heavens, and all the angels, and all those residing in the everlasting dwelling places.[3]

From there, embarking in Ancona, he went to Venice, a city that, if Columbus had not been born, would have no equal in the world; but thanks be

3. Cervantes here refers to the Basilica of the Holy House, a pilgrimage site in Loreto, Italy, that contains the house of Mary, which was believed to have been miraculously transferred from Palestine by angels.

to heaven and the great Hernando Cortés, who conquered great Mexico City so that great Venice would in some way have some competition. These two famous cities resemble each other in their streets, which are all of water: the one in Europe, the admiration of the old world; the one in America, the wonder of the new. Tomás thought its wealth was infinite, its government prudent, its location unassailable, its abundance great, its surroundings lively; in short, all of it as a whole and in its parts deserving the fame of its merits, which extends all over the world and gives reason for crediting even more this truth, the structure of its famous shipyards, where galleys as well as countless other vessels are constructed. The pleasures and pastimes our inquisitive young man found in Venice approximated those of Calypso, because they almost made him forget his primary purpose. But having spent a month there, by way of Ferrara, Parma, and Piacenza, he returned to Milan, the workshop of Vulcan, the envy of the kingdom of France, a city, in short, about which it is said that it both says and does, made magnificent by its own grandeur and the grandeur of its temple, and its marvelous abundance of all things necessary for human life.

From there he went to Asti and arrived on time, for the next day the regiment was leaving for Flanders. He was very well received by his friend the captain, and in his company and comradeship he went to Flanders and arrived in Antwerp, a city no less astonishing than those he had seen in Italy. He saw Ghent and Brussels, and he saw that the entire country was prepared to take up arms and undertake a campaign the following summer.

Having satisfied the desire that moved him to see what he had seen, he decided to return to Spain and Salamanca to complete his studies. And when he thought of it he acted on it, to the great sorrow of his comrade who asked him when they said goodbye to keep him informed regarding his health, his arrival, and his trip. He promised to do so and returned to Spain by way of France without seeing Paris, because it was engaged in a conflict. Finally he reached Salamanca, where he was welcomed by his friends; and with the comforts they provided, he continued his studies until he graduated as a lawyer.

At this time a lady happened to arrive in that city who was all tricks and devices. Then all the birds in the area came after her, lured by decoys and calls, until every student and his book bag had visited her. Tomás was told that the lady said she had been in Italy and Flanders, and to see whether he knew her, he went to visit her, and his visit and the sight of him left her enamored of Tomás. He was unaware of this, and if not of necessity when taken there by others, he did not wish to enter her house. Finally, she revealed to him her desire and offered him her fortune. But since he attended more to his books than to other pastimes, in no way did he respond to the wishes of the lady. She, seeing herself scorned and, in her opinion, despised, and unable to conquer through ordinary, common means the rock of Tomás's affection, decided to find other means—in her opinion more effective and sufficient—to satisfy her desires.

And so, advised by a Moorish convert, she gave Tomás what is called a charm in a Toledan quince, believing that she was giving him something that would force his will to love her, as if there were in the world herbs, enchantments, or words sufficient to force one's free will; and so, those who give these love potions or foods are called malevolent, because all they do is poison the person who takes them, as experience has demonstrated on many diverse occasions.

Unfortunately, Tomás ate the quince and immediately his feet and hands and mouth began to convulse, as if he suffered from epilepsy. And he did not recover for many hours, at the end of which time he was stupefied and said, his tongue confused and stumbling, that a quince that he had eaten had killed him, and he stated who had given it to him. The authorities heard of the case and went to find the malefactor; but she, seeing how badly it had turned out, fled and was never seen again.

Tomás was in bed for six months, and in that time he withered and became nothing but skin and bone, as they say, and all his senses seemed disturbed. Although he was given all the possible remedies, only the disease of his body was cured but not the disease of his mind, because he regained his physical health but was mad with the strangest madness of all the madnesses that had ever been seen. The unfortunate man imagined he was made completely of glass, and because of this, when anyone approached him, he shouted in the most terrible way, begging and pleading with predetermined words and expressions that no one come near because they would break him, that he really and truly was not like other men, that he was all glass from head to toe.

To free him from this strange fancy, many people ignored his shouts and pleas, rushed at him and embraced him, saying that he should look and see how he did not break. But what was gained was that the poor man threw himself to the ground, shouting and then falling into a faint from which he did not recover for many hours, and when he did regain consciousness, he renewed the pleas and entreaties that he not be approached again. He said they should speak to him from a distance and ask whatever they chose, for he would respond to everything with greater understanding since he was a man of glass and not of flesh, and because glass was a subtle and delicate material, the soul could act with greater speed and efficiency than it did in a heavy, terrestrial body.

Some people wanted to test whether what he said was true. And so they asked him many difficult things, to which he replied spontaneously with great sharpness of mind; this astounded the most lettered men of the university, and the professors of medicine and philosophy, seeing that an individual suffering from so extraordinary a madness that he thought he was made of glass would have so great an intelligence that he could answer every question with accuracy and acuity.

Tomás asked to be given some kind of covering in which he could place the breakable glass container of his body so it would not be shattered by a close-fitting piece of clothing when he dressed. He was given drab-colored garments and a very wide shirt, which he put on with extreme caution and tied with a cotton cord. He refused absolutely to wear shoes, and the order he gave for being fed without anyone approaching him was to attach to the end of a rod a case for a chamber pot in which some fruit in season was placed. He did not want meat or fish; he drank only from a fountain or river, and only with his hands. When he walked he stayed in the middle of the street, looking up at the roofs, fearful that a tile would fall down on him and break him. In summer he slept outdoors in the countryside, and in winter he stayed in an inn and buried himself up to his neck in the hayloft, saying this was the most suitable and safest bed that men made of glass could have. When it thundered, he trembled as if he were suffering from mercury poisoning and went out to the countryside and did not enter a town until the storm had passed. His friends kept him locked up for a long time; but seeing that his misfortune got worse, they decided to accede to what he asked of them, which was to let him go free, which they did, and he went out into the city, causing amazement and compassion in all those who knew him. Then boys surrounded him, but he stopped them with his staff and asked them to speak to him from a distance so he would not break, because, being a man of glass, he was very delicate and breakable. Boys, who are the greatest rogues on earth, in spite of his pleas and words began to throw rags at him and even stones to see whether he was made of glass, as he said. But he shouted so much and lamented so loudly that he moved men to scold and chastise the boys to keep them from throwing anything at him. But one day when they pestered him a great deal, he turned to them and said:

"What do you want of me, boys as persistent as flies, as dirty as bedbugs, as insolent as fleas? Am I, by chance, Monte Testaccio in Rome that you throw so many pieces of earthenware and tiles at me?"[4]

---

4. Monte Testaccio is an enormous man-made mound from the Roman Empire composed of broken pottery.

In order to hear him scold and respond to everyone, many boys always followed him and thought and considered it better sport to hear him than to throw things at him.

Once, passing through the district of clothing stores in Salamanca, a clothes dealer said to him:

"Señor Lawyer, my soul aches for your misfortune; but what shall I do if I cannot cry?"

He turned to her and very calmly said:

"*Filiae Hierusalem, plorate super vos et super filios vestros.*"[5]

The clothes dealer's husband understood the malice in the statement and said to him:

"Brother Lawyer Vidriera, or Glass"—for this is what he said his name was—"you are more scoundrel than madman."

"I do not care," he replied, "as long as I am in no way a fool."

Walking one day past the bawdy house and inn, he saw many of its residents in the doorway and said they were mules in the army of Satan, lodged in the inn of hell.

One of them asked him what advice or consolation he would give to a friend who was very sad because his wife had gone off with another man.

To which he responded:

"Tell him to thank God for allowing her to be taken to the house of his enemy."

"Then he shouldn't go to find her?" said another.

"What an idea!" replied Vidriera. "Finding her would mean finding a perpetual and truthful witness to his dishonor."

"If that is so," said the same man, "what should I do to have peace with my wife?"

He replied:

"Give her whatever is necessary. Allow her to command all those in her house, but do not permit her to command you."

A boy said to him:

"Señor Lawyer Vidriera, I want to leave my father's house because he beats me so often."

And he replied:

"Be advised, boy, that the whippings fathers give their sons honor them, while those of the executioner are an insult."

5. Luke 23:28: "Daughters of Jerusalem, weep not for me, but weep for yourselves, and for your children."

At the door of a church, he saw a farmer going in, one of those who always boast of being old Christians,[6] and behind him came one whose reputation was not as good. And the lawyer cried out to the farmer, saying:

"Wait, Domingo, until Saturday passes you."[7]

Regarding schoolmasters he would say they were fortunate since they always dealt with angels, and were most fortunate if the little angels weren't insolent brats.

Another man asked him what he thought of procuresses. He replied that they weren't strangers but neighbors.

The news of his madness and his replies and sayings spread throughout Castilla and came to the attention of a prince or lord at court, who wished to send for him, and he charged a gentleman who was a friend and lived in Salamanca to send the lawyer to court. And running into him one day, the gentleman said:

"You should know, Señor Lawyer Vidriera, that a great noble at court wants to see you and has sent for you."

To which he replied:

"Your grace, please give my regrets to that nobleman, for I am not suited to the palace: I have self-respect and do not know how to flatter."

Despite this, the gentleman sent him to court, and to do so this device was used. The lawyer was placed in straw panniers like those in which glass is carried, balancing the other half with stones, and some articles of glass were placed in the straw so he would understand that he was being carried as if he were a glass container.

He arrived in Valladolid; he came in at night and was removed from the panniers in the house of the nobleman who had sent for him, and who received him very well, saying:

"A very warm welcome to Señor Lawyer Vidriera. How was your journey? How are you?"

To which he replied:

"No road is bad as long as it ends, except the one that leads to the gallows. I am well and in balance, because my heart is in equilibrium with my brain."

6. "Old Christians" was the term used to designate Spaniards who came from families of pure Christian lineage, without any trace of Muslim or Jewish ancestry.

7. Domingo is both a proper name and the word for Sunday in Spanish. Thus, the paradoxical aspect of the statement lies in the fact that Saturday must always come before Sunday.

The next day, having seen a good number of perches for hunting birds and many falcons and goshawks, he said that hunting with these birds was worthy of princes and great lords, but they should be aware that in terms of income derived, it was two thousand times more pleasurable than profitable. He said that hunting hares was very pleasurable, especially when one hunted with borrowed greyhounds.

The gentleman enjoyed his madness and allowed him to go out into the city, under the shelter and protection of a man who made sure that boys would not harm him, for within six days the boys and the entire court knew about him. And at each step, each street, and any corner, he would answer all the questions asked of him. A student asked if he were a poet, because it seemed he had the intelligence for everything. To which he replied:

"Until now I have not been that foolish or that fortunate."

"I do not understand what you say about foolish and fortunate," said the student.

And Vidriera replied:

"I have not been so foolish as to turn out a bad poet, nor so fortunate as to deserve the name of good one."

Another student asked what opinion he had of poets. He responded that he held the science in high regard but had none for poets. When asked why he said that, he responded that, of the infinite number of poets, there were so few good ones that they almost did not amount to a number. And so, as if there were no poets at all, he did not have any regard for them but admired and revered the science of poetry, because it contained all other sciences, because it makes use of all of them, adorns and polishes itself with all of them, and brings its marvelous works to light, filling the world with benefits, delights, and marvels.

And he added:

"I know very well how a good poet should be esteemed, because I recall those verses by Ovid that say:

> *Cum Ducum fuerant olim Regnumque, Poeta,*
> *Premiaque antique magna tulere chori,*
> *Sanctaque Maiestas, et erat venerabile nomen,*
> *Vatibus, et large sape debantur opes.*[8]

8. Ovid, *Ars Amandi* III, 405–8: "When poets were the favorites of leaders and kings, and ancient choirs gained great rewards, Divine Majesty, that name was revered, Poet, and upon them great riches were often bestowed."

"And I certainly have not forgotten the quality of poets, for Plato calls them interpreters of the gods. And Ovid says of them:

Est Deus in nobis agitante calescimus illo.[9]

"And he also says:

At sacri vates, et Divum cura vocamus.[10]

"This is said of good poets, for of the bad ones, the prattlers, what can be said except that they are the idiocy and arrogance of the world?"

And he added:

"Just look at the volleys fired by one of these poets of first impressions when he wants to recite a sonnet to those around him and says: 'Listen, your graces, to a little sonnet I wrote last night for a certain occasion, and though in my opinion it's not worth much, it does have a certain something that's quite nice,' and then he purses his lips, raises his eyebrows, scratches at his purse, and from another thousand pieces of soiled and half-torn papers on which there are thousands of other sonnets, he takes out the one he wants and, finally, reads it in a mellifluous, affected tone! And if, perhaps, those who are listening to him, because they are pranksters or ignorant men, don't praise it, he says: 'Either your graces have not understood the sonnet, or I haven't read it well, and so it would be a good idea to recite it again, and for your graces to pay more attention because the truth is, the sonnet is worth it.' And he recites it again from the beginning with different gestures and different pauses. Just see them criticizing one another. What shall I say of how the modern pups yap at aged and serious mastiffs? And what of those who slander some illustrious and excellent individuals in whom the true light of poetry shines and who, considering it a relief and entertainment after their many important occupations, reveal the divinity of their intelligence and the sublimity of their concepts, in spite of and regardless of the ignorant public that judges what it does not know, and despises what it does not understand, that wants the foolishness that sits beneath the canopies to be esteemed, and the ignorance that moves up to the seats of honor to be highly regarded?"

9. Ovid, *Fasti* VI, 5: "There is a god in us, and we are inflamed by his movement."

10. Ovid, *Amores* III, IX, 17: "And we call poets sacred and the beloved of the gods." The final verb is *vocamur* in Ovid.

Again he was asked the reason for most poets being poor. He responded that they wished to be, for it lay within their power to be rich if they knew how to take advantage of the opportunity, for at times it lay in the hands of their ladies, all of whom were extremely wealthy, for their hair was gold, their foreheads burnished silver, their eyes green emeralds, their teeth ivory, their lips coral, their throats transparent crystal, and the tears they wept liquid pearls; furthermore, wherever their feet stepped, no matter how hard and barren the soil, it immediately produced jasmines and roses; and their breath was pure amber, musk, and civet;[11] all these things were signs and models of their great wealth. These and other things were what he said about bad poets, but he always spoke well of good ones and praised them to the skies.

One day he saw on the wall of San Francisco some very badly painted figures, and he said that good painters imitated nature but bad ones deformed it.

One day he approached, with great caution so he would not break, a bookseller's shop and said to him:

"This trade would please me a great deal if it weren't for one shortcoming it has."

The bookseller requested that he tell him what that was. He replied:

"The affected caution booksellers display when they buy a license for a book, and the way they mock its author if the book is printed at his expense, for instead of fifteen hundred they print three thousand copies, and when the author thinks his books are selling, they are actually someone else's."

On the same day it happened that six prisoners sentenced to a flogging came across the plaza, the crier proclaiming: "The first one for a thief," and he shouted at those in front of him, saying:

"Move aside, brothers, don't let the count begin with one of you."

And when the crier said: "And in the rear . . ."; he said:

"That must be the bondsman for young boys."

A boy said to him:

"Brother Vidriera, tomorrow they're taking a procuress out to be flogged."

He replied:

"If you said they were taking a procuress out to be flogged, I would understand that they were going to flog a carriage."[12]

One of the men who carry sedan chairs happened to be there, and he said:

11. Cervantes is making fun of the commonplaces of Petrarchan love poetry.

12. Carriages were used by prostitutes for their business and, as such, were associated with their illicit acts.

"And us, Lawyer, don't you have anything to say about us?"

"No," responded Vidriera, "except that each of you knows more sins than a confessor, but with this difference: the confessor knows them to keep them secret, and you to proclaim them in taverns."

A mule driver's helper heard this, because all kinds of people were always listening to him, and he said:

"About us, Señor Bad Mouth, there is little or nothing to say, because we're decent people and necessary in society."

To which Vidriera replied:

"The honor of the master brings to light the servant's. And therefore look at whom you serve and you will see how honorable you are. You serve the most despicable rabble on earth. Once, when I was not made of glass, I traveled for a day on a rented mule so flawed I counted 121 defects, all of them major and inimical to the human race. All the helpers have their touch of scoundrel, their bit of thief, their hint of swindler. If their masters (which is what they call those they carry on their mules) are gullible, they play more tricks on them than were played in this city in years past. If they are foreigners, they rob them; if students, they curse them; if religious, they renounce them and blaspheme; if soldiers, they fear them. Soldiers and sailors and carters and muleteers have an extraordinary way of life meant only for them. The carter spends most of his life in less than three feet of space, the approximate distance from the mules' yoke to the front of the cart; half the time he sings, and the other half he blasphemes. And when he says: 'Stay behind me,' that's another pass. And if perhaps a wheel is stuck in the mud, he finds two curses more helpful than three mules. Sailors are not believers or very well-mannered people, and the only language they know is the one used on ships. In fair weather they are diligent, and in a squall they are lazy. During a storm many give orders and few obey. Their God is their ship; their entertainment is seeing passengers seasick. Muleteers are people who have been divorced from sheets and married to packsaddle blankets. They are so diligent and in so much of a hurry that in exchange for not losing a day's travel, they will lose their souls. Their music is the sound of mortars; their sauce, hunger, their matins, getting up to feed the mules, their Masses, not hearing any."

As he was saying this he was in the doorway of a pharmacy. And turning to the owner, he said:

"Your grace has a healthful occupation, if you were not such a great enemy of your lamps."

"In what way am I an enemy of my lamps?" asked the pharmacist.

And Vidriera replied:

"I say this because whenever oil is needed, you supply it from the nearest lamp. And this occupation has something else as well, important enough to undermine the reputation of the most accomplished physician in the world."

Asking what that was, he replied that there were pharmacists who, to avoid saying they did not have the medicines the physician had prescribed, replace the missing drugs with others that, in their opinion, had the same virtue and quality, when that was not so; and therefore, the badly compounded medicine had an effect opposite to the one the correctly combined preparation would have had. Then someone asked what he thought of physicians, and this is what he replied:

"'*Honora medicum propter necessitate, etenim creavit eum altissimus; a Deo enim est omnis medela, et a rege accipiet donationem. Disciplina medici exaltavit caput illius, et in conspectu magnatum collaudabitur. Altissimus de terra creavit medicinam, et vir prudens non aborrebit illam.*'[13] This," he says, "was said in *Ecclesiasticus* about medicine and good doctors. One could say just the reverse about the bad ones, for there are no people more harmful to society. The judge can oppose or defer justice; the attorney defend for the sake of his own interest our unjust demand; the merchant eat away at our fortune; in short, everyone with whom we deal out of necessity can do us some harm, but none can take our lives and not be subject to the fear of punishment. Only physicians can kill us, and kill us without fear, or much effort, or unsheathing any sword other than that of a prescription. And there is no way to uncover their crimes because they are put in the ground immediately. I recall when I was a man of flesh and not glass, as I am now, that a second-rate physician discharged a patient so he could be treated by another doctor, and four days later the first one happened to stop by the pharmacy where the second one filled his prescriptions, and he asked the pharmacist how things were going for the sick man he had discharged, and whether the other physician had prescribed any purge for him. The pharmacist responded that he had a prescription for a purge the patient was to take the next day. He asked that he show it to him and saw that at the end was written: *Sumat diluculo,* or *To be taken at dawn, and*

13. Ecclesiaticus 38:1–4: "Honour a physician with the honour due unto him for the uses which ye may have of him: for the Lord hath created him. For of the most High cometh healing, and he shall receive honour of the king. The skill of the physician shall lift up his head: and in the sight of great men he shall be in admiration. The Lord hath created medicines out of the earth; and he that is wise will not abhor them."

wipe your ass, and the physician said: 'I am happy with everything in this purge except this *diluculo* or wipe-your-ass because it is overly wet.' "[14]

Because of these and other things he said about every occupation, people followed him without doing him harm and without letting him rest. But even so, he could not defend himself against boys unless his guard did not come to his defense. Someone asked him what he should do in order not to envy anyone.

He replied:

"Go to sleep, because all the time you are asleep you will be equal to the man you envy."

Another asked him what solution he had for coming out ahead with a commission, because he had been trying for two years, and he said:

"Go out on horseback and observe very carefully the person who has the commission, and ride in front of him to the city gates, and in this way you will come out ahead."

Once a specifically assigned judge happened to pass in front of him on his way to a criminal hearing, and he had with him a good number of people and two bailiffs. The lawyer asked who he was, and when he was told, he said:

"I'll wager that judge has vipers in his bosom, small pistols in his sash, and thunderbolts in his hands to destroy anything within reach of his assignment. I remember having a friend who, in a criminal assignment, passed so excessive a sentence that it far exceeded the guilt of the criminals. I asked him why he had passed so cruel a sentence and committed so manifest an injustice. He answered that he intended to grant an appeal, and in this way he was leaving the field open to the gentlemen of the Council to display their mercy, moderating and reducing his rigorous sentence to its proper and correct proportion. I replied that it would have been better to have passed a sentence that would have removed him from that work because then they might have taken him for an upright, accomplished judge."

In the crowded circle of people who, as we have said, were always listening to him, was an acquaintance of his in a lawyer's cassock and cloak whom someone called *Señor Licentiate.* And since Vidriera knew that the man did not even have a bachelor's degree, he said to him:

"Be careful, compadre, that the friars who redeem captives don't find your diploma, because they'll take it from you as common property."

To which his friend responded:

14. *Diluculo* literally means "at daybreak" in Latin, but it can be taken as a play on the words *diluo* (to wash) and *culo* (ass).

"Let us treat each other nicely, Señor Vidriera, for you already know I am a man of high and profound letters."

Vidriera replied:

"I know you are a Tantalus of letters, because some get away from you because they are too high and you cannot reach the profound ones."

Once he was near a tailor's shop and saw the tailor with folded hands, and he said to him:

"There is no doubt, maestro, that you are on your way to salvation."

"How do you see that?" asked the tailor.

"How do I see that?" Vidriera replied. "I see it because, since you have nothing to do, you will not have occasion to lie."

And he added:

"Woe to the tailor who does not lie and sews for fiestas; it is a marvelous thing that in almost everyone in this trade you can hardly find one who makes a garment right, let alone one who is righteous, when there are so many who make them and are sinners."

About cobblers he said that they never made, according to them, a bad shoe. If it was tight and pinched, they told the client it had to be that way because it was elegant to wear tight shoes, and after two hours they would be wider than espadrilles, and if they were too wide, they said it had to be that way because of the client's gout.

A clever boy who was a clerk in an office of the civil court hounded him with questions and requests and brought him news of what was going on in the city, because he discoursed on everything and responded to everything. The boy once said to him:

"Vidriera, a banker who was condemned to be hanged died in prison tonight."

To which he replied:

"He did right to hurry and die before the executioner could leave a mark on him."

Some Genoese were on the sidewalk at San Francisco, and as he was walking by one called to him, saying:

"Come over here, Señor Vidriera, and recount a story worth a million."

He replied:

"I do not want to because you will take the million and send it to Genoa."[15]

15. Another stereotype of the greed of Genovese merchants, as seen in "The Little Gypsy Girl."

Once he came across a shopkeeper walking with her daughter who was very ugly but covered with jewels, finery, and pearls. And he said to the mother:

"You did very well to pave her with stones so you could take a stroll."

Regarding pastry cooks he said that for many years they had been cheating at cards without being fined, because they had sold the two-*maravedí* pastry for four; the four-*maravedí* for eight; and the one for eight for half a *real*, simply for their own whim and caprice.

About puppeteers he said a thousand evil things; he said they were tramps who treated divine things indecently, because with the figures shown in their depictions they turned devotion into laughter, and they would pack all or most of the figures from the Old and New Testaments into a sack, and sit on it to eat and drink in cheap restaurants and taverns. In short, he said he was amazed at how it could be that perpetual silence was not imposed on their performances or they were not exiled from the kingdom.

Once an actor dressed as a prince happened to pass by. And upon seeing him, he said:

"I recall seeing this man leave the theater with his face covered in flour, and dressed in lambskin turned inside out. And even so, at each step he takes off the stage, he swears by his faith as a nobleman."

"He must be one," another man replied, "because many actors are wellborn and noble."

"That may be true," replied Vidriera, "but what farce needs least are wellborn people; gallant lovers, yes, and handsome fellows with clever tongues. I can also say about them that they earn their bread by the sweat of their brow, with unbearable labor, constantly committing their roles to memory, turned into perpetual Gypsies going from place to place and from tavern to inn, concerned with pleasing others, because their own well-being depends on the pleasure of others. What is more, with their occupation they deceive no one, because they continuously show their wares on the public square to be judged and seen by everyone. The work of the directors is incredible, and the care they take is extraordinary, and they have to earn a great deal so that at the end of the year they are not so deep in debt they are obliged to begin bankruptcy proceedings. And even so, they are as necessary to society as woods, tree-lined walks, watching entertainment, and the things that provide us with decent amusement."

He said it had been the opinion of a friend of his that the man who served an actress served many ladies in one, for example, a queen, a nymph, a goddess, a scullery maid, and a shepherdess. And often it turned out that he served a page and a groom in her, for all these roles and more are played by an actress.

Another man asked who had been the most fortunate man in the world. He replied *nemo*; because *nemo novit patrem, nemo sine crimine vivit, nemo sua sorte contentus, nemo ascendit in coelum.*[16]

About swordsmen, he once said they were masters of a science or an art though they did not know when it might be needed, and that they touched upon with some presumption, for they wished to reduce to mathematical demonstrations, which are infallible, the choleric movements and thoughts of their opponents.

For men who dyed their beards he felt a particular enmity. And once when two men were quarrelling in front of him, one of them a Portuguese, who said to the Castilian, as he grasped his own beard:

"By dis beard dat covers my face!"

To which Vidriera responded:

"Listen, my man, don't say covers but colors!"

Another man had a beard that was speckled and spotted with many colors, the result of poor dye, to whom Vidriera said that his beard was like a dung heap filled with eggs. To another, whose beard was half white and half black because he had carelessly let his roots grow in, he said he should try not to challenge or quarrel with anyone because he was liable to be told he was a two-faced liar.

Once he recounted that a discerning and intelligent young lady, in order to accede to the will of her parents, agreed to marry an old man whose hair was white, and he, the night before the wedding, went not to the River Jordan, as the old wives say, but to a flask of nitrate of silver, with which he renovated his beard so that when he went to bed it was snow and when he awoke it was pitch. The time came to exchange vows, and the young lady knew the personage by his features and markings, and told her parents to give her the same husband they had shown her, for she did not want any other. They said that the man in front of her was the same one they had shown her and given to her as her husband. She replied that he was not and brought in witnesses who testified that her parents had given her to a mature man with white hair, and since this man did not have white hair, she called it a deception. Attention was paid to this, color that could run was found to be irksome, and the betrothal was broken.

16. *Nemo* is Latin for "no one," and what follows are a collection of biblical and classical aphorisms: "No one knows the father, no one lives without crime, no one is content with his fate, no one ascends to heaven."

Toward duennas he had the same animosity as he had toward men with dyed hair. He said marvels about their "by my faith," the winding sheets of their headdresses, their many affectations, their finickiness, and their extraordinary niggardliness. He was irritated by the weakness of their stomachs, the dizziness of their heads, their manner of speaking with more pleats and folds than their headdresses, and, in short, their uselessness and laziness.

Someone said to him:

"Why is it, Señor Lawyer, that I have heard you speak ill of many occupations and you have never said anything about notaries, when there is so much to say?"

To which he replied:

"Although I am glass, I am not so fragile that I go along with the tide of vulgar opinion, which is most often mistaken. It seems to me that the basic grammar of gossips and the satiric *la la la* of those who sing are notaries; because, just as one cannot go on to other fields of knowledge except through the door of grammar, and just as music murmurs before it sings, in the same way slanderers begin to show the malice of their tongues by speaking ill of notaries and bailiffs and other ministers of justice, the occupation of the notary being one without which truth would go through the world hidden, abashed, and mistreated; as *Ecclesiasticus* says: *In manu Dei potestas hominis est, & super faciem scribe imponet honorem.*[17] The notary is a public person, and the occupation of the judge cannot be exercised comfortably without him. Notaries must be free and not slaves or the children of slaves; legitimate, not bastards or born of any evil race. They swear their fidelity in secret, and will not write any usurious document; neither friendship nor enmity, neither advantage nor harm will move them to not perform their office with a good, Christian conscience. And so, if this occupation requires so many good elements, why would anyone think that of the more than twenty thousand notaries in Spain, the devil takes the entire crop, as if they were the rootstalks of his new vines? I do not want to believe it, and it is not good for anyone to believe it. Because, in brief, I say they are the most necessary people there are in well-ordered societies, and if they charge too many fees, they also commit too many injustices, and from these two extremes a middle way may result that would oblige them to perform their work honorably."

About bailiffs he said it was not surprising they had some enemies, since their occupation was to arrest you or take your riches from the house, or keep

17. Ecclesiasticus 10:5: "In the hand of God is the prosperity of man: and upon the person of the scribe shall he lay his honour."

you in theirs under guard and eating at your expense. He found fault with the negligence and ignorance of prosecutors and solicitors, comparing them to physicians who, whether they cure or do not cure the patient, charge their fee; and the same for prosecutors and solicitors, regardless of whether the case is successful or not.

Someone else asked which was the best land. He replied, one that produces early and is fruitful. The other man responded:

"I'm not asking that, but which is the better city, Valladolid or Madrid?"

And he replied:

"In Madrid, the extremes; in Valladolid, the middle sections."

"I don't understand," repeated the man who had asked the question.

And he said:

"In Madrid, sky and earth; in Valladolid, the entresol."[18]

Vidriera heard one man tell another that as soon as she had entered Valladolid, his wife became very sick because she had sampled the earth. To which Vidriera replied:

"It would have been better if it had swallowed her up, in the event she is jealous."

Regarding musicians and mail delivered on foot, he said they had limited hopes and expectations, because the second finished by being delivered on horseback and the first with becoming the king's musicians.

Regarding the ladies called courtesans, he said that all or most of them were more courteous than sanitary.

One day when he was in a church, he saw them carry in an old man to be buried, a child to be baptized, and a woman to be married, all at the same time, and he said that temples were battlefields where old men die, children conquer, and women triumph.

A wasp once stung him on the neck and he did not dare brush it away for fear he would break, but even so he complained. One man asked him how he felt the wasp if his body was glass. And he replied that the wasp was probably a gossip, and that the tongues and mouths of gossips were enough to shatter bodies of bronze, let alone glass.

When a very fat cleric happened to pass by, one of his listeners said:

"From an excess of ethics the father can hardly move."

Vidriera became angry and said:

"Let no one forget what the Holy Spirit says: *Nolite tangere Christos meos.*"[19]

18. Possibly a reference to the weather in those cities.

19. Psalms 105:15: "Do not touch my anointed ones."

And becoming even angrier, he said they should think about it and they would see that of the many saints canonized in a short time by the Church and placed among the number of the blessed, none was called Captain So-and-so or Secretary What's-his-name or the Count, Marquis, or Duke of Wherever, but Brother Diego, Brother Jacinto, Brother Raimundo; all brothers and priests. Because the religious orders are the orchards of heaven whose fruits are commonly placed on the table of God.

He said that the tongues of gossips were like the eagle's feathers that eat away and damage all the feathers of other birds that get close to them. He said marvels about owners of gambling houses and cardsharps. He said the owners were public prevaricators because, by taking a tip from the one who was winning a game, they wanted him to lose and lose the deal, because his opponent would deal and the owner would collect his fees. He praised to the skies the patience of a cardsharp who spent the entire night playing and losing; and being of a choleric nature and possessed by the devil, as long as his opponent did not stand up, his lips were sealed, and he suffered the martyrdom of Barrabas. He also praised the consciences of certain honored owners of gambling houses who could not be imagined giving their consent for playing any other games in their houses but the slow-moving *polla* and *cientos*; and so, over a slow fire, not fearing or taking any heed of backbiters, at the end of the month they acquired more money than those who consented to the faster games of *estocada, reparolo, siete y llevar,* and *pinta en la del punto.*[20]

In short, he said such things that if it were not for the great shouts he gave when he was touched or approached too closely, the clothes he wore, the scantiness of his meals, the way in which he drank, his wanting to sleep only out of doors in the summer and in haylofts in the winter, as has been mentioned, and because he gave such clear signs of his madness, no one could believe he was not one of the sanest men in the world. For more than two years he endured this sickness, because a cleric of the Order of San Jerónimo who had the grace and extraordinary knowledge to make mutes understand and speak in a certain way, and to cure madmen, was moved by charity to undertake the responsibility of curing Vidriera, and he cured and healed him, and returned him to his earlier judgment, understanding, and discourse. And when he saw that he was cured, he dressed him in the cassock and cloak of a lettered man and had him return to the capital where, giving as many signs of sanity as he

---

20. A *polla* is a bet in a card game, and *cientos, estocada, reparolo, siete y llevar,* and *pinta en la del punto* are various card games.

had of madness, he could exercise his profession and become famous because of it.

This is what he did, and calling himself Attorney Rueda, and not Rodaja,[21] he returned to the capital, and as soon as he did so, the boys recognized him. But since they saw him dressed so differently, they did not dare shout at him or ask questions; but they did follow him and say to one another: 'Isn't this the madman Vidriera? Yes, it's true. And now he's sane, but a madman can be well dressed or badly dressed. Let's ask him something and put this confusion behind us.' The lawyer heard all this and was silent, more confused and irascible than when he was out of his mind.

The information passed from boys to men, and before the lawyer reached the Courtyard of the Advisers,[22] he had more than two hundred people of all kinds following him. With this entourage, larger than that of a university professor, he reached the courtyard, where he was also surrounded by all those in the building. Seeing so many people around him, he raised his voice and said:

"Gentlemen, I am the Attorney Vidriera, but not the one I once was. I am now Lawyer Rueda; certain events and misfortunes that occur in the world with heaven's permission made me lose my reason, and God's mercies have returned it to me. Based on the things people say I said when I was mad, you can consider what I shall say and do when I am sane. I am a graduate in law from Salamanca, where I studied in poverty and obtained a second in my licentiate, from which it can be inferred that skill more than favor gave me the degree I hold. I have come to this great sea of the capital to be a lawyer and earn my living, but if you do not allow me to do that, I shall have come here to ply the oars and come close to death. For the love of God, do not make following me be the same as persecuting me, so that what I achieved as a madman, which is sustenance, I shall lose as a sane one. What you used to ask me in the squares, you can ask me now in my house, and you will see that the man who answered well, they say, and spontaneously, will respond better after some thought."

Everyone listened and some let him be. He returned to his lodgings with a somewhat smaller entourage than before. He went out the next day, and the same thing happened; he gave another sermon, and it did no good. He lost a great deal and earned nothing, and seeing himself dying of hunger, he decided to leave the capital and return to Flanders, where he intended to make

21. A *rueda* is a wheel while a *rodaja* is a slice.
22. A patio at the royal palace in Madrid.

use of the strength in his arms since he could not make use of the strength of his mind. And doing this, he said as he left the capital:

"Oh capital that lengthens the hopes of daring claimants and shortens the hopes of the virtuous and timid! You sustain abundantly the shameless knaves and starve to death the honorable and discerning!"

He said this and went to Flanders, where the life he began to immortalize through letters he ended by immortalizing through arms in the company of his good friend Captain Valdivia, leaving behind, when he died, the fame of being a prudent and very valiant soldier.

THE NOVEL OF THE POWER OF BLOOD

One hot summer night in Toledo, an elderly nobleman with his wife, a small boy, a daughter of sixteen, and a maid were returning from an outing at the river. The night was clear, the time was eleven, the road was lonely, and their pace was slow so they would not pay with fatigue for their efforts at coming up from the river or flatland of Toledo. With the security the ever-present forces of law and order and upright people of that city promise, the good nobleman and his honorable family were far from thinking of any disaster that might befall them. But since most misfortunes are not anticipated, contrary to all their expectations something occurred that disturbed their contentment and gave them reason to weep for many years.

There was a gentleman of that city, some twenty-two years old, whom wealth, illustrious blood, debased inclinations, an excess of freedom, and dissolute company had led to commit acts and display an effrontery unworthy of his birth; as a result, he had a reputation for insolence.

And so this gentleman—whom for now, out of respect and hiding his name, we shall call Rodolfo—with some friends, all of them young, all of them reckless, and all of them audacious, descended the same slope that the nobleman was climbing.

The two groups, the sheep and the wolves, met, and with indecent boldness, Rodolfo and his comrades, their faces covered, looked at the faces of the mother, the daughter, and the maid. This incited the old man, who reproached and censured their presumption. They responded with grimaces and mockery, and with no further rudeness continued on their way. But the great beauty of the face Rodolfo had seen, the face of Leocadia, which is what we shall call the nobleman's daughter, began to be etched so strongly in his memory that desire followed and awakened in him a longing to enjoy her in spite of all the obstacles that might stand in his way. And in an instant he communicated his thought to his comrades, and in another instant they resolved to go back and abduct her, to please Rodolfo, for the wealthy who are generous always find someone to praise their excesses and call their evil pleasures good. And so, the birth of his evil intention, communicating and approving it, deciding to abduct Leocadia, and then abducting her, all happened almost at the same time.

They covered their faces with their handkerchiefs and, unsheathing their swords, went back and in a few steps caught up with those who were still thanking God for having freed them from the hands of those insolent men.

Rodolfo attacked Leocadia, picked her up, and fled with her; she did not have the strength to defend herself, and the shock made her lose her voice and even the light in her eyes, for in a faint and unconscious, she did not see who was carrying her, or where she was being taken. Her father shouted, her mother cried out, her little brother wept, the maid scratched her face; but the shouts were not heard, the cries not listened to, the tears moved no one to pity, and the scratches did no good at all, because everything was hidden by the solitude of the place, the muffled silence of night, and the cruel hearts of the evildoers. In short, some left happily, and the rest were left behind in sadness.

Rodolfo reached his house with no difficulty, and Leocadia's parents reached theirs wronged, afflicted, and desperate: blind, without the eyes of their daughter, who was the light of theirs; alone, because Leocadia was their sweet and amiable companion; confused, not knowing whether it would be a good idea to inform the authorities, fearful of being the principal instrument for making their dishonor public.

As impoverished nobles, they were in need of protection. They did not know about whom to complain if not their unfortunate fate. Rodolfo, in the meantime, clever and astute, had Leocadia in his house and in his room; and since he sensed that she had fainted when he carried her away, he had covered her eyes with a handkerchief so she would not see the streets along which he carried her, or the house or room where she was; and there, not seen by anyone because he had a secluded room in the house of his father, who was still alive, he also had keys to all the rooms—an oversight of parents who want to keep their children safe—and before Leocadia recovered from her faint, Rodolfo had satisfied his desire, for the unchaste urges of youth rarely, if ever, attend to the comforts and requirements that enhance or elevate them. Blind to the light of reason, in the dark he stole Leocadia's most precious possession; and since the sins of sensuality for the most part do not go beyond the boundary marker of their satisfaction, Rodolfo then wanted Leocadia to disappear, and it occurred to him to put her on the street just as she was, in a faint, and as he was about to do this, he realized she had regained consciousness and was saying:

"Where am I, oh unfortunate girl? What darkness is this? What shadows surround me? Am I in the limbo of my innocence or the hell of my faults? Jesus! Who is touching me? Am I in bed and injured? Are you listening, mother, my lady? Do you hear me, dear father? Oh, woe is me, I know my parents don't hear me and my enemies are touching me! I would be fortunate if this darkness would last forever and my eyes would never see again the light of the world, and if this place where I am now, whatever it is, would be the tomb of my honor, for dishonor unknown is better than honor in the opinion of other people. Now I remember, how I wish I would never remember! A little while ago I was in the company of my parents; now I remember that I was assaulted; now I imagine and see that it's not a good idea for people to see me. Oh you, whoever you are, who are here with me!"—and she grasped Rodolfo's hands—"If your soul admits any kind of plea, I beg you, now that you have triumphed over my reputation, that you also triumph over my life! Take it from me now, for it is not a good thing to have when one does not have honor! Consider this: the harsh cruelty you have used in offending me will be tempered by the pity you will use in killing me, and so, at the same time, you will be both cruel and compassionate!"

Leocadia's words left Rodolfo confused, and being a youth with little experience, he did not know what to say or do, and Leocadia wondered at his silence, and attempted with her hands to discover whether she was with a phantom or ghost. But as she touched a body and recalled the force he had used as she walked with her parents, she realized the truth of the tale of her misfortune. And with this thought, she resumed the words that her many sobs and sighs had interrupted, saying:

"Audacious young man, for your actions lead one to judge you as very young, I forgive the transgression you have committed against me if you will only promise and swear that just as you have concealed it in this darkness, you will conceal it in perpetual silence and never tell anyone about it. I ask very little recompense of you for so great an offense; but for me it will be the greatest I can ask of you or that you may want to give me. You should know that I have never seen your face, nor do I want to see it, because if I must remember the offense against me, I do not wish to remember the offender or keep in my memory the image of the author of my injury. My complaints will pass from me to heaven with no wish for the world to hear them, for the world does not judge things on the basis of actual events but according to how they are set in the world's estimation. I do not know how I can tell you these truths, which are usually based on the experience of many cases and the passage of many years, when I am not yet seventeen, which leads me to believe that sorrow at once ties and loosens the tongue of the afflicted person, sometimes exaggerating the injury so it will be believed, other times not saying anything because no one provides a remedy. In any case, whether I am silent or speak, I believe I must move you to believe me or rectify what you have done; not believing me would be ignorance, and if you provide no corrective, it is impossible to find any relief. I do not want to kill myself in despair, because it will cost you so little to provide consolation, which is this: do not wait for or expect the passage of time to temper the just fury I feel toward you, and do not attempt to pile up your offenses: the less you enjoy me, having already enjoyed me, the less your evil desires will be set ablaze. Realize that you offended me by accident, not thinking about what you were doing. I shall pretend I was not born into the world, or if so, it was in order to be unfortunate. Put me on the street, or at least, near the principal church, because from there I shall know how to return to my house, but you also must swear not to follow me, or find out where my house is, or ask me the name of my parents, or my name, or the name of my kinfolk, for if they were as rich as they are noble, they would not be so unfortunate in me. Answer me this, and if you are afraid I shall know you by your speech; I can tell you that outside of my father and my confessor, I have not spoken to any man in all my life, and I have heard so few speak that I could never distinguish them by the sound of their voices."

Rodolfo had no other response to the discerning words of the injured Leocadia than to embrace her, giving signs that he wanted to confirm again in this way his pleasure and her dishonor. Seeing this, with more strength than her tender years promised, Leocadia defended herself with her feet, her hands, her teeth, and her tongue, saying:

"Be aware, you traitorous and heartless man, whoever you may be, that the spoils you've stolen from me are what you could have taken from an insensible tree trunk or pillar whose conquest and triumph will redound to your discredit and scorn. But what you are attempting now you will not achieve except with my death. You trampled on me and dishonored me when I was in a faint, but now that I am conscious, you'll find it easier to kill me than to conquer me; if now, when I am awake, I were to give in to your odious desire with no resistance, you might imagine my swoon was feigned when you dared destroy me."

In short, Leocadia resisted so gallantly and persistently that Rodolfo's strength and desire weakened; and since the shamelessness he had used with Leocadia had no basis other than a lascivious impulse from which true love never is born, what remains in place of the passing impulse is, if not repentance, then at least a feeble desire to repeat it. Rodolfo, then, with no strength, and tired, and not saying a word, left Leocadia in his bed and house and, locking the door to the room, went to find his comrades to consult with them regarding what he should do.

Leocadia sensed she was alone and locked in, and getting up from the bed, she walked around the entire chamber, feeling the walls with her hands to see whether she could find a door to walk through or a window out of which to throw herself. She found the door, but it was locked, and came upon a window she could open, and through it the moonlight came in, so bright that Leocadia could make out the colors of some damasks that adorned the room. She saw that the bed was gilded and so richly made it looked more like the bed of a prince than of some private gentleman. She counted the chairs and cabinets; she noticed where the door was located, and though she saw panels hanging on the walls, she could not see the paintings they contained. The window was large, decorated and guarded by a heavy grating; her eyes fell on a garden that was also enclosed by high walls; these were difficulties that interfered with her intention to throw herself down to the street. Everything she saw and noted regarding the size and rich adornments of the room gave her to understand that its owner must be distinguished and rich, not just moderately but surpassingly so. In a cabinet next to the window, she saw a small crucifix made all of silver, which she took and placed in the sleeve of her dress, not because of devotion or to steal it, but moved by an astute plan of her own. Having done this, she closed the window, just as it had been earlier, and returned to the bed, waiting to see what conclusion the bad beginning of this event would have.

In what seemed to her less than half an hour she heard the door of the room open, and a person approached who, not saying a word, blindfolded her with a handkerchief, and taking her arm, walked her out of the room, and she heard the door close again. This person was Rodolfo, who had gone in search of his comrades but then did not wish to find them, thinking it was not a good idea for him to create witnesses to what had occurred with that girl; instead, he decided to tell them that, regretting his evil deed and moved by her tears, he had left her in the middle of the street. And so he returned as quickly as he could to put Leocadia near the principal church before dawn, as she had requested; daylight would interfere with his taking her out and force him to keep her in his room until the next night, during which time he did not want to use force with her again or give her any opportunity to recognize him.

And so he took her to the square called the Ayuntamiento, and there, in a voice he disguised, and speaking half Portuguese and half Castilian, he told her she could go to her house with full confidence because no one would follow her; and before she had a chance to remove the handkerchief, he went to a spot where he could not be seen.

Leocadia was alone; she removed the blindfold and recognized the place where she had been left. She looked around and saw no one, but suspecting she might be followed from a distance, she stopped constantly as she walked to her house, which was not very far away. And to confound the night patrol in the event they were following her, she entered a house she found open, and from there soon came to her own house, where she found her parents astonished and still dressed, for they had not even thought of sleeping.

When they saw her they ran to her with open arms and welcomed her with tears in their eyes. Leocadia, filled with shock and alarm, asked her parents to withdraw with her so they could speak privately, which they did, and in a few words she recounted the entire wretched affair, with all its circumstances and her ignorance of who her attacker and the thief of her honor might be. She told them what she had seen in the theater where the tragedy of her misfortune had been performed—the window, the garden, the grating, the cabinets, the bed, the damasks—and then she showed them the crucifix she had brought with her, before whose image their tears were renewed, entreaties were made, vengeance was asked for, and miraculous punishments wished for. She also said that, although she had no desire to know her attacker, if her parents thought it would be good to know who he was, they could find out through the image by having all the sacristans say in all the pulpits of all the parishes in the city that whoever had lost the image would find it in the keeping of whichever cleric they might designate, and in this way, knowing the owner of the image, they would know the house and even the person of her enemy.

To which her father replied:

"Well said, daughter, if ordinary malice were not opposed to your discerning discourse, for it is clear that today this image will be missed in the room you describe, and the owner will be certain the person who was with him took it, and when he hears it is in the possession of a cleric, it will help him find out who gave it to the cleric who has it rather than help us learn the owner who lost it, because it may be that someone else to whom the owner has given the address will come for it. And this being so, we shall be confused rather than informed, since we can use the same artifice we suspect, giving it to the cleric through a third person. What you should do, daughter, is keep it and commend yourself to it, for since it was a witness to your misfortune, it may allow a judge to give you justice. And remember, daughter, that an ounce of public dishonor wounds more than a bushel of secret disgrace. And since you can live honorably with God in public, do not grieve over being dishonored with yourself in secret. True dishonor is in sin, and true honor is in virtue; one offends God with one's words, with desire, and with the act; and since neither in words or thought or action have you offended Him, consider yourself honorable, for I shall consider you so and never look at you except as your true father."

With these prudent words, her father consoled Leocadia, and her mother, embracing her again, also attempted to console her. She groaned and wept again and was obliged to resign herself and live a retired life under the protection of her parents, her dress as honest as it was poor.

Rodolfo, in the meantime, had returned to his house, and when he missed the image of the crucifix, he imagined who had taken it; but he did not care, and as a rich man did not have to explain it, nor did his parents ask about it when, three days later, he departed for Italy and gave everything left in the room to one of his mother's maids.

Rodolfo had decided to go to Italy some time earlier, and his father, who had traveled there, persuaded him to go, saying that those who were gentlemen only in their own countries were not gentlemen at all, that one had to be a gentleman in other countries as well. For these and other reasons, Rodolfo's will was prepared to comply with the wishes of his father, who gave him bills of exchange for a great deal of money in Barcelona, Genoa, Rome, and Naples; and he, with two of his comrades, left, enticed by what he had heard some soldiers say about the abundance in the inns of Italy and France, and the freedom that Spaniards had in their lodgings. He liked the sound of that *Ecco li buoni pollastri, piccioni, prosciutto e salcicie*[1] and other words of this nature, which soldiers remember when they return here from those places and endure the austerity and discomforts of the inns and taverns in Spain. In short, he left with so little memory of what had occurred with Leocadia that it was as if it had never happened.

She, meanwhile, spent her life in her parents' house in all possible seclusion, not allowing herself to be seen by anyone, fearful that her misfortune could be read on her forehead. But, in a few months, she found herself obliged to do what until then she had done by choice. She found it advisable to lead a withdrawn and hidden life because she was pregnant, an event that brought tears that had been forgotten for a time back to her eyes, and sighs and laments again began to pierce the air, without the discernment of her good mother able in any way to console her. Time flew, and the moment arrived to give birth in so much secrecy that they did not even dare confide in the midwife. Her mother took over this office, and Leocadia brought into the world one of the most beautiful boys imaginable. With the same caution and secrecy in which he had been born, they took him to a village where he was reared for four years, after which time his grandfather brought him to his house, calling him a nephew, and there he was brought up, if not with great wealth, at least very virtuously.

---

1. "Here are the good chickens, doves, ham and sausages."

The boy—who was named Luis, after his grandfather—had a beautiful face, a gentle disposition, a sharp intelligence, and in everything he could do at that tender age, he gave signs of having been fathered by a nobleman, and his grace, beauty, and discernment inspired so much love in his grandparents that they came to consider their daughter's misfortune good fortune because it had given them a grandchild such as this. When he walked down the street, he was showered with thousands of blessings; some blessed his beauty; others, the mother who bore him; these, the father who had sired him; those, the person who brought him up so well. With this kind of praise from those who knew him and those who did not, the boy reached the age of seven, when he already knew how to read Latin and Castilian and to write a well-formed and very nice hand, because his grandparents' intention was to make him virtuous and learned since they could not make him rich, as if knowledge and virtue were not the riches over which thieves have no jurisdiction and the goddess called Fortune has no power.

And so it happened that one day, when the boy was taking a message from his grandmother to a kinswoman of hers, he passed a street where they were racing horses. He started to watch, and to find a better spot he crossed from one side to the other and could not avoid being trampled by a horse whose owner failed to stop the animal in the frenzy of its gallop. He rode over him and left him as if dead, lying on the ground and bleeding heavily from the head. No sooner had this happened than an elderly gentleman who was watching the race leaped, with uncommon agility, from his horse, went up to the boy, and removing him from the arms of someone already holding him, took him in his own, and ignoring his white hair and his authority, which was considerable, he hurried to his house, ordering his servants to leave and find a physician to treat the boy. Many gentlemen followed him, sorry for the misfortune of so beautiful a child; then someone called out that he was Luisico, the nephew of a gentleman, and then named his grandfather. The news flew from mouth to mouth until it reached the ears of his grandparents and his secret mother; and they, confirming what had happened, rushed out as if mad to find their dear child. And because the gentleman who had taken him was so well known and so distinguished, many of those they encountered told them where his house was, and they arrived when the boy was already in the care of the physician.

The gentleman and his wife, whose house it was, asked the people they thought were the boy's parents not to weep or raise their voices in laments because it would do the child no good. The physician, who was famous, had treated him with great care and skill and said the wound was not as serious as he had thought at first. In the middle of the treatment, Luis awoke, for until then he had been unconscious, and was very happy to see his aunt and uncle, who asked him, weeping, how he felt. He responded that he felt well, though his body and head hurt a great deal. The physician ordered them not to talk to the boy but allow him to rest. They did so, and his grandfather began to thank the master of the house for the great charity he had shown his nephew. To which the gentleman replied that he had nothing to thank him for, because, he said, when he saw the boy on the ground, trampled, he thought he had seen the face of his son, whom he loved dearly, and this had moved him to pick up the boy and carry him to his house, where he could stay as long as the treatment lasted, with all possible and necessary indulgence. His wife, a noble lady, said the same thing and made even more extravagant promises.

The grandparents were amazed at so much Christianity; but the mother was even more amazed because, the physician's comments having calmed somewhat her agitated spirit, she looked carefully at the room where her son was lying, and clearly, by many indications, she knew it was the room where her honor had been ended and her misfortune began. And although it was not adorned with the damasks it once had, she recognized its arrangement and saw the window with the grating and the garden below; because it was closed on account of the injured boy, she asked whether that window overlooked a garden, and the answer was that it did. But what she knew best was that this was the same bed she considered her coffin, and the cabinet that held the image she had taken was still in the same place.

In brief, the truth of all her suspicions was brought to light by the steps she had counted when she had been taken from the room blindfolded; that is, the stairs down to the street, which she had counted with discerning foresight. And when she returned to her house, leaving her son behind, she counted them again and found the number correct. And comparing some characteristics with others, she was convinced of the truth of what she had supposed, which she told in detail to her mother who, being an insightful woman, found out whether the gentleman in whose house her grandson was staying had ever had a son. And she learned that the one we are calling Rodolfo was his son and was in Italy. And calculating the time they said he had been out of Spain, she knew it was seven years, the age of her grandson.

She informed her husband of all this, and the two of them and their daughter agreed to wait to see what God willed for the injured boy, who in two weeks was out of danger and in a month was out of bed; in all this time he was visited by his mother and grandmother, and doted on by the owners of the house as if he were their own son. And at times, when Doña Estefanía, which was the name of the gentleman's wife, spoke to Leocadia, she said the boy so resembled her son in Italy that whenever she looked at him she seemed to see her son in front of her. These words led Leocadia to say to her, once when they were alone, these words, or others like them, which, with the consent of her parents, she had determined to say:

"On the day, Señora, when my parents heard their nephew was so gravely injured, they believed and thought the sky had darkened and the world collapsed. They imagined they no longer had the light of their eyes and the staff of their old age, having lost their nephew, whom they cherish with a love that far exceeds the love other parents have for their children. But as they say, when God wounds He also provides the cure, which the boy found in this house, and in it I have recalled memories I shall not be able to forget for as long as I live. I, Señora, am noble because my parents are, and all my forebears, and in only moderate circumstances they have happily sustained their honor wherever they have lived."

Doña Estefanía was surprised and amazed listening to Leocadia's words, and she could not believe, even though she saw it, that so much discernment could be contained in so few years, since she judged her to be twenty years old, more or less. And without saying a word or answering in any way, she waited to hear all the words Leocadia wanted to say, which were precisely those needed to recount the wrongdoing of Doña Estefanía's son, Leocadia's own dishonor, the abduction, her blindfolding, being brought to that room, the signs by which she had recognized it as being the one she suspected. In confirmation of this she removed from her bodice the image of the crucifix she had taken, and to it she said:

"You, Lord, who were witness to the force used upon me, be the judge of the redress I should receive, I took you from that cabinet with the purpose of reminding you always of my offense, not to ask you for vengeance, which is not my intention, but to beg that you grant me some consolation to help me endure my misfortune with patience. This child, Señora, to whom you have shown the extremes of your charity, is your true grandson. It was with heaven's permission that he was trampled, so that, by bringing him to your house, I might find in it, as I hope to find here, if not the most suitable remedy for my affliction, at least the means by which I can endure it."

Saying this, and embracing the crucifix, she fainted into the arms of Estefanía who, being noble and a woman, in whom compassion and mercy tend to be as natural as cruelty is in a man, placed her face next to Leocadia's as soon as she saw her swoon, shedding so many tears it would not be necessary to sprinkle any other water on her for Leocadia to regain consciousness.

The two women were like this when the gentleman, Estefanía's husband, happened to come in, holding Luisico by the hand, and seeing Estefanía weeping and Leocadia in a faint, he quickly asked them the reason. The boy embraced his mother as his cousin and his grandmother as his benefactor, and also asked why they were crying.

"We have great things to tell you, Señor," Estefanía replied to her husband, "and they can be summarized by saying that the girl in a swoon is your daughter and the child your grandson. This truth that I am telling you the girl has told me, and it has been and is confirmed by the boy's face, in which both of us have seen the face of our son."

"If you do not tell me more, Señora, I cannot understand you," replied the gentleman.

At this point Leocadia regained consciousness, and embracing the crucifix, she seemed transformed into a sea of tears. All of which had the gentleman in great confusion, from which he emerged when his wife told him everything Leocadia had told her; and with the divine permission of heaven he believed it as if many reliable witnesses had proved it to him. He consoled and embraced Leocadia, kissed his grandson, and that same day they sent a letter to Naples, telling their son to come home immediately because they had arranged a marriage for him with an exceedingly beautiful woman, perfectly suited to him. They did not consent to Leocadia or her son going back to the house of her parents, who, extremely happy at their daughter's good fortune, gave constant and infinite thanks to God.

The message reached Naples, and Rodolfo, greedy to enjoy a woman as beautiful as his father had indicated, two days after receiving the letter, and taking advantage of four galleys about to sail for Spain, embarked on one with his two comrades, who had not left him; with favorable winds he arrived in Barcelona within twelve days, and from there in another seven he was in Toledo, and he entered his father's house, so charming and elegant that the extremes of charm and elegance met in him.

His parents rejoiced at the health and safe arrival of their son. Leocadia was afraid, watching him from a hiding place, to stray from the plan and arrangement Doña Estefanía had made for her. Rodolfo's comrades wanted to leave for their houses immediately, but Estefanía did not consent to this, because she needed them for her plan. It was close to nightfall when Rodolfo arrived, and as supper was being prepared, Estefanía called her son's comrades aside, believing beyond any doubt that they must be two of the three men Leocadia had said were with Rodolfo on the night she was abducted, and with many entreaties she asked them to tell her if they remembered her son abducting a woman on such-and-such a night, this number of years ago, because the honor and tran-quility of all his kin depended on knowing the truth about this. And she pleaded with these exhortations and others like them, and with so many re-assurances that no harm would come to them if this abduction were revealed, that they decided to confess it was true that one summer night, when they and another friend were out with Rodolfo, they abducted a girl on the night she had indicated, and Rodolfo had taken her while they held the people in her family, who tried to defend her with their shouts, and the next day Rodolfo had told them he had taken her to his house; and this was the only answer they could give to what they were being asked.

The confession of the two locked away all the doubts anyone might have had in such a case, and so she determined to carry out her good idea, which was this: shortly before they sat down to supper, his mother and Rodolfo went into a room by themselves, and placing a portrait in his hands, she said to him:

"Rodolfo, my son, I want to give you a delicious supper by showing you your wife. This is her true portrait, but I want to tell you that what she lacks in beauty she makes up for in virtue; she is noble and wise, and moderately wealthy. And since your father and I have chosen her, you can be sure she is the right one for you."

Rodolfo looked at the portrait attentively and said:

"If painters, who ordinarily are lavish with the beauty they give to the face they depict, have been so with this one, I believe beyond a doubt that the original must be ugliness itself. By my faith, Señora, dear mother, it is just and good for children to obey their parents in everything they direct them to do; but it is also suitable and even better for parents to give their children the sta-tus they like best. And since the state of matrimony is a knot not untied except with death, it would be good for its bonds to be equal and made of the same strands. Virtue, nobility, discernment, and the goods of fortune can certainly bring joy to the mind of one who has found these in his wife; but that her ugli-ness should bring joy to the eyes of her husband seems impossible to me. I am young, but I understand very well that the sacrament of marriage includes the just and proper delight married people enjoy, and if that is missing, the mar-riage falters and contradicts its second purpose. And so to think an ugly face that one has to see constantly in the sitting room, at the table, and in the bed can bring delight, I say again, I think that is almost impossible. I beg of your grace, dear mother, please give me a companion who will entertain and not irritate me; because without distorting either one, let the two of us share the weight equally of the yoke heaven will place on us and walk a straight path. If this lady is noble, wise, and rich, as your grace says, she will not lack a husband whose temperament is different from mine. Some men look for nobility; others, intelligence; others, money; and others, beauty; and I am one of the latter. Because nobility I already have, thanks to heaven and my forebears, and my parents, who have made it my inheritance; as for good judgment, as long as a woman is not stupid, a simpleton, or a fool, it is enough that her sharp intelligence is not blunted or that she is not taken advantage of as a fool; and as for riches, my parents' wealth makes me unafraid of becoming poor; I am looking for beauty, loveliness is what I want, with no other dowry except modesty and good habits; if my wife brings me this, I shall serve God with pleasure and give my parents a good old age."

His mother was very pleased with Rodolfo's words, because from them she knew her plan was succeeding. She answered that she would attempt to marry him according to his desire and he should not be concerned, it was easy enough to undo the agreements that had been made for him to marry the lady. Rodolfo thanked her, and since it was time for supper, they went to the table. And when his father and mother, and Rodolfo and his two comrades, were already sitting down, Doña Estefanía said as if in passing:

"Sinner that I am, how well I treat my guest! Go now," she said to a servant, "and tell the Señora Doña Leocadia that, without thinking too much about her great modesty, she should come and honor us at this table, for those who are here are my children and their servants."

All of this was a plan of hers, and Leocadia had been told and advised on what she should do. Before long Leocadia came out and made the most unexpected and beautiful appearance that circumspect and natural beauty could ever make.

Since it was winter, she wore a skirt and bodice of black velvet, sprinkled with buttons of gold and pearls, the waist and neckline with diamonds. Her hair, which was long and not too blonde, served as an adornment and headdress, whose invention of loops and curls and the glimmer of interwoven diamonds troubled the light in the eyes of those who looked at it. Leocadia had an elegant and charming disposition. She held her son by the hand, and before her came two maids lighting her way with two wax candles in two silver candlesticks.

Everyone stood to bow to her, as if she were something from heaven that had miraculously appeared. It seemed that none of those who were enthralled looking at her managed to say a word, they were so astonished. Leocadia, with confident grace and elegant good manners, curtsied to everyone, and taking her by the hand, Estefanía sat her in the seat next to hers, facing Rodolfo. They sat the child next to his grandfather.

Rodolfo, having a closer look at Leocadia's incomparable beauty, said to himself:

"If the woman my mother has chosen to be my wife had half this beauty, I should think myself the most fortunate man in the world. Lord save me! What am I seeing? Am I by chance looking at some human angel?"

This was when the beautiful image of Leocadia began to enter through his eyes to take possession of his soul, and she, as the supper was being served, also seeing close to her the man she already loved more than the light of her own eyes, she stole an occasional glance at him, began to turn over in her imagination what had occurred with Rodolfo. In her soul the hope of his being her husband, which his mother had given her, began to weaken, for she feared that his mother's promises would correspond to the meagerness of her own destiny. She considered how close she was to being fortunate or luckless forever. And the concept was so intense and her thoughts so unruly, and they gripped her heart so tightly, that she began to perspire and turn pale in an instant, and was overcome by a swoon that obliged her to lean her head on the arms of Doña Estefanía, who as soon as she saw her in this state received her, disquieted, in her arms.

Everyone was alarmed and, leaving the table, hurried to help her. But the one who displayed the most concern was Rodolfo, for to reach her quickly he tripped and fell twice. Even with her bodice unfastened and water sprinkled in her face, she did not regain consciousness; rather, her elevated bosom and her pulse, which they could not find, were giving precise signs of death; and the maids and servants in the house, being less thoughtful, cried out and proclaimed her dead. This bitter news reached the ears of Leocadia's parents, whom Doña Estefanía had hidden for a happier occasion. They, with the parish priest, who was with them, came into the room, disrupting Estefanía's plan.

The priest hurried to see whether she was giving any signs of repenting her sins so she could be absolved; and where he thought he would find one fainted person he found two, because Rodolfo's face was already on Leocadia's chest. His mother gave him room to approach her as if she already belonged to him; but when she saw that he was unconscious too, she was on the verge of losing consciousness as well, and she would have if she had not seen that Rodolfo was regaining his, embarrassed that everyone had seen him give such extreme demonstrations of sorrow. But his mother, almost as if guessing what her son was feeling, said to him:

"Do not be ashamed, son, of the displays you have made, but of those you did not make when you learn what I do not wish to keep hidden from you any longer, though I intended to leave it for a happier occasion. You must know, son of my soul, that this woman in a faint whom I am holding in my arms is your true wife; I call her true, because your father and I chose her for you; the one in the portrait is false."

When Rodolfo heard this, carried away by his amorous, blazing desire, and the name of husband removing all the obstacles the modesty and decency of the place might impose, he threw himself at Leocadia and, joining his mouth to hers, it was as if he were waiting for her soul to emerge so he could shelter it in his. But when everyone's tears of pity had increased, and the cries of sorrow had grown, and the pulled hair and beard of Leocadia's mother and father had been reduced, and the shouts of her son were reaching heaven, Leocadia regained consciousness, and with it the joy and happiness that had disappeared from the bosoms of those present.

Leocadia found herself in Rodolfo's arms, and she attempted with seemly force to free herself, but he said:

"No, Señora, this cannot be, it is not right for you to struggle to leave the arms of one who has you in his soul."

With these words Leocadia came completely to her senses, and Doña Estefanía decided to go no further with her initial decision, and told the priest to marry her son to Leocadia immediately. He did so, for since these events took place in a time when, with just the will of the partners and without the just and holy proceedings and precautions in use today, the marriage could be made, and there was no difficulty that could impede the wedding vows.

This being finished, we shall leave it to another pen and another intelligence more subtle than mine to recount the universal joy of all those present: the embraces that Leocadia's parents gave to Rodolfo; the thanks they gave to heaven and his parents; the offerings of all parties; and the astonishment of Rodolfo's comrades, who so unexpectedly saw on the very night of their arrival so beautiful a wedding, and even more so when they learned, because Doña Estefanía told everyone, that Leocadia was the young girl her son had abducted in their company, which confounded Rodolfo even more. And to be even more certain of that truth, he asked Leocadia to tell him a sign that led her to full knowledge of what could not be doubted, for it seemed their parents had looked into it very carefully.

She responded:

"When I woke and regained consciousness after another swoon, I found myself, Señor, in your arms, without honor, but I consider it fortunate, for when I woke from the one I was in now, I found myself in the same arms as then, but now with honor. And if this sign is not enough, the image of a crucifix, which no one could have stolen from you except me, will do, in the event you missed it in the morning and if it is the same one my lady has."

"You are the image of my soul, and you will be for as many years as God wills it, my love."

And as he embraced her again, again they were blessed and congratulated by those present.

The supper arrived, along with musicians who had already been informed. Rodolfo saw himself in the mirror of his son's face. The four grandparents wept with joy. There was not a corner of the house that was not visited by jubilation, happiness, and joy. And although the night flew by on rapid black wings, it seemed to Rodolfo that it moved and walked not with wings but with crutches, so great was his desire to find himself alone with his beloved wife.

The longed for hour arrived at last. Everyone went to bed, the entire house was buried in silence, where the truth of this story will not remain, for their many children, and the distinguished lineage they left in Toledo, would not consent to it, and they live now, these two fortunate newlyweds, who for many happy years enjoyed each other, their children, and their grandchildren, all of it allowed by heaven and the power of blood that the valiant, illustrious, and Christian grandfather of Luisico saw spilled on the ground.

THE NOVEL OF THE JEALOUS EXTREMADURAN

Not many years ago a gentleman, born of noble parents, left a village in Extremadura and, like a second Prodigal Son, traveled through Spain, Italy, and Flanders, spending in this way both years and riches; and after many travels, his parents already dead and his patrimony spent, he came to the great city of Sevilla, where he found ample opportunity to finish consuming the little he had left. Finding himself so lacking in money, and not yet possessing many friends, he resorted to the remedy used by many others who had been lost in that city, which is to sail to the Indies, refuge and shelter to the desperate of Spain, church to swindlers, deliverance to murderers, shield and protection to the gamblers called *ciertos* by experts in the art of marking cards, general snare to unattached women, and personal solution to very few.

In brief, after a time a fleet was leaving for Tierra Firme, and having reached an agreement with the admiral, he assembled his possessions and his straw-mat shroud, and embarking in Cádiz, having finished with Spain, the fleet set sail, and to widespread joy unfurled its sails to a gentle, favorable wind that in a few hours hid the land from sight and revealed the broad, spacious plains of the great father of waters, the Ocean Sea.

Our passenger was pensive, turning over in his memory the many different dangers he had faced and the bad judgment he had used in the course of his life, and as a result of this self-examination, he made a firm resolution to change the way he lived, manage differently the goods that God was pleased to grant him, and proceed with more prudence where women were concerned.

The fleet was in a dead calm when this storm broke over Felipo de Carrizales, for this is the name of the man who has provided the material for our tale. When the wind blew again, it impelled the ships forward with so much force that no one was left in his place; and so Carrizales was obliged to leave his imaginings and begin to face the concerns of the voyage, which was so successful that, with no reversals or sudden changes in the wind, they reached the port of Cartagena. And to conclude with everything that does not contribute to our purposes, I say that Filipo's age when he went to the Indies was forty-eight, and in the twenty years he spent there, aided by his ability and perseverance, he acquired more than one hundred fifty thousand pesos in ingots of unadulterated silver.

Finding himself rich and prosperous, and touched by the natural desire that everyone has to return to his homeland, he postponed important business transactions that had been offered to him, left Perú, where he had acquired all his wealth, which he carried in ingots of gold and silver, registered it to avoid difficulties, and returned to Spain. He disembarked in Sanlúcar, arrived in Sevilla, as full of years as of riches, removed his goods with no problem, and looking for his friends, found they were all dead; he wanted to leave for his birthplace, even though he had already heard that death had taken all his kin. And if, when he went to the Indies poor and in need, he had many worrisome thoughts that did not give him a moment's rest in the middle of the ocean, now they troubled him on solid ground, although for a different reason; if he had not slept earlier because he was poor, now he could not rest because he was rich, for wealth is as heavy a burden for the man who is unaccustomed to having it and does not know how to use it as is poverty for the man who suffers it continually. Gold occasions cares, as does the lack of it; but the latter is resolved by acquiring a moderate amount, while the former increase the more gold one has.

Carrizales thought about his ingots, not because he was a miser, for during the years he had been a soldier he had learned to be openhanded, but in regard to what he would do with them, since keeping his wealth in bars was fruitless, and keeping it in the house was fodder for the covetous and a stimulus for thieves.

The desire to return to the troubled business of commerce had died in him, and he thought that, considering his age, he had more than enough money for the rest of his life and wanted to spend it in his country, making investments, living on the interest, and passing the years of his old age in peace and quiet, giving to God what he could since he had already given more than he should have to the world. On the other hand, he thought there was a good deal of penury in his village; the people were very poor, and going to live there meant making himself a target for all the importunities the poor create for the rich man who is their neighbor, especially when there is no one else in the village to turn to with their miseries. He wanted to have someone to leave his fortune to when his life was over, and with this desire he took the pulse of his fortitude and thought he could still bear the burden of matrimony. And when this thought came to him, he was overwhelmed by such great fear that the thought dissipated and dissolved like a cloud in the wind, because he was by nature the most jealous man in the world, even though he was not married, and just imagining he had a wife caused him to be attacked by jealousy, wearied by suspicions, and assailed by fantasies, and this so efficiently and vehemently that he decided once and for all not to marry.

And having resolved this but not what he would do with his life, as fate would have it, one day as he was walking along a street, he raised his eyes and saw at a window a young girl, apparently thirteen or fourteen years old, with so amiable and beautiful a face that, incapable of defending himself, the good old man Carrizales surrendered the frailty of his many years to the few years of Leonora, for this was the name of the beautiful maiden. And immediately, with no further hesitations, he began to reflect unceasingly, and talking to himself, he said:

"This girl is beautiful, and according to the appearance of this house, she cannot be rich; she is a child, and her youth can assuage my suspicions. I shall marry her, keep her in seclusion, train her to my habits and customs, and in this way she will have no tendencies other than those I teach her. And I am not old enough to lose the hope of having children as my heirs. Whether or not she has a dowry is not a consideration, for heaven has given me enough, and rich men should not look for wealth in their marriages but pleasure; for pleasure lengthens life and disagreements between married couples shorten it. Enough: the die is cast, and this is the girl heaven wants me to have."

And so, having had this soliloquy not once but a hundred times, after a few days he spoke to Leonora's parents and learned that, although poor, they were noble; and informing them of his intention and the worth of his person and fortune, he asked that they give him their daughter as his wife. They requested time to look into what he had said, and for him to learn whether what they had said about their nobility was true.

They took their leave of one another, the parties were informed, and they found that what each had said was true; in brief, Leonora was promised as the wife of Carrizales, who first made her a gift of twenty thousand *ducados*: so ablaze was the heart of the jealous old man. As soon as the husband said yes, he was suddenly overcome by a rush of raging jealousy and for no reason at all began to tremble and be more worried than he had ever been before. And the first sign he gave of his jealous nature was his not wanting any tailor to take his wife's measurements for the many dresses he planned to have made for her; and so he searched for another woman more or less the same size and shape as Leonora, and he found a poor woman and had a dress made to her measurements, and when his wife tried it on he found that it fit, and in this way he had the rest of the dresses made, and there were so many, and so richly made, that the bride's parents considered themselves more than fortunate to have chanced upon so good a son-in-law to protect them and their daughter. The girl was astonished to see so many fine clothes, for in her life the ones she had worn did not go beyond a serge skirt and a taffeta jacket.

The second sign Filipo gave was not wanting to be with his wife until he had settled her in a different house, which he prepared in this way: for twelve thousand *ducados* he bought a house in a distinguished area of the city, which had spring water and a garden with many orange trees; he closed off all the windows that faced the street and gave them a view of the sky, and he did the same to all the other windows in the house. At the street entrance, which in Sevilla they call the *casapuerta*, or vestibule, he had a mule shed built, and above that a hayloft and lodging for the man, an old black eunuch, who would tend to the mule; he raised the walls around the flat roofs so that whoever entered the house had to look at the sky in a straight line, unable to see anything else; he had a small revolving door, the kind used in convents, placed in the wall between the vestibule and the courtyard.

He bought rich furnishings to adorn the house, so that the tapestries, reception rooms, and opulent ornamental hangings indicated that he was a great gentleman; he also bought four white slave women who spoke no Spanish and branded them on the face, and two more black slave women who were simpleminded.

He arranged with a steward to purchase and bring home food on the condition he not sleep in the house or enter it past the vestibule wall, where he would have to hand over what he had brought. Having done this, he invested a portion of his wealth in real estate to receive rents from a variety of good properties; another portion he put in the bank; and he kept some for any chance eventuality. He also made a master key for the entire house and put in it everything ordinarily bought either at one time or seasonally, an entire year's provisions; and having arranged and prepared everything in this way, he went to the house of his in-laws and asked for his wife, and they handed her over to him but not without many tears, for it seemed to them she was being taken to her grave.

The tender young Leonora still did not know what had happened to her, and so, weeping with her parents, she asked for their blessing, and taking her leave, surrounded by her female slaves and maidservants and grasping her husband's hand, she came to her house, and when they had entered, Carrizales preached a sermon, entrusting them with guarding Leonora and ordering them that under no circumstances and by no means were they to allow anyone past the inside door, not even the black eunuch. And the person he made most responsible for the guarding and care of Leonora was a very prudent and serious duenna whom he engaged as a kind of governess to Leonora, and to supervise everything that went on in the house and take charge of the slaves and two other maidens the same age as Leonora, whom he accepted so that she could pass the time with girls her own age.

He promised them he would treat and indulge them all so they would not feel their seclusion, and on feast days each one without exception would go to hear Mass, but so early in the morning the light would scarcely be able to see them. The servants and slaves promised to do everything he had ordered without regret and with a ready will and good spirits. And the new wife shrugged, bent her head, and said she had no will other than her husband's and lord's, whom she would always obey.

Having taken these precautions, the good Extremaduran withdrew into his house and began to enjoy as he could the fruits of his marriage; and Leonora, since she had no experience of any others, found these neither pleasant nor unpleasant. And so she passed the time with her duenna, her maidens, and her slaves, and they, to have a better time, turned to gluttony, and few days went by without the preparation of a thousand things made delicious by honey and sugar. They had more than enough of what they needed to do this, and their master more than enough desire for them to do so, thinking this kept them entertained and occupied with no time to begin thinking about their seclusion.

Leonora behaved with her maids as an equal and amused herself with the same things they did, and in her innocence gave herself over to making dolls and other childish pastimes, which showed the lack of guile in her nature and the tenderness of her years, all of which provided great satisfaction to her jealous husband, who thought he had guessed correctly and chosen the best life imaginable, and that in no way could human cunning or malice disturb his tranquility. And therefore his only concern was to bring presents for his wife and remind her to ask for anything that occurred to her, for he would oblige her in everything.

On the days she went to Mass, which, as we have said, occurred at dawn, her parents came too and spoke to their daughter in the church, in the presence of her husband, who gave them so many gifts that although they felt sorry for their daughter because of the confinement in which she lived, their sorrow was tempered by the many presents that Carrizales, their generous son-in-law, gave them.

He would get up in the morning and wait for the steward to arrive; the night before, by means of a note placed in the revolving door, he told him what he was to bring the next day; and after the steward arrived, Carrizales left the house, most of the time on foot, leaving both doors, the one to the street and the one in the middle, locked, and between the two the black man.

He would take care of his business affairs, which were few, and soon returned home; locking the doors behind him, he would spend his time indulging his wife and being kind to her maids, and all of them loved him because his nature was so straightforward and pleasant and, above all, because he was so generous to all of them.

In this way they spent a year of their novitiate and professed their vows in that life, deciding to live this way until their lives had ended; and this is how it would have continued if the astute confounder of humankind had not interfered, as you shall now hear.

Whoever thinks he is more perceptive and circumspect can tell me now what other precautions for his security old Felipo could have taken, for he did not even consent to having any male animal in his house. A tomcat never chased the mice, and a male dog was never heard barking; all the animals were of the female gender. By day Felipo would think, by night he did not sleep; he was the night watch and sentry of his house, the Argos of what he loved dearly. No man ever passed through the door to the courtyard; he did business with his friends on the street. The figures on the hangings that adorned his rooms and antechambers were all females, or flowers, or landscapes. His entire house smacked of purity, seclusion, and modesty; even in the tales told by the maids on long winter nights by the hearth, no kind of lasciviousness could be found because he was present. The silver in the white hair of the old man seemed like pure gold to Leonora, because the first love young girls have is impressed on their souls like a seal in wax. His overzealous guardianship seemed like well-advised prudence to her; she thought and believed that what she was experiencing was experienced by all newlyweds. Her thoughts never strayed beyond the walls of her house, nor did her will long for anything more than what her husband desired; she saw the streets only on the days she went to Mass, so early in the morning that, except for her return from church, there was no light by which to see them.

No convent was ever so walled in, no nuns more cloistered, no golden apples more closely guarded; and even so, there was no way to prevent or avoid the fall into what he so feared; or, at least, the thought that she had fallen.

There are in Sevilla idle, indolent people commonly called *neighborhood boys*. These are the sons of the residents in each parish, the richest among them: useless, well dressed, well spoken, well mannered; there is a great deal to be said about them and their clothing and their way of life, their character and the laws they obey among themselves, but for good reasons we shall put all that aside.

One of these elegant fellows, who among themselves are known as *blades*— young bachelors who call newlyweds *shawls*—happened to look at the house of the cautious Carrizales, and seeing it was always locked, wanted to find out who lived there; and he pursued the task with so much zeal and curiosity that he learned what he wanted to know.

He learned about the old man's character, the beauty of his wife, and the way he kept watch over her; all of this kindled his desire to see whether, through force or through cunning, it would be possible to storm so well-guarded a fortress. And communicating with friends, two blades and a shawl, they agreed to set themselves this task, for there is never any lack of advisers and helpers for tasks like these.

They pondered the difficulties of undertaking so arduous a feat; and having consulted about the matter many times, they agreed on this: Loaysa, which was the blade's name, would pretend he was leaving the city for a few days and remove himself from the sight of his friends, which he did. And having done this, he put on clean linen breeches and a clean shirt, but over these he put clothes so ragged and patched that no poor man in the entire city wore anything more wretched. He removed some of his beard, covered one eye with a patch, tied up one leg very tightly, and leaning on a pair of crutches, successfully transformed himself into a lame beggar unequaled by the truest cripple.

This was how he appeared every night when the Angelus rang, at the door of Carrizales's house, which was already locked, with the black, whose name was Luis, closed in between the two doors. Once there, Loaysa would take out a small, somewhat grimy guitar missing a few strings, and being something of a musician, would begin to play some happy, cheerful melodies, changing his voice in order not to be recognized. Then he quickly turned to an impassioned singing of ballads on Moorish themes, and he did this with so much charm that passersby stopped to listen, and a group of boys would always surround him as he sang. And Luis, the black man, listening between the doors, hung on the blade's music and would have given an arm to open the door and listen to him more at his ease; that is how great the inclination of blacks to be musicians can be. And when Loaysa wanted those who were listening to leave him, he would stop singing and put away his guitar and, taking up his crutches, walk away.

Four or five times he had played for the black—and only for him—thinking the place where he must begin to bring down that building had to lie with

Luis; and his thought was not a foolish one, because one night, coming as usual to the door, he began to tune his guitar and sensed that the black man was already listening, and going up to the door frame, in a quiet voice he said:

"Would it be possible, Luis, to give me a little water? I'm dying of thirst and can't sing."

"No," said the black man, "because I don't have the key to this door, and there's no opening where I could pass it to you."

"Then who has the key?" asked Loaysa.

"My master," responded the black man, "and he's the most jealous man in the world. And if he knew I was here talking to anybody now, he'd kill me. But who is it that's asking me for water?"

"I," responded Loaysa, "am a poor one-legged cripple who earns his living begging for the love of God from good people; and along with that, I teach some dark-skinned slaves and other poor people to play; and I have three blacks, slaves of three councilmen, and I've taught them so they can sing and play at any dance and in any tavern, and they paid me very, very well for that."

"I'd pay you even better," said Luis, "for a chance to take a lesson, but that isn't possible because of my master; when he goes out in the morning, he locks the street door, and does the same thing when he returns, leaving me walled in between two doors."

"For God's sake, Luis," replied Loaysa, who already knew the black man's name, "if you found a way to let me in for a few nights to give you a lesson, in less than two weeks I'd make you so good on the guitar that you could play on any street corner with no embarrassment at all; because I'll tell you that I'm a really skillful teacher, and besides that, I've heard you have very good abilities, and from what I hear and can judge from the instrument of your voice, which is high-pitched, you must sing very well."

"I don't sing badly," responded the black, "but what good does it do me since I don't know any songs except 'The Star of Venus' and 'Through a Green Meadow,' and the one that's so popular now that goes:

> 'The troubled hand that clutches
> at the iron prison bars?'"

"All of those are nothing but air," said Loaysa, "compared to the ones I could teach you, because I know all the songs about the Moor Abindarráez and his lady Jarifa, and all the songs about the history of the great Sofí Tomunibeyo, and the sacred ones in the style of the sarabande that are so good they astonish even the Portuguese. And I teach all this with so good a method and so much facility that, even if you're not in a hurry to learn, by the time you've eaten three or four heaps of salt[1] you'll find yourself a satisfactory musician on every kind of guitar."

At this the black sighed and said:

"What good is all that if I don't know how to get you inside the house?"

"I have the solution," said Loaysa. "Get hold of your master's keys, and I'll give you a piece of wax where you can press them down so that the wards of each key are marked in the wax; because of how fond I am of you, I'll have a locksmith who's a friend of mine make the keys, and then I'll be able to go in at night and teach you better than Prester Juan of the Indies;[2] I think it's a great shame to lose a voice like yours because it lacks the support of the guitar. I want you to know, my brother Luis, that the best voice in the world loses its worth when it isn't accompanied by an instrument, whether it's a guitar or a clavichord, an organ or a harp; but the one best suited to your voice is the guitar because it is the easiest and least expensive of the instruments."

"That seems fine to me," replied the black, "but it's impossible, because the keys are never in my possession, and my master doesn't let go of them during the day, and at night they lie under his pillow."

"Well, then, do something else, Luis," said Loaysa, "if you want to be a superior musician, but if you don't, there's no reason for me to wear myself out giving you advice."

"But I do want to!" replied Luis. "I want to so much that I'll do anything, as long as it's possible to carry it off, in exchange for becoming a musician."

"Well, if that's so," said the blade, "through these doors I'll give you something, if you make a space by taking away some of the earth at the frame; I mean I'll give you pliers and a hammer, and at night you can use them and easily remove the nails of the wolf-tooth lock, and just as easily put the lock back so no one can see it was unnailed. And when I'm inside, locked in with you in your hayloft, or wherever you sleep, I'll do what I have to do so quickly you'll find yourself even more of what I told you about, making use of my person and your ability. As far as eating's concerned, don't worry about that, I'll bring enough fodder for both of us for more than a week; I have students and friends who won't let me suffer."

"As for food," replied the black man, "there's nothing to fear, because with the amount of food my master gives me and the leftovers the slave girls bring me, there will be more than enough food for another two people. Just

1. An ironic remark that makes the task out to be something quite difficult.
2. Prester John was a legendary Christian believed to be the ruler of a lost Christian population in the Orient.

bring that hammer and pliers you mentioned, and I'll make a place where they'll fit, right by this frame, and I'll cover and close it again with mud, and even if I have to hit the lock a few times to get it off, my master sleeps so far from this door, it will either be a miracle or our great misfortune if he hears me."

"Then God's will be done," said Loaysa, "and two days from now you'll have, Luis, everything needed to carry out our virtuous purpose; and be careful not to eat phlegm-producing food, because that's harmful to the voice, not helpful."

"Nothing makes me as hoarse," responded the black, "as wine, but I won't stop drinking it for all the voices in the world."

"I'm not saying that," said Loaysa, "God forbid. Drink, Luis my son, drink and may it do you good, for wine drunk in a measured way never caused any harm at all."

"I drink it by the measure," replied the black man. "I have a jug here that holds two liters exactly; the slave girls fill it for me without my master knowing, and the steward secretly brings me a wineskin that holds exactly four liters, and with that I can supplement whatever's lacking in the jug."

"I say," said Loaysa, "that my life should be as good as I think yours is, because a throat that's dry can't sing or cry."

"Go with God," said the black, "but be sure not to stop coming here to sing on the number of nights it will take you to bring what you have to bring in order to come inside; I'm impatient to see my fingers placed on a guitar."

"Of course I'll come!" replied Loaysa. "I'll even bring new songs."

"That's all I ask," said Luis, "and now be sure to sing something for me, so I can go to sleep happy; as for payment, the poor gentleman should understand that I'll pay him better than a rich man would."

"I don't care about that," said Loaysa, "because you'll pay me according to how I teach you, and for now listen to this little tune, and soon enough you'll see miracles."

"That will be a happy day," answered the black.

And when this long dialogue was over, Loaysa sang a little oxytonic ballad that left the black man so happy and satisfied he could already see the time to open the door.

As soon as Loaysa left, with more speed than his carrying crutches promised, he went to tell his advisers about his good beginning, a prediction of the good ending he hoped for. He found them and recounted what he had arranged with the black, and the next day they found the tools, so strong they could break any nail as if it were made of wood.

The blade did not forget to go back and play music for the black man, just as the black did not forget to make the hole for what his teacher would give him, covering it over so that, unless it was looked at with cunning and suspicion, one could not tell a hole was there.

On the second night Loaysa handed over the tools, and Luis tested his strength, and almost without exerting any he found the nails broken, and with the lock in his hands, he opened the door and received his Orpheus[3] and teacher inside, and when he saw him with his two crutches, so ragged and with his leg so bound, he was astonished. Loaysa was not wearing the patch over his eye because it was not necessary, and as soon as he came in he embraced his good disciple and kissed him on the face, and then he placed a large wineskin in his hands and a case of preserves and other sweet things, which filled some bags he was carrying. And dropping the crutches, as if there were nothing wrong with him, he began to prance about; this astounded the black even more, and Loaysa said to him:

"You should know, my brother Luis, that my lameness and incapacity are the result not of disease but of ingenuity, and with it I earn my bread begging in the name of God, and helped along by this and my music, I live the best life in the world where everyone who isn't clever and a swindler dies of hunger; you'll see this in the course of our friendship."

"We'll see," replied the black man, "but first let's put this lock back where it belongs so the change in it can't be seen."

"I'm happy to," said Loaysa.

And taking nails out of his bags, they set the lock in place so that it was as good as before, which made the black man exceedingly happy; and Loaysa climbed up to the lodging the black had in the hayloft and made himself as comfortable as he could.

Then Luis lit a twist of wax, and with no further delay Loaysa took out his guitar, and playing it quietly and gently, he so enthralled the poor black man that he was beside himself listening. Having played a little, he took out more food and gave it to his pupil, and even though the food was sweet, Luis drank from the wineskin with so much goodwill that it left him in more of a daze than the music did. When he had finished, Loaysa said it was time for Luis to have a lesson, and since the poor man had four measures of wine in his brains, he could not find the frets, and even so, Loaysa made him believe he already knew at least two songs, and the strange thing was that the black man believed

3. In Greek mythology, Orpheus was known as the supreme musician, able to charm stones and animals with his lyre.

it, and all night he did nothing but play a guitar that was out of tune and missing the necessary strings.

They slept for what was left of the night, and at approximately six in the morning Carrizales came down, opened the inner door and the street door, and waited for the steward, who came shortly afterward, passed in the food in the revolving door, and left again; then he called to the black man to come down and get barley for the mule and his own food; after Luis had taken the food, Old Carrizales left, leaving both doors locked, not noticing what had been done to the street door, which pleased both teacher and disciple more than a little.

As soon as his master had left the house, the black seized the guitar and began to play so that all the maids heard him, and through the revolving door they asked him:

"What is this, Luis? How long have you had a guitar, or who gave it to you?"

"Who gave it to me?" responded Luis. "The best musician in the world, the one who will teach me more than six thousand songs in six days."

"And where is this musician?" asked the duenna.

"Not very far from here," answered the black, "and if he wasn't shy and I wasn't afraid of my master, maybe I'd show him to you right now, and by my faith you'd enjoy seeing him."

"And where can he be that we could see him," replied the duenna, "if no man except our master ever entered this house?"

"Well, now," said the black, "I don't want to tell you anything until you see what I know and what he's taught me in the brief time that I've said."

"There's no doubt," said the duenna, "that if the man who's going to teach you isn't some demon, I don't know who could turn you into a musician in such a short time."

"Go on," said the black man, "you'll hear and see him some day."

"That can't be," said another girl, "because we don't have windows to the street where we can see or hear anybody."

"That's true," said the black, "but everything has a remedy except death, even more so if you know how to be silent and want to be silent."

"Oh, we know how to be silent, brother Luis!" said one of the slaves. "We'll be more silent than if we were mutes; for I promise you, my friend, I'm dying to hear a good voice, because after we were walled in here, we haven't even heard the birds singing."

Loaysa listened to this conversation with great joy, thinking all of it was moving toward the attainment of his intention, and that good luck had taken the girls by the hand to lead them according to his will.

The maids took their leave when the black man promised that when they least expected it, he would call them to hear a very good voice; and fearing his master would return and find him talking to them, he left them and withdrew to his cloistered room. He would have liked to have a lesson but did not dare play during the day so he would not be heard by his master, who returned home soon afterward, locking the doors as was his custom and shutting himself away in the house. And that day, when food was passed in the revolving door to the black man, Luis said to the black girl who brought it to him that tonight, after their master was asleep, they should all come down without fail to the revolving door to hear the voice he had promised them. It is true that before he said this, he had pleaded with his teacher to be so good as to sing and play that night at the revolving door so he could keep the word he had given that he would have the maids hear a great voice, assuring him he would be flattered by all of them. The teacher made him beg him to do what the teacher most desired, but finally he said he would do what his good disciple asked, just to give him pleasure, and for no other reason.

The black man embraced him and kissed his cheek to show how much happiness the promised favor had brought him, and that day he fed Loaysa as well as if he were eating in his own house, and perhaps even better, for something may have been lacking in his house.

Night came, and in the middle of it, or perhaps a little earlier, a hissing began at the revolving door, and then Luis understood it was a drove of maids; and calling his teacher, they came down from the hayloft, with the guitar well strung and better tuned. Luis asked who the listeners were and how many there were. They responded that they were all of them except their mistress, who was sleeping with her husband, which Loaysa regretted; but even so, he wanted to begin his plan and make his disciple happy, and gently strumming the guitar, he played melodies that amazed the black man and astonished the flock of listening women.

Well, and what shall I say of what they heard when he played "Pésame dello" and ended with the devilish sound of the sarabande, which was then new to Spain? No old woman was left not dancing, no young one who did not wear herself out, all of it muted and strangely silent, and they placed sentries and spies to let them know if the old man awoke.

Loaysa also sang verses of seguidillas, with which he put the finishing touches on the delight of his listeners, who eagerly asked the black man to tell them who the miraculous musician was. Luis said he was a poor beggar, the most gallant and charming of all the paupers in Sevilla.

They begged him to arrange things so they could see the stranger, and not to let him leave the house for two weeks, and they would treat him very well and give him anything he might need. They asked what means he had used to get him in the house. To this he did not say a word; as for the rest, he said that to see him they should make a small hole in the revolving door, and afterward they could fill it in with wax; as for keeping him in the house, he would do what he could.

Loaysa also spoke to them, offering to serve them with such fine words that they observed the words did not come from the mind of a poor beggar. They pleaded with him to come to the same spot the next night, and they would arrange for their mistress to come down to listen to him in spite of their master's light sleep, which was the result not of his great age but his great jealousy. To which Loaysa said that if they wanted to hear him with no fear of sudden appearances by the old man, he would give them some powders to put in his wine, which would make him sleep deeply and longer than usual.

"Jesus save me!" said one of the maidens. "If this is true, what good fortune has come through the doors to us without our hearing or deserving it. Those would not be sleeping powders for him but living powders for all of us, and for my poor mistress Leonora, his wife, for he pesters her and does not let her out of his sight for a moment. Ah, dear gentleman of my soul, bring those powders and may God grant you everything you desire! Go, and don't be long; bring them, Señor, and I volunteer to mix them into his wine and serve it to him; and may it please God that the old man sleeps three days and nights, and that we have the same number of days of glory."

"Well, I shall bring them," said Loaysa, "and they do nothing else, they do not harm the person who takes them except to induce in him a very heavy sleep."

They all begged him to bring the powders soon, and agreeing to make the hole in the revolving door with an auger the following night, and to bring their mistress to see and hear him, they took their leave. And Luis, though it was almost dawn, wanted to have a lesson, which Loaysa gave him and convinced him there was no better ear than his among all the students he had; and the poor black man did not know, and never learned, how to play the simplest chord.

Loaysa's friends were careful to come at night to listen at the street door and see whether their friend had something to tell them or needed anything; and by giving a signal they had agreed upon earlier, Loaysa knew they were at the door, and through the hole in the frame he gave them a brief account of how well things were going and asked them most earnestly to find something that would induce sleep in Carrizales, for he had heard there were powders that produced that effect. They told him they had a friend who was a physician and would give them the best medicine he could find, if it existed; and encouraging him to persevere in his undertaking, and promising to return the next night with the powders, they quickly took their leave.

Night came, and the flock of pigeons arrived promptly at the call of the guitar. With them came the guileless Leonora, in fear and trembling that her husband would awaken; for although she, overcome by this fear, had not wished to come, her maids, in particular the duenna, told her so many things about the sweetness of the music and the gallant disposition of the poor musician—for, without having seen him, she praised him and placed him higher than Absalom[4] and Orpheus—that their poor mistress, convinced and persuaded by them, would do what she did not choose and never would have chosen to do by herself. The first thing they did was drill a hole in the revolving door to see the musician who no longer was in a poor man's clothes but wore large breeches of tawny silk, wide in the nautical fashion, a doublet of the same fabric with gold braid, and a hunting hat of gold satin, a starched collar with long lace inserts, all of which he had placed in his bags, supposing the occasion might arise when it would be advantageous for him to change his clothes.

He was young, charming, and good-looking; and since all of them had seen no man but their old master for so long, it seemed to them that they were looking at an angel. One peered through the hole to see him, and then another; and to allow them to see better, the black kept moving the twist of lit wax up and down the young man's body. And when all of them had seen him, even the dim-witted black girls, Loaysa picked up the guitar and sang so perfectly that he left them all dumbfounded and amazed, the old woman as well as the girls, and they asked Luis to tell his teacher how to get inside so they could hear and see him up close, not just through a peephole, and without the fear of being so distant from their master that he could take them by surprise to catch them red-handed; which would not happen if they had the musician hidden inside.

Their mistress opposed this most earnestly, saying such a thing should not be done because it would weigh on her soul, for they could see and hear him from there safely and with no danger to their honor.

4. Absalom, the son of King David in the Old Testament, was known for his good looks.

"What do you mean honor?" said the duenna. "We have too much honor; your grace is locked in with your Methuselah, and we are left to enjoy ourselves the best we can. Besides, this gentleman seems so honorable, he will not want anything from us that we do not wish to give."

"My ladies," Loaysa said, "I came here only with the intention of serving all your graces with my soul and my life, commiserating with your unheard of confinement and the times lost in this narrow kind of life. By my father's life, I am a man so candid, so gentle, so good-natured, and so obedient that I shall do only as I am told; and if any of your graces were to say: 'Maestro, sit here; maestro, go there; come over here; go over there,' I should do it like the tamest and best-trained dog that skips about for the king of France."

"If it will be like that," said the innocent Leonora, "how will the maestro manage to get inside?"

"Well," said Loaysa, "your graces make an effort to obtain a wax impression of the key to this door, and tomorrow night I shall have it made into a duplicate that we can use."

"If you make that key," said one of the girls, "you make them for the entire house, because that is the master key."

"It won't be worse because of that," replied Loaysa.

"That is true," said Leonora, "but this gentleman must swear, first of all, that when he is here inside he will not do anything but sing and play when he is told to, and will stay confined and quiet wherever we put him."

"Yes, I swear."

"That oath is worth nothing," responded Leonora, "you have to swear on the life of your father, and you have to swear on a cross and kiss it, so we all can see it."

"On the life of my father, I swear it," said Loaysa, "and on this sign of the cross, which I kiss with my sinful mouth."

And making a cross with two fingers, he kissed it three times.

When he had done this, another of the maids said:

"Look, Señor, be sure not to forget those powders, they're the essential thing in all this."

That night's talk ended, and everyone was very satisfied with the arrangement. And luck, which directed Loaysa's affairs from good to better, brought his friends along the street at that time, which was two in the morning, and they made their usual signal, which was to play a mouth harp, and Loaysa spoke to them and told them about the point he had reached in his plan, and asked them to bring the powders, or something like them, as he had requested, so that Carrizales would sleep. He also told them about the master key. They said the powders would come the next night, or a salve that, applied to the inside of the wrists and the temples, caused a deep sleep from which one could not awaken in two days unless all the parts where it had been applied were washed with vinegar; they also told him to give them the key in wax, and they would make the new key with no difficulty.

And then they took their leave, and Loaysa and his pupil slept the little left to them of the night, Loaysa waiting impatiently for the next night to see whether the promise about the key was kept. And although time seems dilatory and lazy to those who are waiting, it does, after all, run at the same speed as thought, and reaches the desired moment because it never stops or rests.

And so the night came, and the accustomed hour for going to the revolving door, where all the maids in the house—large and small, black and white— came because they all wished to see the musician within their seraglio; but Leonora did not come, and when Loaysa asked after her, they responded that she was lying in bed with her husband, who had locked the door of the room with the key and then placed it under his pillow, and their mistress had told them that as soon as the old man was sleeping, she would do what she could to take the master key from him and make the impression, for she had the wax already prepared and soft, and in a little while they were supposed to call her through a cat hole.

Loaysa marveled at the old man's caution, but that did not weaken his desire; and then he heard the mouth harp. He went to the spot and found his friends, who gave him a vial of ointment with the properties they had described; Loaysa took it and told them to wait a little while and he would give them the pattern for the key. He returned to the revolving door and told the duenna, who showed the most persistent desire for him to come inside, to take the salve to Señora Leonora, telling her the property it had, and that she should attempt to apply it to her husband so cautiously that he did not feel it, and she would see marvels. The duenna did so, and when she reached the cat hole, she discovered that Leonora was waiting, stretched out on the floor with her face to the opening. The duenna approached, and stretching out in the same way, placed her mouth to her mistress's ear and whispered that she had the salve and told her how she was to test its qualities. She took the salve and told the duenna that in no way could she take the key from her husband, because he did not have it beneath his pillow, as he usually did, but between the two mattresses and under almost half his body; but she should tell the maestro that if the salve worked as he said, they would easily obtain the key as often as they wished, and so it would not be necessary to copy it in wax. She told the duenna to go immediately and tell the maestro and then come back to see how the salve was working, because she intended to apply it to her husband right away.

The duenna went down to give Maestro Loaysa the message, and he said goodbye to his friends, who were waiting for the key. Trembling and very tentatively, almost without letting the breath out of her mouth, Leonora succeeding in applying the ointment to the jealous husband's wrists, as well as his nostrils, and when she was about to touch them she thought he quivered, and she was as still as a corpse, thinking he would catch her in the act. But, in fact, she finished applying the salve the best she could to all the places she had been told were necessary, which was the same as having embalmed him for burial.

It did not take the opiate salve long to give manifest signs of its qualities, because the old man soon began to snore so loudly he could be heard in the street; to the ears of his wife, it was music more melodious than that of the black man's teacher; and not yet sure of what she was seeing, she went up to her husband and shook him a little, and then more, and then just a little more to see if he awoke; and no matter how daring she was, he turned from one side to the other without waking. When she saw this, she went to the cat hole in the door, and in a voice louder than the first time, called to the duenna, who was waiting there, and said:

"Good news, sister, Carrizales is sleeping more soundly than a dead man!"

"Well, why do you delay in taking the key, Señora?" said the duenna. "The musician has been waiting for you for more than an hour."

"Wait, sister, I'm going for it now," responded Leonora.

And going back to the bed, she placed her hand between the mattresses and removed the key without the old man feeling it; and holding the key in her hands, she began to jump for joy, and with no further delay opened the door and handed the key to the duenna, who accepted it with the greatest delight in the world.

Leonora told her to open the door for the musician and bring him to the galleries, because she did not dare leave where she was in case something happened; but, before anything else, he had to confirm the oath he had made to do no more than what they told him to, and if he did not wish to confirm it and make it again, she was in no way to open the door for him.

"As you wish," said the duenna, "and by my faith, he will not enter if he does not swear first, and swear again, and kiss the cross six times."

"Don't put a number on it," said Leonora. "Let him kiss it the number of times he chooses, but be sure he swears on the life of his parents and everything he loves, because with that we shall be certain and can listen to him sing and play all we wish, for in my soul I know he will do it beautifully. And go, don't wait any longer, we don't want to spend the night chatting."

The good duenna raised her skirts and with unheard-of speed arrived at the revolving door, where all the people in the house were waiting for her; and after showing them the key she had brought, everyone's joy was so great that they lifted her up as if she had just won a university chair, crying: 'Long live, long live the duenna!' and even more so when she said there was no need to copy the key, because considering how the old man slept with the salve, they could easily use the master key as often as they wished.

"Well, then, my friend," said one of the maidens, "open that door, and have this gentleman come in, for he has been waiting a long time, and let us enjoy the music as much as we want to!"

"But that has to wait," replied the duenna, "for we must take his oath as we did the other night."

"He's so good," said one of the slaves, "he won't even pay attention to oaths."

Then the duenna opened the door, and holding it partially open, called to Loaysa, who had been listening to everything through the hole in the revolving door; and he, coming up to the door, wanted to walk right in, but placing her hand on his chest, the duenna said to him:

"Your grace must know, Señor, that in God and my conscience, all of us behind the doors of this house are virgins like the mothers who bore us, except my mistress; and although I must look forty years old, I am not yet thirty and am still two and a half months away from that age, and I am also a maiden, more's the pity; and if I perhaps seem old, vexations, difficulties, and distresses add a zero to one's age, and sometimes two, according to whim. And since this is so, and it is, it would not be reasonable for us, in exchange for hearing two, or three, or four songs, to risk all the virginity confined here; even this black girl, whose name is Guiomar, is a maiden. And so, gentleman of my heart, before entering our kingdom, your grace has to make a very solemn oath to us that your grace will do only what we command; and if what we are asking seems a great deal, consider that much more is being risked. And if your grace comes with good intentions, swearing will cause very little pain, for a good debtor does not mind guarantees."

"Well said, Señora Marialonso, very well said," said one of the maidens, "spoken like a wise person informed about things, as she should be; and if the gentleman does not wish to swear, let him not come in."

In reponse, Guiomar the black girl, who did not speak Spanish very well, said:

"For me, sure he swear, and in come devil, no matter he swear, if he here, he forget all."

Loaysa listened very calmly to Señora Marialonso's speech, and with solemn composure and authority he replied:

"Certainly, Señoras, my sisters and friends, my intention never was, is, or will be anything other than to give you as much pleasure and delight as I am able to; and so I shall not find this oath you ask of me difficult; but I should like to have some trust in my word, because given by a person like myself, it is the same as a legal obligation; and I want your grace to know you cannot judge a book by its cover, and all that glitters is not gold. But so that all your graces can be certain of my virtuous desire, I have decided to swear as a Catholic and a moral man; and so I swear by uncorrupted efficaciousness, where the complete text is contained at length, and by entrances to and departures from holy Mount Lebanon, and by everything that in its proem contains the true history of Charlemagne, and the death of the giant Fierabrás, not to stray from or pass over the oath that has been taken and the command of the least and most scorned of these ladies, under penalty that if I should do or wish to do anything else, from henceforth and from thenceforth I declare it null and void and nonbinding."[5]

The good Loaysa had reached this point in his oath when one of the two girls who had been listening to him attentively called out in a loud voice, saying:

"Now this is an oath to move stones! Curse me if I want you to swear to more, for with what you have already sworn, you could enter the very abyss of Cabra!"[6]

And grasping his breeches, she pulled him inside, and then all the others surrounded him. One went immediately to give the news to her mistress, who was sentry to her husband's sleep, and when the messenger told her the musician was coming up, she was happy and perturbed at the same time and asked whether he had sworn. She answered that he had and with the newest form of oath she had ever heard.

"Well, if he has sworn," said Leonora, "we have him. Oh, how prudent I was to have him swear!"

At this point the entire crowd arrived together, with the musician in the middle and Luis the black man and Guiomar the black girl lighting their way. And when Loaysa saw Leonora, he showed signs of throwing himself at her feet to kiss her hands. She, keeping silent and gesturing, had him stand, and

---

5. Loaysa's oath is a humorous combination of disparate religious, legal, and literary references.

6. A legendary Spanish site believed to be one of the entrances to Hell.

all the maids were mute, not daring to speak, fearful that their master would hear them; after considering this, Loaysa said they could speak aloud because an attribute of the ointment used on their master was that, without taking his life, it made a man seem dead.

"I believe that," said Leonora, "and if it were not so, he would have awakened twenty times by now, because all his ailments make him a light sleeper; but since I applied the salve, he has been snoring like an animal."

"Well, if that is true," said the duenna, "let us go to that drawing room over there where we can hear the gentleman sing and be glad."

"Let us go," said Leonora, "but have Guiomar stay here to keep watch and let us know whether Carrizales wakens."

To which Guiomar responded:

"Black girl stay, white girls go; God forgive all!"

The black girl remained; the others went to the drawing room that had a richly decorated estrade, and placing the gentleman in the middle, they all sat down. The good Marialonso took a candle and began to look at the good musician from top to bottom, and one of the maids said: 'Oh, what a nice forelock he has, so curly!' And another: 'Oh, what white teeth! Too bad for trimmed pine nuts that are not whiter or prettier!' And another: 'Oh, what big eyes, and so wide open! And by my mother's life, they're green, and they look just like emeralds!' One praised his mouth, another his feet, and all together they made a slow, detailed examination of his anatomy. Leonora alone was silent, and looked at him, and thought his figure was better than her husband's. Then the duenna picked up the guitar, which the black man was holding, and put it in Loaysa's hands, asking him to play and sing some of the verses that were very popular then in Sevilla, which said:

> Mother, O my mother,
> your guards watch over me.

Loaysa complied with her request. All the maids stood and began to wear themselves out dancing. The duenna knew the verses and sang them with more gusto than good voice, and this is what she sang:

> *Mother, O my mother,*
> *your guards watch over me,*
> *if I don't guard myself,*
> *none can watch over me.*
>
> They say it is written,
> and it is surely true,

privation only feeds
desire and appetite;
love that is locked away
grows to infinite size,
therefore it is better
not to lock me away,
if I don't guard myself,
none can watch over me.

If will and will alone
does not guard itself,
nobility or fear
will not watch over it;
in truth it will break through
even death itself,
until it finds the fate
you never did intend,
if I don't guard myself,
none can watch over me.

An affectionate girl
who is used to loving,
like a bright butterfly
will pursue her own light,
and though you place a horde
of guards all around her,
and though they may propose
to do just what you do,
if I don't guard myself,
none can watch over me.

Love's power does not yield;
such is the strength of love
that it turns the fairest
into bold chimeras;
a heart ablaze conquers
a bosom made of wax,
hands that are made of wool,
feet that are made of felt,
if I don't guard myself,
none can watch over me.

The circle of maidens, led by the good duenna, were reaching the end of their singing and dancing when Guiomar, the sentry, came in, completely agitated, her hands and feet and mouth convulsing as if she suffered from epilepsy, and in a voice between a rasp and a whisper, she said:

"Señora, Señor woke; Señora, Señor woke, and got up, and comes!"

Whoever has seen a flock of pigeons feeding without fear in a field planted by other hands, and then at the deafening noise of musket fire are startled and rise up, and forgetting the food, fly through the air confused and bewildered, can imagine the state of the flock and circle of dancers, stunned and fearful at hearing the unexpected news Guiomar had brought, and each one seeking her excuse and all of them a way out, they scattered and went to hide in the garrets and corners of the house, leaving the musician alone; and he, setting aside his guitar and his song, was filled with confusion and did not know what to do.

Leonora wrung her beautiful hands; Señora Marialonso slapped her own face, though gently. In short, there was nothing but confusion, alarm, and fear. But the duenna, being more astute and controlled, ordered Loaysa into her room, while she and her mistress remained in the drawing room, for there would be no lack of excuses to give her master if he found them there.

Loaysa hid immediately, and the duenna listened attentively to hear whether her master was coming, and hearing no noise at all, she plucked up her courage, and little by little, very slowly, approached the room where her master was sleeping and heard him snoring as he had earlier; reassured that he was asleep, she lifted her skirts and ran back to tell her mistress to rejoice at the good news that her husband was asleep, which she did very willingly.

The good duenna did not want to miss the opportunity that fortune had offered her to enjoy the musician's gratitude before anyone else; and so, telling Leonora to wait in the drawing room while she went to call him, she left her mistress and went to the room where he was waiting, as confused as he was thoughtful, waiting to hear what the drugged old man was doing. He cursed the lie of the ointment, and lamented the credulity of his friends and his own lack of caution in not testing it first on someone else before using it on Carrizales.

Then the duenna arrived and assured him the old man was sound asleep. His heart calmed down and he listened carefully to the many amorous words Marialonso said to him, from which he inferred her evil intentions, and he proposed to himself to use her as the bait to catch her mistress. And as the two of them were chatting, the rest of the maids, hidden in various places throughout the house, one here and another there, came back to see whether it was true that their master had awakened. And seeing that everything was buried in silence, they came to the drawing room where they had left their mistress, from whom they learned of their master's deep sleep; and asking for the musician and the duenna, she told them where they were, and all the maidens, as silently as they had come, went to listen at the door to what the two of them were doing.

Guiomar the black girl was not missing from the group, but the black man was, because as soon as he heard that his master had awakened, he embraced his guitar and went to hide in his hayloft, and covered by the blanket on his poor bed, lay sweating and perspiring with fear; and in spite of everything, he did not fail to try the guitar strings, so great was (may he be sent to Satan!) the love he had for music.

The maids overheard the old woman's flirting, and each cursed her in her own way; none called her old without the epithet and adjective of witch, whiskery, fickle, and others not repeated here out of respect, but what would have most amused anyone who heard them then were the words of Guiomar the black girl who, because she was Portuguese and not very Castilian, reviled her in a very strange fashion. In short, the conclusion of their talk was that he would go along with her desires after she had delivered to him her willing mistress.

It was difficult for the duenna to offer what the musician asked for, but in exchange for satisfying the desire that by this time had taken possession of her soul and the bones and marrow of her body, she would have promised every imaginable impossibility. She left him and went to talk to her mistress; and when she saw all the maids crowded around the door, she told them to return to their rooms; there would be time the next night to enjoy the musician with fewer alarms or none at all, for by now that night's disturbance had spoiled their enjoyment.

They all understood very well that the old woman wanted to be alone, but they could not fail to obey her, because she was in charge of them all. The maids left, and she went to the drawing room to persuade Leonora to conform to Loaysa's desires with a long speech so well composed it seemed she had studied it for many days. She praised his gallantry, his valor, his grace, and his many charms. She described for her how much more pleasurable the embraces of a young lover would be than those of her old husband, assuring her of the secrecy and duration of her joy, and many other comparable things, for the demon endowed her tongue with so many rhetorical figures that were so demonstrative and efficacious, they would have moved not only the tender, innocent heart of the ingenuous, incautious Leonora but one of hardened marble. Oh, duennas, born and used in the world for the perdition of a thousand chaste good intentions! Oh, long and folded headdresses, chosen to give authority to the drawing rooms and estrades of distinguished ladies, and how contrary to how you ought to behave in your almost obligatory occupation! In short, the duenna said so much and persuaded so much that Leonora surrendered, Leonora was deceived, and Leonora was lost, toppling all the precautions of the discerning Carrizales, who slept the sleep of the death of his honor.

Marialonso took her mistress by the hands, and almost by force, her eyes filled with tears, took her to Loaysa, and giving them her blessing with a demon's false smile, and closing the door behind her, she left them there and began to doze on the estrade or, rather, to await payment for her services, content with the leftovers. But the wakefulness of the past few nights vanquished her, and she fell asleep on the estrade.

It would have been good at this time to ask Carrizales, if we did not know he was sleeping, what had happened to his clever prudence, his suspicions, his forewarnings, his convictions, the high exterior walls of his house, the exclusion from it of even the shadow of anyone that had the name of male, the narrow revolving door, the thick walls, the windows without light, the notable seclusion, the large dowry he had conferred on Leonora, the constant gifts he made to her, the good treatment of her maids and slaves, not omitting anything of all he imagined they might need or could desire. But we have already said there was no reason to ask him this, because he was sleeping more than necessary. And if he were to hear and perhaps reply, he could not give a better answer than to shrug his shoulders and raise his eyebrows and say: "All of this was demolished down to the foundations, in my opinion, by the astuteness of an idle, licentious young man, the malice of a false duenna, and the carelessness of a cajoled and susceptible girl." God save everyone from such enemies, against whom there is no shield of prudence that defends, no sword of caution that cuts.

But even so, Leonora's merit was such that at the most suitable time she displayed it against the base forces of the cunning deceiver, for they were not enough to vanquish her; he exhausted himself in vain, she was victorious, and both of them slept. At this moment heaven willed that, in spite of the ointment, Carrizales awoke, and as was his custom, felt around the bed, and not finding his beloved wife, leaped from the bed in terror and astonishment, with greater agility and boldness than his many years promised; and when he did not find his wife in the bedroom, and saw the door open and the key between the mattresses missing, he thought he would lose his mind. But, controlling himself, he went out to the hall, and from there, taking very small steps so as not to be heard, he reached the room where the duenna was sleeping, and seeing her alone, without Leonora, he went to the duenna's bedroom, and opening the door very slowly, saw what he had never wanted to see, saw what he would gladly have given his eyes not to see. He saw Leonora in Loaysa's arms, sleeping as soundly as if the ointment had worked on them and not on the jealous old man.

Carrizales was breathless at the bitter sight of what he was seeing, his voice caught in his throat, his arms fell useless at his sides, and he was turned into a cold marble statue; and although anger did its natural work, reviving his almost dead vital spirits, grief was so strong it did not allow him to draw breath; and with it all, he would have taken the revenge that so great an evil required if he had found himself with weapons to take it; and so he determined to go to his room for a dagger and return to remove the stains on his honor with the blood of his two enemies, even with all the blood of all the people in his house. With this honorable and necessary decision, he returned, as silently and cautiously as he had come, to his room, where grief and anguish tightened so much around his heart that, incapable of anything else, he fell on the bed in a swoon.

Day arrived and caught the new adulterers entwined in the net of their arms. Marialonso awoke, and wished to go to receive what, in her opinion, was hers; but seeing it was late, she decided to leave it for the following night. Leonora became agitated when she saw the day so far gone, and she cursed her carelessness and that of her perverse duenna, and the two women, with rapid steps, went to where her husband was, murmuring a prayer to heaven that they would find him still snoring; and when they saw him lying silently on the bed, they believed the ointment was still working because he was asleep, and with great delight they embraced each other. Leonora went up to her husband, and grasping him by the arm she turned him from one side to the other to see whether he awoke with no need to wash him with vinegar, which they said was necessary for him to regain consciousness. But with the motion, Carrizales recovered from his swoon, and sighing deeply, in a sorrowful, faint voice, he said:

"Woe is me, what a sad end my fortune has brought me to!"

Leonora did not really hear what her husband said, but since she saw him awake and speaking, and was surprised to see that the effect of the ointment did not last as long as she had been told, she went up to him, and placing her face next to his, and holding him tightly, she said:

"What is wrong, my lord, for it seems you are complaining?"

The unfortunate old man heard the voice of his sweet enemy, and opening his eyes very wide, as if both astonished and bewitched, he turned them toward

her, and very intently, not blinking, he looked at her for a long time, at the end
of which he said to her:

"If you would be so kind, Señora, please send for your parents right away
on my behalf, because I feel something in my heart that causes me great pain
and anguish; I fear it will take my life very soon, and I should like to see them
before I die."

Leonora undoubtedly believed that what her husband was saying was true,
thinking that the potency of the ointment, and not what he had seen, had
brought him to this crisis; and responding that she would do as he asked, she
told the black man to go immediately for her parents, and embracing her husband, gave him the most intense caresses she had ever given him and asked
him how he was feeling with words as tender and loving as if he were the thing
in the world she loved best. He looked at her as if bewitched, as we have said,
each of her words and caresses the thrust of a lance that pierced his soul.

The duenna had already told the people in the house and Loaysa about her
master's illness, insisting it had to be serious because he had forgotten to order
the street doors locked when Luis went out to summon her mistress's parents;
the request itself surprised them, because neither one had ever entered that
house after they married their daughter to Carrizales.

In short, everyone was silent and astonished, unaware of the true cause of
the indisposition of their master, who from time to time heaved sighs so deep
and so melancholy that his soul seemed uprooted with each one.

Leonora wept to see him in that state, and he laughed with the laugh of a
person who was beside himself as he considered the falsity of her tears.

Leonora's parents arrived, and as they found the street and courtyard doors
open, and the house buried in silence and seemingly empty, they were taken
by surprise and felt quite alarmed. They went to their son-in-law's room and
found him, as we have said, staring at his wife, whose hands he grasped as both
of them shed copious tears; she, simply because her husband was weeping; he,
because he saw how deceptively she cried.

As soon as her parents came in, Carrizales spoke and said:

"Sit down, your graces, and the rest of you, with the exception of Señora
Marialonso, leave this room."

They did as he asked, and when the five of them were alone, and not waiting for anyone else to speak, in a calm voice and wiping his eyes, this is what
Carrizales said:

"My parents and señores, I am certain it will not be necessary to bring in
witnesses for you to believe a truth I wish to tell you. You must remember, it is
not possible it has dropped from memory, with how much love and goodwill

you gave me your beloved daughter to be my legitimate wife one year, one month, five days, and nine hours ago. You also know what a generous dowry I provided, a dowry that more than three girls could use to marry and still be called rich. And your graces must also recall the care I took in dressing and adorning her with everything she could find to desire and I could determine would suit her. And certainly your graces have seen, Señores, how, moved by my nature and fearful of the ailment of which I undoubtedly shall die, and experienced because of my advanced age in the singular and varied occurrences in the world, I wished to guard this jewel that I chose and your graces gave to me with the greatest caution possible. I raised the exterior walls of this house, I removed the view from the windows facing the street, I doubled the locks on the doors, I put in a revolving door as if it were a convent, I perpetually banished from it everything that had the shadow or the name of male; I gave her maids and slave girls to serve her; I never denied them or her anything they wished to ask of me; I made her my equal; I told her my most intimate thoughts; I gave her all my wealth. All this was done so that, if one considers it carefully, I could live sure of enjoying with no surprises what had cost me so much, and she could endeavor to give me no reason for any kind of jealous fear to enter my mind. But since one cannot prevent by human effort the punishment that the divine will wishes to inflict on those who do not place all their desires and hopes in that will, it was not long before I was thwarted in mine and became the producer of the poison that is taking my life. But, since I see the perplexity you all feel, hanging on my every word, I want to conclude the long preambles to this conversation by telling you in a word what it is not possible to say in thousands. I say then, Señores, that everything I have said and done stopped early this morning when I found this woman, born into the world for the perdition of my tranquility and the end of my life"—and he pointed at his wife—"in the arms of a handsome young man hidden right now in the room of this pestilential duenna."

No sooner had Carrizales said these last words than Leonora's heart sank and she fell into a faint across her husband's knees. Marialonso turned pale, and Leonora's parents had lumps in their throats that did not allow them to say a word. But Carrizales continued and said:

"The revenge I intend to take for this affront is not and will not be one of those ordinarily taken, for just as I was excessive in what I did, my revenge should also be immoderate, inflicted on myself as the one most guilty in this transgression; for it must be considered that there should be no compassion for a man who overlooked the disparity between this girl's fifteen years and his own, which number almost eighty. I was the one who, like the silkworm, built the house for my own death, and I do not blame you, oh badly advised child!"—and saying this he leaned over and kissed the face of the unconscious Leonora—"I do not blame you, I say, because the persuasive arguments of crafty old women and the wooing of young men in love easily vanquish and triumph over the limited intelligence that youth possesses. But so that the whole world can see the value and worth of the desire and faith with which I loved you, in this final critical moment of my life I want to reveal it, so that it stays in the world as an example, if not of goodness, at least of innocence never before seen or heard. And so I want a scribe brought here, for I wish to make a new will, in which I shall double Leonora's dowry and ask that when my life is over, for my days are numbered, she arrange to be married, and she can do it easily, to that boy whom the white hairs of this pitiable old man never offended; in this way she will see that, if while I lived I never moved a jot away from what I thought would please her, in death I am doing the same thing, and I want her to be with the one she must love so much. The rest of my wealth I shall use for other pious works, and to your graces, Señores, I shall leave enough for you to live honorably the rest of your lives. Let the scribe come soon, because the emotion I feel presses me so that it is shortening the days of my life."

Having said this, he succumbed to a terrible swoon and fell so close to Leonora that their faces were next to each other: a strange, sad spectacle for the parents who looked at their dear daughter and beloved son-in-law. The wicked duenna did not want to wait for the censure she thought she would receive from her mistress's parents, and so she left the room and went to tell Loaysa everything that had happened, advising him to leave the house immediately, and she would be sure to inform the black man of all that had occurred, for there were no more doors or keys to constrain him. Loaysa marveled at the news, and taking her advice, dressed again as a beggar and went to tell his friends about the strange, never-before-seen outcome of his love affair.

In the meantime, while the husband and wife were both in a faint, Leonora's father sent for a friend who was a scribe, and who arrived when his daughter and son-in-law had regained consciousness. Carrizales made his will as he had said he would, with no mention of Leonora's error except to say that for good reason he asked and requested that she marry, if he should die, the young man he had mentioned to her in secret. When Leonora heard this, she threw herself at her husband's feet, and with her heart pounding in her chest, she said:

"Live for many years, my lord and my love, and since you are not obliged to believe anything I say, you should know that I have not offended you except in my thoughts."

And as she began to ask forgiveness and recount in detail the truth of the matter, she could not move her tongue and fainted again. The grieving old man embraced her, though she was in a swoon; her parents embraced her; everyone wept so bitterly that they obliged and even forced the scribe to join them as he was writing the will, in which Carrizales left enough to support all the maids in the house, freed the slave girls and the black man, and gave the false Marialonso nothing but the salary owed her; be that as it may, sorrow so overwhelmed him that he was buried seven days later.

Leonora was left a widow, weeping and rich; and while Loaysa waited for what he already knew her husband had stated in his will, he saw that within a week she had entered one of the most cloistered convents in the city. He, disheartened and chagrined, went to the Indies. Leonora's parents were left exceedingly sad, although they took comfort in what their son-in-law had left them in his will. The maids were consoled in the same way, the slaves, by their freedom, and the perverse duenna was left poor and disappointed in all her immoral thoughts.

And I was left with the desire to come to the end of this matter, a model and example of how little faith should be put in keys, revolving doors, and walls when the will is free, and even less trust in green and immature youth if their ears are subjected to the exhortations of duennas in their long, black nuns' habits and outspread white headdresses. What I do not know is the reason Leonora did not beg forgiveness with more zeal and let her jealous husband know how pure and without offense she had emerged from these events, but embarrassment tied her tongue, and the speed with which her husband died left no room for her excuses.

THE NOVEL OF THE ILLUSTRIOUS SCULLERY MAID

Two prominent, wealthy gentlemen lived, not long ago, in the illustrious and famous city of Burgos; one was named Don Diego de Carriazo, and the other Don Juan de Avendaño. Don Diego had a son to whom he gave his own name, and Don Juan had another whom he named Don Tomás de Avendaño. Since they will be principal personages in this story, and to eliminate and save letters, we shall simply call these two young gentlemen Carriazo and Avendaño.

Carriazo must have been thirteen years old, or a little older, when, carried away by a picaresque bent and not obliged by any bad treatment from his parents but only by his own pleasure and whim, he broke away, as the boys say, from his parents' house and went out into the world, so happy in the free life that, in the midst of the discomforts and miseries that come with it, he did not miss the abundance in his father's house, nor did going on foot tire him, nor cold displease him, nor heat bother him. For Carriazo, all the seasons of the year were sweet, temperate spring; he slept as well on a pile of unthreshed wheat as on a mattress, and burrowed into the hayloft of an inn with as much pleasure as if he were lying between sheets of Holland linen. In brief, he did so well in the matter of being a rogue that he could have taught classes on the subject to the celebrated Alfarache.[1]

In the three years it took him to return home, he learned to throw knucklebones in Madrid, play rentoy in the Ventillas of Toledo, and lansquenet between the walls of Sevilla;[2] but even though indigence and poverty are intrinsic to this kind of life, Carriazo behaved like a prince in his affairs. Even from a distance he revealed in a thousand ways that he was well born because he was generous and equitable with his companions. He rarely visited the hermitages of Bacchus, and although he drank wine, it was so little he never could enter the company of those called unfortunate whose faces, when they drink too much, look as if they had been painted with vermillion and red ochre. In short, in Carriazo the world saw a rogue who was virtuous, clean,

1. *Guzmán de Alfarache* (1599) was a picaresque novel by Mateo Alemán.
2. The three games correspond to popular sites of picaresque activity in Spain.

well mannered, and more than a little intelligent. He passed through all the ranks of roguery until he graduated with a master's degree in catching tuna with nets in Zahara, the *non plus ultra* of the rogue's life.[3]

Oh kitchen scullions, dirty, fat, and florid, feigned paupers, false cripples, pickpockets of the Zocodover in Toledo and the Plaza in Madrid, blind reciters of prayers who can see, porters of Sevilla, servants of the underworld, along with all the infinite throng that falls under the name of rogue! Deflate your pride, lower your ardor, and do not call yourselves rogues if you have not taken two courses in the academy of fishing for tuna! There, there, work along with idleness are in their element! There is clean filth, rounded corpulence, ready hunger, abundant satiety, undisguised vice, gambling always, quarrels continuously, deaths at each moment, obscenities at every step, dances as if at a wedding, well-known seguidillas, ballads with refrains, poetry unrestrained. Here they sing, there they blaspheme, farther on they quarrel, over here they gamble, and everywhere they steal. There liberty takes the field and work shines. There many distinguished fathers go, or send someone, to look for their sons, and find them, and are as sorry to take them away from that life as if they were taking them to their death.

But all this sweetness I have depicted has an acrid juice that makes it bitter, and it is their not being able to sleep secure from the fear that in an instant they will be transported from Zahara to Barbary.[4] For this reason they gather at nights at the watchtowers and have their squadrons of cavalry and sentries on patrol, and confidence in their eyes allows sleepers to close theirs, although at times it has happened that sentries and cavalry, rogues, their chiefs, boats, nets, and the entire multitude that occupies the place have gone to sleep in Spain and awakened in Tetuán. But this fear was not the reason that after three summers our Carriazo stopped going there to enjoy himself. The last summer he had such good luck that he won close to seven hundred *reales* at cards, and with them he wanted to buy new clothes and return to Burgos and to his mother's eyes, which had shed so many tears for him. He took leave of his friends, for he had many, and many good ones, and promised he would be with them the following summer, if sickness or death did not prevent him. He left half his soul with them, and all his desires he

3. Zahara de los Atunes (literally "Zahara of the Tunas") is a town in Cádiz known for its tuna, which was caught using an ancient technique called the "almadraba."

4. Barbary, on the coast of North Africa, was known for its corsairs who would capture Spaniards for ransom.

fixed on those dry sands, which to him seemed fresher and greener than the Elysian Fields. And being accustomed to traveling by foot, he took to the road and on two espadrilles walked from Zahara to Valladolid singing "Three Geese, Mother."[5] He stayed there two weeks to correct the color of his face, changing mulatto to Flemish, erasing the traces of the roguish life and preparing a clean copy of a gentleman.

He did all this with the possibilities provided by the five hundred *reales* he brought with him to Valladolid, and he set aside a hundred of them to hire a mule and a servant so he could appear before his parents upright and content. They welcomed him with great joy, and all their friends and kin came to congratulate them on the safe arrival of their son, Señor Don Diego de Carriazo. It should be noted that during his travels, Don Diego had changed the name Carriazo to Urdiales, which is what he was called by people who did not know his real name. Among those who came to see the recent arrival were Don Juan de Avendaño and his son Don Tomás, with whom Carriazo, since both were the same age and neighbors, had struck up and confirmed a very close friendship.

Carriazo told his parents and everyone else a thousand long, magnificent lies about things that had happened to him during the three years of his absence. But he never touched on or even dreamed of telling them about catching tuna in nets, although he was constantly imagining it, especially when he saw it would soon be the time when he had promised his friends he would return. He did not enjoy the hunt that occupied his father, nor did he take pleasure in the many decent, agreeable gatherings customary in that city; every pastime bored him, and he preferred tuna fishing to all the principal entertainments offered him.

His friend, Avendaño, often seeing him melancholy and pensive, trusted in their friendship and dared ask him the reason, promising to remedy it if he could, with his very blood if necessary. Carriazo did not wish to hide anything from him in order not to offend the great friendship they professed; and so he recounted in detail the rogue's life, and how all his sadness and pensiveness were born of the desire he had to return to it. He depicted it in such a way that Avendaño, when he finished listening to him, praised rather than condemned his wish.

In short, their talk concluded with Carriazo preparing Avendaño's desire to accompany him and enjoy for a summer the joyful life he had described,

5. A line from a common song for travelers.

which made Carriazo extremely happy, for it seemed to him he had gained a defense witness to vindicate his base resolve. They also planned to obtain all the money they could; and the best way they came upon was that in two months Avendaño was supposed to go to Salamanca, where for three years he had been studying Greek and Latin for his own pleasure, and now his father wanted him to move ahead and study whatever he chose at the university, and he would give him money to do so.

This was when Carriazo proposed to his father his desire to go with Avendaño to study at Salamanca. His father agreed so happily that he spoke to Avendaño's father and they arranged for them to live in the same house in Salamanca, with all the requisites demanded by their being the sons of noble fathers.

The time arrived for their departure, and their fathers provided them with money and sent with them a tutor to guide them, a man who had more kindness in his nature than competence. The fathers gave their sons advice regarding what they should do and how they were to behave to progress in virtue and the sciences, the fruit every student should attempt to obtain from his efforts and studies, particularly those who are well born. The sons showed themselves humble and obedient; the mothers wept; they received everyone's blessing and set out with their own mules and two house servants as well as the tutor, who had allowed his beard to grow to lend authority to his position.

When they reached Valladolid, they told the tutor they wanted to spend two days seeing it, because they had never seen or visited the city. The tutor reprimanded them severely and harshly for the visit, saying that those who were going to study as soon as they were could not stop for even an hour, let alone two days, to look at foolishness, and he would have reason for concern if he were to allow them to stop even for an instant, and so they had to leave immediately, otherwise they would have to face the consequences.

This was the extent of the ability of the tutor, or steward, whatever we choose to call him. The boys, who already had the money they needed, for they had stolen four hundred gold *escudos* their tutor was carrying, said he should let them stay only that day, for they wanted to see the Argales Fountain, where large, wide aqueducts were already beginning to carry water.[6] Though with a sorrowful spirit, he gave them permission, because he wished to excuse the waste of that night by stopping in Valdeastillas and traveling in two days the eighteen leagues from Valdeastillas to Salamanca rather than the twenty-

6. The Argales Fountain was part of an aqueduct built in the fifteenth century and expanded in the sixteenth century to supply water to Valladolid.

two from Valladolid. But since the horse thinks one way and the man saddling him another, everything happened contrary to his wishes.

The young lads, with only one servant and riding on two very good, home-raised mules, rode out to see the fountain of Argales, famous for its age and its water, in spite of the Caño Dorado and the reverend Priora, not to mention Leganitos and the very great Castellana Fountain, and in this competition we can be silent about Corpa and the Pizarra de la Mancha.[7] They reached Argales, and when the servant thought Avendaño was removing from the saddle-bags a vessel to drink from, he saw him take out a sealed letter, and Avendaño told him to return to the city immediately and give the missive to their tutor and then wait for them at the Campo Gate.

The servant obeyed; he took the letter and returned to the city, and they went in the opposite direction and that night slept in Mojados, and two days after that in Madrid, and in another four sold the mules at a public auction, and someone trusted them for a share of six *escudos*, and someone even gave them the full asking price in gold. They dressed as peasants, in short, two-paneled ponchos, wide, baggy breeches, and stockings of drab cloth. A clothes dealer bought their clothing in the morning and by evening had changed them so much that the mothers who bore them would not have recognized them.

Having cast off the trappings of their station, just as Avendaño wished and recognized, they set out for Toledo *ad pedem literae*[8] and without their swords; for the clothes dealer, though they were not pertinent to his business, had bought them too.

Let us leave them for now, for they are traveling contented and happy, and resume the account of what the tutor did when he opened the letter the servant brought him and found that it said this:

> *May it please your grace, Señor Pedro Alonso, to have patience and return to Burgos, where your grace will tell our parents that we, their sons, with mature consideration, having reflected on how much more appropriate arms are to gentlemen than letters, have decided to trade Salamanca for Brussels and Spain for Flanders. We are taking the four hundred* escudos; *we plan to sell the mules. Our noble intention and the long road ahead are a sufficient excuse for our error, although no one will judge it as such*

7. These are all fountains that would have been found around Madrid.

8. Literally, "to the foot of the letter," meaning exactly as something is written. Here, the phrase is used to indicate that they traveled by foot.

unless he is a coward. Our departure is now; our return when it pleases
God, and may He keep your grace as He can and as we your most humble
servants desire. From the fountain of Argales, with our feet in the stirrups
on the road to Flanders.

Carriazo and Avendaño

Pedro Alonso was bewildered as he read the letter and hurried to his travel bag, and finding it empty confirmed the truth of the letter; and then, on the mule he still had, he left immediately for Burgos to give the news to his masters as quickly as possible, because that would allow them to find a solution and discover a way to overtake their sons. But the author of this novel says nothing about these matters, because as soon as he had Pedro Alonso on the back of the mule, he returned to his account of what happened to Avendaño and Carriazo at the entrance to Illescas, saying that when they passed through the town gate they encountered two young mule drivers who looked Andalusian, wearing wide linen breeches, slashed doublets of canvas, sleeveless buckskin jackets, large *quillon* daggers, and swords without belts. Apparently, one was coming from Sevilla and the other was going there. The one going was saying to the other:

"If my masters were not so far ahead of me, I'd stop even longer to ask you a thousand things I want to know; because you've amazed me with what you've said about how the count hanged Alonso Genís and Ribera without the consent of the High Court."[9]

"Oh, sinner that I am!" replied the Sevillan. "The count set a trap for them, and took them under his jurisdiction, illegally because they were soldiers, and passed judgment on them, and the high court couldn't save them. You should know, friend, that this Count Puñonrostro has a Beelzebub inside who pierces our souls with his fingers. Sevilla is swept clean of thugs for ten leagues around; no thief stops inside the city limits. Everybody is as frightened of him as they are of fire, though the word is he'll leave the post of Deputy Governor because it is not in his nature to find himself constantly at odds with the gentlemen of the High Court."

"May they live a thousand years," said the one going to Sevilla, "for they are fathers to the poor and shelter to the unfortunate! How many poor wretches are dead and buried just because of the rage of an arbitrary judge, a badly informed or very impassioned magistrate! But many eyes see more than two can; the poison of injustice does not overpower many hearts as quickly as it does just one."

---

9. Alonso Genís and Ribera were famous criminals in sixteenth-century Spain.

"You've turned into a preacher," said the boy from Sevilla, "and at this rate you won't finish very quickly and I can't wait for you. And tonight don't go to your usual inn but to the Sevillan's inn, because there you'll see the most beautiful scullery maid anyone's ever heard of. Marinilla from the Tejada inn is disgusting compared to her. I won't tell you any more, but it's well known that the Magistrate's son is head over heels in love with her. One of my masters over there swears that when he gets back from Andalucía he'll spend two months in Toledo in that inn just so he can see her as much as he wants. I already gave her a pinch as a sign, and what I got back was a slap on both cheeks. She's as hard as marble, and as stubborn as the peasant of Sayago,[10] and as harsh as a nettle, but she has a face that brings joy and features that make you want to sing; on one cheek she has the sun and on the other the moon; one is made of roses and the other of carnations, and on both there are also lilies and jasmines. I'll say no more except that you should see her, and you'll see that I haven't told you anything compared to what I could have said about her beauty. I'd gladly give her my two gray mules as a dowry if they would give her to me as my wife; but I know they won't, she's a jewel for an archpriest or a count. And I'll tell you again that you can see her there; and goodbye, I'm gone."

And with this the two mule drivers said goodbye; their talk and conversation left the two friends, who had listened to them, speechless, especially Avendaño, in whom the mule driver's simple account of the scullery maid's beauty awoke an intense desire to see her. And in Carriazo too, but not so much that he did not wish to reach his fishing nets more than he desired to stop to see the pyramids of Egypt, or another of the seven wonders, or all of them together.

Repeating the words of the mule drivers and imitating and copying their manner and gestures entertained them on their way to Toledo; and immediately, with Carriazo as guide, for he had been in that city before, going down Sangre de Cristo,[11] they came to the Sevillan's inn; but they did not dare ask for rooms because they were so poorly dressed.

It was dusk, and although Carriazo importuned Avendaño that they go elsewhere to find lodging, he could not get him away from the door to the Sevillan's inn, waiting to see if by chance the celebrated scullery maid would appear. Night fell, and the scullery maid did not come out; Carriazo was losing his patience and Avendaño would not move. To achieve his aim, using the excuse of asking after some gentlemen from Burgos who were going to the city of Sevilla,

10. A common, stereotyped character from Golden Age theater.
11. A stairway in the Zocodover Plaza in Toledo.

Avendaño entered the inn as far as the courtyard. And, as soon as he had, he saw a girl come out of a room off the courtyard; she looked fifteen or so, was dressed like a peasant, and carried a lit candle in a candlestick. Avendaño did not look at the girl's dress or clothes but at her face, and it seemed to him like the faces of angels in paintings. He was overwhelmed and amazed by her beauty, so enthralled and astonished he could not ask her anything. The girl, seeing that man before her, said:

"What are you looking for, brother? Are you by chance a servant to one of the guests in the inn?"

"I'm not anyone's servant but yours," responded Avendaño, so great were his confusion and shock.

The girl, who heard him respond in that manner, said:

"Well, then, brother, luckily those of us who serve have no need of servants."

And calling her master, she said:

"Señor, see what this young man wants."

Her master came out and asked him what he wanted. He said he was looking for some gentlemen from Burgos on their way to Sevilla, one of whom was his master, who had gone ahead to Alcalá de Henares where he had important business, and he had told him to go to Toledo and wait for him at the Sevillan's inn, where he would lodge, and he thought he would arrive tonight or tomorrow at the latest. Avendaño told his lie so well that the innkeeper believed it was true, and told him:

"Stay, friend, at the inn, and you can wait here for your master until he comes."

"You're very kind, innkeeper," responded Avendaño, "and if your grace prepares a room for me and a friend who is traveling with me and is outside, we have money to pay for it as well as any other man."

"That's fine," said the innkeeper.

And turning to the girl, he said:

"Costancica, tell Argüello to take these fellows to the corner room and give them clean sheets."

"I shall, Señor," replied Costanza, for that was the girl's name.

And curtsying to her master, she left them, and for Avendaño her absence was what the setting of the sun and the coming of sad, dark night usually is for the traveler. Even so, he went out to recount to Carriazo what he had seen and what he had arranged; by a thousand signs Carriazo knew his friend had been smitten by the disease of love, but he did not want to say anything to him until he could see whether the person who had engendered the extraordinary praise and great hyperbole with which Costanza's beauty was extolled to the skies actually deserved it.

Finally they entered the inn and Argüello, who was a woman about forty-five years old, in charge of the beds and cleaning the rooms, led them to one that was not for gentlemen or servants but for people somewhere between the two extremes. They asked for supper; Argüello responded that in this inn they did not give food to anyone but cooked and prepared what their guests brought in, but there were taverns and public houses nearby where they could eat whatever they liked with no problem. They took Argüello's advice and went to a tavern where Carriazo dined on what he was given and Avendaño on what he brought with him, which were thoughts and fancies.

The little or nothing that Avendaño ate surprised Carriazo very much. To learn his friend's thinking in its entirety, when they returned to the inn he said to him:

"It's a good idea for us to get up at dawn tomorrow, so that we're in Orgaz before the worst of the heat."

"I'm not thinking about that," answered Avendaño, "because I'm thinking that before I leave this city I should see what it has that's famous, like the Sacrarium,[12] the device that Juanelo built,[13] the Heights of San Agustín,[14] the Orchard of the King,[15] and the Plain."[16]

"That's fine," replied Carriazo, "you can see that in two days."

"The truth is that I plan to take it slow, we're not going to Rome to petition for rank or position."

"Aha!" said Carriazo. "By my life, friend, you want to stay in Toledo more than you want to continue the pilgrimage we've already begun!"

"That's true," responded Avendaño, "and it will be as impossible for me to stop seeing that girl's face as it is not possible to go to heaven without good works."

"Elegant praise," said Carriazo, "and a determination worthy of a heart as generous as yours! Perfectly suited to a Don Tomás de Avendaño, son of Don Juan de Avendaño, gentleman, which is good; rich, which is sufficient; young, which brings joy; discerning, which is admirable; and madly in love with a scullery maid who serves in the Sevillan's inn!"

12. The tabernacle in the Toledo Cathedral.
13. The device is a waterwheel on the Tajo River built by Juanelo Turriano.
14. An area with picturesque views alongside Toledo's Bridge of San Martín.
15. An ancient orchard along the Tajo River.
16. Another famous area of Toledo along the Tajo River.

"I think the same when I consider," responded Avendaño, "Don Diego de Carriazo, son of a father with the same name, the father a knight of the Order of Alcántara, and the son about to inherit his fortune through primogeniture, as gallant in body as he is in spirit, and with all these generous attributes, who do you think he loves? Queen Guinevere? No, of course not, but tuna fishing in Zahara, which is uglier, I believe, than one of the temptations of St. Anthony!"

"Hoisted on my own petard, friend!" responded Carriazo. "You've killed me with the blades I used to wound you; let's leave our dispute here, and go to sleep, and tomorrow we can resolve everything."

"Look, Carriazo, so far you haven't seen Costanza; when you do, I give you permission to insult or reprimand me as much as you wish."

"I already know how this is going to end," said Carriazo.

"How?" replied Avendaño.

"I'll go to my tuna nets and you'll stay with your scullery maid," said Carriazo.

"I won't be so fortunate," said Avendaño.

"And I won't be foolish enough," said Carriazo, "to stop striving for my good because you follow a foolish whim."

They reached the inn having this conversation, and spent half the night in others similar to it. And having slept, it seemed to them, little more than an hour, the sound of many flageolets playing in the street woke them. They sat up in bed and listened attentively, and Carriazo said:

"I'll wager that it's day and there must be a feast day in the nearby convent of Our Lady of Carmen, and that's why they're playing those flageolets."

"It's not that," responded Avendaño, "because we didn't sleep long enough for it to be day already."

As they were talking, they heard a knock at the door to their room, and when they asked who it was, the answer was:

"Boys, if you want to hear some good music, get up and go to the grilled window that faces the street in the room across the way, nobody's in it."

They both got up, and when they opened the door, they did not see anyone and did not know who had given them the news; but because they heard the sound of a harp, they believed the music was real, and so, in their underclothes, just as they were, they went to the room where another three or four guests were standing at the grilled windows. They found a spot, and soon, to the sound of a harp and a *vihuela*, they heard this sonnet being sung in a marvelous voice that remained in Avendaño's memory:

   Singular, humble creature who elevates
   beauty to sublimity so exalted

that in it all nature surpasses herself
and you outdistance even highest heaven;
   if you speak, or if you laugh, or if you sing,
if you show gentleness or asperity,
as the effect alone of your elegance
you enchant the faculties of our souls.
   So that the unmatched beauty you possess
and the pure chastity you celebrate
may be better known and apprehended,
   abandon service, for you should be served
by all who see your hands and see your temples
gleaming because of scepters and of crowns.

It was not necessary for anyone to tell them that the music was being played for Costanza, for the sonnet had revealed that very clearly, and the way the music sounded to Avendaño's ears meant that he would have thought it good if, in order not to have heard it, he had been born deaf and would remain deaf all the rest of his days, because from that point on he began to consider it as bad as the person who finds his heart pierced by the harsh lance of jealousy. And the worst thing was that he did not know of whom he should or could be jealous. But soon that concern was resolved by one of those at the window, who said:

"What a fool this Magistrate's son is to go around playing music for a scullery maid! It's true she's one of the most beautiful girls I've seen, and I've seen many, but that's no reason for him to court her so publicly."

To which another of those at the window added:

"The truth is I've heard it said, and very reliably, that she pays no more attention to him than she would to a nobody; I'll wager she's sleeping like a log now behind her mistress's bed, where they say she sleeps, not thinking at all about music or songs."

"That's true," replied the other man, "because she's the most virtuous girl you can imagine, and it's a miracle that in a house like this, with so much coming and going, and new people every day, and her going into all the rooms, not the slightest misbehavior in the world is known about her."

When Avendaño heard this, he began to come back to life and catch his breath, so he could listen to many other things the musicians sang to the sound of different instruments, all the songs meant for Costanza who, as the guest had said, was sleeping peacefully.

When day came the musicians left, taking their flageolets. Avendaño and Carriazo returned to their room, where whoever could sleep slept till morning;

and then the two of them got up, both desiring to see Costanza, but the desire of one was curious, and that of the other enamored. But Costanza obliged both by coming out of her master's parlor, so beautiful they both thought all the mule driver's praise was scant and not really praise at all.

Her clothes consisted of a skirt and bodice of green cloth with an edging of the same cloth. Her bodice was low cut but her blouse was cut high, with a pleated collar, a collar-band of embroidered black silk, like a necklace of jet stars around a piece of alabaster column, for her throat was no less white; her belt was a cord of St. Francis, and on the right side, on a pendent ribbon, hung a large assortment of keys. She did not wear mules but red shoes with two soles and leggings that could not be seen except for a shadow that revealed they were red as well. Her hair was braided with white silk threads, but the braid was so long it passed over her shoulders to her waist; the color was not quite chestnut, touching on blonde, but, it seemed, so clean, so even, so well combed that none, even if made of threads of gold, could compare. From her ears hung two small pumpkin-shaped pieces of glass that looked like pearls; her hair itself served as her net coif and headdress.

When she left the parlor she crossed herself and made a deep curtsy before an image of Our Lady hanging on one of the walls of the courtyard; and looking up, she saw the two young men with their gaze fixed on her, and as soon as she saw them she withdrew and returned to the parlor, where she called to Argüello to get up.

It remains to be said what Carriazo thought of Costanza's beauty, for we have already said what Avendaño thought of it when he saw her for the first time. I shall say only that Carriazo thought it as perfect as his friend did but fell much less in love, so much less that he did not want night to find him in the inn but wished to leave immediately for his fishing.

When Costanza called, Argüello came out to the passageways with two other hefty young women who were also maids and, it is said, from Galicia; and this number of maids was required because of the many people who frequented the Sevillan's inn, which was one of the best and busiest in Toledo. The guests' mule drivers also came in to ask for barley. The innkeeper came out to give it to them, cursing his maids, for it was because of them that a servant had left who had kept his accounts very well for him and, in his opinion, had not missed a single grain of feed. Avendaño heard this and said:

"Don't be concerned, innkeeper, give me the accounts book, and in the days I'm here I'll have it in such good order, showing the barley and straw that are requested, that you won't miss the servant you say has left you."

"I'm truly grateful, young man," replied the innkeeper, "because I can't take care of this; I have many other matters to attend to in addition to the inn. Come down; I'll give you the book, and be careful, because these mule drivers are the very devil and cheat and steal from a bushel of barley with less conscience than if it was straw."

Avendaño went down to the courtyard and devoted himself to the book, and began dispatching bushels like water, and writing them down in so orderly a way that the innkeeper, who was watching him, was very happy and said:

"May it please God that your master doesn't come and you'll want to stay here; changing your circumstances will change your luck, because the boy who left came here about eight months ago, ragged and skinny, and now he has two very good sets of clothes and is as fat as an otter. Because I want you to know, son, that in this house there is money to be made aside from your food and wages."

"If I stayed," replied Avendaño, "I wouldn't pay much attention to profits, because I'd be happy with anything in exchange for being in this city that I've heard is the best in Spain."

"At least," said the innkeeper, "it's one of the best and richest. But we need something else now, which is to find someone to go to the river for water, because another boy left me too, and with an admirable donkey of mine, he kept the water jars overflowing and the house turned into a lake. And one of the reasons mule drivers like to bring their masters to my inn is because of the abundance of water they always find here, so they don't have to take their animals to the river and their mounts can drink from large tubs here in the house."

Carriazo heard all this, and seeing that Avendaño had found a place and work in the inn, he did not want to be left with nothing, especially when he considered the great pleasure it would give Avendaño if he followed his lead; and so he said to the innkeeper:

"Bring on the donkey, innkeeper, for I'll know how to girth it and load it as well as my friend knows how to record your goods in the ledger."

"Yes," said Avendaño, "my friend Lope the Asturian will carry water like a prince, and I guarantee him."

Argüello, who was listening from the passageway to all this talk, hearing Avendaño say that he guaranteed his friend, said:

"Tell me, good sir, who will guarantee him? In truth it seems to me there is more need to guarantee him than for him to do the guaranteeing."

"Be quiet, Argüello," said the innkeeper, "don't meddle in what doesn't concern you; I guarantee both of them, and on your life you girls better not have any disputes with the boys who work here, because you're the reason all of them leave."

"And what," said another maid, "these young men are staying here now? By my faith, if I were traveling with them, I'd never trust the wineskin with them."

"Enough bad jokes, Señora Galician," responded the innkeeper, "and get back to work, and don't interfere with the boys or I'll give you a beating you won't forget."

"Oh yeah, sure," replied the Galician. "Just see what jewels for me to yearn for! The truth is that my good master hasn't found me so playful with the boys in the inn or on the outside to have so bad a 'pinion of me. They're scoundrels, and they'll leave whenever they feel like it without us girls giving them any reason. Nice people, I'll say, they don't need any encouragement to leave their masters in the lurch when they least expect it."

"You talk a lot, Galician," responded her master. "Stitch up your mouth, sister, and take care of what you have to do."

By this time Carriazo had harnessed the donkey, and leaping onto its back, left for the river, leaving Avendaño very happy to have seen his valiant resolve.

Here it is: we now have—may it be the right time to recount it—Avendaño turned into a servant named Tomás Pedro in the inn, for that is what he said his name was, and Carriazo, with the name of Lope the Asturian, turned into a water carrier; metamorphoses worthy of being placed ahead of those by the sharp-nosed poet, Publius Ovidius Naso.[17]

No sooner had Argüello understood that the two were going to remain at the inn than she fixed her eye on the Asturian and took him for her own, deciding to treat him so well that even if his nature were distant and withdrawn, she would make him more pliant than a glove. The more affected Galician had the same thought regarding Avendaño, and since the two maids were great friends in their dealings and conversation, and because they slept in the same room, one immediately told the other of her amorous decision, and beginning that night they resolved to begin the conquest of their two uninterested lovers. But the first thing they realized was that they would have to ask the boys not to be jealous because of things they might see them do, because the girls cannot treat those inside well if they do not have paying customers on the outside.

"Be still, brothers," the girls said as if they had them present and were already their real fancy men or lovers, "be still and cover your eyes, and let the

17. Publius Ovidius Naso is better known simply as Ovid. The final last name, Naso, is Latin for nose; hence the epithet.

one who knows how play the tambourine, and let the one who understands lead the dance, and there won't be two canons in this city more pampered than you will be by these two earners of yours."

These and other words of the same nature and kind were said by the Galician and Argüello, and in the meantime our good Lope the Asturian was on his way to the river along the Carmen slope, his thoughts on tuna fishing and the sudden alteration in his status. Either for this reason, or because fate so ordained it, in a narrow pass as he came down the hill he encountered a water carrier's donkey on his way up, loaded with water. And since he was going down and his donkey was spirited, well-disposed, and not very tired, it bumped into the tired, skinny one that was going up and knocked it to the ground, and since the jugs broke, the water spilled, and because of this misfortune the old water carrier, resentful and full of anger, attacked the new water carrier who was still astride the donkey, and before he could move and dismount, the old one had hit and settled on him a dozen hard blows with his stick that did not do the Asturian much good.

He got down at last but was so furious he rushed at his enemy, grasped his neck with both hands, threw him to the ground, and hit his head so hard against a rock that it cracked open in two places and gushed so much blood he thought he had killed him.

Many other water carriers came along, and when they saw their friend in that awful condition they attacked Lope and held him tight, shouting:

"Help! Call the law! This water carrier has killed a man!"

Along with these words and shouts, they beat him with sticks and punched him in the face. Others came to help the fallen man and saw that his head was split, and he was about to expire. The news traveled from mouth to mouth up the slope, and in the Plaza del Carmen they reached the ears of a bailiff who, with two constables, came to the place where the fight had occurred more quickly than if he had flown, in time to see the wounded man stretched out across his donkey; they had seized Lope's animal, and he was surrounded by more than twenty water carriers who did not allow him to turn around but were crushing his ribs so that he had more reason to fear for his life than the wounded man, considering how the fists and staffs of those avengers of other people's injuries rained down on him.

The bailiff arrived, moved the people away, handed the Asturian over to his constables, and taking his donkey by the reins and leading the wounded man on his animal, he took them to prison, accompanied by so many people and so many boys following him he could barely make his way along the streets.

At the sound of all those people, Tomás Pedro and his master came to the door of the inn to see what the cause of so much shouting could be and discovered Lope between the two constables, his face and mouth covered in blood. The innkeeper immediately looked for his donkey and saw it being led by another constable who had joined them. He asked the reason for the arrests and was told the truth of what had happened. He felt sorry about his donkey, fearing he would lose it or, at least, have to pay more to get it back than it was worth.

Tomás Pedro followed his friend but could not manage to say a word to him because of the press of people and the zeal of the constables and the bailiff. In fact, he could not even see him placed in the prison and in a dungeon, with two sets of shackles, and the wounded man in the infirmary, where he went to see him treated and saw that the wound was dangerous, very dangerous, and the surgeon said the same thing.

The bailiff took both donkeys to his house, along with five coins of eight *reales* each that the constables had taken from Lope.

Tomás Pedro returned to the inn filled with confusion and sadness. He found the man he now called master no less sorry than he was, and he told him how he had left his friend, and how the wounded man was in danger of dying, and what had happened to his donkey. He told him something else: another misfortune no less vexing had been added to the affliction he already suffered, and this was that he had met a good friend of his first master on the road, who had told him that because his first master was in a great hurry and wanted to avoid two leagues of travel from Madrid, he had crossed the river on the Aceca ferry and would sleep that night in Orgaz, and had given his friend twelve *escudos* to give to his servant, along with the order to go to Sevilla, where he was expecting him.

"But I can't do that," Tomás added, "because it isn't right for me to leave my friend and companion in prison and in so much peril. My master is bound to pardon me for now because he's so good and honorable he'd think any slight I committed against him is fine if it meant I didn't commit one against my friend. Your grace, master, please take the money and attend to this matter; and when it is spent, I shall write to my lord and tell him what has happened, and I know he'll send me enough money to get us out of any danger."

The innkeeper's eyes opened wide, he was so happy to see that the loss of his donkey was being remedied in part. He took the money and consoled Tomás, telling him that he had people in Toledo whose position brought them the respect of the authorities, especially a nun, kin to the Magistrate, with whom she was very close, and that a laundress for this nun's convent had a daughter who was a very close friend to the sister of a friar who was very close to the nun's confessor, and the laundress washed the clothes at home.

"And if she asks her daughter, and she will, to speak to the sister of the friar to speak to her brother to speak to the confessor, and if the confessor speaks to the nun and the nun is willing to give a note (which will be easy) to the Magistrate, asking him kindly to look into the affair, there's no doubt we can expect a good outcome, as long as the water carrier doesn't die and there's no lack of grease for the palms of all the ministers of the law, because if they aren't greased, they squeak louder than an ox cart."

Tomás was amused by his master's offers of assistance and the infinite, complicated twists and turns along which he had led him; and though he knew he had said it with more cunning than innocence, even so he thanked him for his encouragement and gave him the money, with the promise that much more would be available, according to the confidence he had in his first master, as he had already said.

Argüello, who saw her new paramour in chains, hurried immediately to the prison to bring him food, but she was not permitted to see him and came back offended and unhappy, but that did not dissuade her from her virtuous intention.

In short, in two weeks the wounded man was out of danger, and after almost three the surgeon declared him completely healed, and in this time Tomás had found a way to receive fifty *escudos* from Sevilla, and taking them from his shirt, gave them to the innkeeper with letters and the false receipt from his first master. And as the innkeeper cared little about verifying the truth of that correspondence, he took the money, all in gold *escudos*, which made him very happy.

For six *ducados* the wounded man withdrew his complaint; the Asturian was sentenced to a fine of ten *ducados*, the price of the donkey, and judicial costs. He left prison but did not wish to be with his friend again, giving as his excuse that while he had been imprisoned Argüello had visited him and told him of her love, something he found so distasteful and unpleasant that he would rather be hanged than reciprocate the desires of so wicked a woman; what he planned to do, since he was determined to continue and move forward with his purpose, was to buy a donkey and work as a water carrier for as long as they remained in Toledo; and with that disguise, he would not be tried or imprisoned as a vagrant, and with just one load of water he could spend the entire day idly wandering the city and looking at simpleminded girls.

"You'll be looking at beautiful girls, not simpleminded ones in this city, famous for having the most discerning women in Spain, and their beauty matches their intelligence; just look at Costancica, whose scraps of beauty could enrich not only the beautiful girls of this city but the whole world."

"Slow down, Señor Tomás," replied Lope. "Let's go very carefully in prais-ing Madam Scullery Maid unless you want me to think you're a heretic as well as a madman."

"Did you call Costanza a scullery maid, brother Lope?" replied Tomás. "May God forgive you and bring you to a true knowledge of your error."

"Well, isn't she a scullery maid?" replied the Asturian.

"So far I haven't seen her scour the first plate."

"It doesn't matter," said Lope, "whether you've seen her scour the first plate if you've seen her scour the second, and even the hundredth."

"I tell you, brother," replied Tomás, "she doesn't scour or know anything but her needlework, and looking after the silverware in the inn, and there's a good deal of that."

"Well, why is she called the illustrious scullery maid all over the city," said Lope, "if she doesn't scour? But it undoubtedly must be that since she scours silver, and not crockery, they call her illustrious. But leaving that aside, tell me, Tomás, what is the state of your expectations?"

"In a state of perdition," said Tomás, "because for all the days you were in prison I haven't been able to say a word to her, and in response to the many the guests say to her, she only lowers her eyes and doesn't move her lips; her mod-esty and virtue are such that her reserve inspires as much love as her beauty. What makes me lose my patience is that the Magistrate's son, who's a spirited and rather bold young man, is dying of love for her and courts her with music, and few nights go by without his musicians playing for her, and so openly that when they sing they name her, praise her, and celebrate her. But she doesn't hear them, and from nightfall till morning doesn't leave her mistress's room, a shield that doesn't allow the hard arrow of jealousy to pierce my heart."

"Well, what do you plan to do about the impossible challenge you face in conquering this Portia, this Minerva, this new Penelope, who in the figure of a maiden and a scullery maid inspires you to love, be a coward, and become feeble?"

"Mock me as much as you like, Lope my friend, for I know I'm in love with the most beautiful face that nature could shape and the most incomparable purity that one can have in the world now. Costanza is her name, not Portia, Minerva, or Penelope; she serves in an inn, which I cannot deny, but what can I do if it seems to me that destiny with hidden power disposes me, and choice with clear reasoning moves me to adore her? Look, my friend, I don't know how to tell you," Tomás continued, "how Love, the lowly subject of this scul-lery maid, as you call her, honors me and raises me so high that seeing her, I don't see her, and knowing her, I don't know her. It isn't possible, even when

I try, for me to contemplate with rapture, if I can call it that, the lowliness of her social state because then this thought is immediately erased by her beauty, grace, serenity, modesty, and reserve, which allow me to understand that beneath the rough surface must be enclosed and hidden a mine of great value and merit. In brief, whatever she may be, I love her dearly, and not with the vulgar love I've felt for other girls but with a love so pure it does not aspire to more than serving her and striving to have her love me, repaying with a virtuous desire what is owed to my desire, which is also virtuous."

At this point the Asturian gave a great shout and exclaimed:

"Oh, Platonic love! Oh, illustrious scullery maid! Oh, most happy age in which we live, when we see that beauty inspires love without wickedness, virtue ignites without burning, charm gives pleasure without incitement, and the lowliness of a humble state obliges and forces others to raise it to the wheel of what is called Fortune. Oh, my poor tunas, you are spending this year not being visited by this man so in love, so devoted to you. But next year I shall make amends so that the elders of my longed for fishing will not complain."

To which Tomás said:

"I can see, Asturian, how openly you mock me. What you could do is go with my blessing to your fishing while I stay here in my hunt, and here you'll find me when you return. If you want to take with you the money that is yours, I shall give it to you immediately, and go in peace, and let each man follow the path where his destiny leads him."

"I thought you more discerning," replied Lope. "Don't you see that what I'm saying is a joke? But now that I know that what you say is sincere, I shall serve you just as sincerely in any way you choose. I ask only one thing as recompense for the many things I intend to do in your service, and that is that you don't put me in a position where Argüello can flatter or flirt with me, because I'd rather break off our friendship than run the risk of having hers. Good Lord, friend, she talks more than a judge reading a sentence and, from a league away, you can smell the dregs of wine on her breath. All her teeth on top are false, and I think her hair is a wig; and to make up and compensate for these deficiencies, after she revealed her evil thoughts to me, she began to beautify herself with white lead and apply it to her face so it looks like a mask of pure plaster."

"It's all true," replied Tomás, "and the Galician isn't so bad that she makes a martyr of me. What we can do is that just for tonight you stay at the inn, and tomorrow you can buy the donkey and find a place to stay, and in this way you'll avoid encounters with Argüello and I'll remain, subject to the Galician's and to the irreparable lightning flashes of seeing my Costanza."

The two friends agreed to this and went to the inn, where the Asturian was welcomed by Argüello with demonstrations of great love. That night, at the door of the inn, there was dancing by the many mule drivers who were there and at nearby hostelries. The Asturian was the one who played the guitar; the female dancers, in addition to the two Galicians and Argüello, were three other maids from other inns. A good number of men gathered, their faces hidden, wanting to see Costanza more than the dancing, but she did not appear or come out to watch, leaving many desires thwarted.

Lope played the guitar in a way that had people saying he made it speak. The girls asked him to sing a ballad, and Argüello was the most eager. He said that if they danced to it in the way they sing and dance in plays, he would sing it, and to keep them from making a mistake, they had to do everything he sang in the song and nothing else.

There were dancers among the mule drivers, and the same was true of the maids. Lope cleared his throat, spat twice, and in this time thought about what he would say, and since he had a quick, facile, and elegant mind and a felicitous talent for improvisation, he began to sing:

> Let the beauteous Argüello
> come forth, young and a maid no more,
> and then make a curtsy, and then
> take two steps back, where she began.

> Let the one they call Barrabas,
> the Andalusian mule driver,
> canon of cadence in Compás,
> take our Argüello by the hand.

> Of the two Galician maidens
> who live in this inn, let the one
> with the plumpest cheeks come forth
> in underclothes and no apron.

> Let Torote catch hold of her
> and all four all together, with
> a swing and a sway of their hips
> cast off the stepping of the dance.

Everything that the Asturian sang the men and women did exactly; but when he said that they should cast off the stepping of the dance, the dancing mule driver familiarly called Barrabas responded:

"Brother musician, watch what you sing and don't accuse nobody of being badly dressed, because nobody here's in castoffs, and we wear what God gives us."

The innkeeper, who heard the mule driver's ignorance, said to him:

"Brother mule driver, *cast off* is a term in a foreign dance and not an accusation of ragged clothes."

"If that's true," he replied, "there's no reason for us to complicate things; let them play their usual sarabandes, chaconnes, and *folías*, and do whatever they want, for there are people here can stuff them up to their gullets."

The Asturian, not saying a word, continued with his song, saying:

> Then we'll let the trollops enter
> and the fops who are to come in,
> for the dance we call the chaconne
> is wider than the ocean sea.
>
> You must ask for the castanets,
> and then get down and clean and scrub
> your hands in that sand over there,
> or dirt from the dung heap outside.
>
> You have all performed very well,
> there is nothing I must correct,
> cross yourselves, then give the devil
> a finger or two from your fig tree.
>
> Spit in the face of the whoreson
> so that he lets us be happy,
> because we never want to move
> far from this dance, the chaconne.
>
> I'm changing the tune, oh divine
> Argüello, lovelier than a
> hospital, for you my new muse,
> my doxy, grant me your favors.
>
> The dance we call the chaconne
> the good life it holds and contains.
>
> There we find a practice that suits
> the state of our health and vigor,
> shaking idle laziness from
> all our limbs, our parts, our members.

Laughter bubbles in the bosom
of the dancer and the player,
the one who watches the dance and
listens to sonorous music.

Feet rush and spurt like quicksilver,
people dissolve, consumed with love,
and to the joy of their owners
shoes lose their soles made of cork.

Their spirit and agility
become young again in the old,
and in the young are exalted,
and they intone over again

The dance we call the chaconne
the good life it holds and contains.

How many times has this noble
lady attempted and tried
with the joyful sarabande
"*Péseme*" and "*Perra mora*,"

To enter religious houses,
slipping in through the cracks and clefts
to disturb moral decorum
that resides in the holy cells!

How many reviled and censured
by the same ones who adore her!
For the lustful man imagines
and the fool takes a fancy to

The dance we call the chaconne
the good life it holds and contains.

This swarthy mulatta Indian
about whom the rumors proclaim
her guilty of more offenses,
more sacrilege than Aroba,

She, who takes as tributaries
the throng of scullery maids,

> the horde of valets and pages,
> the crowd of lackeys and grooms,
>
> Says, swears, and she does not explode,
> that in spite of the *zambapalo*,
> a haughty dance from the Indies,
> she is the flower of them all.
>
> And that the chaconne alone
> the good life it holds and contains.

While Lope was singing, the mob of dancing mulants and sculletresses, who numbered twelve, stomped the ground into shreds; and as Lope was preparing to move forward, singing other songs of greater importance, substance, and consideration than the ones he had sung so far, one of the many men with muffled faces who were watching the dance said, without removing the part of his cloak that covered the lower part of his face:

"Shut up, drunkard! Shut up, sot! Shut up, toper, poet of the old-fashioned, fake musician!"

After this others spoke up with so many insults and grimaces that Lope decided to be quiet, but the mule drivers took such exception to this that, if it had not been for the innkeeper, who calmed them with reasonable words, there would have been a terrible brawl, and even so, hands would not have been lowered if the law had not arrived at that moment and taken them all away.

No sooner had they left than a man's voice reached the ears of all those who were awake in the area; he was sitting on a rock facing the Sevillan's inn, and singing with such marvelous sweet harmony that he astounded those who heard him and obliged them to listen to the end. But the most attentive was Tomás Pedro, for he was the most moved, not only by the music but by the words, which for him did not mean hearing lyrics but letters of excommunication that afflicted his soul, because what the musician sang was this ballad:

> Where are you, that you don't appear,
> you heavenly sphere of beauty,
> loveliness of divine making
> presented to our human life?
> Empyrean heaven where love
> has his safe and constant abode;
> first mover who brings behind you
> all happiness and good fortune;

crystalline, pellucid setting
where pure, transparent waters can
cool down the blazing flames of love,
amplify them and refine them;
new and beautiful firmament,
where two stars can join and unite,
without taking borrowed light, and
illuminate heaven and earth;
a happiness that opposes
the disordered sorrows of the
father who gives his children
interment in his own stomach;
a humility that resists
elevation to the heights of
great Jove, who is influenced by
your benevolence, which is great;
invisible and subtle net
that places in harsh confinement
the adulterous warrior,
ever triumphant in battles;
oh, fourth heaven and second sun,
the first left in darkness when you
by chance allow a glimpse; the sight
of you brings good fortune and joy;
solemn emissary, you speak
with a wisdom and sense so strange
that you persuade by keeping still,
even more than you propose to.
Of the second heaven you have
no more than its great loveliness,
and of the first, you have no more
than the radiance of the moon.
In this sphere you are, Costanza,
set, most unfortunately, in
a place that, because unworthy,
confounds your joyful good fortune.
Fashion your own destiny, and
consent to rectitude reduced
to treatment according to custom,

cool aloofness to blandishment.
With this you will see, Señora,
that your destiny is envied
by haughty ones for your bloodline,
by great ones for your loveliness.
If you want to shorten the path,
the richest, purest love in me
that e'er saw love in another
soul I offer now to you.

Concluding these final verses and two half-bricks flying toward him were all one; and if, instead of landing at the musician's feet, they had hit the middle of his head, music and poetry could easily have been removed from his skull. The poor man was frightened and started to run up the hill so quickly a greyhound could not have overtaken him. Unhappy condition of musicians, bats, and owls, always subject to similar downpours and misfortunes! All those who had listened to the assaulted man's voice thought it was good; but the one who liked it best was Tomás Pedro, who admired the voice and the ballad. But he would have preferred someone other than Costanza to be the occasion for so much music, although none of it ever reached her ears.

Barrabas, the mule driver, who had also listened attentively to the music, was of the opposite opinion, because as soon as he saw the musician fleeing, he said:

"There you go, you fool, Judas's versifier, I hope fleas eat your eyes! Who the hell taught you to sing about things like spheres and heavens and wheels of fortune to a scullery maid, calling her moons and martyrs! You might've said, and damn you and anybody who thinks your versifying's good, that she's as stiff as asparagus, as puffed up as plumage, as white as milk, as pure as a novice friar, as finicky and stubborn as a rented mule, and harder than a piece of mortar; if you'd said that, she would've understood and been happy, but calling her emissary and net and mover, and highness and lowness is better said to some orphan in a religious school than to a scullery maid. The truth is there are poets in the world who write verses not even the devil can understand; I, at least, though I'm Barrabas, in no way understood the ones this musician sang. Just think what Costancica will do! But she goes him one better, because she's in her bed mocking even Prester Juan of the Indies. At least this musician isn't one of those who play for the Magistrate's son, for there are a lot of them, and every once in a while you can understand them, but this one, I swear, he just makes me angry!"

All those who heard Barrabas were very pleased and thought his criticism and opinion accurate.

After this, everyone went to bed, and as soon as the people were quiet, Lope heard a very slow knock on his door. And asking who it was, the answer came in a low voice:

"It's Argüello and the Galician; open up, because we're dying of the cold."

"Well, the truth is," answered Lope, "we're in the middle of the dog days."

"That's enough jokes, Lope," replied the Galician, "get up and open the door, we're like a couple of archduchesses."

"Archduchesses, and at this hour?" responded Lope. "I don't believe in them, but I do understand you're either witches or scoundrels; go away right now, if not, on the life of . . . I swear that if I get up, with the metal on my shield strap I'll beat your hindquarters as red as poppies!"

When they heard answers so harsh and so far from what they had first imagined, they feared the Asturian's anger, and with their hopes thwarted and their designs frustrated, they returned, sad and unfortunate, to their beds; but, before moving away from the door, Argüello said, putting her mouth to the keyhole:

"Honey isn't for a donkey's mouth."

And then, as if she had uttered a judgment and taken her just revenge, she returned, as we have said, to her sad bed.

Lope, who heard that they had left, said to Tomás Pedro, who was awake:

"Look, Tomás, set me to fighting two giants, and if it so happens that for your sake I must break the jaws of half a dozen or even a dozen lions, I shall do that more easily than drinking a glass of wine; but if you make it necessary for me to fight tooth and nail with Argüello, I shall not consent even if the Holy Brotherhood puts an arrow through my heart.[18] Just see the Maidens of Denmark that fortune offered us tonight![19] Well now, God's in his heaven."

"I've already told you, my friend," said Tomás, "that you can do as you choose, either continue on your pilgrimage or buy the donkey and be a water carrier, whatever you decide."

"I'm firm about being a water carrier," replied Lope, "and let's sleep the short time until daybreak, I'm drunker than a cask of wine and have no desire to chat with you now."

18. The Holy Brotherhood was a law enforcement organization established by the Catholic Monarchs.

19. "Maidens of Denmark" is an ironic sobriquet for the women of the inn, who are likely prostitutes.

They fell asleep, day came, they got up, and Tomás went to feed the mules and Lope went to the animal market, which was nearby, to buy a good-looking donkey.

It so happened that Tomás, led by his thoughts and the opportunity afforded him by the solitude of the siestas, had composed some amorous verses and written them in the same book where he kept the barley accounts, intending to copy them out and tear up or erase the pages of the account book. But before he did, when he was out of the house and had left the book on the container of barley, his master picked it up and, opening it to see the accounts, found the verses, and reading them disturbed and alarmed him.

He took them to his wife, and before he read them to her he called Costanza, and with a good deal of praise mixed with threats, told her to tell him whether Tomás Pedro, the boy who took care of the barley, had paid her any compliments or said anything rude to her or given any indication of being fond of her. Costanza swore that the first word, of that kind or any other, was yet to be said, and that he never, not even with his eyes, had given her any sign of a lewd thought.

Her master and mistress believed her, for they were accustomed to always hearing her tell the truth in everything they asked. They told her she could go, and the innkeeper said to his wife:

"I don't know what to think about this. You should know, Señora, that Tomás has written in this account book some verses that make me suspect he's in love with Costancica."

"Let's see the verses," his wife replied, "and I'll tell you what's in them."

"I'm sure you will, no doubt about that," replied her husband, "since you're a poet, you'll understand them right away."

"I'm not a poet," answered his wife, "but you know I have a good mind and can say the four prayers in Latin."

"You'd do better to pray in Spanish; your uncle the priest already told you that you say a lot of nonsense when you pray in Latin, and that you really weren't praying at all."

"That arrow comes from your niece's quiver, she's envious when she sees me pick up the Book of Hours in Latin and go through them as easy as you please."

"Whatever you say," replied the innkeeper. "Listen carefully, these are the verses:

> Who finds joy and delight in love?
> One who's silent.

Who triumphs over its harshness?
    One who's constant.
Who achieves its felicity?
    One who's steadfast.
And so, in this matter, my soul
might well expect the triumphant
palm of victory if it is
silent, and constant, and steadfast.

How is love nourished and sustained?
    With kind favor.
How is its furor diminished?
    With an offense.
But first, does it grow with disdain?
    No, it grows faint.
Clearly, in this matter it seems
that my love will be immortal,
for the cause and source of my ills
does not offend or show favor.

In despair, what can one hope for?
    Absolute death.
But, which death remedies the ills?
    A partial death.
Well then, can it be good to die?
    Best to suffer.
Because many times it is said,
and may this truth be accepted,
that after the angriest squall
a serene calm always returns.

Shall I confess to my passion?
    When it is apt.
Suppose for me it never is?
    Oh, it will be.
My death will come in the meantime.
    Then let it come,
for your pure faith and honest hope,
when Costanza learns of them, will
transform your tears into laughter.

"Is there more?" said the innkeeper's wife.

"No," answered her husband, "but what do you think of these verses?"

"First," she said, "we have to find out if they're Tomás's."

"There can be no doubt about that," replied her husband, "because the writing in the barley accounts and the verses is the same, and that cannot be denied."

"Look, husband," said the innkeeper's wife, "in my opinion, since the verses name Costancica, and from this one might think they were written for her, we don't have to swear that's true as if we saw him writing them, especially since there are other Costanzas in the world besides ours; but even if they're for her, nothing's said there that dishonors her and nothing's asked for that matters. Let's keep our eyes open and let the girl know, because if he's in love with her, it's certain he'll write more verses and try to give them to her."

"Wouldn't it be better," said her husband, "to rid ourselves of these worries and just throw him out?"

"That," responded the innkeeper's wife," is up to you; but, as you say, the truth is the boy is so useful it would be unjust to dismiss him with so little cause."

"Well then," said her husband, "we'll keep our eyes open, as you say, and time will tell us what we have to do."

They agreed on this, and the innkeeper put the book back where he had found it. Tomás returned, filled with anxiety, to look for his book; he found it, and to avoid another fright, copied the verses, tore up the pages in the book, and proposed to reveal his desire to Costanza at the first opportunity. But since she was always vigilant regarding her purity and chastity, she gave no man the chance to look at her, let alone engage her in conversation; and since there were ordinarily so many people and so many eyes in the inn, the difficulty in speaking to her increased, which caused the poor man in love to despair. But that day Costanza had appeared wearing a headdress that was tight around her cheeks, and said to someone who asked why she had put it on that she had a terrible toothache, and Tomás, whose desires had sharpened his wits, in an instant devised what he should do and said:

"Señora Costanza, I shall give you a written prayer, and after saying it twice your pain will disappear very easily."

"What good fortune," responded Costanza, "and I shall say the prayer, because I know how to read."

"It must be on the condition," said Tomás, "that it not be shown to anyone, because I value it very highly, and it would not be good for many people to know it and then look down on it."

"I assure you, Tomás," said Costanza, "I shall not give it to anyone; and give it to me now, because the pain is bothering me a great deal."

"I shall copy it down from memory," responded Tomás, "and give it to you right away."

These were the first words Tomás said to Costanza and Costanza to Tomás in all the time he had been at the inn, which now amounted to more than twenty-four days.

Tomás withdrew and wrote the prayer, and he had an opportunity to hand it to Costanza without anyone seeing. And she, with much joy and more devotion, went into a room alone, and opening the paper saw that this was what it said:

> *Señora of my soul: I am a gentleman from Burgos. If I survive my father, I inherit as the eldest son six thousand ducados of income. Because of the fame of your beauty, which extends for many leagues, I left my homeland, changed my attire, and in the clothes you see now I came to serve your master. If you should wish to be mine, by whatever means most suitable to your virtue, see what proofs you want me to present so that you can confirm the truth of this; and once you have confirmed it, if it is your pleasure, I shall be your husband and consider myself the most fortunate man in the world. But for now I beg you not to throw thoughts as loving and pure as mine out into the street; for if your master knows them and does not believe them, he will condemn me to exile from your presence, which would be the same as condemning me to death. Allow me, Señora, to see you until you believe me, considering that one who has committed no fault other than adoring you does not deserve the harsh punishment of not seeing you. You can respond with your eyes, hidden from the many men who are always looking at you, for they kill when angry and revive when filled with pity.*

While Tomás considered that Costanza had gone to read his paper, his heart was pounding, fearing and hoping either for his sentence of death or the restoration of his life. At this point Costanza came out, so beautiful, though her cheeks were bound, that if her beauty could be augmented through some unexpected event, it could be deemed that the shock of having seen on Tomás's paper something so far from what she expected had increased her loveliness. She came out with the paper torn into tiny pieces, and said to Tomás, who could barely remain standing:

"Brother Tomás, this prayer of yours resembles witchcraft and deception more than a holy prayer, and so I do not wish to believe it or use it, and that is why I have torn it up, so no one who may be more credulous than I can see it. Learn other, easier prayers, because it will be impossible for this one to be of much benefit to you."

Saying this, she went in to be with her mistress, and Tomás was taken aback but somewhat consoled when he saw that the secret of his desire was in Costanza's bosom alone; it seemed to him that since his master knew nothing of it, at least he was in no danger of being dismissed from the inn. He thought that with the first step he had taken in his plan, he had overcome a thousand difficulties, and that in large, doubtful matters, the greatest difficulty lies at the beginning.

While this occurred at the inn, the Asturian had gone to buy the donkey where they were sold. And although he found many, none satisfied him, though a Gypsy was very solicitous about pressing on him one that walked more because of the mercury put in its ears than its own agility,[20] but though its step was pleasing its body was not, for it was very small and not the size and shape Lope wanted, for he was looking for one large enough to carry him, not to mention the water jugs, whether empty or filled.

Then a boy came up to him and said into his ear:

"Young man, if you're looking for an animal that's right for the trade of water carrier, I have a donkey close by, in a meadow near here, and there's not a better or bigger one in the city; and I advise you not to buy an animal from Gypsies, because even though they look healthy and good, they are all false and full of hidden aches and pains. If you want to buy the one that's right for you, come with me and keep your mouth closed."

The Asturian believed him and told him to take him to the donkey he was praising so much. The two of them went shoulder to shoulder, as they say, until they reached the Huerta del Rey, where, in the shadow of an irrigation waterwheel, they found many water carriers whose donkeys were grazing in a nearby meadow. The seller showed the Asturian his donkey, which looked good to him; and everyone there praised the donkey as strong, good at walking, and an exceptional runner. They completed their transaction, and with no other security or information, and with the other water carriers acting as agents and mediators, the Asturian paid sixteen *ducados* for the donkey and all the implements of the trade.

He paid in gold *escudos*. They congratulated him on his purchase and entrance into the trade, and affirmed that he had purchased an excellent donkey

---

20. Putting mercury in animals' ears to make them move faster was a common practice among the Gypsies.

because the owner who was letting it go, after having supported himself and the donkey in an honorable fashion without crippling or killing it, in less than a year had earned two sets of clothes as well as those sixteen *escudos*, with which he intended to return home where a marriage had been arranged for him with a distant relation.

In addition to the agents for the donkey, there were four other water carriers playing cards on the ground, using the earth as their table and their cloaks as the tablecloth. The Asturian began to watch them and saw that they gambled not like water carriers but like archdeacons, making wagers of more than one hundred *reales* in copper and silver. All of them staked everything on one hand, and if one did not give the advantage to another, he would take all his money. Finally, two of them lost all their money in that wager and got to their feet. Seeing this, the seller of the donkey said that if there were four he would play, because he did not like a three-handed game. The Asturian, as sweet as sugar, said he would not spoil the stew, as the Italians say, and would be the fourth player. They all sat down; matters were going smoothly, and preferring to gamble money rather than time, in a short while Lope lost the six *escudos* he had, and finding himself without a *blanca*, said that if they wanted him to wager the donkey, he would. They agreed, and he wagered a fourth of the donkey, saying he wanted to bet the donkey in quarters. The game went so badly for him that in four consecutive hands he lost the four fourths of the donkey, and the same man who had sold it to him won it back. And standing in order to hand the donkey over to him, the Asturian said they should be aware that he had wagered only the four quarters of the donkey, but they had to give him the tail, and then they could lead the animal away.

His demanding the tail made them all laugh, and the erudite men who were there were of the opinion that what he was asking for was unjustified, saying that when a sheep is sold, or any other animal, the tail is not cut off or removed but of necessity remains with one of the hindquarters. To which Lope replied that the sheep of Barbary ordinarily have five quarters, and the fifth is the tail, and when these sheep are quartered, the tail is worth as much as any other fourth; and as for the tail remaining with the live animal when it is sold and has not been quartered, he conceded that; but his was not sold but wagered, and it never was his intention to wager the tail, and they should return it to him at once, along with everything related and connected to it, from the top of the head and including the spine, where the tail begins and then comes down until it stops at the end of the last hairs on it.

"Let's suppose," said one of them, "that it is as you say, and they give you the tail as you request and settle for what remains of the donkey."

"That's it exactly!" replied Lope. "Let me have my tail; otherwise, by God, they won't take my donkey even if all the water carriers in the world come for it. And don't think because there are so many of you here you can swindle or scare me, because I'm a man who knows how to get close to another man and plunge two spans of dagger into his belly without his even knowing who did it, or where, or how; what's more, I don't want to be paid in installments, a little from each of you, but want the tail complete, in one piece, and cut from the donkey as I've said."

The winner and the others did not think it a good idea to use force in the matter, because they judged the Asturian to be so spirited that he would not agree to their doing so; and he, accustomed as he was to fishing for tuna, in which all kinds of dangers and threats were common, as well as extraordinary boasts and demonstrations of bravado, tossed aside his hat and grasped a dagger he had under his short cape and assumed a posture that instilled fear and respect into all that water-carrying company. Finally, one of them who seemed the most reasonable and rational, had them agree to play the tail against a quarter of the donkey in a card game called *quinola* or *dos y pasante*. They agreed, and Lope won at *quinola*; the other man tried, wagered the other quarter, and in another three hands was left without a donkey. He wanted to play for money; Lope did not want to; but all of them insisted that he had to, and so he took all his honeymoon money from the betrothed man, leaving him without a single *maravedí*; and the man who had lost everything was so despondent that he threw himself down and began to bang his head against the ground. Lope, being wellborn and generous and compassionate, picked him up and returned all the money he had won from him as well as the sixteen *ducados* for the donkey, and what he had left over he distributed to the others, and his singular generosity astonished all of them; and if these had been the days and times of Tamerlane, they would have made him king of the water carriers.[21]

To great accompaniment, Lope returned to the city, where he told Tomás what had happened and Tomás in turn recounted his good news. There was no tavern, eating place, or gathering of scoundrels where they did not hear about the game for the donkey, the retaliation of the tail, and the Asturian's spirit and generosity. But since the evil beast of the rabble is ill-behaved, ill-fated, and ill-spoken, it did not bring to mind the generosity, spirit, and good qualities of the great Lope, but only the tail; and so, after less than two days

21. Tamerlane was a nomadic conqueror who became King of Persia in the fourteenth century.

carrying water in the city, he found many people pointing fingers at him and saying: 'This is the water carrier with the tail.' All the boys were attentive, they knew what had happened, and no sooner did Lope enter any street than all along it they were shouting, from near and far: 'Asturian, let's have the tail! Let's have the tail, Asturian!'

Lope, who found himself harassed by so many tongues and so many voices, said nothing, thinking his prolonged silence would negate so much insolence; but not even that had an effect, for the more he was silent, the more the boys shouted. And so, he tried transforming his patience into anger; he got down from the donkey and began beating the boys with a stick, which simply was grinding the gunpowder even finer and setting fire to it, or cutting off the heads of the snake, since for each one he cut off by beating a boy, at the same moment not another seven but another seven hundred grew back, and the boys called for the tail with even greater eagerness and frequency. Finally, he decided to withdraw to an inn different from the one where his friend was staying, thinking he would escape Argüello and stay there until the influence of the evil planet had passed and their demand for the tail would have been wiped from the boys' memory.

Six days went by without his leaving the inn except at night, when he went to see Tomás to ask how he was, and Tomás recounted that after giving the paper to Costanza, he had not been able to say another word to her, and she seemed even more aloof than usual, although once he had occasion to approach her and speak to her, and when she saw him she said, before he could come any closer:

"Tomás, my tooth doesn't hurt at all, and so I have no need of your words or prayers; be glad I'm not denouncing you to the Inquisition, and don't be wearisome."

But she said these words without showing anger in her eyes or any other harshness that could give rise to further severity. Lope told him about the boys' provocations when they demanded the tail because he had asked for his donkey's tail to make his famous wager. Tomás advised him not to go out, at least not on the donkey, and if he did go out to use side streets that were not busy, and if this were not enough, all he had to do was leave the trade, the final remedy for ending so unseemly a demand. Lope asked if the Galician was still pursuing him. Tomás said no, but she never stopped enticing him with gifts and presents of what she had stolen in the kitchen from the guests. Then Lope returned to his inn, determined not to leave it with the donkey for another six days at least.

It must have been eleven at night when suddenly and unexpectedly many officers of the law came into the inn, followed by the Magistrate. The innkeeper became agitated, and even some of the guests, because just as comets—when they show themselves—always cause fears of miseries and misfortunes, it is exactly the same when a crowd of officers enters a house without warning, alarming and terrifying even clear consciences. The Magistrate entered a parlor and called for the innkeeper, who came in trembling to see what the Magistrate wanted. And as soon as the Magistrate saw him, he asked with a great deal of dignity:

"Are you the innkeeper?"

"Yes, Señor, and I am completely at your service."

The Magistrate asked that everyone in the parlor go out and leave him alone with the innkeeper. They did so, and when they were alone, the Magistrate said to the innkeeper:

"Innkeeper, what service people do you have working in your inn?"

"Señor," he responded, "I have two Galician maids, and a housekeeper, and a boy who keeps the barley and straw accounts."

"Anyone else?" replied the Magistrate.

"No, Señor," replied the innkeeper.

"Well tell me, innkeeper," said the Magistrate, "where is a girl who people say works in this house, so beautiful that the entire city calls her the illustrious scullery maid, and I have even heard that my son, Don Periquito, is in love with her and not a night goes by that he does not serenade her?"

"Señor," said the innkeeper, "it is true that the one they call the illustrious scullery maid is in this house, but she is not my servant girl and never was."

"I do not understand what you are saying, innkeeper, about the scullery maid being and not being your servant girl."

"I have told you the truth," added the innkeeper, "and if your grace gives me leave, I shall tell him about this, which I have never told to anyone."

"First, before hearing anything else, I want to see the scullery maid; call her here," said the Magistrate.

The innkeeper went to the parlor door and said:

"You, woman, have Costancica come in here!"

When the innkeeper's wife heard that the Magistrate was calling for Costanza, she became perturbed and began to wring her hands, saying:

"Oh, woe is me! The Magistrate with Costanza, and alone. Something terrible must have happened; the beauty of this girl bewitches men."

Costanza, who heard this, said:

"Señora, don't be distressed, I'll go to see what the Magistrate wants, and if something terrible has happened, your grace can be certain I'm not to blame."

And then, not waiting to be called again, she took a lit candle in a silver candlestick, and with more shyness than fear, went to where the Magistrate was waiting.

As soon as the Magistrate saw her, he told the innkeeper to close the door to the parlor; when this was done, the Magistrate stood, and taking the candlestick Costanza was holding, he brought the light up to her face and looked at her from head to toe; and since Costanza was frightened, the color rose in her face, and she looked so beautiful and so chaste that it seemed to the Magistrate he was looking at the beauty of an angel on earth; and after having looked at her attentively, he said:

"Innkeeper, this jewel does not belong in the low setting of an inn; from this I say that my son Periquito is discerning, for he has known how to direct his thoughts very well. I say, maiden, that people not only can and should call you illustrious, but most illustrious; and these titles should not be used with the name of scullery maid, but with that of duchess."

"She isn't a scullery maid, Señor," said the innkeeper, "for her only work in this house is to keep the keys to the silver; I have some, thanks to the Good Lord, and I use it to serve the honored guests who come to this inn."

"Even so," said the Magistrate, "I say, innkeeper, it is neither right nor proper for this girl to be in an inn. Is she by some chance related to you?"

"She is neither my kin nor my servant; and if your grace would like to know who she is, if she were not present your grace would hear things that not only would please you but astound you as well."

"Yes, I would like to," said the Magistrate, "and let Costancica go outside, and I can promise what her own father could promise: that her great chastity and beauty oblige all who see her to offer her their service."

Costanza did not say a word, but with great composure made a deep curtsy to the Magistrate and left the parlor, and found her mistress eagerly waiting to find out from her own lips why the Magistrate had summoned her. She told her what had happened, and how her master had stayed with him to tell him "I don't know what" things that he didn't want her to hear. The innkeeper's wife still was not calm and did not stop praying until the Magistrate left and she saw her husband come out a free man; he, as soon as he was alone with the Magistrate, had said to him:

"Today, Señor, according to my count, it has been fifteen years, one month, and four days since a lady dressed as a pilgrim and carried in a sedan chair came to this inn, accompanied by four servants on horseback, and two duennas and a lady's maid who rode in a carriage. She also had two mules covered in rich caparisons and carrying a costly bed and kitchen condiments; in short, the trappings were notable and the pilgrim appeared to be a great lady; and although her age seemed to be a little over forty, she still looked extremely beautiful. She was ill, and pale, and so exhausted she ordered her bed prepared immediately, and her servants did so in this very parlor. They asked me who the most famous physician in the city was. I told them Dr. de la Fuente. They went for him without delay, and he came without delay. She told him about her illness when they were alone, and the result of their conversation was that the doctor said her bed should be placed elsewhere, in a place free of noise. They moved her immediately to another room, upstairs and isolated, and with the advantages the doctor had requested. None of her male servants entered their mistress's room, and only the two duennas and the lady's maid served her. My wife and I asked the servants about the lady, what her name was, where she had come from, and where she was going, whether she was married, widowed, or a maiden, and why she was wearing pilgrim's attire. We asked all of these questions many times, but none of the men would tell us anything except that this pilgrim was a rich, prominent lady from Castilla la Vieja, a widow who had no children as her heirs; and since for some months she had been suffering from dropsy, she had vowed to make a pilgrimage to Our Lady of Guadalupe, and because of that promise she wore those clothes. As for saying her name, they had been ordered to call her only the pilgrim. That's what we learned then, but after three days, during which time the pilgrim stayed in the inn because she was ill, one of the duennas called for my wife and me on her mistress's orders. We went to see what she wanted, and with the door closed and before her female servants, almost with tears in her eyes, she said what I believe are these exact words:

" 'My friends, heaven is my witness that through no fault of mine I find myself in the harsh predicament I shall tell you about now. I am pregnant, and so close to term that the pains have already begun to afflict me. None of the male servants traveling with me know of my need or my misfortune; I have not been able to hide it from my women, nor have I wished to. For the sake of escaping malicious eyes in my homeland and not giving birth there, I vowed to go to Our Lady of Guadalupe; she must have wished the birth to take place in your inn; it is now up to you to help and attend to me with the secrecy that the lady who places her honor in your hands deserves. The reward for the good turn you do me, for that is what I wish to call it, if it does not correspond to the great benefit I expect, will at least give proof of a very grateful will; and I want the two hundred gold *escudos* here in this purse to begin to give that proof.'

"And taking from beneath her bed pillow a purse embroidered in gold and green, she placed it in the hands of my wife who, like a simpleton unaware of what she was doing because she was enthralled by the pilgrim and hanging on her every word, took the purse without a single courteous word of thanks. I remember telling her that none of that was necessary; that we were not people who, for the sake of self-interest rather than charity, were moved to do good when the opportunity presented itself. She went on, saying:

"'It is necessary, my friends, that you think about where to take the baby I shall give birth to any moment now, and think too of lies to tell the person to whom you give the infant; for now it will be in the city, and later I want it to be a village. What needs to be done afterward, if it pleases God to guide me and help me fulfill my vow, you will know when I return from Guadalupe, because time will have allowed me to think and decide what is best for me to do. I have no need of a midwife, nor do I want one; for other, more honorable births I have had assure me that with only the help of my maids I shall make short work of any difficulties and be spared another witness to my misfortunes.'

"Here, the unfortunate pilgrim stopped speaking and began weeping copiously and was consoled in part by the many virtuous words that my wife, who had regained her civility, said to her. In short, I went out to find a place to take the newborn no matter the hour; and between twelve and one that same night, when everyone in the inn was asleep, the good lady gave birth to a girl, the most beautiful my eyes had ever seen, who is the same girl your grace has just seen now. The mother did not even groan during the birth and her daughter was not born crying; there was a marvelous calm and silence in everyone, which perfectly suited the secret of that strange case. She was in bed for another six days, and on all of them the physician came to see her, but not because she had told him the origin of her ailment; and she never took the medicines he prescribed, because she was simply attempting to deceive her male servants with the doctor's visits. She herself told me this when she was out of danger, and after a week she got out of bed with the same swollen shape, or with another that resembled the one she had lain down with.

"She went on her pilgrimage and returned in twenty days, almost cured, because she was gradually removing the device that made her look dropsical after the birth. When she returned, the girl whom I called my niece was already with a wet nurse in a village two leagues from here. At her baptism she was given the name Costanza, following the orders of her mother who, pleased with what I had done, gave me a gold chain when she took her leave, which I still have, and from it she removed six fragments, which she said the person who came for the girl would have with him. She also cut a blank piece of parchment on which she had written something into an irregular zigzag shape, just as when one's fingers are interlaced and something is written on the fingers that can be read when one's hands are together and when they are apart the message is divided because the letters have been separated, but when the fingers interlace again the letters come together and correspond and all the letters can be read; I say that one half of the parchment serves as the soul of the other, and together they can be read, but divided it is not possible except by guessing the other half; almost the entire chain remained in my possession, and I have all of it, waiting for the countersign all this time, for she told me that within two years she would send for her daughter, and asked me to rear her not like the person she was but in the way one rears a peasant. She also requested that if by some chance it was not possible to send for her daughter so quickly, and even though she grew and reached the age of reason, that I not tell her how she had been born, and that I forgive her for not telling me her name or who she was, but she was saving that for another more important occasion. In short, giving me another four hundred gold *escudos* and embracing my wife, she departed weeping tender tears, leaving us astonished by her good judgment, valor, beauty, and discretion. Costanza spent two years in the village, and then I brought her here, and have always dressed her as a peasant, as her mother told me to. Fifteen years, one month, and four days I have been waiting for the person who will come for her, and the long delay has consumed all my hope of seeing that person; and if no one comes this year, I have decided to adopt her and give her my entire estate, which is worth more than six thousand *ducados*, God be praised.

"All that remains, Señor Magistrate, is to tell your grace, if it is possible for me to know how to say it, about the perfections and virtues of Costancica. She is, first and foremost, completely devoted to Our Lady; she confesses and takes Communion every month; she knows how to write and read; there is no better lace-maker in Toledo; when she's alone she sings like an angel; in purity there is no one to equal her, and as for beauty, your grace has already seen that. Señor Don Pedro, your grace's son, has never spoken to her; it is true that from time to time he plays music for her, which she never listens to. Many noble gentlemen have stopped at this inn, and have halted their journey for many days to see more of her; but I know very well that none can truthfully boast that she has given him the opportunity to say a single word to her—or many, for that matter. This, Señor, is the true history of the illustrious scullery maid who does no scrubbing, and in it I have told nothing but the truth."

The innkeeper fell silent, and the Magistrate said nothing to him for a long time, for the events the innkeeper recounted had left him dumbfounded. Finally, he told him to bring the chain and the parchment, for he wished to see them. The innkeeper went for them and brought them back, and the Magistrate saw they were just as he had said. The chain was made of carefully wrought fragments; on the parchment these letters were written, one beneath the other, in the space that was supposed to fill the blank of the other half: E T E L S N V D D R, and with these letters he saw the necessity of joining them with the ones on the other half in order to understand them. He thought this sign of recognition was very sensible and he judged the pilgrim who had left such a chain with the innkeeper to be very rich; and having in mind the idea of taking the beautiful girl out of that inn when he had arranged for the convent where he would take her, for the moment he was content to take only the parchment, telling the innkeeper that if by chance anyone came for Costanza, he should inform and tell him who the person was who came for her before showing the chain, which he left in his possession. And then he left, marveling as much at the story and circumstances of the illustrious scullery maid as at her incomparable beauty.

For the entire time the innkeeper spent with the Magistrate, and the time Costanza was with them when they called her, Tomás was beside himself, his soul torn by a thousand different thoughts and unable to hit upon a single one he liked. But when he saw the Magistrate leaving and Costanza staying, his spirit was restored and he could breathe again, for his heart had almost stopped. He did not dare ask the innkeeper what the Magistrate had wanted, and the innkeeper did not tell anyone except his wife, and with that her spirits were restored, and she thanked God that she had been freed of so much apprehension.

The following day, at about one o'clock, two old gentlemen of venerable appearance entered the inn, along with four men on horseback, having first asked one of two boys who accompanied them on foot if this was the Sevillan's inn; and when the answer was yes, they all came in. The four dismounted, and went to help the two old men get down, indicating that those two were gentlemen on the council. Costanza came out with her usual courtesy to see the new guests, and as soon as one of the old men had seen her, he said to the other:

"I believe, Señor Don Juan, that we have found all that we came to search for."

Tomás, who came to give feed to the animals, immediately recognized two of his father's servants, and then he recognized his father and Carriazo's, for they were the two old men whom the others respected. And though he was surprised at their arrival, he thought they must have gone looking for him and Carriazo fishing for tuna, for someone would have told them they would find their sons there and not in Flanders; but he did not dare show himself in those clothes; instead, risking everything, with his hand up to his face, he passed before them and went to find Costanza, and as his good luck would have it, he found her alone, and quickly and with his tongue confused, fearing she would not give him a chance to say anything to her, he said:

"Costanza, one of the two old gentlemen who have just arrived here is my father, the one you will hear called Don Juan de Avendaño; ask one of his servants if he has a son named Don Tomás de Avendaño; I am he, and from this you can infer and ascertain that I have told you the truth regarding the quality of my person and shall do the same regarding everything I have offered you. May God be with you, for until they leave I do not intend to return here."

Costanza did not reply, and he did not wait for her to respond, but turning to leave, his face covered just as he had come in, he went to inform Carriazo that their fathers were at the inn. The innkeeper called for Tomás to come give barley to the animals; but since he did not appear, he did it himself. One of the two old men called one of the Galician maids aside and asked her the name of the beautiful girl they had seen, and whether she was the daughter or a relation of the innkeeper or the innkeeper's wife. The Galician responded:

"Her name's Costanza; she's not related to the innkeeper or his wife, and I don't know what she is; I'll just say a plague on her, I don't know what's wrong with her, she doesn't give any of us maids at the inn a chance. Well, the truth is we have the features that God gave us! A guest doesn't come in without asking right away who the beautiful girl is and saying: 'She's pretty; she looks good; by my faith she's not bad; bad luck for the ones with paint on their faces; may I never do worse!' And nobody says to us: 'What have you got there, devils or women or whatever you are?'"

"Then this girl, according to you," replied the gentleman, "must allow the guests to touch and flatter her."

"Yes," responded the Galician, "you'll find out what she's like! You've picked the right one! By God, Señor, if she even allowed herself to be looked at, she'd wallow in gold; but she's harsher than a hedgehog; she's holier-than-thou, doing needlework all day and praying. The day she performs any miracles I'd like to have some of the profits. My mistress says she wears a hair shirt next to her skin; you can believe that if you want to, father of mine!"

The gentleman was very pleased with what he had heard from the Galician, and not waiting for his spurs to be removed, he called the innkeeper, and taking him aside in a parlor, he said to him:

"Innkeeper, I have come to take a jewel of mine that you have had in your possession for some years; to take it from you I have brought a thousand gold *escudos*, these fragments of chain, and this parchment."

And saying this, he took out the countersign of the six chain fragments, as well as that of the parchment; the innkeeper, overjoyed at the offer of a thousand *escudos*, responded:

"Señor, the jewel you wish to take is here in the inn, but not the chain or the parchment needed to prove the truth, which I believe your grace is concerned with; and so I beg your patience, and I shall return immediately."

And he went straight to the Magistrate to inform him of what had happened and that there were two gentlemen in his inn who had come for Costanza.

The Magistrate had just finished eating, and he wanted so much to see the end of that story that he mounted his horse immediately and went to the Sevillan's inn, taking with him the parchment of the countersign. And as soon as he saw the two gentlemen he opened his arms and went to embrace one of them, saying:

"Lord save me! How welcome you are, Señor Don Juan de Avendaño, my cousin and my lord!"

The gentleman returned his embrace, saying:

"No doubt, cousin, about my welcome, for I see you enjoying the health I always wish for you. Cousin, embrace this gentleman, Señor Don Diego de Carriazo, a great lord and a good friend of mine."

"I already know Señor Don Diego," responded the Magistrate, "and I am his humble servant."

The two men embraced after greeting each other with great love and courtesy, and they went into a room where they were alone with the innkeeper, who had the chain with him, and said:

"The Magistrate knows why your grace has come, Señor Don Diego de Carriazo; if your grace will take out the fragments missing from this chain, and the Magistrate takes out the parchment in his possession, we can have the proof I have been awaiting for all these years."

"That means," replied Don Diego, "there will be no need to tell the Magistrate again about our arrival, for it will be very clear it has been for the reason, innkeeper, that you have said."

"I was told something, but there was a good deal I didn't know. I have the parchment here."

Don Diego took out the other piece, and bringing the two parts together they made one, and the letters on the piece the innkeeper had were, as we have said, E T E L S N V D D R, and corresponded to the ones on the other parchment, which were: S A S A E A L E R A E A, and put together it said: ÉSTA ES LA SEÑAL VERDADERA (THIS IS THE TRUE SIGN). Then they compared the fragments of the chain, and they found them to be true signs.

"This is finished!" said the Magistrate. "We still have to determine, if possible, the parents of this most beautiful jewel."

"I am her father," stated Don Diego, "and her mother is no longer alive; it is enough to know she was so distinguished I could have been her servant. And because, as her name is concealed, her renown should not be concealed nor should what seems to be a manifest error and evident fault in her be blamed, you must know that the mother of this jewel, being the widow of a great gentleman, withdrew to live in a village of hers, and there, with great discretion and virtue, she led a quiet, tranquil life with her servants and vassals. As fate would have it, one day, as I was passing through her village on my way to the hunt, I wanted to visit her, and it was siesta time when I reached her castle, which is what her large house could be called. I left my horse with a servant of mine; I went in without encountering anyone, all the way to the room where she was taking a siesta on a black estrade. She was extremely beautiful, and the silence, the solitude, and the opportunity awoke in me a desire more bold than virtuous, and with no moral reflection I closed the door after me, and going up to her I woke her, and grasping her tightly I said: 'Your grace, my lady, do not cry out, for your screams will proclaim your dishonor. No one saw me enter this room, because my luck, so that it would be excellent in enjoying you, has rained down sleep on all your servants, and when they come in response to your cries they will have to take my life, and that will be in your arms, and my death will not remove the doubt surrounding your reputation.' In short, I enjoyed her against her will by dint of my strength. She, defeated, exhausted, and shaken, could not or would not say a word to me, and I, leaving her stupefied and bewildered, went out again, retracing my steps, and came to the village of another friend of mine, two leagues from hers. This lady moved from that village to another, and without my ever seeing her, or trying to, two years went by, at the end of which I learned that she was dead. And some twenty days ago, writing very insistently and saying it was a matter that was very important to my well-being and my honor, a steward of this lady sent for me. I went to see why he had summoned me, for I was far from thinking what he told me. I found him on the verge of death, and to make a long story short, he told me very briefly how at the time his mistress died, she had told him everything that had happened with me, and how the rape had left her pregnant, and to hide her shape she had gone on a pilgrimage to Our Lady of Guadalupe, and how she had given birth in this house to a girl who would be named Costanza. He gave me the signs with which to find her, that is, the chain and parchment that you have seen. And he also gave me thirty thousand gold *escudos*, which his mistress had left to marry her daughter. He told me as well that he had not given them to me as soon as his mistress died or told me what she had confided to him in secret out of sheer greed, and to make use of that money, but now that he was about to settle accounts with God, to ease his conscience he was giving me the money and telling me where and how I could find my daughter. I took the money and the countersigns, and recounting this to Señor Don Juan de Avendaño, we set out for this city."

As Don Diego was saying this, they heard someone shouting at the street door, saying:

"Tell Tomás Pedro, the boy with the barley, that they've arrested his friend the Asturian; and he should go to the prison, he's waiting for him there."

At the words "prison" and "arrested," the Magistrate said the prisoner and the bailiff who arrested him should come in. They told the bailiff that the Magistrate, who was inside, ordered him to bring in the prisoner, and that is what he had to do.

The Asturian came in with his teeth covered in blood, in very poor condition but very well gripped by the bailiff; as soon as he entered the room, he recognized his father and the father of Avendaño. He was disquieted, and in order not to be recognized, as if he were wiping away blood with a cloth, he covered his face. The Magistrate asked what the boy had done to receive such a beating. The bailiff responded that the boy was a water carrier named the Asturian, and in the street the boys called after him, 'Let's have the tail, Asturian, let's have the tail!' And then very briefly, he recounted the reason why they asked him for the tail, and everyone laughed quite a bit at the story. He also said that coming off the Alcántara Bridge, hurrying because of the boys demanding the tail, he got down from his donkey, and running after all of them, caught one, whom he left half dead from a beating with a stick; and when he attempted to detain him he had resisted, and that was why he was in such poor condition.

The Magistrate ordered him to show his face, and when he insisted on not showing himself, the bailiff approached and removed the cloth; his father recognized him immediately and said in great agitation:

"My son, Don Diego, why are you in this state? What clothing is this? You still have not left your roguery behind?"

Carriazo fell to his knees at the feet of his father who, with tears in his eyes, held him in his embrace for some time. Don Juan de Avendaño, since he knew that Don Diego had traveled with his son, Don Tomás, asked after him, and he responded that Don Tomás de Avendaño was the servant in charge of barley and straw in the inn. The Asturian's words filled everyone present with astonishment, and the Magistrate told the innkeeper to bring in the boy in charge of the barley.

"I don't believe he's here," said the innkeeper, "but I'll look for him."
And he left to find him.

Don Diego asked Carriazo to explain these transformations and what had moved him to be a water carrier and Don Tomás a servant in an inn. To which Carriazo replied that he could not answer those questions so publicly and would respond in private.

Tomás Pedro was hiding in his room to see, without being seen, what his father and Carriazo's father would do. He was intrigued by the arrival of the Magistrate and the uproar that reigned in the house. Naturally, someone told the innkeeper where he was hiding. The innkeeper went up for him, and more by force than willingly, he obliged him to go downstairs; but he would not have gone down if the Magistrate himself had not come out to the courtyard and called him by name, saying:

"Come down, your grace, my kin, bears and lions are not waiting for you here."

Tomás went down, and with lowered eyes and great humility kneeled before his father, who embraced him with great joy, like the father of the Prodigal Son when he celebrated his return.

By now the Magistrate's carriage had come to take him home, for the great occasion did not allow him to return on horseback. He sent for Costanza, and taking her by the hand, presented her to her father, saying:

"Señor Don Diego, receive this jewel, and esteem her as the richest you can ever desire. And you, beautiful maiden, kiss the hand of your father and give thanks to God that so honorable an event has corrected, raised, and improved the lowliness of your social position."

Costanza, who did not know and could not imagine what had happened to her, was troubled and trembling and could think of nothing else to do but kneel before her father, and grasping his hands began to kiss them tenderly, bathing them with infinite tears that flowed from her beautiful eyes.

In the meantime, the Magistrate had persuaded his cousin Don Juan that everyone should return with him to his house, and although Don Juan refused, the Magistrate's words were so persuasive that he had to concede; and so everyone got into the carriage. But when the Magistrate told Costanza to get in the carriage as well, her heart began to ache, and she and the innkeeper's wife held each other and began to weep such bitter tears that it broke the hearts of all those who heard them. The innkeeper's wife said:

"What is this, child of my heart, you're going and leaving me? How do you have the heart to leave this mother who has brought you up with so much love?"

Costanza wept and replied with words no less tender. But the Magistrate was moved and told the innkeeper's wife to get in the carriage too, and not to leave the side of her daughter, for that is what she considered her, until she left Toledo. And so the innkeeper's wife and everyone else got in the carriage and went to the Magistrate's house, where they were warmly welcomed by his wife, who was a distinguished lady. They ate splendidly and sumptuously, and after their meal Carriazo told his father how, for love of Costanza, Don Tomás had begun to serve in the inn, and that he was so in love with her that, without knowing she was as distinguished as she was, being his daughter, he would have taken her as his wife while she was still a scullery maid. Then the Magistrate's wife dressed Costanza in clothes that belonged to a daughter of hers who was the same age and size as Costanza, and if she looked beautiful in a peasant's clothes, in those of a noblewoman she looked like something from heaven; they suited her so well that it seemed as if she had been a lady ever since she was born and had always worn the best clothing.

But among so many joyful people, there was one who was sad, and this was Don Pedro, the son of the Magistrate, who imagined then that Costanza would not be his, and this was true; because the Magistrate and Don Diego de Carriazo and Don Juan de Avendaño agreed among themselves that Don Tomás should marry Costanza—her father giving her the thirty thousand *escudos* her mother had left her—and the water carrier Don Diego de Carriazo should marry the Magistrate's daughter, and Don Pedro, the Magistrate's son, should wed a daughter of Don Juan de Avendaño, for his father offered to obtain a dispensation because they were cousins.

In this way everyone was content, joyful, and satisfied, and news of the weddings and the good fortune of the illustrious scullery maid spread through the city, and infinite numbers of people came to see Costanza in her new attire, in which she demonstrated that she was the great lady we have said. They saw Tomás Pedro, the boy who took care of the barley, turned into Don Tomás de Avendaño and dressed like a gentleman; they noted that Lope the Asturian was noble after he had changed his clothes and abandoned the donkey and water jugs; but even so, there were still those who, in the midst of all the display, asked for the tail when he went down the street.

They spent a month in Toledo, and then Don Diego de Carriazo and his wife, his father, and Costanza with her husband, Don Tomás, and his father, returned to Burgos, along with the Magistrate's son, who wanted to go there and see his kinswoman and wife. The Sevillan was rich with the thousand *escudos* and the many jewels that Costanza gave to her mistress; for she always called the woman who had reared her by that name. The history of the illustrious scullery maid gave the poets of the golden Tajo the opportunity to wield their pens to solemnize and praise the unequaled beauty of Costanza, who still lives accompanied by her good servant at the inn, and Carriazo the same, with three sons who, without imitating their father or thinking whether there is tuna fishing in the world, today are all studying at Salamanca; and their father only has to see some water carrier's donkey to remember and recall the one he had in Toledo, and when he least expects it, he will again encounter in some satire, 'Let's have the tail, Asturian! Asturian, let's have the tail!'

THE NOVEL OF THE TWO MAIDENS

Five leagues from the city of Sevilla is a village called Castilblanco, and at nightfall a traveler riding a handsome foreign pony entered one of its many inns. He had no servant with him and did not wait for anyone to hold the stirrup, but dismounted with great agility.

The innkeeper appeared immediately, a diligent and obliging man, but he was not quick enough and the traveler was already sitting on a stone bench in the entrance, very quickly unfastening the buttons at his chest, and then his arms dropped to his sides, clearly indicating that he had fainted. The innkeeper's wife, a charitable woman, went to him and sprinkled water on his face, so that he regained consciousness; and he, evincing his regret that they had seen him in that state, did up his buttons again and asked to be given a room right away where he could rest and, if possible, be alone.

The innkeeper's wife told him there was one room left in the entire inn and it had two beds, and if a guest were to come, they would be obliged to accommodate him in the other one. To which the traveler responded that he would pay for the two beds whether or not another guest arrived. And taking out a gold *escudo*, he gave it to her on the condition that she not give anyone the empty bed.

The innkeeper's wife was not displeased with the payment, but offered instead to do what he asked even if the dean of the cathedral in Sevilla came that night to her inn. She asked whether he wanted supper and he answered that he did not, but wished only that they be very careful with his pony. He asked for the key to the room, and taking with him some large leather bags, he went in and locked the door behind him and even, as they learned later, placed two chairs against it.

As soon as he had locked himself in, the innkeeper and his wife, and the boy who gave barley to the animals, and two villagers who happened to be there came together to talk; and all of them mentioned the great comeliness and gallant disposition of the new guest, concluding that they had never seen such handsomeness. They considered his age and determined he must be sixteen or seventeen years old. They went back and forth and to and fro, as they say, regarding what might have been the cause of his faint but could not decide, and were left with their wonder at his good looks.

The villagers left for their houses, and the innkeeper went out to give the pony some feed and his wife to prepare something for supper in case other guests arrived. And that did not take very long, for a guest came in a little older than the first, and no less charming; and as soon as the innkeeper's wife saw him, she said:

"Lord save me! What does this mean? Have angels come to stay at my inn tonight?"

"Why does the innkeeper's wife say that?" asked the gentleman.

"I say it for good reason, Señor," she replied. "All I'm saying is that your grace shouldn't dismount because I don't have a bed to offer you, for the two that I had were taken by a gentleman in this inn, and he paid me for both, though he had no need for more than just one, so that no one else would stay in the room; he must like to be alone, though by God and my soul I don't know why, because he doesn't have a face or a disposition that ought to be hidden but should be seen and blessed by everyone."

"Is he so good-looking, Señora?" replied the gentleman.

"He certainly is good-looking!" she said. "And even more than very, very good-looking!"

"Hold this, boy," the gentleman said then, "because even if I sleep on the floor, I have to see a man so warmly praised."

And indicating the stirrups to a groom who was traveling with him, he dismounted, and told them to serve him supper immediately, and they did. And as he was eating, a bailiff from the village came in, which is common in small villages, and sat down to converse with the gentleman while he ate supper, and between one word and the next he did not fail to drink down three cups of wine and gnaw on a partridge breast and thigh that the gentleman offered him; and the bailiff paid for it all by asking for news of the court and the wars in Flanders and the advances of the Turks, not forgetting the deeds of the Transylvanian, may the good Lord keep him.[1]

The gentleman ate and was silent, because there was no pause when he could answer the questions. By now the innkeeper had finished feeding the pony, and he sat down to make a third in the conversation and to try no fewer cups of his own wine than the bailiff. And with each drink he turned and leaned his head on his left shoulder and praised the wine to the skies, though he did not dare leave it in the clouds for very long to keep it from being watered. From one topic to another, they returned to praises of the secluded guest

---

1. Most likely a reference to Sigismund Báthory, who abdicated his throne as Prince of Transylvania and then reversed his decision on more than one occasion.

and recounted his fainting and withdrawal and his not wanting any supper at all. They considered the sumptuousness of his bags, the quality of his pony, and the luxurious traveling clothes he wore, all of which contrasted with his not having a boy to serve him. All these exaggerations increased the gentleman's desire to see him, and beseeching the innkeeper to arrange for him to sleep in the other bed, he said he would give him a gold *escudo*. And even though the innkeeper coveted the money, which definitely inclined his will to accede, he found it impossible because the door was locked on the inside, and he did not dare waken the one who slept there, for he had also paid for both beds. All of which facilitated the bailiff's saying:

"What we could do is this: I'll knock at his door saying I'm the law and that, under orders from His Honor the Magistrate, I've brought this gentleman to stay here at the inn, and since there's no other bed, he's ordered to give us that one. To which the guest will reply that this is an affront since the bed is already rented and it isn't right to take it from the one who has it. In this way the innkeeper won't be responsible and your grace will achieve your purpose."

Everyone thought the bailiff's plan was a good one, and he was paid four *reales* for it.

They put it into effect, and so, with a show of great feeling, the first guest opened the door to the law and the second, begging his pardon for the offense that apparently had been done to him, went to lie down in the empty bed. But the first guest did not say a word or let his face be seen, because as soon as he opened the door, he went to his bed and turned his face to the wall, pretending to sleep so he would not have to reply. The second guest lay down, hoping his desire would be fulfilled in the morning, when they got up.

It was one of those long, sluggish December nights, and the cold and the weariness of travel forced a person to attempt to pass it in rest, but the first guest had no rest, and a little after midnight he began to sigh with so much bitterness that each sigh seemed to be his soul's last, to the extent that even though the second guest slept, he had to waken to the heartbreaking sound of the other's lamentations. And surprised at the sobs that accompanied his sighs, he began to listen attentively to what the other man appeared to be murmuring to himself. The room was dark and the beds far apart, but even so he could hear these words, among others, which in a thin, feeble voice the unhappy first guest was saying:

"Oh woe! Where is the irresistible force of my fate taking me? Which road is mine, or what escape can I hope for from the intricate labyrinth in which I find myself? Oh my few, unhappy years, incapable of wise deliberation and counsel! How will this secret pilgrimage of mine end? Oh, honor scorned! Oh, love disdained! Oh, respect for honored parents and kin trampled underfoot! And woe is me a thousand and one times, who so freely let myself be carried away by my desires! Oh, false words that so truly obliged me to respond to you with deeds! But about whom do I complain, unfortunate girl? Am I not the one who wanted to be deceived? Am I not the one who took the knife in my own hands and with it slashed and threw to the ground my reputation, along with the one my elderly parents had because of my worth? Oh false, despicable Marco Antonio! How is it possible that mingled with the sweet words you said to me was the bitter gall of your discourtesy and scorn? Where are you, ungrateful man? Where did you go, oh thankless one? Answer me, I am speaking to you; wait for me, I am following you; hold me up, I am swooning; pay me, you are in my debt; help me, for you are obliged to me in so many ways."

Saying this, she fell silent, indicating in quiet exclamations and sighs that she had not stopped shedding tender tears. All of which in calm silence the second guest listened to, gathering from what he heard that the plaintive guest was undoubtedly a woman, which further piqued his desire to meet her, and he decided several times to go to the bed of the person he believed to be a woman, and would have done so if he had not heard her get up, open the door, and call to the innkeeper to saddle the pony because she wished to leave. To which, after a good long time when the innkeeper let himself be called, he replied that the guest should be quiet because it was not yet past midnight, and it was so dark that setting out on the road would be foolhardy. The first guest became still, and closing the door again, threw herself on the bed, heaving a deep sigh.

It seemed to the one listening that it would be a good idea to speak to her and offer whatever assistance he could, obliging her in this way to allow herself to be seen and to recount her pitiable story, and so he said:

"Certainly, my esteemed Señor, if your sighs and words had not moved me to sorrow for the injury you lament, I would understand that I lacked natural feeling, or that my soul was of stone and my heart of hard bronze; and if this compassion I have for you, and the intention that has been born in me to devote my life to finding a remedy to your injury, if it has one, merit the recompense of some courtesy, I beg you to use it with me, telling me, without concealing anything, the reason for your sorrow."

"If it had not impaired my judgment," responded the one who was lamenting, "I certainly should have remembered that I was not alone in this room, and so I would have curbed my tongue and restrained my sighs; to pay for having my memory fail when having it mattered so much to me, I want to do as you ask, because by repeating the bitter history of my misfortunes, it may be that the new feeling will disappear. But if you wish me to do as you ask you must swear, by the faith you have shown in making the offer you have made to me, and for the sake of who you are, which you reveal in your words, to promise me a great deal, which is that in response to things you will hear in what I say you will not move from your bed, or come to mine, or ask me more than I shall wish to tell you, because otherwise, at the moment I hear you move, I shall run myself through the heart with a sword I have at the head of the bed."

The other guest, who would have promised a thousand impossibilities to learn what he so wished to know, said he would do precisely what he had been asked, affirming this with a thousand oaths.

"With this assurance, then," said the first guest, "I shall do what I have not done until now, which is to tell another person my life, and so, listen carefully. You should know, Señor, as you undoubtedly have already been told, that I entered this inn in a man's clothes but am an unfortunate maiden, at least one who was a maid until a week ago, and stopped being one through carelessness and madness, and belief in the beautiful false words of treacherous men. My name is Teodosia; my home a principal town of Andalucía, whose name I shall not say because it is not as important to you to know it as it is for me to hide it; my parents are noble and more than moderately wealthy, and they had a son and a daughter: he for their support and honor, and she for just the opposite; they sent him to study in Salamanca; they kept me at home, where they brought me up with the seclusion and prudence their virtue and nobility demanded, and I, with no regret at all, was always obedient to them, adjusting my will to theirs completely, in every way, until my impaired fate or my great brazenness placed me before the eyes of the son of a neighbor of ours, richer than my parents, and as noble as they. The first time I looked at him, the only thing I felt was that it was more than a pleasure to have seen him; and this was not a great deal, because his grace, elegance, face, and habits were praised and esteemed in the town, along with his singular good judgment and courtesy. But what good can it do me to praise my enemy or prolong with words the misfortune that befell me or, to be precise, the beginning of my madness? I say, in brief, that he saw me once and many times through a window across from one of mine. From there, it seemed to me, he sent me his soul through his eyes, and mine, with a happiness different from the earlier one, enjoyed seeing him and even compelled me to believe that everything I read in his gestures and face was pure truth. Sight was the intercessor and intermediary of speech, speech to declare his desire, his desire to ignite mine and attest to his. This was the goal of the promises, oaths, tears, sighs, and everything else that in my opinion a steadfast lover can do to indicate the morality of his will and the constancy of his heart, and to me, unfortunate girl, who never had found myself in similar circumstances or critical moments, each word was artillery that demolished part of the fortress of my honor; each tear a fire in which my modesty burned; each sigh a furious wind that increased the blaze, so that in the end it consumed the virtue that until then had not been touched. Finally, with the promise he would be my husband, in spite of his parents, who wanted him to marry someone else, I threw all my propriety to the ground, and without knowing how, gave myself to him without my parents' knowledge, with no other witness to my folly than a page of Marco Antonio, for this is the name of the disturber of my peace; and no sooner had he taken from me the jewel he coveted than he disappeared from the town two days later and neither his parents nor any other person could say or imagine where he had gone. Let whoever has the power to do so say the state I was in, for I do not, and do not know how to, say what I felt. I castigated my hair, as if it were responsible for my error; I martyrized my face, for it seemed to me it had been the occasion of my misfortune; I cursed my fate; I denounced my hasty decision; I shed many, infinite tears; I almost drowned between them and the sighs from my wounded heart; I complained in silence to heaven; I pondered it in my imagination to see whether I could discover a road or path to a remedy, and the one I found was to dress in a man's clothes and leave my parents' house and go in search of this second deceiving Aeneas,[2] this cruel, perfidious Bireno,[3] this defrauder of my virtuous thoughts and legitimate, well-founded hopes. And so, without delving deep into my thoughts, and taking advantage of a set of traveling clothes of my brother's, and saddling a pony of my father's, one very dark night I left the house intending to go to Salamanca where, as was said afterward, it was believed Marco Antonio might have gone, because he too is a student and a friend of my brother's. I did not fail to take with me a quantity of gold coins for everything that might occur on my unforeseen journey. And what concerns me most is that my parents will follow and find me because of the clothing and the pony I have with me; and when I don't fear this, I fear my brother in Salamanca, for if he recognizes me, it is clear my life is in danger; because even if he listens to my excuses, the smallest point of his honor pierces all the excuses I could give him. Despite all this, my principal determination

2. A reference to Aeneas's abandonment of Dido in Carthage, which caused her to commit suicide and allowed him to go on to found Rome.

3. In Ludovico Ariosto's *Orlando furioso*, Bireno was the lover of Olimpia. He abandoned her on an island near Scotland after falling in love with the daughter of the King of Frisia.

is, though I lose my life, to find my pitiless husband, for he cannot deny that without denying the token he left me, a diamond ring with an inscription that says: 'Marco Antonio is the husband of Teodosia.' If I find him, I shall learn from him what he found in me that moved him to leave me so soon; in brief, I shall make him keep his word to me and the faith he promised, or I shall take his life, showing I am as quick to vengeance as I was easy when I allowed him to offend me; for the noble blood my parents gave me has awakened in me the spirit that promises either the solution or the vengeance for the offense against me. This is, Señor, the true and unhappy history you wished to know, which should be sufficient excuse for the sighs and words that woke you. What I ask and beg of you is that, since you cannot give me a solution, at least you will give me advice to help me avoid the dangers that assail me and temper the fear I have of being found, and facilitate the means I should use to achieve what I so desire and need."

The man who had been listening to the history of the enamored Teodosia did not say a word for a long time, so much time that she thought he had fallen asleep and had heard nothing, and to affirm what she suspected, she said to him:

"Are you asleep, Señor? And it would not be a bad thing if you were, because the tormented person who recounts his misfortunes to one who has not felt them tends to cause more fatigue than compassion in the person listening."

"I am not asleep," said the gentleman, "rather, I am so awake and feel your misfortune so deeply that I do not know whether to say it afflicts and pains me as much as it does you, and for this reason the advice you ask of me not only will not end in my advising you but in helping you to the full extent of my power; for the manner in which you have recounted what happened to you has displayed the exceptional understanding you possess, and accordingly your conquered will must have deceived you more than the persuasions of Marco Antonio, and yet I still want to consider as an excuse for your error your youth, which did not allow you to know of the many deceptions of men. Be calm, Señora, and sleep if you can for the little that remains of the night, for when day comes, the two of us shall talk and see what path will lead us to a solution."

Teodosia thanked him as profusely as she could and attempted to rest a while to allow the gentleman to sleep, but he was not still for a moment and began to toss and turn in the bed and sigh, so that Teodosia was obliged to ask him what was wrong, for if it was some affliction she could remedy she would do so as willingly as he had made the same offer to her. To which the gentleman responded:

"Since you, Señora, are the one causing the restlessness you have heard, you are not the one who can remedy it, for if you were, I would have no sorrow at all."

Teodosia could not understand where that confused reasoning was going, but still she suspected that some amorous passion was troubling him, and she still thought she was the reason, and it was sensible to suspect and think so, for the convenience of the room, the solitude, the darkness, and his knowing she was a woman, all could easily have awakened in him some unchaste thought. And fearing that, she dressed very quickly and silently, and girded on her sword and dagger, and in that way, sitting on the bed, she waited for day, which in a short while gave signs of its arrival with the light that entered through the many spaces and openings that rooms in hostelries and inns have. And the gentleman had done exactly what Teodosia did, and as soon as he saw the room studded with the light of day, he got up from the bed, saying:

"Get up, Señora Teodosia, for I wish to accompany you on this journey and keep you by my side until you have your Marco Antonio as your legitimate husband, or he and I have lost our lives; and here you will see the obligation and will your misfortune has created in me."

And saying this, he opened the windows and doors of the room.

Teodosia had wanted day to come so she could see in its light the figure and appearance of the man to whom she had been speaking all night. But when she looked at him and recognized him, she wished dawn had never broken but that there, in perpetual night, her eyes had been closed; because as soon as the gentleman turned to look at her, for he too wished to see her, she knew he was her brother, whom she feared so much, and at the sight of whom she almost lost her own eyesight, and she was paralyzed and mute, with no color in her face; but deriving strength from her fear and discernment from the danger, and placing her hand on her dagger and holding it by the blade, she went to kneel before her brother, saying in a perturbed and fearful voice:

"Take this, Señor, my dear brother, and use this weapon to punish me for the error I have committed, and satisfy your anger, since for guilt as great as mine it is not right for any mercy to be shown toward me. I confess my sin, and I do not wish my repentance to serve as an excuse. I beg only that the penalty be the kind that takes my life and not my honor, for since I have placed it in clear danger by leaving my parents' house, my good name will be saved if the punishment you give me is secret."

Her brother looked at her, and although the boldness of her audacity provoked him to vengeance, the very tender and effective words with which she had expressed her guilt softened his heart so much that, with a pleasant expression and conciliatory appearance, he raised her from the floor and consoled her as well as he could, telling her, among other things, that since he could not find a punishment equal to her madness, he had suspended the search; and for that reason, and because it seemed to him that fortune had not yet closed completely all the doors to a remedy, he wanted to attempt to find one by all possible means before he took his revenge for the offense, which her great profligacy had imposed on him.

With these words Teodosia recovered her lost vital spirits, the color returned to her face, and her almost dead hopes revived. Don Rafael, which was her brother's name, did not wish to talk any further about what had happened. He told her only to change her name from Teodosia to Teodoro, and that the two of them should return immediately to Salamanca to find Marco Antonio, although he imagined he was not there, for since he was his friend he would have spoken to him, although it might be that the offense Marco Antonio had committed against him had silenced him and taken away his desire to see Don Rafael. The new Teodoro agreed with what her brother wished. Then the innkeeper came in, and they asked him for some breakfast because they wanted to leave right away.

While the groom was saddling the animals and they were waiting for breakfast, a nobleman came into the inn; he had been traveling, and Don Rafael knew him immediately. Teodoro also knew him and did not dare leave the room in order not to be seen. The two men embraced, and Don Rafael asked the recent arrival for news from home. To which he replied that he was coming from the Port of Santa María where he had left four galleys on their way to Naples, and he had seen Marco Antonio Adorno, the son of Don Leonardo Adorno, embark on one of them, and the news made Don Rafael happy, for it seemed that hearing news about what mattered to him so much without even thinking about it was a sign this matter would end well. He asked his friend to trade his father's pony, which he knew very well, for the mule he was riding, not telling him he was coming from but going to Salamanca and did not want to take such a good pony on so long a trip. The other man, who was a good friend and very prudent, was pleased with the trade and promised to return the pony to Don Rafael's father. They had breakfast, and Teodoro ate alone in the room, and when it was time to leave, the friend took the road to Cazalla, where he had a large estate.

Don Rafael did not leave with him, and to deceive him said he had to return that day to Sevilla; and as soon as he saw that he had gone, their mounts being ready and the innkeeper paid, he and his sister took their leave and rode away from the inn, leaving everyone in it marveling at their comeliness and gallant disposition, for Don Rafael had no less charm, elegance, and circumspection than his sister had beauty and grace.

Then, as they were leaving, Don Rafael told his sister the news he had been given about Marco Antonio, and he thought they should ride as quickly as possible to Barcelona, where the galleys sailing to Italy or arriving in Spain ordinarily stop for a few days, and if they had not arrived yet, they could wait, and there they undoubtedly would find Marco Antonio. His sister said to do whatever he thought best, because she had no will other than his.

Don Rafael told the groom he had brought with him to be patient because he had to stop in Barcelona, and assured him he would be paid to his satisfaction for the time he had been with him. The boy, who was one of those in the trade who enjoyed traveling and knew Don Rafael was generous, said he would accompany him and serve him to the ends of the earth. Don Rafael asked his sister how much money she had with her. She replied that she had not counted it, all she knew was that she had put her hand into their father's strongbox seven or eight times and taken it out filled with gold *escudos*; and accordingly Don Rafael supposed she might have up to five hundred *escudos*, and with the two hundred he had and a gold chain he was wearing, it seemed to him they were in no great need, and was more certain than ever they would find Marco Antonio in Barcelona.

And so they hurried in order not to lose a day's travel, and without mishaps or obstacles they came within two leagues of a town called Igualada that is nine leagues from Barcelona. They had learned on the way that a gentleman traveling as the Ambassador to Rome was in Barcelona waiting for the galleys, which had not yet arrived, a piece of news that made them very happy. And with that happiness they rode into a small wood along the road, and from it they saw a man running out and looking back, as if he were frightened. Don Rafael stopped before him, saying:

"Why are you running, my good man, or what has happened that you show signs of fear and move so quickly?"

"Why wouldn't I run quickly and in fear," replied the man, "since only by a miracle have I escaped a company of bandits in the wood?"

"That's bad," said the groom, "bad. Lord save us! Bandits at this time of day? By my faith, they won't be nice to us."

"Don't be distressed, brother," said the man from the wood, "the bandits have gone and left more than thirty travelers in their underclothes, tied to the trees of this wood. They left only one man free so he could untie the rest after they had gone behind a hill, which they said would be his signal."

"If that's true," said Calvete, which was the groom's name, "then we can go through safely, because bandits don't come back to a place where they've made an assault for several days, and I can say this as someone who has been in their hands twice and knows their habits and customs very well."

"That's true," said the man.

Having heard this, Don Rafael decided to go on. And they had not gone very far when they came across the people tied to the trees, who numbered more than forty, and the one who had been left free was untying them. They were a strange sight: some, completely naked; others, dressed in the bandits' ragged castoffs; some, weeping at finding themselves robbed; others, laughing at the strange garb of the others; one recounting in detail what they had taken from him; another saying that of the infinite number of things they had taken from him, he most regretted a box of Agnus Dei images he had brought from Rome. In short, everything there was the weeping and wailing of the miserable people who had been stripped and robbed. All of which the brother and sister observed, not without great sorrow, and thanking heaven they had been saved from so great and proximate a danger. But what prompted their greatest compassion, especially Teodoro's, was seeing a boy who seemed to be sixteen or so tied to an oak in just a shirt and canvas breeches, but with a face so beautiful it moved deeply everyone who looked at him.

Teodoro dismounted to untie him, and he gave very courteous thanks for the good turn, and to make a good turn even better, Teodoro asked Calvete, the groom, to lend him his cape until they could buy another in the next town for that charming youth. Calvete gave his cape to Teodoro, who covered the boy with it, asking where he was from, where he had come from, and where he was going.

Don Rafael witnessed all this, and the boy responded that he was from Andalucía, from a town that, when he named it, they realized was no more than two leagues from theirs. He said he had come from Sevilla and his plan was to travel to Italy to try his luck in the practice of arms, as many other Spaniards had done; but he had been dealt a losing hand with his unfortunate encounter with the bandits, who had taken from him a good deal of money and clothes so good they could not be bought for three hundred *escudos*; but in spite of everything he intended to continue his journey because his was not a lineage in whom the heat of a fervent desire would cool at the first unfortunate turn of events.

The boy's fine speech, together with hearing that he came from a town so close to theirs, not to mention the letter of recommendation of his comeliness, moved the brother and sister to favor him in every way they could. And, distributing money to those they thought had the greatest need, especially friars and clerics, and there were more than eight of them, they had the boy get up on Calvete's mule, and with no further stops, in a short time they reached Igualada, where they learned that the galleys had arrived in Barcelona the day before and would sail in two days if the insecurity of the beach did not oblige them to do so earlier.

This news meant that the following morning when they woke before the sun, although they had not slept much during the night, the brother and sister were subjected to more of a surprise than they had expected, because at the table where they were eating with the boy they had untied, Teodoro looked fixedly and with some curiosity at his face, and it seemed to her he had pierced ears, and this along with his very timid glance made her think he must be a woman, and she wanted to finish supper in order to confirm her suspicions when they were alone. During the meal, Don Rafael asked him whose son he was, because he knew all the leading people in his town if it was the one he had mentioned. To which the youth replied that he was the son of Don Enrique de Cárdenas, a well-known gentleman. Don Rafael said he knew Don Enrique de Cárdenas very well but knew and was certain he had no son, but if the boy had said this in order not to reveal the identity of his parents, it did not matter and he would never ask him the question again.

"It is true," replied the boy, "that Don Enrique has no sons, but a brother of his named Don Sancho does."

"He doesn't have sons either," responded Don Rafael, "but he does have one daughter, and they say she is one of the most beautiful maidens in Andalucía, and I know this only through hearsay, for although I have been in her town many times, I never have seen her."

"Señor, everything you say is true," said the youth, "and Don Sancho has only one daughter, but she is not as beautiful as they say; and if I said I was the son of Don Enrique, it was, Señores, so you'd think I was somebody, for I'm only the son of a steward of Don Sancho's who has served him for many years, and I was born in his house, and because I made my father angry when I took a good amount of money from him, I wanted to go to Italy, as I told you, and follow the path of war, by means of which, as I have seen, even those of obscure birth can become famous."

His words and the manner in which he said them were carefully noted by Teodoro, whose suspicions were being confirmed.

They finished supper, the table was cleared, and while Don Rafael was undressing, Teodoro, who had told him what she suspected about the youth, with her brother's agreement and permission walked with the boy to the balcony of a wide window that faced the street, and there, with both of them leaning their chests against the balustrade, Teodoro began to speak to the boy:

"I should like, Señor Francisco," for that is what he said his name was, "to have done you so many good turns you would be obliged not to deny me anything I could or might wish to ask of you, but the short time I have known you has not allowed for that. It may be that in the future you will know what my desire deserves, but if you do not wish to satisfy the one I have now, I shall not for that reason stop being your servant, as I am now; before I reveal that desire to you, you should know that although I am as young as you, I have more ex-perience in worldly matters than my few years might indicate, and that has led me to suspect you are not a man, as your clothing indicates, but a woman, and as well born as your beauty proclaims, and perhaps as unfortunate as this change in clothing denotes, for such changes never benefit the one who makes them. If what I suspect is true, tell me so, and I swear to you, by the faith of a gentleman, which I profess, to help and serve you in every way I can. You cannot deny you are a woman, for this truth is seen clearly in your ears, and you were careless not to close and disguise those holes with some flesh-colored wax, for it might be that someone else as attentive as I, but not as honorable, would bring to light what you have hidden so badly. I say that you should not hesitate to tell me who you are, taking it as a given that I am offer-ing you my help. I assure you the secret will be kept as long as you wish."

The youth listened very attentively to what Teodoro was saying, and seeing that she had finished, before answering took her hands, brought them up to his mouth, kissed them forcefully, and even bathed them in a great quantity of tears that fell from his beautiful eyes, causing a strange sentiment in Teo-doro, who could not help but join in (it is an inborn and natural condition of noblewomen to be moved by the sentiments and travails of others); but after she withdrew her hands with difficulty from the mouth of the young man, she was attentive to how he would respond, and groaning deeply and heaving many sighs, he said:

"I do not wish to nor can I, Señor, deny that your suspicion is true; I am a woman, and the most unfortunate one that women have brought into the world, and since what you have done for me and the offers you have made oblige me to obey you in whatever you may command, listen, and I shall tell you who I am, if you are not already tired of hearing the misfortunes of others."

"May I live always in them," replied Teodoro, "if the pleasure of learning them does not overcome the sorrow caused in me by their being yours, for I feel them as if they were my own."

And embracing Teodoro again and reiterating his offers, the youth, some-what more tranquil, began to say these words:

"As for my homeland, I have said the truth; as for my parents, I did not; because Don Enrique is not my father but my uncle, and his brother Don Sancho is my father; for I am the unfortunate daughter your brother says

Don Sancho has, so celebrated for her beauty, whose deception and disillusionment can be seen in my lack of beauty. My name is Leocadia; the reason for my change of clothing you will hear now. Two leagues from my town is another, one of the richest and noblest in Andalucía, where a distinguished gentleman lives who traces his lineage to the noble and ancient Adornos of Genoa. He has a son who, unless praise has exaggerated his fame, as it has in my case, is one of the most gallant men one could desire. And because of the proximity of our towns and because, like my father, he is a hunting enthusiast, he sometimes would come to our house and stay five or six days, and all of them, and even part of the nights, he and my father would spend in the countryside. This opportunity was taken by fortune, or love, or my carelessness, and it was enough to throw me down from the height of my virtuous thoughts to the lowliness of the situation in which I find myself, for having contemplated Marco Antonio's elegance and discernment more than was licit for a modest young maiden, and having considered the quality of his lineage and his father's large fortune, it seemed to me that acquiring him as a husband was all the happiness my desire could hold. With this thought in mind, I began to look at him more carefully, and no doubt it must have been more carelessly as well, because he became aware that I was looking at him, and the traitor did not want nor did he need any other entrance to penetrate the secret of my heart and steal from me the finest tokens of my soul. But I don't know why I've started to recount to you, Señor, point by point, the trifling details of my love, since they are so beside the point, but I must tell you once and for all what he, with many shows of solicitude, acquired from me, which was that having faithfully sworn and given his word, with great and, to my mind, firm and Christian vows to be my husband, I offered myself to him to do with as he wished. But still not really satisfied by his vows and words, I had him write them on a paper that he gave to me, signed with his name, and with so many written pledges and obligations that I was satisfied. Having received the document, I devised a plan for him to go from his town to mine and come over the garden wall to my bedroom where, with no interruption of any kind, he could pick the fruit destined for him alone. At last the night I so desired arrived."

Until this point Teodoro had been silent, her soul hanging on Leocadia's words, for each of them pierced her soul, especially when she heard the name of Marco Antonio, and saw Leocadia's rare beauty, and considered the greatness of her valor and her singular judgment, which was clear in the way she recounted her story. But when she said, "at last the night I so desired arrived," Teodoro almost lost patience and could not help speaking, saying:

"And so, as soon as he arrived on that joyous night, what did he do? Did he come in, by chance? Did you enjoy him? Did he again confirm your document? Was he happy to have obtained from you what you said was already his? Did your father learn the outcome of such chaste, wise principles?"

"The outcome," said Leocadia, "was to put me in the situation you see, because I did not enjoy him, and he did not enjoy me, because he never came to the meeting we had arranged."

Teodosia breathed when she heard this and her vital spirits returned; they had gradually been leaving her, stimulated and heightened by the ravening pestilence of jealousy, which had begun to enter the marrow of her bones and take complete possession of her patience; but it did not leave her so free that she did not listen again with great surprise as Leocadia continued, saying:

"Not only did he not come, but a week later I learned from a reliable source that he had left his town and taken from her parents' house a maiden from the same town, the daughter of an eminent gentleman, named Teodosia, a maid of extreme beauty and singular discernment. And because her parents were so noble, in my town they knew of the abduction, and then it reached my ears, and with it the cold, fearful lance of jealousy, which pierced my heart and burned my soul in so great a blaze that in it my honor turned to ash, my standing was consumed, my patience dried up, and my good sense came to an end. Ah, woe is me, unfortunate woman! Immediately I imagined Teodosia more beautiful than the sun and more discerning than discernment itself, and above all, luckier than I, who had no luck. Then I read the words on the paper, firm and binding ties that could not fail in the faith they proclaimed, and although my hope took refuge in them as if they were something sacred, when I realized the suspect company that Marco Antonio took with him, I threw them all to the ground. I scratched my face, tore at my hair, cursed my fate; and what I regretted most was not being able to perform these sacrifices constantly because of my father's unavoidable presence. In short, to lament without impediment, or to end my life, which is more accurate, I determined to leave my father's house. And as if to bring an evil thought into action, it seems that opportunity facilitates and smooths away all difficulties, and fearing nothing, I stole clothes from one of my father's pages, and from my father a large amount of money, and one night, wrapped in its black cloak of darkness, I left the house and walked a few leagues and reached a town called Osuna; I found a seat in a cart, and two days later I entered Sevilla, which meant entering the certainty I would not be found even if they looked for me. There I bought other clothes and a mule and traveled until yesterday with some gentlemen hurrying to Barcelona in order not to lose the advantage of some galleys sailing to Italy, and then the bandits must have told you what happened to me: they took everything I had, among other things the treasure that sustained my well-being and alleviated the burden of my efforts, which was Marco Antonio's document, which I intended to take with me to Italy, and finding Marco Antonio, present it to him as a testimony to his faithlessness and to my great constancy, and somehow make him keep his promise to me. But at the same time I have considered that the man who denies the obligations that should be engraved in his soul could easily deny the words written on a paper; and it is clear that if he has with him the incomparable Teodosia, he will not want to look at the unfortunate Leocadia, but even so I plan to die or come into their presence so that the sight of me upsets their tranquility. That enemy of my rest should not think she can enjoy at so little cost what is mine! I shall look for her, find her, and take her life if I can."

"But how can Teodosia be blamed," said Teodoro, "if she perhaps was deceived by Marco Antonio, as you have been, Señora Leocadia?"

"Can that be true," said Leocadia, "if he took her with him? And when people who love each other are together, what deception can there be? None, of course; they are happy because they are together, whether they are, as they say, in the remote burning deserts of Libya or in the lonely distant wastes of frozen Scythia. She no doubt enjoys him wherever they are and she alone must pay for what I have suffered until I find them."

"It might be that you are deceived," replied Teodosia, "for I know this enemy of yours very well and know her character and virtue, and she would never risk leaving her parents' house or comply with the will of Marco Antonio; and if she had, not knowing you or anything about what you had with him, she did not offend you in any way, and where there is no offense, there should be no vengeance."

"As for her modesty," said Leocadia, "there's no need to talk to me about that, for I was as modest and virtuous as any maiden you could have found, and even so I did what you have heard; that he took her away, there is no doubt, and that she has not offended me, looking at it without passion, that I confess. But the pangs of jealousy I feel represent her in my memory just like a sword that has passed through my entrails, and before long, as if she were a weapon that hurts me, I shall attempt to pull her out and break her into pieces; moreover, it is prudent to remove those things that harm us, and it is natural to hate those that harm us and interfere with our well-being."

"This being as you say, Señora Leocadia," responded Teodosia, "and I see that the passion you feel does not allow you to speak more reasonably, you are not ready to accept beneficial advice. As for me, I can tell you what I have already told you, that I shall help and favor you in everything that is just and in any way I can, and I promise the same of my brother, for his character and nobility will not allow him to do otherwise. We are going to Italy; if you would like to come with us, you already have a fair idea of the nature of our company. What I ask is that you give me permission to tell my brother what I know of your condition so that he treats you with the courtesy and respect to which you are entitled and is obliged to look after you properly. Together with this, it does not seem a good idea for you to change clothes, and if in this town it is possible to dress you differently, in the morning I shall buy you the best clothes available, the ones that suit you best, and as for the rest of your intentions, leave them to time, which is the great master of giving and finding a remedy for the most desperate cases."

Leocadia thanked Teodosia, whom she thought was Teodoro, for her many offers, and gave her permission to tell her brother whatever she wished, begging that she not be abandoned, for she could see all the dangers she would be subject to if she were recognized as a woman. With this they took their leave and went to bed, Teodosia to her brother's bedroom and Leocadia to another that was beside it.

Don Rafael was not yet asleep, waiting for his sister to find out what had happened with the man she thought was a woman, and when she came in, before she lay down, he asked her, and she, point by point, recounted everything Leocadia had told her: whose daughter she was, her love, Marco Antonio's document, and her intentions. Don Rafael was amazed and said to his sister:

"If she is who she says she is, I can tell you, sister, that she is one of the most eminent persons in her town and one of the most noble ladies in all of Andalucía. Her father is well known by ours, and the fame she had as a beautiful girl corresponds very well to what we see now in her face. And what I think is that we should go carefully, so that she does not speak to Marco Antonio before we do, for I am somewhat concerned about the document she says he signed even if it has been lost. But be calm and go to bed, sister, and we shall find a remedy for everything."

Teodosia did as her brother said as far as going to bed was concerned, but being calm was beyond her control, for the raging disease of jealousy had already taken possession of her soul. Oh, how much greater than they really were did the beauty of Leocadia and the disloyalty of Marco Antonio appear in her imagination! Oh, how many times did she read, or pretend to read, the document he had given her! What words and phrases did she add to it, which made it certain and very effective! How many times did she not believe it had been lost! And how many did she imagine that, without it, Marco Antonio would not fail to fulfill his promise, not thinking of his obligations to her!

She spent most of the night thinking about this, not sleeping. And Don Rafael, her brother, did not get more rest that night, because as soon as he heard who Leocadia was his heart began to burn with love for her, as if he had met her long ago; for beauty has this power, that in an instant, a moment, it brings with it the desire of whoever sees and knows it, and when it reveals or promises some way of reaching and enjoying it, with powerful fervor it sets fire to the soul of whoever contemplates it, just like the means whereby dry prepared gunpowder is easily lit by any spark that touches it.

He did not imagine her tied to the tree, or dressed in torn men's clothing, but in her own women's clothes and in the house of her wealthy parents, with a lineage as eminent and rich as they were. His thoughts did not linger, nor did he wish them to linger, on the cause that had brought her to his meeting with her. He wanted day to arrive so he could continue his journey and find Marco Antonio, not so much to make him his brother-in-law as to prevent his becoming Leocadia's husband, and love and jealousy already had so much control over him that he would have thought it a good outcome to see his sister without the remedy he was seeking for her and Marco Antonio without his life, in exchange for not finding himself with no hope of winning Leocadia; this hope was already promising him a happy conclusion to his desire, either by means of force or by means of gifts and good works, for the time and occasion offered him every possibility.

Having promised himself this, he calmed down somewhat, and a short while later day broke, and they left their beds, and calling the innkeeper, Don Rafael asked if it would be possible in that town to obtain clothes for a page whom the bandits had stripped. The innkeeper said he had a moderately priced outfit to sell; he brought it, and it fit Leocadia very well. Don Rafael paid him and she put it on, and girded on a sword and dagger with so much grace and spirit that even in those clothes Don Rafael's senses were enthralled and Teodosia's jealousy doubled. Calvete saddled the animals, and at eight in the morning they left for Barcelona, not wishing at that moment to go up to the famous monastery of Monserrat, leaving it for a time when God would be pleased to return them to their homeland with more tranquility.

We cannot give a good account of the thoughts of the brother and sister, or with what different spirits they both looked at Leocadia, Teodosia desiring her death and Don Rafael her life, both of them jealous and impassioned,

Teodosia searching for faults in her so as not to be disheartened in her hope, and Don Rafael discovering perfections that, point by point, obliged him to love her more. In spite of all this, they did not fail to ride quickly, so that they reached Barcelona a little before sunset. They admired the beautiful location of the city and judged it the flower of beautiful cities in the world, the honor of Spain, the dread and terror of its neighboring and distant enemies, the pleasure and delight of its residents, a sanctuary to foreigners, a school of chivalry, an example of loyalty, and the satisfaction of everything a judicious and cultivated desire can ask of a great, famous, rich, and well-founded city.

As they entered it, they heard a loud noise and saw a great throng of people running and making a huge uproar, and asking the reason for that noise and movement, the reply was that the people from the galleys that were at the beach had risen up and entered into battle with the people of the city. Hearing this, Don Rafael wanted to see what was going on, although Calvete told him not to, for it made no sense to place himself in clear danger, and he knew very well how badly those who became involved in such disputes fought, for they were common in the city when the galleys arrived. Calvete's good advice was not enough to hold back Don Rafael, and so they all followed him. And when they reached the beach, they saw many swords unsheathed and many people slashing and stabbing with no pity at all. In spite of this, without dismounting, they came so close they could clearly see the faces of those who were fighting, because the sun had not yet gone down.

An infinite number of people from the city had gone there and many were disembarking from the galleys, even though the man in command of the ships, a Valencian nobleman named Don Pedro Vique, from the stern of the flagship threatened those in skiffs going to help their people. But seeing that his shouts and threats did no good, he had the prows of the galleys turned to face the city and fired a gun without a cannonball, a sign that if they did not leave, the next shot would be sure to have one.

At this point Don Rafael was attentively watching the cruel and bitterly fought dispute, and he saw and noted that among those from the galleys who most distinguished themselves was a youth of twenty-two or so, dressed in green, with a hat of the same color adorned with a rich band, apparently made of diamonds. The skill with which the young man fought and the elegance of his clothing made everyone watching the dispute turn to look at him, and the eyes of Teodosia and Leocadia looked in such a way that at the same time both said:

"Lord save me, either I have no eyes or the one in green is Marco Antonio!"

And saying this, with great agility they jumped down from their mules, and putting their hands on their daggers and swords, with no fear whatsoever went right to the middle of the crowd, and with one of them on each side stood beside Marco Antonio, for he was the young man in green.

"Do not be afraid, Señor Marco Antonio," said Leocadia as soon as she reached him, "for at your side you have one who will make a shield of his life to defend yours."

"Who can doubt it," replied Teodosia, "when I am here?"

Don Rafael, who saw and heard what was happening, followed them as well and fought on Marco Antonio's behalf. Marco Antonio, occupied in attacking and in defending himself, did not notice the words the two women said to him; rather, absorbed in the fight, he did things that seemed incredible. But since the number of people from the city was growing by the moment, those from the galleys were forced to retreat until they were in the water. Marco Antonio retreated unwillingly, and in step with him, at either side, the two valiant and new Bradamantes and Marfisa[4] or Hippolytas and Penthesileas.[5]

Now a Catalan knight of the famous Cardona family appeared on a powerful horse, and placing himself between the two factions, made those from the city retreat, for they respected him as soon as they recognized him. But from a distance some threw rocks at those retreating to the water, and as bad luck would have it, one hit Marco Antonio in the temple with so much force that it knocked him into the water, which was already up to his knees; and as soon as Leocadia saw him fall she embraced him and held him up in her arms, and Teodosia did the same. Don Rafael was at a slight distance, defending himself against the infinite stones raining down on him and wishing to assist Leocadia, his soul, and his sister and brother-in-law, but the Catalan knight placed himself in front of him, saying:

"Calm yourself, Señor, for the sake of what you owe a good soldier, and be so kind as to place yourself at my side, for I shall free you from the insolence and audacity of this ill-mannered rabble."

"Ah, Señor," replied Don Rafael, "let me pass, for I see the things I love most in this life placed in great danger!"

---

4. Bradamante and Marfisa were female warriors from Matteo Boiardo's *Orlando innamorato* and Ariosto's *Orlando furioso*.

5. Hippolyta and Penthesilea were Amazonian queens from Greek mythology.

The knight let him pass, but he did not arrive so quickly that Marco Antonio and Leocadia, who never let him out of her arms, had not already been picked up by the skiff from the flagship; and Teodosia wanted to embark with them, but either because she was tired, or because of the sorrow of having seen Marco Antonio wounded, or because she saw him leaving with her greatest enemy, she did not have the strength to get into the skiff and undoubtedly would have fainted into the water if her brother had not come in time to help her, and he felt no less sorrow than his sister to see Leocadia leaving with Marco Antonio; for he too had already recognized Marco Antonio. The Catalan knight, liking the gallant presence of Don Rafael and his sister, who he thought was a man, called to them from the shore and asked them to come with him, and they, forced by necessity and fearful that the people, who were not yet peaceful, would commit some offense against them, were obliged to accept his offer.

The knight dismounted, and keeping them at his side, with his sword unsheathed he passed among the turbulent crowd, asking them to withdraw, which they did. Don Rafael looked all around to see if he could find Calvete with the mules, and he did not see him because the groom, as soon as they had dismounted, took the mules by the reins and went to an inn where he had stayed at other times.

The knight reached his house, which was one of the most prominent in the city, and asked Don Rafael in which galley he was traveling; he responded that he had been in none of them, for he had reached the city at the very moment the dispute began, and because in the fight he had met the gentleman who had been wounded by a stone and taken away in a skiff, he had placed himself in that danger, and he asked the knight to have the wounded man brought ashore, for on that his happiness and his life depended.

"I shall do that willingly," said the knight, "and I know the general will surely give that order, for he is an eminent gentleman and my kin."

And without stopping again, he returned to the galley and discovered that they were treating Marco Antonio, whose wound was dangerous, for it was on the left temple and the surgeon said he was in peril; he obtained the general's permission to have him treated on land, and placing him with great caution in the skiff, they took him away, and Leocadia refused to leave him and embarked with him as if following the polestar of her hope. When they reached land, the knight had a sedan chair brought from his house for him. In the meantime, Don Rafael sent for Calvete, who was at the inn, concerned about what fate had befallen his masters, and when he learned they were all right, he was very happy and went to join Don Rafael.

At this point the master of the house arrived and accommodated Marco Antonio, Leocadia, and everyone there with great lavishness and care. The knight immediately sent for a famous surgeon in the city to treat Marco Antonio again. He came but did not want to treat him until the following day, saying that the surgeons in armies and armadas were always very experienced because of the many wounds they constantly had before them, and so it was not advisable to treat him until the next day. What he ordered was that he be placed in a warm room and allowed to rest.

The surgeon from the galleys arrived and described the wound to the surgeon from the city and told him how he had treated it, and that in his opinion, the wounded man's life was in danger; which led the surgeon from the city to conclude he had been properly treated; at the same time, according to what he had been told, he exaggerated the danger Marco Antonio was in.

Leocadia and Teodosia heard this with the same emotion they would have felt if they had heard his death sentence, but, in order not to display their sorrow, they repressed it and were silent, and Leocadia determined to do what she thought necessary to satisfy her honor. And so, as soon as the surgeons had left, she entered Marco Antonio's room, and before the master of the house, Don Rafael, Teodosia, and other persons, she went to the head of the wounded man's bed, and taking his hand, said these words to him:

"This is not the time, Señor Marco Antonio Adorno, when we can or should say many words to you; and so I wish only for you to hear a few that are necessary, if not for the health of your body than for that of your soul, and to say them it is necessary for you to give me your permission and tell me if you are capable of listening to me; for it would not be right, after having tried from the moment I met you to always please you, to cause you grief at this moment, which I take to be your last."

At these words Marco Antonio opened his eyes and turned them attentively to Leocadia's face, and having almost recognized her, more from the organ of her voice than from the sight of her, in a weakened and afflicted voice, he said:

"Tell me, Señor, whatever you wish, for I am not so close to death that I cannot listen to you, nor is your voice so disagreeable that it causes me annoyance to hear it."

Teodosia was very attentive to this conversation, and each word Leocadia said was a sharp arrow that pierced the heart and even the soul of Don Rafael, who was listening as well. And continuing, Leocadia said:

"If the blow to your head, or, I should say, the one to my soul, has not taken from your memory, Señor Marco Antonio, the image of the woman who not long ago you said was your glory and your heaven, you must certainly remember who Leocadia was and the promise you made to her in a document signed by your own hand, nor can you have forgotten the worth of your parents, the integrity of their prudence and virtue, and the obligation you have toward them for having attended to your whims in everything you desired. If you have not forgotten this, even though you see me in these strange clothes, you will easily know I am Leocadia who, fearing that new events and situations would take from me what is rightfully mine, as soon as I heard that you had left your home, overcoming infinite difficulties I decided to follow you dressed like this, intending to search for you everywhere on earth until I found you. None of this should startle you, if you have ever heard of the power of true love and the fury of a deceived woman. I have suffered some hardships in my quest, all of which I judge and deem restful, considering the compensation they have brought of seeing you, and since you are in the state you are in, if it is God's will to take you to a better life, if, before you pass, you do what you owe to the person you are, I shall believe myself more than fortunate, promising you, as I do promise you, to lead such a life after your death that I soon will follow you on this final, obligatory journey. And so I beg you, first for the sake of God, to whom my desires and intentions are directed, and then for your sake, for you owe a great deal to being who you are, and finally for my sake, to whom you owe more than to any other person in the world, that here and now you take me as your legitimate wife, not permitting justice to do what reason, with so many truths and obligations, persuades you to do."

Leocadia said no more, and all those in the room maintained a marvelous silence while she was speaking. And in the same silence they waited for Marco Antonio's response, which was this:

"I cannot deny, Señora, that I know you, for your voice and face will not allow me to. Nor can I deny how much I owe to you, nor the great worth of your parents, together with your incomparable virtue and modesty, nor do I think, nor shall I think, any less of you for what you have done in coming to find me in clothing so different from your own; rather, I esteem you for this and shall esteem you to the greatest degree possible; but, since my bad luck has brought me to this state, as you say, which I believe will be the final one of my life, and since such critical moments overflow with truths, I wish to tell you a truth, and if it is not to your liking now, it might be to your benefit later on. I confess, beautiful Leocadia, that I loved you dearly and you loved me, and along with that I confess that the document I wrote for you was more to satisfy your desire than mine; because many days before I signed it, I had given my will and my soul to another maiden from my own town, whom you know well, and whose name is Teodosia, the daughter of parents as noble as yours;

and if I gave you a document signed by my hand, to her I gave my hand signed and accredited by so many actions and witnesses that it was impossible for me to give my freedom to any other person in the world. The love I had with you was a pastime, with which one does not attain anything but the courting you already know, which did not offend nor can it offend you in any way; what happened to me with Teodosia meant obtaining the fruit she could give me and that I wanted her to give, with the faith and certainty of being her husband, as I am. And if I left her and you at the same time, you perplexed and deceived, and she fearful and, in her opinion, without honor, I did so without thinking very much about it and with the judgment of a young man, which I am, believing that all those things were of small importance and that I could do them with no scruples of any kind, with other thoughts that came to me and inclined me to whatever I wished, which was to come to Italy and spend some of the years of my youth there and return afterward to see what God had done with you and my true wife. But heaven, grieving over me, undoubtedly has allowed me to be brought to this state in which you see me so that, confessing these truths, born of my many faults, I could pay what I owe in this life, and you would be undeceived and free to do what you think best. And if at some time Teodosia learns of my death, she will know from you and from those here present how in death I kept the word I gave her in life. And if in the little time remaining to me, Señora Leocadia, I can serve you in anything, tell me, and as long as it is not making you my wife, for I cannot, I shall not fail to do anything I possibly can to please you."

While Marco Antonio was saying these words his head was on his elbow, and as he finished speaking his arm dropped, indicating that he had fainted. Don Rafael hurried to his side and, embracing him closely, he said:

"Regain your consciousness, Señor, and embrace your friend and brother, for you wish me to be both. I am Don Rafael, your friend, who will be the true witness to your will and the good turn you wish to do his sister by receiving her as your own."

Marco Antonio regained consciousness, immediately recognized Don Rafael, and embracing him closely and kissing his face, said:

"Now I believe, my brother and my lord, that the great joy I have received in seeing you cannot bring any less abatement than a great grief, for people say that after pleasure sadness follows, but I shall consider any that might come to me well deserved in exchange for having enjoyed the pleasure of seeing you."

"Well, then, I want to make your happiness more complete," replied Don Rafael, "by presenting to you this jewel who is your beloved wife."

And looking for Teodosia he found her weeping behind all the people, astonished and torn between sorrow and joy because of what she had seen and heard. Her brother grasped her hand and she, not resisting, allowed herself to be led wherever he wished, and that was to Marco Antonio, who recognized and embraced her, both of them weeping tender, amorous tears.

Everyone in the room was astonished at seeing so singular an event. They looked at one another without saying a word, waiting to see where those matters would end. But the undeceived and luckless Leocadia, who saw with her own eyes what Marco Antonio was doing and saw the one who she thought was Don Rafael's brother in the arms of the man she considered her husband, and together with this seeing her desires thwarted and her hopes lost, avoided the eyes of everyone (who were looking attentively at what the patient was doing with the page he held in his arms), and left the room or bedchamber and in an instant was in the street, intending to go, lacking all hope, through the world or wherever people could not see her. But no sooner had she reached the street than Don Rafael missed her, and as if he were missing his soul, asked for her but no one could tell him where she had gone. And so, not waiting for anything else, desperate, he went out to find her, and went to where they said Calvete was staying, in case she had gone there to obtain a mount for her departure; and not finding her there, he ran through the streets like a madman looking for her everywhere; and thinking she might by chance have returned to the galleys, he went to the beach, and shortly before he arrived he heard someone calling from land for the flagship's skiff, and knew that the one calling was the beautiful Leocadia; she, hearing footsteps behind her and wary of some mishap, gripped her sword and waited, prepared, until Don Rafael reached her, and then she recognized him and was sorry he had found her, especially in so solitary a place; for she already understood, from more than one sign Don Rafael had given her, that he did not think badly of her but so highly that he would consider it a good match even if Marco Antonio had loved her a little more.

With what words can I tell now the words Don Rafael said to Leocadia, opening his soul to her? There were so many and of such quality that I do not dare to write them. But since I must say some, these were a few of the many he said to her:

"If with the good fortune I lack I were to lack now, oh beautiful Leocadia, the boldness to reveal to you the secrets of my soul, the most loving and chaste will ever born or that ever can be born in a loving heart would be buried in the bosom of perpetual oblivion. But in order not to commit that offense again my legitimate desire, let come what may, I wish, Señora, for you to know, if your impassioned thought will allow it, that Marco Antonio is not better than me in anything except in the great good fortune of being loved by you. My lineage is as good as his, and in what are called the goods of this world he does not have much of an advantage; as for those of nature, it is not proper for me to praise myself, even more so if in your eyes they have no worth. I say this, devoted Señora, so that you can take the solution and the means that fate offers you in the extremity of your misfortune. You see now that Marco Antonio cannot be yours because heaven made him my sister's, and the same heaven that today has taken Marco Antonio away from you, wishes to compensate you with me, and I desire no other good in this life than to offer myself to you as your husband. Look and see that good fortune is knocking at the door of the bad you have had until now, and do not think the boldness you have shown in looking for Marco Antonio will be a reason not to esteem and value you as much as you deserve, if you have ever had such a thought, for when I decide I am your equal, choosing you for my everlasting lady, at that same moment I shall forget, and have already forgotten, everything about this that I have learned and seen; for I know very well that the powers that have forced me to so impetuously and unrestrainedly adore you and give myself to you, are the same ones that have brought you to the state in which you find yourself, and so there will be no need to find excuses where there has been absolutely no error."

Leocadia was silent while Don Rafael said everything he had to say, except that from time to time she heaved deep sighs that came from the very bottom of her heart. Don Rafael was daring enough to take her hand and she did not have the strength to prevent it, and so kissing her hand over and over again, he said:

"Lady of my soul, be finally the lady of all of me in the sight of the star-filled heaven that covers us, and this quiet sea that listens to us, and these sea-bathed sands that sustain us. Say yes, which no doubt will benefit your honor as well as my contentment. I tell you again that I am a gentleman, as you know, and wealthy, and I love you dearly, which is what you must value most, and instead of finding you alone and in clothes unworthy of your honor, far from the house of your parents and kin, with no one to provide what you may need, and no hope of achieving what you were seeking, you can return to your homeland in your own honored and true clothing, accompanied by a husband as good as the one you could choose for yourself, rich, happy, esteemed, served, and even praised by all those made aware of the facts of your story. If this is so, as it is, I don't know what makes you hesitate. Finally be (once again I say it to you) the one who raises me from the earth of my misery to the heaven of deserving you, and in doing this you will act in your own best interest and obey the laws of courtesy and good understanding, showing that you are both grateful and discerning."

"Well, then," the hesitant Leocadia said at this point, "if heaven has ordained this, and it is not in my hands or those of any living being to oppose what He has determined, let what He wishes and you desire, Señor, be done; and heaven itself knows with what discomfort I acquiesce to your will, not because I do not understand how much I gain by obeying you, but because I fear that, in fulfilling your desire, you will look at me with eyes different from those with which you have perhaps seen me until now, and looking at me, you will see that they have deceived you. But in short, however that may be, the name of the legitimate wife of Don Rafael de Villavicencio is one that cannot be lost; and only with this title shall I live content. And if the customs you see in me after I am yours play a part in your finding me even a little worthy of your esteem, I shall thank heaven for having brought me by such strange and roundabout ways and by means of so many evils to the good of being yours. Give me, Señor Don Rafael, your hand as a token that you are mine, and here you see that I give you mine in return, and let those you mentioned be witness to this: heaven, sea, sand, and this silence interrupted only by my sighs and your pleas."

Saying this, she allowed herself to be embraced and gave him her hand, and Don Rafael gave her his, celebrating this new nocturnal betrothal only with the tears that happiness, in spite of past sadness, drew from their eyes. Then they returned to the knight's house, which was in great sorrow because of their absence, and Marco Antonio and Teodosia were just as sad; they had already been married by a priest, for persuaded by Teodosia, fearful that some unexpected obstacle would interfere with the good she had found, the knight sent immediately for a cleric to marry them, so that when Don Rafael and Leocadia came in and Don Rafael recounted what had happened with Leocadia, the joy in the house was increased as if they were close kin, for it is a natural and typical characteristic of the Catalan nobility to know how to be friends and favor strangers who may have need of them.

The priest, who was present, ordered Leocadia to change her clothes and put on her own; and the knight saw to this quickly, dressing the two girls in two rich dresses that belonged to his wife, an eminent lady from the ancient line of the Granolleques, famous in that kingdom. He advised the surgeon who, out of charity, pitied the wounded man, who was talking a great deal, for they would not leave him alone; the surgeon came and ordered what he had at first, which was that Marco Antonio be left in silence. But God, who had ordained this, taking as the means and instrument of His works—when He wishes to perform for our eyes some miracle—what nature itself cannot achieve, ordained that Marco Antonio's joy and lack of silence were instrumental in healing him, so that the next day, when they treated him, they found him out of danger, and two weeks later he got up so healthy that with no fear whatsoever he could travel again.

It should be noted that while Marco Antonio was in bed he made a vow that if God cured him, he would go on a pilgrimage, by foot, to Santiago de Galicia, and in this promise he was joined by Don Rafael, Leocadia, Teodosia, and even Calvete, the groom—an act rarely performed by those in similar trades; but the goodness and open-heartedness he had found in Don Rafael obliged him not to leave him until they returned to their homeland; and seeing that they would go on foot, like pilgrims, he sent the mules to Salamanca along with the one that belonged to Don Rafael, for there was no lack of people with whom to send them.

The day of their departure arrived, and having obtained their pilgrims' capes and everything they needed, they took their leave of the generous knight who had favored and treated them so well, whose name was Don Sancho de Cardona, celebrated because of his lineage and famous because of his person. They all said that they and their descendants, for whom they would leave orders, would keep perpetually the memory of the singularly good treatment they had received from him as a way of thanking him, since they could not return the favor. Don Sancho embraced them all, saying it was part of his nature to perform those and other good deeds for all those he knew or imagined were Castilian nobles.

The embraces were repeated twice, and with joy mixed with some feelings of sadness, they took their leave, and traveling as quickly as the delicacy of the two new pilgrims permitted, in three days they reached Monserrat, and staying there another three days, doing what good Catholic Christians ought to do, in the same amount of time they resumed their journey, and with no setbacks or mishaps arrived in Santiago. And after fulfilling their vow with the greatest possible devotion, they did not wish to remove their pilgrims' capes until they entered their houses, to which they traveled slowly, rested and content. But before they arrived, when they were within sight of Leocadia's town which, as we have said, was a league from Teodosia's, from the top of a rise they could see them both, unable to hide the tears of joy that seeing their homes brought to their eyes, at least the eyes of the two brides, for the sight of them brought back memories of past events.

From where they were standing, a broad valley between the two villages could be seen, and there they saw, in the shade of an olive tree, a gallant knight on a powerful horse, and a pure white shield on his left arm, and a long, heavy lance resting across his right; and looking at him attentively, they saw two other knights come riding through the olive grove with the same weapons and the same grace and elegance, and then they saw that the three came together, and after a short while separated, and one of those who had come later moved away with the one who had been beneath the olive tree first; and spurring their horses, they charged each other with signs of being mortal enemies, beginning to attack with fierce and skilled thrusts of their lances, now avoiding the blows, now blocking them on their shields with so much proficiency that they made it clear they were masters of that calling. The third one was watching, not moving from the spot; but Don Rafael, unable to endure being so far away, and looking at that hard-fought and singular battle, rode down the slope as fast as he could, followed by his sister and his wife, and in a short time he was near the two combatants who by now were slightly wounded. The hat of one of the knights fell off, and with it a steel helmet, and when he turned his face Don Rafael recognized his father, and Marco Antonio knew that the other was his. Leocadia, who had looked carefully at the one not fighting, recognized the man who had fathered her, and this sight left all four perplexed, astonished, and beside themselves; but shock gave way to the power of reason, and the two brothers-in-law, without stopping, placed themselves between the two who were fighting and called out:

"No more, gentlemen, no more, and those who ask and entreat this are your own sons. I am Marco Antonio, my father and lord," said Marco Antonio, "I am he for whose sake, I imagine, your venerable white head is placed in this difficult situation. Temper your rage and throw down your lance, or turn it against another enemy, for the one before you now will be your brother from today on."

Don Rafael said almost the same words to his father, and when they heard them the knights stopped and began to look carefully at those who were saying them, and turning around, they saw that Don Enrique, Leocadia's father, had dismounted and was embracing the man they thought was a pilgrim. For Leocadia had approached him, and making herself known had begged him to make the combatants stop fighting, telling him briefly that Don Rafael was her husband and Marco Antonio was Teodosia's.

Hearing this, her father dismounted and embraced her, as we have said; but leaving her, he went to make peace between the two men, although it was not necessary, for they had already recognized their sons and were on the ground, holding them in their arms, all of them shedding tears born of love and joy. They all came together and looked at their children again, and did not know what to say. They touched their bodies to see whether they were phantoms, for their unexpected arrival gave rise to this and other suspicions; but disabused somewhat of their uncertainty, they returned to their tears and embraces.

Then, along the same valley, there appeared a large number of armed men, on foot and on horse, who had come to defend the gentleman from their town. But when they arrived and saw them embracing those pilgrims, their eyes filled with tears, they dismounted and were amazed and bewildered, so that Don Enrique had to tell them briefly what Leocadia, his daughter, had told him.

Everyone went to embrace the pilgrims with such great signs of happiness they can hardly be described. Don Rafael again recounted to everyone, as briefly as the moment required, the history of all their loves and how he came to be married to Leocadia, and his sister Teodosia to Marco Antonio, news that once again caused great joy. Then, from among the horses of the people who had come to help, they took the ones needed for the five pilgrims and agreed to go to Marco Antonio's town, his father offering to celebrate everyone's weddings there, and with this they left; and some of those who had been present rode ahead to ask the kin and the friends of the newlyweds to come and celebrate. On the way, Don Rafael and Marco Antonio learned the reason for the dispute, which was that Teodosia's father and Leocadia's had challenged Marco Antonio's father, because he had known about his son's deceptions, and since both of them had come and found him alone, they did not wish to fight with any advantage but one on one, like gentlemen, in combat that would have ended in the death of one or both if their children had not arrived.

The four pilgrims thanked God for the happy outcome. And the day after their arrival, with wonderful and splendid magnificence and sumptuous expense, Marco Antonio's father celebrated the wedding of his son and Teodosia, and the wedding of Don Rafael and Leocadia. And they lived long and happy years with their wives, leaving behind a distinguished progeny and lineage, which still exist in the two towns, which are among the best in Andalucía; and if we do not name them it is to protect the honor of the two maidens, for evil tongues, or foolishly scrupulous ones, might charge them with having frivolous desires and suddenly changing into men's clothes; and these I entreat not to launch into vituperation of such liberties until they look into themselves and see whether they have ever been shot with what is called Cupid's arrow, which in fact is an invincible force, if it can be called that, brought by appetite against reason.

Calvete, the groom, kept the mule Don Rafael had sent to Salamanca, and the many other gifts the two bridegrooms gave him. And the poets of that time had occasion to use their pens to exaggerate the beauty and history of the two maidens, as chaste as they were bold, the principal subjects of this singular tale.

THE NOVEL OF SEÑORA CORNELIA

Don Antonio de Isunza and Don Juan de Gamboa, notable gentlemen of the same age, very discerning, great friends, and students in Salamanca, decided to abandon their studies and go to Flanders, moved by the fire of young blood, the desire, as they say, to see the world, and because it seemed to them that the practice of arms, though it ennobles and is advantageous to everyone, principally suits and is even more advantageous to the wellborn of eminent lineage.

And so they arrived in Flanders at a time when there was peace, or agreements and treaties to achieve it soon. In Antwerp they received letters from their fathers, who wrote of how troubled they were by their sons having abandoned their studies without notifying them, so that they could have traveled in the luxury demanded by their being who they were. In short, recognizing the grief of their fathers, they agreed to go back to Spain, since there was nothing to do in Flanders, but before they returned they wanted to see all the most famous cities in Italy. And having seen them all, they stopped in Bologna, and admiring the curricula offered at that celebrated university, they wished to continue their own studies there.[1] They notified their fathers of their intention, which made their parents extremely happy, and they showed this by providing for their sons magnificently, in a way that would demonstrate who they were and the kind of fathers they had. And from the first day they went to the schools, everyone knew they were gentlemen: gallant, intelligent, and well bred.

Don Antonio must have been twenty-four, and Don Juan no more than twenty-six; and they graced this good age by being very charming men who were musicians, poets, and skilled, valiant swordsmen, talents that made them loved and valued by everyone who had dealings with them.

They soon had many friends, not only Spanish students of the many studying in that university but also students from the city as well as other places.

1. The University of Bologna was founded in 1088 and is considered to be the oldest university in the world. In the fourteenth century, the Royal Spanish College was founded for Spanish students to study abroad under Royal Spanish patronage as part of the university.

They were generous and courteous with everyone—very far from the arrogance often attributed to Spaniards. And since they were young and lighthearted, they were not displeased to hear about the beautiful women in the city; and although there were many ladies, maidens, and married women, famous for their virtue and beauty, they were all surpassed by Signora Cornelia Bentivoglio of the ancient and noble family of the Bentivoglios, who had once been the lords of Bologna.

Cornelia was exceptionally beautiful and lived under the guardianship and protection of Lorenzo Bentivoglio, her brother, an exceedingly honorable and valiant gentleman, for their father and mother were both dead; and although they had been left alone, they had been left wealthy, and wealth is an immense consolation to orphans.

Cornelia's modesty was so great and her brother so solicitous in guarding her that she did not allow herself to be seen nor did her brother consent to her being seen. These reports made Don Juan and Don Antonio desirous of seeing her, even if only in church. But their efforts in this regard were in vain, and their desire for the impossible, the power of hope, began to wane. And so, with only love of their studies and the entertainment of some seemly youthful adventures, they had a life as joyful as it was honorable. They rarely went out at night, and if they did, they went together and well armed.

And so it happened that, having planned to go out one night, Don Antonio told Don Juan that he wanted to stay and say certain prayers, but his friend should go and he would follow.

"There's no need," said Don Juan, "I'll wait for you, and if we don't go out tonight, it doesn't matter."

"No, on your life," replied Don Antonio, "go and take the air, and I'll be with you right away if you go where we usually do."

"Do as you like," said Don Juan. "Stay here in peace, and if you do go out tonight, I'll be at the usual places."

Don Juan left, and Don Antonio remained. It was a fairly dark night, and the time was eleven; and having walked two or three blocks and finding himself alone, with no one to talk to, he decided to return home, and as he did, he passed along a street that had doorways with marble pillars and heard someone hissing at him from a door. The darkness of the night and the shadows cast by the doorways did not allow him to guess where the hiss was coming from. He stopped for a moment, was very attentive, and saw a door open slightly. He approached and heard a quiet voice that said:

"Are you by any chance Fabio?"

Don Juan, just to see what would happen, replied:

"Yes."

"Well, take this," came the answer from inside, "and hide it in a safe place, and come right back, it's important."

Don Juan put out his hand and touched a bundle, and wanting to take it, saw that it required two hands, and so he had to grasp it with both hands. As soon as he had, the door closed and he found himself carrying something in the street without knowing what it was. But almost immediately a baby began to cry, apparently a newborn, whose cry left Don Juan confused and bewildered, not knowing what to do or what decision to make, for if he knocked at the door again, he might be in danger no matter to whom the infant belonged, and if he left the baby there, then it would be at risk; if he took it home, there was no one there to help, and he did not know anyone in the city to whom he could bring a baby. But since he had been told to hide it in a safe place, he decided to take it home and leave it with a housekeeper who worked for them, and return immediately to see whether his help was necessary in any other way, since it was obvious he had been taken for someone else and the infant given to him in error.

Finally, without another thought, he went to his house, and Don Antonio was no longer in. He went into a room and called the housekeeper, uncovered the infant, and saw that it was the most beautiful he had ever seen. The swaddling clothes indicated it had been born to rich parents. The housekeeper unwrapped the clothes and they discovered the baby was a boy.

"This child," said Don Juan, "must be nursed, and this is how it has to be done: you have to remove these rich clothes and replace them with more humble ones, and without saying I brought him here, you have to take him to the house of a midwife, for they can always give help and assistance in these matters. Take enough money to satisfy her, and give the baby whatever parents you choose in order to hide the truth of my having brought him here."

The housekeeper said she would, and Don Juan, as quickly as he could, returned to see whether he was hissed at again; but a little before he reached the house where they had called him, he heard a great clanging of swords, as if many people were dueling. He listened carefully and did not hear a single word. The sword fight was silent; and in the light of the sparks that rose from the stones struck by swords, he could almost see that many men were attacking one, and he confirmed this as true when he heard someone say:

"Ah, traitors, so many of you and I am alone! But even so, your treachery will do you no good."

Hearing and seeing this, Don Juan, moved by his valiant heart, in two leaps stood at the man's side, and placing his hand on his sword and on a small shield he was carrying, said to the man defending himself, speaking Italian so he would not be recognized as a Spaniard:

"Do not be afraid, for help has come that will not fail until life is lost; wield your blades, for traitors can do little even if they are many."

To these words, one of the opponents replied:

"You lie! There is no traitor here; the wish to regain lost honor permits all excess."

He did not say another word because the speed with which his enemies (Don Juan estimated there were six) attempted to wound him did not give him the opportunity. They pressed his companion so hard that, with two simultaneous thrusts to his chest, they knocked him to the ground. Don Juan thought he had been killed, and with agility and uncommon valor he stood in front of them all and made them retreat before a downpour of slashes of his dagger and thrusts of his sword. But his diligence would not have been enough to attack and defend himself at the same time, if good luck had not come to his assistance when the residents of the street brought lights to the windows and called in loud voices for the law; seeing this, his opponents left the street, turned their backs, and disappeared.

By now the fallen man was on his feet, because the sword thrusts had hit a small breastplate he wore that was as hard as a diamond. Don Juan's hat had fallen off in the skirmish, and as he looked for it he found another one that he put on without thinking about it, not looking to see whether it was his or not. The man who had fallen came up to him and said:

"Signore, whoever you may be, I confess I owe you my life, which, with all that I am worth and am capable of, I shall spend in your service. Be good enough to tell me who you are and your name, so that I may know to whom I owe my gratitude."

To which Don Juan responded:

"I do not wish to be discourteous, since I am impartial. In order to do, Signore, what you ask, and only to give you pleasure, I shall tell you that I am a Spanish gentleman and a student in this city. If it matters to you to know my name, I shall tell it to you; but if by some chance you should like to use me in any other matter, you should know that my name is Don Juan de Gamboa."

"You have done me a very good turn," said the man who had fallen, "but I, Signor Don Juan de Gamboa, do not wish to tell you who I am or my name, because I shall be very pleased if you hear it from someone other than myself, and I shall take care that you do."

Don Juan had first asked if he was wounded, because he had seen him receive two great sword thrusts, and he had replied that, after God, an excellent breastplate he was wearing had defended him; but even so, his enemies would have finished him if Don Juan had not been at his side. Then they saw a large number of people coming toward them, and Don Juan said:

"If these are your enemies returning, prepare yourself, Signore, and act like the man you are."

"I believe these men coming toward us are not enemies but friends."

And that was the truth, because those who approached—there were eight men—surrounded the one who had fallen and exchanged a few words with him, but so quietly and secretively that Don Juan could not hear them.

Then the man he had defended came back to Don Juan and said:

"If these friends had not come, Señor Don Juan, in no way would I have left you until you had finished rescuing me; but now I beg most earnestly that you go and leave me, and this matters a great deal to me."

Saying this, he put his hand to his head and discovered he did not have a hat, and turning to those who had arrived, he asked them to give him a hat because his had fallen off. As soon as he said this, Don Juan placed on his head the hat he had found. The man who had fallen felt it, and turning to Don Juan, he said:

"This hat is not mine; on your life, Señor Don Juan, take it as a memento of this skirmish and keep it, for I believe it is well known."

They gave another hat to the man he had defended, and Don Juan, to comply with what had been asked of him, and exchanging a few more courtesies, left without knowing who the man was, and came to his house, not wanting to pass by the door where he had been given the infant, because it seemed to him the entire neighborhood was awake and aroused because of the altercation.

And it so happened that returning to his lodgings, he encountered his friend, Don Antonio de Isunza, in the middle of the street, and having recognized each other, Don Antonio said:

"Come back with me, Don Juan, up this way, and I'll tell you something strange that happened to me, and you won't have heard anything like it in your entire life."

"I could tell you one of those stories too," answered Don Juan, "but let's go wherever you like, and tell me yours."

Don Antonio led the way and said:

"You should know that a little more than an hour after you left the house I went out to look for you, and not thirty steps from here I saw a black figure coming right toward me, and coming very quickly; and when it was close, I saw it was a woman in a long habit, and she, in a voice interrupted by sobs and sighs, said to me: 'Signore, are you a foreigner, by chance, or are you from the city?' 'I am a foreigner, a Spaniard.' And she: 'Thank heaven, which does not want me to die without the sacraments.' 'Are you wounded, Signora,' I replied, 'or have you suffered some fatal wrong?' 'It might be that the one I have suffered will be fatal if I don't find a remedy quickly; for the sake of the courtesy that always reigns in those of your nationality, I beg you, Spanish gentleman, to get me off these streets and take me to your lodgings as quickly as you can, and there, if you so wish, you will hear of the wrong I have suffered and who I am, even at the cost of my reputation.' Hearing this, and thinking she had a real need for what she was asking, without saying anything else I took her by the hand and brought her to our lodgings by deserted backstreets. Santisteban, the page, opened the door, I had him withdraw, and without his seeing her I took her to my room, and when she entered she fell onto my bed in a swoon. I went to her and uncovered her face, which she had concealed with her cloak, and discovered there the greatest beauty human eyes have ever seen; I thought she was eighteen, perhaps younger, but surely not older. I marveled at seeing such extraordinary beauty; I sprinkled a little water on her face, and she regained consciousness, sighing tenderly. And the first thing she said to me was: 'Do you know me, Señor?' 'No,' I said, 'I have not enjoyed the great good fortune of knowing so much beauty.' 'Woe to the girl,' she answered, 'to whom heaven gives it, to her great misfortune; but Señor, this is not the time for praising beauty but for remedying misfortune. For the sake of who you are, leave me here, locked in, and do not permit anyone to see me, and then return to the place where you found me and see if any people are fighting, and do not favor any of those who are fighting but make peace, for any harm to those involved will increase my own.' I left her locked in and came to settle the dispute."

"Do you have anything else to say, Don Antonio?" asked Don Juan.

"Well, don't you think I've said enough?" replied Don Antonio. "Haven't I said that I have under lock and key, in my room, the greatest beauty human eyes have ever seen?"

"The incident is undoubtedly strange," said Don Juan, "but listen to mine."

And then he recounted everything that had happened to him, and how the infant they had given him was at home in the care of the housekeeper, and how he had told her to change the rich swaddling clothes into poor ones and to take the baby where he would be nursed or at least provided for in the present necessity. And he said that the dispute he had gone looking for was already ended and resolved, and that he had found himself in the middle of it, and he imagined that all those involved in the dispute were rich, powerful men.

They were each amazed at what had happened to the other and quickly returned to their lodgings to see what the locked-in girl might need. On the way, Don Antonio told Don Juan that he had promised the lady he would not let her be seen by anyone, nor would anyone else enter that room except him, for as long as that was her preference.

"It doesn't matter at all," responded Don Juan, "for there will be no lack of opportunity to see her, which I desire very much after hearing you praise her beauty."

At this point they arrived, and in the light brought by one of their three pages, Don Antonio looked up at the hat Don Juan was wearing, and he saw it bright with diamonds. He took it off his friend's head and saw that the lights came from many gems on the rich band around the hat. They both looked at it and looked at it again and concluded that if all of them were of fine quality, as they seemed to be, it was worth more than twelve thousand *ducados*. Now they knew with certainty that important people were involved in the dispute, especially the man helped by Don Juan, whom he remembered saying that he should take the hat and keep it because it was well known. They had the pages withdraw, and Don Antonio opened the door to his room and found the lady sitting on the bed, her hand on her cheek, shedding tender tears. Don Juan, with the desire he had to see her, put his head in the doorway as far as he could, and the gleam from the diamonds immediately shone in the weeping girl's eyes, and looking up, she said:

"Come in, Signor Duke, come in. Why do you wish to be so miserly with the happiness of my seeing you?"

And Don Antonio said:

"Signora, there is no duke here trying to avoid seeing you."

"What do you mean?" she replied. "The man who looked in now is the Duke of Ferrara, who can hardly hide the richness of his hat."

"The truth is, Signora, that the hat you saw is not worn by any duke; and if you wish to be undeceived by seeing who is wearing it, give him permission to enter."

"He is welcome to come in," she said, "although if he is not the duke, my misfortunes will be even greater."

Don Juan heard everything, and seeing he had permission to go in, with the hat in his hand he entered the room, and as soon as he stood before her and she realized that the man with the rich hat was not the one she had said, in a troubled voice and hurried speech, she said:

"Oh, woe is me! Signore, tell me now, without keeping me in suspense: do you know the owner of this hat? Where did you leave him, or how did it come into your possession? Is he alive or is this the news of his death? Oh, my treasure! What has happened? Here I see your clothing, here I find myself without you, locked in and in the power of two men, and if I did not know they were Spanish gentlemen, the fear of losing my virtue would have cost me my life."

"Be calm, Signora," said Don Juan, "for the owner of this hat is not dead, nor are you in a place where you will be wronged in any way but served in everything we are capable of, even laying down our lives to defend and protect you; for it would not be right for the faith you have in the goodness of Spaniards to be in vain; and since we are Spaniards, and prominent ones (for here what seems arrogance is appropriate), you can be sure the propriety your presence deserves will be maintained."

"That is what I believe," she replied, "but even so, tell me, Signore, how did that rich hat come into your possession, or where is its owner, who is none other than Alfonso de Este, Duke of Ferrara?"

Then Don Juan, in order not to keep her in suspense any longer, told her how he had found himself in an altercation, and in it he had favored and helped a gentleman who, from what she had said, undoubtedly was the Duke of Ferrara, and during the skirmish he had lost his hat and found this one, and the gentleman had told him to keep it, for it was well known, and the dispute had ended without the gentleman or himself being wounded, and when it was over, people had arrived who apparently were servants or friends of the man he thought was the duke, who had asked him to leave and had seemed 'very grateful for the help I had given him.'

"And so, my lady, this rich hat came into my possession in the manner I have said, and its owner, if he is the duke, as you say, was fine, safe and sound, when I left him less than an hour ago. Let this truth be a reason for you to take comfort, if that will be the result of your knowing the good condition of the duke."

"So that you may know, gentlemen, whether I have reason and cause to ask about him, pay attention and listen—I don't know whether I should call it this—to my unfortunate story."

While all of this was happening, the housekeeper was busy rubbing the infant's lips with honey and replacing his rich wrappings for poor ones. And when she had him ready, she wanted to take him to the house of a midwife, as Don Juan had told her to. And when she walked with him past the room where the lady was about to begin her story, the infant cried so that she heard him, and getting to her feet, the lady began to listen carefully, and when she heard his cry more distinctly, she said:

"Signori, what infant is that? It sounds like a newborn."

Don Juan answered:

"It's a child left tonight at our door, and the housekeeper is going to find someone to nurse him."

"Bring him here, for the love of God," said the lady, "for I shall perform that act of charity for other people's children, since heaven does not wish me to do it with my own."

Don Juan called the housekeeper, took the child from her, approached the one who had asked for him, and placed him in her arms, saying:

"Here you see, Signora, the gift we were given tonight, and he is not the first, for few months go by that we don't make similar discoveries at our door."

She took him in her arms and looked at him intently, at his face as well as the poor but clean swaddling in which he was wrapped, and then, unable to contain her tears, she placed her headdress over her breasts so she could nurse the infant with modesty, and placing him there she put her face next to his, and with her milk she nourished him and with her tears she bathed his face. And she did not raise her face but stayed this way for as long as the child wanted to stay on her breast. During this time the four of them kept silent. The child nursed, but not really, because new mothers do not produce milk, and so, when she realized this, she turned to Don Juan, saying:

"I've been charitable for nothing; I'm clearly new to these matters. Signore, have this child's lips rubbed with a little honey, and don't allow him to be carried through the streets at this hour. When day comes, and before they take him away, bring him back to me; it's a great comfort for me to see him."

Don Juan returned the child to the housekeeper and told her to take care of him until morning, and to put back the rich swaddling he had on at first, and not to take him out without first telling him. And entering the room again, with the three of them alone, the beautiful lady said:

"If you wish me to speak, first give me something to eat, I feel faint, and with good reason."

Don Antonio went quickly to a cabinet and took out a good number of preserves, and the lady who felt faint ate some, and drank a glass of cold water, and this brought her around; and somewhat calmer, she said:

"Sit down, Signori, and listen to me."

They did so, and settling on the bed and wrapping herself carefully in the skirts of her dress, she lowered a veil she had been wearing from her head to her shoulders, leaving her face uncovered and unveiled and looking the same as the moon, or rather, the sun itself when it is most beautiful and bright. Liquid pearls rained from her eyes, and she wiped them with a snowy white linen handkerchief and hands so white that between them and the handkerchief not even the best judge could tell which was whiter. Finally, after heaving many sighs and attempting to calm her bosom somewhat, in a sorrowful and troubled voice, she said:

"Signori, I am the one whose name you undoubtedly have heard here, because the fame of my beauty, such as it is, is proclaimed by many tongues. I am, in effect, Cornelia Bentivoglio, sister of Lorenzo Bentivoglio, and in telling you this, perhaps I have told you two truths: one, regarding my nobility; the other, regarding my beauty. When I was still very young my father and mother both died, and I was cared for by my brother, who, from the time I was a little girl, guarded me with absolute discretion, although he trusted my honorable disposition more than the solicitude with which he protected me. In short, surrounded by walls and solitudes, accompanied only by my maids, I grew, and with me grew the fame of my comeliness, made public by servants and those who had spoken to me in secret, and by a portrait by a famous painter, which my brother had made so that, as he said, the world would not be left without me if heaven were to call me to a better life. But all of this would have played a very small part in hastening my perdition if it had not happened that the Duke of Ferrara was best man at the wedding of a female cousin of mine, to which my brother took me with the best of intentions and to honor our kin. There I looked and was seen; there, I believe, I conquered hearts and subjugated wills; there I felt that praise gave pleasure, even when spoken by flattering tongues; there, in short, I saw the duke and he saw me, and the result of that seeing is the state in which I find myself now. I do not wish to tell you, Signori, because it would mean proceeding into infinity, the terms, the schemes, and the means by which, after two years, the duke and I eventually satisfied the desires born at that wedding, because neither guardianship, nor prudence, nor honorable admonitions, nor any other human precaution was enough to keep us from coming together, which finally had to be under the promise he made to be my husband, because without that it would have been impossible to surrender the rock of the valued and honored presumption of my own honor. A thousand times I told him to publicly ask my brother for me, for it was not possible he would refuse, and there was no need to give explanations to the rabble for whatever blame they would put on him for the inequality of our marriage, since the nobility of the Bentivoglio line did not diverge in any way from that of the Este line. He responded to this with excuses, which I considered sufficient and necessary, and as self-assured as I was vanquished, I believed as a woman in love believes and gave myself with all my will subject to his, through the intercession of one of my maids, more susceptible to the duke's gifts and promises than she should have been, given the confidence my brother had in her loyalty. In short, after a few days I knew I was pregnant, and before my clothes could reveal my improprieties, to call them by their only name, I pretended I was sick and melancholic and had my brother take me to the house of that cousin whose best man had been the duke. There I let him know my condition, and the danger that threatened me, and how insecure I felt my life was, for I conjectured that my brother suspected my audacity. The duke and I agreed that I would inform him when I was beginning my ninth month, and he would come for me with other friends of his and take me to Ferrara, where he would marry me publicly. Tonight was when we had arranged that he would come for me, and this very night, as I was waiting for him, I heard my brother pass by with many other men, apparently armed, as indicated by the clatter of their weapons, and that sudden fright brought on the birth, and in an instant I delivered a beautiful boy. That maid of mine, aware of my actions and their intermediary, and already prepared for the event, wrapped the infant in swaddling different from the cloths around the baby left at your door; she went to the street door and gave him to a man she said was a servant of the duke. A short while later, taking with me what I could in light of my present needs, I left the house thinking the duke was on the street, and I should not have done that until he came to the door; but the fright my brother's armed band had given me, and my belief that he was already wielding his sword on my neck, did not allow me to make a better decision; and so, rash and crazed, I went out, and what you have seen happened to me. And although I find myself without my son and without my husband, and fear something worse, I thank heaven for bringing me under your protection, and from you I hope for all the Spanish courtesy I can hope for, and even more from your own, which you will surely enhance if you are as noble as you seem."

Saying this she let herself fall onto the bed, and the two men hurried to see whether she had fainted and saw that she had not, but was weeping bitterly, and Don Juan said to her:

"If until now, beautiful lady, I and Don Antonio, my friend, felt compassion and pity for you because you are a woman, now, knowing your nobility, pity and compassion have become the clear obligations to serve you. Take heart and do not faint, and even though you are not accustomed to situations like these, the more patience you can bring to bear, the more you will show who you are. Believe me, Signora, for I imagine that these singular events will have a happy ending, since heaven will not allow so much beauty to be unhappy and such virtuous thoughts to come to naught. Go to sleep, Signora, and take care of yourself, for you need that, and a maid of ours will come in to serve you, and you can have the same trust in her as you do in us. She will know how to be silent about your misfortune as well as she knows how to tend to your needs."

"My need is so great that it obliges me to even more difficult things," she replied. "Señor, let whomever you wish come in, for guided by you I cannot fail to have the assurance that someone so needed will be very good; even so, I beg you not to let anyone but your maid see me."

"No one will," said Don Antonio.

And leaving her alone, they went out, and Don Juan told the housekeeper to go in and bring the infant wrapped in the rich clothes if she had already put them back on him. The housekeeper said she had, and he was exactly as he had been when they brought him home. The housekeeper, already instructed in how she should respond to what the lady she would find inside would ask her about the infant, entered the room.

Seeing her, Cornelia said:

"You are very welcome, my friend; give me the baby and bring that candle over here."

The housekeeper did so, and taking the child in her arms, Cornelia became very perturbed and looked at him fixedly, and said to the housekeeper:

"Tell me, Señora, are this child and the one you brought to me, or that was brought to me not long ago, the same?"

"Yes, Señora," answered the housekeeper.

"Well, then, why is his swaddling so different?" replied Cornelia. "The truth is, my friend, it seems to me that either these are different clothes or this is not the same infant."

"Everything's possible," responded the housekeeper.

"Sinner that I am!" said Cornelia. "What do you mean that everything's possible? Housekeeper, what does that mean? My heart will burst in my bosom until I know about this change. Tell me, my friend, for the sake of everything you love best. I mean, tell me where you found such rich swaddling, because I'll tell you that they are mine, if my eyes do not deceive me and my memory is not confused. In these same clothes or others exactly like them I gave my lady-in-waiting the dearly loved darling of my soul; who took them away? Oh, woe is me! And who brought them here? Oh, luckless woman!"

Don Juan and Don Antonio, who were listening to all these complaints, did not want them to go any further, and would not allow the deception of the changed swaddling to cause her more grief, and so they came in, and Don Juan said:

"These cloths and this child are yours, Señora Cornelia."

And then he recounted point by point how he had been the person to whom her lady-in-waiting had given the child, and how he had brought him home and told the housekeeper to change the swaddling and why he had done that, although after she told him about the birth he always was certain this was her son; and if he had not told her so, it had been so that the fright of doubting whether she knew him would be replaced by the joy of having known him.

Then came Cornelia's infinite tears of joy, infinite kisses to her son, infinite thanks offered to those who had favored her, calling them her human guardian angels and other titles that clearly revealed her gratitude. They left her with the housekeeper, whom they told to look after Cornelia and serve her as well as possible, reminding her of the condition she was in so that she could offer solutions, for she, being a woman, knew more about those needs than they did.

Then they went to sleep for what remained of the night, intending not to enter Cornelia's room unless she called them or there was a pressing need. Day arrived, and the housekeeper brought the woman who secretly and covertly would nurse the baby, and the two men asked about Cornelia. The housekeeper said she was resting a little. They left for the university and walked down the street where the skirmish took place and past the house Cornelia had come out of to see whether her absence was already known or whether people were gossiping about it; but they heard nothing at all about either the skirmish or Cornelia's absence. And so, having attended their lectures, they returned to their lodgings.

Cornelia sent for them through the housekeeper, to whom they responded that they had decided not to set foot in her room so that the decorum owed to her virtue would be maintained. But she replied with tears and pleas that they come in to see her, saying this was the best decorum, if not for her remedy at least for her consolation. They obeyed, and she received them with a joyous face and a great deal of courtesy; she asked them to be so kind as to go out in the city to see whether they heard anything about her audacity. They responded that this task had already been taken care of very carefully, but no one was saying anything.

At this point one of their three pages came to the door of her room, and from outside he said:

"A gentleman is at the door with two servants and he says his name is Lorenzo Bentivoglio and he's looking for my master Don Juan de Gamboa."

At this message Cornelia made two fists and brought them up to her mouth, and through them came a faint, timorous voice that said:

"My brother, Señores, that's my brother! Undoubtedly he must have learned that I'm here and he's come to kill me. Help me, Señores, protect me!"

"Calm yourself, Señora," Don Antonio said to her, "for you are in the home and under the protection of one who will not allow the slightest offense in the world to be committed against you. Go, Señor Don Juan, and see what this gentleman wants, and I shall stay here to defend Cornelia, if that proves necessary."

Don Juan, with no change of expression, went downstairs, and then Don Antonio had two loaded pistols brought to him and told the pages to take their swords and be ready. The housekeeper, seeing these preparations, trembled; Cornelia, fearing some awful act, shivered. Only Don Antonio and Don Juan were calm and collected and very well prepared for what they had to do. At the street door Don Juan found Don Lorenzo who, seeing Don Juan, said:

"I entreat your *signoria*"—which is how "your grace" is said in Italy—"to be so kind as to come with me to that church across the way, for I have a matter to discuss with your *signoria* that involves my life and my honor."

"I shall do that gladly," responded Don Juan. "Let us go, Señor, wherever you wish."

This being said, they went to the church together, and sitting on a bench where they could not be overheard, Lorenzo spoke first and said:

"I, Señor Spaniard, am Lorenzo Bentivoglio of, if not the richest, then one of the most prominent families in this city. This truth being so widely known will serve as an excuse for my praising myself. I was orphaned a few years ago, and a sister was left in my care, so beautiful that, if she were not so closely related to me, perhaps I would praise her in such a way that I would lack superlatives, because none can correspond completely to her beauty. Since I am honorable and she is a lovely girl, I was very solicitous in guarding her, but all my precautions and diligence have been thwarted by the rash will of my sister Cornelia, for that is her name. In brief, to make what could be a long story short and not weary you, I shall say that the Duke of Ferrara, Alfonso de Este, with his lynx's eyes defeated those of Argos, overthrew and vanquished my purpose, conquered my sister, and last night took her from the house of a kinswoman of ours, and some say she had just given birth. I learned this last night, and last night I went out to find him, and I believe I did find him and stab him with a knife; but he was aided by some angel who did not allow his blood to wash away the stain of the offense against me. My kinswoman told me, for she is the one who has told me all of this, that the duke deceived my sister by promising to take her as his wife. I don't believe this, for the marriage is unequal in terms of material riches, although in natural riches the world knows the quality of the Bentivoglio family of Bologna. What I believe is that he relied on what the powerful always rely on when they wish to violate a timid, chaste maiden, placing before her the sweet name of husband, making her believe that for certain reasons he could not marry immediately, telling her lies that have the appearance of truth but are false and malicious. Be that as it may, I find myself without my sister and without my honor, for until now I have kept all this under the lock and key of silence and have not wished to tell anyone about this offense until I could determine whether I could remedy and satisfy it in some way. For it is better for dishonor to be presumed and suspected rather than known with certainty and clarity, for between the yes and no of doubt, each person can favor whichever he chooses, and each will have its defenders. In short, I have decided to go to Ferrara and demand of the duke himself that he make amends for the offense, and if he refuses, to challenge him with regard to this matter. And this will not be with squadrons of people, for I cannot form or sustain them, but with individuals, and for this I should like your help, and hope that you accompany me on this path, confident you will do so because you are a Spaniard and a gentleman, as I have been informed, and because I do not wish to explain anything to any kinsman or friend, from whom I expect nothing but advice and dissuasion, and from you I can expect what is good and honorable, fearing no danger. You, Señor, must do me the kindness of coming with me, for with a Spaniard at my side, and one like the man you seem to be, I shall assume I have the armies of Xerxes behind me. I am asking a great deal of you, but you are more obliged by the responsibility to respond to what the fame of your nation proclaims."

"No more, Señor Lorenzo!" said Don Juan, who until then had not interrupted but had listened to every word. "No more! From this moment on I assume the position of your defender and adviser and take as my own the duty to satisfy or avenge the offense against you. And not only because I am Spanish but because I am a gentleman and you are one as eminent as you have said, as I know and everyone knows. Decide when you want us to leave, and the sooner the better, because the iron must be struck when hot, and the fervor of anger increases the spirit, and a recent injury awakens vengeance."

Lorenzo stood and embraced Don Juan warmly, and said:

"A heart as generous as yours, Señor Don Juan, does not need to be moved by placing before it any interest other than the honor that will be won in this deed, which I grant to you now if we are victorious in this matter, and furthermore, I offer you all I have, can do, and am worth. I want to depart tomorrow, because today we must prepare what we shall need for the journey."

"I think that is a good idea," said Don Juan, "and allow me, Señor Lorenzo, to recount this deed to a gentleman, a friend of mine whose valor and silence you can count on even more than mine."

"Well, Signor Don Juan, you have, as you said, made yourself responsible for my honor; dispose of it as you wish and speak of it as you choose and to whomever you wish, for, being a friend of yours, what else could he be but very good?"

With this they embraced and said goodbye, agreeing that the next day, in the morning, Lorenzo would call for him so that they could mount their horses outside the city and continue their journey in disguise.

Don Juan returned and recounted to Don Antonio and Cornelia what had occurred with Lorenzo, and the agreement they had reached.

"God save me!" said Cornelia. "Great, Señor, is your courtesy, and great is your confidence. What? So quickly you have ventured to undertake an action filled with difficulties? And how do you know, Señor, whether my brother will take you to Ferrara or somewhere else? But wherever he takes you, you can be sure that fidelity itself goes with you, although I, wretch that I am, trip over the motes in the sun and am afraid of any shadow; and why shouldn't I be afraid since my life or death depends on the duke's response, and how do I know whether he'll respond with so much moderation that my brother's rage will be contained within the limits of his good judgment? And when he comes out, does it seem to you that you have a weak enemy? And does it not seem to you that for the days until you come back I shall be in suspense, fearful and afflicted, waiting for the sweet or bitter news of what has happened? Do I love the duke or my brother so little that I do not fear the misfortunes of either one and feel them in my soul?"

"You speak a great deal and fear a great deal, Señora Cornelia," said Don Juan, "but find room among so many fears for hope, and trust in God, in my skill and good wishes, for you will see yours fulfilled with every happiness. Going to Ferrara cannot be avoided, nor can I fail to help your brother. So far we do not know the duke's intention or whether he knows of your absence, and all of this has to be heard from his mouth, and no one will be able to ask him as well as I. And understand, Señora Cornelia, that the reputation and happiness of your brother and the duke are placed in the pupils of my eyes; I shall look out for them just as I look through them."

"If heaven grants you, Señor Don Juan," said Cornelia, "the power to remedy and the grace to console me in the midst of my misfortunes, I count myself as very fortunate. I should like to see you leave and come back no matter how fear afflicts me in your absence, or hope torments me."

Don Antonio approved of Don Juan's decision and praised the exact reciprocity Lorenzo Bentivoglio's confidence had found in him. And he also said he wished to accompany them, just in case something happened.

"No, not that," said Don Juan, "not only because it's not a good idea for Señora Cornelia to be left alone, but because I don't want Señor Lorenzo to think I wish to make use of somebody else's efforts."

"Mine is yours," replied Don Antonio, "and so, although in disguise and in secret, I shall follow you, and I know Señora Cornelia will like that, and she will not be so alone that she will lack those who serve her, protect her, and accompany her."

"It will be a great consolation to me, Señores, if I know you are going together, or at least in a way that you can help each other if the situation demands; and since your going seems dangerous to me, be so kind, Señores, as to take these relics with you."

And saying this, she took from her bosom a cross of diamonds of inestimable value, and a gold Agnus Dei as rich as the cross. They looked at the rich jewels and appreciated them even more than they had appreciated the hatband; but they returned them to her, not wanting to take them under any circumstances, saying they would carry relics with them, if not as beautifully adorned then at least as good in their quality. Cornelia was sorry they would not accept them, but in the end it had to be as they wished.

The housekeeper was very attentive in caring for Cornelia; she knew of the departure of her masters, which they had told her about, but not the purpose of their journey or where they were going, and she made herself responsible for looking after the lady, whose name she did not yet know, so that she would not miss the favors of the two men. The next day, very early in the morning, Lorenzo was at the door, and Don Juan was dressed for traveling; he wore the hat with the band, which he adorned with black and yellow plumes, and he covered the band with a black scarf. They took their leave of Cornelia who, imagining her brother very close by, was so fearful she could not manage to say a word as they said goodbye to her.

Don Juan left first, and with Lorenzo he went outside the city, and in a somewhat remote field they found two very good horses, and two grooms who held them by the reins. They mounted with the grooms in front of them and by footpaths and unused roads traveled to Ferrara. Don Antonio, on a small horse and in different clothes, followed them covertly; but it seemed to him they were avoiding him, especially Lorenzo, and so he decided to follow the straight road to Ferrara, certain he would find them there.

As soon as they had left the city, Cornelia told the housekeeper everything that had happened, and how the baby was hers and the Duke of Ferrara's, with all the points of the story we have recounted so far, not hiding that her masters' journey was to Ferrara and that they were accompanying her brother, who was going to challenge Duke Alfonso. Hearing this the housekeeper, as if the devil were in control of her, and in order to confuse, hinder, or delay Cornelia's remedy, said:

"Oh, Señora of my soul! You've gone through all these things and you're here so carefree and unconcerned? Either you have no soul, or yours is so indifferent it doesn't feel anything. Do you really think your brother is going to Ferrara? You're wrong; you should think and believe that he wanted to take my masters away from here and get them out of the house so he could come back here and kill you, and he could do that as easily as drinking a glass of water. What protection and help do we have except for the three pages! They're too busy scratching the mange that covers them to get involved in somebody else's problems; as for me, I can tell you I won't have the heart to wait for the ruin that threatens this house. Señor Lorenzo, an Italian, trusting in Spaniards and asking for their favor and help! By my eyes, I don't give a fig for that!"—and she made the gesture right there. "My child, if you want to take my advice, I'll give you some that will benefit you."

Cornelia was dumbfounded, astonished, and confused as she listened to these words of the housekeeper, who said them so fervently and with so many signs of fear that Cornelia thought everything she said was true, and that perhaps Don Juan and Don Antonio were dead and her brother was coming through these doors to stab her to death; and so she said:

"And what advice would you give me, my friend, that would be helpful and prevent this looming misfortune?"

"Of course I'll give you good advice! So helpful and so good it couldn't be better," said the housekeeper. "I, Señora, have served a *piovano*, I mean a priest, from a village two miles from Ferrara. He's a good and saintly person who would do anything I asked because his obligations to me are more than those of a master. Let's go there, I'll find somebody to take us right away, and the wet nurse is a poor woman who'll follow us to the ends of the earth. And if we suppose, Señora, that you'll be found, it will be better for you to be found in the house of an old and honorable priest than with two young students, and Spaniards to boot, for they, and I'm a good witness to this, never miss a trick. And now, Señora, since you're not well, they've treated you with respect, but if you get better and convalesce under their protection, God alone can help you. Because the truth is, if my refusals, reproaches, and resolve had not protected me, they would already have tossed me and my honor onto the trash heap; because not all that glitters in them is gold, they say one thing and think another; but they met their match in me, because I'm smart and know what side my bread is buttered on, and above all I'm well born, for I'm a Crivelli from

Milan, and my point of honor is ten miles above the clouds.[2] And in this, Señora, you can see the calamities I've endured, for in spite of being who I am,
I've become a *masara* to Spaniards, whom they call housekeeper; although the
truth is I have nothing to complain about with my masters, because they're
simple if they're not angry; in this way they resemble Basques, which is what
they say they are. But perhaps with you they'll be Galicians, a nation that
people say is a little less diligent and honorable than the Basque."

In effect, she said so much that poor Cornelia was prepared to do as she
said; and so, in less than four hours, the housekeeper disposing and Cornelia
agreeing, they found themselves, along with the wet nurse and the baby, in a
carriage, and without being heard by the pages, they set out for the priest's village. And all this was done on the housekeeper's advice and with her money,
because not long before her masters had given her a year's salary, and so it was
not necessary to pawn a jewel that Cornelia gave her. And since they had heard
Don Juan say that he and her brother would not follow the straight road to Ferrara but travel the back roads, they wanted to follow the straight one, and
travel slowly so as not to meet up with them; and the owner of the carriage
accommodated to the pace they wanted, because they had paid him what he
asked.

Let us leave them here, for they are boldly going on the right road, and let
us find out what happened to Don Juan de Gamboa and Señor Lorenzo Bentivoglio; it is said that on the road they learned that the duke was not in Ferrara but in Bologna. And so, abandoning the roundabout route they were
following, they reached the royal road, or the *strada maestra*, as they call it over
there, thinking that would be the road taken by the duke on his way back from
Bologna. And a short while after they came onto the road, looking toward Bologna to see whether anyone was coming that way, they saw a throng of people
on horseback, and Don Juan said to Lorenzo that he should leave the road,
because if it happened that the duke was among those people, he wanted to
speak to him before he took refuge in Ferrara, which was fairly close. Lorenzo
did so, agreeing with Don Juan's opinion.

As soon as Lorenzo rode away, Don Juan removed the scarf that covered
the rich hatband, accompanied by careful consideration, as he himself said
afterward.

At this point the crowd of travelers approached, and among them was a
woman on a dappled horse, dressed for traveling and her face covered by a

2. The Crivelli family was an illustrious Milanese family who could claim relation to Pope Urban III, born Uberto Crivelli (d. 1187).

mask, either to better her disguise or for protection against the sun and wind. Don Juan stopped his horse in the middle of the road, and waited, his face uncovered, for the travelers to reach him; and when they were near, his figure, his spirit, his powerful horse, the elegance of his clothes, and the brilliance of the diamonds meant that all their eyes were on him, especially those of the Duke of Ferrara, who was among them, and as soon as he laid eyes on the hatband he knew that the man wearing it was Don Juan de Gamboa, who had helped him in the skirmish; and he perceived this truth so deeply that without thinking twice he spurred his horse toward Don Juan, saying:

"I do not believe I shall be at all deceived, Señor, if I call you Don Juan de Gamboa, for your gallant disposition and the adornment on your hat tell me so."

"That is true," answered Don Juan, "for I never knew how nor wished to hide my name; but tell me, Señor, who you are, so that I do not fall into some discourtesy."

"That would be impossible," replied the duke, "for in my opinion I believe you could never be discourteous under any circumstance. Even so I shall tell you, Señor Don Juan, that I am the Duke of Ferrara and the man obliged to serve you all the days of his life, for not four nights ago you gave it back to him."

The duke had not finished saying this when Don Juan, with unusual agility, leaped from his horse and hurried to kiss the feet of the duke; but in spite of how quickly he moved, the duke was already out of the saddle so that he dismounted into the arms of Don Juan.

Señor Lorenzo, watching these ceremonies from some distance, thought they were not courteous but choleric and spurred his horse; but in the middle of the gallop he stopped because he saw the duke and Don Juan in a close embrace, for the duke had recognized him. The duke saw Lorenzo over Don Juan's shoulder and recognized him, which startled him, and as they were embracing, he asked Don Juan if Lorenzo Bentivoglio, who was there, had come with him. To which Don Juan responded:

"Let us move away from here, and I shall tell Your Excellency great things."

The duke did so, and Don Juan said to him:

"Señor, Lorenzo Bentivoglio, whom you see there, has a serious complaint about you. He says that four nights ago you took his sister, Señora Cornelia, from the house of a cousin and that you deceived and dishonored her, and he wants to learn from you what satisfaction you intend to give him so that he can determine the proper course of action. He asked me to be his patron and mediator. I agreed because, from the indications he gave about the skirmish, I knew that you, Señor, were the owner of this hatband, which because of your generosity and courtesy you wanted to be mine; and seeing that no one could defend your interests better than I, as I have said, I offered him my help. Now, Señor, I should like you to tell me what you know about this matter, and if what Lorenzo says is true."

"Oh, my friend!" said the duke. "It is so true that I would not dare deny it even if I wanted to. I have not deceived or taken Cornelia away, although I know she is missing from the house you mentioned; I haven't deceived her because I consider her my wife; I haven't taken her because I don't know where she is. If I did not celebrate my wedding publicly, it was because I was waiting until my mother, who is in her final moments, passes from this life to a better one, for she wants my wife to be Señora Livia, the daughter of the Duke of Mantua, and because of other difficulties perhaps weightier than the ones I have alluded to, and which cannot be mentioned now. The fact is that on the night you helped me, I was to bring her to Ferrara, because she was about to give birth to the precious jewel heaven arranged to place in her; either because of the fight, or my carelessness, when I went to her house I found that the woman who had arranged our meetings was going out. I asked for Cornelia and she told me she had already left, and had given birth to a boy that night, the most beautiful in the world, and had given him to Fabio, my servant. The lady-in-waiting is there; Fabio is here; and the child and Cornelia are not to be seen. I have been in Bologna these past two days, investigating and hoping to hear news of Cornelia, but I haven't learned anything."

"And so, Señor," said Don Juan, "when Cornelia and your son appear, you won't deny she is your wife and he your son?"

"Certainly not, because although I value being a gentleman, I value being a Christian more; besides, Cornelia is such that she deserves to be mistress of a kingdom. If she would appear, whether my mother lives or dies, the world will know that if I knew how to be a lover, I also knew how to keep in public the promise I gave in secret."

"Then, will you also say," said Don Juan, "what you have said to me to your brother Señor Lorenzo?"

"It grieves me, in fact," replied the duke, "that it has taken so long for him to hear it."

Don Juan immediately signaled to Lorenzo to dismount and come to where they were standing, which he did, far from thinking of the good news that awaited him. The duke came forward to receive him with open arms, and the first word he said was to call him brother.

Lorenzo hardly knew how to respond to so loving a greeting and so courteous a reception; and being somewhat indecisive, before he could speak a word, Don Juan said to him:

"The duke, Señor Lorenzo, admits the secret dealings he had with your sister, Señora Cornelia. He also admits she is his legitimate wife, and what he says here he will say publicly when the opportunity arises. He also concedes that four nights ago he went to take her from her cousin's house to bring her to Ferrara and wait for the occasion to celebrate their marriage, which was delayed for just cause, which he has told me. He has also spoken of the dispute he had with you, and that when he went for Cornelia he met Sulpicia, her lady-in-waiting, who is that woman there, from whom he learned that Cornelia had given birth not an hour before, and that Sulpicia had given the infant to a servant of the duke, and then Cornelia, believing the duke was there, had left the house fearful because she imagined that you, Señor Lorenzo, already knew what she had done. Sulpicia did not give the baby to the duke's servant but to another man instead. Cornelia is not here, he blames himself for everything, and says that whenever Señora Cornelia appears he will receive her as his true wife. Decide, Señor Lorenzo, whether there is more to say or more to desire, except to find the two jewels as rich as they are unfortunate."

Señor Lorenzo responded by throwing himself at the feet of the duke, who insisted on raising him up:

"From your Christianity and greatness, my sister and I could not hope for less than what you are doing for both us, my most serene lord and brother: she by your making her your equal, and I by your considering me one of yours."

Then his eyes filled with tears, as did the duke's, both of them moved, one by the loss of his wife, and the other by the gain of so good a brother-in-law. But they thought that giving signs of so much feeling with tears seemed like weakness, and they repressed them and enclosed them again in their eyes; and Don Juan's eyes were joyful, almost asking them for a reward for the good news that Cornelia and her son had appeared, for he had left them in his house.

And then Don Antonio de Isunza made his presence known, though from some distance his small horse had been recognized by Don Juan; but when he came nearer he stopped and saw Don Juan's and Lorenzo's horses, which the grooms held by the reins, and a little farther away he recognized Don Juan and Lorenzo, but not the duke, and he did not know whether he should ride up to where Don Juan stood. Approaching the duke's servants, he asked whether they knew the gentleman with the other two, pointing at the duke. They replied that he was the Duke of Ferrara, which left him more confused and less certain what to do; but Don Juan rescued him from his bewilderment, calling him by name. Don Antonio dismounted, seeing that everyone was standing, and went up to them; the duke received him with great courtesy, because Don Juan said he was his friend. In short, Don Juan recounted to Don

Antonio everything that had happened with the duke until the moment of his arrival. This made Don Antonio extremely happy, and he said to Don Juan:

"Why, Señor Don Juan, don't you make the joy and contentment of these gentlemen complete by requesting a reward for the good news that Señora Cornelia and her son have been found?"

"If you hadn't arrived, Señor Don Antonio, I would have asked for it, but you should do it, and I'm sure they would give it to you very gladly."

Since the duke and Lorenzo heard them mention finding Cornelia and the reward for good news, they asked what they were discussing.

"What could it be," said Don Antonio, "except that I want to play a part in this tragic comedy, and it has to be the one of the man who requests a reward for the good news of finding Señora Cornelia and her child, who are in my house?"

And then he told them point by point everything that has been said so far; and from this the duke and Señor Lorenzo derived so much pleasure and delight that Don Lorenzo embraced Don Juan and the duke embraced Don Antonio. The duke promised his entire estate as celebration of the good news, and Señor Lorenzo his inheritance, his life, and his soul. They called for the lady-in-waiting who had handed the infant to Don Juan, and she, having recognized Lorenzo, began to tremble; they asked if she knew the man to whom she had given the child. She said no, but she had asked him if he was Fabio, and he had responded that he was, and in good faith she had handed him the baby.

"That's true," said Don Juan, "and then you, Señora, told me to keep the baby safe and turned around and closed the door."

"That's true, Señora," the lady-in-waiting answered, weeping.

And the duke said:

"Tears are no longer necessary here, but rejoicing and celebrations are. The fact is that I don't have to go into Ferrara but shall return immediately to Bologna, because these joys are mere shadows until the sight of Cornelia makes them real."

And without another word, by common consent they returned to Bologna. Don Antonio rode ahead to prepare Cornelia so she would not be frightened by the sudden arrival of the duke and her brother. But since he did not find her, and the pages could not give him any information about her, he was the saddest and most confused man in the world; and when he saw that the housekeeper was not there either, he imagined she had arranged Cornelia's absence. The pages told him that the housekeeper had left the same day they did, and that they never saw the Cornelia he was asking about. Don Antonio was beside himself because of this unexpected situation, fearing that perhaps the duke would take them for liars or swindlers, or perhaps imagine other things even worse that would reflect badly on Cornelia's honor and good name. He was thinking about this when the duke, Don Juan, and Lorenzo came in; they had come to Don Juan's house along deserted backstreets, leaving the others outside the city, and found Don Antonio sitting in a chair, his cheek resting in his hand, the color of a corpse.

Don Juan asked him what was wrong and where Cornelia was. Don Antonio replied:

"What isn't wrong? Cornelia isn't here, she went away on the same day we did with the housekeeper we left here to be her companion."

The duke almost expired, and Lorenzo almost committed suicide when they heard this news. In short, they were all perturbed, indecisive, and lost in thought. Then a page came up to Don Antonio and whispered in his ear:

"Señor, Santisteban, Señor Don Juan's page, has kept a very pretty woman locked in his bedroom since the day your graces left, and I believe her name is Cornelia, because I've heard him call her that."

Don Antonio became agitated again, and rather than find her in such a place, he wished Cornelia had not appeared, for he undoubtedly thought she was the woman the page had hidden. He said nothing, but keeping silent he went to the page's room and found the door locked and the page not in the house. He went up to the door and said in a quiet voice:

"Open the door, Señora Cornelia, and come out to receive your brother and the duke, your husband, who are coming to see you."

The answer came from behind the door:

"Are you making fun of me? Well, the fact is I'm not so ugly and worthless that I couldn't find some dukes and counts on my own, but that's what a person deserves who spends her time with pages."

With these words Don Antonio realized that the woman who answered was not Cornelia. At this point the page Santisteban came home, went to his room, and there he found Don Antonio, who asked him to bring all the keys in the house to see if any fit the door. The page, kneeling and with the key in his hand, said:

"The absence of your graces and my own sinfulness, to call it what it is, made me bring in a woman to be with me these past three nights. I beg your grace, Señor Don Antonio de Isunza, and may you hear good news from Spain, that if my master Don Juan de Gamboa doesn't know about it that you don't tell him, and I'll get rid of her right now."

"And what's this woman's name?" asked Don Antonio.

"Her name's Cornelia," said the page.

The page who had revealed the secret, who was not very fond of Santisteban, and we do not know whether he was simpleminded or malicious, went down to where the duke, Don Juan, and Lorenzo were waiting, and said:

"Devil take that page! By God, they made him spew out Señora Cornelia; he had her hidden away, and you can be sure he didn't want the gentlemen to come home so he could stretch out his *gaudeamus* another three or four days."

Lorenzo heard this and asked:

"What are you saying, my good man? Where is Cornelia?"

"Upstairs," replied the page.

As soon as the duke heard this he ran up the stairs like a lightning flash to see Cornelia, whom he imagined had appeared, and he immediately came to the bedroom where Don Antonio was, and going in, he said:

"Where is Cornelia? Where is the life of my life?"

"Here's Cornelia," answered a woman who was wrapped in a sheet on the bed, and had covered her face, and who went on to say:

"Lord save us! What a fuss about nothing! Why all the excitement? Haven't you ever heard of a woman sleeping with a page?"

Lorenzo, who was present, with indignation and anger pulled one end of the sheet and revealed a young woman who was not bad looking, and she, in embarrassment, put her hands over her face and picked up her clothes, which she had used as a pillow because there was none on the bed, and from her clothes they saw that she must have been a tramp, one of the world's harlots.

The duke asked if it was true that her name was Cornelia; she said it was, and that she had very honorable kinsmen in the city, and no one should say that's something I'd never do. The duke was so irritated that he almost began to wonder whether the Spaniards were mocking him; but to avoid such evil suspicions, he turned his back without saying a word, Lorenzo following him, and they mounted their horses and rode off, leaving Don Juan and Don Antonio much more irritated that they were leaving, and they decided to do everything possible, and even impossible, to find Cornelia and satisfy the duke as to their truthfulness and honest desires. They dismissed Santisteban for insolence and threw out the scapegrace Cornelia, and at that moment they recalled that they had forgotten to mention to the duke the jewels of the Agnus Dei and the diamond cross that Cornelia had offered them, and with these signs he would believe that Cornelia had been under their protection, and if she was not there they were not responsible. They went out to tell him this but did not find him in Lorenzo's house, where they thought he would be; but Lorenzo was there, and he told them that without stopping for an instant the duke had returned to Ferrara and ordered him to search for his sister.

They told him what they were going to say to the duke, but Lorenzo said the duke was very satisfied that they had behaved properly, and that he and the duke had attributed Cornelia's absence to her great fear, and God willing she would reappear, because the earth could not have swallowed the child, the housekeeper, and her. They were all comforted by this and did not wish to search for her publicly but rather in secret, for no one except her cousin knew of her absence; and among those who did not know, the duke's intention, if it were made public, might put his sister's reputation at risk, and it would be very difficult to satisfy the suspicions that an ardent overconfidence can instill.

The duke continued his journey, and good luck, which was arranging his fortune, had him come to the village of the priest where Cornelia, the child, and the housekeeper, her adviser, already were; they had recounted their history and asked his advice on what to do.

The priest was a great friend of the duke, who would often come from Ferrara to visit, staying at the priest's house, which reflected the taste of a wealthy and cultured cleric, and from there he would go hunting, for he enjoyed very much both the culture of the priest and his wit, which he brought to everything he said and did. He was not disconcerted to see the duke in his house because, as we have said, this was not the first time; but he was concerned see him so sad, because he saw immediately that his spirit was preoccupied.

Cornelia overheard that the Duke of Ferrara was there, and she became extremely perturbed, not knowing why he had come; she was wringing her hands and pacing back and forth like someone who had lost her mind. She would have liked to speak with the priest, but he was conversing with the duke and did not have the opportunity to talk to her.

The duke said to him:

"I've come here feeling very sad, father, and I don't want to go to Ferrara today; I'd like to be your guest; tell the men traveling with me to return to Ferrara and have only Fabio stay."

The good priest did so, and then he went to give instructions on how to serve and attend to the duke, and this was when Cornelia could speak to him, and taking him by the hands, she said:

"Oh, Señor, father! What is it that the duke wants? For the love of God, Señor, intercede for me and try to find out what his intention is; in effect, guide him in the way you think best, and with your great wisdom counsel him."

To which the priest replied:

"The duke has come here sad; so far, he has not told me the reason. What you must do, Señora, is dress the child very nicely and put on him all the jewels you have, especially those the duke might have given you, and let me do what I can, for I hope to heaven that we shall have a good day today."

Cornelia embraced him and kissed his hand, and withdrew to prepare the child. The priest went to converse with the duke while they waited for the midday meal, and in the course of their talk the priest asked the duke if it was possible to know the reason for his melancholy, because there was no doubt one could see from a league away that he was sad.

"Father," said the duke, "it is obvious that the sorrows of the heart appear on one's face. In the eyes one can read what is in one's soul, and the worst thing is that for now I cannot communicate my sadness to anyone."

"Well, the truth is, Señor," the priest replied, "that if you were disposed to see pleasing things, I would show you one that in my opinion would please you very much."

"The man would be simpleminded indeed," responded the duke, "who, offered relief from his affliction, refused to accept it. By my life, father, show me what you have mentioned, for it must be one of your rare objects, which in my opinion offer great pleasure."

The priest stood and went to Cornelia, who had adorned her son and put on him the rich jewels of the cross and the Agnus Dei, with three other very precious pieces, all of them given to Cornelia by the duke, and taking the baby in his arms, he went out to the duke, and telling him to stand and come to the light from the window, he put the child in the duke's arms, and he, when he looked at and recognized the jewels and saw they were the same ones he had given Cornelia, was astounded; and looking closely at the child, it seemed to him he saw his own face, and filled with wonder he asked the priest whose infant this was, for in his adornments and finery he seemed to be the son of a prince.

"I don't know," responded the priest. "All I know is that I don't know how many nights ago a gentleman from Bologna brought him to me and asked me to look after him and rear him, and that he was the child of a valiant father and a distinguished and very beautiful mother. A wet nurse also came with the gentleman, and I have asked her whether she knows anything about the baby's parents, and her answer is that she does not know a thing; and in truth, if the mother is as beautiful as the nurse, she must be the most beautiful woman in Italy."

"Couldn't we see her?"

"Yes, of course," said the priest. "Come with me, Señor, and if you marvel at the finery and beauty of this infant, as I think you do, it is my understanding that the sight of his nurse will have the same effect."

The priest wanted to take the baby from the duke, who did not want to let him go; instead, he held him tighter in his arms and gave him many kisses. The priest walked a little ahead of him and told Cornelia to come with no uneasiness at all to receive the duke. Cornelia did so, and the shock colored her face so intensely that her beauty seemed immortal. The duke was dumbfounded when he saw her, and she, throwing herself at his feet, tried to kiss them. The duke, not saying a word, handed the child to the priest, and turning his back, hurried out of the room; Cornelia, seeing this, turned to the priest and said:

"Oh Señor! What if the duke was horrified to see me? What if he despises me? What if he thinks I'm ugly? What if he's forgotten the obligation he has to me? Won't he say even a single word to me? He finds his son so tiresome that he throws him out of his arms?"

The priest did not say a word in reply, surprised at the duke's flight, for it seemed a flight more than anything else; the duke did not leave, however, but went out to call for Fabio and say:

"Fabio, my friend, hurry as fast as you can back to Bologna and immediately tell Lorenzo Bentivoglio and the two Spanish gentlemen, Don Juan de Gamboa and Don Antonio de Isunza, to offer no excuses and come to this village immediately. Look, friend, fly and don't come back without them, because I can't tell you how important it is for me to see them."

Fabio was not a lazy man, and he immediately followed the orders of his master.

Then the duke returned to Cornelia, who was shedding beautiful tears. He took her in his arms, and adding tears to her tears, kissed the breath of her mouth a thousand times, happiness having tied both their tongues; and so, in virtuous, loving silence the two happy lovers and true spouses enjoyed each other.

The baby's nurse, and the one with the last name Crivelli, no less, as she said, who had been watching the duke and Cornelia through the doors to the next room, began to bang their heads against the walls with happiness, though it seemed as if they had gone mad. The priest gave the child in his arms a thousand kisses, and with the right hand, which he had freed, could not give enough blessings to the embracing couple. The priest's housekeeper, who had not been present at the great event because she had been busy preparing the food, came in to call them to the table since the meal was ready. This separated the close embraces, and the duke relieved the priest of the child and took him in his arms, where he held him all through the simple and well seasoned, rather than sumptuous, meal. And while they were eating, Cornelia recounted everything that had happened to her before she came to this house on the advice of the housekeeper to the two Spanish gentlemen who had served, sheltered, and protected her with the most virtuous and proper decorum anyone could imagine. By the same token the duke told her everything that had happened to him until that moment. The two servants were present, and the duke offered and promised the women a great deal. Joy was renewed in everyone with the happy ending of the matter, and they waited only for the arrival of Lorenzo, Don Juan, and Don Antonio to complete it and make it better than anyone could desire; three days later they arrived, concerned and wanting to know whether the duke knew anything about Cornelia; for Fabio, who had gone for them, could not tell them anything about her being found, since he did not know anything about it.

The duke went out to receive them in an antechamber to the room where Cornelia was, showing no signs of happiness at all, which made the recent arrivals very sad. The duke had them sit down, and he sat with them, and addressing Lorenzo, he said:

"You know very well, Señor Lorenzo Bentivoglio, that I never deceived your sister, and to this both heaven and my conscience can testify. You know as well how diligently I have searched for her and the desire I have to find her so that we can marry, as I promised her. She has not appeared, and my word cannot be eternal. I am young, and not so experienced in the things of this world that I don't allow myself to be carried away by those that are constantly offered to me for my delight. The same desire that made me promise to be Cornelia's husband also led me to give my word earlier to marry a peasant girl in this village, whom I planned to deceive to turn to the worth of Cornelia, though I did not turn to what my conscience demanded, which would not have been a small demonstration of love. But nobody marries a woman who is not there, nor is it reasonable for anyone to look for the woman who leaves him to find one who despises him; and so I ask you, Señor Lorenzo, what reparation I can make to you for the offense I never committed against you, for I never intended to do so, and I want you to give me permission to keep my first promise and marry the peasant girl, who is now in this house."

While the duke was saying this, Lorenzo's face was changing a thousand colors, and he could not remain seated in the chair; clear signs that rage was taking possession of all his senses. The same thing was happening to Don Juan and Don Antonio, who immediately proposed not to allow the duke to carry out his intention even if it cost them their lives. And the duke, reading their intentions on their faces, said:

"Calm down, Señor Lorenzo, for before you say a word, I want the beauty you will see in the woman I wish to take as my wife to oblige you to give me the permission I ask of you, because it is so fine and so great that it would excuse even greater errors."

Having said this, he stood and went to where Cornelia was richly adorned with all the jewels the child had and many more. When the duke turned his back, Don Juan stood, and with both hands leaning on the two arms of the chair where Lorenzo was sitting, he whispered in his ear:

"By Santiago de Galicia, Señor Lorenzo, and by my faith as a Christian and a gentleman, I am as likely to let the duke carry out his intention as I am to become a Moor! Here, here in my hands, he will leave his life or keep the promise he made to Señora Cornelia, your sister, or at least he has to give us time to find her, and until it is known for certain that she is dead, he will not marry!"

"I am of the same opinion," said Lorenzo.

"As my friend Don Antonio will be," replied Don Juan.

At this point Cornelia came into the room between the priest and the duke, who led her by the hand, and behind them came Sulpicia, Cornelia's lady-in-waiting, for the duke had sent to Ferrara for her, and for the two servants, the child's wet nurse and the housekeeper to the two gentlemen.

When Lorenzo saw his sister, and was sure he had recognized her, for at first what seemed to him the impossibility of anything like this happening had kept him from accepting the truth, he stumbled over his own feet and threw himself at the feet of the duke, who raised him up and put him in the arms of his sister; I mean to say, his sister embraced him with all possible demonstrations of joy. Don Juan and Don Antonio told the duke that it had been the most clever and delightful joke in the world. The duke took the child, whom Sulpicia was carrying, and giving him to Lorenzo, he said:

"Receive, my dear brother, your nephew and my son, and decide whether you wish to give me permission to marry this peasant, the first one to whom I gave my promise of marriage."

We would never conclude were we to tell how Lorenzo responded, what Don Juan asked, what Don Antonio felt, the rejoicing of the priest, the joy of Sulpicia, the happiness of the adviser, the jubilation of the housekeeper, the astonishment of Fabio, and, in short, the general delight of everyone.

Then the priest married them, their best man being Don Juan de Gamboa; and all of them agreed to keep the marriage secret until they saw the outcome of the sickness that had brought the duchess, the duke's mother, to the verge of death, and in the meantime Señora Cornelia would return to Bologna with her brother. Everything was done this way: the duchess died; Cornelia entered Ferrara bringing joy to everyone who saw her; mourning turned into festivities; the servants were rich; Sulpicia married Fabio; Don Antonio and Don Juan were very happy to have served the duke, who offered to marry them to two cousins of his with rich dowries. They said that the gentlemen of the Basque nation generally married in their homeland, and not because of disdain, for that was not possible, but to obey a praiseworthy custom and the will of their parents, who must have already arranged their marriages, and so they did not accept so distinguished an offer.

The duke accepted their reasoning, and by virtuous and honorable means, and looking for licit occasions, he sent many presents to Bologna, some so rich and sent in so timely and opportune a way, that although they could not be accepted to avoid the appearance that they were being paid, the time when they arrived facilitated everything; especially those sent at the time of their departure for Spain, and the ones he gave them when they went to Ferrara to take their leave; by then Cornelia had two other babies, both girls, and the duke was more in love than ever. The duchess gave the diamond cross to Don Juan and the Agnus Dei to Don Antonio, who, finding it impossible to do anything else, accepted them.

They arrived in Spain and their homeland, where they married rich, distinguished, and beautiful women, and maintained a constant correspondence with the duke and duchess, and with Señor Lorenzo Bentivoglio, to the great enjoyment of them all.

THE NOVEL OF THE DECEITFUL MARRIAGE

A soldier was leaving the Hospital of the Resurrection in Valladolid, just outside the Campo Gate, and because he used his sword as a cane and his legs were thin and his face yellow, he gave very clear indications that, although the weather was not very hot, he must have sweated out in twenty days all the humor he had perhaps acquired in an hour.[1] He took the small, hesitant steps of a convalescent, and as he entered the city through the gate, he saw coming toward him a friend he had not seen in more than six months, who, crossing himself as if he had seen some diabolical sight, approached him and said:

"What, Señor Lieutenant Campuzano? Is it possible that your grace is in this country? On my life, I thought you were in Flanders, fighting with your lance there instead of dragging your sword here! What a color you have! How skinny you are!"

To which Campuzano replied:

"As to whether or not I am in this country, Señor Licentiate Peralta, seeing me here is your answer; I have nothing to say to your other questions except that I have left this hospital after sweating out fourteen gallons of pustules given to me by a woman I took as my own and shouldn't have."

"Does your grace mean he is married?" replied Peralta.

"Yes, Señor," responded Campuzano.

"It must have been for love," said Peralta, "and such marriages have an act of repentance attached to them."

"I cannot say whether it was for love," responded the lieutenant, "although I can state it was for my sorrow, for when I took my wife, or should I say my life, I suffered so many pains in my body and soul that to alleviate the ones in my body has cost me forty sweat treatments, and I cannot even find a remedy for those in my soul. But since I am in no condition to have a long conversation on the street, your grace will pardon me, and tomorrow I can

1. The four humors—blood, yellow bile, black bile, and phlegm—were part of an ancient Greek medical theory still prevalent in Cervantes's time which posited that one's health and temperament were the result of the combination of humors in the body.

more comfortably recount the events that have occurred, which are the strangest and most unusual your grace has heard in all the days of his life."

"That will not be necessary," said the licentiate, "for I want you to come with me to my lodgings, and there we can suffer through my poor supper together, for the stew is meant for two but my servant will have a meat pie instead, and if you can eat it in your condition, some slices of Rute ham will be our first course, and above all the goodwill with which I offer it, not only this time but as many times as your grace might wish."

Campuzano thanked him and accepted the invitation and the proposal. They went to the Church of San Llorente, heard Mass, Peralta took him home, gave him what he had promised, made his offer again, and when they had finished eating asked him to recount the events he had described so extravagantly. Campuzano did not have to be begged but began to speak, saying:

"Your grace must remember, Señor Licentiate Peralta, what good friends I was with Captain Pedro de Herrera, who is now in Flanders."

"I remember very well," answered Peralta.

"Well, one day," continued Campuzano, "we had just finished eating at La Solana Inn where we were living, when two women of wellborn appearance came in with two maids. One began to talk to the captain, as both of them were standing near a window; the other sat in a chair next to mine, her shawl lowered to her chin, not allowing more of her face to be seen than that permitted by the thinness of the fabric. And although I asked her for the sake of courtesy to be so kind as to uncover her face, I could not persuade her, which simply inflamed my desire to see her. And to increase that desire even more (whether intentionally or by chance), the lady revealed a very white hand wearing very good rings. I was elegantly dressed at the time, with the heavy chain your grace would recognize, the hat with plumes and a band, my outfit in a soldier's colors, and so gallant in the eyes of my madness that I could catch birds in midflight. And so I asked her again to uncover her face, to which she replied: 'Do not be insistent. I have a house; have a page follow me, for although I am more honorable than what this reply promises, provided your good judgment corresponds to your gallantry, I shall be happy to let you see me.'

"I kissed her hands for the great kindness she was doing me, and as payment I promised her mountains of gold. The captain concluded his conversation; the ladies left; a servant of mine followed them. The captain told me the lady wanted him to carry some letters to Flanders to another captain, her cousin, she said, although he knew he had to be her lover.

"I was inflamed by the snowy hands I had seen and dying for the face I desired to see. And so the next day, led by my servant, I was freely admitted to her very nicely decorated house, and found a woman of about thirty, whom I recognized because of her hands. She was not extremely beautiful, but her beauty was of the kind that could inspire love in one who knew her, because she had so gentle a way of speaking that it entered the soul through one's ears. I had long, amorous colloquies with her; I boasted, hewed, hacked, offered, promised, and demonstrated everything I thought necessary to make her favor me. But since she was accustomed to hearing similar or greater wooing and words, it seemed she listened attentively but did not believe any of it. In brief, I spent our conversation paying compliments for the four days I visited her and never plucked the fruit I desired.

"During the time I visited her, I always found the house empty, and had no glimpse of feigned kinsmen or true friends; she was served by a maid more clever than simpleminded. Finally, treating my love as if I were a soldier on the eve of being transferred, I pressed my Señora Doña Estefanía de Caicedo (for this is the name of the woman who brought me to this state), and she responded: 'Señor Lieutenant Campuzano, it would be foolish if I tried to present myself to your grace as a saint. I have been a sinner and still am one, but not in a way that makes my neighbors gossip nor those more remote to take notice of me. I inherited nothing from my parents or any other kin, and even so the furnishings in my house are worth twenty-five hundred *escudos*, and these things, put up for public auction, would take no time at all to convert into currency. With this property I am looking for a husband to whom I shall give myself, and to whom I shall owe obedience, and to whom I shall offer, along with the rectification of my life, an incredible solicitude in caring for him and serving him, because no prince has a better cook or one who knows as well as I exactly how long to cook stews when I set my mind to it and want to show how well I tend house. I know how to be a steward in the house, a maid in the kitchen, and a lady in the salon. In short, I know how to give orders, and I know how to have people obey them. I waste nothing and save a great deal; my fortune is worth not less but much more when it is spent as I direct. My house linens, and I have a large quantity of them, and of very good quality, were not acquired from shops or dealers: these hands and those of my maids stitched them; and if we could spin at home, we would have woven them. I say these things in my own praise because to do so is not improper when the need to say them is obligatory. In short, I mean that I am looking for a husband who will protect me, command me, and honor me, and not a lover who will serve and revile me. If your grace would like to accept the gift that is offered him, here I am, true and tried, subject to everything your grace orders, no longer for sale, which is the same as being talked about by matchmakers, and there's not one of them as good as the parties themselves to make arrangements.'

"I, who at that time had my good sense not in my head but in the soles of my feet, delighted in the picture painted in my imagination, and in her offering so openly the amount of her estate, which I already was contemplating converted into money, and thinking of nothing except what pleasure gave rise to, had my understanding in shackles, and I told her I was the fortunate and felicitous one since heaven had given me, almost as if by miracle, such a companion to make mistress of my will and estate, which was not so small that it was worth nothing, for with the chain I wore around my neck and some other little jewels I had at home, and by selling off a few soldier's trappings, it amounted to more than two thousand *ducados*, which together with her twenty-five hundred was enough for us to go to live in the village I came from and where I owned some property; a farm that, well managed, selling the fruits at an opportune time, could give us a happy and restful life. In short, on that occasion our betrothal was arranged and we planned how the two of us would publish the banns, which we did together on a feast day, then there were the three days of celebration, and on the fourth day we were married, those present being two friends of mine and a young man she said was her cousin, to whom I offered myself as a kinsman with very courteous words, as were all the words spoken until then by my new wife, with so twisted and traitorous an intention that I would like to conceal it, because although I am telling you the truth, these are not the truths of the confessional, which must be said.

"My servant moved my chest from my lodgings to my wife's house; in her presence I locked my magnificent chain inside; I showed her three or four others, if not as large, then better made, along with another three or four rings of different kinds; I showed her my military finery and trappings and gave her the four hundred *reales* I had for household expenses. For six days I enjoyed the early days of marriage, idling in the house like the despicable son-in-law in the house of the wealthy father-in-law. I walked on rich carpets, rumpled sheets of Holland linen, lit my way with silver candlesticks; I had breakfast in bed, got up at eleven, had lunch at twelve, and at two o'clock napped in the drawing room; Doña Estefanía and the maid anticipated all my desires. My servant, who until then had been known as lazy and slow, became as fleet as a deer. When Doña Estefanía was not at my side, she could be found in the kitchen completely solicitous about arranging for stews that would awaken my delight and enliven my appetite. My shirts, collars, and handkerchiefs were a new Aranjuez of flowers considering their fragrance, for they were washed in water perfumed with orange blossoms. Those days flew by as the years pass that are under the jurisdiction of time; and during those days, finding myself so indulged and so well served, the evil intention with which that business had begun was transforming into good. And then, one morning when those days had come to an end, and I was still in bed with Doña Estefanía, there came a loud knocking at the street door. The maid looked out the window, instantly moved away, and said:

"'Oh, let us welcome her! Have you seen how she came here faster than she wrote she would the other day?'

"'Who is it that has come, girl?' I asked her.

"'Who?' she responded. 'My Señora Doña Clementa Bueso, and with her Señor Don Lope Meléndez de Almendárez, with two servants and Hortigosa, the duenna she took with her.'

"'Run, girl, and Lord bless me! Open the door for them,' said Doña Estefanía at this point, 'and you, Señor, for my sake, do not become agitated or come to my defense no matter what you may hear said against me.'

"'But who can say anything to offend you, especially when I am present? Tell me who these people are, for it seems to me their arrival has upset you.'

"'I can't answer you now,' said Doña Estefanía. 'Just know that everything that happens now is false and directed toward a certain purpose and effect that you will know about afterward.'

"And although I wanted to reply, Señora Doña Clementa Bueso did not give me the opportunity, for she entered the room dressed in green satin decorated with a good deal of gold passementerie, a short cape of the same cloth and the same adornment, a hat with green, white, and pink plumes, a rich hatband of gold, and a thin veil covering half her face. Señor Don Lope Meléndez de Almendárez came in with her, no less elegantly and richly dressed for travel. Duenna Hortigosa was the first to speak, saying:

"'Jesus! What is this? The bed of my Señora Doña Clementa occupied, and what is worse, by a man? Today I am seeing miracles in this house; by my faith, Señora Doña Estefanía, trusted with the friendship of my señora, was given a hand and has taken an arm.'

"'I assure you, Hortigosa,' replied Doña Clementa, 'that I am to blame, for I never learned not to take as friends women who don't know how to be friends, unless they find it useful.'

"To which Doña Estefanía replied:

"'Your grace should not feel regret, my Señora Doña Clementa Bueso, and realize that what you see in this your house is not without mystery, for when you unravel it, I know I shall be forgiven and your grace will have no complaints.'

"By this time I had put on my breeches and doublet, and taking me by the hand, Doña Estefanía led me to another room, and there she told me that her friend wanted to play a joke on Don Lope, who had come with her, and whom she intended to marry. And the joke was to make him understand that the house and everything in it all belonged to Doña Clementa, concerning which she planned to make a dowry document, and once they had married she would quickly disclose the deception, trusting in the great love Don Lope had for her.

" 'And then she will return everything that is mine and will not be judged harshly, nor will any other woman who attempts to find an honorable husband, even if it is by means of some fraud.'

"I replied that what she wanted to do was pressing the limits of friendship, and that she should think carefully first because later she might have need of the law to recover her property. But she responded with so many justifications, alleging so many obligations to serve Doña Clementa, even in matters of greater importance, that very reluctantly, and with many doubts in my mind, I had to yield to Doña Estefanía's wishes, and she assured me the deception would last only a week, during which time we would be in the house of another friend of hers.

"She and I finished dressing, and then, coming in to take her leave of Señora Doña Clementa Bueso and Señor Don Lope Meléndez de Almendárez, she had my servant pick up the chest and follow her, and I also followed, not taking my leave of anyone. Doña Estefanía stopped at the house of a friend of hers, and before we went in she spent a long time inside talking to her, and then a maid came out and told my servant and me to go in. She took us to a narrow room where there were two beds so close together they seemed to be one, because there was no space between them and the sheets were kissing.

"And in effect, we were there six days, and in all that time not an hour went by when we weren't arguing and I wasn't telling her how foolish she had been to leave her house and property, even if it had been for her own mother. I kept returning to this subject so often that one day, when Doña Estefanía said she was going to see how her affairs were progressing, the mistress of the house wanted to know why I was moved to argue so much with her, and what she had done that I spoke so harshly, telling her it had been patent foolishness rather than perfect friendship. I told her the entire story, and when I said I had married Doña Estefanía and mentioned the dowry she had brought with her, and how simpleminded it had been for her to leave her house and property to Doña Clementa, even with so honest an intention as acquiring a husband as distinguished as Don Lope, she began to cross herself so quickly and with so many exclamations of 'Jesus, Jesus, what an evil woman!' that she threw me into great confusion, and finally she said to me:

"'Señor Lieutenant, I don't know whether it goes against my conscience to reveal to you what I also think would weigh on it if I concealed it from you; but may God and luck be with me, however it turns out, long live truth! And death to lies! The truth is that Doña Clementa Bueso is the true owner of the house and estate that formed the dowry presented to you; the lie is everything Doña Estefanía has told you, for she has no house, no wealth, and no dress other than the one she's wearing. Her having had the opportunity and time to create this deception was because Doña Clementa went to visit some kinsmen in the city of Plasencia, and from there she went on her nine-day pilgrimage to Our Lady of Guadalupe. While she was away, she had Doña Estefanía stay in her house and look after it because, in fact, they are great friends; though if you think about it, one cannot blame the poor lady, for she managed to acquire a person like the lieutenant as her husband.'

"Here she finished speaking and I began to think about killing myself. And undoubtedly I would have if my guardian angel had been just a little negligent in helping me, coming to tell me in my heart to remember I was a Christian, and that the greatest sin among humans is suicide, because it is a sin of demons. This consideration or good inspiration was some consolation, but not so great that I did not take my cape and sword and go out to look for Doña Estefanía, with the purpose of inflicting upon her an exemplary punishment. But as luck would have it, and I cannot say if this made matters worse or better for me, I did not find Doña Estefanía in any of the places where I thought I would. I went to San Llorente, put myself in the hands of Our Lady, sat on a bench, filled with regret, and fell into so deep a sleep that I would not have awoken very quickly if I had not been awakened. Filled with anguish and distress, I went to Doña Clementa's house and found her to be the very calm mistress of her house. I did not dare say anything to her because Don Lope was also there; I returned to the house where I had been staying, and the owner said she had told Doña Estefanía how I knew all about her tricks and lies, and that she had asked how I looked when I heard the news, and she had said awful, that in her opinion I had gone out with a bad intention and worse determination to find her. Finally, she told me that Doña Estefanía had taken everything in the chest, leaving me nothing but one traveling outfit.

"Just imagine! Once again God had me by the hand. I went to look at my chest, and I found it open and like a grave waiting for a corpse, and there was good reason for it to be mine if I had the understanding to feel and ponder so great a misfortune."

"It was more than great," Licentiate Peralta said at this point, "for Doña Estefanía to have taken so many chains and hatbands, for, as the saying goes, sorrows are easier to bear on a full stomach."

"I had no trouble in that regard," replied the lieutenant, "for I could also say: Don Simueque thought he would deceive me with his one-eyed daughter, and by God, I'm crippled on one side."[2]

"I don't know to what end your grace can say that," answered Peralta.

"The fact is," said the lieutenant, "that all that jumble and show of chains, hatbands, and jewels couldn't have been worth more than ten or twelve *escudos*."

"That isn't possible," replied the licentiate, "because the one the lieutenant wore around his neck seemed to be worth more than two hundred *ducados*."

"It would be," responded the lieutenant, "if truth corresponded to appearances, but since all that glitters is not gold, my chains, hatbands, gems, and jewels were pleasing, though false, but so well made that only an assayer or a foundry could have revealed their fraudulence."

"That means," said the licentiate, "that your grace and Doña Estefanía both gave as good as you got."

"So good," responded the lieutenant, "that we could deal the cards and start all over again! But the trouble is, Señor Licentiate, that she can get rid of my chains but I can't get rid of the falsity of her status; in effect, though it grieves me, she is my prize."

"Give thanks to God, Señor Campuzano," said Peralta, "that she was a prize with feet and has left you, and you are not obliged to look for her."

"That is true," answered the lieutenant, "but even so, even without looking for her, I always find her in my imagination, and wherever I am, the offense against me is present."

"I don't know how to respond," said Peralta, "except to remind you of two lines of Petrarch, which say:

> *Ché qui prende diletto di far fiode,*
> *Non si de lamenter si altri l'ingana.*

"Which in our Castilian means: 'The man who custmarily takes pleasure in deceiving another, should not complain when he is deceived.'"

"I'm not complaining," said the lieutenant, "but I do feel sad that the guilty man, knowing his guilt, does not stop feeling the pain of the punishment.

---

2. A popular saying referring to the deception of the deceiver.

I see very clearly that I wanted to deceive and was deceived, and was wounded by my own blade; but I cannot so control my feelings that I don't complain on my own account. In short, what is most relevant to my tale, and you can give that name to this recounting of what happened to me, is that I learned that Doña Estefanía went off with the cousin I said was present at our wedding, who in any case had been her lover for a long time. I didn't want to look for her and then find the harm I was missing. I changed lodgings and in a few days changed my hair, because I began to lose my eyebrows and lashes, and gradually my hair fell out, and I became bald before my time, having a disease called alopecia. I was really hairless and penniless, because I didn't have a beard to groom or money to spend. The disease moved at the pace of my need, and since poverty tramples honor underfoot and takes some to the gallows and others to the hospital, and makes others walk through the gates of their enemies with courtesy and humility, which is one of the greatest miseries that can befall an unfortunate man to avoid paying for his cure by pawning his clothes, which had to cover and honor me in health, and when the time came for sweating in the Hospital of the Resurrection, I went in and have had forty sweat treatments. They say I'll be fine if I take care of myself; I have a sword, and may God take care of the rest."

The licentiate offered his services again, amazed at the things that had been recounted.

"Well, your grace marvels at very little, Señor Peralta," said the lieutenant, "for I still have other things to tell you that surpass all imagination, for they are outside all the boundaries of nature. Your grace should not want to know more, except they are such that I consider all my misfortunes well spent, for they were part of what placed me in the hospital where I saw what I shall tell you now, which is what your grace cannot now, or ever, believe, and there is no one in the world who will believe it."

All the lieutenant's preambles and praise before recounting what he had seen inflamed Peralta's desire, so that with no less praise he asked him immediately and without delay to tell him the marvels he still had to tell.

"Your grace must have seen," said the lieutenant, "two dogs that with two lanterns walk at night with the Brothers of the Basket, lighting their way when they beg for alms."[3]

"Yes, I have."

---

3. The Brothers of the Basket were members of the religious order started by San Juan de Dios (1495–1550) who would accept alms in woven baskets to help the sick.

"And your grace also must have seen or heard," said the lieutenant, "what is said about the dogs: that if someone tosses their coins from a window and they fall to the ground, they go immediately to light the spot and look for what has fallen, and they stop in front of the windows where they know people customarily give alms. And though they do this so meekly that they resemble lambs more than dogs, in the hospital they are like lions guarding the house with great care and vigilance."

"I have heard," said Peralta, "that all this is true, but it can't and shouldn't cause me to marvel."

"But what I shall say now about them is something that does, and without crossing myself or alleging impossible or difficult things, your grace should be prepared to believe it. And it is this: I heard and almost saw with my own eyes these two dogs, one named Cipión and the other Berganza, stretched out on some old straw mats behind my bed on the next to the last night of the sweat treatment, and in the middle of that night, when I was in the dark and awake, thinking about my past adventures and present misfortunes, there close by I heard talking, and I listened attentively to see whether I could learn who was talking and what they were talking about. And I soon realized, because of what they were saying, that the speakers were the two dogs, Cipión and Berganza."

As soon as Campuzano said this, the licentiate stood and said:

"Your grace, go in peace, Señor Campuzano, for until now I wondered whether to believe what you told me about your marriage, but what you're telling me now, that you heard dogs speaking, has made me decide that I don't believe anything you say. For the love of God, Señor Lieutenant, don't tell this foolishness to anyone except someone who is as good a friend to you as I am."

"Your grace should not think I am so ignorant," replied Campuzano, "that I don't understand that, except for a miracle, animals cannot speak; I know very well that if starlings, magpies, and parrots speak, it is nothing but words they learn and remember, and because they have the right kind of tongue these animals can pronounce them; but that doesn't mean they can speak and respond in reasoned discourse as these dogs spoke. And so, quite often after I heard them, I have not wanted to believe it myself, wanted to believe I had dreamed things that I heard, listened to, made note of, and, in brief, wrote down when I and all my five senses were awake, just as Our Lord was pleased to give them to me, not omitting a single word, and you should take this as a real indication that can move and persuade you to believe this truth I am telling you. The things they talked about were important and varied, more to be spoken of by wise men than said by the mouths of dogs. And so, since I could not invent them on my own, in spite of myself and contrary to my own opinion, I have come to believe that I was not dreaming and the dogs were talking."

"By my soul!" replied the licentiate. "The days of old have returned, when pumpkins could talk, or the time of Aesop, when the rooster reasoned with the fox, and brutes reasoned with other brutes."

"I would be one of those brutes, the greatest one," replied the lieutenant, "if I believed that time had returned. Or if I stopped believing what I heard and what I saw and what I'll dare to swear to with an oath that obliges and even forces incredulity itself to believe. But, even supposing I have been deceived and my truth is a dream and insisting that it is true is foolishness, wouldn't your grace, Señor Peralta, like to see written in a colloquy the things these dogs, or whoever they were, talked about?"

"So that your grace," replied the licentiate, "does not exhaust himself persuading me that he heard the dogs speak, I'll listen to this colloquy very gladly, which, being written and noted by the lieutenant's good intellect, I already judge to be good."

"There's something else in this," said the lieutenant, "for since I was so attentive and my mind was sharp, and my memory refined, subtle, and clear, thanks to the many raisins and almonds I had eaten, I took it all from memory, and the next day I wrote almost the same words I had heard, not looking for rhetorical colorings to adorn them or adding or taking away anything to make them more pleasing. Their conversation was not on a single night but on two consecutive nights, though I did not write down more than one, which is the life of Berganza, and the life of his companion Cipión (that was the one recounted on the second night) I plan to write down when I see whether this one is believed or, at least, not treated with scorn. I have the colloquy here in my shirt; I put it in the form of dialogue to avoid repeating 'said Cipión,' 'replied Berganza,' which usually lengthen a piece of writing."

And saying this, he took a notebook from his bosom and placed it in the hands of the licentiate, who took it, laughing, as if he were mocking everything he had heard and intended to read.

"I shall lie back," said the lieutenant, "in this chair while your grace reads these dreams or, if you like, this nonsense, their only recommendation being that you can put them aside when they annoy you."

"Your grace should do whatever he pleases," said Peralta, "for I shall finish this quickly."

The lieutenant reclined, the licentiate opened the notebook, and at the beginning he saw this title written:

THE NOVEL OF THE COLLOQUY OF THE DOGS

Dogs of the Hospital of the Resurrection, which is in the city of Valladolid,
outside the Campo Gate, who are commonly called the dogs of Mahudes.

CIPIÓN: Berganza, my friend, tonight let us leave the hospital guarded by trust
and withdraw to this solitude and these mats, where without being heard
we can enjoy this unheard of grace that heaven has granted both of us at
the same time.

BERGANZA: Cipión, my brother, I hear you speak and I know I am speaking to
you, and I cannot believe it, because it seems to me that our speaking goes
beyond the limits of nature.

CIPIÓN: This is true, Berganza, and this miracle is even greater because we
not only are speaking but speaking with intelligence, as if we were capable
of reason, though we are so lacking in it that the difference between the
brute animal and man is that man is a rational animal, and the brute, ir-
rational.

BERGANZA: I understand everything you say, Cipión, and your saying it and
my understanding it makes me wonder and marvel yet again. It is true that
in the course of my life I have heard on many different occasions about our
great virtues; so much so, it seems, that some have wanted to feel we have
a natural instinct, very lively and sharp in many things, that gives indications and signs of our being close to demonstrating that we have some kind
of understanding capable of speech and reflection.

CIPIÓN: What I have heard lauded and praised is our remarkable memory, our
gratitude, and great fidelity, so that we are often painted as symbols of
friendship; and you'll have seen, if you have looked, that on alabaster tombs
with figures of those buried there, when they are husband and wife, between the two, at their feet, the figure of a dog is placed as a sign that in life
their friendship and fidelity were inviolable.

BERGANZA: I know very well there have been dogs so grateful that they have
thrown themselves into the grave along with the dead body of their master.
Others have remained on the graves where their masters are buried and not
moved away from them, eating nothing, until they die. I also know that

after the elephant, the dog occupies first place in appearing to possess understanding, followed by the horse, and finally, the monkey.

CIPIÓN: That is true; but you must also confess that you have never seen or heard of any elephant, dog, horse, or monkey who spoke; and from this I assume that our speaking so unexpectedly falls into the category of things called portents, which, when they appear and reveal themselves, as experience has shown, some great calamity threatens the world.

BERGANZA: In that case it won't be difficult for me to take as a portentous sign what I heard a student say recently as I passed through Alcalá de Henares.

CIPIÓN: What did you hear him say?

BERGANZA: That of five thousand students enrolled in the university that year, two thousand of them were studying medicine.

CIPIÓN: And what do you infer from that?

BERGANZA: I infer that these two thousand doctors will either need to have sick people to cure, which would be a great plague and a misfortune, or they will starve to death.

CIPIÓN: But whichever it is, we're speaking, whether it's a portent or not; what heaven has ordained will happen, and no human effort or knowledge can foresee or prevent it; and so there's no reason for us to argue about how or why we're speaking; it would be better on this fine day, or fine night, that we take advantage of the opportunity, and since it's so comfortable on these mats and we don't know how long our good fortune will last, let us make use of it and talk all night long, not surrendering to the sleep that will interfere with this pleasure, which I have long desired.

BERGANZA: As have I, for ever since I had the strength to gnaw a bone I have wanted to speak, to say things that settled in my memory, and there, being old and numerous, either moldered away or were forgotten. But now, finding myself so unexpectedly enriched with this divine gift of speech, I plan to enjoy it and make use of it as much as I can, rushing to say everything I can think of, even if it's hurried and confused, because I don't know when I'll lose this benefit that I assume is only a loan.

CIPIÓN: Let's do it this way, Berganza, my friend: tonight you tell me your life and the events that have brought you to the point where you are now, and if tomorrow night we still can speak, I shall tell you mine; because it will be better to spend the time recounting our own lives rather than attempting to learn about other people's.

BERGANZA: Cipión, I have always considered you wise, and a friend, and now I think that more than ever, for as a friend you want to tell me your life and know about mine, and as a discerning creature you will parse the time when we can recount them. But first see whether anyone can hear us.

CIPIÓN: No one, as far as I can tell, although nearby there is a soldier taking a sweat treatment; but at this time, he must be more interested in sleeping than in listening to anybody.

BERGANZA: Well, if I can speak with that certainty, then listen; and if what's being said becomes tiresome, either reprimand me or tell me to be quiet.

CIPIÓN: Speak until dawn or until someone hears us; I shall listen to you very gladly and won't stop you except if it seems necessary.

BERGANZA: It seems to me I first saw the sun in Sevilla, in its Slaughterhouse, which is outside the Gate of Meat, and from this one would imagine, if not for what I shall tell you later, that my parents must have been hounds, the kind raised by those ministers of chaos called slaughterers. The first person I knew as a master was one named Nicolás the Snub-nosed, a robust young man, short, stocky, and choleric, like all those who engage in slaughter. This Nicolás taught me and other pups, accompanied by old hounds, to attack bulls and seize them by the ears. In this I easily became an eagle.

CIPIÓN: I'm not surprised, Berganza; since doing evil is a consequence of nature, one easily learns to do it.

BERGANZA: What could I tell you, Cipión, my brother, about what I saw in the slaughterhouse and the excesses that go on there? First, you must take it for granted that all those who work there, from the youngest to the oldest, are people without scruples, heartless, unafraid of either the king or his justice; most live in sin. They are bloodthirsty birds of prey; they and their girlfriends live on what they steal. Every morning before dawn on the days you can buy meat, a great number of low women and boys are at the slaughterhouse, all of them with bags that come in empty and return filled with pieces of meat, and the maids get the testicles and entire half loins. No cattle are killed without these people taking tithes and first fruits of the most delicious and best parts. And since in Sevilla there is no one person in charge of setting the price of meat, each man can sell what he chooses, the first one slaughtered, or the best, or the cheapest; and with this arrangement there is always an abundant supply. The owners entrust themselves to the good people I've mentioned, not so they won't steal from them, for that is impossible, but so they'll moderate the cuts and shavings they inflict on the dead animals, for they trim them and prune them as if they were willows or grapevines. But nothing surprised me more, or seemed worse to me, than seeing that these slaughterers would kill a man as easily as a cow; in the blink of an eye and without thinking twice, they take a knife with a yellow hilt and slit open a person's belly as if they were slaughtering a bull. A day without fights and wounds and sometimes without deaths is exceptional; all boast of being brave and still have their pimp's habits; not one of them lacks his guardian angel on the Plaza de San Francisco, bribed with beef loins and tongues.[1] In short, I heard a discerning man say that the king had three things to conquer in Sevilla: the Calle de la Caza, the Costanilla, and the Slaughterhouse.

CIPIÓN: If you're going to spend as much time as you have just now recounting the condition of the masters you've had and the evils in their trades, we shall have to ask heaven to grant us speech for at least a year, and even so I fear, at the rate you're going, you won't get to half your story. I want to advise you of something, and you'll see the truth of it when I tell you the events of my life; and it is that some stories hold and contain their charm inside themselves, and others have theirs in the way they're told; I mean there are some that give pleasure even though they're told without preambles and ornamentations of words; others need to be dressed in words and told with facial expressions and hand gestures and changes of voice to make something of a trifle, turning poor, weak things into something clever and pleasing; and don't forget this advice and use it in recounting what you still have to say.

BERGANZA: I shall, if I can and if the great temptation I have to speak will let me, although I think it will be very difficult to control myself.

CIPIÓN: Then control your tongue, for there lie the greatest ills in human life.

BERGANZA: I was saying, then, that my master taught me to carry a basket in my mouth and defend it against anyone who tried to take it from me. He also showed me the house of his girlfriend, and her maid did not have to come to the slaughterhouse because at dawn I brought what he had stolen at night. And one day at dawn, when I was diligently taking her the daily portion, I heard someone calling my name from a window; I looked up and saw an extremely beautiful girl; I stopped for a moment, and she came down to the street door and called me again. I went up to her as if I were going to see why she had called me, which was simply to take what I was carrying in the basket and put in its place an old clog. Then I said to myself: 'Flesh has gone to flesh.' The girl said to me as she took the meat: 'Go on, Hawk, or whatever your name is, and tell Nicolás the Snub-nosed, your

1. The Plaza de San Francisco was the center of administrative activity in Sevilla. The guardian angels are a tongue-in-cheek reference to corrupt government officials.

master, not to trust in animals, and not to play games with wolves, or to do so as little as possible.' I could easily have taken back what had been taken from me but did not want to so as not to put my dirty, slaughterhouse mouth on those clean, white hands.

CIPIÓN: You did the right thing, for it is a prerogative of beauty to always be respected.

BERGANZA: That is what I did; and so I went back to my master without the portion and with the clog. He thought I had returned quickly; he saw the clog; he imagined the gibe; he took a knife with a hilt and hurled it at me, and if I hadn't moved out of the way, you'd never be hearing this story now, or the many others I intend to tell you. I ran away as fast as I could, and taking the route into my own hands and feet, I went behind San Bernardo through fields of God wherever fortune wanted to take me. That night I slept outdoors, and the next day a herd or flock of ewes and rams presented me with good luck. As soon as I saw them, I believed I had found the center of my well-being, thinking it was the proper and natural occupation of dogs to guard livestock, for it is work that contains a great virtue, which is protecting and defending the humble and weak against the powerful and proud. As soon as one of the three shepherds guarding the flock saw me, he began to call me with a clicking sound. And I, who wanted nothing else, went up to him, lowering my head and wagging my tail. He ran his hand along my back, opened my mouth, spat in it, looked at my teeth, knew my age, and said to the other shepherds that I had all the signs of being a good breed. At this moment the owner of the flock rode up on a gray mare with short stirrups, a lance and shield, looking more like a coast guardian than the owner of livestock. He asked the shepherd: 'What dog is this? He looks like a good one.' 'Your grace can well believe that,' replied the shepherd, 'for I've looked him over, and there's nothing about him that doesn't show and promise that he'll be a great dog. He just came here, and I don't know who he belongs to, though I do know he doesn't belong to any of the flocks around here.' 'Well, if that's so,' said the owner, 'hurry and put a collar on him, the one that belonged to Leoncillo, the dog that died, and give him the same ration of food as the others, and pet him so he begins to love the flock and stays with it.' Saying this, he left, and the shepherd put around my neck a spiked collar, having first given me a large amount of bread and milk in a trough. He also gave me a name and called me Barcino. I found myself full and happy with my second master and my new occupation; I showed myself to be solicitous and diligent in guarding the flock, not leaving it except for siestas, which I spent in the shade of a tree, a slope, a crag, or a bush at the edge of one of the many streams that flowed there. And I didn't spend these hours of tranquility doing nothing, because during that time I occupied my memory in recalling many things, especially the life I had led in the Slaughterhouse, and the life led by my master and all those like him, subjected to satisfying the impertinent desires of their girlfriends. Oh, what things I could tell you now that I was taught in the school of my master's slaughterhouse lady! But I shall have to be quiet about them so you don't consider me long-winded and a gossip.

CIPIÓN: Since I have heard that one of the great poets of antiquity said it was difficult not to write satires, I shall consent to your gossiping a little, with light but not blood; I mean that you can aim but not wound or expose anyone with what you have thrown; for even if it makes many people laugh, gossip is not good if it exposes someone; and if you can please without it, I'll think you very discerning.

BERGANZA: I shall take your advice and wait impatiently for the time to come when you recount your life to me; from someone who knows so well how to perceive and correct the faults I have in recounting mine, we can certainly expect an account that both teaches and delights. But, tying up the broken thread of my story, I say that in the silence and solitude of my siestas, I considered among other things that what I had heard about the life of shepherds probably wasn't true; at least, the ones my master's lady read in books when I would go to her house, because they all dealt with shepherds and shepherdesses, saying that they spent their whole life singing and playing bagpipes, panpipes, rebecs, and flageolets, and other extraordinary instruments. I would stop and listen to her read, and she read about how the shepherd Anfriso sang exceedingly, divinely well in praise of the matchless Belisarda without there being, in all the woodlands of Arcadia, a single tree against whose trunk he had not sat down to sing, from the time the sun rose in the arms of Aurora until it set in those of Thetis, and even after raven night had spread its black, dark wings across the face of the earth, he did not cease his well sung and better wept complaints. And she did not forget about the shepherd Elicio, more in love than he was daring, of whom it was said that without tending to either his love or his livestock, he concerned himself with other people's cares. She also said that the great shepherd Filida, the most excellent painter of a portrait, had been more confident than fortunate. Regarding the dismay of Sireno and the repentance of Diana she said she thanked God and the enchantress Felicia, who with her enchanted water undid that collection of entanglements and clarified that labyrinth of difficulties. I thought of many other books of this sort that I had heard her read, but they weren't worthy of being brought to mind.

CIPIÓN: Berganza, you're taking advantage of my advice as you go along; hurry along and continue, and may your intention be virtuous, though your tongue doesn't seem to be.

BERGANZA: In these matters the tongue never stumbles if the intention doesn't fall first, but if it happens that through carelessness or malice I gossip, I shall reply to the person who reprimands me with the response of Mauleón, a foolish poet and mock academic of the Academy of Imitators, to one who asked him the meaning of *Deum de Deo*; and he replied 'Dare do derring-do.'

CIPIÓN: That was the answer of a simpleton; but you, if you are wise or wish to be so, should never say anything that you have to excuse. Proceed.

BERGANZA: I say that all the thoughts I've mentioned, and many others, made me see how different the manners and actions of my shepherds and all the others on that piece of land were from those of the shepherds in the books I had heard;[2] because if mine sang, they weren't refined, nicely composed songs but 'The wolf is watching where Juanica goes' and others like it; and this was not to the sound of flageolets, rebecs, or bagpipes but the one made by hitting one shepherd's crook with another or bringing together small tiles held between the fingers; and not sung by delicate, sonorous, admirable voices but ones that were hoarse and, alone or together, sounded not as if they were singing but shouting or growling. They spent most of the day delousing themselves or repairing their sandals; and none of them was named Amarilis, Filida, Galatea, or Diana, and there were no Lisardos, Lausos, Jacintos, or Riselos; they were all Antones, Domingos, Pablos, or Llorentes; and so I came to understand what I think everyone must believe: that all those books are well-written dreams meant to entertain the idle, and have no truth in them; if they did, among my shepherds there would have been some remains of that supremely happy life, and of those pleasant meadows, spacious woodlands, sacred mountains, beautiful gardens, clear streams, and crystalline fountains, and of that wooing as virtuous as it was well spoken, and of that shepherd swooning here, that shepherdess swooning there; someone playing a reed pipe over yonder, and nearby someone else playing the flute.

CIPIÓN: Enough, Berganza; return to your path and keep walking.

2. Berganza here contrasts the reality of shepherds with their idealistic interpretation in pastoral literature, the kind he recalled hearing at the house of his master's lady.

BERGANZA: I thank you, Cipión, my friend; because if you hadn't warned me, my mouth was heating up so much that it wouldn't have stopped until it had painted you an entire book of the kind that had deceived me; but the time will come when I shall say it all with better words and better reasoning than I do now.

CIPIÓN: Look at your feet and you'll fold up your tail, Berganza. I mean you should see that you're an animal that lacks reason, and if you show some now, the two of us have already decided it's something supernatural and unheard of.

BERGANZA: That might have been true if I were in my earlier ignorance; but now that what I was going to tell you at the start of our talk has come to mind, I not only am not surprised at speaking but am amazed at what I'm not saying.

CIPIÓN: Well, can't you say now what you've just remembered?

BERGANZA: It's a certain story of what happened to me with a great sorceress, a disciple of Camacha de Montilla.

CIPIÓN: I say that you should tell it to me before you go any further in the account of your life.

BERGANZA: I certainly won't do that until it is time. Be patient and listen to these things in their proper order, and you'll enjoy them more if you're not worn out by wanting to know middles before beginnings.

CIPIÓN: Be brief, and tell whatever you want and however you want to tell it.

BERGANZA: I'll say, then, that I was happy with my occupation of guarding livestock, because it seemed to me that I was eating the bread I had earned by the sweat of my brow, and that idleness, root and mother of all the vices, had nothing to do with me, because if during the day I rested, at night I didn't sleep, since wolves attacked us often and put us on the defensive; and as soon as the shepherds said to me: 'Get the wolf, Barcino,' I came running, before the other dogs, to the place where they indicated the wolf was lurking; I ran through the valleys, I investigated the mountains, I dug up the woods, I jumped across ravines, crossed roads, and in the morning I returned to the flock not having found the wolf or any trace of him, gasping for breath, tired, overcome by fatigue, my paws torn by broken branches; and in the flock I would find either a dead ewe or a ram with its throat torn open and half eaten by the wolf. It made me angry to see how little good my care and diligence accomplished. The owner of the flock came; the shepherds came out to receive him with the hides of the dead animals; he accused the shepherds of negligence and ordered the dogs punished for laziness; blows with sticks and reprimands rained down on us; and so, finding myself punished one day when I was blameless, and seeing that my care, speed, and valor were of no use in catching the wolf, I decided to change my style, not going away to search for him, as I usually did, far from the flock, but staying close, and if the wolf came, it would be easier to attack him. Each week the alarm sounded, and on a very dark night I was on the lookout for wolves, though the flock couldn't be protected from them. I crouched behind a bush, the dogs, my friends, went out, and from there I observed that two shepherds seized one of the best rams in the fold and slaughtered it in such a way that in the morning it really looked as if a wolf had been the killer. I was dumbfounded, astonished when I saw that the shepherds were the wolves; the ones who were supposed to protect the sheep were tearing them to pieces. They immediately informed their master of the wolf's kill, gave him the hide and part of the meat, and kept the best for themselves. Again the owner reprimanded them, and again the dogs were punished. There were no wolves; the flock was shrinking; I would have liked to bring this to light; I was mute. All of which filled me with amazement and distress. 'Lord save me!' I said to myself. 'Who can remedy this evil? Who is capable of revealing that the defense offends, the sentinels are asleep, trust is a thief, and your guardian is killing you!'

CIPIÓN: And you were correct, Berganza, because there is no greater or more subtle thief than a servant; and so, many more of the trustful die than the suspicious; but the bad thing is that it's impossible for people to get along in the world if they don't trust and have confidence in one another. But let's leave this for now, I don't want us to seem like preachers. Continue.

BERGANZA: I'll continue and say that I decided to leave that occupation even though it seemed so good, and choose another where, if I did the work well, even if I weren't remunerated, I wouldn't be punished. I returned to Sevilla and began to serve a very rich merchant.

CIPIÓN: What method did you use to gain access to a master? Because, in general, it is very difficult these days for an honest man to find a master to serve. The earthly masters of the Master of heaven are very different; for them to accept a servant they first scrutinize his lineage, examine his skill, study his person, and even want to know the clothes he has; but to begin to serve God, the poorest is the richest; the humblest has the best lineage; and anyone prepared to serve Him with a pure heart is immediately entered in the book of His benefits, marking them as so important that, being so many and so great, they surpass all our desires.

BERGANZA: All that is preaching, Cipión, my friend.

CIPIÓN: It seems that way to me too, and so I'll be silent.

BERGANZA: As for what you asked regarding the method I used to find a master, I'll say that you already know that humility is the basis and foundation of all the virtues, and that without it no virtue exists. It levels obstacles, overcomes difficulties, and is a means that always leads us to glorious ends; it makes friends of enemies, tempers the rage of the wrathful, and diminishes the arrogance of the proud; it is the mother of modesty and sister of temperance; in short, with it the vices cannot find an opportunity to triumph, because the arrows of sins are blunted and break in its softness and gentleness. And so I made use of it when I wanted to enter the service of a house, having first considered and verified very carefully that it was a house that could support and take in a large dog. Then I stayed at the door and when, in my opinion, a stranger went in, I barked at him, and when the master came I lowered my head and, wagging my tail, approached him and cleaned his shoes with my tongue. If they beat me with a stick, I endured it, and with the same gentleness I showed affection toward the man who gave me the beating, which was never repeated, seeing my persistence and noble behavior. In this way, after two attempts I stayed in the house; I served well, they soon had affection for me, and no one sent me away unless I sent myself away, I mean to say, unless I left; and I even found a master and would be in his house today if bad luck had not pursued me.

CIPIÓN: In the same way that you've recounted, I entered the houses of the masters I've had, and it seems we can read their thoughts.

BERGANZA: We've had similar experiences along those lines, if I'm not mistaken, and I'll tell you about them in time, as I've promised; and now listen to what happened to me after I left the flock in the care of those villains.

I returned to Sevilla, as I said, which is a shelter to the poor and a refuge to the scorned, for in its greatness there is room for the humble, and they don't even notice the great. I approached the doorway of a large house that belonged to a merchant, took the usual steps, and in a short while was inside. They took me in to keep me tied behind the door during the day and untied at night; I served with great care and diligence; I barked at strangers and growled at those who weren't very well known; I didn't sleep at night, visiting the corrals, going up to the flat roofs, becoming the general guardian of my house as well as other people's houses. My master was so pleased with my good service that he gave orders for me to be well treated and fed a ration of bread, the bones from his table, and leftovers from the kitchen, for which I showed my gratitude, jumping up and down over and over again when I saw my master, especially when he came in from outside; I gave so many demonstrations of joy and jumped so much that my master gave orders for me to be untied and allowed to walk free both day and night. When I found myself free, I ran to him, ran all around him, not daring to touch him with my forepaws, remembering the fable of Aesop in which an ass was such an ass that he tried to give his owner the same caresses that a spoiled lapdog of his gave, and was severely beaten. It seemed to me that this fable lets us know that the charms and graces of some don't suit others; let the court jester invent nicknames, the actor do sleight-of-hand and acrobatics, the rogue bray like a donkey, and the lowborn man who has devoted himself to it imitate the song of birds and the various gestures and actions of animals and men, and let the eminent man avoid these things, for none of these abilities can be a credit to him or give him an honorable name.

CIPIÓN: Enough. Go on, Berganza, your point has been made.

BERGANZA: I only hope that just as you understand me, those for whom I'm saying this understand me too! I don't know what kind of good nature I have, but it pains me greatly when I see a gentleman tell indecent jokes, and boast of knowing how to play cups and balls,[3] and brag that no one dances the chaconne as well as he. I know a gentleman who prided himself on the fact that, implored by a sacristan, he cut thirty-two paper rosettes that were attached to black cloths and placed on a monument, and he attributed so much importance to this that he took his friends to see them as if he were taking them to see the banners and spoils of enemies on the tomb of his parents and grandparents. This merchant, then, had two sons, one twelve and the other almost fourteen, who were studying grammar in the school of the Company of Jesus. They went to school with a great deal of show, with a tutor and with pages who carried their books and what is called a *vademécum*.[4] Seeing them go so ostentatiously, in canopied seats if the weather was sunny, in a carriage if it was raining, made me consider and remark on the simplicity with which their father went to the exchange to tend to his affairs, because the only servant he took was a black, and sometimes he even rode on an unadorned old mule.

CIPIÓN: You should know, Berganza, that it is the custom and condition of the merchants in Sevilla, and even in other cities, to show their authority and wealth not in their own persons but in those of their children; because

---

3. A version of the shell game where a cone from a cypress tree is hidden under a cup and passed between others using sleight of hand.

4. *Vademécum* is Latin for "goes with me" and refers to a small book or notebook.

merchants are greater in their shadows than in themselves. And if they make an exception and attend to something other than their deals and contracts, they do so modestly; and since ambition and wealth long to show themselves, they explode in their children, and so they treat them and empower them as if they were the children of some prince. And there are some who obtain titles for them and place on their bosoms the sign that distinguishes eminent people from plebeians.

BERGANZA: It is ambition, but a generous ambition, of someone who attempts to improve his status without harming another.

CIPIÓN: Rarely, if ever, can ambition be satisfied with no harm to another.

BERGANZA: We've already said that we weren't to gossip.

CIPIÓN: Yes, and I'm not gossiping about anybody.

BERGANZA: Now I've just confirmed as true what I've heard so often. A slanderous gossip has just ruined ten lineages and defamed twenty good men, and if anyone reproves him for what he has said, he replies that he hasn't said anything, and if he has said something, it wasn't all that bad, and if he thought anyone would be offended, he wouldn't have said it at all. The truth is, Cipión, that whoever wants two hours of conversation without touching on the boundaries of gossip has to know a great deal and take great care; because I see in myself that, being an animal, which is what I am, after a few phrases words come rushing to my tongue like mosquitoes to wine, and all of them malicious and slanderous; and for this reason I'll say again what I have said before: we have inherited doing and saying evil from our first parents and drink it in with our mother's milk. We can clearly see that as soon as the child has freed his arm from his swaddling, he raises his hand with indications that he wants to take his revenge on whoever in his opinion has offended him; and almost the first articulated word he says is to call his wet nurse or mother a whore.

CIPIÓN: This is true, and I confess my error, and I want you to forgive me for it, as I have forgiven you for so many; let's make up, as the children say, and not gossip from now on; and continue your story, for you left off at the display made by the children of the merchant, your master, when they went to the school of the Company of Jesus.

BERGANZA: I commend myself to Him in everything; and although I consider not gossiping anymore very difficult, I intend to use a remedy that I heard was used by a man who swore constantly and, repentant over his bad habit, whenever he swore he would pinch his arm, or kiss the ground as a punishment for his fault; but even so, he still swore. And so, each time I go against the precept you have given me to stop gossiping and against the intention I

have not to gossip, I shall bite the tip of my tongue so that it hurts and re-
minds me of my fault so I don't repeat it.

CIPIÓN: If you use that remedy, I expect you'll bite yourself so many times
you'll be left without a tongue, and therefore incapable of gossiping.

BERGANZA: At least I shall do what I must, and may heaven overlook my faults.
And so I say that my master's children left a portfolio one day in the courtyard, where I happened to be; and since my master had taught me to carry
the slaughterer's basket, I took hold of the portfolio and went after them,
intending not to let go of it until I reached the school. Everything happened
as I wished: my masters, who saw me coming with the portfolio in my
mouth, held gently by the straps, sent a page to take it from me; but I did
not consent and did not let go of it until I went into the classroom with him,
something that made all the students laugh. I went up to the older of my
masters and, with what I thought was great courtesy, placed it in his hands
and remained sitting in the doorway of the room, staring fixedly at the
teacher who was lecturing from his desk. I don't know what there is in virtue, for I have so little of it, or nothing at all; but I immediately rejoiced at
seeing the love, the manner, the solicitude, and the care with which those
blessed fathers and teachers taught those children, straightening the tender
stalks of their youth so they would not twist or go the wrong way on the
path of virtue, which they showed them along with letters. I considered how
they reprimanded them gently, punished them with mercy, animated them
with examples, motivated them with prizes, overlooked their misdeeds with
wisdom, and, finally, how they painted for them the ugliness and horror of
vices, and sketched for them the beauty of virtues so that, despising the first
and loving the second, they might achieve the end for which they were
brought up.

CIPIÓN: You have spoken the truth, Berganza, because I have heard it said of
those blessed people that as teachers there are none as prudent anywhere
in the world, and as guides and leaders on the road to heaven, few can rival
them. They are mirrors where one can see righteousness, Catholic doctrine,
a rare prudence, and, finally, profound humility, the foundation on which
the entire edifice of heavenly bliss is erected.

BERGANZA: Everything is just as you say. And continuing with my story, I shall
say that my masters liked me to carry the portfolio for them, which I did
very willingly; with this I led the life of a king and even better, because it
was restful; the students liked to play with me and I made myself so gentle
with them that they would put their hands in my mouth and the littlest
ones would climb on my back. They would throw their caps or hats, and

I would return them unharmed and with signs of great joy. They would feed me as much as they could, and they liked to see that when they gave me walnuts or hazelnuts I would open them like a monkey, leaving the shells and eating the meat. And it so happened that to test my ability, they brought me in a handkerchief a large quantity of mixed greens, which I ate as if I were a person. It was winter, a season when soft rolls and butter are outstanding in Sevilla, and in this I was so well served that more than two Latin grammars were pawned or sold so that I could have a meal. In short, I led a student's life without hunger or scabies, which is the greatest praise one can give to say that it was good; because if scabies and hunger were not so closely associated with students, there would be no other life more pleasant and amusing, because in it virtue and pleasure go together, and one spends one's youth learning and enjoying oneself. From this glory and this tranquility a lady came to take me away who, I believe, they call reason of state, and when one's obligations toward her are fulfilled, one must unfulfill many others. The fact is that those honorable teachers believed that the half-hour period between lessons was being used by the students not to review the lessons but to amuse themselves with me; and so, they ordered my masters not to bring me to the school anymore. They obeyed, returned me to the house and to my former guarding of the door, and because my older master did not recall the kindness he had done me earlier when he let me walk free both day and night, I again offered my neck to the chain and my body to a straw mat they put down for me behind the door. Oh, Cipión, my friend, if you knew how hard it is to suffer the change from a happy to an unhappy state! Look: when miseries and misfortunes have been usual for a long time and are continuous, either they end quickly with death, or their continuation becomes a habit and suffering them a custom, and usually when harshest they can be a kind of relief; but when, from an unfortunate and calamitous fate, one suddenly and without thinking begins to enjoy another kind of fate that is prosperous, fortunate, and happy, and then a little while later one suffers again one's earlier travails and misfortunes, it is so harsh a sorrow that if one's life does not come to an end, it is only to increase one's torment by continuing. In short, I returned to my doggish portion and the bones that a black woman in the house threw to me, and even these were tithed by two Roman cats that, untied and lithe, found it easy to take from me whatever did not fall into the area my chain could reach. Cipión, my brother, may heaven grant you the good you desire, and without being annoyed let me now philosophize a little, because if I fail to say the things that at this moment have come to mind regarding what happened to me then, I think my story would be neither exact nor worthwhile.

CIPIÓN: Take care, Berganza, that this desire to philosophize which you say has come over you is not a temptation of the devil; because gossip has no better disguise to extenuate and conceal its dissolute evil than for the gossiper to let it be known that everything he says are the aphorisms of philosophers, and that speaking ill of someone is a reprimand, and revealing the defects of others is admirable zeal. And no gossip has a life that, if you consider and analyze it carefully, is not filled with vices and insolence. And knowing this, you can philosophize now all you want.

BERGANZA: You can be sure, Cipión, that if I gossip it is because I intend to. Well, the fact is that since I was idle all day, and idleness is the mother of the imagination, I began to review in my memory some Latin phrases that remained in my mind of the many I heard when I went with my masters to school, so that, in my opinion, I found myself somewhat improved in my understanding, and I decided, as if I knew how to speak, to take advantage of them when the occasion arose, but in a way that was different from the one used by some ignorant people. There are those who do not know Latin but in conversation occasionally blunder with some brief, concise Latin expression, letting those who don't understand know that they are great Latin scholars when they barely know how to decline a noun or conjugate a verb.

CIPIÓN: I think that does less harm than the injury inflicted by those who really do know Latin, for some of them are so imprudent that when speaking with a cobbler or a tailor, they sprinkle Latin phrases as if they were water.

BERGANZA: From this we can infer that the man who says Latin expressions to one who doesn't know them sins as much as the man who says them but doesn't know them.

CIPIÓN: Well, there's something else you can give advice about, which is that there are some whose knowledge of Latin does not excuse them from being asses.

BERGANZA: Well, who can doubt it? The reason is clear, because when in the time of the Romans everybody spoke Latin as their mother tongue, there must have been among them one simpleton whose speaking Latin did not excuse him from being a fool.

CIPIÓN: To know how to be silent in the vernacular and speak in Latin, discernment is needed, Berganza, my brother.

BERGANZA: That is true, because you can say something idiotic in Latin as well as in the vernacular, and I have seen erudite fools, and tedious grammarians, and ignorant writers in the vernacular who weave in their lists of Latin words, so they very easily can annoy the world not just once but many times.

CIPIÓN: Let's drop this; you can begin to tell me your philosophies.

BERGANZA: I've already told them to you. They're the ones I've just said.

CIPIÓN: Which ones?

BERGANZA: The ones about Latin and vernacular words, which I began and you finished.

CIPIÓN: You call gossip philosophizing? Well, well, well: applaud, applaud, Berganza, the accursed plague of gossip! Call it whatever you like, it will call us cynics, a word that means gossiping canines; and by your life, be quiet now and go on with your story.

BERGANZA: How can I go on with it if I'm quiet?

CIPIÓN: I mean just go straight ahead, without making the story look like an octopus with all the tails you keep adding to it.

BERGANZA: Speak properly; the appendages of an octopus are not called tails.

CIPIÓN: That was the mistake of the man who said that it wasn't witless or vicious to call things by their own names, as if it weren't better, since it is obligatory to name them, to use circumlocutions and evasions that moderate the disgust caused by hearing their names. Decorous words are an indication of the decorum of the one who says or writes them.

BERGANZA: I want to believe you; and I say that my fate, not content with removing me from my studies and the life I led pursuing them, so joyous and composed, and tying me behind a door, and exchanging the generosity of the students for the stinginess of the black woman, ordered that I be disturbed in what by then I already considered tranquility and peace. Look, Cipión, you can consider it true and proven, as I do, that misfortunes search out and find the unfortunate man even if he hides in the farthest corners of the world. I say this because the black woman was in love with a black man who was also a slave in the house; and this black man slept in the portico between the street door and the one in the middle, behind the one where I was, and they couldn't be together except at night, and for this they had stolen or copied the keys; and so, most nights the black woman came down, and covering my mouth with a piece of meat or cheese, opened the door to the black man, with whom she spent a long time, facilitated by my silence, and at the cost of many things she stole. Some days her gifts clouded my conscience, making me think that without them my flanks would grow thin, and I would look more like a greyhound than a mastiff. But in fact, led by my better nature, I wanted to be responsible for what I owed my master, since I received benefits from him and ate his bread, which is what should be done not only by honorable dogs, giving them their reputation for gratitude, but also by all those who serve.

CIPIÓN: This, Berganza, is what I want to be taken as philosophy, because these are words made up of good truth and good understanding; continue your story, and speak plainly, not going round in circles.

BERGANZA: First I beg you to tell me, if you know, what philosophy means; because even though I say it, I don't know what it is. I simply assume it's something good.

CIPIÓN: I shall tell you briefly. This word is composed of two Greek nouns, and they are *philos* and *sophia*; *philos* means love, and *sophia* means knowledge; and so philosophy means love of knowledge, and a philosopher is a lover of knowledge.

BERGANZA: You know a great deal, Cipión. Who the devil taught you Greek nouns?

CIPIÓN: Really, Berganza, you're a simpleton, because you take notice of this; these are things that schoolchildren know, and there are also those who presume to know Greek and don't know it, just like Latin and those who are ignorant of it.

BERGANZA: That's what I say, and I'd like those people to be placed in a press, and by turning the handle the juice of what they know would be squeezed out of them, as the Portuguese do with the blacks of Guinea, and then they wouldn't go around deceiving everybody with the glitter of their false Greekisms and false Latinisms.

CIPIÓN: And now, Berganza, you can bite your tongue and slice off mine, because everything we're saying is gossip.

BERGANZA: Yes, for I am not obliged to do what I have heard that a certain Corondas, a Tyrian did, when he decreed that no one could enter the council chambers of his city with weapons, under pain of death. Then he forgot and the next day he entered the council meeting wearing his sword; realizing what he had done, and remembering the penalty, he immediately unsheathed his sword and passed it through his chest, and was the first man to decree and break a law and pay the penalty. What I said was not decreeing a law but promising I would bite my tongue when I gossiped. But nowadays matters do not follow the tenor or rigor of ancient times; today a law is passed, and tomorrow it is broken, and perhaps it is better this way. Now one promises to correct his vices and the next moment falls into even greater ones. It is one thing to praise discipline and another to submit to it, and, in effect, there's many a slip 'twixt the cup and the lip. Let the devil bite himself,

I don't want to bite my tongue or do fine things behind a straw mat, where I'm not seen by anyone who can praise my honorable determination.

CIPIÓN: According to that, Berganza, if you were a person, you'd be a hypocrite, and every action you took would be pretense, feigned, and false, covered with the cloak of virtue just so you would be praised, which is what every hypocrite does.

BERGANZA: I don't know what I would do then; what I do know is that what I want to do now is not bite myself, when there are so many things yet for me to say that I don't know how or when to finish saying them, and even more so when I'm fearful that when the sun comes up we shall be left in darkness and not have speech.

CIPIÓN: Heaven will do better than that. Go on with your story and don't leave the short, smooth road with presumptuous digressions; in this way, no matter how long it may be, you'll soon finish it.

BERGANZA: I'll say, then, that having seen the insolence, thievery, and dishonesty of the blacks, I decided, as a good servant, to hinder them by the best means I could; and I could so well that I achieved my purpose. The black woman would come down as you have heard, to take her pleasure with the black man, certain that the pieces of meat, bread, or cheese that she threw to me would keep me silent. Gifts can accomplish a great deal, Cipión!

CIPIÓN: A great deal; don't digress; go on.

BERGANZA: I remember that when I was studying I heard the teacher cite a Latin proverb, which they call an adage, and it said: *Habit bovem in lingua.*

CIPIÓN: Oh, it was an evil hour when you slipped in your Latin! Have you forgotten so soon what we said just a short while ago against those who insert Latin phrases into vernacular conversations?

BERGANZA: This Latin phrase fits perfectly; you should know that the Athenians used, among others, a coin stamped with the figure of an ox, and when a judge failed to say or do what was reasonable and just because he had been bribed, they would say: 'This one has an ox on his tongue.'

CIPIÓN: Its relevance falls short.

BERGANZA: Isn't it perfectly clear, if the gifts from the black woman kept me silent for many days, so that I didn't want or dare to bark at her when she came down to be with her black lover? For this reason I repeat that gifts can accomplish a great deal.

CIPIÓN: I've already replied that they can, and if it weren't to avoid a long digression now, with a thousand examples, I'd prove how much gifts can accomplish; but perhaps I shall if heaven grants me the time, the place, and the speech to tell you the story of my life.

BERGANZA: God grant what you desire, and listen. In brief, my good intentions were broken by the black woman's evil gifts; one very dark night, when she was coming down for her customary amusement, I attacked her without barking so the household would not be disturbed, and in an instant I ripped her blouse to shreds and tore off a piece of her thigh; a bit of fun that was enough to keep her in bed for more than a week, pretending some illness or other for her masters. She got better, returned on another night, and I renewed the fight with my bitch, and without biting her I scratched her entire body, carding her as if she were a blanket. Our battles were silent, and I always came out the victor, while she was always injured and not at all happy. But her anger was certainly noticeable in my fur and my health. She cut off my ration and the bones, and mine slowly began to appear along my spine. With it all, though they took away my food, they couldn't take away my bark. But to finish me off once and for all, she brought me a sponge fried in lard; I recognized the evil act; I saw it was worse than eating poison paste, because if you eat it your stomach swells and there's no way out except to die. And thinking it was impossible to defend myself against the snares of such unworthy enemies, I thought of putting land between us, removing them from my sight. One day I found myself untied, and without saying goodbye to anyone in the house, I went into the street and in less than one hundred paces, luck presented me with the bailiff I mentioned at the beginning of my story, who was a great friend of my master Nicolás the Romo;[5] as soon as he saw me he recognized me and called me by name. I knew him too, and when he called me, I went up to him with my usual ceremonies and caresses. He seized me by the collar and said to two of his constables: 'This is a famous guard dog that belonged to a great friend of mine; let's take him home.' The constables were delighted, and said if I was a guard dog it was a benefit to everybody. They wanted to seize me to take me away, and my master said it wasn't necessary, that I would go because I knew him. I've forgotten to tell you that the spiked collars I took when I left and abandoned the herd were taken from me by a Gypsy in an inn, and in Sevilla I went around without them; but the bailiff put a collar on me decorated with Moorish copper. Just consider, Cipión, the changeable wheel of my fortune: yesterday I was a student, and today you find me a constable.

CIPIÓN: That's the way the world is, and there's no reason for you to start exaggerating the mutability of fortune, as if there were a great deal of difference

5. There is no bailiff mentioned in the story, a possible oversight on Cervantes's part.

between serving a slaughterer and serving a constable. I can't endure and don't have patience for hearing the complaints about fortune from men whose greatest good was having prospects and hopes of becoming squires. With what curses they curse her! With how many insults do they dishonor her! And only so that whoever hears them will think they have fallen from a high, prosperous, and good position into the unfortunate, low state in which they are found now.

BERGANZA: You're right. And you should know that this bailiff was the friend of a notary, and they were often together. The two of them were the lovers of two worthless women, not a little more or less but totally less in everything. The truth is their faces were rather pretty, but there was a good deal of whorish ease of manner and slyness in them. They served as the net and hook for fishing on dry land in this way: they would dress so that their appearance was like the mark that indicates the picture card,[6] and from a distance one could see they were free-living ladies; they were always on the prowl for strangers, and when the autumn fair came to Cádiz and Sevilla, the scent of their earnings arrived with it, and there was no foreigner they did not pursue; and when some foreign libertine fell in with these pure ladies, they would tell the bailiff and the notary the inn they were going to, and when they were together the two would take them by surprise and arrest them for having illicit relations; but they weren't taken to prison, because the foreigners always redeemed their humiliation with money.

It so happened, then, that Colindres, which was the name of the notary's girlfriend, caught a lustful and licentious foreigner; she agreed to have supper and spend the night at his inn; she gave the information to her friend; and no sooner had they undressed than the bailiff, the notary, two constables, and I found them. The lovers were in an uproar; the bailiff exaggerated the offense and ordered them to dress immediately so he could take them to prison; the foreigner was very distressed; moved by charity, the notary intervened, and by sheer pleading reduced the fine to only one hundred *reales*. The foreigner asked for a pair of chamois trousers he had put on a chair at the foot of the bed, where he had money to pay for his release, and the trousers did not appear and could not appear, because as soon as I entered the room the aroma of bacon reached my nostrils and consoled me for everything; I found it by smell in a pocket of his trousers. I say I found a piece of famous ham, and to enjoy it and take it out with no noise,

6. A reference to a mark made on a playing card to indicate secretly that it is of high value.

I took the trousers to the street and devoted myself to the ham with all my heart and soul, and when I returned to the room, I found the foreigner shouting in an adulterated and bastardized language—though he could be understood—that they had to return his trousers, for in them he had fifty *escuti d'oro in oro*. The notary supposed that either Colindres or the constables had stolen them; the bailiff thought the same; he called them aside; no one confessed; and they created a huge commotion. Seeing what was going on, I went back to the street where I had left the trousers so I could return them, for the money was of no use to me at all; I didn't find them, because some fortunate passerby had already taken them. When the bailiff saw that the foreigner had no money for a bribe, he was infuriated and intended to extract from the landlady what the foreigner did not have. He called for her, and she came in half dressed, and hearing the shouts and complaints of the foreigner, and finding Colindres naked and crying, the bailiff in a rage, the notary in a fury, and the constables stealing whatever they found in the room, she was not very happy. The bailiff told her to get dressed and come with him to prison, because she allowed disreputable men and women in her house. And then there really was a commotion! This was when the shouting increased and the confusion grew. Because the landlady said: 'Señor Bailiff, Señor Notary, don't try any tricks with me, I see through all of them; no threats with me, and no bluster; shut your mouths and go with God; if not, by my faith, I'll make such a fuss that we'll get to the bottom of this and expose everybody; for I know Señora Colindres very well, and I know that for many months she's been working with Señor Bailiff; and don't force me to say any more but return his money to this gentleman, and let us all be regarded as good people; because I am an honorable woman and have a husband with his patent of nobility and his *a perpenan rei de memoria* with all its dangling stamps and seals,[7] God be praised, and I follow this trade very honorably and without harm to anyone else. I keep my price list nailed up where everybody can see it, and no tricks with me, because by God I know how to disentangle myself from everything. I'm just the right one to send women to the rooms of guests! They have the keys to their rooms, and I'm not a lynx that can see through seven walls.'

---

7. These were documents that attested to one's lineage as an old Christian and a noble; the landlady, who mispronounces the Latin phrase *ad perpetuam rei memoria*, most certainly does not have such documents.

My masters were dumbfounded hearing the landlady's harangue and seeing how she read them the story of their lives; but as they saw that they had no one from whom to extract money if not from her, they insisted on taking her to prison. She complained to high heaven of the unreasonableness and injustice being done to her when her husband, so eminent a nobleman, was absent. The foreigner howled for his fifty *escuti*. The constables insisted they hadn't seen the trousers, God forbid. The notary insisted surreptitiously to the bailiff that he search Colindres's clothes, for he suspected that she must have the fifty *escuti* because she was in the habit of inspecting hiding places in the underwear and pockets of those with whom she went to bed. She said the foreigner was drunk and must be lying about the money. In short, everything was confusion, shouts, and oaths, with no way of calming them down, and they would never have calmed down if at that moment the Auxiliary Magistrate, who was visiting the inn and was attracted by the shouting, had not walked into the room. He asked the reason for the shouting; the landlady responded with a minimum of details; she identified the prostitute Colindres, who was already dressed, declared publicly Colindres's public friendship with the bailiff, exposed his tricks and method of stealing, apologized that a woman of questionable reputation had ever entered her house, canonized herself as a saint and her husband as a blessed man, and called to a maid to run and bring from a chest her husband's patent of nobility, so that the Señor Auxiliary Magistrate could see it, saying that once he saw it he would know that the wife of so honorable a husband could not do anything wrong, and if her inn was a brothel it couldn't be helped; for God knew how much it grieved her, and if she wanted to have some income and her daily bread she had no choice but to follow this profession. The Auxiliary Magistrate, annoyed at her inexhaustible talk and boasting of the patent of nobility, said: 'Sister Landlady, I'll believe your husband has a patent of nobility when you confess to me that he is an innkeeping gentleman.' 'And with great honor,' replied the landlady. 'And what lineage is there in the world, no matter how good, that doesn't have some blemish or other?' 'What I'll tell you, Sister, is that you get dressed, because you have to go to prison.' At this news, she fell to the floor; she scratched her face and began to shout; but, even so, the Auxiliary Magistrate, excessively harsh, took them all to prison, which is to say, the foreigner, Colindres, and the landlady. Afterward I learned that the foreigner lost his fifty *escuti*, in addition to ten more that he was fined for costs; the landlady paid the same amount, and Colindres walked out the street door a free woman. And on the very day they released her, she fished a sailor, who paid for the foreigner, with the same deception of the informer; so you can see, Cipión, how many and how great were the difficulties born of my gluttony.

CIPIÓN: You should say, born of the roguish desires of your master.

BERGANZA: Just listen, then, for it got even worse, since it grieves me to speak ill of bailiffs and notaries.

CIPIÓN: Yes, for speaking ill of one does not mean speaking ill of all; yes, for there are many, more than many, notaries who are good, faithful, and legal, and friends of pleasing without harming anyone; yes, for not all of them delay lawsuits, or give information to the parties, or charge more than is lawful, and not all of them go looking into and inquiring about other people's lives to cast doubt upon them, or join with the judge for 'you scratch my back and I'll scratch yours,' and not all bailiffs collude with tramps and cardsharps, and not all of them have the girlfriends for their swindles that your master had. Many, and more than many, are noble by nature and have noble dispositions; many are not impetuous, insolent, badly behaved, or thieves, like those who go through inns measuring the swords of foreigners, and if they find them a hair longer than prescribed, they arrest the owners. Yes, not all of them arrest and release, and are judges and lawyers whenever they wish.

BERGANZA: My master aimed higher than that; he took another path; he thought of himself as brave, arresting famous criminals; he kept up his valor with no danger to his person, but at the cost of his purse. One day at the Jerez Gate he set upon six famous scoundrels by himself, and I couldn't help him at all because my mouth was restrained by a bit made of rope that he had me wear during the day, though at night he removed it. I was astonished to see his daring, his spirit, and his courage; he charged and attacked the six swords of the ruffians as if they were reeds; it was a marvelous thing to see the agility with which he rushed forward, his thrusts and feints, his care and alert eye so they could not attack him from the rear. In short, in my opinion and in the opinion of everyone who watched the fight and had the knowledge, he was considered a new Rodamonte,[8] having taken his enemies from the Jerez Gate to the marble columns of Master Rodrigo's Academy,[9] more than one hundred paces. He left them confined and re-

8. Rodamonte was a Saracen cavalier from Boiardo's *Orlando innamorato* and Ariosto's *Orlando furioso* known for his excessive strength and arrogance.

9. Master Rodrigo's Academy is the antiquated name for the University of Sevilla inspired by its founder, Master Rodrigo Fernández de Santaella.

turned to pick up his battle trophies, three sheaths, which he then took to show to the Auxiliary Magistrate, who at that time, if I remember correctly, was Licentiate Sarmiento de Valladares, famous for the destruction of Sauceda. People looked at my master as he walked down the streets, pointing at him as if to say: 'That's the brave man who dared to fight alone against the best of the toughs of Andalucía.' As he went around the city so he could be seen, what was left of the day passed, and night found us in Triana, on a street next to the powder mill; and my master, having observed, as they say in the ballad, whether anyone could see him, entered a house, and I went in after him, and in a courtyard we found all the thugs from the fight, without their cloaks or swords, and with their vests unbuttoned; and one, who must have been the host, had a large jug of wine in one hand and in the other a large tavern goblet, and filling it with an excellent foaming wine, he drank to the health of everyone present. As soon as they saw my master, they all went toward him with open arms, and everyone toasted him, and he drained his glass with all of them, and would have done so with others if he had been interested, since he had an affable nature and did not want to anger anyone over trifles. I want to tell you now what they talked about there, the supper they had, the fights they recounted, the thievery they referred to, the ladies they knew and how they ranked them and the ones they scorned, the praise they heaped on one another, the absent thugs who were named, the skill that was pondered there, getting up in the middle of the meal to put into practice the fencing moves that occurred to them, fencing with their hands, the exquisite words they used, and, finally, the figure of the host, whom they all respected as their leader, and that would mean my entering a labyrinth I couldn't get out of when I wanted to. In short, I came to understand with full certainty that the owner of the house, whom they called Monipodio, harbored thieves and led pimps, and that my master's great fight had been agreed upon first with them, along with the circumstance of their fleeing and leaving behind the sheaths, which my master immediately paid for, along with all that Monipodio said the supper had cost, which concluded almost at dawn, and which everyone had enjoyed. And dessert was to inform my master of a brand new foreign scoundrel who had arrived in the city. He must have been braver than they were, and out of envy they betrayed him. My master seized him the following night, naked in his bed; if he had been dressed, I saw in his figure that he would not have allowed himself to be taken so easily. With this arrest, which came after the dispute, my cowardly master's fame increased, and my master was more cowardly than a hare, and by dint of meals and drinks he maintained his reputation for valor, and everything he earned with his office and his schemes emptied into the canal of his valor. But have patience, and listen now to a story that happened to him, and I won't add or take away anything from the truth.

Two thieves in Antequera stole a very fine horse; they brought it to Sevilla, and to sell it with no danger they used a trick that, in my opinion, was both clever and discerning. They went to stay at different inns, and one went to the authorities with a petition that said Pedro de Losada owed him four hundred *reales* that he had borrowed, as could be seen in a receipt, signed with his name, which he offered as proof. The lieutenant ordered this Losada to certify the authenticity of the receipt and his signature; and if he did, to pay the amount in guaranties or go to prison. This task fell to my master and his friend, the notary. The thief took them to the inn where the other thief, who immediately certified his signature and confessed to the debt, was staying, and offered as a guarantee the horse; when my master saw it, he burned with greed and marked it as his own in the event it was sold. The thief declared the legal time limit past, the horse was put up for auction at a price of five hundred *reales*, and the bailiff induced another person to buy it for him. The horse was worth at least one-and-a-half times the amount paid for it, but since the advantage to the seller was in making a quick sale, he accepted the first bid for his merchandise. One thief collected the debt that was not owed him, the other retrieved the receipt that was not necessary, and my master kept the horse, which brought him worse luck than Seyano had brought to its owners.[10] The thieves fled immediately, and two days later, after my master had refurbished the trappings and other items the horse needed, he rode it into the Plaza de San Francisco, more pompous and vain than a villager dressed for a festival. He was congratulated a thousand times on his good purchase, affirming that it was worth one hundred fifty *ducados* as surely as an egg was worth a *maravedí*, and he, turning and pirouetting the horse, played out his tragedy in the theater of the aforementioned plaza. And as he was twirling and whirling, two men with fine figures and better clothes arrived, and one said: 'By God, this is Piedehierro, my horse that was stolen in Antequera a few days ago!' Everyone accompanying him—that is, four servants—said this was true, that the horse was Piedehierro and had been stolen. My master was dumbfounded,

10. According to Aulus Gellius's *Attic Nights* (III, 9), Seyano (Seianus) was Gnaeus Seius's magnificent Argive horse that brought ruin to its successive owners.

the owner filed a complaint, there was a trial, and the owner's evidence was so good that the sentence came down in his favor, and my master lost the horse. People heard about the thieves' mockery and skill, for through the intervention of the law itself, they had sold what they had stolen, and almost everyone was pleased that, because of my master's greed, in the end he was left with nothing.

And this was not the end of his misfortune, for that night the Auxiliary Magistrate himself went out on patrol with him because he had been told there were thieves in the district of San Julián; they passed a cross-roads where they saw a man running, and the Auxiliary Magistrate, grasping me by the collar and urging me on, said: 'Get the thief, Gavilán! Hey, Gavilán, good dog, get the thief, get the thief!' I was already wearied by the iniquities of my master, and in order to carry out Señor Auxiliary Magistrate's commands without disobeying him in anything, attacked my own master, who could not defend himself, and threw him to the ground; and if someone hadn't pulled me off, I would have avenged more than a few; I was pulled off to the great sorrow of both of us. The constables wanted to punish me and even beat me to death, and they would have if the Auxiliary Magistrate had not said to them: 'No one touch him, for the dog did what I ordered him to do.' His slyness was understood, and I, without taking my leave of anyone, went out into the countryside through a hole in the wall, and before daybreak I was in Mairena, a town four leagues from Sevilla. As my good luck would have it, I found a company of soldiers there who, according to what I heard, were going to embark for Cartagena. Four scoundrels, friends of my master, were in the company, and the drummer had been a constable, and a great cardsharp, as most drummers tend to be. They all recognized me and spoke to me; and so they asked me about my master, as if I could have responded; but the one who showed me the most affection was the drummer, and so I decided to stay with him, if he wanted me to, and follow that expedition even if it took me to Italy or Flanders; because it seems to me, and you must agree, that since the adage says: 'A fool at home is a fool in Rome,' traveling through different countries and communicating with different people educates a man.

CIPIÓN: That is so true that I recall hearing from one of my masters, who was extremely clever, that the famous Greek named Ulysses was known as a prudent man only because he had traveled through many lands and communicated with different people and several nations; and so I extol your intention of going wherever they took you.

BERGANZA: And so it happened that the drummer, having the opportunity to demonstrate even more of his deviltry, began to teach me to dance to the sound of the drum and to do other tricks that no other dog would have been able to learn, as you shall hear when I tell you about them. To shorten the route, they marched very slowly. There was no commissioner watching us; the captain was young, but a very fine gentleman and a great Christian; the lieutenant had left the court and his servants not many months before; the sergeant was experienced and astute and a great leader of companies, for he could lead them from where they started off to the port of embarkation. The company was filled with ruffians and rogues, who offended some of the towns we passed through, which led to cursing some who did not deserve it. It is the unhappiness of the good prince to be blamed by his subjects because of his subjects, since some are the assassins of others, through no fault of the lord's; for even if he wishes and endeavors to, he cannot remedy these injuries, because all or most matters of war bring with them asperity, harshness, and vexation. In short, in less than two weeks, with my good wit and the diligence of the man I had chosen as my master, I had learned to jump for the king of France and not for the wicked wife of the tavern owner. He taught me to walk on my hind legs like a Neapolitan horse and in a circle like a mule in a flour mill, along with other things that, if I had not determined not to step forward and display them, would have caused some to wonder whether a demon in the shape of a dog was performing them. They called me the *learned dog*, and we hadn't reached our billet yet when, playing his drum, he walked through the town proclaiming that all persons who wished to see the marvelous grace and talents of the learned dog could do so for eight *maravedís* or four, depending on whether it was a large town or a small one, in such-and-such a house or hospital. With this kind of public praise, there was not a person in the town who did not come to see me, and none who did not leave amazed and happy at having done so. My master made a great deal of money and supported six comrades as if they were kings. Greed and envy awoke a desire in the scoundrels to steal me, and they kept looking for the opportunity, for this idea of earning a living without doing any work has many admirers and enthusiasts; that is why there are so many puppeteers in Spain, so many who display retables, so many who sell pins and poems, since their entire property, even if they were to sell everything, is not enough to support them for one day; and even so they don't leave the hostels and taverns all year; which leads me to conclude that the current of their drunkenness flows from a source other than their trades. All these people are idlers, useless, ne'er-do-wells, sponges of wine and weevils of bread.

CIPIÓN: Enough, Berganza, let's not return to the past; continue, the night is passing, and when the sun comes up I wouldn't want us to be left in the darkness of silence.

BERGANZA: Don't worry, and listen. Since it's an easy thing to add to what has already been invented, and seeing how well I could imitate the Neapolitan charger, my master made me some tooled-leather trappings and a small saddle, which he placed on my back, and on it he sat a small figure of a man with a slim lance for running the ring, and taught me to run directly at a ring he hung between two poles;[11] and the day I was to run, he proclaimed that on that day the learned dog would run the ring and perform other new and never before seen tricks, which I did because I chose to, as they say, in order not to prove my master a liar. And so, in the planned number of days, we reached Montilla, a town belonging to the famous and very Christian Marquis of Priego, a lord of the house of Aguilar and Montilla. My master was billeted, because he requested it, in a hospital. Then he made his usual proclamation, and since fame had preceded him and brought the news of the skills and charms of the learned dog, in less than an hour the courtyard had filled with people. My master was happy to see that the harvest would be a good one, and that day he showed himself to be too much of a scoundrel. The fiesta began first of all with my jumping through the hoop of a sieve so large it looked as if it came from a barrel. He commanded me by means of the usual requests, and when he lowered a rod of quince wood that he held in his hand, it was the signal to jump; and when he raised it, I was to remain still. The first of that day, memorable among all those I've had in my life, was his saying to me: 'Well, Gavilán, my friend, jump for that dirty old man you know who dyes his gray beard; and if you don't want to, jump for the pomp and show of Doña Pimpinela de Plafagonia, who was a friend of the Galician girl who served in Valdeastillas. Don't you like the command, Gavilán, my son? Then jump for Bachelor Pasillas, who calls himself licentiate without having any degree at all. Oh, how lazy you are! Why don't you jump? But now I see, now I understand your tricks: now jump for the wine of Esquivias, as famous as that of Ciudad Real, San Martín, and Ribadavia.' He lowered the rod, and I jumped,

11. Running the ring was a courtly exercise in which horsemen would try to snag hanging rings with a lance.

and I noted his cunning and malicious nature. Then he turned toward the people and said in a loud voice: 'Don't think, oh valiant senate, that what this dog knows is anything to sneer at. I've taught him twenty-four pieces, and a sparrow hawk would go flying for the least of them; I mean that before seeing the least of them, one could go thirty leagues. He knows how to dance the sarabande and the chaconne better than the woman who invented them; he can drink two liters of wine without leaving a drop; he intones a *sol fa mi re* as well as a sacristan; all these things, and many others I could mention, your graces will see in the days the company is here; and for now, let our learned dog give another jump, and then we shall take up the principal subject.' With this the audience, which he had called senate, was enthralled, and he set fire to their desire to see everything I knew. My master turned to me and said: 'Go back, Gavilán, my son, and with great agility and skill do in reverse the jumps you have already done; but it must be with devotion to the famous witch who once lived, they say, in this town.' As soon as he had said this, the person who tended the sick, an old woman who seemed older than sixty, raised her voice and said: 'You wicked swindler, liar, and whoreson, there's no witch here. If you say there is because of Camacha, she's already paid for her sin and is in the place that God knows about; if you say so because of me, you indecent trickster, I am not now nor have I ever in my life been a witch, and if I have the reputation of being one, it was due to false witnesses and a one-sided agreement and a thoughtless and badly informed judge; everybody knows the life I lead now, repentant, not for spells I did not cast but for many other sins, sins I committed as a sinner. And so, you crafty drummer, leave the hospital, and if you don't, on my life, I'll make you leave pretty fast.' And with this she began to shout so much and direct so many insults one after the other at my master that she left him in a state of confusion and indecision; in short, she did not allow the fiesta to continue in any way whatsoever. My master was not sorry about the uproar because he kept the money and postponed the rest of the performance until the next day in another hospital. The people left cursing the old woman, adding to 'sorceress' the name of 'witch' and 'bearded old hag.' With it all, we stayed in the hospital that night; and the old woman, finding me alone in the corral, said to me: 'Is it you, Montiel, my son? Can it be you, my son?' I raised my head and looked at her very slowly, and she, seeing this, came toward me with tears in her eyes and threw her arms around my neck, and if I had allowed her to, she would have kissed me on the mouth; but I felt disgusted and did not allow it.

CIPIÓN: You did the right thing, because it's not a gift but a torment to kiss or let oneself be kissed by an old woman.

BERGANZA: What I want to tell you now I should have told you at the beginning of my story, and then we could have avoided the astonishment we felt when we found ourselves able to speak. Because you should know that the old woman said to me: 'Montiel, my son, follow me and you'll know where my room is, and tonight try to see me there alone, and I'll leave the door open; I have many things to tell you about your life, and to your benefit.' I lowered my head as a sign I would obey her, and from this she definitely understood that I was the dog Montiel she had been looking for, as she told me afterward. I was astonished and surprised, waiting for nightfall to see what the mystery or marvel was that the old woman had mentioned; and since I had heard her called a witch, I expected great things from seeing and talking to her. At last it was time for me to go to her room, which was dark and narrow and had a low ceiling, and the only light was the weak illumination of an earthenware oil lamp; the old woman trimmed it, sat on a small chest, pulled me to her, and without saying a word embraced me again, and I had to make an effort to keep her from kissing me. The first thing she said to me was:

'I trusted in heaven that before these eyes of mine closed for their final sleep, I would see you again, my son, and now that I have, let death come and take me from this wearisome life. You should know, son, that the most famous witch in the world, whom they called Camacha de Montilla, lived in this town; she was so excellent at her work that the Erichthos, the Circes, and the Medeas were not her equal, and I have heard that histories are filled with them. She froze the clouds when she wanted to, covering the face of the sun with them; and when she felt like it, she could calm the most turbulent sky; she brought men from distant lands in an instant; with marvelous skill she could repair young maidens who had been somewhat careless in defending their virginity; she covered up widows so they could be indecent with decency; she unmarried married women and married those she wished to. In December she had fresh roses in her garden, and in January she was reaping wheat. And making watercress grow in a kneading trough was the least of what she could do, or having the living or dead that someone asked to see appear in a mirror or an infant's fingernail. It was said that she turned men into animals and for six years had used a sacristan in the form of a jackass, really and truly, but I have never been able to understand how it's done, because what they say about those old sorceresses, that they turned men into animals, according to those who know best, was simply that they, with their great beauty, and their flattery, attracted men so that the men fell in love with them, and then the sorceresses enthralled them and made use of them for anything they wished, so that they seemed like animals. But in you, my son, experience shows me the opposite, for I know you are a rational person and I see you in the semblance of a dog, unless this is something done with that science called prestidigitation, which makes one thing look like another. Whatever it may be, what grieves me is that neither I nor your mother, disciples of the good Camacha, ever learned as much as she did; and not because of a lack of wit, or ability, or spirit, which we had in abundance, but because of her excessive perversity, for she never wished to teach us the big things but kept them solely for herself.

'Son, your mother was named Montiela, second in fame only to Camacha; my name is Cañizares, if not as wise as them, at least with desires as good as those of either one. The truth is that not even Camacha herself could equal the desire your mother had to draw and enter a circle and shut herself in with a legion of devils. Always somewhat fearful, I was satisfied with conjuring up half a legion of demons; but bless them both, and as for preparing the ointments that we witches use on ourselves, of all those who follow and keep our rules today, none could do it better. For you should know, my son, that since I have seen and see that the life that flies on the swift wings of time is coming to an end, I've wanted to leave behind all the vices of witchcraft in which I was mired for many years and have retained only the inquisitiveness of being a witch, which is an extremely difficult vice to abandon. Your mother did the same, left many vices behind and did many good deeds in this life, but in the end she died a witch, not of any disease but of sorrow when she learned that Camacha, her teacher, resented her lack of respect in wanting to know as much as she did, or perhaps they had some other jealous squabble I never found out about. Your mother was pregnant, the time to give birth had arrived; Camacha was her midwife and received in her hands what your mother delivered, and showed her that she had given birth to two puppies; and as soon as Montiela saw them she said: 'There's wickedness here, there's trickery here!' 'But Montiela, my sister, I'm your friend; I'll hide this birth; you take care of recovering and know that this misfortune of yours will be buried in silence; don't worry at all about it, for you know that I know that except for your friend Rodríguez, the porter, you haven't had anything to do with any other man; so that this doggish birth comes from elsewhere and contains a mystery.' Your mother and I, for I was present throughout, were astonished at this strange event. Camacha left and took the pups; I stayed with your mother to help care for her, and she could not believe what had happened to her. Camacha's end came, and in her final hour she called for your mother and told her that she had turned her children into dogs because she had been annoyed with her; but she shouldn't grieve, for they would return to their true form when least expected; but it could not be before they saw this with their own eyes:

> They will return to their true shape and form
> when they witness the overthrow, with swift
> and ready care, of the haughty on high
> and the raising of the humble and low
> by a powerful, a most potent hand.

'Camacha, at the time of her death, said this to your mother just as I have said it to you. Your mother wrote it down and memorized it, and I fixed it in my memory in the event the time came when I could tell it to one of you; and to recognize you, I call all the dogs I see with your color by your mother's name, not because I think dogs will know it, but to see whether they respond to being called something so different from what other dogs are named. And this afternoon, when I saw you doing so many things, and that you were called 'the learned dog,' and that you raised your head to look at me when I called to you in the corral, I believed you were the child of Montiela, whom I have told with great pleasure about yourself, and how you will regain your original form; and I hope it is as easy as the one told about Apuleius in *The Golden Ass*, which consisted of simply eating a rose. But in your case it is based on the actions of others and not on your own efforts. What you must do, my son, is commend yourself in your heart to God and hope that these—I don't want to call them prophecies—riddles happen quickly and prosperously; and since the good Camacha pronounced them, they undoubtedly will happen, and you and your brother, if he is alive, will see each other just as you desire.

'What troubles me is that I am so close to my end that I won't have the opportunity to see it. I've often wanted to ask my goat how your misfortune will turn out, but I haven't dared to because he never answers what we ask directly but uses twisted and equivocal phrases; and so one mustn't ask our lord and master anything, because he mixes a thousand lies with one truth. And what I've gathered from his answers is that he doesn't know anything certain about the future but can only conjecture. Even so, he has so deceived those of us who are witches that even though he constantly mocks us, we cannot leave him. We go to see him very far from here, in a large field, where an infinite number of people, wizards and witches, gather, and there he gives us unpleasant food to eat, and other things occur that in truth and in God and in my soul I don't dare tell, they are so filthy and disgusting, and I do not wish to offend your chaste ears. Some think we don't go to these celebrations except in our fantasy, where the demon represents images of all those things that we later say have happened to us. Others say no, that we really go in body and in spirit; and I think both theories are true, since we don't know how we go, because everything that happens to us in fantasy is so intense that there's no way to distinguish it from when we go really and truly. The gentlemen of the Inquisition investigated this with some of us whom they had arrested, and I think they found that what I have said is true.

'I would like, son, to move away from this sin, and I have made my efforts toward that end: I work in a hospital; I treat the poor, and some die but give me life with what they leave me or with what they have left among their rags because of how careful I am to delouse their clothes; I pray little, and in public; I gossip a great deal, and in secret; it's better for me to be a hypocrite than a public sinner; the appearance of my present good works are erasing from the memory of those who know me my evil past deeds. In short, feigned saintliness harms no one except the person who uses it. Look, Montiel my son, I'll give you a piece of advice: be good in every way you can; and if you have to be bad, do your best not to seem so in every way you can. I'm a witch, I won't deny it; your mother was a witch and a sorceress, and I can't deny that either; but a good appearance gave us both a good reputation with everyone. Three days before she died we had both been at an outing in a valley in the Pyrenees; and even so, when she died, it was with such calm and tranquility that if it hadn't been for some faces she made a quarter of an hour before she gave up the ghost, it would have seemed as if the bed she was in was a bed of roses. Her two sons were a pain in her heart, and even at the moment of her death, she refused to forgive Camacha; that's how steadfast and firm she was in her affairs. I closed her eyes, and accompanied her to the grave; there I left her, never to see her again, though I haven't lost the hope of seeing her before I die because they say in the town that some have seen her wandering cemeteries and crossroads in different forms, and perhaps sometime I'll run into her and ask if she wants me to do something to ease her conscience.'

Each of these things the old woman said in praise of the woman she said was my mother was a blow of a lance that pierced my heart, and I would have liked to attack her and tear her to pieces with my teeth; and if I didn't, it was so death would not take her in so sinful a state. Finally, she said that on that very night she planned to apply ointment to go to one of her usual gatherings, and when she was there she intended to ask her master what was going to happen to me. I wanted to ask what ointments they were, and it seemed as if she read my mind, for she responded to my desire as if I had asked the question and said:

'This ointment we witches apply is composed of the sap of hallucinatory herbs and is not, as the ignorant say, made of the blood of the children we murder. You could also ask me now what pleasure or profit the demon derives from making us kill tender infants, for he knows that since they are baptized, and innocents without sin, they go to heaven, and he experiences a particular punishment with each Christian soul that escapes him; all I can reply is what the old saying tells us, that 'there are those who would lose both eyes as long as their enemy lost one,' that is, the grief he inflicts on parents by killing their children, which is the greatest one can imagine. And what matters to him most is to have us constantly commit so cruel and perverse a sin; and God allows it all because of our sins, for without His permission I have seen in my own experience that the devil cannot offend even an ant; and this is so true that once I asked him to destroy the vineyard of an enemy of mine, and he responded that he could not touch a leaf of it because God did not wish it; and therefore you'll understand, when you're a man, that all the misfortunes that come to peoples, kingdoms, cities, and nations, sudden deaths, shipwrecks, downfalls, in short, all the ills called harmful, come from the hand of the Almighty and His approving will; and the ills and misfortunes they call culpable come from us and are caused by us. God is faultless; from this it can be inferred that we are the authors of sin, forming it in intention, in word, and in deed; and God permits it all because of our sins, as I have said. You'll ask now, son, if you even understand me, who made me a theologian, and perhaps you'll say to yourself: For God's sake, the old whore! Why doesn't she stop being a witch if she knows so much, and return to God, for she knows He is more given to pardoning sins than to permitting them? And my reply to this, as if you had asked me, is that the habit of vice becomes one's nature, and being a witch turns into our flesh and blood, and in the midst of its ardor, which is great, it brings a cold that enters the soul and chills it and deadens even faith, which gives rise to a forgetting of oneself, and one does not even recall the fear with which God threatens or the glory with which He invites; in effect, since it is a sin of the flesh and its pleasures, it is a force that muffles all the senses and enthralls and entrances them, not allowing them to function as they should; and so the soul, being useless, feeble, and careless,

cannot even consider having a good thought; allowing itself to be sub-
merged in the profound abyss of its misery, it does not wish to raise its hand
to the hand of God, Who offers it only for the sake of His mercy so that the
soul can rise up. I have one of the souls I've depicted for you. I see everything and understand everything, and since sin has shackled my will, I always have been and shall be evil.

'But let us leave this and return to the subject of the ointments; I say they
are so cold that they deprive us of all our senses when we apply them, and
we are left lying naked on the floor, and then they say that in fantasy we
experience everything we think we really have experienced. Other times,
when we have applied the ointment, we think we change shape and are
transformed into roosters, owls, or crows; we go to the place where our master is waiting for us, and there we recover our original form and enjoy pleasures I shall not tell you about because they are such that one's memory is
scandalized recalling them, and so one's tongue avoids recounting them;
and even so, I am a witch and cover all my many faults with the mantle of
hypocrisy. The truth is that if some esteem and honor me as a good woman,
there are quite a few who call me witch right to my face, which is what the
fury of a choleric judge who dealt with me and your mother in the past
made them think, depositing his rage in the hands of an executioner who,
because he had not been bribed, used all his power and full severity on our
backs. But this passed, as all things pass; memories come to an end, lives do
not come back, tongues grow tired, new events make one forget old ones. I
work in a hospital; I give good indications of how I behave; my ointments
give me some good times; I am not so old I cannot live another year, since
I am seventy-five; since I can no longer fast, because of my age, or pray,
because of my dizzy spells, or go on pilgrimages, because of the weakness in
my legs, or give alms, because I am poor, or think of the good, because I like
gossiping and to do that one must think about it first, so that my thoughts are
always evil; with it all, I know that God is good and merciful and knows what
will become of me, and that's enough, and let this talk end here, for it truly
is making me sad. Come, my son, and you can watch me use my ointments,
for all sorrows are bearable with bread; bring the good day in the house, for
as long as you laugh you're not crying; I mean that even though the pleasures
the devil gives us are only apparent and false, they still seem like pleasures to
us, and imagined delight is much greater than the one that is enjoyed,
though in true pleasures it must be just the opposite.'

Having said this long harangue she got up, and taking the lantern went
into another small room that was even narrower. I followed her, torn by

different ideas and amazed at what I had heard and what I expected to see. Cañizares hung the lantern on the wall, and quickly undressed down to her chemise, and taking from a corner a pot of glazed earthenware, she put her hand in it, and murmuring to herself, applied the ointment from her feet to her head, which was bare. Before she finished she told me that whether her senseless body remained in that room or disappeared from it, I should not be frightened or fail to wait there until morning, because she would know what I still had to go through before I became a man. Lowering my head, I indicated that I would, and then she finished her application and stretched out on the floor like a dead woman. I brought my mouth up to hers and saw that she wasn't breathing, either lightly or heavily.

I want to confess a truth to you, Cipión, my friend: it filled me with fear to find myself enclosed in a narrow room with that figure in front of me, which I shall describe for you to the best of my ability. She was more than seven feet long, her anatomy was all bones covered by black skin that was hairy and rough; her belly, like soft leather, covered her shameful parts and even hung down to the middle of her thighs; her teats resembled two dry, wrinkled cow bladders; her lips were black, her teeth rotten or missing, her nose curved and rigid, her eyes contorted, her head disheveled, her cheeks emaciated, her throat narrow, her breasts sagging; in short, she was skinny and possessed by the devil. I looked at her for a time and soon felt overwhelmed by fear, considering the evil sight of her body and the worse possession of her soul. I tried to bite her to see if she regained consciousness, and everywhere on her body I was hindered by disgust; but even so, I seized her by a heel and dragged her out to the courtyard, but still she gave no signs of consciousness. There, looking at the sky and finding myself in an open space, my fear lifted; at least, it moderated so that I had the courage to wait and see how the going and coming of that evil female would turn out, and what she would tell me of my life. At this point I asked myself: who made this evil old woman so wise and so wicked? How does she know which are harmful ills and which are culpable? How does she understand and talk so much of God, and do so much of the devil's work? Why does she sin so willfully and not even excuse herself by claiming ignorance?

The night passed in these deliberations, and day came and found the two of us in the middle of the courtyard; she had not come to, and I was sitting beside her, concentrating, looking at her frightening, ugly face. People from the hospital arrived, and seeing that display, some said: 'The blessed Cañizares is dead! Look how distorted and skinny she was from penitence'; others, more thoughtful, took her pulse, saw that she had one and was not dead, from which they gathered that she was in an ecstasy, a rapture, because she was so good. There were others who said: 'This old whore, she must be a witch and smeared with her ointment; saints never have such indecent transports, and until now, among those of us who know her, she's known more as a witch than a saint.' There were the curious who came to stick pins in her flesh, from head to toe; not even that woke the sleeping woman, who did not regain consciousness until seven in the morning; and since she felt herself riddled with pins, and bitten on the heel, and bruised by being dragged from her room, and before so many pairs of eyes looking at her, she believed, and believed the truth, that I had been the cause of her dishonor; and so she attacked me, and putting both hands around my throat attempted to strangle me, saying: 'Oh, you ungrateful, ignorant, malicious villain! Is this the reward deserved by the good turns I did for your mother, and the ones I planned to do for you?' I, who found myself in danger of losing my life between the nails of that ferocious harpy, shook her off, and seizing her by the long folds of her belly, tore at her with my teeth and dragged her around the courtyard; she shouted for someone to free her from the teeth of that malignant spirit.

With these words of the evil old woman, most of the people thought I must be one of those demons that have a constant grudge against good Christians, and some hurried to sprinkle holy water on me, others did not dare approach to detach me from her, others called for someone to exorcise me; the old woman growled; I clamped down my teeth; the confusion grew; and my master, who had come when he heard the noise, became exasperated when he heard people say I was a demon. Others, who knew nothing about exorcisms, brought three or four sticks with which they began to make the sign of the cross on my back. The joke began to smart, I let go of the old woman, and with three leaps I was on the street, and with a few more I left the town, pursued by an infinite number of boys who ran, shouting in loud voices: 'Make way, the learned dog has rabies!' Others said: 'He doesn't have rabies, he's the devil in the shape of a dog!' Considering the blows I had received, I ran out of the town as fast as I could, followed by many who undoubtedly believed I was a devil because of the things they had seen me do, as well as the words the old woman said when she awoke from her accursed sleep. I fled and disappeared from their sight so quickly they thought I had disappeared like a demon. In six hours I ran twelve leagues and came to an encampment of Gypsies in a field near Granada. I stopped there for a while because some of the Gypsies recognized me as the learned dog, and with no small pleasure they welcomed me and hid me in a cave so I would not be found if anyone came looking for me, intending, as I realized later, to earn money with me as my master the drummer had done. For twenty days I was with them, during which time I learned about and observed their life and customs, and since they are notable, I am obliged to tell you about them.

CIPIÓN: Before you go any further, Berganza, it would be good for us to pay some attention to what the witch told you and find out whether the great lie you believe can be true. Look, Berganza, it would be very foolish to believe that Camacha changed men into animals and that the sacristan in the shape of a donkey served her for all the years they say he served her. All these things and others like them are deceptions, lies, or falsifications of the devil; and if it seems to us now that we have some understanding and reason, since we speak when we are really dogs, or have taken on their shape, we have already said that this is an amazing, never-before-seen case, and even if we touch it with our hands, we won't believe it until the fact of its happening shows us what we ought to believe. Do you want to see it more clearly? Consider what trivial and foolish points Camacha said our restoration consisted of, and what must have seemed like prophecies to you are nothing but the words of fairy stories or old wives' tales, like the ones about the horse with no head and the magic wand, told to pass the time before the fire on long winter nights; because, if they were anything else, they would already have been done, unless her words are to be taken in a sense I have heard called allegorical, and this sense does not mean what the words sound like but something else that, although different, contains a resemblance; for instance, if one says:

> They will return to their true shape and form
> when they witness the overthrow, with swift
> and ready care, of the haughty on high
> and the raising of the humble and low
> by a powerful, a most potent hand.

Taking it in the sense I've said, I think it means we shall recover our form when we see those who were at the top of the wheel of fortune yesterday trampled and humbled at the feet of misfortune and ignored by those who most esteemed them. And by the same token, when we see others, who not two hours ago had no portion other than to be one more in a growing number of people in this world, now so elevated in their good fortune that we lose sight of them; and if at first they did not appear because they were small and shrinking, now we cannot reach them because they are large and lofty.

And if, as you say, our return to our former shape depends on this, we have already seen it and see it constantly; from this I gather that Camacha's verses are to be taken not in the allegorical sense but in the literal; but our remedy does not lie in this either, for we have often seen what they say and we are still as dog as you can see; therefore, Camacha was a false deceiver, Cañizares a liar, and Montiela foolish, malicious, and a scoundrel, and excuse my saying so in the event she is our mother, or yours, for I do not want her as my mother. And so I say that the real meaning is a game of ninepins in which with speed and diligence the ones standing are knocked down and those that have fallen are raised up again, and this by the hand of the person who can do it. Consider, then, whether in the course of our lives we have ever seen a game of ninepins, and if we have, did we therefore turn back into men, if that's what we are.

BERGANZA: I say you're right, Cipión, my brother, and that you are wiser than I thought; and from what you have said I've come to think and believe that everything we have experienced so far and what we are experiencing now is a dream, and that we are dogs; but for that reason we should not stop enjoying this gift of speech that is ours and the extraordinary benefit of having human discourse for as long as we can; and so, don't tire of hearing me recount what happened to me with the Gypsies who hid me in the cave.

CIPIÓN: I'll listen to you gladly if only to oblige you to listen to me when I tell you, if it please heaven, the events in my life.

BERGANZA: The life I led with the Gypsies was to consider during that time their many perversities, their deceptions and lies, the thefts they commit, women as well as men, almost from the moment they're out of swaddling and can walk. Do you see their multitude scattered across Spain? Well, they all know one another and hear about one another, and transfer and move what they've stolen back and forth from one group to another. They give their obedience not to the king but to one they call count, and they give the surname Maldonado to him and to all who succeed him; and not because they are descendants of that noble line but because a page of a gentleman with that name fell in love with a Gypsy girl who refused to give him her love until he became a Gypsy and took her as his wife. The page did so, and the rest of the Gypsies liked him so much they chose him to be their leader and gave him their obedience; and as a sign of their vassalage they offer him part of what they steal if it is valuable. To hide their idleness, they forge objects of iron, making tools they use in their thefts; and so you will always see the men in the street selling pincers, augers, hammers, and the women trivets and pokers. All the women are midwives, and in this they have an advantage over our women because with no cost or assistance they give birth to their children and wash the infants in cold water as soon as they're born; and from birth to death they are hardened and inured to suffer the inclemencies and rigors of the weather; and so you will see that they are all strong, and good jumpers, runners, and dancers. They always marry within the group so their evil ways will not be known by others; the women are loyal to their husbands, and very few are unfaithful with outsiders. When they beg, they obtain more with disguises and ribaldry than with devotions; and with the excuse that no one trusts them, they are not in service, and tend to be idlers; if I remember correctly, rarely if ever have I seen a Gypsy woman taking communion at the altar, even though I've gone into churches quite often. Their thoughts are imagining how they'll deceive and where they'll steal; they tell one another about their thefts, and how they did them; and so, one day a Gypsy man told others, in front of me, about a deception and theft he had once committed against a farmer, and it was this: the Gypsy had a donkey whose tail had been cut off, and to its hairless piece of tail he attached a shaggy one so that it looked like the donkey's natural tail. He took the animal to the market, a farmer bought it for ten *ducados*, and having sold it to him and taken the money, he told the farmer that if he wanted to buy the brother of this donkey, an animal just as good as the one he had bought, he would sell it to him for a better price. The farmer replied that he should go for it and bring it back, and he would buy it, and while he was waiting he would take the one he had bought to his lodging. The farmer left, the Gypsy followed him, and for whatever reason, the Gypsy was crafty enough to steal the donkey, the one he had sold him, from the farmer, and at the same time he removed the false tail so the donkey was left with the hairless one. He changed the saddle and bridle and was bold enough to look for the farmer so he could sell it to him, and the Gypsy found him before the farmer had missed the first donkey, and after a brief negotiation the farmer bought the second one. He intended to pay him at his lodgings, but the donkey could not find his donkey, and though he was a great dunce, he suspected that the Gypsy had stolen it and did not want to pay him. The Gypsy looked for witnesses, and brought those who had collected their sales tax for the first donkey and swore the Gypsy had sold the farmer an animal with a very long tail, one very different from the tail on the second donkey. A bailiff happened to be present for all this, and he took the part of the Gypsy with so much evidence that the farmer had to pay for the same donkey twice. They recounted many other thefts, all or most of them of animals, in which they hold advanced degrees, and these are the kinds of theft they commit most often. In short, they are an evil people, and even though many very discerning judges have ruled against them, they have not reformed as a result.

After twenty days they wanted to take me to Murcia. I passed through Granada, where the captain whose drummer was my master was located. When the Gypsies learned this, they shut me up in a room at the inn where they were staying; I heard them say the reason; I didn't like the journey they were taking, and so I decided to get free, which I did, and leaving Granada, I found myself in an orchard owned by a Morisco,[12] who was happy to take me in, and I was even happier, thinking he didn't want me for anything more than guarding the orchard, work, in my opinion, less arduous than guarding livestock; and since it was not possible to haggle over my salary, it was easy for the Morisco to find a servant to command and I a master to serve. I was with him for more than a month, not because I liked the life I had, but because I liked knowing about my master's life, and from that about the life of all the Moriscos living in Spain. Oh, how many different things I could tell you, Cipión, my friend, about this Morisco rabble, if I weren't afraid I couldn't finish in two weeks! And if I went into detail, I wouldn't finish in two months; but, in fact, I'll have to say something, and so listen to what I saw in general and noticed in particular about these good people.

It is a miracle to find among so many even one who believes honestly in sacred Christian law; their entire intention is to lock away and keep minted money; and to obtain it they work and do not eat; if a *real* of any value comes into their power, they condemn it to perpetual prison and eternal darkness; so that by always earning and never spending, they accumulate the largest amount of money in Spain. They are the moneybox, the clothes moth, the magpie, and the weasel; they acquire everything, hide everything, and swallow everything. Consider that there are many of them, and each day they earn and hide a little or a lot, and a slow fever like typhus ends life; and since they are growing, the number of concealers is increasing, and they grow and will grow into infinity, as experience has demonstrated. Among them there is no chastity, and neither men nor women enter the religious life; they all marry, they all multiply, because a sober life increases the causes of procreation. War does not consume them, and no work wearies them too much; they steal from us very calmly, and with the

12. Moriscos were Muslims who had converted (sometimes by force) to Christianity.

fruits of our inheritance, which they sell back to us, they become rich. They have no servants, because they are all their own servants; they don't spend money on their children's studies, because their only knowledge is stealing from us. Of the twelve sons of Jacob that I've heard went into Egypt, when Moses led them out of that captivity 600,000 men left, not counting children and women; from this one can infer how the Morisca women will multiply, for they undoubtedly have greater numbers.

CIPIÓN: A remedy has been sought for all the evils you have noted and suggested; I know very well that the ones you don't speak of are greater and more numerous than those you recount; so far they have not found the right solution; but our nation has very discerning caretakers who, considering that Spain rears and has in its bosom as many vipers as there are Moriscos, with the help of God they will find a certain, rapid, and secure solution to so much harm. Go on.

BERGANZA: Since my master was miserly, as are all those of his kind, he maintained me on millet bread and leftover soup, his ordinary fare; but heaven helped me bear this misery in a very strange way, which you will hear now. Each morning at dawn a young man sitting beneath one of the many pomegranate trees in the orchard would waken, apparently a student, dressed in heavy flannel, not as black or thick as it was drab and threadbare. He wrote in a notebook and from time to time would smack his forehead and bite his nails, while looking up at the sky; at other times he would become so pensive that he did not move his foot, his hand, or even his eyelashes, so great was his enthrallment. Once I went up to him without his seeing me and heard him murmuring to himself, and after a long while he gave a great shout, saying: 'By God, this is the best octave I've made in all the days of my life!' And writing quickly in his notebook, he gave signs of great contentment; all of which led me to assume that the unfortunate man was a poet. I gave him my usual caresses to assure him of my gentleness. I lay down at his feet, and he, with this reassurance, continued with his thoughts and scratched his head again, and returned to his ecstasies and to writing down what he had thought. While this was going on, another young man, gallant and elegantly dressed, came into the orchard with some papers in his hand, from which he read from time to time. He went up to the first young man and said: 'Have you finished the first act?' 'I just did,' responded the poet, 'the most exquisite act that one can imagine.' 'In what way?' asked the second young man. 'In this way,' said the first: 'His Holiness the Pope comes out in full pontifical dress, with twelve cardinals, all dressed in purple, because when the event occurred that my play recounts, it was the time of *mutatio caparum*, when the cardinals dress not in red but in purple; and so in every way, and in defense of accuracy, it is right and proper that my cardinals come out in purple; and this is a point of great importance for the play, and people would stumble over this and make a thousand rude remarks and foolish comments. I can't be wrong in this, because I've read the entire Roman ceremonial just to be certain about their dress.' 'Well,' replied the other man, 'where do you want my director to find purple clothes for twelve cardinals?' 'Well, if you take out even one,' responded the poet, 'I'll sooner fly than let you have my play. Good Lord! This magnificent effect will be lost! Imagine, right here, how it will seem in a theater when a Supreme Pontiff, with twelve somber cardinals and the other prelates who must accompany him, appear on stage. By heaven, it will be one of the greatest and most sublime spectacles ever seen in a play, even the *Ramillete de Daraja!*'[13]

At this point I realized that one was a poet and the other an actor, who advised the poet to reduce the number of cardinals unless he wanted to make it impossible for the director to put on the play. To which the poet said they ought to thank him for not having included the entire conclave present at the memorable ceremony that he sought to have people recall in his excellent play. The actor laughed and left him to his work to pursue his, which was to study a role in a new play. The poet, having written, very calmly and slowly, a few verses of his magnificent play, took a few crusts of bread from his pouch along with something like twenty raisins, I believe, because I counted them and am still not sure if there were so many, because they were mixed with some crumbs of bread, which he blew away, and one by one he ate the raisins and the stems, because I didn't see him discard anything, helped along by the crusts that were purplish with the lint from his pouch and looked moldy, and they were so hard that although he attempted to soften them, putting them in his mouth over and over again, he could not make them more tender; all of which was to my benefit, because he tossed them to me, saying, 'Here, boy! Take this and I hope you enjoy it.' 'Look,' I said to myself, 'look at the nectar or ambrosia this poet is giving me, the ones they say nourish the gods and Apollo there in heaven!' In short, the poverty of most poets is great, but my need was greater, for it obliged me to eat what he threw away. For as long as the composition of his play lasted, he did not fail to come to the orchard and I did not lack for

13. *Ramillete de Daraja* is a lost play, likely of a Moorish theme, that was popular during the Golden Age in Spain.

crusts, because he shared them with me very liberally, and afterward we would go to the waterwheel, and I on my stomach and he with a scoop would satisfy our thirst like monarchs. But then the poet failed to appear, and there was such a surfeit of hunger in me that I decided to leave the Morisco and go into the city to seek my fortune, for the one who changes finds it. When I entered the city, I saw my poet coming out of the famous monastery of San Jerónimo,[14] and when he saw me he approached with open arms, and I went to him with new signs of rejoicing at having found him. Then he immediately began to pull out pieces of bread, softer than those he used to take to the orchard, and offer them to my teeth without passing them first along his, a kindness that with new pleasure satisfied my hunger. The tender crusts, and seeing my poet come out of the monastery, made me suspect that he had embarrassing muses, as do many others. He walked toward the city and I followed, determined to have him for a master if he so wished, imagining that the leavings of his castle could support my army; because there is no greater or better purse than that of charity, whose generous hands are never poor; and so I don't agree with the adage that says: 'The stingy man gives more than the naked one,' as if the hard, avaricious man gave anything comparable to what the generous naked man gives who, in effect, gives his good wishes when he has nothing else. From one adventure to another, we came to the house of a director who, if I remember correctly, was named Angulo el Malo, and not the other Angulo, not a director but a performer, the wittiest the theater had, then or now.[15] The entire company gathered to hear my master's play, for I already considered him my master; and in the middle of the first act, one by one and two by two everyone left except me and the director, who served as the audience. The play was such that, even though I'm an ass as far as poetry is concerned, it seemed to me that Satan himself had written it for the total ruin and perdition of the poet himself, who was gritting his teeth when he saw the solitude in which the audience had left him; and before long his prophetic soul told him of the misfortune that was threatening him, which was that all the performers, who numbered more than twelve, returned, and without a word seized my poet, and if it had not been because the authority of the director and his entreaties and shouts came between them, they undoubtedly would have

14. The monastery of San Jerónimo in Granada was founded by the Catholic Monarchs.

15. Angulo el Malo was an actor and owner of a theater company whom Cervantes also mentions in *Don Quixote*.

tossed the poet in a blanket. The incident left me stunned; the director, surly; the actors, joyful; and the poet, gloomy; and he, very patiently, though his face was distorted, took his play, placed it in his shirt, and said, half-whispering: 'One must not cast pearls before swine'; and with this he left very calmly. I was so embarrassed I couldn't and wouldn't follow him, and I was right not to, because the director gave me so many caresses that they obliged me to stay with him, and in less than a month I became a great actor in interludes, and a great performer of mute characters. They put a cloth muzzle on me and taught me to attack in the theater anyone they wanted; and since most of the interludes end with a drubbing, in my master's company they would incite me and I would knock down and trample everyone, which gave the ignorant something to laugh at, and a large profit to my master. Oh, Cipión, I wish I could recount what I saw in this and two other companies of actors where I worked. But since it isn't possible to reduce it to a succinct, brief narration, I shall have to leave it for another day, if there is another day when we communicate with each other. Do you see how long my talk has been? Do you see the many diverse events of my life? Have you considered the many paths and masters I have taken? Well, everything you have heard is nothing compared to what I could tell you of what I noted, found out, and saw in these people: their behavior, their life, their customs, their activities, their work, their leisure, their ignorance, their cleverness, with an infinite number of other things, some to be whispered in your ear, and others to be hailed in public, and all to be remembered in order to bring the truth home to many who idolize false characters and the beauty of artifice and transformation.

CIPIÓN: I can see all too clearly, Berganza, the broad field that lies before you for extending your talk, and it is my opinion that you should leave it for a separate tale and a moment of undisturbed tranquility.

BERGANZA: Let it be so, and listen. I came with a theater company to this city of Valladolid, where in an interlude I received a wound that almost ended my life; I could not take my revenge because I was muzzled at the time, and afterward I did not want to in cold blood, for vengeance that is planned implies cruelty and a malicious spirit. That enterprise began to weary me, not because it was work but because I saw in it things that all together called for rectification and punishment; and since I could feel it more than remedy it, I decided not to see it, and so I took refuge in religion, as do those who abandon their vices when they can no longer practice them, though better late than never. And so, I say, that seeing you one night carrying the lantern with the good Christian Mahúdes, I considered you content and occupied by something just and holy; and filled with virtuous envy, I wanted to follow in your footsteps, and with this praiseworthy intention I placed myself in front of Mahúdes, who chose me as your companion and brought me to this hospital. What happened to me here is not so insignificant that there is no need for time to recount it, especially what I heard from four patients whom luck and necessity brought to this hospital, all four being together in four paired beds. Forgive me, for the story is brief, and has not been expanded, and fits here like a glove.

CIPIÓN: Yes, I forgive you. And finish up, because I believe it won't be long until daybreak.

BERGANZA: I say that in the four beds at the end of this ward, there was an alchemist in one, a poet in the second, a mathematician in the third, and in the fourth one of those they call mad reformers.

CIPIÓN: I remember having seen those good people.

BERGANZA: And so, I say that during a siesta last summer, when the windows were closed and I was taking the air under one of their beds, the poet began to complain most pitifully of his luck, and when the mathematician asked what it was he was complaining about, he answered that it was his bad luck. 'How could it not be reasonable for me to complain?' he continued; 'for I, having obeyed what Horace decrees in his *Poetica*, that one should not publish a work until ten years after its composition, spent twenty years writing a work, and that was twelve years ago; its subject is noteworthy, its inventiveness admirable and new, its verse serious, its episodes entertaining, and its structure wondrous, because the beginning corresponds to the middle and to the end, so that together they form a poem that is lofty, sonorous, heroic, delightful, and substantial, and with it all I find no prince to whom I can dedicate it. A prince, I say, who is intelligent, generous, and magnanimous. Oh, ours is a miserable age and a depraved time!' 'What is the book about?' asked the alchemist. The poet replied: 'It deals with what Archbishop Turpin did not write about King Arthur of England,[16] with another supplement to the *History of the*

---

16. Archbishop Turpin was the Archbishop of Reims in the eighth century and was believed to be the author of the *History of the Life of Charlemagne and Roland*, also known as the *Chronicle of (Pseudo-) Turpin*, which tells the tale of how Charlemagne came to Spain to liberate the tomb of St. James from the Arabs. That text has nothing to do with the Arthurian legend that Cervantes comically has the poet mention.

Search for the Holy Brail,[17] and all of it in heroic verse, part of it in royal octaves, part in hendecasyllabic blank verse, but all of it dactylishly, I mean, dactyls in the nouns but not in any verbs at all.' 'I understand little of poetry,' said the alchemist, 'and so I cannot properly evaluate the misfortune your grace complains of, since, even if greater, it would not be equal to mine, which is that because I lack the instruments, or a prince to support me and give me the requisites that the science of alchemy demands, I am not now brimming over with gold and more riches than Midas, Crassus, or Croesus.' 'Has your grace,' the mathematician said at this point, 'Señor Alchemist, performed the experiment of deriving silver from other metals?' 'So far I have not,' replied the alchemist, 'but really, I know that it can be derived, and in two months I shall obtain the philosopher's stone, with which one can derive silver and gold from the stones themselves.' 'Your graces have certainly exaggerated your misfortunes,' said the mathematician, 'but, after all, one of you has a book to dedicate, and the other is in potential propinquity to the philosopher's stone; but what shall I say about my misfortune, which is so unique it has nowhere to lay its head? For twenty-two years I have been searching for the fixed longitudinal point, and here I leave it and there I take it up again and think I have found it and that it is impossible for it to get away, and then when I least expect it, I find myself so far from it that I am astonished. The same thing occurs with the squaring of the circle, for I have come so close to finding it that I do not know and cannot imagine why I don't already have it in my purse; and so, my suffering is like that of Tantalus, who is close to the fruit and dies of hunger, and near the water and dies of thirst. For moments I think I have come upon the nature of truth, and for minutes I find myself so far from it that I again climb the mountain I have just descended with the stone of my work on my back, like another Sisyphus.'

Until now the mad reformer had been silent, and here he began to speak, saying: 'Poverty has gathered together in this hospital four complainers so accomplished they could appear before the Great Turk, and I disdain occupations and practices that neither entertain nor feed their practitioners. I, Señores, am a reformer, and at different times I have offered His Majesty many diverse schemes, all to his advantage and harmless to the realm; and now I have prepared a written petition asking him to indicate the person to

17. *History of the Search for the Holy Brail* is a satirical allusion to the stories concerning the Arthurian legend of the Holy Grail.

whom I should communicate a scheme I have that would result in the total restoration of his debts and obligations; but considering what has happened to other petitions of mine, I realize that in the end this one too will die and be buried. But so that your graces do not consider me a fool, even if my scheme is made public, I shall tell it to you now: the parliament must demand that all of His Majesty's vassals, from the age of fourteen to sixty, be obliged to fast on bread and water once a month, on a chosen, specified day, and all the expenditure for other foodstuffs such as fruit, meat, fish, wine, eggs, and vegetables that would have been made on that day should be converted into money and given to His Majesty, down to the last penny, under oath; and by so doing, in twenty years he will be free of all debts and difficulties. Because, if you count it up, as I have done, there are in Spain more than three million people of that age, aside from the sick and those who are older and younger, and not one will fail to spend at a minimum a *real* and a half a day; and I want it to be no more than a *real*, and it cannot be less unless the person eats fenugreek. Well, do your graces think it would be insignificant to have three million *reales* a day as if they had fallen from heaven? It would benefit and in no way be harmful to those who fast, because the fast would please heaven and serve the king; and each one could fast in a way that would be advantageous to his health. This is a straightforward scheme, and it could be collected by parishes, free of the cost of tax collectors, who destroy the nation.' Everyone laughed at the scheme and the mad reformer, and he too laughed at his foolishness, and I was amazed at having heard them and seeing that, for the most part, those with similar inclinations came to die in hospitals.

CIPIÓN: You're right, Berganza. See if you have anything left to say.

BERGANZA: Just two more things, and then I shall end my talk, for I think day is almost here. One night, when my master went to beg at the house of the Magistrate of this city, who is a great gentleman and a very great Christian, we found him alone and it seemed a perfect opportunity to tell him certain information I had heard from an old patient in this hospital concerning how to solve the glaring disgrace of the vagrant girls who, in order not to go into service, do so many wicked things, things so wicked that in summer they populate all the hospitals with the dissolute men who follow them, an intolerable plague that demanded a quick and effective solution. And I, wanting to tell him this, raised my voice, thinking I could speak, and instead of pronouncing rational words I barked so rapidly and so loudly that the Magistrate became angry and called for his servants to drive me out of the room with a beating; and one lackey who came at the sound of his master's voice—and it would have been better for me if for the moment he had been deaf—picked up a copper vessel and hit me with it so hard on my ribs that to this day I bear the scars of those blows.

CIPIÓN: And did you complain about that, Berganza?

BERGANZA: How could I not complain if even now it hurts, just as I have told you, and if it seems to me my good intentions did not deserve so harsh a punishment?

CIPIÓN: Look, Berganza, no one should go where he is not called, nor try to do the work that is not his. And you must remember that the poor man's advice, no matter how good, never is accepted, and the poor, humble man should never presume to advise the great and those who think they know everything. Wisdom in the poor man is obscured, and need and poverty are the shadows and clouds that darken it; and if it happens to be revealed, it is judged as foolishness and treated with contempt.

BERGANZA: You're right, and learning from my mistakes, from now on I shall follow your advice. By the same token, on another night I entered the house of a distinguished lady who had in her arms one of those little things called lapdogs, so small she could hide it in her bosom; and when the dog saw me, she jumped from her mistress's arms and ran at me, barking, and with so much boldness that she did not stop until she bit me in the leg. I looked at her again, fixedly and with annoyance, and said to myself: 'If I were to catch you, you miserable little beast, on the street, I would either ignore you or tear you to pieces with my teeth.' I thought that even cowards and the fearful are daring and insolent when they are protected, and they come forward to offend those who are worth more than they.

CIPIÓN: An example and sign of the truth you have said is given by some small men who in the shadow of their masters dare to be insolent; and if by chance death or another accident of fate knocks down the tree where they are leaning, then their lack of courage is revealed and made manifest; because, in effect, their gifts have no greater value than that given by their masters and protectors. Virtue and a good understanding are always one, always the same, naked or dressed, alone or accompanied. It is certainly true that they can suffer in the estimation of other people but not in the true reality of what they deserve and are worth. And with this let us end our talk, for the light coming in these cracks shows that it is already day, and tonight, if this great gift of speech has not abandoned us, it will be my turn to tell you about my life.

BERGANZA: So be it, and be sure you come to this same place.

The conclusion of the colloquy by the licentiate and the waking of the lieutenant happened at the same time, and the licentiate said:

"Even if this colloquy is imagined and never happened, it seems to me so well composed that the lieutenant can go ahead with the second."

"With this opinion," responded the lieutenant, "I shall gather my courage and prepare to write it, without disputing any further with your grace as to whether the dogs spoke or not."

To which the licentiate replied:

"Señor Lieutenant, let us not return to that dispute. I grasp the artfulness and inventiveness of the colloquy, and that's sufficient. Let us go to the Plaza de Espolón to entertain the eyes of our bodies, for I have already entertained those of my understanding."

"Let us go," said the lieutenant.

And with this, they left.

THE END

The first question that probably occurs to readers of Cervantes's *Exemplary Novels* is how—and whether—this collection of twelve novellas differs from *Don Quixote*, Cervantes's universally admired masterwork. Some differences, based on genre, are palpable, starting with the contrast between short and extended fictions. Others are subtler and have to do with style and intention. The question of difference, or possible similarity, certainly occurred to me as I took on the daunting project of bringing these captivating but not particularly well-known works into English. This volume, it seems, is the first publication in many decades of the complete collection in English—a fact that is both astonishing and appalling. Astonishing because these twelve stories range from exceptional to extraordinary, and their author is a fundamental presence in the saga of the world's literature: the creator of the modern novel and the great luminary of all literature written in Spanish. Appalling because for far too long the English-speaking public has been deprived of a contemporary version of all twelve tales in a translation based on a reliable text in Spanish. I can't begin to account for the vagaries of literary history, but I can share some of my thoughts and observations as I became immersed in the task of translating these wonderful stories.

First, I have a confession to make: I had read these novellas when I was in school, as an undergraduate and as a graduate student, and the truth is that back then, many decades ago, the novellas made my eyes glaze over. They seemed superficial, lacking in relevance, lightweight, and not especially significant or memorable. I remember thinking that they were a prime example of a literary tradition that was not to be trusted, and it was clear to me that these works had ridden into prominence not on their own merits but on the back of *Don Quixote*.

Years later, when I reencountered them for this translation, I was surprised and deeply chagrined, in retrospect, to find myself charmed, amused, engaged: reading them was almost like listening to one of Mozart's lighter operas. And I think there is relevance in that comparison. These novellas do not

have the gravitas of a longer fiction—they are certainly not *Don Giovanni*—
but they are clearly entertainments, meant to be precisely what they seem to
be: temporary respites from the daily grind, works intended to amuse and instruct in that sly way that all European Renaissance literature is meant to
instruct—through delighting and entertaining the reader.

What is more, as if the *Exemplary Novels* were a family recipe treasured
over the generations, they are enriched and heightened by the tang of Cervantes's constant yet kind-hearted irony, the lemon zest that enhances the fla-
vor of all these tales. In *Don Quixote*, Cervantes paints a remarkable portrait of
sixteenth- and seventeenth-century Spain: an early modern society that is also
a vast imperial power. In that novel, the protagonists travel through the countryside, through cultivated terrain, through forests, mountains, small towns,
and large cities, and they encounter and interact with people from practically
every stratum of society: mad beggars, bandits, prisoners, scoundrels, charla-
tans, peasants, ladies of easy virtue, mule drivers, innkeepers, soldiers, the rural
and urban bourgeoisie, the forces of law and order, university students, clerics,
nobles, and even a royal magistrate. And in Cervantes's novellas, I believe the
communal portrait is even more acutely observed and depicted, though I suspect the writer's task is eased because there is no need to accommodate or account for the irrationality of a mad seventeenth-century provincial who thinks
he's a fictional fifteenth-century knight errant. In other words, in Cervantes's
shorter works of fiction, the upper, middle, and lower classes can go about their
several businesses—legal, suspect, or downright criminal—with no fear of interruption by a middle-aged lunatic from somewhere in La Mancha. Their
only concern is that sooner or later they will eventually be brought down by
the weight of the law, or public opinion, or malevolent gossip, or their own failings and idiosyncrasies. But a constant, unstated thread in all the novellas is
that God is exactly where He should be and all's right with the world—or will
be very soon.

Don Quixote gives the impression of being written in broad, freehand
strokes, an expansive style that accretes phrases and clauses as it winds its leisurely way down the page. It is a beautiful and complex baroque style, burnished by the taut relationship between Don Quixote and Sancho Panza as
they evolve over the course of the novel, at times as dissimilar as two characters can be, at other times drawing close enough to begin, like an old married
couple, to resemble each other. The novellas, on the other hand, give the impression of being terse, compact, not expansive but concise, and as a consequence, they leave us with a sense of modernity wondrously achieved through
stylistic economy. Written with urbane good humor, they are comfortable in

a gamut of settings ranging from the splendors of the English court of Elizabeth I to the lively yet unforgiving haunts of the Sevillan underworld. The characters and settings change significantly from novella to novella, while the level of diction moves from high to low and back again, and I think this allows us to develop the feeling that we are reading a unique literary creation twelve times over. In fact, Cervantes's originality and stylistic innovation support our perception of having encountered a singular literary experience in each of the novellas.

Love and honor are the great motivators in these tales that are full of plot twists, strange encounters, astonishing coincidences, and even a pair of talking dogs. I think each of them could be a very successful soap opera, better written than any soap opera the world has ever seen. Be happy you picked up this book: I know you'll enjoy it.

Edith Grossman
New York

MIGUEL DE CERVANTES (1547–1616) was a Spanish writer best known for *Don Quixote*, considered by many to be the first and greatest modern novel.

EDITH GROSSMAN has translated major contemporary and classic authors, including Gabriel García Márquez, Mario Vargas Llosa, Carlos Fuentes, Álvaro Mutis, Luis de Góngora, Sor Juana Inés de la Cruz, and Miguel de Cervantes. Both Carlos Fuentes and Harold Bloom have praised her version of *Don Quixote* (Ecco Press, 2003) as one of the best in English.

ROBERTO GONZÁLEZ ECHEVARRÍA is the Sterling Professor of Hispanic and Comparative Literature at Yale. The author of many books, he is a member of the American Academy of Arts and Sciences, and received the National Humanities Medal in 2011 from President Barack Obama. His lectures on *Don Quixote* are available through the Open Yale Courses through Yale University.